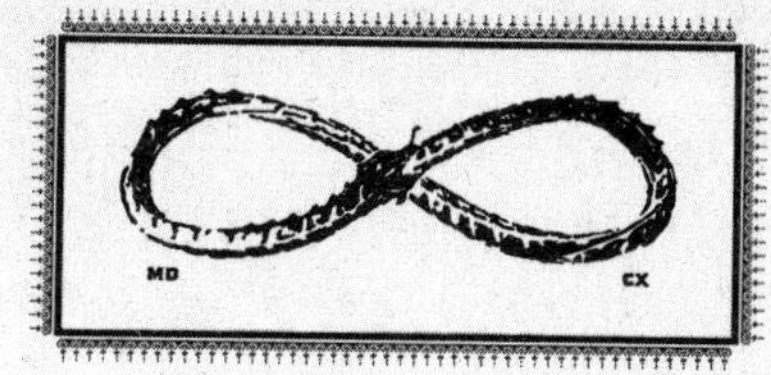

E. G.

The EXPLORERS GUILD

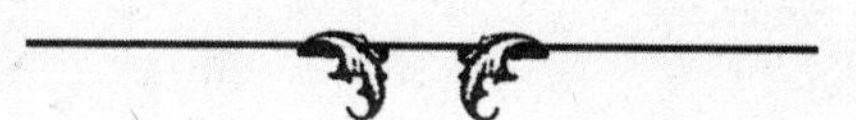

Volume One: A Passage to Shambhala

by

JON BAIRD

with

KEVIN COSTNER

and STEPHEN MEYER

. . .

Illustrated by

RICK ROSS

ATRIA BOOKS

New York London Toronto Sydney New Delhi

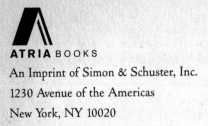

ATRIA BOOKS
An Imprint of Simon & Schuster, Inc.
1230 Avenue of the Americas
New York, NY 10020

This book is a work of fiction. Any references to historical events, real people, or real places are used fictitiously. Other names, characters, places, and events are products of the author's imagination, and any resemblance to actual events or places or persons, living or dead, is entirely coincidental.

First Atria Books hardcover edition October 2015

ATRIA BOOKS and colophon are trademarks of Simon & Schuster, Inc.

For information about special discounts for bulk purchases, please contact Simon & Schuster Special Sales at 1-866-506-1949 or business@simonandschuster.com.

The Simon & Schuster Speakers Bureau can bring authors to your live event. For more information or to book an event contact the Simon & Schuster Speakers Bureau at 1-866-248-3049 or visit our website at www.simonspeakers.com.

Interior design by Jon Baird

Manufactured in the United States of America

10 9 8 7 6 5 4 3 2 1

Library of Congress Cataloging-in-Publication Data is available.

ISBN 978-1-4767-2739-4
ISBN 978-1-4767-2741-7 (ebook)

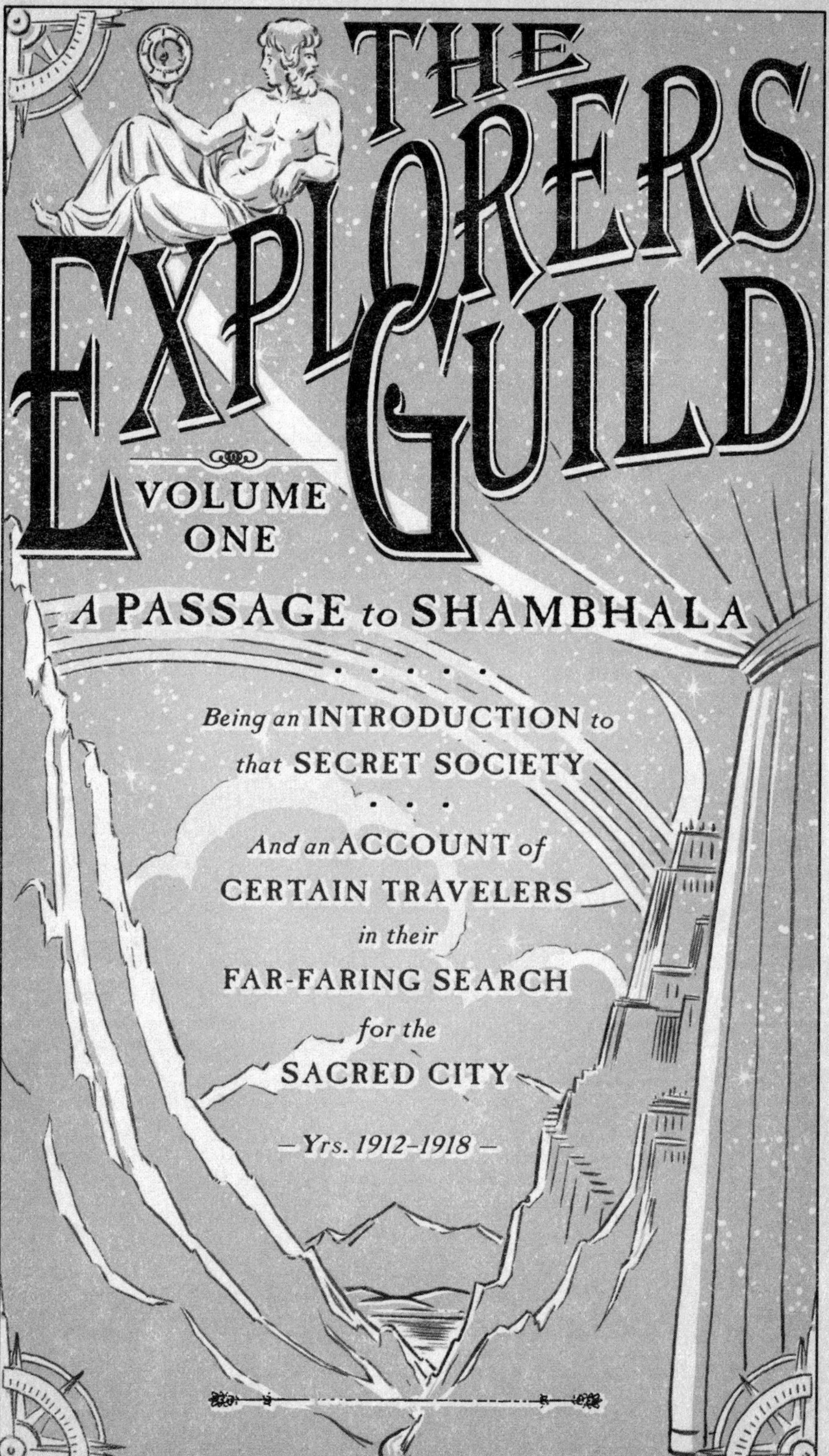
THE
EXPLORERS GUILD
VOLUME ONE
A PASSAGE to SHAMBHALA
Being an INTRODUCTION to
that SECRET SOCIETY
And an ACCOUNT of
CERTAIN TRAVELERS
in their
FAR-FARING SEARCH
for the
SACRED CITY
– Yrs. 1912–1918 –

'THERE IS A QUALITY IN THESE ANCIENT VISTAS, AS THEY BREAK UPON THE LONE RIDER IN THE STILL HOURS OF THE MORNING...'

for ALI, BEN *&* WINNIE
and for TRISHA

Gentle Reader:

The cities of the world–or the decent ones, I should say–have in common a certain unassuming door, and you may find it if you are hunting in the quieter districts with an eye to things that are not exactly hidden, but designed rather to discourage notice. The tourist's literature will carry nothing about it, and it will be so familiar to the mind of the local that he would not dream of pointing you there. But I can tell you, by way of marking one out for you, that there are typically three things on or about this door: a flagstaff, a weather-effaced coat-of-arms and, always, some representation of the Latin motto *Cognoscere*.

Your next discovery, unless you are only noting the door and passing on (which I understand counts for sport among a certain class of traveler)–But I say, you will find next that the door has no lock; and that no matter where you are, in whatever corner of the world, once you have entered through it you will set foot on a Turkey runner, and you will hear a muffled creaking as the planks beneath it take your weight. You will be assailed by smells of sandalwood, cigar smoke, gun oil, aged paper and preserved animal hide. And you will see all about you the trophies and

Scarab compact case with false bottom, from Mozayaf Castle, Marrakech. Held poisoned pastilles given to Moulay ben Walad, 'The Boy Pasha,' by his Sudanese concubine.

. . . .

From Explorers Guild Collection, Hong Kong Lodge

mementos of travel, and recurring motifs of cartography and navigation. There is, in fact, such a pronounced uniformity to the scene that if you have relived it in more than one city you will experience a moment's dislocation or *déjà vu*, as though there were a thousand doors from Boston to Bangalore all giving in to this same vestibule.

In the colder latitudes, there will be a fire kept in the front hall; if ice is available, you will hear it rattling in tumblers. The language of conversation—for there is always a drone of conversation—will vary by locale, as will the complexion of the speakers (though not, again, as much as you might suppose). Otherwise the gentlemen of the outer rooms tend to be 'citizen of the world' types, inclining to stoutness and to age, most of them considerably well-off and all with at least one story of personal exploit they are keen to share.

They will tell you (certainly if asked; even odds if not) that *Cognoscere* means 'to know,' from the Latin. They may also tell you this motto comes from an old fable, in which a boy vanishes from a cathedral in Manila and appears three days later, calling up from a storm drain outside the Bruneian summer palace. The boy, pulled from the drain and carried half-dead to his mother, utters the word *Cognoscere* and faints into that good lady's arms.

It is not the most entertaining fable, as these things go. But the gentlemen who tell it say it is the very model of adventure, and a fine illustration of *Cognoscere* as they construe the word in these halls: a boy, you see, desires *to know* where the Spanish catacombs lead. And with no more motive than this, carrying his life in his hands, expectant of I know not what, he goes headlong into the darkness. For his pains he finds not only the answer to the catacombs' riddle but an old escape tunnel of the maharajahs, a thing disused for centuries that you can pay eight Philippine pesos for a tour of today.

'And the boy's name,' the old men will conclude, with a portentous lift of eyebrow, dipping a match to a pipe-bowl–'...That boy's name was Augustus.' Which I don't suppose will mean very much to you. But they will take a few meditative puffs and add: 'Founder of our *little club*, you know.'

That is to say, it is not just a fable, this story. Some very real boy had had this selfsame adventure beneath the Philippine city–and a great many other adventures besides–and had lived eventually to found this not-altogether-secret order of kindred souls into which you have stumbled. For you are among *explorers* now, if you have not yet guessed it. It is their object, and the *raison d'être* of this society, to throw light into the shadowed corners of the earth, just as the boy Augustus felt he must map out the darkness beneath Manila in his own day. The desire *to know* as the impetus to *action*, you see. Ideally with an element of risk, and crowned with some revelation or discovery in some yet-unknown portion of the world.

It may surprise you, as you survey the rather settled old types in the club's outer rooms, that each man here has inked in his own blank space on one map or another. Indeed, it is a requisite of membership that he would have done so; and I believe most here can represent credibly that they *have*. It may be that some of the newer memberships were won by dint of 'discovering' a novel way up Kilimanjaro, or by standing for a portrait in some square of desert or jungle where Christian man had so far, strictly, omitted to set his foot. But what of that? We needn't all be da Gamas. And you may appreciate, what with the advance of man and the

Miniature sarcophagus from the tomb of Pharaoh Semerkhet II. Stolen shortly after excavation and believed accursed. Appeared 1907, Vakhil Bazaar (Persia). Trader who had re-fashioned relic into a cigarette lighter had also presumably died in result. His name & date of decease inscribed on reverse.

Explorers Guild Collection, San Francisco Lodge

Pickled death's-head soldier from 'Terry's Breadfruit Army.' Mannikin of carved breadfruit, reeds and boot-polish, used in the rescue of Sir Terrence Glyde, Tonga Islands, 1789.

. . . .

Explorers Guild Collection, Rangoon (Burma) Lodge

dwindling of the undiscovered places and so forth, that the opportunities for today's explorer mightn't be what they once were.

Now: you are free to form your own opinion of these men. I hesitate to call them ridiculous, myself—I find them to be first-rate dinner company for one thing, and I say this having a wide experience of tables; nor have they misled you, exactly, on the origins or the purpose of our club (though the story of young Augustus is on several points fallacious; let us set that aside). Yet I wouldn't leave you too long with them, either. For just as all about the place you'll discover wheels within wheels and meanings within meanings, so you'll see a distinction between our outer rooms and the inner, and the corresponding memberships of each. To know what truly goes on here, I say, we will have to leave these bluff old men to their pipes and papers, and venture in a bit deeper....

You will learn, for instance, on penetrating to the quiet inner rooms of the club, that the motto *Cognoscere* is imperfectly rendered as 'to know.' For the Greeks and Romans it meant something more like 'to acknowledge a thing *already known*.' Which will give you a slightly developed sense of our mission. We are constituted to explore and to extend man's knowledge of the world, it is true; but never with the sense that the Unknown is unknown to anyone but man himself.

It is modernity's boast, of course, that man has mapped and measured, claimed and contested this earth down to its last inch. He has tamed its moods and subdued its monsters, and lit it from end to end with the fires of his ingenuity. So we are assured. Yet we who have been canvassing this same earth through the centuries—who have been every place on it that you would care to go, and many more that you would not—we incline to a different view. We find there are elements and beings and systems of intelligence no less baffling to the modern mind than they were to the ancients. And we find these not only to exist but to *co*-exist with the ones we know, in places and in ways that our Sciences cannot predict nor our Reason explain. There is a whole Unknown World, as we see it, that does not diminish with the advance of man; it rather waits, whether in recognition of us or no, till our inquisitive spirits, our pioneers and (inevitably) our blunderers rend that veil between our world and theirs, and bring humanity into communion with the Dark Unknown.

This will all sound a bit wild to you, I do not doubt. Yet I have been myself in the margins of the earth and have seen such things at first-hand. I would tell you this Unknown World is like nothing you have ever dreamt, but that you might have dreamt it exactly. I would tell you it lies far removed from you, dear reader, but that it features in all things, and the night like a tide brings it right to your window.

And just as this Unknown World lies at the heart of all enquiry in the inner chambers of our club, so it represents the subject of the accounts that follow. I would give you, in these pages, a glimpse into *Terra Incognita* and a view of its inhabitants, now that you have discovered your own door, as it were, into the Explorers Guild.

– E. W. Blake
Series Curator
Loire Valley, France
19—

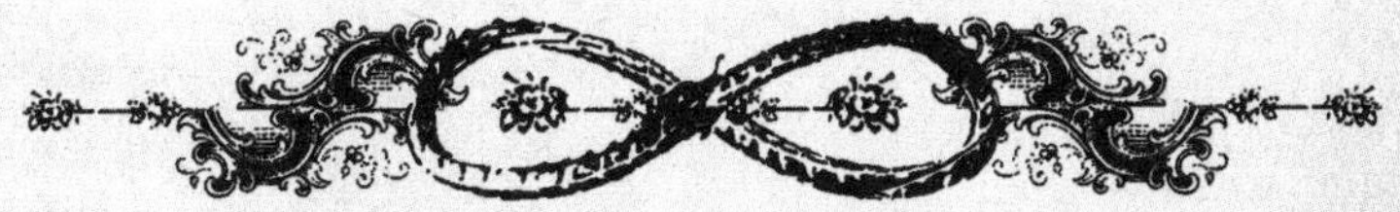

PROLOGUE

On the

ICE FIELDS

WIDE

and

WICKED

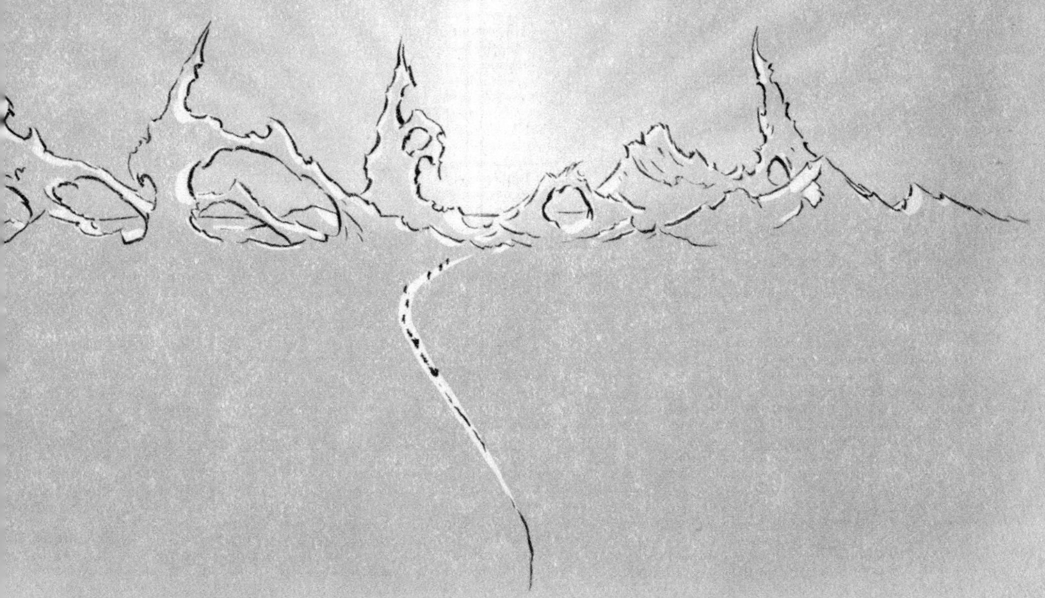

YOU WILL RECALL THAT ARTHUR OGDEN AND HIS PARTY WERE LOST AT OR ABOUT THE POLE IN THE WINTER OF 1912.

CERTAINLY IT WAS ALL OVER THE PAPERS AT THE TIME.

YET THERE ARE ASPECTS OF THIS EXPEDITION THAT WOULD NOT HAVE BEEN GUESSED AT HOME.

THERE IS THE MATTER OF THESE LIGHTS, FOR ONE.

72º 56' 43" N Lat

136º 56' 12" E Long

BEAUFORT SEA, CANADIAN ARCTIC

DECEMBER, 1912

OGDEN...?
STAY BACK. JUST A MOMENT.
WHAT IS IT?
YOU CAN...JUST MAKE THEM OUT.
WHAT–?
POINTING, I THINK. MIGHT HAVE SEEN US, YOU KNOW.

OGDEN HAS LAIN HIMSELF BELLY-DOWN OVER THE LIGHTS' SOURCE, WHEN THE ICE GIVES BENEATH HIM.

STEADY, THEN.
ALL RIGHT, PULL NOW. READY...?
AND: PULL!
STILL, IT IS OGDEN ALONE WHO WILL RETURN TO CIVILIZATION

–THAT'S IT... PULL NOW...
PULL...
TO RELATE SUCH WONDERS AS WE WILL PRESENTLY HEAR.

ALL OF THIS IN ITS
PLACE, DEAR READER.
WE MUST WORK BACK ROUND TO OGDEN
AND HIS DISCOVERY IN THE NORTH...

...BY WAY OF A YOUNG RIDER
AND HIS OWN ADVENTURES

IN A VERY DIFFERENT
QUARTER OF THE WORLD.

'THE BRAVERY OF THE COMPANY'S RUNNERS IS SOMETHING OF A BY-WORD IN INDIA, BUT IT DOES HAVE ITS LIMITS; AND HERE, IF YOU LIKE, IS ONE OF THEM.'

BOOK ONE

- of Five -

Introduces a

STRANGE DIVERSION

alongside the

ROAD OF HISTORY

. . .

While the

GREAT WAR

proves

INSUFFICIENTLY GREAT

for one

CORPORAL BUCHAN

30° 29' 33" N Lat | 47° 50' 39" E Long

Southeast Mesopotamia

CEYLON COMPANY FIELD CAMP
AT MUSALLAM
–DHIRE DHIRE CALIYE–
–SAHIB? THIS IS FAR ENOUGH, YOU UNDERSTAND...

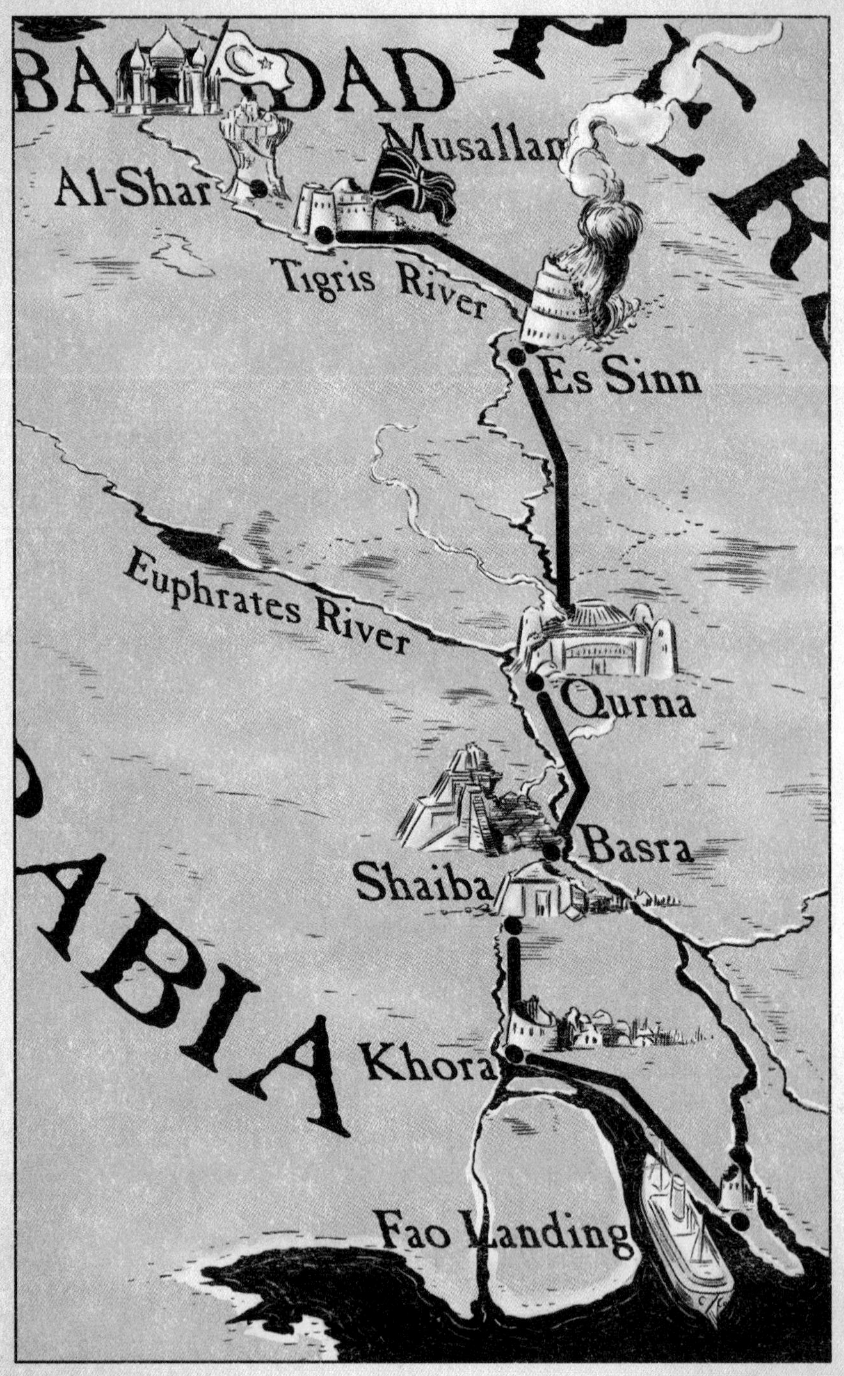
BA DAD
Musallan
Al-Shar
Tigris River
Es Sinn
Euphrates River
Qurna
Basra
Shaiba
ABIA
Khora
Fao Landing

I.

AUGUST, 1917. Balmy days, as you may recall, for the Ceylon Company and the Anglo-Indian Arms. The 6th (Poona) Rifles have landed at Fao and chased the Sultan up through his crumbling forts on the Tigris, howling behind him like the loosed inmates of Bedlam. The Ottoman 38th, put to school under General Nixon, lies strewn now across the sands in ones and twos. Their commander has presented himself alone and barefoot at the gates of the capital, and will shoot himself there before the week is out.

The Company, in fine, is having a good run so far in Mesopotamia. And as the Near-East sun salaams to the tents and pavilions of her Indian guests, as the sentries challenge a young rider on the Basra Road, we find Lieutenant-General Sir John Nixon, our red-phized John Bull, commander of the Company armies in the theater, behaving precisely as he would at this hour at his club in Madras. Which is to say, he has got himself staggering tight.

Sir John sifts through old intelligence reports, German propaganda fliers and bawdy prints from France, alternately scowling over one or another or holding them to the light...which is strictly for show, you understand. Reading is out of the question for a man with this much liquor on board. Anyway, he has left his reading glasses at cantonments in India.

Seated beside General Nixon is his second, a Major-General Sir Charles Townshend, K.C.B., still known in 1917 as the hero of Chitral Fort. Like Nixon, Sir Charles is regaling himself with 'Kabul whiskey,' an unholy brand of arrack or palm wine browned with tobacco juice. Unlike Nixon, Sir Charles is making no other pretense of effort.

It is easy–it is tempting–to see nothing out of the way here. Just two officers of the Company, taking their ease in the approved manner, as little excited as two bachelor baronets (which they are) whiling the evening at some country shooting lodge (which you're aware this is not).

But stay a moment. You may find the quiet a bit too perfect, and not just in the commanders' tent: silence, you will observe, overhangs the camp like a pall. And now you'll see Sir John is shifting in his seat, gnawing a section of his lip, his face flushed not just with drink but with a strain of effort, as though he were struggling to subdue his thoughts.

You'll see that even the mild eyes of Sir Charles apprehend the view outside with something like dread.

For the road to Baghdad is long, gentle reader, and the signs are everywhere tonight that Nixon and Townshend are headed the wrong way on it.

There is an Ottoman division, for one, whispered coming south from the Dardanelles at speed. Two thousand fighting Turkmen sprung from their trenches at Gallipoli, with a vanguard reported already at Al-Shar, just a day's march north of Nixon's position. Berlin, too, has issued a rather lurid account of the Hindu-Christian crusade under way on the Tigris, and the German propaganda seems to have run the width of Araby. Jihadis from as far away as Palestine and the Caspian coast are arriving at Al-Shar with the Kaiser's broadsheets in hand. And it is said there are Jangalis from the Persian Plateau, Kurds from the Zagros foothills, Tatars from the Caucasus and all manner of loose elements from the Empty Quarter poking in to see what the racket is.

It may be that Lord Pomeroy, Director of the Ceylon Company, Viceroy and Governor-General of India, has reached too deep into the desert this time. He may find, and quickly, that he has ventured too small a force, or stretched their lines of supply too far. Certainly this is the prevailing opinion at Musallam, where the young men on picket can already hear the drums of Mohammedan armies, borne into camp on the wind....

Yet there are other sounds at Musallam, too. And if the men are merely quiet–if they have not yet deserted outright–you may credit another rumor that has come in with the late watches.

A mixed detail of sepoy and Midlands companies (and they all are mixed now, irrecoverably) had returned to camp short one lieutenant of grenadiers, you see. Questioned by the relieving officer, men of the detail had proved 'indisposed to speak, not to say dodgy,' and the mystery of the missing grenadier was not solved till he had rolled with an empty bottle of *eau-de-vie* from a credenza in the enlisted mess, rather surprising a steward who was laying tables for breakfast.

The grenadier's testimony had perforce been slight and not of the clearest, but he seemed to have witnessed a company of cavalry skirting the camp by night, some two-score men wildly turned out and bristling with weapons, heading north and bent (according to the grenadier) on 'Satan's earthly errands.' It was demonstrated that the name *Ogden*, pro-

nounced in the grenadier's hearing, would send him into a kind of fugue; but he'd little more to add, and on sobering he had ceased to speak altogether. His fellows on picket had denied his account out of hand and recommended him for discipline at Fao, but by now the camp were readying an advance, and the inquest was closed without any finding as to Ogdens or phantom cavalrymen. Thus, anyway, for the matter on record.

Now, Lord Pomeroy is known—is *believed*, I should say—to have chartered a company of deserters and mutineers under a man called John Ogden (brother of the same Arthur Ogden we have met in these pages). The Fifth Dragoon Guards—known widely as 'Ogden's Horse,' and as utter devils—are said to represent just forty-odd men from the frontiers of India, yet they are credited with horrors out of counting on five continents and on the ships at sea. And though Pomeroy disclaims any knowledge of Ogden's dragoons, he is believed capable of raising them at any time and in all corners of the empire, like his own *djinn* of the lamp.

It may be, then, that he has conjured these men once more for his Mesopotamian venture. Certainly the number counted by the grenadier, and their appearance, and the state of the witness—these were all consistent with the Fifth's reputation. They might be reducing Al-Shar at this very hour, beating a path north for Nixon's advance. Though again, as Nixon must reflect, they would be as apt to wait and train their guns at *him*, for this was their reputation also....

In any event—and here is the point—Nixon has been ordered ahead without delay. It is this fact rising out of all his calculations and looming incontrovertibly over all these shades and rumors. Tomorrow, Sir John will march into whatever happy mess the fates have prepared for him. And if his little expeditionary force isn't swallowed whole, if he doesn't end his war on the Sultan's rack or pegged out on the roadside by Ogden and his merry band, he will be spurred on to Baghdad, where Pomeroy would have him by the Christmas holiday, leading a choir of Imams in 'Silent Night,' I do not doubt.

It is an unhealthy and undignified state of affairs all round, thinks Sir John, who was still entertaining ideas this morning of a leisurely run to the capital, a tour of the landmarks, laurels from H.R.H., speeches and portraits, &c. &c. And who by now, if you must know, has had quite all the Mesopotamia he needs for this life.

...BEG YOUR PARDON?
MM? DIDN'T SAY ANYTHING.

NO. HE DID.

WHO'S THAT?

SAID HE'S...WHAT DID YOU SAY?

ME? CORPORAL BUCHAN,* SIR. THIRD LIGHT CAVALRY.
THEN HE WANTS A MAP. THIRD LIGHTS ARE IN AFRICA.
*PRONOUNCED BUCK-AN

OH—NO, I SHOULD SAY— I'M RUNNING A DISPATCH FROM BOMBAY, SIR. FOR A MAJOR OGDEN—
—BEG PARDON?

YES, SIR. I'D JUST GOT TO THIS POINT WITH HIM.
WHICH?
I TOLD MAJOR-GENERAL TOWNSHEND I WAS AFTER OGDEN, AND HE SAID 'I BEG YOUR PARDON.' THAT'S WHEN YOU PIPED IN—

CAREFULLY, SON.
AYE. THAT SOUNDS LIKE CHEEK, OUT OF YOU.
ANYWAY, WE HAVEN'T GOT ANY OGDENS, I'M SURE.

NO, SIR. I WAS TOLD I MIGHT CATCH HIM AT AL-SHAR, IF I LEGGED IT.
WHO TOLD YOU THAT?
BOMBAY, SIR.
HRM. I SUPPOSE THEY MENTIONED, WE'RE ALL GOING TO AL-SHAR?

YES, SIR.
THOUGH HE'S NOT INTERESTED IN OUR COMPANY, YOU KNOW. HE'S ONLY COME TO GET A HORSE.
FROM US? OH, NOT TONIGHT, HE WON'T.

BUT–IF OGDEN'S GONE AHEAD–
THEN HE'S LED HIS FORTY AGAINST A TURK DIVISION, HASN'T HE.
WITH THE SHARIF'S GUARD, AND ALL THE LOCAL RABBLE, BESIDES–
AYE, AND ALL THE SORCERERS OF ARABY, FOR ALL YOU KNOW–

–SEEM TO THINK THEY'RE INVOLVED IN ANOTHER CRUSADE, THESE PEOPLE–
–THAT'S RIGHT. WE KNOW OGDEN'S REPUTATION, SON. MAYBE HE'S KILLED THE LOT. MAYBE HE'S ONLY GOT TO SHOW HIS FACE AND THEY ALL RUN RAVING INTO THE DESERT.

BUT IF HE HASN'T WON OUT–
–OR IF HE'S DONE HIS JOB AND GONE ON, MORE LIKELY–
AYE, EITHER WAY YOU RIDE SMACK INTO A...WELL A HIVE OF RATHER EXCITED ARABS, DON'T YOU.

...NOT THAT YOU'RE MUCH BETTER OFF IN OGDEN'S HANDS.
–HEAVENS, NO. LET THE GYPS HAVE YOU, GIVEN THE CHOICE.
I SAY, WE KNOW OGDEN'S REPUTATION, MR. BUCHAN. I WONDER IF YOU DO.

...NONETHELESS–

NONETHELESS YOUR GRANNY, SON.
–THAT'S RIGHT–

YOU REALIZE, IF IT ISN'T ALL HELL UP THAT ROAD, MR. BUCHAN, IT'LL BE A FAIR IMITATION.
ANYWAY, YOU'RE NOT GOING.
IF THE VICEROY WANTS TO FEED A COMPANY OF HORSE TO HIS ENEMIES, THAT'S HIS BUSINESS. BUT THIS IS REALLY TOO MUCH.

–AND I'LL HAVE A LOOK AT THAT DISPATCH.
SIR, MY ORDERS–
KEEP IT, THEN, D–MN YOU. BUT YOU'LL WAIT AND MARCH WITH US, AND THERE'S AN END OF IT.
NOW: YOU'LL HAVE A DRINK, CORPORAL, AND TELL US WHAT NEWS FROM BOMBAY.

OH–NO, I COULDN'T. JUST CAME FOR THE CHANGE OF HORSE, REALLY–
HAVE YOU? BY G–D, WE'LL SEE ABOUT THAT–
STAFF SERGEANT? COME–WE'VE A...

...A MUTINY IN HERE.
WHERE'S HE GONE?
«CRRACK!»

THERE.

THIS IS HOW THEY'RE TRAINING THEM IN BOMBAY, I SUPPOSE.
«CRRACK!»
BUCHAN HAS TAKEN LT.-GEN TOWNSHEND'S MUNIQI ARABIAN

YOU WANT AFTER THAT ONE, SIR?
QUITE THE FITTEST HORSE AT MUSALLAM, AS HE HAD JUDGED ON SIGHT.

...GENERAL SAHIB?
MM? OH: NO-NO, THANK YOU.

...*EHH*, BUT GIVE IT AN HOUR, THEN FALL THE OTHERS IN. WE'LL GO AND SEE WHAT'S UP THAT RIVER.
GOOD, SIR.

AND IF THERE'S ANYTHING LEFT OF THAT BOY AT AL-SHAR...

...I'LL PIN A VICTORIA CROSS TO IT.

II.

THE CITADEL AT AL-SHAR commands a bend in the Tigris River about fifty kilometers south of Baghdad. Here was once an important river crossing and a spur of the old Silk Road, but it has long withered under the shadows of Ctesiphon and Baghdad, and the village today is probably much as it was when it greeted the eyes of Saladin.

The gun at Al-Shar is called the *Akh-Siru*, and, like many guns christened with a name, it is a weapon of some repute. Cast in Yuan China and made to throw a 98-cm stone ball, the *Akh-Siru* is a 'bombard' or monstrous forerunner of the cannon, and was already long obsolete when rolled west by the Mongols and sunk by them in the Caspian Sea. Whatever their reasons, or their method, it appears they did not sink the thing far enough, for it was recovered by the Mamluks; and it was these great scavengers who dragged it home and installed it God-knows-how on the heights at Al-Shar, where it remains in 1917, too big to shift and virtually indestructible. Today the *Akh-Siru* sees use officially on occasions of state, and less officially when it suits the moods of the Sharif Al-Shar,

whose birthdays and romantic conquests and spells of boredom are all equally represented in the smashed huts and river-vessels below.

Of course, the real wonder of the *Akh-Siru* is that it doesn't topple the garrison when it's deployed, and this you would appreciate on seeing the gun's situation over the town.

The Al-Shar garrison—or palace, if you like—sits perched on a sandstone column once merely vertical but cut into by the Romans and the weather until the butte, as you see it today, is actually wider at its crest than it is a third of the way down. And as its base diminished over the centuries, so the garrison itself grew under the Parthians, Sassanids, Turkmen and Ottomans, with each new tenant enlarging on the plans of the last. The bulwarks and towers and apartments of the latest design crowd right to the edge of the precipice, where they sit in defiance of Newtonian physics, needing just that last gust of wind—or that last bird settling on just the right flagstaff—to send the whole works crashing to the desert floor.

Till then, as we say, the garrison at Al-Shar presents one of the more arresting sights on the Tigris. Something like a view of Noah's Ark landed on Mount Ararat…Or so it strikes one Corporal Buchan, as he bears down on the village this morning. Here, Buchan thinks, knuckling sweat from an eye—Here is where Ogden waits, if only because he could not be elsewhere. It seems the great heap of domes and towers and minarets has been raised expressly to mark the end of this long ride. And somewhere in it, surely, there will be Major Ogden, whether he lies fettered in the Caliph's dungeons, or stands upstairs drinking from the man's skull. Perhaps, even now, Ogden is sporting with his men in the seraglio, or drinking from the Grand Vizier's jewel-crusted goblet, as long-nailed courtiers and almond-eyed houris look on, and the music of unseen players builds to a frenzy....

Mr. Buchan, I should say, is not usually given to flights like this of the imagination, and particularly not when he is riding under orders. But you will recall he is bringing a sealed dispatch from the Viceroy into the land of the *Arabian Nights*, and that he is awaited here by John Ogden, a man as much figment as fact and introduced by all manner of lurid tales. There is a quality, too, in these ancient vistas, as they break upon the lone rider in the silent hours of the morning, that revives some of the more romantic notions of youth. And where our rider is still just nineteen and a son of the Eastern Colonies, I doubt these notions are so deeply buried in him in the first place.

We find Mr. Buchan, therefore, entering Al-Shar in a mode of abstraction this morning, with the long and gainly stride of the Arabian beneath him, a warming breeze coming off of the river and a high, whining sound overhead that would seem to be some desert bird proclaiming the dawn.

...Though, on second thought, it isn't a very likely spot for birds.

«THOOOM!»

HOAH...HOAH-HOAH!

–HEH-HEH...
ACCHA HAI.

‹...WIDE TO RIGHT, EIGHTEEN YARDS. LEAD A BIT MORE. HE'S COMING ON.›*
*TRANSLATED FROM THE HINDI, AND NOT ONE OF YOUR LOCAL TONGUES.

–HYEUGH-HYEUGH–

STAY RIGHT... *EHH*, JUST LIKE THAT. THAT'S...

...HUH.

–DOOFH!

VAHĀM USĒ PAKARŌ.

I'M–SIR, I'M A ROYAL SUBJECT, ENTITLED TO–*HYEK*–!

–ENTITLED TO–
...THIS IT FOR CARTRIDGES?
CUPA RAHŌ.

HEY–
UNH–! THAT'S ALL, YES. BUT–YOU SPEAK ENGLISH.

ENGLISH, YAH. AN' PASSABLE KURDISH, THROUGH NO FAULT O' MINE.
'TWEEN THAT AN' HIM LOOKIN' PASSABLE ARAB, WE'RE STUCK OUT HERE FOR A REARGUARD, AN' NOT OVERJOYED ABOUT IT. SO YE'LL ANSWER QUESTIONS AND SHUT YER MOUTH OTHERWISE.
OGDEN'S GUARD, YOU MEAN–
–SAID QUIET.

–THEN IT'S TRUE. YOU RODE IN WITH HIM LAST NIGHT, AND KILLED THESE MEN AND TOOK THEIR CLOTHES...
BUT: WHO WAS FIRING AT ME, JUST NOW?

...HOW D'YOU MEAN, LAD?
I MEAN SOMEONE'S BEEN AT THIS MORTAR. QUITE NEARLY KILLED ME ON THE WAY IN–
OH: YAH. THAT WAS US. HIM, REALLY.
–ON HIS ORDERS–

MAJOR'S ORDERS. THEY TOLD YOU NO ONE CROSSES THAT PLAIN, HEY?
BUT I'M IN UNIFORM–
–NO ONE, I SAYS.

NOT TILL THE MUEZZIN SINGS IN YON MINARET. THAT IS THE SIGNAL.
AYE, YOU MUST LET US DO OUR WORK.
WELL. NO HARM DONE, I– SORRY, WOULD YOU MIND TERRIBLY IF I STOOD UP?

IN A MOMENT. WE'RE SENDING YOU BACK ON MR. GURUNG'S MARE, OVER THERE.
OH–NO, I'M AFRAID I COULDN'T.
NONSENSE. FINE KASHMIRI. YOU'LL BE THE ENVY OF YOUR UNIT. 'SPECIALLY IF THEY TURN YOU UP A MOUNTAIN.
I MEAN I CAN'T GO BACK. I'VE GOT ORDERS TO FIND MAJOR OGDEN.

AND WHAT, BRING 'IM THIS?

SIR, I CAN'T ALLOW YOU TO–
NEVER MIND WHAT YE'LL ALLOW. WHEN IT'S YOUR BOOT ON ME, I'LL ASK.

«CRACK!»

WHAT IS THAT?
MEAN, YOU DON'T KNOW?

NO, SIR. THEY TOLD ME IT CAME DOWN TO POMEROY, THROUGH SOME HIGHER CHANNEL–
–HIGHER'N THE VICEROY? AN' WHO'D THAT BE?
I DON'T KNOW, SIR. DO YOU THINK IT'S TRUE?

Y'KNOW I'LL VENTURE, GOING STRICTLY ON YOUR LOOKS, CORPORAL, THAT VERY LITTLE OF WHAT PEOPLE TELL YOU IS TRUE.

...UNLESS THAT'S THE COMPANY'S NEW SEAL, HEY?
'CAUSE IT AIN'T 'IS MAJESTY'S.
WHOSE DO YOU THINK IT IS, THEN?

KYĀ ĀPA YAHA CĀHATĒ HAIM?
...ALL RIGHT.
THE SYMBOL WORKS A SWIFT CHANGE OF MOOD IN OGDEN'S MEN. THE GURKHA, IN PARTICULAR, WANTS NOTHING TO DO WITH IT.

YA SEE THAT MINARET, SON? AND RIGHT BELOW IT, THE GATE?
YES, SIR–

I WATCHED MAJOR GO THROUGH THAT GATE LAST NIGHT, AND NO ONE'S COME BACK OUT YET, WORSE LUCK FOR THE GYPS. YOU GO AND KNOCK, AND ASK FOR HIM.
HE OUGHT TO KNOW WHAT THAT IS.

III.

...THUS A COLONEL WREN AND A LT.-COLONEL MASTERS, 8TH DRAGOON GUARDS, ON THEIR WAY TO FAO ON THE TRANSPORT CRUISER *HMS COMPUNCTION.*

THE OTHER VIEW ON THE *COMPUNCTION* WAS VOICED IN STEERAGE, AND HELD GENERALLY FOR THE ENLISTED MEN:

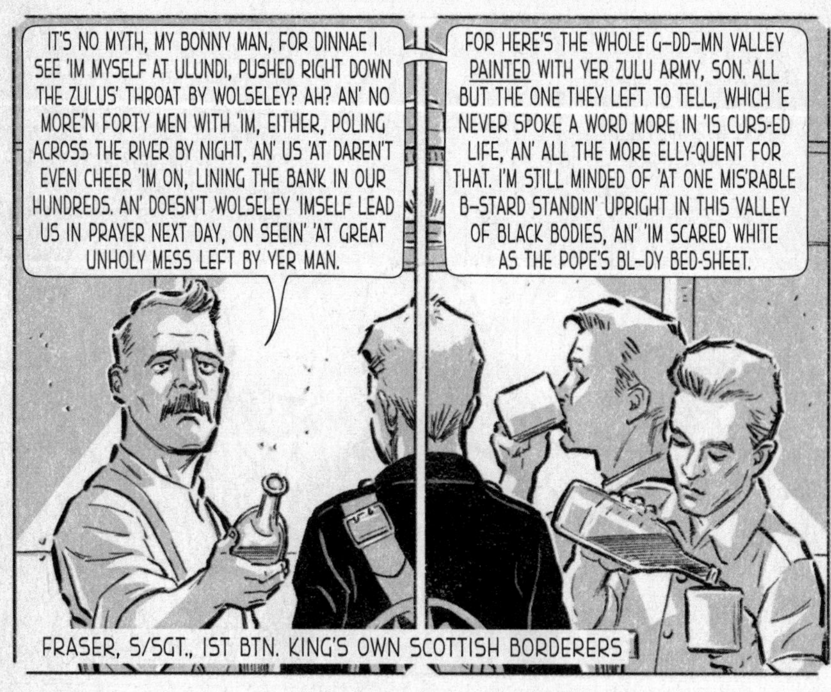

IT'S NO MYTH, MY BONNY MAN, FOR DINNAE I SEE 'IM MYSELF AT ULUNDI, PUSHED RIGHT DOWN THE ZULUS' THROAT BY WOLSELEY? AH? AN' NO MORE'N FORTY MEN WITH 'IM, EITHER, POLING ACROSS THE RIVER BY NIGHT, AN' US 'AT DAREN'T EVEN CHEER 'IM ON, LINING THE BANK IN OUR HUNDREDS. AN' DOESN'T WOLSELEY 'IMSELF LEAD US IN PRAYER NEXT DAY, ON SEEIN' 'AT GREAT UNHOLY MESS LEFT BY YER MAN.
FOR HERE'S THE WHOLE G–DD–MN VALLEY PAINTED WITH YER ZULU ARMY, SON. ALL BUT THE ONE THEY LEFT TO TELL, WHICH 'E NEVER SPOKE A WORD MORE IN 'IS CURS-ED LIFE, AN' ALL THE MORE ELLY-QUENT FOR THAT. I'M STILL MINDED OF 'AT ONE MIS'RABLE B–STARD STANDIN' UPRIGHT IN THIS VALLEY OF BLACK BODIES, AN' 'IM SCARED WHITE AS THE POPE'S BL–DY BED-SHEET.
FRASER, S/SGT., 1ST BTN. KING'S OWN SCOTTISH BORDERERS

...NO, IF OGDEN EVER LIVED—AND I MUCH DOUBT IT—HE'S SUPPOSED DEAD IN A HUNDRED DIFFERENT OUTPOSTS.
BUT—THEN WHY WOULD THEY SEND ME AFTER HIM, IF HE WEREN'T ANYTHING REAL?
HOW SHOULD WE KNOW THAT?
MM. THE LORD POMEROY, YOU KNOW: RATHER KNOWN FOR THIS SORT OF THING.
SOME...UNFATHOMABLE SORT OF JOKE, I SHOULD THINK.

THE STORIES HAD ONLY MULTIPLIED AS BUCHAN NEARED THE FRONT, WITH NO TWO OF THEM AGREEING. BY MUSSALAM, THE CAMP HAD BEEN FULL OF NOTHING ELSE.

NO–I WOULDN'T CREDIT IT EITHER, THEM SENDING FORTY-ODD OF US NORTH AHEAD OF THE VAN. BUT I DREW PICKET LAST NIGHT, YOU MIND, AND SEEN THE WHOLE G–D-AWFUL SHOW MYSELF.
LEAROYD, PTE.
103RD MAHRATTA LGT. INFANTRY

OH, AYE, SO'D WE ALL SEE IT, NOT JUST YOUR MR. LOFTUS OF GRENADIERS. NOT THAT I COULD EXPLAIN IT, QUITE. OTHER THAN...WELL YOU WOULDN'T CALL THIS FORTY OF US, WOULD YOU.
MULVANEY, CPL.
14TH KING'S HUSSARS

MORE LIKE FIGGERS IN SOME BL–DY AWFUL DREAM. ALL DEAD WEARY IN THE SADDLE AND DRESSED ANY-OLD-HOW. PASSED ON LIKE THAT WITH NIVVER A WORD FOR US.
ORTHERIS, SGT.
7TH HARIANA LANCERS

DESERTERS AND MUTINEERS, CAPTAIN SAID, OUTTA INJA AN' THEREABOUTS, AN' THAT GREAT HAMMERHEAD MARE UP TO FRONT, WITH THE DEVIL HIMSELF RIDING FOR A OFFICER.

AYE, THAT WAS HIM, SON. THE 'FLAIL OF INDIA,' AND QUITE ENOUGH FOR ANYONE OUTSIDE THAT PLACE, TOO.
–WHO AS I HAPPEN TO KNOW IS WORSHIPPED AS A DIVINITY BY CERTAIN SECTS ON THE INJAN FRONTIERS–
AN' WHO BUT JOHN OGDEN TO RIDE AT ALL THE NORTHERN ARMIES, WITH JUST HIS FORTY MEN BEHIND 'IM?
YE'LL SEE THE PATH THEY CUT THROUGH AL-SHAR, MR. BUCHAN. AN' IT WON'T BE A STORY FER THE JOONIOR BUCHAN'S BEDTIME, NEITHER...

...This last view, at least, being borne out already. It is the morning after John Ogden's visit to this place, and the destruction of Al-Shar village is total. A few Canaan dogs nose through the rubble, and here and there a vulture squats in the scant shade, too engorged to fly. But there isn't a soul stirring otherwise, not even to draw water or to minister to the dead. It would be impressive work for any army; but if this is the record of just forty men passing, they were men possessed of unnatural gifts.

And it is not altogether in the physical damage that Ogden and his men have written their account. The village, as Buchan reflects, was likely little more than a ruin to begin with. It is rather this horrible *quiet*, which is not the early-morning lassitude of the desert towns, and is not the holy stillness of the ancient places. It is as though the village itself had been stricken dead of fright, or stood in a kind of shock–its living and its dead, the walls and the very ground beneath them all frozen, with breath held, against the return of this horror. Not even the breezes that beat about the Tigris and cut across the plains have followed Buchan down these silent paths, through the rows of battered and fire-blackened huts.

Al-Shar village really might, to borrow General Nixon's phrase, have been shown some fair imitation of hell.

PAUSED AT THE PALACE GATES,
BUCHAN HEARS A PISTOL-SHOT
FROM SOMEWHERE INSIDE.

QUIETLY, HE UNSHEATHES HIS ENFIELD.

Buchan crosses a shallow courtyard, picking his way through blocks of fallen stonework and statuary in the shade of the giant sandalwood gates, which have been blasted off their hinges and thrown aslant against the castle walls. As in the village below, there is not a soul stirring anywhere here, and the very air is eloquent of the violence that has lately passed this way.

There are urns and fountains and hedgerows on the walkway's sides, providing cover for any castle invader desirous of it. But Buchan keeps to the center of the path, coming on steadily–as he has done, indeed, since Bombay–through the courtyard, to where two iron-studded doors stand parted outside the dim castle interior.

Moments later, the barrel of his Enfield is pushing into the darkness, just ahead of the runner's own wary and wide-eyed face....

The men of this house, since the day of the Caesars and likely long before that, have received their tributes and collected their tithes here, and sifted in the currents of trade that crossed from the extremes of East and West at their door. And though the star of this house has long set, the castle still preserves an opulence out of all proportion to the peasant village below. The parlors and sitting-rooms where we find young Buchan are so crowded with art and ornament that he must shoulder his way carefully from room to room, and more than once he starts back from some human or animal likeness, excusing himself.

Signs of Ogden and his men, too, have become even plainer here than in the village. It seems no opportunity has been lost to break, burn, slash or otherwise despoil these rooms. Even the statues have had their heads shot from their shoulders. And here we see the first of the palace guards and servants, who might have breathed their last just hours ago.

Buchan is lowering himself to one of them when he freezes and draws the bolt of his rifle. He has cocked an ear to the ceiling before he is quite conscious of the sounds drifting down from overhead.

He pads up a snaking flight of stairs, then, and down another hall, with the sounds rising before him. This is not what you and I would call *music*, exactly; and if you have never heard a Near-East mangling of an Anglo-Saxon dance hall standard, this is not a thing easily described. For Mr. Buchan it calls to mind images of gypsy performers bouncing in an eccentric-wheeled cart, or of a mob of mismatched, diabolically tuned instruments animated by the castle genius and forced to couple until dead. It is a sound exotic and unnerving and, as it strikes him, perfectly in keeping with the surroundings and with his own strange mood.

There are feet, too, somewhere ahead, beating out a tattoo on wooden planks, and the chaos is compounded by the shouts and whistles of men, and by bursts of singing at random, all audible now in the second-floor gallery.

Edging silently, steadily forward, Buchan begins to make out the ringing and crashing of glassware, the rattling of silver and china, and snatches of English over a gruff Babel of tongues and gusts of laughter, all of it tumbling in with the music and the tread of feet, re-echoing dreamlike through the bloodied and bullet-pocked halls and swelling to a terrific din as he draws up to a figured archway....

The archway gives in to a banquet hall or theater, where the bulk of Ogden's men sit gathered—or stand, perhaps—it is difficult to make much sense of things at first. A few low-set oil lamps make silhouettes of the dragoons and throw them, multiplied and enlarged, across the pillars and walls behind them, till it seems Mr. Buchan has caught a whole demon army at their revels. Nor do the shapes resolve into anything especially human as he advances into the hall.

There seems to be a perfect dog's dinner here of Sikhs, Gurkhas, Pashtuns, Marathas, Afghans, &c., with the fighting castes of India and criminal classes of Europe equally represented, and a few Boers and Chinese thrown in with some others who could really be anything. They are all an order of magnitude taller and burlier than your Company regulars, and all turned out like no earthly cavalry Mr. Buchan has seen, who has ranged over a good bit of the Commonwealth. They seem rather like bogeymen of the hills who have dunked themselves in pitch and rolled along the length of India's borders, picking up all manner of weapons and vesture and ribbons and insignias of rank—and sticks and brambles and the very aura of blood and havoc from those desperate places. And Buchan finds them all howling and jeering now like men demented, stamping on tables and chairs and flags with their rowelled boots, and lobbing bottles and the castle plate at some performance at the hall's far end.

The performance is worth mentioning, too, for here stand (so far as they can) remnants of the Ottoman 9th and 19th–the heroes of Gallipoli, flower of the empire, &c.–on a bow-shaped proscenium, rouged and corseted and groaning their way through 'Good-bye, Dolly Gray' in phonetic English. Ogden's men have not even bothered to disarm them, so comprehensive is the fear and exhaustion of these captives.

The scene will look something barbarous, I do not doubt, to the modern eye. And it may be Mr. Buchan feels some seemly bit of revulsion that he is at pains to conceal. But we only see him drifting deeper into the room with his rifle carried loose at his thighs and a grin enlivening his features, as though he were under some spell of enchantment. And we are reminded that he is a child of the frontier provinces himself (his father being a civil servant at Peshawar); and it is likely that the first glimpses he'd have had, as a boy, of the Ceylon Company army and its exploits–these visions of war that first quickened a purpose in him, and sent him running after the drum when he was scarcely out of his short-pants–I say, it is likely these scenes would share some hue of barbarism with the one before him now. And there may therefore, in his introduction to the Fifth Dragoons, be a certain note of homecoming, as one might experience on re-entering one's own half-forgotten dream.

YAHA! THEY BEG THE EFFENDI TO UNDERSTAND, SIR, WE ARE A THOUSAND LEAGUES FROM LONDON AND THE MUSIC-HALLS–
AYE, THAT'S SO. BUT YOU TELL 'EM LONDON'S COME TO YOU.

–AND COUNTY DORSET, HUGH!
–TH'WELSH MARCHES, D–MN YER EYES–
–KHALSA-JI!–
–AN' LUCKNOW BARRACKS–!
–AYE AND ALL THE NINE BOROUGHS O' HELL, AND AS THESE MEN VALUE LIFE THEY'LL STEP TO LIKE GOOD HEATHENS, AH?

NOW–
–THASSIT, HUGH, YOU TAKE COMMAND, LAD!–
SAID ALL'A YOU, QUIET.
HEH-HEH-HEHHH!
NOW–FOR THE LOVE'A CHR–ST: DOES ANY MAN HERE KNOW ANY OF THE NEW DANCES?

UP-UP, MR. PATEL–YOU SHOW 'EM WHAT HUGH'S MUM TAUGHT YER!–
–TAUGHT ALL'A YOUSE INJYANS–
HRAW-HRAWW!
OI! –WHO'RE YOU?
CORPORAL BUCHAN IMAGINES HE IS WATCHING UNOBSERVED, TILL A VOICE PIPES UP BESIDE HIS EAR.

THIS THE VAN? YOU'RE A BIT EARLY.
OH—NO, I'M LOOKING FOR A MAJOR OGDEN—
WELL, HE AIN'T HERE. YOU THINK 'E'D STAND FOR THIS?

'OO'S THAT, MR. RENTON?
SAYS IS MAJOR 'ERE?
WHO WANTS TO KNOW?

THIS YOUNG JUGGINS.
BUCHAN, SIR. THIRD LIGHT CAVALRY—
WANTS HIS REGI-MENT, RATHER.
SORRY?

THIRD LIGHTS IS GONE TO THE SUDAN, AS WE HAPPEN TO KNOW.
WHO'S HE REALLY, MR. RENTON?
YA—WHO'RE YOU REALLY?

I SAY: THAT'S A HESSIAN SPY, MR. RENTON, OR I'M ONE.
WHAT?
LAY HOLD OF 'IM, LAD.

ALL RIGHT– ENOUGH–!

OW!
HEY! LEAVE THAT–

LOOK: I'M NOT A SPY, I'M SURE.
AH, BUT WOULD HE SAY IF HE WAS?
HE WOULD UNDER TORTURE, AYE.

I'M A STAFF RUNNER FOR LORD POMEROY, AND YOU MEN–
WHAT'S 'AT, THEN?
SOMEHOW, IN THEIR STRUGGLE, MR. RENTON HAS FISHED THE CANISTER FROM BUCHAN'S DISPATCH BAG.

GIVE IT 'ERE, MR. RENTON.
YOU–! CAPTAIN, I'LL HAVE THAT–
INDEED YOU WON'T, SON.
STAY, LAD. YOU THINK MR. SHAW TAKES ORDERS FROM A SPRAT LIKE YOU?

CAPTAIN SHAW IS SOME MOMENTS IN INSPECTING THE CANISTER. HE SPEAKS AGAIN IN A MORE THOUGHTFUL MODE.
SAID YOU'RE ONE OF POMEROY'S?
I AM.
HMM.

...BECAUSE I SAY YE'RE A MESSENGER OF FATE.
WHAT IS IT, JACKIE?
WELL. IT'S NOTHING VERY HEALTHY, I PROMISE YOU THAT.

YE'LL OPEN IT AT LEAST...?
AUGGH, YOU'RE A SU-PERSTITIOUS OLD FISHWIFE. GIVE IT 'ERE–
QUIET.

THERE Y'ARE, SON.
HOLD IT. MR. BUCHAN? LOOK 'ERE:

BUCHAN, ON POINT OF LEAVING, FINDS HE IS LOOKING INSTEAD INTO SERGEANT PENSETTE'S SIDEARM.
IN ALL SERIOUSNESS, NOW:
HAVE YE ANY O' THE NEW DANCES? YOU CAN SEE WHAT THE LADS'RE UP AGAINST...

THE GUN GOES OFF AS CAPTAIN SHAW SWATS IT AWAY.
OI! QUIT THAT, YOU.
«CRRACK!»
AND A SHOT THAT COULD AS EASILY HAVE CRIPPLED BUCHAN HAPPENS ONLY TO MAIM A TABLE-LEG.

WATCH IT, JACKIE–'AT'S ONE O' POMEROY'S. *HRAW-HRAWW!*
GO ON, SON. MAJOR'S 'AT WAY.
THIS COUNTS AS GOOD SPORT WITH THE DRAGOONS, WHO SEE BUCHAN OFF WITH SPIRITS REVIVED.

–YAH, *AUF WIEDERSEHEN,* LAD–*HEH-HEHH...*

♪ *IT'S A LONG WAY TO TIPPERARE-E-E / IT'S A LONG WAY TO GO...* ♪

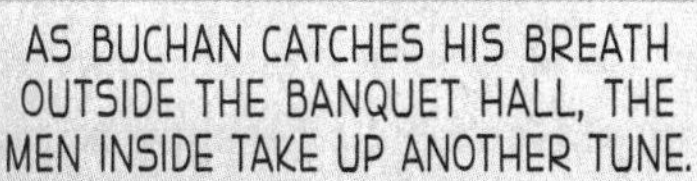
AS BUCHAN CATCHES HIS BREATH OUTSIDE THE BANQUET HALL, THE MEN INSIDE TAKE UP ANOTHER TUNE.

♪ *...IT'S A LONG WAY TO TIPPERARY / TO THE SWEETEST GIRL I KNOW...* ♪
IT SEEMS UNLIKELY ANY OF THEM WOULD COME OUT IN PURSUIT; THOUGH BEST NOT TO LINGER, IN ANY CASE.

What with the types running loose in the Al-Shar garrison, with the hour advancing and Ogden himself, finally, in prospect, it would be a rare piece of art that would call young Buchan from his work. But that is just what the palace decorators have put in his way. There is a tapestry, you see, running between two of the arches and reaching from the fretwork overhead down to the baseboards. And it presents, in these impressive dimensions, a forest scene of dizzying complexity—A depiction, perhaps, of some historic hunt... No, hold that. It isn't a hunt. A celebration *afterward*, then, with young ladies arrived among the men, and even some of the beasts circulating about, all quite collegial. Really the whole forest is a tangle of limbs, arboreal and human and... Some of them would appear... Oh, in fact they're *all*...

Well. The desert races, you know, have not always turned to the loom with the saintliest thoughts. But here someone has rendered such a catalogue of perversions, such a comprehensive merging of sexes and species—many times in the same *person*, mind you, with antlered heads of *this* upon several-legged bodies of *that* and so forth—

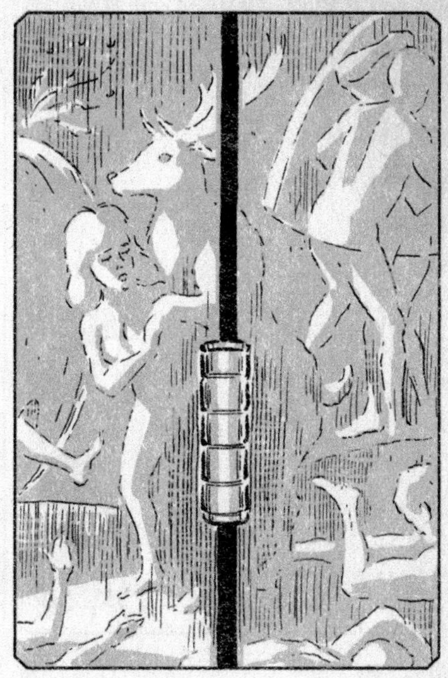

but such a scene, I say, that even the hardiest characters of the *Kama Sutra* or the *Inferno* might give this woodland *mêlée* a pass.

As Buchan's eyes travel from one grouping to the next, he is prey to wonder, horror, outrage, envy, a kind of scholarly doubt and various other currents of mood that are not my business to relate; while what the revelers themselves might be thinking is really anyone's guess. This one here, for instance, if you close right in on his face, might be working out a sum; these two nymphs who've saddled the woodsman seem vaguely to regret the enterprise; this fellow with the balalaika and his foot in the chimp-faced maid could do with a nap, I think; while this young lady here is scarcely bothered by the...How's this? There appears to be a *hinge*, doesn't there, between her and this stag. And I don't mean to say they're using some hinge-like device in...in whatever that is they're doing. I mean there is an *actual* brass hinge, with another above it, and a little brass pull, over the tapestry. And–Something just stirred back there.

Buchan, on his guard again, backs up and levels his rifle at the wall. A minute passes in silence and then, decidedly, from somewhere behind the tapestry there is a rustling sound and possibly a human voice.

He closes on the tapestry now with an ear foremost, trying not to think what he might be placing his cheek against...

And here we are: another castle secret. Hidden door, you see. This segment of the tapestry is bound over a wooden panel that is not much heavier than the hanging itself. To Buchan's surprise, and then horror, the door is unlatched, and it gives to the least pressure.

The Sharif's harem, then. In hindsight, the forest scene on the tapestry outside seems rather an obvious clue. The place seems to have gone undiscovered by Ogden's men, and it sits unguarded now but for the

Sharif's *haseki*, this painted harridan waving the pike, with her charges shrinking behind her.

And here is young Buchan back on his feet, holding his rifle by its forestock and making a close study of his boots. He backs slowly from the room until he feels himself in the cool air of the hallway, and then this young man—who has ridden through fire all over the continent and closed with Ogden's dragoons only today—I say, this same young man goes sprinting for all he is worth, away from the Sharif's harem and into the darkness.

Corporal Buchan continues away from the harem, following one torch-lit hall to the next and so deeper into the castle, until he spies a turbaned castle servant in the unmistakable act of dragging a body behind him. A sound of blows carries back, too, from somewhere ahead, a repeated thumping with a metallic ring, as of a heavy blade driving through something into stone.

Crouched again in readiness, Buchan rounds the corner behind the servant and enters a perpendicular-running, open-air colonnade that fronts the eastern plains. The hall is lit weakly by the sun, which must have climbed past the garrison by now and put this face of the castle back in shadow. Ahead, an exhausted-looking gang of Azap infantrymen are lowering some weight on a rope over the castle's side, and they have left each of the columns behind them tied with a similar rope. Buchan crosses the hall with his eyes and rifle trained on the soldiers, and pokes his head between two of the columns for a look down:

The ropes, as he had guessed, are being used to exhibit the late friends of the Sharif to the settlement below, this to advertise the castle's change of management and to indicate how any relief force might be received. The bodies are hung by wrist and ankle and waist, but not by the neck, you see—each being absent its *head*—which casts rather a dreadful light on those thumping sounds coming from the end of the hall...Still, the way for Mr. Buchan is clearly forward, and on he goes with eyes wide and rifle at the high port.

The soldiers take a brief note of his uniform as he passes, and fall quietly back to work. Buchan gives them a nod of encouragement (which is wholly ignored) and continues to the end of the colonnade, where the sunlight winks out behind him and he can see more distinctly the glow of a fire and a commotion of figures in the dark rotunda ahead. The Sharif's servants are engaged here in piling bodies next to a giant, bull-shouldered dragoon, who is stripped to the waist and blacked with soot. The dragoon takes each of the bodies in turn, clubs it with his *Tulwar* and tosses some object (which Buchan identifies with a flutter of stomach) into a vat of boiling water, before kicking the body aside. Servants then drag the headless bodies back toward the colonnade, while others stir the cauldron with long rods and bank up the fires beneath it.

Now, the bravery of the Ceylon Company's runners is something of a by-word in India, and so far we have no reason to doubt young Buchan's mettle. But this bravery does have its limits, and here, if you like, is one of them. This monster at the end of the hall frightens Mr. Buchan hollow; and he hasn't quite got command of his voice as he snaps a salute and speaks to the man's back.

MAJOR OGDEN, SIR?
...EHH: MAJOR?
MULCAIRN. CONNAUGHT RANGERS.
-OH. I BEG YOUR-

MAJOR'S UP 'EM STAIRS.
NOW F-CK OFF.

...YOU'RE NOT–
–NO, SAHIB.
WELL–I NEED TO SEE HIM.

WE'RE BOTH TALKING ABOUT MAJOR OGDEN, HEY?
I'D LIKE TO SPEAK WITH HIM.
WITH OGDEN.
IF I MAY.
...YES. AND WHAT HAVE YOU DONE, SAHIB, THAT YOU SHOULD BE SO HONORED?

NO, IT'S NOT THAT I–I'VE SOMETHING TO GIVE HIM, IS ALL.
MY ORDERS ARE TO DELIVER THAT INTO MAJOR'S HAND, SIR.
AND...*EHH*, TO OFFER MY ASSISTANCE, IF ANY OF YOU HAVE NEED.

CORPORAL SAHIB: YOU HAVE COME AS NEAR TO MAJOR OGDEN AS A COMPANY REGULAR MAY COME. IF YOU LIKE, YOU MAY...
...YOU MAY WAIT HERE...

SURELY THERE ARE SIGNS IN THIS, FOR A THINKING MAN.
–SORRY?

YOU ARE A DISPATCH-RUNNER FOR THE CEYLON COMPANY.
YES, SIR.
BUT THIS IS NOT THE COMPANY'S.

NO, SIR. BUT YOU RECOGNIZED THAT DEVICE, THERE, ON THE CAP–?
IT IS *GIDDARI RATTARA.* THE EXPLORERS GUILD.
AH.
...AND WHAT'S THAT?

THE MUEZZIN WILL SING IN THIS HOUR, SAHIB. WE'LL NOT STAY TO HEAR HIM.
YOU WILL FIND JOHN OGDEN BEHIND THAT DOOR.
YES, SIR. THANK YOU, SIR.

ALL RIGHT, THEN...

IV.

THE *ZUHR*, OR AFTERNOON CALL to prayer—which will be the first the muezzin will intone today, and is the agreed-upon signal for General Nixon to advance—this has no fixed hour in the Muslim world; but one generally listens for it after the sun has passed its zenith and the shadows on the ground represent, in their length, twice the height of the objects casting them.

Not that Corporal Buchan is in any position to gauge shadows and objects just now. He has turned from the dim palace halls into the full blinding force of the sun, and must stand for a moment blinking and knuckling his eyes and presenting, to any lingering palace guards, an irresistible target.

Happily, there are none of Mr. Buchan's enemies about, and not much stirring otherwise. The chattering of a fountain and the calls of tropical birds reach him as he inches down a short flight of stairs to a foot-path, and here something shifts beside him and darts around an urn, straightening a silver chain behind it. He squints at the paving stones that edge the path until he can make out the old Roman tracery on them; and he sees, now, that the urn has been burst by the roots of a great palm, and that it is a chained capuchin monkey rounding the urn to screech oaths at him. He seems to have wandered onto a terrace garden or promenade, and this impression is confirmed when he draws up to a picturesquely broken arch and takes in the garden's full sweep.

To his right, inside the arch, sits a stepped court, bound on three sides by the porticoed palace walls. A flagstaff projects from a verandah a few stories up, and a pair of hands are busy here withdrawing the palace arms into darkness. To the left of the arch, as Buchan stands, the court opens out into a lawn of wildflowers and wiry grass. Iron rails, overgrown from disuse but marked out by the sun, part the lawn in long white arcs and converge at none other than the *Akh-Siru*, that storied cannon of the Sharif's, which is crouching at the terrace's outer rim like a guardian afreet of the ancient world.

Buchan crosses the lawn, stepping over the heated cannon-rails. He lifts his eyes to the magnificent old weapon and to the view beyond it of the palace's western approach. And what with the murmur of the fountains, the fife-notes of birdsong and the yawning of animals in their niches, with the ferns and palms rising among the ruins and flowered vines spilling from the balconies above, it's as though some Romantic landscape has sprung into being around him, with this ancient cannon as its crowning glory.... Or it might be so, but for Buchan's sense that something here is deeply amiss.

You will note, for instance, that beneath the pleasing woodland sounds there is also a telltale droning of flies. On one of the gravel walks, too, there is a western cavalry boot standing alone and full of bad omen. There is a wire cage lying on its side behind an upset stone pedestal, and beside these a hamadryad cobra stares out from a cleft in a stone wall. Over the cracked lip of a fountain you will see a slippered foot dangling; and lest you miss *that*, a palace guard is lying stretched at full length by the fountain's base.

By the time Mr. Buchan sees the bodies at the fountain, the idyll has vanished. And for a panicked moment the garden seems full of nothing *but* bodies—palace guards and Ottoman regulars and a miscellany of fighting men in and out of uniform, splayed about as men will be who have met death of a sudden and drastic character.

Buchan sees that the stonework around them has not fallen in any slow and picturesque way into ruin, but has been cracked and gouged and toppled by the same guns that took the garrison and village below. And he senses now that Ogden himself is still here. He must have registered the old dragoon somehow—subconsciously perhaps—in his first sweep of the garden, for when he rounds on Ogden's figure now he knows just where to look.

We discover Major John Ogden of the Fifth Dragoon Guards seated on a stone bench in the shade of the garden's inner court, where he winds a soiled length of linen around a bloodied left hand. If he is aware of Corporal Buchan he gives no sign. He only dresses his hand and studies a mosaic at his feet.

For Buchan's part, though his straight approach lies between the standing halves of the arch, he obeys some instinct and draws quietly to the side, reaching to his belt-case to open the flap over his revolver. He stalks toward Ogden with a hand on the gun's grip, careful to keep a stone balustrade between them.

Mr. Buchan has spent the better part of his life running articles between India's outposts, and in this time he has met most of the Company's leading lights and a few of its more noteworthy enemies. He has dined out on his accounts of Lord Pomeroy (who looks like a drowsy Savile Row clerk until he opens his mouth) and the thirteenth Dalai Lama (who was not in the course of a long luncheon observed to blink). Indeed, Buchan considers his list of acquaintance one of the chief perquisites of his job. So while he approaches Ogden with due caution, he is also gauging him with

a connoisseur's eye, and with a view to sharing his impressions later in the barrack-room.

He sees, in particular, a man tall and broad even for a dragoon, but lithe and raw-boned like the hillmen of the Hindu Kush, with the sun-cured skin to match. Like his uniform, Ogden's cavalry whiskers are long estranged from their parade-ground cousins. There is some surprise, perhaps, in his hair being tawny and not black. But he presents a fitting picture for a man of his accomplishments, and the portrait is made complete with the Union Jack–which looks as though it has been dragged across Asia–nodding aloft in place of the castle's standard behind him.

Buchan is still collecting these impressions (and thinking how well they will play at home) when the old dragoon looks up and fixes him for a five-count. It is really only that. Ogden returns his gaze just as quickly to the mosaic, with the younger man apparently forgotten. But the look is enough to root Buchan to the spot, and he sees his pat observations have been none to the point.

Rather, he is eight years old again and at the zoological gardens at Peshawar. He has slipped free from his *amah*'s hand and is running for the elephant wallow, when he spots a male lion in his cage and slows to study it, thinking it asleep. He sees that the lion's keeper has entered the cage without securing the door behind him and is busy drawing tools from his cart; and in this same instant, he meets eyes with the lion. He realizes with a thrill of horror that there is an open path between the animal and himself, and that the lion has learned this just ahead of him.

So too these years later, he considers, in the gardens at Al-Shar. He has looked straight into a wild and murderous nature and seen, somewhere within it, the prospect of his own death. Which is one thing to consider in the abstract, I should say, and quite another to weigh in immediate relation to oneself.

And yet, just as the boy walked with a whole skin from the lion's cage and found himself fortified by the experience, so today does Mr. Buchan find room for encouragement. For this Major Ogden approves of him, at least to the extent that he has forborne to *kill* him. And if that isn't an entrée to friendship, exactly, still it must count for *something*.

MAJ–*HRM*–
–MAJOR OGDEN...? CORPORAL BUCHAN, SIR. RUNNER FOR LORD POMEROY.
HE GIVES YOU THIS, SIR.

I'LL...SET IT OVER HERE.

HOW'S YOUR ARABIC?
SORRY? DO I SPEAK IT, YOU MEAN?
...NO, SIR. THE ODD PHRASE ASIDE–
LIKE WHAT?

WELL: *EHH*, THINGS FOR TRAVEL, MOSTLY–'WHICH WAY'; 'HOW MUCH IS THAT'; ODD BIT OF THE *QUR'AN*–
GIVE HIM THAT.

YES, SIR.
...BUT, GIVE WHO, SIR...?

FOLLOWING OGDEN'S EYES, MR. BUCHAN SEES WHAT MUST BE THE SHARIF HIMSELF, CHAINED TO THE MUZZLE OF HIS OWN GREAT CANNON.

WHEN YOU REACH BOMBAY AGAIN–
OH–AS TO THAT, SIR–THE GOVERNOR-GENERAL'S SAID IF I CAN BE OF ANY USE HERE, HE'D GAZETTE ME WITH YOUR MEN.
–NOT THAT–HE MAYN'T HAVE SAID IT OUTRIGHT, NOW THAT I THINK OF IT–BUT I'M QUITE SURE THAT WAS OUR UNDERSTANDING...

...SORRY. GO ON.
WHEN YOU REACH BOMBAY, TELL THEM WE COULDN'T GET AN ANSWER OUT OF THIS MAN.

YES, SIR. COULDN'T GET AN ANSWER TO WHAT, SIR?
...I SEE. VERY GOOD.

THE REASON I WAS SENT, ALL OF THIS ASIDE...
...WAS TO ASK THAT MAN A QUESTION. SOMETHING ONLY HE'D KNOW.

TO IMPRESS HIM WITH THE IMPORTANCE OF ANSWERING, WE LOADED HIS CANNON AND PRIMED IT, AND PUT HIM WHERE A MISS WAS IMPROBABLE.

I TOLD HIM WHEN THEY SOUNDED THE CALL TO PRAYER I'D ASK HIM MY QUESTION. HE COULD ANSWER, OR HE'D SPEAK HIS NEXT AT ALLAH'S TABLE. AND I SAT DOWN TO WAIT.

THE REST WAS A FREAK OF CHANCE.

<<CRRACK!>>
<<FTOO!>>

<<CRRACK!>>
<<CRRACK!>>
<<CRRACK!>>
<<CRRACK!>>

SOMEHOW THAT ASSASSIN'S DART FOUND THE OLD RISALDAR SEATED BESIDE ME. THIS WAS A MAN WHO'D FOUGHT WITH MY UNCLE.
WATER, SAHIB. I FLUSH IT OUT.

ONLY *USHAR* POISON, I THINK. NOTHING VERY SERIOUS.
I SHALL HAVE TO LIE UP.

YOU, SAHIB, CAN ENJOY CARRYING ME–

WE'D HIT THE FORT WITH ARTILLERY THROUGH THE NIGHT. THE OLD STONEWORK WAS STILL FALLING.

...WELL. VERY SORRY, SIR. FOR THE LOSS.
EHH—BUT THERE'S TIME YET. I'LL UNGAG THE SHARIF, IF YOU'D LIKE TO TRY HIM WITH YOUR QUESTION.

...HE SEEMS RATHER KEEN TO HEAR IT–
THIS WAS MY TRANSLATOR.
...OH.

IT APPEARS OGDEN AND THE SHARIF HAVE PASSED THE DAY AT A STALEMATE, WITH NO WAY TO COMMUNICATE BETWEEN THEM.
♪...*ALLAHU AKBAR. ASH-HADU*...♪

THOUGH AFTER THE DEATH OF HIS FRIEND, OGDEN DOES NOT SEEM VERY MUCH CONCERNED WITH THE SHARIF OR HIS SECRETS.
AND THAT'S THE...I TAKE IT THAT'S THE CALL TO PRAYER?
YES. YOU CAN GIVE HIM THAT BIT OF THE *QUR'AN* NOW.

MEANWHILE, GENERAL NIXON'S EXPEDITIONARY FORCE SITS POISED OUTSIDE THE VILLAGE.
YOU SEE THIS, SIR JOHN? SOMEONE'S GOT OUR COLORS UP OVER THE FORT.

♪...AN LA ILAHA ILL-ALLAH...♪
MAYBE YOUR YOUNG CORPORAL'S DONE IT, SIR.
MM. ABOUT TO SUGGEST THE ENEMY'D DONE IT, BY WAY OF A TRAP.
THE MUEZZIN'S SONG, AS YOU WILL RECALL, IS THEIR SIGNAL TO ADVANCE.

NO, QUITE RIGHT. CAN'T PUT THAT PAST THEM, CAN YOU?
WHAT'S THE ORDER, THEN, SIR?
WELL.

...FORWARD, I S'POSE.

ON THE TERRACE, OGDEN SHAKES A JOURNAL AND A HAND-WRITTEN NOTE FROM HIS CANISTER.
'...NARF ALTLIQNAT MIN RAWAH.'
THERE. DON'T EVEN KNOW WHAT IT MEANS, REALLY.

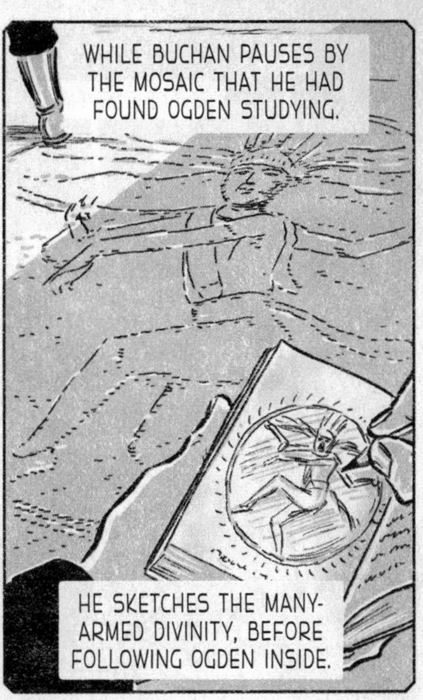
WHILE BUCHAN PAUSES BY THE MOSAIC THAT HE HAD FOUND OGDEN STUDYING.
HE SKETCHES THE MANY-ARMED DIVINITY, BEFORE FOLLOWING OGDEN INSIDE.

OOFH!

YOU.
–WHA'D THE GYP SAY?
THE SHARIF? NOTHING. MAJOR'S TRANSLATOR DIED.
WE'LL GET 'IM A NEW ONE.
WAIT, WHY'M I TELLING YOU?

MAJOR–?
'EY–PLACE IS FULL O' WOG TRANSLATORS, IN'NIT?
WE'RE DESERTING.
OGDEN SHARES THE CANISTER'S CONTENTS WITH SUBADAR PRIDDISH, HIS SIKH ADVISOR.

DESERTING?
NOT YOU.

WHAT, 'CAUSE O' YER NOTE, HERE? WHAT'S IT SAY?
AWW COME ON!

FIND A GIRL OF THE HOUSEHOLD. LET HER CARRY THAT TO THE SHARIF.
GOOD, SAHIB. AND NO MORE INSTRUCTION FOR HER?
SHE'LL UNDERSTAND WHEN SHE SEES HIM.

HE OUGHT TO BE JUDGED BY SOMEONE WHO KNOWS WHAT HE IS. I ONLY KNOW HE HASN'T EARNED A MARTYR'S DEATH.
FIND US IN THAT BANQUET HALL WHEN YOU'RE DONE.
AND MAKE CERTAIN IT'S A GIRL.
YES, SAHIB.

HELP ME, D–MN YOU.
BUT–THAT'S NOT FOR US.
P–SS OFF, THEN.
MR. RENTON IS ABLE TO STAMP OUT THE NOTE BEFORE IT IS WHOLLY CONSUMED.

WOT'S IT SAY, NOW?
GO ON, YOU CAN READ...

THERE'S SOMETHING ABOUT '...THROUGH THE ICE, AND HE'S SEEN A THING BENEATH IT...'
...WELL?
MR. BUCHAN'S CURIOSITY GETS THE BETTER OF HIS JUDGMENT.

...THEN IT JUST SAYS, '–BEEN UNABLE TO DESCRIBE, SAVE TO SAY HE'S MADE THE DISCOVERY OF THE AGE, AND THIS WITH A MOST UNWHOLESOME...' SOMETHING.
...HUH.
GO AHEAD.

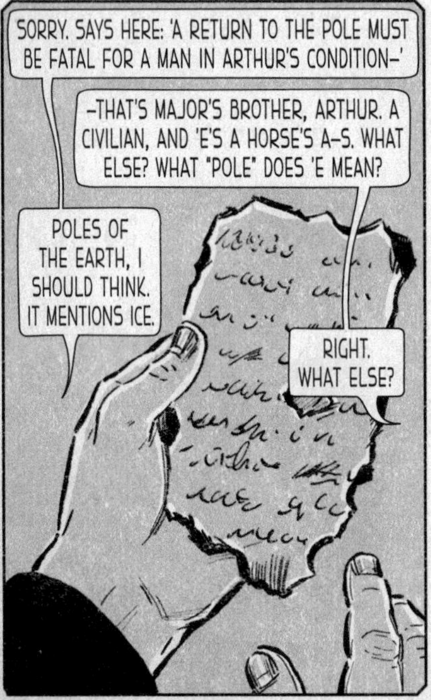
SORRY. SAYS HERE: 'A RETURN TO THE POLE MUST BE FATAL FOR A MAN IN ARTHUR'S CONDITION–'
–THAT'S MAJOR'S BROTHER, ARTHUR. A CIVILIAN, AND 'E'S A HORSE'S A–S. WHAT ELSE? WHAT "POLE" DOES 'E MEAN?
POLES OF THE EARTH, I SHOULD THINK. IT MENTIONS ICE.
RIGHT. WHAT ELSE?

IT'S PRETTY WELL LOST, THE REST OF IT. ENDS WITH SOMETHING ABOUT '...MY LOVE TO YOU, WITH THIS PLEA THAT I DARE NOT CALL A HOPE.' SIGNED 'FRANCES,' WITH NO SURNAME.

Hurrying back through the castle, Mr. Renton finds the banquet hall again and slips inside, throwing the doors to behind him with a glare of warning for Mr. Buchan. The instruments in the hall wheeze out a last, prolonged note of almost perfect dissonance, and the musicians and captive soldiers are run out and introduced not to the firing-squad but to the empty hall and to Mr. Buchan. It seems the dragoons would have a bit of quiet, inside.

Buchan smiles and *hullo*s and pulls these dazed creatures past him, rather like an orderly at Broadmoor letting the inmates out for air. He is a moment in finding the door again, but when he has got it and put an ear to it, he can hear the voice of Ogden raised in a gruff address:

He has just received (has Ogden) a communication from his sister, one Frances Ogden, whose name these dragoons will recall from the Punjab. (Here a voice asks, in a feeling tone, whether Miss Ogden were quite well. Ogden coughs and says he expects she is doing well enough, thank you; and we guess that her time in the Punjab fell something

short of a country ball.) At any rate, this good lady has enlisted Ogden's *help*, and not for herself but for their older brother Arthur, a man who will also be known to the dragoons, at least by reputation (with signs that Arthur's reputation does not do him, or Ogdens anywhere, overmuch credit).

Now, just what Arthur or Miss Ogden desires their younger brother to *do* is not yet clear, other than that he should gather what men he can and make for a certain port in Syria, where a ship and further instruction await him. It seems in Syria he will be set a *task*, and one of no little complexity, involving no little risk. Arthur's very *life*, he is told, may turn on his success in this venture. But more to the point, it is Frances's wish that he go, and so he means to, without delay.

(Here, rather in contrast to what he has just said, Ogden takes a few thoughtful turns up and down the stone floor and comes again to rest.)

This is undeniably (he resumes) a personal matter, and one of which he has only the dimmest outlines. He would sooner travel with men around him, if only to guard against the hazards of the road in wartime. But beyond their salaries and the benefits in spoils and blood that tend to accrue to men in his company, he expects no great material advantage will come out of Frances's 'task.' Certainly he assigns no weight to his brother's claims of discovery in the North, nor to this *secret knowledge* Arthur is represented as holding and waiting to share. The men who follow him from Al-Shar will do so in an expression of friendship, quite as simply as that. Not but he sees every man here as his friend; it is only that, from those who come with him now, he must draw upon what credit he has built in this regard.

And there is one thing more (of which Ogden, quieting a cry from these ready-enough dragoons, goes on to speak): he is under orders to return directly from Al-Shar to India. Any action of his west of the Tigris, after today, will represent rather a clear case of *desertion.* And this will be used–if not by Lord Pomeroy, then certainly by his rivals–as grounds for Ogden's long-delayed hanging. Just as any man found in his company would hang, and their friends in Bombay would only sleep the better for it.

...Now, I should think this warning put the matter in an appropriately serious light; yet it seems to go over as a rare sort of *joke*, with much guffawing and stamping from the dragoons and a crashing of the remaining plate. In an hour's time, says Ogden, he and Mr. Priddish will be found saddled by the postern gates. The dragoons are welcome to join them or to fall in with General Nixon's command. But he has ill-trained them indeed if, after an hour, he should see a thing of value left in this castle that can be carried, dragged or thrown from it by horse or man.

I don't know that this is the end of his speech, either. But we will hardly hear more of it, after such a challenge as this.

HIS RELIEF, ON SEEING HER, IS SHORT-LIVED.

♪...ALLAHU AKBAR. LA ILAHA ILL-ALLAH...♪
«FSSSSSS!»
IN HER GAZE ARE GRIEVANCES OUT OF COUNTING, MOST OF THEM UNPRINTABLE, I SHOULD THINK.

«FWOOOM»
THE SHARIF IS LAST SEEN AS A DARK FEATHER OF BLOOD OVER THE VILLAGE SQUARE.

THE BALL BOUNCES THROUGH THE COMPANY VANGUARD

GOOD G–D.
AND ROLLS TO A STOP AT THE GENERALS' FEET.

WELL...?
SIR?
GENERAL NIXON WONDERS IF THIS WERE FIRED IN WARNING, IN SALUTE, OR AS SOME UNSEASONABLE JOKE.

HAVE WE TAKEN THE TOWN OR NOT?

AND WITH NIXON STALLED IN THE OUTSKIRTS, THE LOOTING OF THE CASTLE GOES ON APACE.
...YOU'RE OFF, THEN. JUST LIKE THAT? AND NO IDEA WHERE TO?
HUMPIN' 'IS INTO YON WAGON, IS WHERE. THEN WE MAKE FOR SYRIA.
BUT, BEYOND THAT–

–BEYOND 'AT, MAJOR AIN'T SAID. WE'LL FOL-LOW 'IM, AND PRESENTLY KNOW WHERE TO.
I SEEN MAJOR'S LOOK TODAY, SON. WHATEVER'S COMING, IT'S NO ADVENTURE. NOT LIKE YOU THINK.

BUT–HIS BROTHER'S MADE SOME DISCOVERY, YOU KNOW–
ARTHUR OGDEN? DON'T YOU BELIEVE IT.

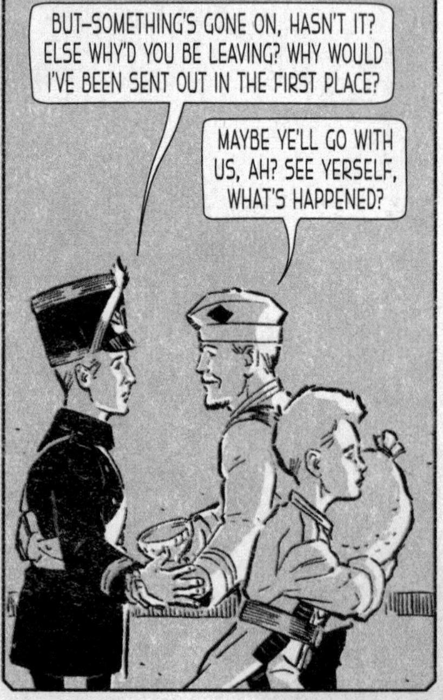
BUT–SOMETHING'S GONE ON, HASN'T IT? ELSE WHY'D YOU BE LEAVING? WHY WOULD I'VE BEEN SENT OUT IN THE FIRST PLACE?
MAYBE YE'LL GO WITH US, AH? SEE YERSELF, WHAT'S HAPPENED?

...OR MAYBE NOT, NOW YOU THOUGHT ABOUT IT.
WELL, I–

–HOW OLD ARE YEH, SON? LOOK AT ME.
ME? TWENTY-THREE, SIR.
AYE, YOU AN' YER GRANNY'S MUKLUKS IS TWENTY-THREE.
NINETEEN, THEN.

WELL: YOU AIN'T INVITED. WHAT HAVE YOU TO SAY TO THAT?
HOLD THE CASTLE TILL YER FRIENDS GET HERE, 'SWHAT YE'LL DO.

SEE WHAT THIS IS, SAHIB. IT IS A KINDNESS TO YOU.
BUT YE'LL REMEMBER US TO THE LORD POMEROY, WON'T YA?
GIMME THAT.

SAT SRI AKAL, CORPORAL.
PEACE GRANT YOU PEACE, THAT YOU MAY MULTIPLY IT.
GO ON, YOU.

WE RECOGNIZE THE BOOK
IN OGDEN'S HANDS AS HIS
BROTHER'S EXPEDITION LOG.

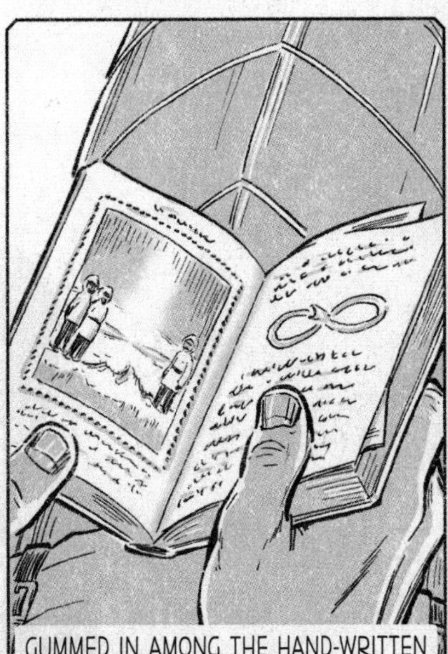
GUMMED IN AMONG THE HAND-WRITTEN
PAGES ARE A PORTRAIT OF ARTHUR
OGDEN WITH HIS MEN AT THE POLE...

...AND AN ENGRAVING OF A MYTHICAL
CITY IDENTIFIED AS 'SHAMBHALA.'

EPILOGUE

Bids Farewell to

MESSRS. NIXON & TOWNSHEND

and to

RECORDED HISTORY, GENERALLY

• • •

HISTORY MAKES LITTLE MENTION of Al-Shar in connexion with the war. Where the town is named at all, it is listed among those river settlements where General Nixon stopped to rest and to resupply on his way to Baghdad. There seems to have been no resistance offered here to the Company's march, and only a few shots fired in the village outskirts (this according to a surprisingly thorough regimental archive, which has Major-General Townshend shooting an insulator from a telegraph pole, to impress Ottoman deserters).

Now, you and I, gentle reader, have just been through Al-Shar ourselves, and we've seen the

place fairly picked apart by Company bullets. We know whose handiwork this is, just as we know whom Sir John may thank if he finds himself opposed by no more than telegraph poles as he passes through. We can look from the garrison even now, and see the dust settling behind John Ogden and his Fifth Dragoon Guards as they ride west for the Syrian coast. Yet for all this, dear reader, I can tell you the Historical Record is markedly silent on the subject of Ogden and his dragoons and their exploits at Al-Shar. Their visit is not recorded in any modern journal or war memoir, not in any staff report, newspaper dispatch or sentry log of the day–Not *anywhere*, so far I know, outside of these pages. Likewise Mr. Buchan, whom we see pacing the citadel in the grips of a dilemma, though the Company rolls list him, at this hour, as dead of nephritis in the Sudan.

History has its uses, I cannot doubt, and I will not debate them here. I would only suggest these uses have their limits. I might even argue–as it has been my experience–that in order to get at the truth in any one matter, one must look *past* the written lines of History, to the blank spaces

in between. Certainly this is where we'll find continuing record of John Ogden and his men. It is where, very soon, we'll run across the orphan Barnes and Mr. Sloane, and the vanished actress Evelyn Harrow and the black-robed men of the Novitiate. It is where, beneath the polar ice and in the Mongolian deserts, on the wastes of Tierra del Fuego and on the summits of Nepal, we will discover the secrets of a hidden City and the true origins of the Great War. And it is where, when we're quite ready, we will penetrate the deeper mysteries of the Explorers Guild and the Three Jackals.

But I get ahead of myself. Let us say, for now, that there are two ways out of Al-Shar, and that like Corporal Buchan we stand at a crossroads.

That way go generals Nixon and Townshend, north to Baghdad. With them go an army of correspondents and biographers, diarists and photographers and chroniclers of all stripes, leaving a path well-marked behind them through library and university, war office and royal archive and so forth. *That* way, in other words, goes the March of History.

There is a second way out of Al-Shar, of course…

...But this road is for you, gentle reader, to discover.

END *of* BOOK ONE

IN BOOK TWO:

ARTHUR OGDEN *deals Uncharitably with the* INUIT;

EVELYN HARROW *receives Instruction from the* DECEASED;

MR. SLOANE *enlists the* ORPHAN BARNES *in a* PREPOSTEROUS ENTERPRISE.

. . .

— Also —

THE POLAR ICE FIELDS;
TIERRA *del* FUEGO;
ROMANIAN CASTLES.

MYSTERY *and* DISCOVERY
on a Widening Scale.

REVELATIONS *to do with This and That.*

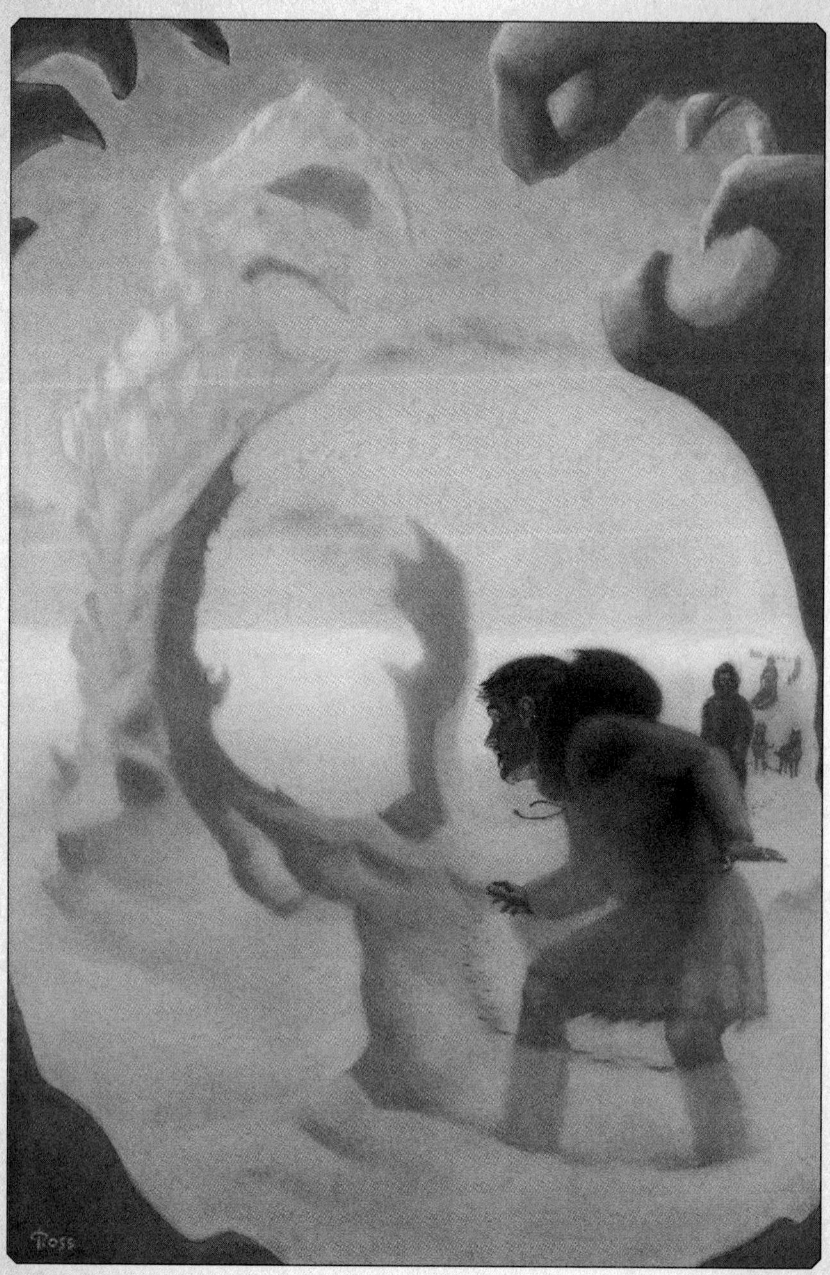

'I AM SO FREQUENTLY FLINCHING AND TURNING IN NERVOUS TERROR FROM THE COMMONPLACE OBJECTS OF THE ROAD THAT I MUST WONDER IF, AFTER ALL, I AM NOT ALREADY SEEING THIS DEVIL.'

BOOK TWO
- of Five -

I.

32º 10' 47" N Lat | 46º 03' 03" E Long

Al-Shar Citadel, Mesopotamia

August, 1917

) Aug 1917

o the Finder of this Note—& I think you will be that
sh Staff Sgt whose bullets followed me out of Musallam
is morning: I leave record to-day of my decampment
rom Al-Shar with intent to follow after the 5th Dragoon
uards, & I should not be awaited in Bombay as I may
s well tell you now.

Whether it is some influence of the Near-East air, or
the mysterious nature of my Charge; whether it is the
example of the 5th Dragoons (who live independent of
our Race, let alone the Company) or their Maj Ogden
(beyond all comparison the Wildest Character & the
Soundest I have met, and mind you I've sat down with
Kings and Dacoits and High Lamas)—And whether
or not they will have me (as is not at all clear)—I am
resolved to see for myself what lies ahead of these
men—To what Thing, that is, the Despatch I have
brought them is the Avenue.

You will call this Folly & worse and I cannot disagree.
I trade a good Commission for hardships unknown, for
Dishonour & Death perhaps beyond the tracing of men &
without the sympathy of friends; & I bear you no ill will,
who must serve out the Justice of King and Company
in my case, even if (as I hope) you would wish me luck
as between men. But I do not stand as I write at some
threshold striving with Conscience—I am past any threshold
and clear of mind, & could no more ride for Bombay
to-day than fly there, being under the influence of the
Intensest Curiosity and already Late for these new
appointments of Providence.

With my Apologies, therefore, & awaiting your Judgme
n Good Faith, I remain

James Mountstuart Buchan
Cpt, 3rd Bombay Light Cavalry
Ceylon Co., Ltd

THERE IT IS, THEN. BOY'S GONE FOR THE CIRCUS.
AND FOR WHAT, SIR?
WULL. YOU KNOW ALL I DO ABOUT IT, PRIVATE.

IT MAY BE JOHN OGDEN'S REALLY BEEN HERE, AND THE BOY FOUND HIM. RATHER MADE A CAREER OUT OF INSPIRING THESE YOUNG MEN TO ACTS OF LUNACY, HAS OGDEN. S'POSE HE'S GOT ANOTHER ACOLYTE, NOW, IN HIS SERVICE.
AYE, THOUGH—SOUNDS AS THOUGH OGDEN WERE DRAWN ON BY SOMETHING HIMSELF, SIR.
LAD SEEMS JUST AS KEEN TO FOLLOW OGDEN AS HE IS TO KNOW WHAT THE MAN'S AFTER.

YES, THIS 'THING,' HE MENTIONS, WITHOUT SAYING WHAT IT IS.
I DO WONDER...
AH, BUT YOU SHOULDN'T WONDER, MR. GLEASON. IT'S NO GOOD FOR MEN IN OUR LINE. YE'LL SEE THIS BUCHAN HANGED FOR WONDERING.
AYE. THAT MAY BE.

ANYWAY HE'S SEEN SOME CHANCE OPEN UP, AND HE'S GONE AFTER IT. THERE'S SOMETHING IN THAT, AIN'T THERE?
THOUGH I MIGHT NOT HAVE CONFESSED TO WHAT I WAS DOING, IN WRITING.
OH, WE WERE ALL HIS AGE ONCE— SOME NOT SO FAR PAST IT. YOU GET RATHER CAUGHT UP IN THESE THINGS, WHAT? FEEL YOU MUST LAY YER CASE BEFORE THE WORLD. MUCH AS HE MAY LIVE TO REGRET DOING IT, THIS BOY.

BUT HE DOESN'T MAKE A CASE TO THE WORLD. HE PUTS THIS IN YOUR HANDS, SERGEANT.
THROWS HIMSELF ON YOUR MERCY, I SHOULD SAY.
SO HE DOES, AYE. AND–WHAT?– SHOULD WE GO ARGUE FOR THIS BOY IN BOMBAY, DO YOU THINK?
PERHAPS WE FORGET HIS NOTE, AND REPORT THIS JACKANAPES DEAD?
WELL. IF WE DID, SIR, IT'D ONLY BE WE MEN WHO KNEW HE WASN'T.

HOW'S THAT, PRIVATE? DO YOU SUGGEST WE PARTICIPATE IN THIS BOY'S CRIMES, WHO'S STOLE A GENERAL'S HORSE AT MUSALLAM, AND NOW DESERTED LORD POMEROY'S ARMY?
ARE YOU SO WROUGHT-UP BY HIS EXAMPLE THAT YE'D CLIMB THE SCAFFOLD WITH HIM? I'M SURE THEY'D MAKE ROOM FOR ALL OF YOU.
EHH–NO INDEED, SIR.
NO? GOOD. I THOUGHT THIS NOTE MIGHT'A SCRAMBLED YER WITS, MAN.

NOW: FALL IN THROUGH THESE GATES, AND WE'LL HEAR NO MORE OF BUCHANS AND THESE BL–DY NOTES.
YES, SIR.

...YOU BE GONE, TOO, BOY. AND HIDE YOU WELL.

I.
♪...SEE, THE BOYS IN BLUE ARE MARCHING / AND I CAN NO LONGER STAY / HARK, I HEAR THE BUGLE CALLING / GOOD-BYE DOLLY GRAY...♪

♪...WITH HIS FACE TOWARD THE FOE / AS HE DIED HE MURMURED LOW...♪

♪...'I MUST SAY GOOD-BYE AND GO, DOLLY GRA-A-Y'...♪

{The Expedition Log of Arthur Ogden, excerpted below – E.W.B.}

. . .

18 OCTOBER, 1912.

We are not Explorers, and so I tell you plainly. Just what we *are*, and what we've got up to, it will be the purpose of this little history to set forward.

I can tell you straight out that we are the victims of an ill-judged boast on my part, made in a spasm of jealousy and wrath and of all things *patriotism*; which boast has flung us far from the pleasures of Society and put us on terms of intimacy with Death, as I say without exaggeration. But just as I have got us here, so will I plot our way out. I will restore us to civilization and reveal our struggles in a heroic light to the multitudes and, you may be assured, I will do all I can to end this chronicle on a bright note of *revenge*. But of all this you must hear presently.

For now, if I were to characterize the group of us—the half-dozen, that is, at the core of this expedition—I should say we are leisured bachelors, heirs most of us, bounders and *flâneurs* and dilettantes and motoring enthusiasts and you probably get the picture. What brought us to the Explorers Guild in the first place none of us properly recalls, except that it was one of those impulses that sweep now and then through our set, like a brush-fire through the dry, empty, neighboring fields that are our idle minds. I needn't say that of the explorer's qualifications—those freaks of constitution or intellect, or reserves of daring, or belief in oneself as a figure of destiny or what-have-you—I say, of these magnificent qualities we are quite unapologetically free. What progress we have made through the world we have done on moral axes rather than geographical ones (though we have covered a good bit of the globe withal), and we have stuck our flags in any number of spots where your gentleman explorer would tremble to set foot. But for all that, I suppose, to the conventional view we represent just six men of middling wit and enterprise, and we succeeded to the Guild in the way we gain most things in this life, viz., by buying our way in and supporting one another's lies.

After myself there is Malthrop, a boyhood friend with whom I have matured, as you would say, a good deal less than I've aged. I tout this man as one of my rowing eight at college, though we differ as to where we were supposed to have matriculated and, as to rowing, neither of us ever made the Boat and we both dislike the sport intensely.

Malthrop got a brother-in-law called Apsley out of a bad marriage of his sister's, and the three of us convened ages ago on the turf at Belmont. Apsley is a solid enough sort, with an inheritance in iron or steel and a useful propensity to forget what he's done while in drink—Useful lately to *myself* I should say, as I have convinced Apsley this infamous boast was *his*, and I have, accordingly, shifted much of the blame for the expedition onto him. This provides a great bit of sport to Malthrop (who is in on the joke and chaffs his brother-in-law relentlessly), just as it is an excellent relief to me.

The rest of our group we have picked up at various stops in the demimonde, and their names are not ones you will need to commit to memory unless they distinguish themselves in these pages, which event I deem unlikely. For the record, they are Thierry, a French Belgian who styles himself the naturalist of the group and has affected a few books to this purpose; and Numm-Smythe, a disinherited lord pressed into service by my forgiving him a debt. There is Gaddis, too, who'd already installed himself at the Guild by the time of our arrival, and God knows how for he has ventured no deeper into this world than Dark Harbor, Maine. But he'd won himself the post of 'Strappado' or Master of the Grog at our own New York lodge, and was welcomed into our number for that obvious reason.

Dickson, the photographer, has a *profession* and is therefore eyed by the rest of us with suspicion, and it helps very little that he is young and appears to have religion as well. I am told he is a first-rate portraitist, and certainly he takes the job with a god-awful seriousness. But we are careful not to discuss our plans or much of anything in front of him, for we must account for the possibility of *scruples* on the young man's part.

Rounding out the group, and strangely enough, there is this man Mr. Vitti (or Fidis), an Italian I believe, who might equally be Greek or Levantine, and whom we all supposed to be someone else's man till we held conference on the subject and discovered he had really come with none of us. We seem to have gained him on our way north, then, and far from showing any inclination to leave, he has sworn himself to our quest with his wild-sounding foreign oaths. I feel he must be a desperate character indeed to have attached himself to us in this way, and, knowing the Mediterranean temperament, whereby your boon companion of one minute is lodging a dagger in your ribs in the next, I have bunked Mr. Vidis in with Dickson, and I will avoid the pair as best I can till they can be made useful or gotten rid of.

There is one other man who does not feature in this expedition, as such, and whom I do not anticipate your meeting in this history, unless it is perhaps once at the very end. Yet there would be no expedition at all but for him, and I feel that a line or two on my Cousin Cyril, the British ambassador, are therefore in order.

On Cyril

. . .

My father was a British subject who enlarged his fortunes and his family together in the Hudson River Valley, where he has likewise committed his bones to the earth (though not his heart, which you may seek out at the family seat in Cheltenham, if that is the sort of thing you would do). Of the many blessings Arthur Ogden *pater** heaped upon his children, our dual citizenship was the one of which I never willingly availed myself. Sister Frances, like her mother, thought it best to flit between coasts and to preserve her British airs; while brother John installed himself in the northern wilds of Scotland and acted very much the Britisher, so he could enroll at Sandhurst and kill as many critics of the Commonwealth as his time on earth might permit.

But I myself, as I say, never saw much good in the place, and my opinion of it did not improve very much as I was dragged through the country manors and seaside resorts of Gloucestershire and Anglesey in the summers of my youth. Still, it was these movements that brought me into collision with one Cyril Aiken, a cousin on my mother's side. And I must make some sketch of this person if you would understand what follows.

Mostly you will have to appreciate what a deeply *irksome* man this is. You must understand what it is like to argue a point with Cyril when he holds the high ground–and I should say, this is the form *all* social intercourse with him takes, whether you are informed on your subject or not, or whether you are even arguing in the first place. I have known him to trump me in argument with just an exchange of *looks*, for that matter, before we had let out a word between us.

There is in this man, you see, that developed sense of confidence or preeminence, that mien of immovable self-satisfaction so particular to the British, and which is never on fuller display, I believe, than when they are set before their American cousins. That sense of cultural superiority we find so galling–and not least of all because we suspect it is in some way warranted–I say, in Cyril you will find its living, smirking embodiment. That singsong condescension is his established mode of speaking; that supercilious gaze and raked eyebrow are writ permanently on his face. You may hurl whatever you like at him–verbally, physically, I have tried it all–and you will not discompose him in the least. Whether he be pitched in argument or telling a joke, whether eating a chop or thrashing a maid or being boiled in a pot by Polynesians–you will see

. . . .

* *My father was the third of this name, as I am the fourth.*

that same bemused look about him, of a cultured man indulging the harangue of a six-year-old boy.

Here—says this look—here is a man living in consciousness of his many advantages; yet indulge me for a moment and we'll examine Cousin Cyril on the point of these *advantages*. I can tell you he is no gentleman, for starters, not in his manner (which is entirely too contentious) nor by birth (all the titles descend on my father's side, and Cyril's mother was a stage actress). You would not call him a *handsome* man, either, not in the meaning commonly applied to that word. I should say he is greatly—outrageously—vain of his *feet*—and they are the feet of a Chinese maiden, to do strict justice to Cyril—But these aside, with his waxy Celtic skin, his bulging eyes and rubbery lips, he strikes one as something that has graduated from the water to land, like a supremely self-assured variety of deep-sea fluke. I have always had the advantage of looks over Cyril, and shall, until we all start walking on our hands. I have more money, too, though I hardly boast of it; and I have always kept the wider circle of friends. You may with good reason, therefore, write down some of his pleasure in baiting me to a consciousness of his *disadvantages*, at least with regard to myself. And you might even think I would allow him a bit of his chaffing, given the way things stand between us. To this I say, just you let my Cousin Cyril make an afternoon's sport out of *you*, and see how well you like it.

Certainly my better nature was not uppermost the last time Cyril and I parted company as young men. I had been to see him at his school, you see, and caught him among his fellows in some debating or dramatic society or another, and he had come at me straightaway. I cannot recall now the subject of our *tête-à-tête*, but I know when my arguments failed me I let drive at Cyril's ear with a fist; and being the only American present and six years Cyril's junior, I made out no better in this than in our contest of wits. I came to some time later and, seeing no further advantage in staying among these scholars, I marched off without my hat or stick. I did not stop, either, till I'd met the Cunard ticketer and told him I had done with his rubbish country once and forever. (And it is an oath on which I have so far made good. Decidedly I will never visit the Downing school again unless it is at the head of an army.)

At any rate, I did not reach New York Harbor with my passions very much cooled, but a boy can only rant and seethe for so long before they lock him up. The years would eventually do their healing work, and the ocean would continue to hold Cyril and me separate. As the millennium approached I was able to hear mention of him without, say, snapping the stem of my wineglass in my fingers.

And the first news out of England was heartening enough. After university, Cyril had stood once and then several more times for his borough, getting no closer to Parliament than Fawkes did, though he hopped from party to party without scruple and left a pile of money at the hustings. By the time he chucked politics and took up in the diplomatic service he was no longer a young man, though he must start at the very bottom anyway, in one of those desperate-sounding outposts of the third world. I was rejoiced at this, of course, and wished all the plagues of Africa on him, though only, by this time, in a passing way. I don't think I preferred him *dead*, but I was prepared to leave him in his Congolese bog, lording it over those poor natives as he might.

It was not until he surfaced at the consulate of some country I'd actually *heard* of, and the event made the *Times* (by which I mean the paper of New York), that I began watching Cyril's movements with renewed concern. You will think it is only hindsight when you've read more, but I was seized by an idea that he was working his way toward *me*. And not in any figurative sense: if you quite literally traced a line across the globe from one of Cyril's appointments to the next, you would see that line tending ever closer to New York (and I would know this, having *done* it at the time). When I read he'd got Bermuda, I threw down the paper with an oath. He was just six hundred miles now from the American coast, waggling a slippered foot at some magistrate in short-pants. And he must go farther, as I now felt certain. Indeed, it was scarcely a year after Bermuda when that fool of an Asquith let the American ambassadorship fall to him. I could have fainted dead away with the letter in my hand.

Picture for a moment the Lord Chelmsford, the one who'd such trouble in Africa as a young man. Imagine he is shooting billiards in his West End home on some quiet evening in his retirement, when he hears a rap at the door. He sets down his stick and drink and crosses the hall, mindful not to wake the old wife, and then opens his door to the entire hooting Zulu nation. They have come like avenging Fates through the decades to stand assembled at his place of sanctuary, ready to finish their appointed work. Well: the news of Cyril's appointment struck me in just the same fashion.

I would have to fly the country, there was no other way about it. I wondered when exactly he would come, and packed a few cases against a surprise visit. I sounded Malthrop and the others out on sojourning abroad–Monaco and the Riviera; my Aunt Tally's in Fiesole; anywhere else they might propose.... I fear I greatly amused them at the time, running from one to the next in such a state. Yet in no case would they consent to leave the City with me. We'd all just come back from our summer rambles, they said, and to leave Manhattan with the weather just getting fine and the social season begun–I could rule it right out. And what *really* had I to fear from my cousin anyway? Weren't our positions neatly reversed, and wasn't it *Cyril* now, alone and friendless and on foreign ground, who ought to be treading carefully round *me*? This, they begged to remind me, was no more of your Cambridge Nimblewits Society; this was no country salon for young lords and wags: *this* was New York City and it was *America*, you see, and we had long since chased out all the clever people. Here you flaunted your titles and your foreign airs at your own peril. Here you could only *badinage* your way so far. Here that fellow you crossed up with your fine speech awaited you later in the street with his horse-whip. And here, ultimately, standing on my chair at some dinner club or gambling hell or brothel, I don't recall which–and it might have been all three–here I vowed in high-flown speech to join arms with my brothers and call upon my own manly resources and make a defense of my home. And if this turned out not to be practical (as I may have reasoned privately), it was a big enough country that I should be able to avoid one man without too much bother.

There followed on this declaration a war of correspondence, conducted on those terms, at least, from my end. Cyril wrote (as though I'd asked) to apprise me of his movements through London and across the Atlantic, then all about the Capital and into his new lodgings in Delaware. Soon enough he was making his sallies into New York, and wouldn't I join him with this or that illustrious person (whose name I would have to look up in *Debrett's*), at such-and-such a club (whose names, to my horror, were not all familiar to me either). His notes were all perfectly blameless, but how I must labor over my replies! I would present myself, you see, as engaged in some task or another that ruled out our meeting absolutely; yet I would convey my regrets in such terms as to say I didn't really regret the circumstance at all. I would praise him for a man of affairs and deprecate my own dawdling life, but only by way of classing him with all those sweating, striving professionals and myself with their betters. And I would look heartily ahead to our next meeting, while giving him to understand that there would be men to see about paintings and horses and the new motors from Italy, and these things must naturally rule out any such meeting.

Whether Cyril felt snubbed or slighted in the least, of course, he left me to guess. His letters had all the same breezy civility no matter how I exerted myself. And what more could I expect? The phrase does not exist in English that will move Cyril from that feline complaisance of his, much less drive him out of one's country. I was forced to admit this, just as I knew, and perhaps had known from the beginning, that I would get no real satisfaction from letters.

I must arrange to meet him and cut him in person, you see. That was the thing. I must be there to see the blows land, and if it were at all practical my friends must see it, too. There was always the chance—what you might call the strong *probability*—of this all going horribly wrong; but I was convinced I must try *something*. The letters were having no effect, and Cyril's visits to the city would bring us together sooner or later. The longer I put off our meeting, the plainer it became that I was avoiding him out of fear (as he may have guessed already). I must confront this *bête noir* of mine and soon, else become a shut-in altogether. So I reasoned.

And here, happily, inspiration struck—really it struck Malthrop first, but he conveyed it quickly to me—and I will tell you what we did:

It began with another letter to Cyril, this one naming a day when he should meet me in the city (and even this invitation, as I like to think, was exquisitely rude). He would call on me at my address, where I would receive him for cordials, and we would proceed together to Chipping's, one of my clubs in mid-town. The plan was, of course, rapturously endorsed by Cyril. He would already be in the city on the date in question and was only too glad to shift the duties of state in order to renew our acquaintance (though he did confess to his ignorance of Chipping's, as well he might, for I had invented the name that day).

Well: he arrived punctual to the minute, d–mn him. I had staked a pair of footmen at windows north and south and we caught him turning onto our square, and I was able to bolt from my door at just the right moment with the air of a man running a last-minute errand. The trim little figure down the walk was Cyril and no doubt, but I must squint at him and call his name, and bellow my surprise to the city at large, then advance on him for a clout on the back and a hale handshake (though his was not a hand I would ordinarily hold in a pair of *tongs*). I saw he was affecting a little Van Dyke beard of the sort you might see at the court of Elizabeth, but that otherwise the years had made little imprint on him. He'd that sort of elfin face and figure that lend middle age a false sheen of youth, which some might call attractive but I find disingenuous and off-putting in the extreme.

He had brought a pair of gifts for me, too, which I tucked away unopened, and he mentioned having a spot of fever, which I felt was encouraging. But I was taking in none of this, you see, I was too busy talking nineteen to the dozen–Welcome to the city, what a disgraceful host I'd been and how well he looked and so forth. I said he'd caught me going to fetch a pair of gloves where I'd left them this morning–at another club of mine hard by, as it happened, and *here* was an idea: why didn't he take the air with me now, then we could have our drinks at this other club and when we were ready for Chipping's I would call for my driver and we'd leave from *there*. I took care to move him along while I put the question to him, so that it wasn't really a question at all (not that he would have refused me, the little diplomat). And before he'd quite got his feet beneath him I was bundling him into the front hall of none other than the Explorers Guild.

Now, Malthrop and his brother-in-law had been at work here since noon, gathering the old men and standing them drinks and putting it about that I'd a guest in town, a cousin from out of the country who was anxious to meet the Quality of the city and to impress them favorably. Of all the haunts in Old Manhattan, they said, I had proposed to start the fellow's education here; so you can imagine in what a genially self-important state we found the Guild membership on that night.

My hope was that in springing so many jabbering old men on Cyril at once, he must be set on his heels. He would have to contend with conversation on all sides, and they would be heaping topics upon him of which he would have a slight experience, if any. He must sink, I felt, under the sheer volume of words and the gathered mass of years, while I, being familiar with most of the old stories, could listen for his points of ignorance and pile on where we'd caught him at a loss. And I would keep him here and toast the King's health till we'd drunk and talked him into some kind of concession, using his own excellent manners against him.

These were my plans and my hopes for the evening, anyway. I will tell you what I can of the results, but I don't suppose anything is more eloquent on this point than that Cyril is still in New York laughing with those puffed-up old trouts at the Guild, while I am *here*, with Cyril's fever into the bargain (I ought not, in hindsight, to have shook his hand while pretending to have lost my gloves).

But, to resume: I brought Cyril to one of the lesser smoking rooms at the Guild and seated him with his back to the door. I was careful to put him at a draped table where he would not have the advantage of his feet, and I went from there to the hearth to rake up the fire and wait on events. Cyril no doubt thought my conduct bizarre–I would not risk a word or even look at him till we were joined and I had got a few more Dresden Sours in me. But I *did* note that he'd rescued his gifts from the coat-room, where I'd tried to check them, and that he'd got these out again on the table. Both were neatly wrapped in crepe, and I judged one to be about the size of a hat-box, while the other was most certainly a stick. I knew immediately what these were, too: they were the very hat and walking-stick I had left at his rooms at Cambridge some twenty years past. And here was Cyril, now, meeting my gaze over these items, with one of his silly French cigarettes plugged into his lips, as much as to say: here are the symbols of your failures in youth, Arthur, and they are still yours, and I do not perceive them much changed, as indeed *you* are not much changed, and this will be our understanding. Nor was I reassured to see he'd got his legs out from beneath the tablecloth and, with one knee hinged over the other, was bouncing one of those d–mned feet where half the room would be free to admire it.

Yet I was in this thing now for good or ill, for here came Malthrop and Apsley, driving the herd of dusty white heads before them, tankards and wineglasses and snifters and hollowed-out horns spilling over and a haze of all the world's tobaccos establishing itself in the cramped room. Malthrop and Apsley, to judge from their beefy and squinting faces, had not stinted themselves a bit of either leaf or grape, but that was all well. They had got us a good crop of old men, whom Cyril marked now with a seraphic smile and a gradual elevation of his brows.

The lion of our group was a grand old soak from the plains states with the lank white hair of Buffalo Bill Cody and the superb name of Dr. Bulstrode Peck. Dr. Peck was a onetime rover of the North Seas and had been dining out on his adventures there since the middle of the last century. He had the habit, too, of ending his long gusts of narrative with conjunctive phrases, so that even while he was getting his breath there was no proper place to insert one's own comments, and he could go on in this way for hours with nothing but the *ooh*s and *ahh*s of his audience to interrupt the rolling baritone of his doctorly voice. You will understand, therefore, that when I saw Dr. Peck stride in and begin studying the familiar objects of the room with the air of a man who is a little drunk and is waiting to be recognized, that I got him as quickly as I could in front of Cyril, shooing away some lesser lights and sweeping that *bl–dy* hat and stick off the table. And with this done, I considered I had got a big gun indeed trained upon my rival.

Now, Dr. Peck was known to be one of the first rescuers on hand when the excursion steamer *City of Rockland* ran aground off the Hook of Holland, and this he told Cousin Cyril (at my instigation) by way of getting to his greater point about a giant deep-sea squid that capsized his own boat near Zeeland in the summer of that year. Knowing the story well enough through repeated hearings, I was able to add details here and there for Cyril's edification, without distracting the doctor beyond the occasional '*hrm*, quite' and 'yes, rather'; and all in all my cousin was getting a long and thorough lesson out of it until I drew his attention to the two half-corroded narwhal horns the doctor had drawn from the squid's digestive tract and presented to the Guild on his initiation. As the doctor turned to look on these prizes himself—they hung crossed over the mantel, behind him—Cyril had just enough space to ask what the doctor had been doing in Zeeland.

Birding, you know, was the reply, as the doctor re-settled in his chair.

And without further prodding he gave out an inventory of his sightings from that year. I was watching Cyril keenly now, and I saw a cloud pass over his face the moment Dr. Peck began naming his birds. The look evolved into one of pain–dyspepsia, I thought, maybe a recrudescence of that fever. Cyril could even be seen elevating a finger as though he might, with extreme reluctance, ask to be let out for a bit of air. The doctor (bless him) was having none of it, and had leapt from birds straight back to his contest with the squid. But here some ass from the gallery asked if there weren't something the matter with the ambassador...?

The doctor blinked just once, letting Cyril jump into the breach again: why, yes, you know, as he understood it, the *Rockland* had been refitted to run petrol through the Dutch blockade, and had been doing so on the night she went down; it was indeed her extra weight that carried her into the rocks. Just so, returned Dr. Peck. This was consistent with his own view, and brought to mind remembrances of the Belgian struggle and of William and Leopold–Only now Cyril's anxiety was so great he must continue, albeit in *convulsions* of politeness. It was his understanding, too, *ahem*, that oil from the wreck had washed down the Dutch coast into Belgium, sweeping all fish and bird migration before it. The Zeeland peninsula had been destitute of birds that summer, and for all the following decade. Add to which, the Cape Gannett, the White-tailed Shrike and the Pied Starling were never seen out of Africa, unless they were brought out shot and stuffed.

Well. He'd taken a terrible liberty, we felt, calling a man's facts into question at the Guild; but there it was. And we must absorb it for a few ticks of the clock, then look to Dr. Peck for a riposte. There were any number of ways through this, of course. He might just *ignore* Cyril's comments, or cite some jumble of dates or species or general defects of memory (I believe I have mentioned he was *old*). One of his grunts, signifying *anything*, would have sufficed. But all he actually *did* was shrink into his collars, which I had thought to be a figure of speech up to that moment.

And now the silence lengthened into something truly awful. A thought flashed through my mind, and in that moment I could see it reflected on all the faces around me: our Dr. Peck was a *fraud*. There had been no giant squid and no Zeeland, and he'd got his narwhal horns out of a Sears catalogue. Just what he was supposed to be a doctor *of* we could no longer guess, but we suddenly and heartily wished this man and his stories at the bottom of the North Seas, whether or not he'd ever roved them or could even point to them on a map.

When the silence eventually did break, it broke in tumult. Seeing Dr. Peck brought down with such a neat shot to his weak point, the others must scramble for their lives. They must prove that *they* at least had done some real adventuring in this world. So it was out with all the old stories at once: tales of *this* subterranean lake and *that* river navigated to its source, *this* species chased to its tree-top canopy and *that* jewel returned to this other crown. And whose approval were they seeking now, who would judge the daring and veracity of these old adventurers but my Cousin Cyril, sitting lofty and serene and self-satisfied as the Buddha, you may be sure. His thrust at Dr. Peck had pricked us all, and didn't he just know it? For we were all of us frauds in this room; we had just never been forced to confront the fact.

From this point on the evening comes to me in snatches, for it was my determination on seeing the collapse of my plan that I should become disgracefully drunk. I have an image of my hollering at Apsley that I d–mn well *could* leave my cousin here (this as I struggled into someone else's coat in the vestibule). I must not have made good an exit, though, for I was back in the sitting-room at some later point, stoking the fire with such a will that the club stewards must ease the poker from my hand.

Dr. Peck had left by this time, else he had disintegrated right into his shoes. The seat next to Cyril, empty before, was filled by a long and languorous foreigner–the guest of another member, I took it–with the pouched eyes of an aristocrat, who affected not to follow the conversation. The rest of the group had drawn tight round Cyril, who held court with improving success, and if you have ever seen the old wives squawking at a country fair as some judge, with chilling dignity, inspects their tulip beds and fatted animals and so forth, you will have a fair impression as to the scene. Cyril contended easily with all of them, making quiet asides to his foreigner (a Russian, I think, for I had seen that complexion before only on drowned men and Russians). He directed a few comments at me, too, as though to draw me into his joke, but I was drawing moodily on a Royal

Ibis cigar—unsnipped, as it happened—and I warned him off with snarling comments of my own (which he seemed perversely to enjoy). Still I must have been listening and waiting my chance, for when I heard one of them mention the Canadian Northwest Passage, I chimed in.

Now, you cannot spend too much time at the Explorers Guild without absorbing the odd bit of worldly-sounding information, whether you would or no. I myself had overheard two young members in debate over this same Northwest Passage, and recently enough that I could still call one of their points to mind. What was better, the fellow I was prepared to quote had been reading from a *newspaper* when the thing started, so there was the off chance that his point had some grounding in fact. This being the case, I put by my cigar and charged the field.

The Northwest Passage? I coughed at Cyril. I was sure he meant *a* northwest passage (and never mind that the original comment had not been his). There were any *number* of ways through the Canadian archipelago, I said, and I could not believe for a *minute* that the last and definitive route had been mapped by a *Swede.*

I was mistaken on the point of Amundsen's nationality—he was Norwegian—but no matter. I was taking issue with Cyril, you see. Giving these other men a moment to regroup. My observation drew a round of raised glasses and *hear-hears*, and a tiny exclamation from Cyril himself. Even his Russian turned to squint at me, as though trying to make me out at a distance.

A passage, yes, Cyril agreed, motioning me to the table (again I declined)...And no doubt we Americans would keep the article vague till one of our own had hit upon the correct route.

Just so, I said, quicker perhaps than he'd expected. It was our continent and we ought to find our own way through it. (Here I discovered my mistake with the cigar, too. I bit off its end and accepted a light from Malthrop). And I *say* (I said), if we were quick enough about it we might save English lives, wot-wot...?

The English, as I took it, had tried more than once for the passage and had met with tragedy and failure. And when I had flung this fact at my cousin, I had exhausted my knowledge of northwest passages. I puffed at my Royal Ibis and fixed Cyril with a look, knowing I must rely on bluster and aid from my fellows from here on.

At first, Cyril only dipped his head and conceded what a shambles his countrymen had made of the job. After Cook and Parry and Franklin, he said, all the others had work enough just to find their frozen forerunners in the ice. (A scattering of laughs here, though I could see his mind working to some malign purpose.) The trick, he said, as practiced by the Americans, was to sail *just* far enough north, to where a man could report on his *own* doings, and where there would be no other English-speaking witnesses to call what he'd seen or supposed he had seen into question. He must, of course, avoid any serious risks with the cold or privation, and he must have a body at home like the American Geographical Society, that would trumpet his findings to the world whether or not they had the backing of proof or even of plausibility. *That* was how a man made a splash in the papers and still lived to enjoy his reputation, said Cyril. And how like Britain—how *unpatriotic*, really—to hold *scientific rigor* over the heads of these poor sons whom she had sent out to the frigid ends of the earth, and likely to their deaths.

The speech drew a snort from Cyril's Russian, while the rest of us must puzzle over what, precisely, he was driving at.* We had sustained an insult of some kind, though none of us was sure on what quarter he'd been hit. Malthrop, in the confusion, slurred something about just *seeing* whether or not it was an American who hit upon the passage, and this rallied our side a bit. A second gentleman laid *odds* it would be an American, and Cyril rose straight to this fly, being an Englishman with a wager in the air. He backed the world against us and added—after conferring aside with his Russian, as I noticed—that even if an American *were* destined to take the Arctic grail, it would certainly not be one of the present company.

Now, why he should have added this last bit I cannot say. It seemed too directly provocative for Cyril. And if it came from his Russian, I will never know that man's motivations, for he excused himself and withdrew just then, his behavior being mysterious from first to last. We were left to pursue the matter with Cyril alone. And indeed, here were his 'present

. . . . .

**Mr. Aiken likely makes reference to Admiral Peary and his disputed sightings in Greenland, 1889–1902. Though we note that London's Royal Geographical Society supported the claim as well.*

company' in full throat now, with mine the loudest voice among them, demanding just what in all h–ll he'd meant by *that*?

Cyril only blinked at us, all innocence. Begging our pardon, he said, but hadn't each of us had enough adventure for *several* lifetimes already? Hadn't he been hearing all about it?

Take this remark as you may. It was enough to mollify certain of our members, it is true. But I was there to hear it spoken and to see that flash of humor in Cyril's eye as he lit a new cigarette; and, taking it all together, it was my unconsidered instinct of that moment to blurt out more or less as follows: that I would not speak for the country at large, but that more than a few of *those present* had strength and wit enough to find any passage he liked. If he required proof of it, if he were in a humor to *wager*, well: he could bet what he liked against *me*. I would find a better way through the Arctic than had Amundsen or any poltroon of the British navy, and I would return with a map of the passage within the sixmonth. When I *did*, Cyril could fête me in the Guild's Great Hall dressed as Yankee Doodle. And he could name his terms if I *failed*, as indeed I would *not*.

I added a good deal more, I am sure, for I shouted myself hoarse before Cyril got in his first word of reply (indeed, we were all of us hooting and hopping like chimps). But I have told you the substance of this speech, anyway, and it is the selfsame boast I mentioned earlier, the one that has landed us in so much difficulty.

What followed–what I can recall of it, anyway–hardly bears going into. Cyril accepted my wager with every appearance of good grace (he would impose no penalty, for instance, if I returned a failure), and we settled on terms with all assembled bearing witness. I was made the hero of the hour, and my health was drunk all round, over and again, into the small hours. There was an undignified rendition of 'The Star-Spangled Banner' in which I may or may not have joined. I dare say the old men would have had me up on their bony shoulders for a run into the East River if any of them could have stood it.

But through all the shouting, through all the gaiety forced and genuine, I was careful not to let my eyes meet Cyril's. For I would only see confirmed there what he and I both knew fully well: that in a life of lesser missteps, I had just committed the mother of them all.

34° 41' 23" N Lat | 35° 57' 11" W Long
Al Hamidiyah, Syrian Coast
November, 1917

ARTHUR'S SUFFERING SOME SORT OF...AILMENT. FAN SAYS WE CAN EXPECT TO FIND HIM VERY MUCH CHANGED WHEN I GET HOME.
OR DEAD, IF WE TAKE OUR TIME ABOUT IT.
BUT WE DO NOT GO DIRECTLY TO YOUR HOME.

NO. THERE ARE A DOZEN OR SO OTHERS WITH THIS CONDITION, STREWN ALL ABOUT. WE'RE TO GATHER UP AS MANY AS WE CAN AND BRING THEM BACK TO ARTHUR, FOR STUDY.
THIS FIRST ONE WE'RE SUPPOSED TO FIND IN SOME TEMPLE RUIN ON THE SINAI.
CHR–ST. I'M A DUTCHMAN IF WE DO.

IF WE DO, YOU MAY CREDIT THE NEXT REPORT, TOO. CER-TAINLY THEY ARE THOROUGH.
...IT IS ARTHUR-SAHIB, WHO MAKES THEM? AND HE'LL CONDUCT THIS STUDY HIMSELF?

ARTHUR? SNORT–!
MY BROTHER COULDN'T DRAIN A BATH HIMSELF IF HE WERE DROWNING IN IT.
THERE'S A FELLOW CALLED SLOANE TREAT-ING HIM IN SOME OLD WING OF THE HOUSE. IT'S ALL VERY QUEER. FAN HASN'T ACTUALLY MET THIS MAN, ONLY HIS ASSOCIATES.

BUT IT DOES SEEM THERE'S NO HELP FOR ARTHUR WITHOUT SLOANE, OR WITHOUT THESE HERMITS OF HIS.
...REALLY I DON'T KNOW WHAT I'M LETTING US IN FOR, MR. PRIDDISH.
YOU ARE TRYING BY THE ONLY MEANS AT HAND TO SAVE YOUR BROTHER'S LIFE. IT IS NOTHING UNREASONABLE.

AH, BUT SEE HOW REASONABLE ARTHUR'S WRITING IS. THEY SAY HIS...CONDITION SPRINGS FROM THIS GREAT DISCOVERY HE'S MADE BENEATH THE POLAR ICE.
...HM. I THINK HIS CONDITION IS NO GREAT MYSTERY. HE LOST HIS PARTY IN THE NORTH AND WANDERED ALONE TILL HE WENT MAD FROM IT.

AND I THINK YOU'D RATHER COMPOUND HIS MADNESS THAN CURE IT, BY BRINGING HIM MORE MADMEN.
STILL: MADNESS OR NO, GREAT DISCOVERY OR NO, I DON'T SEE IT SIGNIFIES. IT IS NOT WHY WE GO.

NO. WE GO BECAUSE OF FAN'S WEAKNESS FOR HER BROTHER, AND MINE FOR HER. YOU SHOULD NOT THINK THAT DOESN'T WEIGH ON ME.

OH? THOUGH I SHOULDN'T LET IT, SAHIB. THESE WEAKNESSES, AS I UNDERSTAND, ARE WHAT KEEP OUR KIND TOGETHER. THEY MAY BE A SIGN OF OUR BETTER NATURE.
–WHICH IS ALL WELL FOR FAMILIES, I S'POSE...

AH. BUT YOU THINK IT IS OUR STRENGTHS THAT BIND THE KING'S GREAT ARMIES, AND YOUR OWN DRAGOONS...?

RESPECTFULLY, SAHIB, I TRUST YOU KNOW BETTER WHY THESE MEN FOLLOW YOU.

LATER, OGDEN IS READING IN HIS CABIN ON THE *VIRAGO*, WHEN A CRY GOES UP FROM THE MEN ON DECK.

VIRAGO
BATAVIA

...THE HORSE? WELL, YOU CAN SEE SHE'S HARDLY NEW. BUT MR. GURUNG'S WAS LAMED IN A FALL. I WAS FORCED TO TRADE FOR THIS LITTLE CASPIAN.
HEH HEH HEHHH!
...SORRY? OH—YES, I HAD TO GIVE THEM EVERYTHING—EVEN MY BOOTS, YOU SEE—
HRAWW-HRAWW!

HAVE HER UP, SON.
OH. REALLY?
YA-YA. JUST SHOW HER THAT'S WHAT YOU WANT.

QUICK, LAD.
—OH—
BRING HER ROUND—STEADY—TAKE HER MANE, NOW, AND GIVE A PULL—SHE'LL CLIMB IT—

DON'T LOOK DOWN, SON—LOOK AT US—
—LET GO THE REINS, NOW—
QUICK, BOY—YE'RE RUNNIN' OUTTA DOCK!

THAT'S IT–PULL–
PULL AND GIVE HER YOUR HEELS–
–MOVE IT, LAD–

–GRAB 'IM, JACKIE!
–A-HAAA!–
VIRAGO

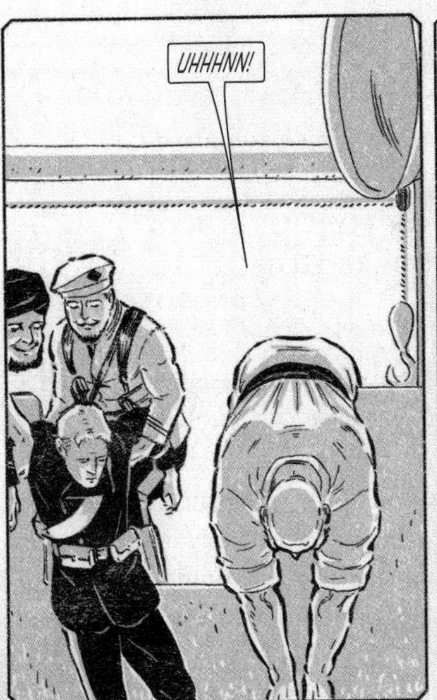
UHHHNN!

HURRRK!

{The Expedition Log of Arthur Ogden, continued.}

I AM REWARDED FOR MY OUTBURST AT THE EXPLORERS GUILD

. . .

Tonight, as I may now tell you, I am seated at a plank desk in the Canadian Yukon. They have me in a 'state room' (instancing the local humor, I think) in a chinked-log shambles that the Canadian authorities are pleased to call 'Fort Defiance.' The name may not signify much to you, and certainly it did not to me just a week ago. But I can tell you we are in the extreme northwest of contiguous Canada, just short of seventy degrees latitude. And a more desperate or pointless act of *defiance* than the erection of a fort on this endless and unfeatured waste can hardly be conceived.

Reaching the fort from civilization is an ordeal of weeks, involving steam and rail and aeroplane and, finally, the ubiquitous dog-drawn *sledge*, all of this removing you not just over the miles but backward through the aeons, to an earth that had not yet dreamt of man and to which he is distinctly unwelcome. Apsley, I think, spoke for us all on our arrival, when he deplaned our shuddering little Curtiss Magpie, spat upon the pack-ice and announced: 'This thing has got pretty far past a joke.'

The fort commands a headland on the Beaufort Sea, and I suppose in a time of thaw it would present the heroic prospect of a seaside bastion. In colder months, of course, the bay freezes over, and there is nothing to show you where the land ends and sea begins, there is just the one unvaried plane of white in all directions, as far as the eye can compass; and then, absurdly, smack in the middle of this great emptiness you see our little fort, stuck fast like Lucifer in his bottommost circle of hell.* Happily, the sun keeps only a quick, grudging engagement here during the day, and we are but briefly reminded of how alone we are.

I would not go on about the cold or the desolation, as you cannot dwell on these things for very long here before you are reaching for your sidearm, and I wonder how edifying a travel-log would be that consisted of nothing but the phrase *'we are cold'* repeated over and over, much as that might represent my daily train of thought. But I would have you reflect for just a moment on how hospitable to the individual is a cold that petrifies very *oceans*. Our fathers did not believe brackish water even *capable* of freezing, mind you; and not very far north from here the sea has *never been otherwise*. I say, it is a deadly, dispiriting, relentless cold. There is not timber or animal-skin thick enough to ward it off, and not enough mortar, mud or pine-tar in the world to chink it away from the body; there is no diversion powerful enough to drive it from the mind, and for the rest of my stay in this forlorn place, unless I state otherwise you may assume I am trembling in every limb and half mad with the cold and am contemplating the attractions of a death by fire.

But, to continue: I share my room and desk at Fort Defiance with

. . . . .

**The deepest hell of the* Divine Comedy *is not a level of fire but of everlasting ice and darkness. Satan, for his treachery against God, is fixed here at the center of a great frozen lake, where he devours Brutus, Cassius, and Judas Iscariot with his three mouths.*

Malthrop, and we are at the latter now seated *vis-à-vis*, close enough to shake hands (or to gouge one another's eyes, if it comes to that). They have us directly above the fort's commanding officer, and the room is heated—to the extent that it is—by a conduit from that gentleman's peat-stove. This is the hour when the commander's gramophone sees use, and we might have the pleasure of his new piano reels from the States were it not for our Mr. Gaddis, who is sneezing next-door to us like a man dynamiting the barracks.

Malthrop is smoking, meanwhile, with his reading neglected, and I suppose he is mulling the plan I have just put across to him. I will hear his reaction presently, but while there is this pause I may as well tell you what I've given him to consider.

Oddly enough, the kernel of my idea came to me from Cousin Cyril himself. You will recall Cyril's view of the American explorer as a fame-seeking amateur who slips outside civilization, dreams up his stories and palms them off on his public with the help of the press and the Geographical Society. Well: I've reflected a good deal on these remarks lately, and drawn two conclusions from them: first, that his description of the American *modus operandi* is actually a fair view of exploration generally, up to the last half-century; and second, that if I were ever fool enough to take up as an explorer myself—as it seems I have—this is exactly how I would go about it.

Now, I can see I am about to give offense to the moral-minded among you. But I must undeceive you on a point or two before (or at least *as*) you rush to judge me and my enterprise:

I begin with the statement that—historically at least—there has been no surer method of defrauding the public and profiting by it than setting oneself up as an *Explorer*. Nor should you think this has not been done, or that the names you've recited in the classroom were not founded just as surely on humbug as upon new-found coasts and Incan gold. Exploration is above all things a *romantic* calling, you see, and it has always selected the veriest of dreamers (who tend also to be our veriest *liars*) for its champions. It is our great curiosity, our incurable *anxiety*, about the Unknown World that brought exploration into being, it is true; but it is our love of being *entertained* that has given the practice its shape.

Look again, I say, at the men who've succeeded to the heights of the profession. You will find the type is much more a fiery sort of stage-hero than the patriot or evangelist or adventurer-cum-scientist or whatever else was held up by his age. These were vagabonds and egoists, disinclined to honest work, wheedlers at court and tyrants of the galley, outwardly suave, inwardly desperate, occasionally bold and enduringly cunning and, above all, the minstrels of their own deeds.* The lies of the pre-Enlightenment explorers are axiomatic, of course, and by the time your Pizarros and Magellans put forth their accounts you might look to the *Voyages of Sinbad* for a more sober relation of facts. Spices and maps and waterways and trade-routes were all well enough, you see, but if your Explorer returned from the Unknown without a good *story*, he'd really missed the point.

And what else really would you have, from your heroes? Where is the harm, I say, in adding a bit of lyricism, a bit of hyperbole—a bit of *fraud*, if you like—to the stories of our men of action, in the places we are not ever likely to visit? I say, there are any number of professions open to the bookish, the modest, the scrupulous: let them keep them all. But the name of Explorer, to my mind, has always been charged with a sort of romance, and I hope it will ever be so. When we dream, we are Marco Polo—aren't we?—coming to grips with the serpents of the China Seas. Certainly we are not shivering beside Parry in his ice-bound frigate, with half our crew got up as ladies of Paris and clomping about the frozen deck-boards with the other half, while the concertina wheezes out songs from the faraway beer-halls and winter closes in.

It is no happy picture, this. But you see: this is just what exploration has come to now that the Anglo-Saxons have got a hold of it. This is where the rise of cynicism and of Cyril's *scientific rigor* have landed us. In place of the old basilisks and glowing grails and cliffs at world's end we must now 'quest' in the name of ethnology and botany and transits of Venus and I know not what else. All the fun and romance have gone right out of the thing. And if you have met any of today's explorers you will know why even the actuary and the missionary find his company insupportably dull.

Now, I have not asked to be made an explorer in this modern mold, and so shall I not be. I may be circumstanced like one at the moment—certainly I am as *miserable* as Parry or Shackleton or Franklin ever wished to be—Yet

. . . .

**And if this is not a fair description of the southern races generally, you may note how many of these men sailed from Spain and Portugal, and make of that what you will.*

from here forward, their paths and mine diverge. From this point, as I tell only you and the men of my party, I aim to revive a great tradition in the field of exploration. I am planning a *hoax*, you see. That is what I'll bring back to civilization—*That* will be my gift to the ages!

. . .

Now: do not misunderstand. This is no easy job, hoaxing the modern public on a matter of exploration. You must first (as Cousin Cyril points out) remove yourself from the sight of men; and if this sounds like no great challenge, then just you try it. Try to find a proper horizon to slip over, as the ancients did. You'll find we don't much have them any more. You will feel eyes upon you *everywhere*, and you will find this is the case from your living room all the way to the blackest pit of Africa. No: in order to create any official-looking hoax of exploration you must establish yourself first at some legitimate outpost of the world. You must write your dispatches to the papers, have your portrait taken with the local worthies and so forth, and

then let them see you striking out into *terra nova* (or at least into *terra vacua*). And you must *stay* out there for a space of weeks or even months, depending on what claims you plan to make on your return.

In my own case, we have Fort Defiance to give you some idea of what these outposts of the world are like. And it lies before me now to abandon even *this* poor refuge, and to try to keep myself and my party alive on the pack-ice without once letting Christian man get sight of us or offer us aid. I think I may say, therefore, and with some justification, that whether we are planning a legitimate enterprise or no, the effort is still more than *you* are likely to undertake, who are reading this in your place of leisure, in full enjoyment of civilization's comforts (as I must assume). I say, if you would *begin* a journey in the margins of the world, if you would continue out of man's sight to where he has seldom or never gone, and is unlikely to follow—to where you might account for your own doings, in other words, and burnish a fact or two without fear of exposure—to do this, you must not only be mad (it hardly bears saying), you must *build upon* or *excel* the madness

of the hundred madmen who've gone before you, and who've pushed the borders of the world into their current, imponderable shape. You must contemplate a *perfect feat* of madness, for which the standard is ever rising. And this applies just as forcefully to your dead-earnest explorers and martyrs like Parry and Franklin, as it does to scoundrels like myself.

Really, I should have thrown the whole business up by now if not for the surprise emergence of a new plan–this thing I've put before Malthrop, you know. And the idea runs something as follows:

Now, we have all been gathering supplies these last three weeks, partly to maintain the outward show of outfitting an expedition, and partly to avoid thinking about what we might really be doing. I have bought sextant and surveyor's transit and have charged Numm-Smythe with learning something of their use, so that at least we might be looking in the right end when Dixon makes his photographs. We've got rope and crampons and tinned beef and pemmican, and we have sledges that will serve, after a bit of tinkering, as canvas-hulled canoes. But above all we have been herding up native guides and trappers and translators, and these of a particular kind. I require that our guides either do not understand our enterprise, or if they do understand it that they not form any negative judgment about it, or if they understand *and* disapprove that they not be anyone whom the white man will listen to or take seriously. Which is to say, I have been trolling about for guides of an especially *disreputable* sort. And you mightn't think, on first surveying the Esquimaux of these parts, that this would narrow the field by a single body. Yet my search has drawn me into the uglier haunts of the local Inuit, where I have met such depictions of disrepute as would put your Delhi untouchable off his food. And it is in these places that I've heard mention of a place called 'Ikkumaaluk.'

Ikkumaaluk, as I gather, is the name given to a permanent encampment in the lee of Banks Island. It is unknown to the Europeans and dismissed as a vulgar myth by the white men of this continent, who seldom range so far north and would never admit to finding a thing like this anyway. For, Ikkumaaluk, you see, is held to be a kind of Gomorrah of the snows, where anything that passes for vice among the northern primitives may be found. And it seems that when once these simple and indolent people choose a path of dissipation, they become just as inventive and thoroughgoing in it as do their fellows in the better-known fleshpots of Europe and Asia. I find it significant that in a culture so plainly free of shame, a man visiting Ikkumaaluk will carry its stigma with him for all his days, and that if an Esquimaux be known to leave his tribe for the forbidden 'city' he is spoken of as if dead. This may be said with some foreknowledge, too, as most pilgrims to Ikkumaaluk do not anticipate making the return passage. It is more common for those hearing its Siren-song to drink, whore and otherwise exert themselves to death, or at least to stay until they are in no condition to leave.

You will understand, therefore, given Ikkumaaluk's isolation from white men, its proximity to our current spot and above all its mode of industry, that I was more than usually attentive on the subject. Could we reach Ikkumaaluk without too much bother? I asked. Yes, it seemed we could, for these men all knew its location and could deliver us there inside the month. Would we be received, though we were white men? Yes again, assuredly. There were none turned away at Ikkumaaluk, they said, and if we came with liquor and pelts we could live like mandarins for as long as our supplies held. Would the 'city' provide for a comfortable existence between bouts of excess–That is, could we count upon food, shelter, warmth, and not, say, getting our throats slit in the night over liquor and sealskins? Yes of course, they answered, the quotidian pleasures of Ikkumaaluk were among its chief attractions. There were excellent personal guards for hire, too. And if a man were wise and cached his trade items in the outlying ice fields he might guarantee his preservation in perfect comfort, if not luxury outright....

All of this I have related now to Malthrop, trying to hold rein on my enthusiasm as I pictured our trading this drafty barrack-room for a cozy igloo at Ikkumaaluk. I have proposed to him that we set out into the North as soon as the sledges can be made ready, and that we spend the winter in a prolonged *debauch*, quartered safely out of sight. What pioneering we do in this time we can do in the realms of *vice*, where though we are already most of us well-traveled, we may yet come to stand with the Magellans and da Gamas of the field. If we happened to spot a northwest passage in our travels, so much the better. But in the weeks of sojourn we'd have time to craft a story of Arctic adventure that would thrill the journals at home without committing us to any untenable claims of *science*, which sort of exercise I felt we might enjoy.

Here, judging from Malthrop's face, I felt an example story to be in order, so I gave him this: We might arrange, I said, in our fictional wanderings, to run across some high-born queen of trackers, an arctic Sacajawea with the face of a Manchurian sphinx, who will lead us to a sacred and hidden waterway of the Esquimaux on the promise that she and I will wed there. We may find the straits are only navigable in certain tides, or that they appear only under a certain phase of the moon or some such. And perhaps I will honor my vows to this woman, perhaps not. But I feel she ought to be stolen back in a raid of natives, anyway, when we have just glimpsed this new passage. And these natives will put our maps to the torch and expose our photographic plates and so forth, so that the location and description of my wedding-place will be committed to no more than memory. We might, then, be dragged from this place to the camp of the raiding Esquimaux, and be in line for execution there till we recognize one of their bearded elders as a lost cabin boy of Parry's crew. And then we will stun the proceedings and save our own lives by calling out this man's long-forgotten Christian name....

This was how I illustrated the point to Malthrop, anyway–Though I rushed to add, seeing his face lengthen in that way of his, that these were only preliminary ideas, on which we'd have time enough to improve.

The greater point is that I am not really *proposing* anything to him, in the sense of waiting on his permission to act. I'd sooner have his help, of course, and am fairly assured he will give it. But if he takes a dim view of my plan I would honestly just as soon leave him here.

In the same way, and meaning no offense to you (whoever you turn out to be), I have led you to this point as carefully as I can. I have placed our expedition in its historical context, and shown myself as a man taking a reasoned and deliberate and time-honored approach to a practice that just happens, by the fault of his birth, not to be honored in his own time. I have argued that there is a decided element of risk and even a savor of heroism to the thing, shameless as it all may sound. I have given you my personal reasons for entering into it, and shown my Cousin Cyril to be a man richly deserving his comeuppance, if not something greatly worse. But again, if you should take all this into calculation and judge me a plain criminal and my project no more than fraud, I am content that you should do so.

I will have my day with Cyril, at all events. I will see that rubber-lipped grin stricken just once, but forcibly, from his face. And I will put my life and my comforts to no unwarranted risks while I am about it. Let you who have not wandered abroad in these god-forgotten latitudes judge me as you may.

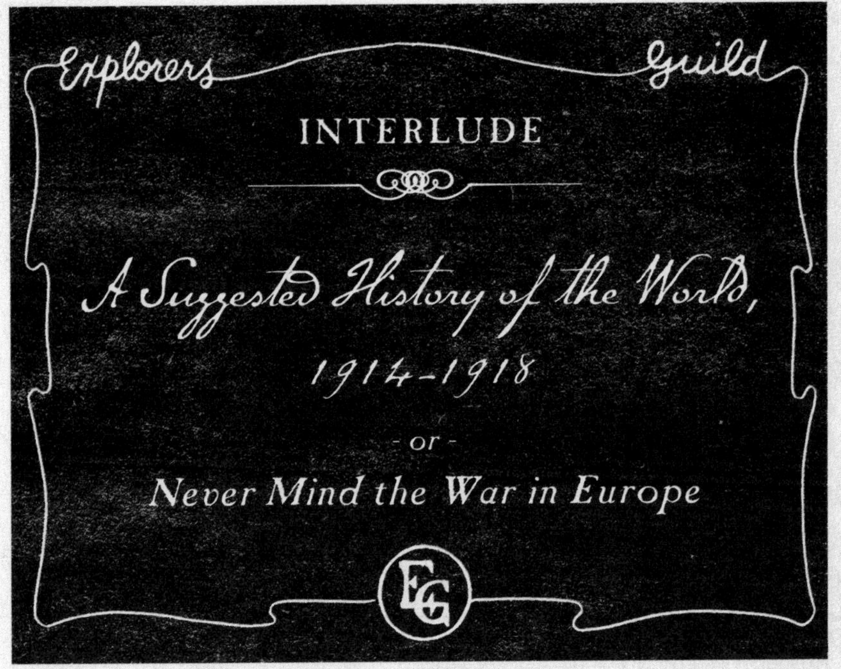
Explorers Guild
INTERLUDE
A Suggested History of the World,
1914-1918
- or -
Never Mind the War in Europe
EG

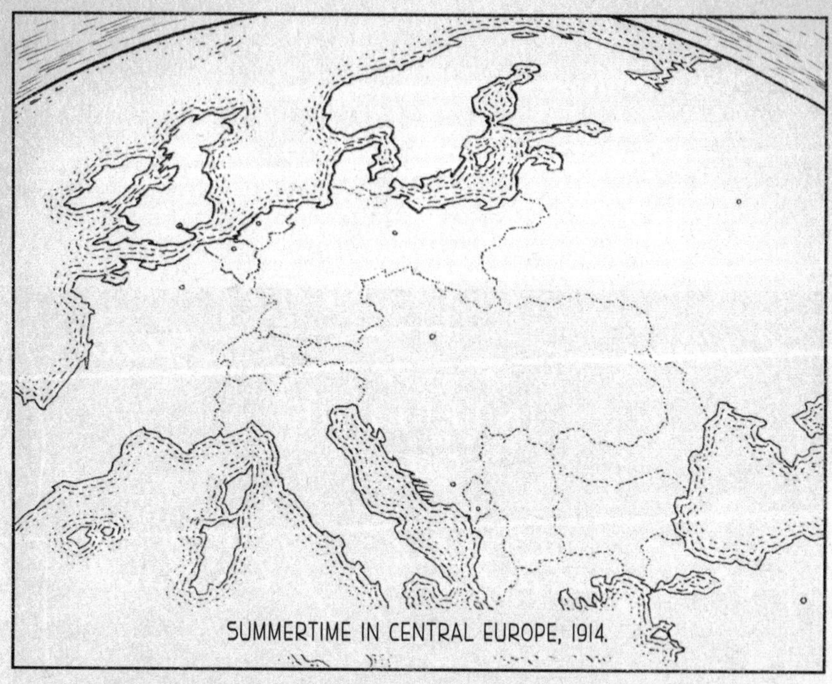
SUMMERTIME IN CENTRAL EUROPE, 1914.

THROUGH THE WINDOWS OF A SARAJEVO CAFÉ, A GRÄF & STIFT CONVERTIBLE MOTORCAR MAY BE SEEN RUNNING ALONG FRANZ JOSEF STREET IN REVERSE.

INSIDE THE CAFÉ, A PENNILESS NINETEEN-YEAR-OLD STUDENT HAS JUST FINISHED HIS CHEESE SANDWICH, AS WILL SOON BECOME KNOWN TO THE WORLD.

ON THE STREET, MOMENTS LATER, THE YOUNG MAN RECOGNIZES THE ARCHDUKE OF AUSTRIA AND DUCHESS OF HOHENBERG.

THEY HAVE LOST THEIR MOTORCADE, TAKEN A WRONG TURN AND NOW STALLED, AS IF BY APPOINTMENT, FIVE FEET IN FRONT OF HIM.

THE COUPLE FAIL TO RECOGNIZE GAVRILO PRINCIP, A SERBIAN NATIONALIST WITH A FABRIQUE NATIONALE PISTOL IN HIS COAT POCKET. THEIR ACQUAINTANCE IS BRIEF.

IN VIENNA, THE AUSTRIAN EMPEROR HONORS HIS
NEPHEW WITH A DECLARATION OF WAR ON SERBIA.

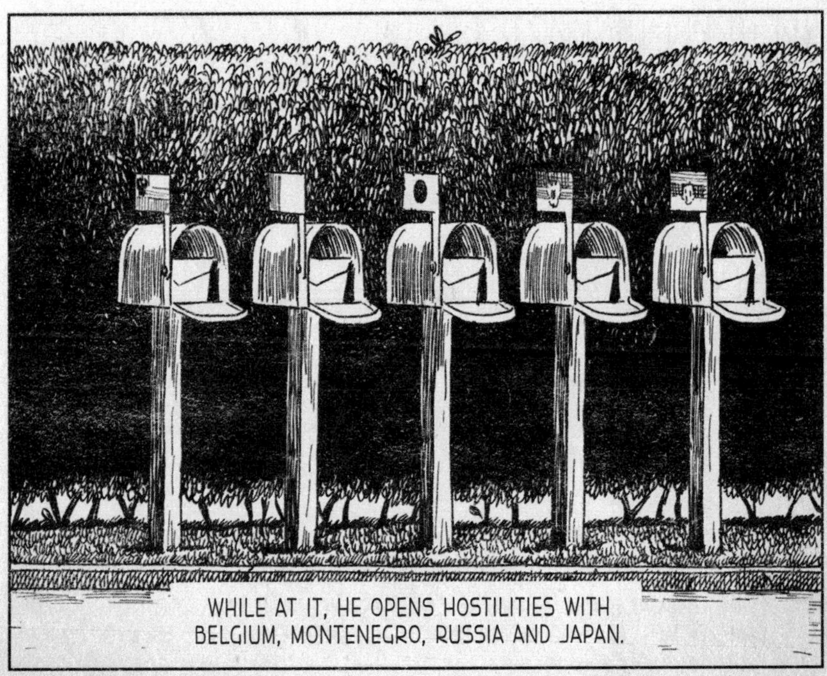
WHILE AT IT, HE OPENS HOSTILITIES WITH
BELGIUM, MONTENEGRO, RUSSIA AND JAPAN.

FRANCE AND ENGLAND, TAKING SERBIA'S PART, ADD THE
GERMAN AND OTTOMAN EMPIRES TO HER LIST OF ENEMIES.

THE GERMANS AND TURKS ANSWER FRANCE AND ENGLAND IN THE
SAME SPIRIT, NOT NEGLECTING PORTUGAL, GREECE OR ITALY. SO IT GOES.

SCARCELY A HUNDRED DAYS AFTER THE SHOTS IN SARAJEVO, WAR HAS OPENED ON SIX CONTINENTS.

<–IN THE CITIES, THERE WILL NOT BE FOUND ONE BRICK AT REST UPON ANOTHER–!>
DOOMSAYERS EVERYWHERE DO A ROARING TRADE.

AND WITH MAN CONTEMPLATING THE END OF HIS DAYS,
WITH EMPIRES FALLING AND POPULATIONS LOST

IT WILL HARDLY ATTRACT NOTICE WHEN A
DOZEN SOULS, HERE AND THERE, GO MISSING.

AND LEAST OF ALL THESE.

THEY ARE THE INDIGENT AND THE INSANE, HERMITS, PRISONERS AND INEBRIATES.

THAT THEY WOULD BE SELECTED FOR SOME PURPOSE, SOUGHT OUT IN THE MIDST OF WAR, GATHERED BY NIGHT ONTO A SHIP FROM THE INDIES: IT WOULD ALL SEEM RATHER ODD–EVEN SINISTER–TO ANYONE WATCHING. WHICH, OF COURSE, NO ONE IS.

AND I WOULD NOT TROUBLE YOU WITH THE RUMORS THAT ARE SPROUTING UP ALONG THE MEDITERRANEAN COASTS, AND FROM THE HUTS OF ABYSSINIA TO THE PORTS OF BISCAY...

...EXCEPT THAT THIS SHIP is one we know. We know several of the men on it, too—or at least, we have met them before in a different part of the world.

Tonight we are three years and a thousand leagues from Sarajevo, in the Caliphate of Jatum, coastal Africa. Six men have put ashore as quietly as a detail of dragoons might, and when they have dragged their boat past the tide line they march inland on an old goat track.

They have come to find and remove a Colonel Riebling, former aerialist of the *Schutztruppe* in German Southwest Africa. It is the sort of job they are well-used to, having sought through these tumbledown ports by moonlight now for the better part of a year. They carry a map of the locale and an etched portrait of *Herr* Riebling, though you will not see Subadar Priddish, who keeps these papers in a fold of his tunic, bring them out once. He and the others proceed by instinct past a walled Berber settlement, around an old well and toward a collapsed schoolhouse on the port's eastern outskirts. As to *Herr* Riebling, they anticipate finding him alone in the ruined building, though indeed, they would recognize him in a crowd of thousands.

Mr. Priddish arrives first at the school, padding quietly past its fallen cupola and through a roofless vestibule into a courtyard, where he scents smoke from a taper that was snuffed, he thinks, just moments ago. Buchan lights a hurricane lantern outside and lifts it to a sign that dubs this ruin the '*Saint-Vitus École de Diverses Activités Sacrées*.'* The drollery

. . . . .

*'*St. Vitus's School of Varied Sacred Pursuits.' The Directoire architecture and French legend are not out of place in Jatum, which is still at this time a French protectorate.*

of the sign, the candle-smoke, and this pervading sense of a watchful, unseen presence–these would all mark the school for the right spot, if indeed the dragoons needed any assurance of the kind. As it is, they let Mr. Buchan climb a rotted staircase while they debouch into the courtyard, sitting and smoking and kicking through the place for valuables. Unseen presence or no, they have learned there is no great danger in these stops, and have come to view them as opportunities to stretch one's legs while Mr. Buchan goes about his work.

And the young man's search, tonight, is brought quickly to a result.

I have said the dragoons know these men and women they are collecting on sight, but what they have really learned to recognize is a sort of malady common to these people. Major Ogden, who continues to receive his briefings and his maps from New York, calls this disease 'the Complaint,' and says little more about it; but the dragoons know to look for it about one's eyes. The disease, you see, rings the eyes in pockets of black and necrotic flesh, either physically enlarging them or else mimicking that effect. There is also very often hemorrhaging in the sclerae, so that the whites of the eyes go black or a deep wine color, and if the irises be light blue or green they will seem to hover, glowing over the black cavities on the sufferer's face, a thing truly awful to behold.

Beyond this, the symptoms of the Complaint show a bit of range. Gnawed lips and nails are common, as are hemorrhaging in the ears and tongue. Aphasia, echolalia and degeneration of the sensory organs are often noted, along with all varieties of fugue and waking nightmare. Loss of memory is nearly universal, too, as is a persistent sense of unreality or disbelief in one's surroundings. And, strange as it will sound, not all victims of the Complaint are ill-pleased by its effects. Truly, for all those discovered in howling misery, there are others who greet the dragoons in tremendously high spirits, and such a one is our Colonel Riebling tonight.

When Mr. Buchan's lantern picks him out, *Herr* Riebling is making a comic show of searching the empty chamber for his effects. He stands, grinning, bows nearly double and snaps back erect, and rattles out some incomprehensible greeting. Buchan is essaying some response when the German hooks the young man's arm in his own and marches him out to the landing. There seems nothing more natural or agreeable to *Herr* Riebling tonight than that he be plucked from his room and led to a waiting ship; though his gaiety, as we see, works to opposite effect on Mr. Buchan and the others downstairs. Truth be known, the soldiers prefer their madmen violent and terror-stricken, and there is something in the pairing of this yammering skeleton and the dazed young trooper beside him that strikes them too much like an allegory of Death.

The dragoons follow at a distance, then, as Riebling walks Buchan through the ruin and out onto the path, declaiming in what I really do not think is German. He carries on like this, chattering and cackling without pause through the sleeping port town, where for all this racket not a single light is raised in a window. We can assume that, whatever business is going forth between the old school in the outskirts and this mysterious ship in the harbor, the locals want no part in it.

The *Virago*'s dinghy is found again where it was beached, and when the dragoons have dragged it back to the water, they begin filing in. Corporal Buchan, as the last aboard, must steady the boat with one hand and *Herr* Riebling with the other, and he has just handed Riebling in when he is addressed by a rag-clad figure on the strand. This would seem to be another alms-beggar or beachcomber (the night in this port is full of them), but that this one hands him a folded note and presents quietly, in English, the compliments of his Lord Pomeroy. The stranger slips into the night, and for a moment it is all Mr. Buchan can do to look after him with the note in his palm and mouth agape. But he shakes off his daze just as quickly. It will not do to be caught tonight with a communiqué from Lord Pomeroy, not with half the dragoons suspecting him still of working under secret orders from the Company. He *hasn't* been, of course—he's had no contact at all with Bombay since leaving that good city—but how would the others know it? Already they are glaring back at him—all of them, Riebling included—as though to demand an explanation for *something*. And Buchan is on point of handing over the note and protesting his innocence when Sergeant Pensette cuts him off with a wicked oath and asks if he wouldn't mind terribly *casting them off*. Ah—very good: Buchan apologizes for the delay—a bit overloud, perhaps—and runs the little wherry out into the surf, not neglecting to drop the note behind him.

The dawn sees the *Virago* gathering way out of the harbor, and *Herr* Riebling settled inside it with the eleven other passengers who have preceded him here. Mr. Buchan's run-in with his messenger seems to have passed unnoticed, and if the dragoons have any other questions or doubts about the night's enterprise they know better than to give these thoughts expression. They lounge on the decks, content to have seen another commission through. So goes the *Virago* out of Jatum.

And we are soon to follow them, dear reader. But I'd direct you first to a bluff overlooking the water, where a man in a black robe and hat has just appeared at the door of a telegraph station. The man lifts the door's latch and settles himself by a salt-eaten instrument inside, and presently we hear the clicking of the station's transmitter.

Moments later, from a second hut—this one on the Black Sea—another black-robed man breaks at a dead run. This second man looks so like his African counterpart, too, that we might almost think he'd transmitted himself from booth to booth, leaving only his hat.

43° 48' 08" N Lat | 28° 34' 39" E Long

Feritiva Settlement

Durere River Estuary, Romania

January, 1918

II.

THIS PILED-UP EDIFICE that frowns on the Black Sea from its rocky height is the Castle Feritiva, seat of the boyar Duhul and Selescu houses of Moldavia. The castle's first stones were set in the time of Charlemagne, and it has risen steadily through the centuries until its latest Count but one—a Count Grigor Selescu—crowned it with the domed observatory you see sitting so incongruous among the ancient turrets and sentry walks. Selescu and his son (whose name is variously recorded) were known to have kept voluminous records here, like modern Tyco Brahes, but never to have published their maps of the cosmos or to have made any findings of note. Today you will find the old observatory shuttered, and any noble inhabitants of the castle long departed.

In place of the latter we find only more of these black-robed men; and you might think, on first look, that the castle has been left in the hands

of the Church. Yet you will not find any religious effects or insignia anywhere about the place. The robes and the hats of the men are unadorned, and even the old Christian texts and symbols cut into the castle's stonework have been effaced.

Tonight, through these halls, we see our telegraph operator go sprinting with his slip of paper, and he stops only when he has got to a two-storied gate of studded oak and presented himself to the tall and officious-looking men standing guard there. These men take the dispatch and consult one another in hushed French (and if you recognize the halting and bookish French that is picked up later in life, you will hear it from these two). Having satisfied themselves of something, they conduct the operator through the gate, securing it behind them.

The sun has not yet risen over the estuary and the transmission from Jatum is not yet two hours old when the black-robed men of Castle Feritiva begin assembling in a theater or lecture hall in another dark quarter of the castle. If this room were better-lit and spruced up we could imagine the old French farces and Italian operettas staged here, as indeed they once were. Yet the new tenants have silenced all the gay old echoes and the assembly this morning looks more like some mix of the English high court and a hearing of the Spanish Inquisition. There is a simple wooden dais in place of the judge's (or Inquisitor's) bench, and raised on this, in a high-backed chair, is a drawn and put-upon-looking young man in a robe and shovel hat of deep burgundy–the only raiments of their kind in the hall, and likely a sign of the young man's station. Before this figure, at a brass rail, sits the telegraph operator, with a second man—a senior representative of this order, it would seem—standing beside him. Behind these two are an audience of black robes, about three-score of them at the stage level and as many more in the galleries above, with others seated in the aisles, in niches and on sills and wherever there is space on the floor. We would guess from the disposition of bodies that this is very nearly the full population of black robes in the castle and outlying buildings, and that gatherings of this magnitude, in this room, are not common.

The dark figures in the audience wait in silence as the young man on the dais mutters a word or two to the senior black robe and receives that man's response with eyes closed. The young man slouches for greater comfort in what seems a rather comfortless chair, and then falls silent like the others, waiting perhaps for the inspiration to speak. And his inspiration comes, to be sure, but in a form more literal than we might have guessed.

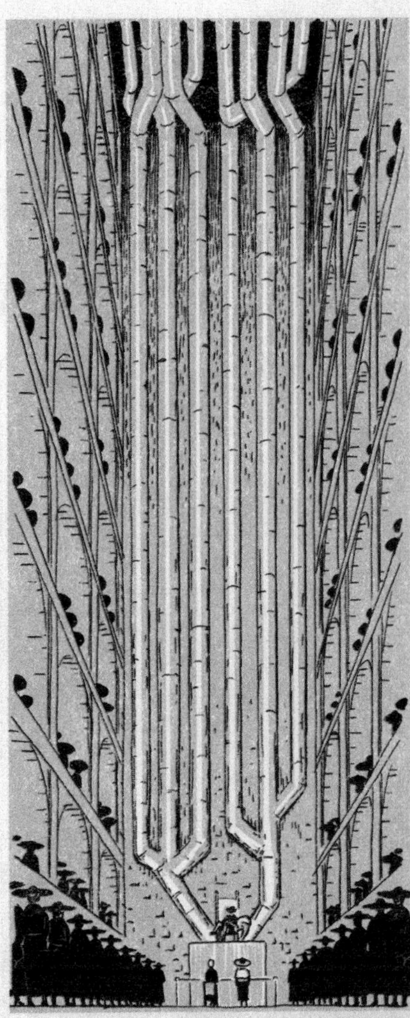

If, gentle reader, you have ever slept in one of those homes of the cold North that has been fitted with modern duct-work, you'll be acquainted with a certain sound the ducts make, in the walls, when they adjust to swings in temperature. It is less a *sound*, I suppose, than an awful groaning that shakes these stout homes and frightens the children and visitors. The 'ghost in the pipes,' as we say.

Well: all through the theater at the Castle Feritiva, climbing the walls and spanning the vaulted spaces overhead, you will see a great network of brass ducts. And the sound that begins to issue now from these (whether from one or all of them, it is not clear) is something like the sound I have described, albeit this is no quaint household ghost. It is rather like we are in the belly of a giant stone demon, and he's begun to speak. And you may even pick out the rhythms and phrasings of human speech—French, I should say—as you listen to these unholy rumblings.

The smaller conduits at the back of the theater and overhead feed into a single, giant brass artery, and this runs beneath the dais and comes up beside our young man, flaring out at its end like the bell of a tuba. It seems the sounds are brought from somewhere else in the castle, through these ducts, to the stage; and that the young man, who rests his fingertips on the vibrating metal, has a talent for deciphering them. It is like the Greeks consulting the spirits at Cumae, and hearing them through the sybils there: our two black-robed men have come to raise the castle's demon, and if we settle in with their audience, we may yet get some clue as to what this gathering is about.

YES. AT ANY RATE WE'VE LOST SIGHT OF THEM AGAIN, AND IT IS NOT YET KNOWN WHERE THAT SHIP IS BOUND.
WE DO FIND IT HAS BEEN HIRED OUT OF THE INDIES, BY A CONCERN REPRESENTING ARTHUR OGDEN'S INTERESTS IN THE SOUTH PACIFIC. MUCH AS WE'D IMAGINED.

IT WILL BE MR. OGDEN'S SHIP, BUT THE WORK IS MR. SLOANE'S.
YES, OF COURSE. THOUGH I DON'T SUPPOSE YOU COULD ENLIGHTEN US AS TO WHERE MR. SLOANE'S SHIP IS GOING?

I CANNOT, BROTHER. I SUSPECT MR. SLOANE IS IN OR ABOUT NEW YORK, AND IF THE SHIP WERE CROSSING DIRECT TO HIM, YOU MIGHT SEE IT NEXT IN THE CANARIES.
BUT YOU DO NOT THINK WE WILL....

NO. I THINK YOU'LL SEE IT AT THE CAPE VERDE ISLANDS, HEADING SOUTH AND WEST, IN A DAY'S TIME. THEY WILL DOCK AT AMBUSCADA AND REFIT FOR THE CROSSING TO SOUTH AMERICA.
...THEN THEY MEAN TO COLLECT THE BOY.

THAT IS MY SURMISE. HE WILL BE THE LAST. AND THEN WE WILL KNOW SOMETHING.
I'LL PREPARE THEM FOR A VISIT, THEN, IN THE ARGENTINE.
BETTER YOU DIDN'T. THERE IS LITTLE ENOUGH OUR BROTHERS THERE COULD DO.

RESPECTFULLY, BROTHER, JOHN OGDEN IS DOWN TO A HANDFUL OF MEN ON THAT SHIP. I THINK THEY COULD BE MANAGED WITHOUT MUCH BOTHER, WHATEVER THEIR REPUTATION–

JOHN OGDEN HAS KEPT ALL THE MEN HE REQUIRES. I WOULD HESITATE TO DEAL WITH SUCH MEN.
I'M AWARE, BUT–A SHIP, YOU KNOW, MAY BE SCUTTLED, NO MATTER WHOM IT CARRIES–
AND TO WHAT PURPOSE, BROTHER?

WELL. I SHOULD SAY IT WOULD PUT A WRINKLE IN MR. SLOANE'S PLAN, AT THE VERY LEAST.
BUT IF WE DO NOT KNOW HIS PLAN, WE CANNOT KNOW IF WE AND MR. SLOANE ARE WORKING AT CROSS-PURPOSES. THERE MAY BE A GREATER DANGER IN THWARTING HIM THAN YOU RECOGNIZE.

WHAT I RECOGNIZE, BROTHER, IS A FEAR OF MR. SLOANE, AND NOW A FEAR OF HIS INSTRUMENTS, IN YOU. I DO NOT THINK THESE ARE FEARS THAT MOST OF US SHARE.
I SEE. I SHOULD HOPE, *PÈRE* MARCHAND, THAT ALL OF US HAVE LIVED DOWN FEAR OF ANY KIND.

IF I COUNSEL PATIENCE, AND WATCHFULNESS, IT IS BECAUSE I BELIEVE MR. SLOANE KNOWS SOMETHING, OR WILL LEARN SOMETHING, THAT IS MORE THAN WE KNOW. AND WHAT HE LEARNS HE WILL TELL US, WHETHER HE VOLUNTEERS IT OR NO.
AND WHOM ELSE WILL HE TELL? THIS IS MY CONCERN.

I THINK YOU ARE TRUSTING A GOOD DEAL TO MR. SLOANE'S DISCRETION.
SO I AM.
AND I SHOULD SAY, IT IS MORE THAN I WOULD RISK, LEAVING THOSE MEN ON THEIR SHIP TO PONDER WHAT THEY ARE DOING, WITH PEOPLE WHO MIGHT PERHAPS FIND A WAY TO TELL THEM.

THEY ARE SOLDIERS, BROTHER. THEY ARE NOT INQUISITIVE LIKE YOU OR ME. THEY DO NOT MAKE INFERENCES OR DEDUCTIONS. AND WHATEVER THEIR PASSENGERS TELL THEM IS NOT LIKELY TO BE BELIEVED, THE TRUTH LEAST OF ALL.
AND IT DOES NOT CONCERN YOU THAT—VERY SOON, PERHAPS—JOHN OGDEN MUST MEET HIS EMPLOYER?

IT CONCERNS ME, BROTHER, BUT NOT FOR THE REASONS YOU HAVE IN MIND.
YOU WILL SEE THAT MR. SLOANE TAKES GREAT PAINS TO AVOID MEETING JOHN OGDEN. AND IF THEY EVER SHOULD MEET, IT WILL NOT BE TO EXCHANGE CONFIDENCES. OF THIS I AM REASONABLY SURE.

THEN YOU HAVE MADE YOUR CALCULATIONS. I SUPPOSE IT IS IN VAIN THAT I EXPRESS MY DOUBTS.

YOUR DOUBTS ARE NOTED. I BELIEVE THEY ARE COMMON TO MANY OF THOSE BEHIND YOU.
IS THAT ALL, THEN...?

I–YES. SO IT APPEARS.
I THANK YOU, BROTHER ABBOT.

LATER, OUTSIDE THE CASTLE WALLS, *PÈRE* MARCHAND WAVES DOWN ANOTHER SENIOR MEMBER OF THE BLACK-ROBED ORDER.
BROTHER DESMARAIS–? A WORD, PLEASE.

...SORRY, BUT THERE ISN'T A WHISPER INDOORS THAT DOESN'T REACH THE ABBOT'S EAR. I TRUST THIS IS NOT THE CASE OUT HERE, WITH YOURSELF?
NO INDEED, BROTHER. YOU MAY SPEAK FREELY.

GOOD. WE ARE SENDING WORD INTO THE WEST THIS MORNING. I WILL EXPLAIN WHAT WE HAVE DONE TO THE ABBOT, IN MY OWN TIME. BUT RIGHT NOW THERE IS LITTLE PROFIT IN DELAY.
NO, I SEE. YOU ARE WAKING THEM IN THE ARGENTINE, THEN?

WELL–YES, BUT I WASN'T THINKING QUITE SO FAR WEST. I WOULD LIKE TO MEET THAT SHIP OF OGDEN'S IN THE CAPE VERDES, IF WE CAN.
I BELIEVE WE HAVE HAD QUITE ENOUGH OF THESE PEOPLE RUN-NING LOOSE IN THE WORLD.

16º 39' 01" N Lat | 22º 00' 41" W Long
North Atlantic Ocean
55 Miles North-east of Boa Vista, Cape Verde

STILL THERE, MR. PRIDDISH?
YES. BUT STILL NO CLOSER.

MM. PERHAPS WE SLOW DOWN FOR HER.

WHO'S IT FOLLOWIN' US, THEN?
WHAT Y'ASKING HIM FOR, TOM?
RIGHT. WE KNOW F–CK-ALL ABOUT THIS, DO WE, BOY?
KNOWS ALL WE DO, I SUSPECT.
PARDON ME, JACK, BUT I'LL HEAR IT FROM HIM.

I–NO, I'M SURE I DON'T KNOW ABOUT ANY SHIPS, PRIVATE.
I MIGHT HAVE ASKED ONE OF YOU THE SAME THING, IF I DIDN'T THINK YOU'D JUST CURSE ME FOR ASKING QUESTIONS.

THAT WE WOULD, SON. YOU KEEP YER QUESTIONS, QUITE RIGHT.
THERE IS NO ONE TO ASK BUT MAJOR, ANYWAY. AND HE CANNOT HEAR YOU, WHERE HE SITS.

...IT IS A FOOLISH DISCUSSION.
AYE, WE'RE THAT. WE'RE FOOLS SURE.
AND DESERTERS NOW, WHAT? MR. BUCHAN?
YOU WERE THAT BEFORE, TOM.

AYE, BUT YOU WEREN'T. YOU WEREN'T HUNTED FOR A CAPITAL CRIME BEFORE, AS Y'ARE NOW. AND YOU MAY D—MN ME IF I SEE IT'S MADE THE LEAST DIFFERENCE IN YOU.
AND WHAT'S THAT MEAN?
YOU ASK HIM WHAT.
SORRY, I DON'T FOLLOW—

...P'RAPS HE DOUBTS HE WOULD HANG FOR THIS, AH? IS THAT IT, TOM? AS HE WOULDN'A INDEED, IF HE AN'T REALLY DESERTED AFTER ALL.
THOUGH I SEE HIM HERE WITH US, MARTIN. AS I SUSPECT YOU DO.
I MEAN IF HE WAS HERE ON ORDERS, SAY, FROM HIS LORD POMEROY.
AHH. THOUGH IT'S A DEAL OF SPECULATING, FOR BOTH YOU MEN. YOU OUGHT NOT TO STRAIN YOURSELVES.

NO—JACKIE, NOW, YE'LL MIND, YEH NEAR SHOT THIS BOY YERSELF FOR A SPY, DINN'YEH?
A SPY?
I SAYS YE'LL TELL US WHAT THAT SHIP IS. OR THEY'LL WATCH, AN' I'LL TRAMPLE AN ANSWER OUT OF YOU.

ALL RIGHT. THAT WILL DO, MR. MULCAIRN.
AYE, AN' I'LL HAVE THAT BOTTLE NOW.
INDEED YOU WILL NOT, JACK.

LET HIM ANSWER, JACK. IF IT AN'T POMEROY SENT HIM AMONG US, THERE'S PLENTY OTHERS'D LIKE TO KNOW WHAT WE'RE UP TO.
AND WHO KNOWS THAT, MR. PENSETTE?
AYE, DOES THIS BOY STRIKE YOU AS SOMEONE WHO KNOWS VERY MUCH THAT HE COULD TELL TO POMEROY, OR TO THE KING OF SIAM? BEGGING YOUR PARDON, CORPORAL.
NOT AT ALL– THAT'S RATHER MY POINT–

THOUGH WHAT HE DON'T KNOW AN'T FOR NOT ASKIN', IS IT?
MAJOR'S TOOK HIM IN, MARTIN, AND THAT'S WHAT YOU KNOW, WHICH IS PLENTY.
NOW: UP WITH YOU. MR BUCHAN, AND HAND ME THAT BOTTLE.
AN' I TELL YOU, SIT.

NAW, JACKIE. WE'LL HEAR WHAT HE KNOWS ABOUT THAT SHIP, FIRST.
MR. BUCHAN? I TOLD YOU TO GO ON.
REALLY, I'D RATHER YOU DIDN'T INVOLVE ME–

BUT Y'SEE, SON: YOU'RE INVOLVED.
THOUGH I DON'T ANSWER FOR YOUR SAFETY, IF YOU CANNOT MOVE YOURSELF.

AS BUCHAN INCHES TOWARD THE BOTTLE AND THE MEN QUIETLY FINGER KNIVES AND PISTOLS, NONE NOTICE MR. RENTON COMING ON.
ALL RIGHT. IF I JUST–PRIVATE: IF YOU'LL PERMIT ME TO...
–I SHOULDN'T DO THAT, MR. BUCHAN–

WHAT'S 'IS? THAT AIN'T FOR HIM.

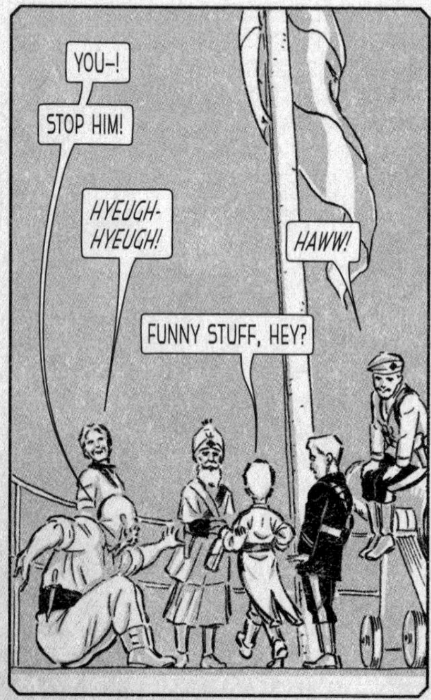
YOU–!
STOP HIM!
HYEUGH-HYEUGH!
HAWW!
FUNNY STUFF, HEY?

HERE'S SOME MORE, THEN–
LAUGH THIS OFF.

YOU MEN SOBER UP. MAJOR SAYS WE'RE BEIN' TRAILED.
WELL YOU SMART LE'LL–

HYAAAH!
RRR-OOFH!
COME ON.

WATCH IT NOW–WATCH IT–!
–GET HIS GUN, JACK–!

YA, IT'S THE CHIMPS MINDIN' THE ZOO, IN'NIT?
WATCH THE STEP THERE.

THEY SEEM TO THINK I'M A... SPY, FOR THE COMPANY.
YA? DOWN THERE AND HAVE A SEAT.
YOU'RE WITH THE LOONIES TONIGHT. MIND YOU STAY AWAKE.

BUT–I JUST CAME FROM HERE. THIS CAN'T BE MY WATCH–
NAW, IT'S MINE. BUT I GOTTA LOOK AFTER MAJOR.

OR GO BACK OUT TO THE GUN-DECK IF YE'D RATHER, WITH YER FRIENDS. YOU WAS GETTIN' ON FAMOUSLY, LOOKED LIKE.
SOMEONE THERE...?
OI! BE STILL, YOU!
«THOOM!»

NOW: KEEP 'EM QUIET TILL WE SPELL YA. THERE'S A GOOD MAN.
MR. RENTON? YOU'LL TELL THEM I'M NOT A SPY...?
AIN'T YOU, THOUGH?

We will not judge Mr. Buchan too severely, I hope, if we find him turning to his watch with no great relish tonight. It is his second of the evening in this dim, dripping corridor, with the grunts and groans of the ship and the cries of her human freight echoing all about him. It is pardonably difficult for the young Corporal, alone on such a night in the belly of the *Virago*, to see his enterprise in any very wholesome light. It seems rather that he and his new friends have been trespassing where they ought not to go; that they are dabbling in the mysteries of an unearthly or unholy intelligence, and that as they venture farther on these mysteries, they will find their steps cannot be retraced nor their ignorance reclaimed, as they may come soon to regret.

With thoughts like these upon him, then, and such company as he has, locked behind these doors, it is small wonder that we find Mr. Buchan wishing earnestly for some interruption of his watch. And there is an interruption coming, to be sure. Though we will have to decide presently whether he is very much the better for it.

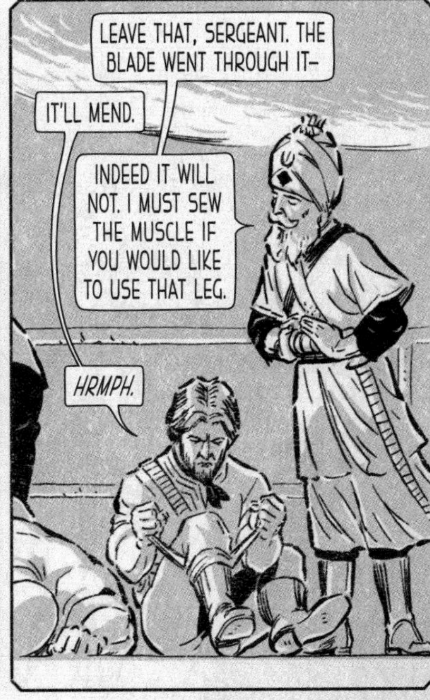

ALL RIGHT. YEH MAY DO YER WORST, MR. PRIDDISH.
BUT HELP ME OVER TO TOM FIRST, WOULD YEH?

THERE Y'ARE. F--CKING BOG-IRISH.
I CAME IN ON YER SIDE, YEH REALIZE.
«STOMP!»

THAT WILL NOT HELP.
BUT YE'R WRONG, SIR. IT IMPROVES MY MOOD. AND YEH SEE WHERE IT IMPROVES HIS LOOKS.

COME. I WOULD LIKE TO DO THIS QUICKLY. I MUST GET ME TO BED.

SIR?
MR. DYAK: YOU'RE ON WATCH WITH THAT HEAP OVER THERE, WHICH YOU'LL FIND IS PRIVATE MULCAIRN.

MR. PRIDDISH HAS HELPED HIM OFF TO SLEEP JUST NOW WITH A BELAYING PIN. BUT YOU MAY WAKE HIM WHEN YOU'RE FEELING MAN ENOUGH.
USE THIS, LAD.

EHH: BUT YOU'LL WAIT TILL I'M BEHIND THAT DOOR, WON'T YOU?

AUGHH.
HONEST TO CHR–ST, SIR, WI' YER D–MN BOOK...

{The Expedition Log of Arthur Ogden, continued.}

6 NOVEMBER.

Another day's rambling over the pack-ice, not at all improved by a lordly hangover. We follow our guides through a landscape in which I can identify no distinctive or permanent markings of any kind. And I have gone from wondering at the perception of these men, to recognizing myself some of these markings they might use for navigation, to developing a misgiving that we have passed not just similar but *the same* formations of ice, and finally to wondering in a very different sense whether these guides have any skills *at all.* And if this is true–if they really are leading us in a wide circle–then I must question whether they are doing it to some *purpose*, or only because they have no earthly idea what they are about....

I have so far hesitated to voice these thoughts, and I hold them even at a distance from myself, as I fear that panic will come quickly in train with them. But I *did* set one of Mr. Thierry's gloves out on a stake this morning as we left camp. I suppose if we run across this item again I shall have to begin worrying in earnest.

. . .

EVENING, 6 NOV.

No reappearance yet of the glove, and we bump along in this white hellscape hoping for the best. Another thing has come up, though, and since I am feeling neither very tired nor sociable and have only the empty hours to fill before sleep, I may as well describe it to you:

Now, I am not usually given to dreaming, and still less to recording my dreams or studying them for meaning. I think that no gentleman considerate of another's time would introduce his dreams into conversation, and I tend to discourage other men when they try. Yet I have been visited for three nights running, and again today as I dozed in the sledge, by a fancy of unusual consistency and power. And I thought I would set it down here if only that I might, through the exercise, either flush it out of my mind or else come properly to grips with it.

In the dream, I am lodging at the Explorers Guild in New York. The Guild, as you may know, maintain rooms above their common areas in most of the larger cities, and they let these rooms free of charge to visiting members. I have never boarded at the New York establishment for obvious reasons, and have made only brief and impromptu use of the upstairs rooms with guests of the gentler sex, which I should say is forbidden by club rules and none of your business anyway. But I stray from my point.

The monastic, oak-paneled room in my dream is not one you would find at the New York Guild, but is borrowed from a boyhood summer home at Anglesey. This is a persistent setting of my bad dreams and a sign that this one, too, will not end well.

As the dream opens I can hear Cousin Cyril holding court downstairs, and it occurs to me that this is the night of his initiation into the Guild. I have with me some undefined comment or bit of information that I feel will spoil the occasion for him and possibly keep him out of our number, yet as keen as I am to get downstairs and have this out I find that in the familiar trope of dreams I am held fast to my bed. A window has been left open in the room and the paralyzing cold of the Arctic is stealing in, which I suppose is what inhibits my movement. And the window, I find, has become my chief concern. I must get to it and close it, for there is some presence of evil outside–something of a piece with the cold, I think, unless the cold is its introduction, as an anaesthetic will precede the surgeon's knife....

My room has sunk by now to the level of the street, and there is a darkened street-lamp framed in the window. The lamp exudes shadow like a photographic negative of itself, and for all that I am looking away I know there is a tall and narrow figure waiting beneath the lamp, with the shadows pooling around him. This man has been looking in through my window and is near enough that he might thrust his face into the room, if indeed he is not already doing it.

In the dream's final stages I am being turned by some perverse impulse toward this man. And whether I see him or not I gather he is the long and languid foreigner I once saw beside my Cousin Cyril at the

Explorers Guild. He is not doing anything, particularly, only watching and waiting on some action of mine. But the recognition of him is so powerful that it jars me from sleep, and I will lie awake till I rise with the camp.

And there you have it—*voilà*, yes—that is all. My apologies, that a dream begun with at least some hint of greater meaning should fizzle out so abruptly. But what more would you have from dreams? I believe I introduced them as a subject that ill became gentlemen. I give you this dream of mine in support of the statement, and I suppose we can end its interpretation there.

III.

14º 13' 31" N LAT | 25º 12' 33" W LONG

ATLANTIC OCEAN, SOUTH OF PORTA DE EMBOSCADA
CAPE VERDE ISLANDS

. . .

JANUARY, 1918

THEY'RE ALL SECURED IN THERE, OGDEN'S MEN.
PARAR! CALE A BOCA!
«DOOM! DOOM!»

IT WAS ONLY THESE TWO HERE, OUT ON WATCH. SLEEPING WHEN THEY WERE BOARDED, I'M TOLD.
WHAT'RE WE UP TO THIS MORNING, FATHER?
QUIET, PLEASE.

AND THIS ONE: IS HE DEAD...?
ONLY BADLY HURT, BROTHER; BUT IT IS NOT OUR DOING. WE DISCOVERED HIM LIKE THIS.
AH. GOOD. AND JUST AS WELL, IF HE STAYS LIKE THIS. I DON'T ESPECIALLY LIKE THE LOOK OF HIM.
...P–SS OFF I SAID!

WHAT'S THIS?
HE SAYS IT'S THE BOY.
IT'S NOT THE BOY. GET AWAY FROM ME, BOTH OF YOU.

DAIEEE!
STOP THIS! WHAT IS HE DOING?
YOU—PEGUE ELE—GRAB HOLD OF HIM!
«STOMP!»

WHAT ABOUT OGDEN? IN HERE, TOO, IS HE?
OFF ME! -DOOFH–!
BETTER HE DON'T COME OUT, FATHER.
«THUNK-THUNK!»

SORRY?
BETTER FOR YOU, I MEAN. MAJOR'S APT TO BLAME YOU LOT FOR SLOWING DOWN HIS SHIP.
I IMAGINE HE WILL, YES. THANK YOU.
HELLO? MR. OGDEN...?

AH: Y'SEE, NOW—YE'RE ON YER OWN, FATHER.

THEY STOLE UP ON OUR WATCH, SIR, PAINTED ALL BLACK, AS YOU SEE 'EM. THEN THESE PRIESTS COME AFTER.
I WOULDN'T FEAR THEIR OLD WEAPONS, SIR. ONLY THOUGHT WE MIGHT HEAR OUT THE ONES IN THE CAFTANS BEFORE WE THREW 'EM BACK IN THE SEA.
JOHN OGDEN?

SIR: YOU HAVE TEN MEN BELOW-DECKS AND TWO WOMEN WHO ARE NOT YOURS AND NOT PART OF THE SHIP'S COMPANY. IF YOU CAN PRODUCE THEM, I WILL TAKE THEM AND LEAVE THE REST OF YOU AS YOU WERE.
I WOULD RATHER NOT GO LOOKING FOR THEM DOWN THERE MYSELF, IF YOU PLEASE.
MAJOR–I SAY–I FEAR YOU'RE INVOLVED IN A BUSINESS THAT HAS NOT BEEN PROPERLY EXPLAINED TO YOU.

I AM HERE TO RELIEVE YOU OF YOUR PART IN IT.
AND IF YOU UNDERSTOOD YOUR POSITION, SIR, AND MINE, YOU WOULD SEE I AM DOING YOU AN EXCELLENT SERVICE.
MR. OGDEN...?

HEAD'S BROKE, SIR. BUT THAT'S MR. PRIDDISH AND MR. PENSETTE, DID THAT.
YES, THAT'S RIGHT.
THROW THAT WATER OVER HIM.

I DARE SAY YOU ARE ONLY FOLLOWING YOUR BROTHER'S ORDERS, MR. OGDEN. BUT YOU CANNOT KNOW WHOM YOU ARE REALLY SERVING, OR WHAT YOU ARE HELPING TO ACCOMPLISH.
«SPLOOSH!»
THEY'VE TOLD YOU THERE'S A WAR GOING, I SUPPOSE...?
HADN'T YOU ALL BETTER BE IN THAT?
HYEKK–!
WAIT–! NO-NO! LET HIM GO–!
SOMEONE HELP HIM!
WHAT'S HE DONE? IS THAT MAN ALL RIGHT?
HE'S–NO, I BELIEVE HE'S DEAD, BROTHER.
«THONK!»

HE'S—WHAT? MY G—D, MAJOR, WHAT ARE THESE MEN, ANIMALS?
AH-WELL: IT'S YOU WHO'VE BOARDED US, FATHER.
BUT—WE CAME WITH NUMBERS, AND GUNS—WE CAME IN OVERWHELMING FORCE, YOU SEE, SO THERE WOULD BE NO QUESTION OF KILLING.

AND NOW IT'S DONE, MAJOR. LOOK AROUND YOU AND COUNT. YOU CAN ONLY BEG TERMS, AND THAT'S—
...WHAT ARE YOU DOING?
I'LL TELL YOU A STORY, FATHER.
A...? NO—I'M NOT IN A HUMOR FOR STORIES, I THANK YOU.

I'LL HAVE THOSE MEN AND WOMEN OUT ON DECK THIS MINUTE, IF YOU PLEASE. OTHERWISE I'M AFRAID I MUST SCUTTLE THE SHIP.
I'D COME WITH AN IDEA OF PRESERVING THEIR LIVES AND YOURS. BUT I WOULD JUST AS SOON LET YOU ALL DROWN TOGETHER, AT THIS POINT.

...IT'S A STORY ABOUT OVERWHELMING NUMBERS, LIKE YOURS.
WHAT?
LISTEN, FATHER. YOU'LL LIKE THIS.

I WAS A BOY OF ABOUT MR. RENTON'S AGE, ATTACHED TO MY UNCLE IN THE INDIAN SERVICE. HE WAS SENT OVERLAND INTO CHINA, WHERE WE SURPRISED A PARTY OF GURKHAS IN A HEAVY FOG, SOMEWHERE NEAR REGONG. WE WERE TEN OR MORE TO THEIR ONE, ARMED WITH SCAVENGED MATCHLOCK RIFLES, AS YOUR MEN HAVE THIS MORNING.

A GURKHA WILL SOONER FIGHT YOU THAN NOT, OF COURSE. BUT THESE, STRANGE TO SEE, WENT BELLY-DOWN IN THE ROAD AT THE SIGHT OF US. MY UNCLE STUDIED THIS FOR SOME MINUTES, THEN ORDERED THE CANNON ROLLED OVER THEM AND ALL BE D–MNED.

WELL, THEY WAITED TILL HIS CHARGER HAD JUST ABOUT TREAD OVER THE FIRST OF THEM. THEN UP THEY ALL JUMPED, AND THEY FELL ON US WITH THEIR KNIVES.

THE REST WAS DONE QUICKLY ENOUGH. I STOOD TO SEE THE ROAD STOPPED UP WITH THE BODIES OF MEN AND HORSES, AND THE NEPALESE ALREADY MILES AWAY. IT WAS ME THEY SPARED, TO BRING THE NEWS BACK TO INDIA.

THE GURKHAS RUSHED YOU BEFORE YOU'D A CHANCE TO FIRE, I SUPPOSE.
WHAT THEY DID WAS LIE IN THE DIRT. WHEN MY UNCLE GAVE THE ORDER, HIS FIFTY GUNS MISFIRED, EVERY ONE OF THEM.
IMPOSSIBLE.

YES, BUT INTERESTING. DO YOU THINK YOU COULD PERFORM THIS TRICK FOR US TODAY, MAJOR?
I CAN TEACH YOU WHAT I LEARNED AS A BOY. THAT THE MATCHLOCK WON'T FIRE IN A HEAVY FOG. AND IT'S EVEN LESS USE IN THE RAIN.
THE ONLY 'TRICK' IS IN KEEPING THE GUNNER STILL WHILE HIS MATCH AND POWDER SOAK. BY LYING IN HIS WAY.
«SNAP»
BROTHER...?

...OR BY TELLING A STORY.
–NO. NO-NO. WAIT–
WE'RE THROUGH WAITING, FATHER. NOW I SEND YOU TO GLORY.
SHOOT! ATIRE! MATÁ-LO!

«PFFFTT»
«PFFFTT»
«PFFFTT»
«PFFFTT»

...HM.

HYEKK!

«SPLOOSH!»

«THWOKK!»
HYEHH!

«FFTINNG!»

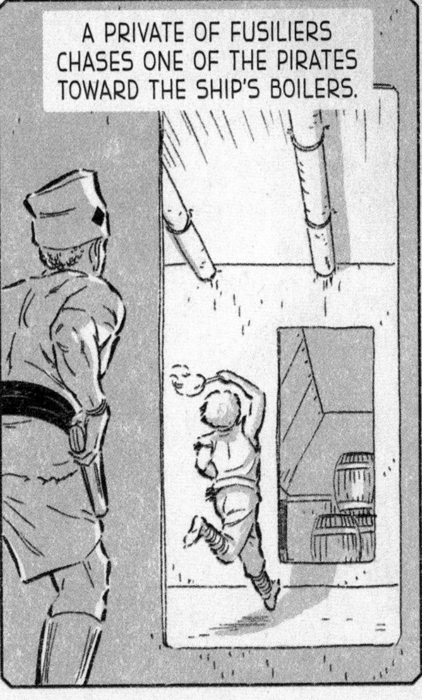
A PRIVATE OF FUSILIERS
CHASES ONE OF THE PIRATES
TOWARD THE SHIP'S BOILERS.

HE FINDS, TOO LATE, THAT THE
POWDER HAS BEEN SET HERE.
«POP!»

«BAVOOOM!»

IT'S NO GOOD WITH THE PUMPS, SIR. WE'VE TOOK ON TOO MUCH WATER.
ALL RIGHT, CALL THE MEN UP. AND CHECK AGAIN FOR HORSES. I CAN HEAR ONE DOWN THERE.
AYE, IT'S MULCAIRN. WON'T COME UP WITH-OUT THAT NAG MR. BUCHAN GAVE HIM.

AH: THERE THEY COME, MAJOR, OUT YON HATCH. THE MAN'S A LOT TOO STUPID TO DIE, IN'NE? MUST GO FOR THE HORSE AS WELL.
MM. OR IT MAY JUST SHOW YOU, SER-GEANT, WHAT A MAN WILL DO FOR A GIFT, WHO ISN'T USED TO GETTING THEM.

THROW THEM OUT A LINE, ANYWAY. MULCAIRN'S NO SWIMMER.
AYE, SIR. AND THEN WHAT?
THEN WE'LL SEE WHAT THEY WANT.
WHO, SIR?

...OH, AYE.

MOMENTS LATER, A YOUNG LADY'S HEAD POKES OVER THE RAIL OF THE WHITE YACHT.
SORRY: THERE ISN'T A MR. SLOANE DOWN THERE...?
SLOANE? AFRAID NOT, MISS.
YOU WOULDN'T MIND CHECKING AGAIN, WOULD YOU? THIS IS AN AWFUL DISAPPOINTMENT.
AH...QUITE SURE, MISS. NO SLOANES ABOARD.

...AUGH. D–MN IT.
HUH. FINE WAY FOR A LADY TO TALK.
WHERE'D SHE GO, NOW?

THERE SHE IS, JACK.
SORRY: IF YOU'D LIKE TO DRY OFF, WE'VE GOT PLENTY OF ROOM.
AH: GOOD. BE MUCH OBLIGED TO YEH, MISS.
YES. THANK YOU, MISS HARROW.

HOW'S THAT, MR. BUCHAN?
I S'POSE YOU KNOW THIS GIRL?
OH, YOU'RE JOKING–THAT'S EVELYN HARROW, ISN'T IT?
WHO?

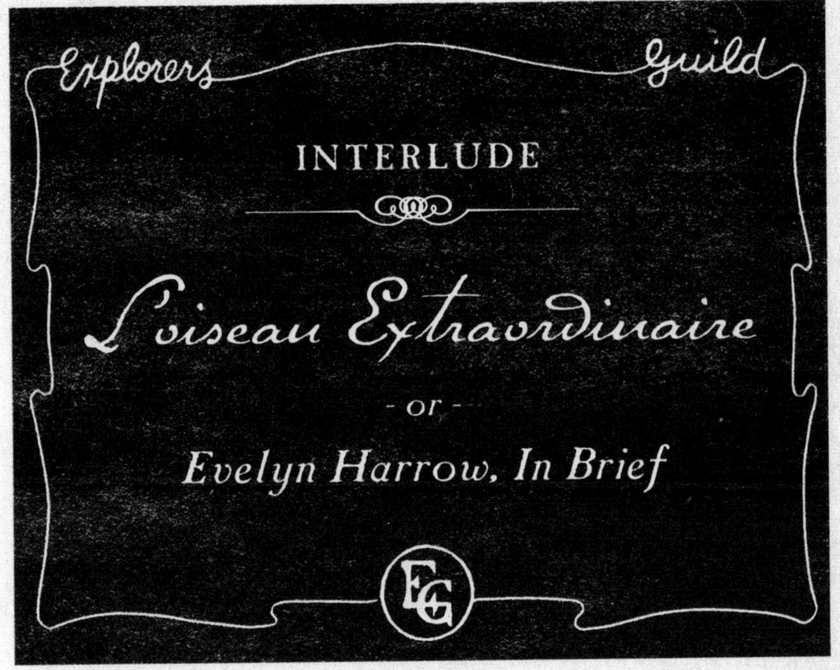
Explorers Guild
INTERLUDE
L'oiseau Extraordinaire
- or -
Evelyn Harrow, In Brief
EG

1898. ILYENA SIROTSKAYA IS BORN TO A FAMILY OF MODEST MEANS IN THE PROVINCES.

«FLING!»

Великий день
Вольфрам мины
HER FATHER AND UNCLES ARE LOST IN A MINE COLLAPSE

AND HER WIDOWED MOTHER GOES QUICKLY TO THE BAD.

AT FIFTEEN, ILYENA IS ALREADY A WORLDLY AND SELF-POSSESSED YOUNG BEAUTY WITH A WIDE EXPERIENCE OF MEN. SHE IS TOURING WITH THE DUKE OF WAPPING WHEN HE IS KILLED AT THE FIFTH TURN OF LE MANS.

HER IMAGE ON A NEWSREEL CAPTIVATES FILM DIRECTOR BASIL SPRAGUE. SHE WILL BE HIS GREATEST DISCOVERY.

ILYENA'S BEAUTY AND SANGFROID MAKE HER A STAR OF THE YOUNG CINEMA.

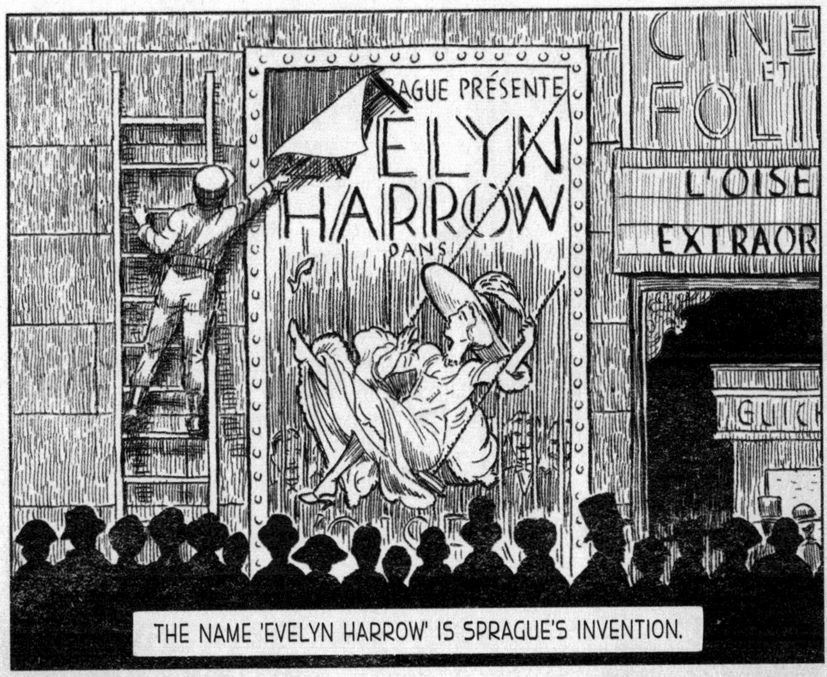
AGUE PRÉSENTE
ELYN
HARROW
DANS
CINE
ET
FOLI
L'OISE
EXTRAOR
THE NAME 'EVELYN HARROW' IS SPRAGUE'S INVENTION.

HER AFFAIRS WITH PROMINENT MEN ARE MANY AND SIMULTANEOUS.

MM. I THOUGHT YOU WERE GETTING ME A MANGO.
IN 1914, SHE IS THE SUBJECT OF SIX DUELS, WAGED ON THREE CONTINENTS IN THE SPAN OF A WEEK. GIVEN THE NEWS ON HOLIDAY IN GREECE, MISS HARROW MAKES HER FAMOUS REPLY.

EVELYN HARROW
ARCHBISHOP'S FOLLY
HER STAR CONTINUES TO RISE. THERE ARE BOX-OFFICE RIOTS IN BUDAPEST; TRAMPLINGS IN ITALY. LATE WITH A PRINT OF 'ARCHBISHOP'S FOLLY,' A VIENNESE CINEMA IS BURNED BY A MOB, ITS MANAGER HURLED INTO THE DANUBE.

SICK OF IT ALL
London Tribune
SICK OF IT ALL!
SAYS HARROW
SICK OF IT ALL
LE JOUR
Sick of it all
SICK OF IT AL
THE CLAMOR SPREADS UNTIL, AT THE HEIGHT OF HER CELEBRITY, MISS HARROW PRONOUNCES HERSELF 'SICK OF IT ALL.'

SHE WITHDRAWS FROM POLITE SOCIETY, AND IS REPORTED IN VARIOUS UNDERGROUND AND OCCULT CIRCLES. IN PRAGUE, SHE TRADES THE ST. ERASMUS RUBY FOR AN INTERVIEW WITH THE DECEASED MADAME BLAVATSKY.

BUT IT IS IN THE EAST, WITH THE MYSTICS OF TIBET, THAT MISS HARROW DISCOVERS HER LIFE'S PURSUIT.

EVER A FICKLE LOVER AND AN INDIFFERENT ACTRESS...

...SHE TAKES UP THE SEARCH FOR SHAMBHALA
WITH A WILL THAT VERGES ON OBSESSION.

WHILE ELSEWHERE, QUIETLY, BASIL SPRAGUE IS BURIED
WITH A PRINT OF YOUNG ILYENA AT LE MANS.

IV.

HWUHH!
<<CRACK!>>

CE SONT DES SAUVAGES!
IN ENGLISH, MESS-YURE.
YE'R UNDER NEW MANAGEMENT.
<<PLONK!>>

LOVELY SHIP, MUM, REALLY. 'PRECIATE THE LOAN OF IT.
IT BELONGS TO THE PASHA OF MARRAKECH. I'M ONLY BORROWING IT MYSELF.
THEN YOU TELL 'IM WHAT I SAID.

SIR: WE'RE ABOUT UNDER WAY. GOT THE LOONIES LOCKED UP BELOW; BIT EXCITED BUT ALL ACCOUNTED FOR.
MM.
...'GOOD WORK, MR. RENTON.'
NOT AT ALL, SIR. MY PLEASURE TO SERVE.

DON'T MIND 'IM, MUM. LOSIN' THE SHIP'S A HARD ONE FOR MAJOR TO SWALLER. 'SIDES WHICH: BIT UNUSED TO THE SERCIETY O' LADIES.
...WHAT?
COME HERE. GO ON, I WON'T PINCH YOUR CHEEK.
NO YOU BL–DY WILL NOT–

HA! YOU'RE WITH THE EXPLORERS GUILD.
ME–? A LOT YOU KNOW. THAT BELONGS TO MAJOR'S BROTHER. FOUND IT IN THE POCKET OF THIS TUNIC, WHEN MAJOR GIVE IT TO ME.
LOOK 'ERE–THIS BULLET-HOLE ON THE RIGHT SHOULDER...

ONLY TIME MAJOR'S BEEN SHOT, THAT WE KNOW OF. THE BALL'S STILL OVER THERE IN HIS SHOULDER. PAINS HIM ON NIGHTS LIKE THIS, WHEN IT RAINS. AND THEN HE DRINKS, AND GETS PARTICKLER ABOUT HIS MUSIC–
YOU'RE JOHN OGDEN.
ARTHUR OGDEN'S BROTHER.
'COURSE 'E IS.

ALL THOSE MAD-LOOKING PEOPLE BELOW: YOU'VE BEEN COLLECTING THEM–HAVEN'T YOU?–FOR YOUR BROTHER. AND NOW YOU'VE GOT INVOLVED WITH MR. SLOANE–
WITH WHO–? MAJOR WOULDN'T BE FOUND DEAD IN A DITCH WITH ANY MR. SLOANES. WOULD YOU, SIR?
'OO'S 'E, THEN?
I'M NOT SUPPOSED TO KNOW THESE THINGS, HM? WELL, I DO. AND IF YOU'D LIKE TO MAKE USE OF MY SHIP–
WE ARE USING IT.

THEN I'M SORRY, DEAR. WE'LL JUST HAVE TO GET ALONG, YOU AND I.
I SAY, YOU CAN GROUSE ABOUT YOUR OLD BOAT ALL YOU WANT. BUT I SHOULD THINK YOU'D LIKE TO KNOW WHO SANK IT FOR YOU, MM? I MEAN THOSE MEN IN THE DARK ROBES, OF COURSE. WOULDN'T YOU JUST LIKE TO KNOW WHO THEY ARE?
...MR. OGDEN?
SEE HER TO HER ROOM, MR. RENTON. IF SHE WON'T GO QUIETLY, LOWER A BOAT FOR HER.
OH, YOU'RE NOT SERIOUS...?

IT'S PIRACY, YOU KNOW–NOT TO MENTION AWFULLY RUDE–LOCKING A YOUNG WOMAN AWAY IN HER OWN SHIP–
–EHH: THOUGH, IN A POINT OF FACT–
WHOEVER'S SHIP IT IS, THEN. I HAD IT FIRST.

11 NOVEMBER, 1912.

I think you cannot hand in your monograph on Arctic travel these days without attempting some anthropological survey of the polar region and its native groups. This history of mine makes no pretense of scholarship, as you are aware; yet I thought I might record a few thoughts and observations on the Inuit, this being a subject that is ever present in my thoughts and always quite literally before my eyes, much as I could desire it elsewhere.

Now, the Inuk male, as I believe, is the very type and expression of his landscape, in that both are an unrelieved *bore*. We praise him for his cleverness and his persistence in regions where we find the living intolerable; yet, as far as that goes, he has made no accommodation to his environment that your reasonably adept sportsman would not think up in a day's outing, and this despite his having some several *millennia* to mull these things over. That it should take so many Englishmen meeting death by cold in their frock coats and gaiters before Perry deigned to dress in the local mode–this, I think, is less a comment on the genius of the Inuit than on the eccentricities of the English, and on the hazards of holding one's dignity too dear.

As to the 'noble savage,' there is not the least evidence of any such creature anywhere in the North. The idea that the Inuk exhibits *wisdom*–or excellence in any form–in his primitive goings-about is strictly a western inference, and is dispelled immediately on one of these fellows' opening his mouth, which he does seldom enough and perhaps for this reason. The Inuk's 'wisdom' derives from emulating the beasts in the field, and before you roll out your odes to *man in a state of nature* I would have you invite one of these sages to your home for the week-end, and see how well you admire him come Monday. You will find, as I have, that his language is preposterous, his manners are a scandal, and for company you are better set with the carved Inuk idol at the Explorers Guild, which at least wore a garter for the Queen's jubilee.

As to the women, just you try to pick them out from the men in a gathering of Inuit. They are all the same waddling, unwashed, walnut-faced heaps of sealskin, with that same animal cunning and instinct to treachery showing about the eyes. It is only when the Inuit fall to work that the gentler sex distinguishes itself, for the ones doing the work will invariably be your females, with the idle remainder being the men. The women are also marginally quieter than the men, which is to say, marginally chattier than the fish they eat; and what conspiratorial grunts and clicks and whispers they do share among them are clearly not for the *Kabluunak*'s (that is to say, our own) hearing.

So: comely and companionable these ladies are not. But industrious? I should say rather. It is they who, when their men have called the day's end and appointed a site, will do everything else of value till we are moving again (and then it is the dogs who do us the greater service). Nights the women unload and moor the sledges, sculpt the ice into berms or windbreaks, set up our tents, kindle the fires and lay out our stores, mend clothes and canvas and rope and splint the sledges and so forth; and all this before setting up camp for their sullen, smoking men. We wake to see the needed items struck and packed, the dogs in harness and bowls of hot water set out for shaving. We do not leave a *neat* camp, for the Inuit strew their refuse everywhere and this cannot be helped. But we spend the hours between one bone-rattling hike and the next in what gentlemanly ease the place affords. And if we have any reserves of strength or will to continue, if any of our wits or a single passably fond recollection remain to us after this journey, it will have been through the agency of these ladies.

I should say, I was not at all conscious of hiring women when we equipped at Fort Defiance, and I was a bit surprised when Mr. Fidis pointed out that these busy ones were females. I asked him, given that we are headed to this Arctic Babylon of Ikkumaaluk, if our guides weren't perhaps carrying their coals to Newcastle, as the saying goes. But it appears the men have brought their ladies as we've brought our own pelts and liquor—that is, as articles of *trade*; and that this is done not only with the ladies' knowledge, but quite possibly at their *instigation*. I suppose I should object to some aspect or other of the arrangement, but I cannot work myself up to the proper pitch of indignation; and I can hardly object to having women about the camp generally, when they are of such manifest use.

Now: you might suppose, with the white men of our party and the Inuit ladies living on such intimate terms and in such prolonged isolation, that some natural affection might spring up between the two. Yet here you would be in error. The miles seem only to erode their trust and to heighten their distaste for us, and it is difficult not to return these sentiments in kind. We see exhibited none of the childish playfulness or freedom from inhibition that excited the unpardonable behaviors of Parry and his men (indeed, I begin to judge his expeditions with a deepening severity); and what kindnesses my men do offer are declined on such terms that they will not renew the attempt. This is odd indeed, given that in some short weeks, if Mr. Vidis be correct, these kindnesses and a good deal more will be exchanged as a matter of commerce. With any other race I would guess the women are only hiking up demand against a time when these withheld favors will become available for purchase. But as I say, the Inuit are never so clever as this. And if you could see the revulsion they exude when among us you would know this to be wholly unfeigned.

At camp, therefore, we maintain a strict division between the Inuit and ourselves, and it is only Mr. Vidis who acts the ambassador between the two. This remarkable man has told me he is a member of the 'international brethren,' by which I think he means he is a *gypsy*. But whatever the case, he is short and dark enough to pass for an Inuk, in his furs, and it is just as well he has established himself at their cook-fire and can be heard clucking away with them in a *patois* of English, Amerindian and Inuktitut—Just as well, I say, since I seem to be growing steadily more aloof from them myself, and do not even consult any longer with the translators.

I should think this evolution had mostly to do with the views and feelings I have described above. But as regards the women, I own an additional perversity that makes any approach to them unthinkable. It is a thing I have discovered in myself as I've traveled the world and sampled its women, notching my share of triumphs, to be sure, but also lying up in places where your most desperate and indiscriminate lover might fear to tread. To be plain, I have some imp in me where once I have set my bottom-most moral boundary or identified some line that I cannot cross or, to be plainer still, marked out some lady as utterly and safely beneath my dignity–and generally with a flood of relief, as though *here* at least were something I needn't fear doing, no matter what my straits–I say, no sooner have I staked out this limit than I realize, with a dread certainty, that I will cross it at my first opportunity.

Just how, or why, the Unthinkable becomes the Inevitable I am sure I don't know; you will have to ask my imp (and you may meet some lesser version of him in yourself, when I tell you, for instance, that you are under no circumstance to think of *orchids*). Yet I know from my history with him how he operates, and that in the current circumstance the more repellant I find these Inuit ladies the greater my certainty that somewhere on the road to Ikkumaaluk I must throw myself at the worst of the lot.

Malthrop and Apsley are familiar with this failing of mine, too, and they find my struggles with the Inuit powerfully amusing. They lay odds on which of them I shall pay court to (a farce, since we've no idea which of them is which), and they suggest I go to Ikkumaaluk bound to a sledge like Odysseus passing the Isle of Sirens. I can appreciate the humor in this, of course. But I find at the same time that I cannot see one of these ladies pass my tent opening without a premonitory thrill of horror.

. . .

15 NOV. Our route continues haphazard into the North. More huddling and conspiracy and darkening looks from these Inuit. What their behavior portends I should not like to guess. But we have mounted an informal guard over the stores and will no longer on any account let the Esquimaux ladies handle our food or drink.

I begin to suspect that our guides are as like to *guides* as we are to *explorers*, which I suppose is only us getting our desserts. In future, when I am settled back at my home and have leisure to reflect on our travels, I will no doubt find some rare joke in this; but tonight I only find it tiresome and in some part alarming.

I have not re-discovered that glove of Thierry's I set outside our old camp, but I cannot, withal, suppress this idea that we have become *lost.* And I am hearing the same suspicion echo now among my men.

I have put some pointed questions to Vidis as to the state of our guides and the prospects for our journey, and he is with the Inuit tonight probing for answers. We await news from him and try to keep our thoughts in happier channels. I will try not to dwell, for instance, on how a group of silent, treacherous primitives are carrying our lives in their hands, nor consider that my one link to these people and their thoughts is a stowaway gypsy....

Gaddis suggests I set down my writing and have a drink, and it is the first sensible proposal anyone has put to me today.

. . .

16 Nov.: Revelations from Mr. Fijdis!

It is because the cold and privation are not challenge enough, that I must deal with this day's madness: our Inuit have become convinced we are being *followed*.

There is a man, they say—or some *thing*, or a party of them—out roaming the wastes; and it—or he, or they—have been dogging our steps since we left the Fort Defiance settlement. I must say, I have never seen these people so exercised as when they entered on the subject of our stalker. And much as it has made a bedlam of camp, it also brings a welcome change from the weeks of sulking silence.

Now, the Inuit have no developed idea of spirits or deities or the occult generally. They evaluate their world, insofar as they do, in the most literal and immediate terms. Yet there is some facet of this thing following us that they cannot quite square with their notions of men. They cannot, for one thing, raise any sign of him, these people who can (when they are of a mind to do it) spot a vole's burrow at half a mile with the dogs in full charge. When pressed to explain what this thing might actually *be*—if not a man or beast—they begin yammering all at once, and recurring to words like *nikpartok*—waiting thing; and *aimerpok*—visitor, foreigner, or 'other'; yet even I could tell they hadn't the words in their lexicon to suit their meaning. This 'Other' was flesh and blood, they said, yet he did not present himself to view in the daylight, and he could not be tracked by any means. He was not always behind us, either, but just as often ahead, keeping well wide of us—Save of course at night, when he went through the camp and featured in their dreams.

We had, up to this last remark, been listening to their ravings with a kind of avuncular concern, not unmixed with amusement and a few winks aside. But I saw this mention of dreams strike a note with my men (and I saw, too, that I was not the only one in camp with an incubus). Our guides stood arrested for a moment, as children do who have suddenly brought a room full of adults to attention; and then they were clamoring again and tugging at us with their excitement redoubled. I felt I must kill this thing before the camp fell wholesale into hysterics, and I stood, therefore (we preferred to address them sitting, while they stood about us), and waved them all to silence. If there were truly a man out on the ice, I said, tossing a hand at the wide white vista, this fellow must introduce himself and beg our aid sooner or later—he must light a *fire* at the very least—else he must perish. And in any case, a full score of vigilant and well-armed men had not the least thing to fear from him. *If*, however—I hastened add, as murmurs rose through the camp—*If* this thing were something other than human, why then I supposed it could only be the Devil himself, late to meet us at Ikkumaaluk.

I needn't tell you I meant this last bit as a little joke. But a more ill-conceived, ill-timed joke I have never made, and I speak from a lifetime's experience in these things. I let forth a shrill, operatic laugh that was not at all the offhand thing I'd intended, and signaled for my men to do the same, which they did. And there we all were, for a long minute that I should dearly like to have back, cackling like Holinshed's witches, to the horror of our Inuit audience.

I understood in that moment—just a moment too late—what it is that veils the eyes of our Inuit. I saw the reason for the gloomy silences, the haunted looks and the huddled, whispering palavers: there is a deep and unshakable *fear* upon these people. It has been gnawing at them since we left Fort Defiance, nor do I doubt that this fear was what chased them from the settlement in the first place.

I have told you the Inuit have very few ghosts or spirits or demons in their tradition. What I suppose I ought to have said is that they have few ghosts or demons that are their own invention. What they *do* have is a proper terror of the Christian Devil, and this as a by-product of living beside the *Kabluunak* for as long as they have (indeed, you will find the Devil well at home in several far-flung populations of the world, whether his creators have arrived yet or no). The Inuit's Devil, as I take it, is a living thing who visits from either the deeps of the sea or the torrid zones of the South, appearing in different guises–some material and corporeal, others less so–but bent always upon deeds of evil, in service of the Christian sorcerers who drum him up. In other words, *precisely* the sort of fellow to lurk about on the wastes, hounding our expedition until his white hosts should call him into service. My laughing invocation of his name has, quite naturally, fixed the matter once and for good in the minds of these people. It is not only the Devil stalking us across the snows, now: it is *my* Devil, you see.

And there we are. We'd a great exchange of shouts after my joke, most of it useless recanting on my part, leading up to Numm-Smythe's firing his pistol into the air and crying out 'Just get us to *f–ing* Ikkumaaluk, can you?'

...But now all of this has passed. We have used up our scant daylight in discussion of this *Other*, as he is called, and we bed down in last night's camp with no progress made toward Ikkumaaluk (or, to think positively, we were led no farther away from it). The Inuit revert to their shrinking silences of yesterday, and not even Mr. Fidis will make bold to sit at their fire tonight.

Yet I am not prepared to count the day a total loss. I have got *something*, after all, to account for our guides' behavior. Not that, absent this fear of theirs, they would be performing acts of vaudeville or declaiming Ovid. I think you take my meaning. It is this *fear* that is driving them pell-mell into the North like a horse with its tail burning, and with no object before them but escaping it. We must discover some way to remove this fear or else make use of it, before we really are lost beyond recall.

Tonight, too, to be practical, and since I have got my own name mixed up in the fears of this camp, I have had the indispensable Mr. Fidis string a trip-wire to a box of flares outside the tent I share with Malthrop. We will make it lively for anyone, man or otherwise, who would call on us unannounced in the night. Though we must endeavor, too, to remember we've set this trap before exiting the tent in the morning.

GOOD MORNING–
WHICH ONE ARE YOU?
CORPORAL BUCHAN, MA'AM–
AUGHH. DON'T ANY OF YOU HAVE CHRISTIAN NAMES?
NO, I DON'T THINK MOST OF US DO; OR NOT THAT WE'D REMEMBER. BUT MY MUM CALLED ME JAMES.

THEN YOU'RE NOT REALLY ONE OF THEM, ARE YOU. I KNEW IT. HOW OLD ARE YOU?
I'M–NO, ONLY A DESPATCH-RUNNER OUT OF BOMBAY, MA'AM. AND I'VE JUST TURNED TWENTY, WHEN WE WERE IN ALGIERS.
YOU DIDN'T. DID YOU? YOU DON'T LOOK ANY OLDER THAN ME.
WELL THAT'S CLEAN LIVING, YOU KNOW.
–*HRM.* I'M SURE IT IS. ANYWAY: I'M EVELYN.

YES, OF COURSE. I SHOULD SAY WHAT A LUCKY THING IT WAS, MISS HARROW, YOUR FINDING US WHEN YOU DID–
–THOUGH YOU KNOW LUCK HAD NOTHING TO DO WITH IT–
–WELL, YOU WERE A GODSEND IN ANY CASE. I HOPE WE'VE ALL CONVEYED OUR THANKS.
HAVEN'T YOU, JUST?
HAVE WE?

WHY, YES. YOU'RE ALLOWING ME MEALS, AREN'T YOU? AND I'M LET OUT ON THE DECK FOR MINUTES AT A TIME, SO YOUR FRIENDS CAN OGLE ME. I SUPPOSE THEY'RE GATHERING UP THERE NOW...?
OH: ONLY CORPORAL O'HARA.
AH! MY MINDER. AND VOLUNTEERED FOR THE JOB, I DON'T DOUBT. HE'S BEEN ESPECIALLY KEEN TO 'CONVEY HIS THANKS' SINCE WE FISHED YOU ALL FROM THE OCEAN, FOOLS THAT WE ARE. YOU WOULDN'T BE A DEAR AND SHOOT THAT MAN FOR ME, WOULD YOU?

...ONLY JOKING, MR. BUCHAN. YOU CAN KEEP YOUR HAIR ON.
–NO, I REALIZE. I JUST DON'T THINK MR. O'HARA APPROVES OF OUR SPEAKING.
OH NEVER MIND WHAT HE APPROVES OF.
WHAT'S THAT? ARE YOU KEEPING A DIARY OF YOUR ADVENTURES?

IT'S–WELL, BITS HERE AND THERE–
AM I IN IT? I AM. OH, AND PICTURES, TOO–YOU'VE GOT TO LET ME LOOK–
STOP IT. STOP.
NO, BUT I TELL YOU WHAT: YOU STAND THERE, AND I'LL DRAW YOU RIGHT NOW.
YOU'LL–? DON'T BE FOOLISH.

GO ON. OR DON'T YOU THINK I CAN?
I HADN'T FORMED AN OPINION ABOUT IT, ONE WAY OR THE OTHER.
I TELL YOU, I'VE TRAINED WITH EUROPEAN MASTERS. I'VE HAD GENERALS' WIVES SIT FOR ME, AND EMPRESS CONSORTS AND THE MAHARANIS OF THE PUNJAB–
–LIAR. WHAT SHOULD I DO? LIKE THIS?

WHATEVER YOU LIKE. BUT QUICKLY: I THINK YOUR MR. O'HARA'S COMING.
...THERE. AH: YOU KNOW, I MAY HAVE GOT YOU TOO WELL.
NO–I DAREN'T LET YOU HAVE THIS.

GIVE IT–! COME ON.

ALL RIGHT. BUT YOU'LL SHOW THIS TO NO ONE ELSE.
YOU'RE MAD.
QUITE SERIOUS. OPEN THAT IN PRIVATE, IF YOU PLEASE.

B–GGER OFF 'ER, BOY.

WHAT IS THIS?
ARE YOU INSANE?

I SUPPOSE THAT'S ME?
West, you man –
And quick about it!

SORRY–OUGHT TO HAVE SAID, IT'S MORE OF AN ALLEGORY–
IT'S A D–MNED IMPERTINENCE. YOU'VE GOT ME AS...CLEOPATRA?
–THAT'S RIGHT. CARRIED ALONG BY THE REST OF US–

BY THE MEN HOLDING ME CAPTIVE, YOU MEAN, ON MY OWN BOAT? WHO LOCK ME IN MY ROOMS, WHENEVER THEY GO ASHORE? HAVE YOU NOTICED AT ALL, MY STANDING AMONG YOU MEN?
WELL–THOUGH YOU KNOW WE ONLY ACT UNDER ORDERS. REALLY, TO HEAR IT FROM THE MEN, I SHOULD SAY IT'S YOU WHO'VE CONQUERED US–APPEARANCES ASIDE, OF COURSE–

–AUGHH, WHAT NONSENSE. AND HERE I THOUGHT WE MIGHT BE FRIENDS, JAMES.
WELL–LOOK: IF YOU DON'T LIKE IT, I'LL TAKE IT BACK AND WE'LL TRY AGAIN–

NO, YOU'VE HAD YOUR CHANCE, AND THIS IS MINE, NOW. I ONLY WANTED TO CORRECT YOU ON THAT ONE POINT.
...AND YOU HAVE MY APOLOGIES.

18 NOVEMBER. Have canalized my thoughts on the Inuit and their 'Other' and set down a course of action in three parts, thus:

First, building on the assumption that we are lost: we ought to calculate just *how* lost we have become (if you can really speak of such a thing in shades or degrees). Can we reach Ikkumaaluk, for instance, or any known settlement, before we are eating the dogs? This is a question I will put to the guides, whether they are in a mood for questions or no.

Second, I must convince the Inuit that there is no one *following* us, or leading us, or whatever they imagine he is doing. It must be borne in on them what an impossible, absurd and potentially dangerous idea this is.

Third–and I am aware this runs counter to last point, so I will call it a last resort–*Third*, I will put it out that it most assuredly *is* the Devil behind us, and he has come at my calling to keep these guides honest about their work. Our wanderings, I will say, have increased his displeasure, and if we cannot right our course and get to Ikkumaaluk *post haste*, we will have *Him* to reckon with.

. . .

20 NOV Inuit remain impenetrable, and we continue to bear the costs of their delusion and panic. Fear of this Other mounts with passing days & they will not accept the idea that he is in my control (which threat I did resort to though in vain). They feel he is here to visit a terrific punishment on *someone*, waiting only on the propitious moment.

If they have not left us in the night it is only because they are not sure which party he would continue to haunt. They will not be shifted with arguments of reason nor bribes or threats of any kind. The effort is exhausting. I bounce along like a babe in swaddling, my Inuk standing behind at the sledge's handles bringing us God-knows-where, his face fixed as a carving.

Struggling on my part to maintain a *fear* that we are lost, as against the *certainty* of it. The struggle against despair, persistence of bad dreams, monotony of the landscape, the h–llish cold all sapping vigor, scattering wits, dulling resolution. Bouncing along into the North, that is all. We cease even to count our stores. We cleave to the Inuit in hopes that they would not at least let *themselves* die, but who can say?

Thierry announced we had crossed 80° based upon his readings of the temperature and some g–dd–mned almanack or other. Madness, and so I told him. We'd have overshot Banks Island by four hundred miles. And anyway I am sure I would die strictly on principle if I'd got to within ten degrees of the Pole. Suggested he throw his almanack onto the fire and jump in after it. Heartily endorsed by the others, though I fear what ought to have been a quiet, cutting remark was shrieked out by myself.

. . .

22 NOVEMBER, 1912. Woke determined to rid us of this Other. Sent Apsley up an especially tall feature with two of the Inuit, a spyglass, Fidis, and Dickson our photographer (never mind that he cannot make his prints out here; the heathen show an awed regard for his instrument & I will keep it in use). Instructed them, simply enough, not to come back down till the Inuit had pointed out sign of some other figure on the ice or had abandoned the idea altogether.

Party seem to have spent their day in a prolonged standoff, watching shadows lengthen and trekking down only with the coming of night. Needn't tell you they had not got the least proof of anything untoward.

Inuit pointing repeatedly south to where this thing had been peering over the skyline at them! Madness, to be certain. But the exercise meant to shake their conviction has only strengthened it. Worse, I believe Apsley, Fidis and Dickson have come down nurturing doubts of *their own*.

As I record this I see the three of them huddled by their fire conferring in undertones. They have asked that they not be disturbed.

. . .

26 (?) NOV The Inuit lying down with the dogs tonight as their Other makes ready to reveal himself. We laugh this off manfully enough yet I see our own tents drawing closer. Surprised Dickson tonight—the Quaker among us, if there is one—cleaning his Martini-Henry.

. . .

[Undated Entry] It is characteristic of the great unfeatured landscapes that we must populate them with our own ghosts. We must send these things *somewhere*, after all. They are not welcomed in our own, civilized portions of the globe; we haven't room for them in our waking minds. What better setting for them, really, than here?

You will think I am trying to be clever, or making some lyrical point; but decidedly I am not. You will point out that men in our enlightened world who argue in earnest about ghosts are locked up for it, and quite so. Yet you will observe I am no longer *there*, in civilization, with you—I am *here*, in this Limbo. And the extraordinary thing about being here is that you quite *expect* to run across these figments you exiled from your conscious mind when you were *there*, and your better self.

I have left off joking that I would welcome the Devil's company to this place. I see that I am careful not to look behind the formations of ice as we pass them, particularly where they are large enough to conceal a man. I mistrust all shadows and take pains never to look at the trail behind us. And I am so frequently flinching and cutting my eyes about and turning in nervous terror from the commonplace objects of the road that I must wonder if, after all, I am not already seeing this Devil.

. . .

DEC 1912. Doubled company back on own trail today; would show by this we are not stalked or followed. Had mad idea to keep going all the way back to Defiance. Unclear how far I would really pursue this, till we reached a very obvious stopping point and here we are. You may imagine with what perturbation of mind *I look on remains of a camp not our own.*

. . .

DEC 1912. Unusual markings on ice in vicinity of strangers' camp. Low wall of ice raised crater-like, perhaps 2-3 miles across, charred shape at the center (what is there to burn?). Dickson will have use of his camera and plates at last.

. . .

DEC 1912. LIGHTS appear at sunset. Presume related to markings, but no accounting for either. Holding back for fear infirmity of ice. Weather kicking up as well. Buckling sounds beneath, perhaps motion of tides.

. . .

[Undated Entry] Fifty-odd shapes–one repeated really–thrown up against the lights. Tapering isosceles form with short stroke near top like crosstrees on a ship's mast. Moving unless it is a trick of the lights. Waking and dreaming this half-resolved image before my mind's eye. S. records it in our interviews though if shapes suggest anything to him he keeps his counsel.

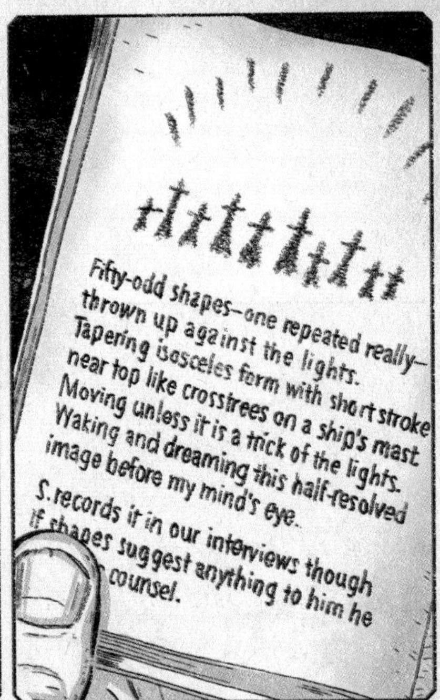
Fifty-odd shapes—one repeated really—
thrown up against the lights.
Tapering isosceles form with short stroke
near top like crosstrees on a ship's mast.
Moving unless it is a trick of the lights.
Waking and dreaming this half-resolved
image before my mind's eye.
S. records it in our interviews though
if shapes suggest anything to him he
counsel.

18-1.
Begin to suspect
S. is the 'other' we
perceived in the
North.

S.

V.

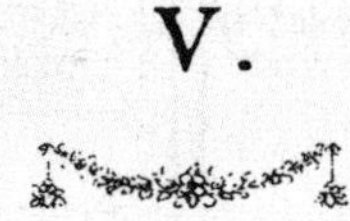

–BY ALL MEANS, COME IN–
I'D LIKE TO KNOW YOUR BUSINESS WITH MR. SLOANE.
DOES THIS MEAN WE'RE SPEAKING, MAJOR?
IT DOES SEEM WE AREN'T KNOCKING.

MY BUSINESS WITH MR. SLOANE IS A PRIVATE MATTER. WHAT I'D LIKE TO KNOW IS HOW YOU'VE GOT INVOLVED WITH HIM.
I HAVEN'T SAID THAT I AM.
AH, BUT YOU ARE, YOU SEE.

THERE ARE ONLY TWO PEOPLE WHO COULD HAVE PLOTTED THIS TRIP OUT FOR YOU, MAJOR. ONE IS MR. SLOANE, AND THE OTHER YOU WOULDN'T LIKE TO KNOW.
IS THERE A REASON WE CAN'T SPEAK CIVILLY ABOUT THIS?
IS IT THE SUBJECT YOU FIND DISTASTEFUL, OR IS IT ME?

BELIEVE THE CONVENTION IS FOR ME TO PUT QUESTIONS TO YOU, MISS HARROW.
AH. WELL, SUPPOSE YOU TRY YOUR CONVENTIONS ON THAT SIDE OF THE ROOM, AND I'LL HAVE MINE OVER HERE, AND WE'LL SEE HOW FAR WE GET. HOW'S THAT, MAJOR?
SORRY, THAT WAS ANOTHER QUESTION. BUT IT WAS RHETORICAL, YOU SEE.

YOU SEEM TO MISUNDERSTAND YOUR POSITION–
YOU MEAN AS A YOUNG LADY, AMONG YOU MEN. YES, YOU'VE GOT ME AT A GREAT DISADVANTAGE, HAVEN'T YOU?

PERHAPS YOU'LL TELL ME WHAT YOU'D LIKE TO KNOW.
I'VE ASKED ABOUT MR. SLOANE. WHO IS HE?
OH I CAN'T POSSIBLY ANSWER THAT. REALLY, I DON'T THINK HE KNOWS HIMSELF.
MAJOR, I'M SORRY. YOU'RE VERY NEW TO THIS. AND UNLESS I'M MISTAKEN, THERE'S MUCH YOU WON'T BE ABLE TO GRASP.

...NO, YOU'RE RIGHT.
I'VE BEEN STRUGGLING WITH THIS, THAT MY SISTER'S SENT ME.
I'VE HAD A THOUGHT ON IT–
I SEE. YOU THINK THE 'S.' IN THE LAST ENTRIES MIGHT BE MY MR. SLOANE.

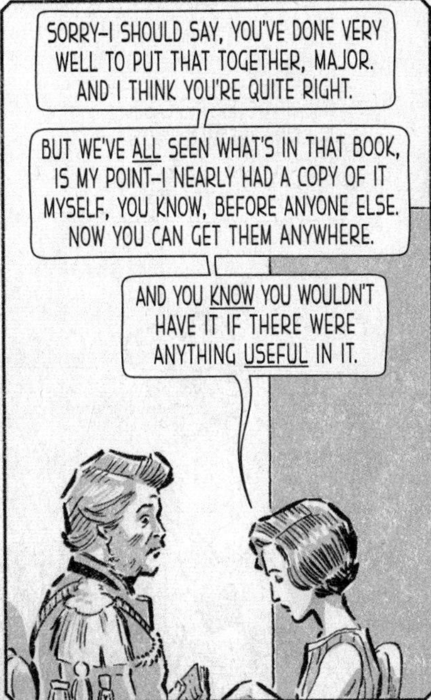
SORRY–I SHOULD SAY, YOU'VE DONE VERY WELL TO PUT THAT TOGETHER, MAJOR. AND I THINK YOU'RE QUITE RIGHT.
BUT WE'VE ALL SEEN WHAT'S IN THAT BOOK, IS MY POINT–I NEARLY HAD A COPY OF IT MYSELF, YOU KNOW, BEFORE ANYONE ELSE. NOW YOU CAN GET THEM ANYWHERE.
AND YOU KNOW YOU WOULDN'T HAVE IT IF THERE WERE ANYTHING USEFUL IN IT.

'USEFUL...' ABOUT SHAMBHALA, YOU MEAN.
YES, THAT'S WHAT I MEAN. IF YOUR BROTHER SAW IT, HE DIDN'T RECORD THE FIRST THING ABOUT IT.
THERE ARE ONLY HIS CLIPPINGS, AND HIS DRAWING OF...WHATEVER THESE SHAPES ARE. NO ONE KNOWS.

...THE WRITING BENEATH THEM IS EFFECTIVELY NONSENSE.
YOU KNOW, YOUR BROTHER'S NO EXPLORER, MAJOR. THOUGH I DO THINK HE'D BE AMUSING IF HE FORGOT ABOUT HIS MYTHICAL CITIES AND GOT HIS LOOKS BACK.
I DON'T SUPPOSE YOU'VE SEEN HIM, LATELY? I UNDERSTAND HE'S NOT LOOKING WELL.
BUT THIS MR. SLOANE–
–YES–SORRY: IT WAS HIM LEADING YOUR BROTHER ABOUT THE ARCTIC. AND FINDING HIM LATER AT HOME, AND ALL THE REST.
MAY I WALK OUT ON THE DECK, NOW?
...AND THE RUSSIAN AT THE EXPLORERS GUILD, WITH OUR COUSIN.
INTERESTING. YES, IT'S ALL UNDERSTOOD TO BE THE SAME MAN. YOU MIGHT SEE HIM YOURSELF IN THE ARGENTINE, IF THAT'S WHERE WE'RE GOING.
...ARE WE?
MM. WHATEVER THE CASE, IF I FIND THE MAN WHO'S BROUGHT ALL THIS ON ARTHUR, I'LL KILL HIM.

WAIT, YOU–BUT YOU CAN'T DO THAT.
...MAJOR?
WE'LL LEAVE YOU SOMEWHERE SAFE AFTER THIS STOP. THAT'S FOR RESCUING US.
WHAT? NO-NO. YOU'RE NOT TO HARM MR. SLOANE.
MAJOR–STOP. LOOK AT ME, IF YOU PLEASE.

SERGEANT? HELP THE YOUNG LADY.
AUGHH–! YOU'VE NO IDEA WHAT YOU'RE DOING–ANY OF YOU–!
«SMASH!»

AH–THAT'LL DO. YOU CAN PUT THAT DOWN, MISS.
GENTLY, NOW. THERE'S A GIRL.

MISS HARROW? IF YOU LIKE, I CAN GET YOU–
CLOSE THE DOOR, PLEASE.
YES. EHH...TERRIBLY SORRY, MA'AM.
COME ON OUT, LAD. SHE'S HAD ENOUGH O' GENTLEMEN CALLERS.

-SOB-
...AYE, YOU GET IT OUT, LASS. THEN WE'LL LAY OUR HEAD DOWN, WOT?
SNIFF–BUT THAT'S THE TROUBLE, YOU SEE. AT HOME I'VE A...OH, NEVER MIND.
YOU TELL ME, DEARIE. GO ON.

YOU'RE VERY KIND–SNIFF–MISS WHITE, YOU KNOW, WHEN I'M WROUGHT-UP LIKE THIS, SHE GIVES ME A TEASPOON OF BRANDY AND THEN I CAN SLEEP.
AH-WELL. 'AT'S THE SOVEREIGN REMEDY, IN'NIT.

...THOUGH WE'VE NO' EVEN A TEASPOON'S-WORTH ABOUT HERE, HAVE WE? NOT SO'S WE FOUND, ANYWAY.
OH THAT'S NOT THE PROBLEM. THE PASHA'S A GREAT COLLECTOR OF SPIRITS, YOU KNOW.
OH?

WELL OF COURSE. HE'S GOT ENOUGH FOR THE MOROCCAN FLEET DOWN THERE.
THOUGH G–D KNOWS WHY, HE NEVER TOUCHES IT.
OH, AYE?
...THOUGH I S'POSE IT'S ALL VERY WELL-HID, IS IT?

WELL...I'LL HAVE TO TRUST YOU, SERGEANT. CAN I TRUST YOU?
ME? I SHOULD SAY SO.
THEN—HERE: I'VE GOT THE PASHA'S KEY...
...AND I CAN GUIDE YOU THERE, IF YOU'LL BRING ME BACK ONE LITTLE BOTTLE OF ANISETTE.

...SERGEANT?
YA. MM?
I SAY, YOU MAY HAVE TO ROOT AROUND A BIT.
THERE ARE JUST ACRES OF CHAMPAGNE, AND RUM, AND SCOTS WHISKEY. GREAT CASKS OF GIN...OUZO... COCONUT ARRACK...

...OH, THE SMELL ALONE MAKES YOU ILL...
AYE. SOUNDS PERFECTLY HIDEOUS...

SOME TIME LATER, SERGEANT PENSETTE IS FOUND ABSENT ON HIS WATCH.
DOWN 'ERE, BOYS.
♪... TOO RA LOO RA LOO RA LOO / THEY'RE LOOKING FOR MONKEYS UP IN THE ZOO... ♪

♪... AN' IF I HAD A FACE LIKE YOU / I WOULD JOIN THE BRITISH ARME-E-E! ... ♪

WHAT-HO!
«PIFF!»
STEADY, MARTIN.
«CRAAAK»

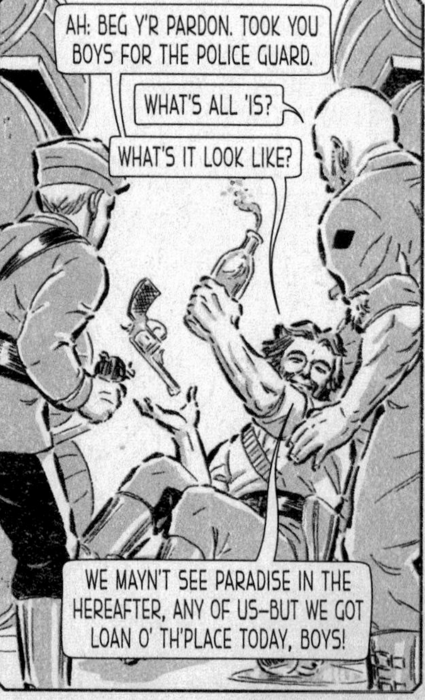
AH: BEG Y'R PARDON. TOOK YOU BOYS FOR THE POLICE GUARD.
WHAT'S ALL 'IS?
WHAT'S IT LOOK LIKE?
WE MAYN'T SEE PARADISE IN THE HEREAFTER, ANY OF US—BUT WE GOT LOAN O' TH'PLACE TODAY, BOYS!

I KNOW YOU'D RATHER I KEPT TO QUARTERS, MAJOR, AND LET YOU GO ON AND RUIN EVERYTHING.

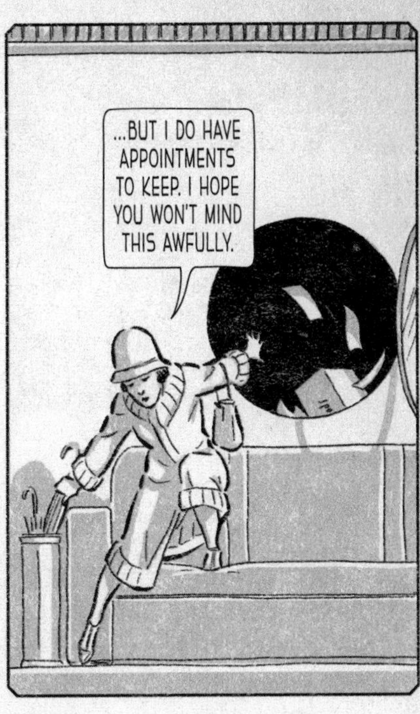
...BUT I DO HAVE APPOINTMENTS TO KEEP. I HOPE YOU WON'T MIND THIS AWFULLY.

AH!

RRRMPH!

GASP!
«SNAP!»

HEHH–WELL!–HEHH–THERE!
NOT THE ARRIVAL WE'D PLANNED, BUT... IT CAN'T BE LONG NOW, ANYWAY. I DO HOPE YOU'VE WAITED FOR US, MY LOVE.

VI.
55° 15' 14" S Lat | 66° 31' 19" W Long
Tierra Del Fuego, South America
February, 1918

WE CALL TONIGHT AT A WORK-HOUSE FOR YOUNG ORPHANS AT THE SOUTHERN TIP OF THE CONTINENT
TSST! –EY! BERTRAM.
MIRA ESTO. MÍRAME. CERCA. POCO MÁS.

WHERE WE FIND CHILDREN PAINTING CLOCK AND WATCH FACES WITH A RADIUM-INFUSED PAINT.
HA–! ARRRH!
...HUH-HUH-HUHH.

LO SIENTO, SEÑOR. PERDÓNEME, SEÑOR.
«THWACK!»

«RRRRRINGG»

«RRRRRINGG»

'...THE LONG RED-LEGGED SCISSOR-MAN / HAD CUT THE THUMB FROM GRIGOR'S HAND...'

'...HIS MOTHER GAVE A FROWN AND SHRUG / AND PICKED HIS THUMB UP FROM THE RUG. / "NOW," SHE SAID, "YOU SEE WHAT COMES / TO NAUGHTY BOYS WHO SUCK THEIR THUMBS."

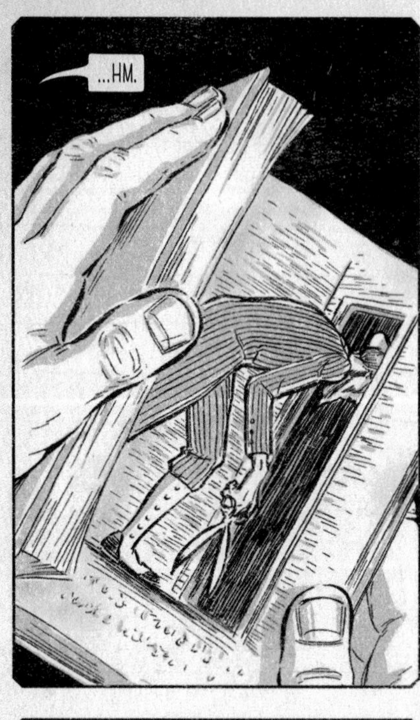
...HM.

DORMID AHORA.
Y NO HABLÉIS.

NO HAY LUCES MÁS.

BEG PARDON.
LOOKING FOR A
BERTRAM BARNES.

COME ON.
YOU DEAF?
¿QUIÉN
ERES?

ME? I'M MR. RENTON. NAME'S FAMILIAR? DARE SAY?
I SAY, YOU HEARD O' ME...?

SEÑOR...'RENTON,' AH? MM... NO. I NEVER 'EAR OF 'EEM.
REALLY? NO?
...NO, I DON'T. *LO SIENTO. HAWW! HAWW!*

WELL: HERE'S SO YOU DON'T FORGET.
«CRRACK!»

ALL RIGHT. WHICH ONE OF YOU'S BARNES, HEY?
AIYAAA-EEE!

HOLD ON–I GOT IT HERE IN THE ESPAN-YOLL...
...LET'S SEE–AHRM:
«TWEEET!»

–DOOFH!

«RRRRRINGG!»

«RRRRRINGG!»
THERE–YOU SEE? THIS WILL BE OGDEN.
UP NOW, YOU MEN– AND HURRY!

YOUR MR. RENTON, SIR.
MM.
«RRINGG»

THE MEN ARE READY.
ALL RIGHT.

THERE Y'ARE–NOT ONE O' YER LE'LL WAIFS, AM I?
«POP! POP!»

«CRAAASH!»
«CRAAASH!»
«THWOK!»

YOU! HOLD STILL–
–AHH...'ESS'...AH, 'SOO NOMBRAY BERTRAM BARNES?'
WELL?
AUGH. GO ON, THEN.

¡–FUEGO! ¡–SE ARDE!
BL–DY USEFUL YOU ARE. TRANSLATORS IS WHAT I NEED.
<<KICK!>>

ACUNA...
¡AQUÍ!
AGUILAR...
¡SÍ, AQUÍ!
BARNES...?

BERTRAM BARNES...?

We have heard the name 'Sloane' repeated here and there, by various of our players. And I can tell you his influence extends over this volume from first to last, though in ways that may take some time yet to explain. I would not try to follow all his many movements for you, nor to describe in any but the broadest terms what he gets up to when he does not come directly under our lens. Yet there are moments, as now, where we've no good way forward except through Mr. Sloane; and I have been anxious anyway that you should meet him (as far as 'meeting' him is really possible). So I will have him out, gentle reader, and we'll make what we can of this....

We are in the dormitory of our workhouse, this long and high-peaked hall that was moments ago filled with sleeping boys and their nodding guardians. The room shows signs of a hasty evacuation now in its empty beds and strewn bedclothes, and the fire from Mr. Renton's lantern is edging quickly along the worm-eaten planks. The fire is only about ten minutes old, but the flames have already ascended to the rafters and climbed the old eaves to the ceiling's sagging peak. I should think we had ten minutes more–at most–before the roof crashes in wholesale. And it is therefore with some surprise that we see a man walking quite deliberately *into* the room.

I would say he stands about six foot, this man, in his black frock coat and Wellington boots, though he might not weigh ten stone. And whatever he is doing, he is in no great rush to do it. He drifts over to the hearth, selects a harpoon-shaped poker from a rack of fire-irons and hefts it, and then, carrying this item over to the rightmost row of beds, he thumps each bundle of bedclothes in turn, one after the next, passing thus down the room. He keeps a fair pace, striking each bed firmly enough with the iron to flush any children out of hiding, and not without broken bones. Yet our impression of his movement is still one of languor, and of great calm. He seems to travel through a thicker effluvium than air, and his motion seems to carry forward in a slow swing of his coat when he stops short at one of the beds.

Here, in the rising firelight, over a stand of starched collars and a substantial piling of neck-cloth, we perceive a fey and finely wrought face with the pouched eyes of the aristocracy and a slight Oriental cast of feature.

There is a slim nose dropping straight as a plumb-line to a brief mouth that is saved from severity or primness by a shadow of humor. His complexion is much as Arthur Ogden has described it, being pale in the extreme and inclining to blue in the furrows, like smoke-tinged porcelain; while his hair is just this side of unruly and black as jet, save for where time has silvered it at his temples. Taking it in generally, I would not call this an unhandsome face, except that at some point you must consider the eyes.

The eyes of Mr. Sloane are the sort that stick casual remarks in one's throat and make mothers reach reflexively for the hands of their children. They are dark and deep-set eyes with an antic sort of light in them, and their gaze cannot be held for very long, which I suppose is why we haven't got more reliable accounts of what he looks like. I have seen eyes like this just once before, when I was a younger man and there was cholera in the provinces of the South. A *campesino* who had not stirred a limb in months would sit suddenly upright, ask for a cigarette, make inane conversation. This behavior, we knew, marked a man in his hour of death. The missioners would say that in the eyes of such men you would see Paradise reflected, though I felt, if this were the case, then Paradise was no place I would ever wish to visit.

You will see this same sort of abstraction, anyway, in the eyes of Mr. Sloane, as if he were looking past our material world into some unholy light beyond. And it is this way now, as we find him studying one of the beds in our burning dormitory, making we know not what of it.

He drops his poker, careless of how it clangs and chatters across the wood planks, and steps in sidelong between the beds, lowering himself to a seat and crossing one leg over the other at the knee. He stares fixedly at the seedy-looking blanket before him, and it is this blanket he addresses when he finally does speak.

'So, Bertram: you and I meet.' Mr. Sloane speaks English without accent, but with the faintest trace of a dry, singsong humor.

There is no response from beneath the blanket, and Mr. Sloane's smile widens infinitesimally. He tips back and roots about in the pockets of his coat and ulster.

'You're aware, there's a…*fire* of sorts out here.' His various pockets yield a cheroot, a box of matches and a small collection of weathered prints. He is sorting through the last of these when he adds, as if to himself: 'While I've got you, though, while it's just the two of us, I was hoping you would do me a favor.'

He sets the cheroot in his teeth and selects a photograph from among the prints. 'There,' he mutters. 'Now, you look at that....'

He extends the photograph toward the next bed, and here at last we see a stir of activity from beneath the blanket. A child's hand, and his wary eye, poke up from beneath the frayed hem, just enough at first to see and take hold of the print. But then, as his curiosity overtakes his fear, he sits upright with the print, and we find this is the same boy we'd spotted earlier at his work-table. This is young Bertram Barnes.

Mr. Sloane holds a match to his cheroot and takes a few meditative puffs, his eyes narrowing as he studies the bandages on Bertram's head. Bertram, for his part, seems as little conscious of Mr. Sloane as he is of the fire climbing around them. He is making a close inspection of the print, which seems to be an image of expeditioners in the Arctic, arranged in two groups on a ridge of ice. Between the groups, in the distance, we can just make out a dim figure-eight symbol burned or somehow etched upon a field of ice.

'You can ignore the men,' Mr. Sloane remarks, tossing his lit match aside. 'They died just after that was taken. It's the symbol on the ground... Here:'

He unclasps a silver tab from his lapel and hands it to Bertram. Embossed on the tab is another figure-eight symbol, this in the form of a snake doubled upon itself, devouring its own tail.

'Is this shape something you've run across? Bertram? In your travels...?' A few sparks wheel through the air as Mr. Sloane exhales smoke. 'And what about talking,' he adds. 'Is that something you do?'

'Sir?' the boy answers, just audibly.

'Never mind. What about this:'

He hands Bertram an engraving of what appears to be a walled Oriental city, or at least, one of these as it may have been dreamt up in the *Arabian Nights*. The city rises in strange twisting tiers, with the minarets and onion domes of the Near East and Central Asia sprouting fantastically from between stupas and pagodas, and the whole of it snugged into a mountain pass. The reclining figure-eight symbol is reproduced across the city's gates and raised on its spires, and rippling lines seem to indicate that the city, or the mountains, or the whole scene were radiating light.

'I don't suppose you've heard of Shambhala. This place you're looking at…?' asks Mr. Sloane.

'No, sir,' come the little fife-notes of Bertram's voice. 'Though it's very nice. Where is it?'

'"Where is it," yes,' says Mr. Sloane, with the quiet, sibilant sound that represents his laugh. 'Here's one more.'

In the next print, a young European man and woman in topees squint against an equatorial sun. The woman holds a black infant in her arms; the man's hands are draped over the shoulders of two older children. A score of dark, close-gathered, bare-skinned bodies fills out the image. A hut behind the smiling group appears to serve as a classroom or chapel, or both.

'Nothing…?' suggests Mr. Sloane, reading Bertram's face. 'Interesting. They tell me those are your parents.' He leans forward and taps on the image with a forefinger, dropping ash onto it from his cheroot. '…Those two in the hats.'

Bertram looks briefly to Mr. Sloane. He wipes the ash away with immense care and studies the print again, drawing it right to his face this time.

«TWEEEET!»
«TWEEEET!»
GUARDS! ¡GUARDIAS, RÁPIDO!
CALMLY, BROTHER POLISSON. WE'VE GOT THEM OUT–ALL BUT LITTLE BARNES. HAVE YOU–

NO-NO–THEM!
GUARDS! STOP THEM!

OI! AIN'T WE MET, FATHER?
MAN CAN SWIM, ANYWAY–WOT, JACK?
'OO CALLED FOR GUARDS, HEY?
«SNAP!»

GOT 'EM ALL HERE–HOW MANY YOU NEED?

The dormitory over the workhouse, as Ogden rightly judges, has only a few minutes more to stand. A section of the roof has fallen in and the beds on either side of Bertram Barnes are going up like tapers. A timber crashes to the floor not ten feet away him and he twitches in reflex, though his eyes hold fast to the picture of his parents. Mr. Sloane does not register the sound at all.

'... Yes, one's parents,' Mr. Sloane comments. 'Very exciting.'

There is the slightest hitch in his movement as he taps the ash from his cheroot: a sound has caught his ear—a heavy tread on the wooden stairs somewhere beneath the room. Yet he continues to smoke as before. His eyes travel back to the dressing on Bertram's head.

'What about *that*, Bertram,' he asks. 'What do you suppose happened to your head?'

'Oh. I'm not... really sure.'

'No? Maybe we'd better have a look—'

Sloane makes as if to stand, but Bertram kicks himself suddenly to a far corner of the bed.

'Oh–sir,' he says, 'if you could possibly stay over there. I'm to keep these on.' He holds the bandages in place with one hand, gathering the blanket to his chest with the other.

'Interesting,' mutters Mr. Sloane. He scans the rooms and clears his throat. 'Bertram–You'll allow me to be frank with you?'

'Yes, sir.'

'–Good. I think it suits us both.' He waves a few long fingers. 'I've taken in a bit of your surroundings here, and I've seen you and your friends about your work. The life has its advantages, I dare say–but I must wonder if this is really the *place* for you. I should think it had all grown a bit *tired* by now.'

Bertram makes a noncommittal shrug, his eyes still wary on Mr. Sloane.

'Well. You can see it's undergoing a transformation in any event. Not the sort of thing we generally like–is it?–a man's house falling down around his ears. But I tell you, there may be opportunity in this. Or a *sign*, perhaps. If you believe in that sort of thing.'

'Sir, I–'

'You don't follow. And here I'd promised to be frank.' Mr. Sloane squares himself to Bertram with his hands on his knees. 'Tell you what, Bertram: you don't take a man by storm, do you? But you *do* have a certain spirit, that's clear enough. And fond as you are of this place, I wonder if you wouldn't rather be out *there*, you know. Seeing a bit more of the world.'

'The world?'

'That's right. This world and a good deal more, if you're the boy I think you are.' Mr. Sloane pitches his cheroot aside and stands. 'This could be just the thing for you, Bertram. Close rather a dull chapter in your life. Embark on something new. You'll see they've brought you a ship.'

'Who have, sir? Tonight, they have?'

'Tonight, yes.' Mr. Sloane scoops up his prints and the silver collar-tab from Bertram's bed. If he knows he is pocketing one less print than he gave out, he makes no sign of it.

'But–You'll tell them I'm only seven?'

'You can remind them yourself.' He lowers a hand to Bertram and looks idly around at the rising fire. 'Though I suppose you ought to hurry, if you'd make it there in one piece.' Bertram gnaws his lip for just a moment more before he snatches the hand and hops from beneath his blanket. In the next instant–and manifestly to Mr. Sloane's surprise–he is standing in boots and a suit of mismatched tweeds, with a man's ragged overcoat rolled up to his wrists and waisted with a length of rope.

'I say,' Sloane remarks, 'overdressed you a bit for bed, didn't they?'

'I was told I ought to be ready to travel.' Bertram with something of a boy's pleasure, now, at having confounded an adult. 'I've had a dream about this, you know.'

'You've dreamt about...someone visiting you tonight.'

'Yes.'

Mr. Sloane sinks to his haunches and studies the boy with renewed interest. This just as a boot kicks in a door at the far end of the hall, and two tall, wild-looking figures enter.

'Out wit'yeh now, my mannie, and quick about it.' It is the burr of Sergeant Pensette calling over the fire. 'Yeh may leave the boy.'

Mr. Sloane makes no pretense of hearing. '...And where did you dream you were going?' he asks Bertram, setting another cheroot in his teeth.

'Oh, I didn't know that. I had hoped *you* would tell me.'

'Sir?' The voice of Pensette closer now.

Sloane lets out a dry laugh, and stands to face Pensette and Subadar Priddish.

Now: I have mentioned that these dragoons–perfectly sturdy men otherwise–may be put off by the uncanny or unnatural. And you may imagine a man of Mr. Sloane's looks touching right upon this weakness. But to any general superstitious aversion you may add a very specific impression, shared instantly by both these dragoons, that the man before them is one they had known some years ago in India, and have long believed dead.

In any event, the sight of Mr. Sloane stops them short. And in much less time than it takes to tell it, Mr. Pensette has got out his sidearm, and Priddish has leveled his Afghan rifle and drawn back its bolt.

'An' what're you?' Pensette demands, at the same time that Priddish states, in a softer voice, 'You will be Mr. Sloane.'

Pensette cuts his eyes over to Priddish, then back to Mr. Sloane. The latter raises an eyebrow and says: 'Then we've met.'

'I surmise, Sahib.'

'An' you know *us*, hey?' Pensette demands.

'Well. I think you either follow John Ogden, or you've killed two men who did and taken their uniforms. In any case, if you see him, you may give him my regards.'

Sloane digs out his matches, and the soldiers tense and sight their weapons on him. Pensette thumbs back the hammer of his Webley.

'I dunno how yeh come here, sir,' he says, 'or how yeh come by this new name. But if ye're called Sloane now, there's a young lady lookin' for yeh, much as we wasn't.' He indicates Bertram with his pistol. 'If that be le'll Barnes, sir, you may send him over. An' jest you take a step after him, I'll clap a bullet right in that fiend's head o' yours.'

Mr. Sloane's smile spreads as he lights his cheroot. 'There you are, Bertram,' he says. 'Fine new pair of friends for you. Go on.'

Bertram looks to the dragoons and back to Mr. Sloane, as though weighing the one prospect against the other without a decided preference. But Mr. Sloane nudges him ahead, as the dragoons motion him on. Bertram, on a sudden impulse, takes Mr. Sloane's wrist.

'How's 'is?' booms Pensette. 'You can't tell me he's grown fond of yeh?'

'Of course not.' Bertram has drawn Mr. Sloane's hand closer to him, and Sloane opens the hand to disclose his silver collar-tab, with its figure-eight device. Bertram taps the symbol with a finger and says, barely above a whisper: 'That is in my dream, too.' He gives Mr. Sloane a solemn nod, as to make certain he has been understood, and then pads away toward the soldiers.

The fire has risen now to the height of the men, and with only a few lanes through it. Embers, glowing bolts, bits of glass and burning shingles rain freely from the ceiling.

'Carefully,' says Pensette. He and Priddish guide Bertram away, keeping their guns trained on Mr. Sloane. 'When we're gone, sir,' he calls, 'ye're free to go hang, as yeh prolly will.'

Mr. Sloane chuckles back at them over the din. His image is already wobbling and rippling in the heat. 'I suspect you're right, Sergeant. Though we've both got our work to do, first. You'll get that boy over safely, won't you? I've been told there's a war going.'

'Oh the Kaiser we can handle, sir. It's you I'll keep an eye on.'

In Bertram's last view of him, Mr. Sloane is seated again on one of the beds, refastening the silver escutcheon to his coat. He is almost wholly obscured by the fire and the beams that have fallen crisscross into the room, though he shows no inclination to leave.

LOOK AHEAD OF YOU NOW, BERTRAM. YOU DO NOT KNOW WHAT THAT MAN IS.
WULL IT'S OUR MAN FROM THE PUNJAB, IN'NIT? HE'S ABOUT SAID AS MUCH.

...THOUGH HOW YEH S'POSE HE GETS HISSELF HERE–AH? AN' HIM WALKIN' UPRIGHT AGAIN, AND MIXED UP IN OUR AFFAIRS BESIDES?
I AM SURE I DON'T KNOW, SERGEANT.
NO MORE DO I.

I DO KNOW IF IT BE EITHER MAN– LET ALONE BOTH–MAJOR'LL SHOOT THAT B–STARD ON SIGHT. AS I'M HALF-MINDED TO DO MYSELF.
YES? THOUGH IT SEEMS YOU JUST PASSED UP AN EXCELLENT CHANCE TO DO IT, SERGEANT.
AH F–CK OFF, YOU. AN' SEE IF I MISS THE NEXT ONE.

WHAT'S HAPPENED TO YOU TWO? LOOK AT'CHA!
WHEEST, LAD.

UP-UP, NOW. THERE Y'ARE, SON.
THAT'S BARNES? WHERE'S THE REST OF 'IM?
AFRAID THIS IS ALL THE BARNES WE GET, MR. RENTON.

THEY MIGHT'A SENT HIM WITH THE MAIL, AND SAVED US A TRIP.
AH-WEEL. YEH MAY BE GLAD ENOUGH FOR NOW, WE GET TO QUIT THIS BOGGIN' PLACE.

AS THE OTHERS RIDE OUT TO THE SHORE, CAPTAIN SHAW GATHERS THE ORPHANS OUTSIDE THE WORKHOUSE.
THERE YOU ARE, LADS. I LEAVE YOU THE FIELD.
IF YOU FEEL LIKE IT, YOU MAY COVER OUR RETREAT.

AND ARMS THEM WITH THE STAVES OF THEIR GUARDIANS.
WHEN THIS IS DONE, BROTHER, I SHALL WANT PAPER AND PEN.
YES, BROTHER POLISSON.

MISS HARROW ELUDES OGDEN'S DRAGOONS, BUT COMES JUST TOO LATE TO INTERCEPT MR. SLOANE.
AUGHH. IT REALLY WOULD HAVE KILLED YOU TO STAY FIVE MINUTES MORE....

ALL RIGHT.
YOU'LL JUST HAVE TO HAVE A CRASH, MY LOVE. NOTHING TOO AWFUL.

YOU'LL STAGGER BACK TO ME, OUT OF THE WOODS, ON FOOT.
...THERE, IT'S DONE. YOU WILL APPEAR...NOW.
I SAY...NOW.

NOTWITHSTANDING HER EFFORTS, MR. SLOANE'S CAR SPEEDS SAFELY AWAY.
NO? THEN I'M NOT A CLAIR-VOYANT. BUT YOU'LL CREDIT A GIRL FOR TRYING.

It is not in Miss Harrow's nature to dwell upon defeat, nor even to stay still for very long. She is only giving herself the space of this cigarette to decide which end of the road offers her the better prospect. And she is in the course of this calculation when her eyes come to rest on the burning compound behind her.

The black-robed prefects have freed themselves by now and, with nothing more to do about the fire, they have gathered in silence on the grounds. They may be scanning around for stray children, or looking up the forest lane after Mr. Sloane; but what they are doing is beside the point. It is rather this *picture* they present, these slender, black triangles standing a dozen or so abreast, with a faint, horizontal stroke—presumably their hat-brims—at the top of each shape: a thing you might liken, in the abstract, to the crosstrees on a ship's mast....

. . .

END *of* BOOK TWO

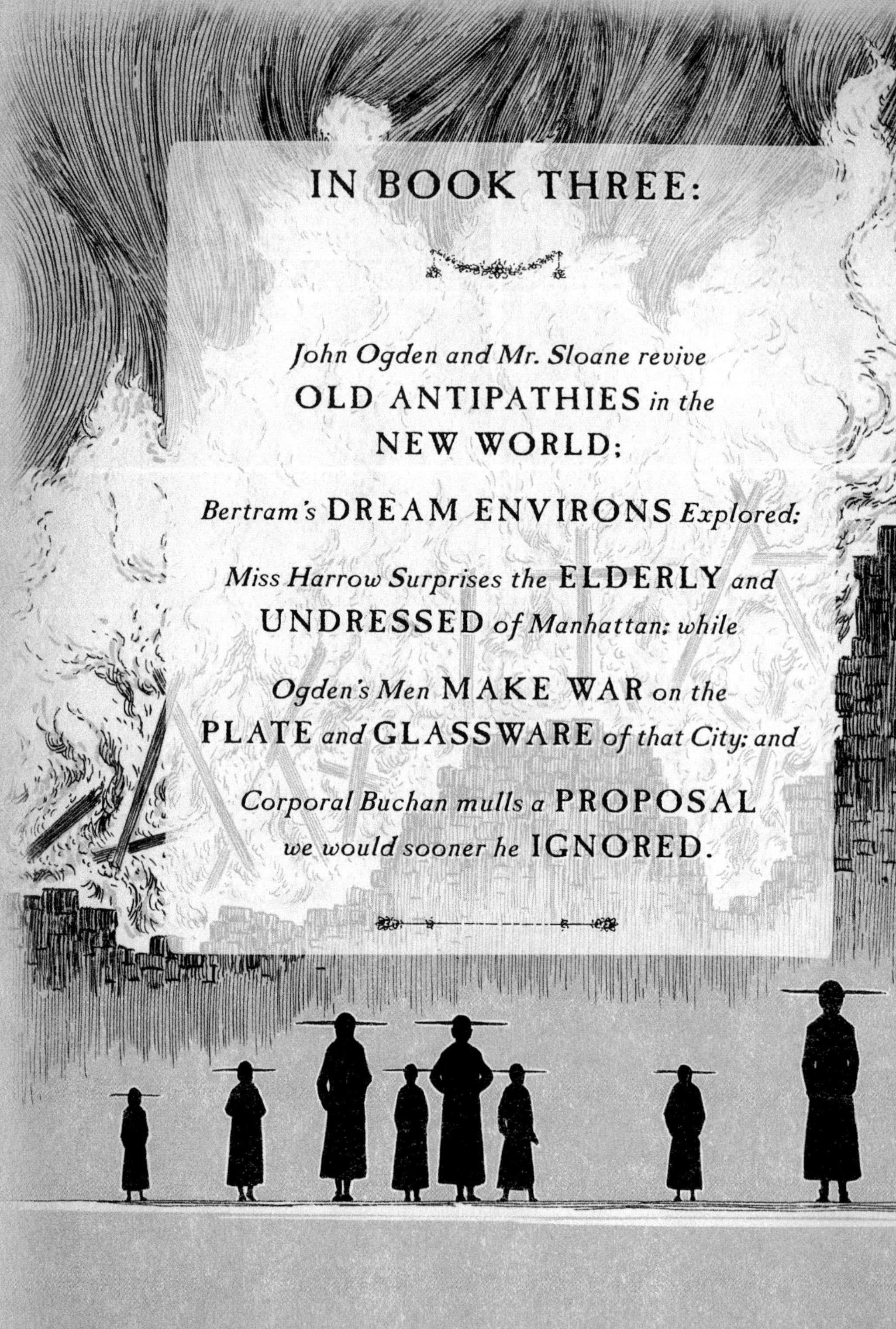
IN BOOK THREE:
John Ogden and Mr. Sloane revive OLD ANTIPATHIES in the NEW WORLD;
Bertram's DREAM ENVIRONS Explored;
Miss Harrow Surprises the ELDERLY and UNDRESSED of Manhattan; while
Ogden's Men MAKE WAR on the PLATE and GLASSWARE of that City; and
Corporal Buchan mulls a PROPOSAL we would sooner he IGNORED.

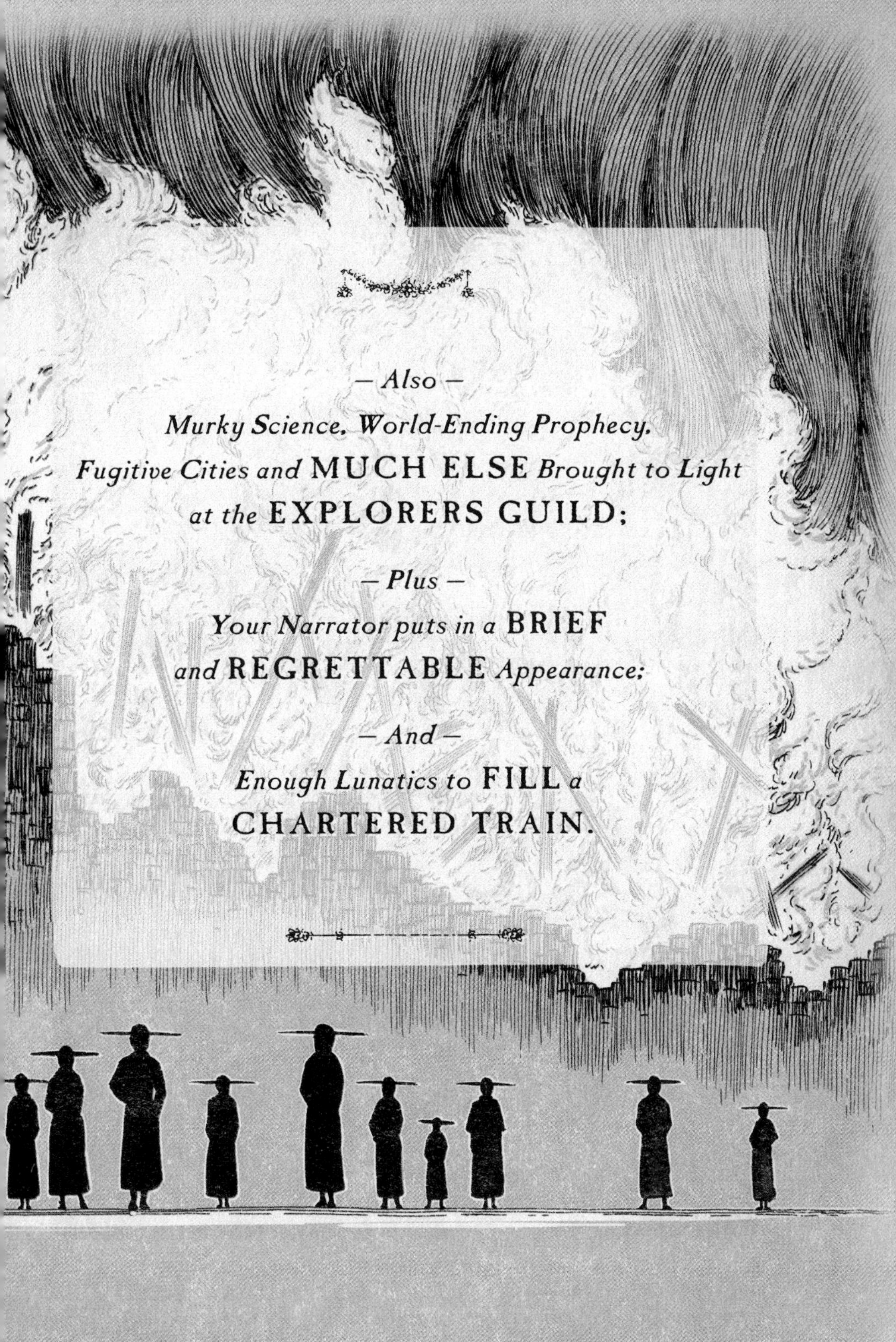
— Also —
Murky Science. World-Ending Prophecy.
Fugitive Cities and MUCH ELSE Brought to Light
at the EXPLORERS GUILD;
— Plus —
Your Narrator puts in a BRIEF
and REGRETTABLE Appearance;
— And —
Enough Lunatics to FILL a
CHARTERED TRAIN.

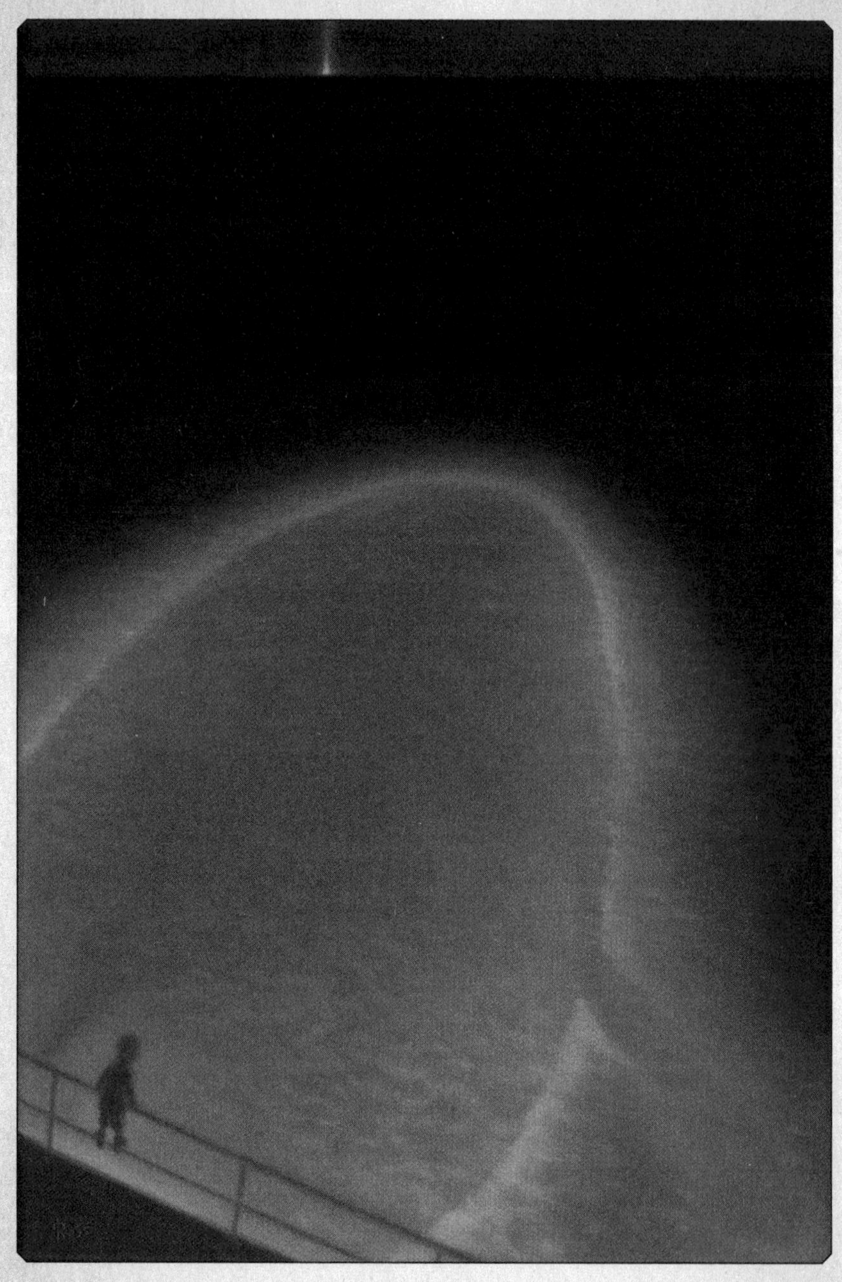

'THE BODY OF A WHALE, PROCEEDING WITH AN AWFUL SLOWNESS FROM UNDER THE SHIP'S HULL, WREATHED IN PHOSPHORESCENCE...'

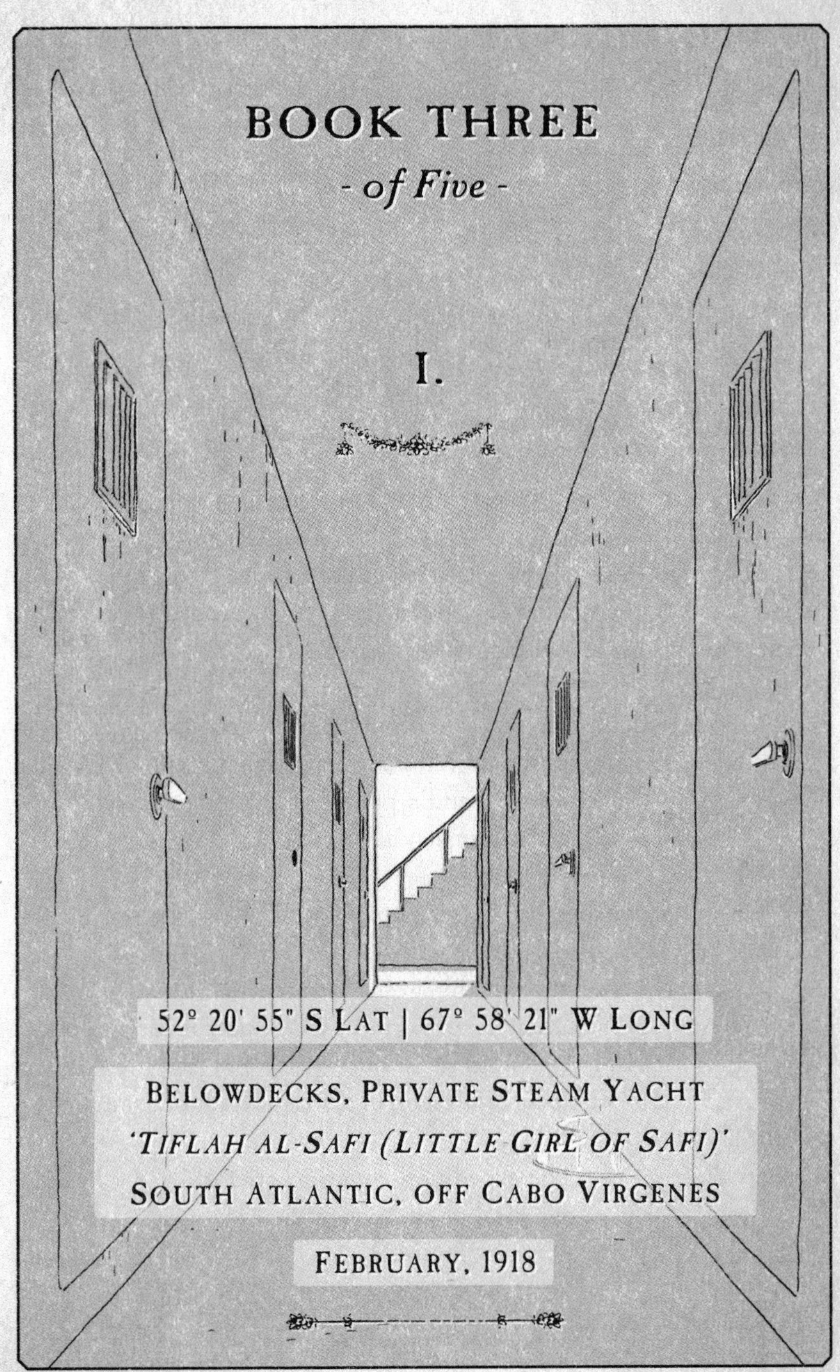

BOOK THREE

- of Five -

I.

52º 20' 55" S LAT | 67º 58' 21" W LONG

BELOWDECKS, PRIVATE STEAM YACHT

'TIFLAH AL-SAFI (LITTLE GIRL OF SAFI)'

SOUTH ATLANTIC, OFF CABO VIRGENES

FEBRUARY, 1918

Summary Introductions *to the* Passengers *in the* No. 6 Hold:

. . .

In the Machinery Closet

1.

Mr. Devang

1891. A mystic of Nepal makes a brief and sensational tour of Europe's resort towns. 'Mr. Devang' is fêted by an occult-mad idle class at Torquay, St. Moritz, Baden-Baden, the Riviera &c. By most accounts he is small and retiring, vulgar when in drink, and surpassingly ugly.

. . . .

His looks, more than anything, lend credence to his wild stories and assertions, among them a tale of 'hidden' mountains and a pathway to the 'Pure Land' in the Tibetan Himalayas.

. . . .

Inevitably, his star in Europe fades.

. . . .

Six months after his western début, Mr. Devang's return to the Orient is arranged by a disreputable branch of the Explorers Guild at Strasbourg. He will lead two Alsatian climbers into Tibet, in search of his hidden mountain.

. . . .

The expedition comes to grief of one kind or another in the Mahabharat foothills.

. . . .

Mr. Devang

A traveler's log, thought to have been kept by the alpinists and detailing, among other things, a 'bridge of viscid light,' is discredited at Strasbourg.

. . . .

Mr. Devang is recognized and seized at Kathmandu and jailed for the alpinists' murder.

• • •

In the Boatswain's Closet

2.

Lodewijk Geerts

1901. Lualaba River basin, Congo Free State. Rubber collectors go missing from the Duivelden Plantation and are believed hiding in tunnels beneath Mahali-pa-siri, an extinct volcano deep in the surrounding jungle.

. . . .

The Anglo-Belgian India Rubber Company send local militia into the caves, provisioned for two days' search. A small, weedgrown arch conducts the party from the jungle into channels of inconceivable depth and complexity.

. . . .

Lost for thirteen days beneath the volcano, the party approach an 'underground hive of light and activity,' unseen but reflected in a hallway of quartz or vitrified stone. Dr. Geerts misplaces a foot at the mouth of the tunnel, cracking and dislocating any number of bones. He is held immobile as the rest of the party, 'struck dumb by the apparition…proceed toward the thing as if beguiled.' He will eventually lose the foot.

. . . .

Dr. Geerts records signs of a 'vast and populous and many-steepled city, with outer gardens' reflected in the lustrous stone, though he will later recant the vision as a morphine-dream inspired by Plato's *Allegory of the Cave*.

On reaching civilization, months later, a transformed Dr. Geerts falls in with the dispossessed tribes of the Lualaba Basin.

. . . .

No more is heard of the missing rubber collectors or the Abir militia, and the caves of Mahali-pa-siri are sealed. Dr. Geerts fades from record after stabbing a Jesuit missionary at Stanley Falls.

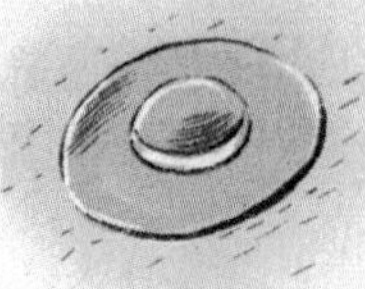

. . .

In Dry-Goods Storage

3.

COLONEL OTTO RIEBLING

1886. German South-West Africa.

. . . .

Colonel Otto Riebling, aerialist of the *Schutztruppe*, falls from his reconnaissance balloon after spotting a strange symbol on the floor of the Kalahari.

. . . .

Riebling vanishes mid-air in a flash of phosphorescence, and appears moments later on the Micronesian isle of Fo'a-Fo'a, rather surprising a few natives on the strand.

. . . .

He describes a symbol on the trunk of a banyan tree and retires into the forest. His movements over the next twenty-two years remain obscure.

. . . .

Col. Riebling

• • •

In the Linens Closet

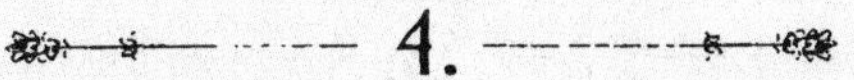

4.

Wilhelmina Van Doessler

1888. Academics, occultists and explorers descend on the Amazon forest when fluttering lights are reported in the skies over Rondônia.

. . . .

The visitors pose with guides and elders by a strange figure-eight symbol they have found burned or etched in the tree canopy, some half a mile over the forest floor.

. . . .

Wilhelmina Van Doessler, botanist and photography enthusiast of the University at Leipzig, backs along a kapok bough in order to widen her view of the gathering.

. . . .

One imagines a portrait characterized by outstretched arms and cries of warning.

. . . .

Miss Van Doessler's fall is broken by the lesser branches below. She is marveling at her luck when her camera and tripod come crashing after her, laming her and exposing her photographic plates in the same instant.

. . . .

She is the only one of her party ever to reach the forest floor again.

. . . .

Miss Van Doessler

• • •

In the Paint Closet

5.

EMIL LØGNER

1896. Emil Løgner, engineer and lecturer at the University at Aarhus, tests an experimental diving bell in the Kattegat Strait.

. . . .

An assistant of Løgner's, manning a floating bellows after a night's hard drinking, is unable to wave off the *SMY Hohenzollern II* as it returns from a sojourn in Norway. The yacht snares the submersible by its suspension cable and drags it from the Danish coast to the German port of Kiel.

. . . .

A regatta at Kiel is brought to a halt as Løgner and the tangled remains of two marine biologists are pulled from beneath the *Hohenzollern*. The scientists' decease and the wild appearance of the three men are written down to a hastened decompression.

. . . .

Løgner's ravings about a 'bright undersea manifestation' (*undervandsstøj lyser*) in the Jutland Trench are ascribed, likewise, to the strain of the ordeal.

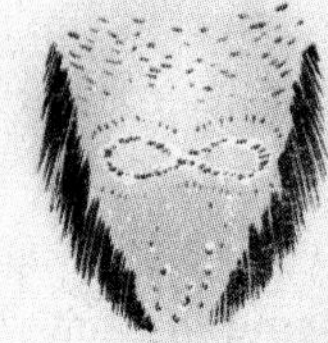

. . . .

Held down by rescuers and onlookers, the engineer falls into a cataleptic state, and the regatta is resumed.

. . . .

Herr Løgner

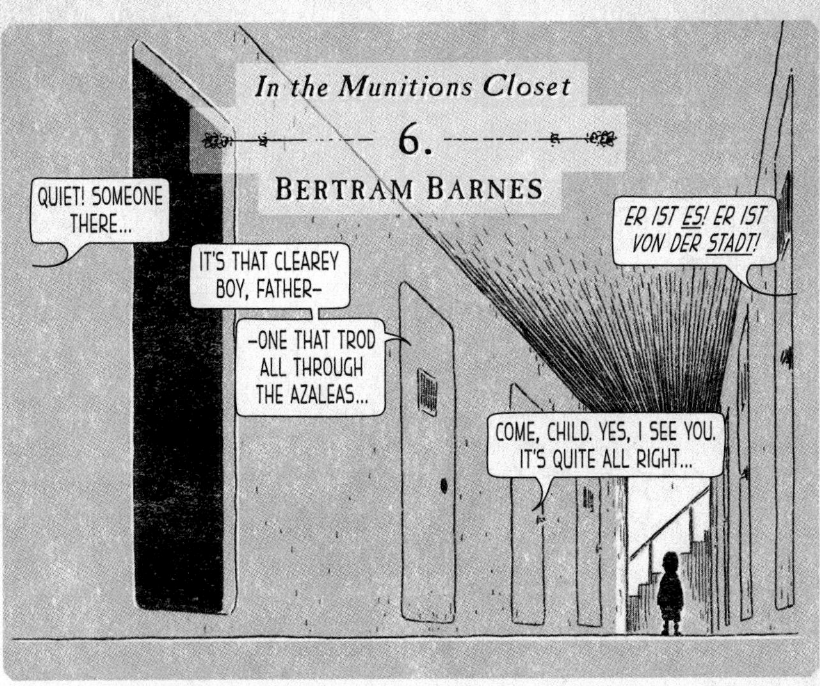
In the Munitions Closet
6.
Bertram Barnes
QUIET! SOMEONE THERE...
IT'S THAT CLEAREY BOY, FATHER–
–ONE THAT TROD ALL THROUGH THE AZALEAS...
ER IST ES! ER IST VON DER STADT!
COME, CHILD. YES, I SEE YOU. IT'S QUITE ALL RIGHT...

COME. COME...
THERE'S A GOOD BOY...CLOSER, YES...

HA! GOT HIM!
HOLD STILL, NOW, AND SHOW ME THAT TONGUE!
DAAAH!
COME–I'LL SHOW YOU THE FORK IN IT!

WELL: HOW YA LIKE THIS, BERTRAM? IT'S YER FELLOW PASSENGERS, IN'NIT?
SHOW ME, OR I'LL TEAR THE EAR RIGHT OFF YER POXY HEAD, D–MN YOU!
PLEASE, MISS–!

WO GEHT ER HIN? ER IST ES!
YOU ALL GET THE GRAND TOUR O' THE WORLD, AND NONE'A THE SHIP'S WORK, YOU LUCKY DUCKS.
QUIET, ALL OF YOU!
ACH! COME, YOU BLACK DEVIL!

I S'POSE YE'R IN ON THIS SECRET WITH 'EM, BERTRAM? THIS PLACE YOU ALL SEEN...?
WHAT PLACE?
WELL. IF I KNEW THAT I'D BE DOWN 'ERE WITH YOU, WOULDN'T I?

MR. BUCHAN SAYS YOU ALL BEEN TO SOME GLORIOUS CITY, AND DON'T YOU JUST LOOK IT.
...YOU SURE YOU AIN'T BEEN TO THIS PLACE, BERTRAM? PASSED RIGHT THROUGH IT, P'RAPS?
YOU'RE NOT SURE?
NO.
NO–I DON'T KNOW ANY SECRET PLACES.

WELL, SOMEONE THINKS YOU DO. AND YE'R GOING UP IN FRONT OF MAJOR'S BROTHER AT THE END OF THE TRIP, SO BEST THINK OF SOMETHING TO TELL 'IM.
'COURSE I'LL TELL 'IM HE'D LEARN MORE AT THE ZOO THAN FROM YOU ZANIES. NEXT TIME HE CAN GO COLLECT YOU ALL 'IMSELF.
...AND 'ERE WE ARE:

MY, BERTRAM: IT'S ROOMS FOR A TRAVELIN' EMPEROR, IN'NIT?
EWER AND BASIN; TICK FOR SLEEPING; PUNCHEONS TO KEEP YOU UP FROM SHIP'S VERMIN; STOOL FOR...ENTERTAINING GUESTS, I S'POSE. SHIP'S RIGGING AND TACKLE, WHICH YOU'RE NOT TO TOUCH.
AND LOOK 'ERE: SOME LITTLE GIRL'S DOLL IS MISSIN' ITS PEA-COAT, WOT?

MR. RENTON? I'M NOT MAD, AM I?
MM? OH, HOW WOULD I KNOW THAT?
YOU EAT UP, NOW. MAYBE TRY A SPRITZ AT THE BASIN FIRST. SET AN EXAMPLE FOR THESE OTHERS.
ALL RIGHT.

I'LL SEND SOMEONE IN THE MORNING TO AIR YOU OUT.
THANK YOU, MR. RENTON.
YOU...ARE...WELCOME, SIR.

LO! WE ARE IN THE SNAKE THAT DEVOURS ITS OWN TAIL! AND IT GIRDS THE WORLD, FROM POLE TO POLE!
WHERE'D HE GO, D—MN HIS EYES?

AS SOON AS HE IS LEFT ALONE, BERTRAM EXAMINES THE PRINT HE HAS TAKEN FROM MR. SLOANE.
...I'LL SNATCH THAT TONGUE OUT 'IM AND BOIL IT, S'HELP ME!

IN THE HALL, SERGEANT PENSETTE SEEMS TO HAVE ARRIVED FOR HIS WATCH.
«THOOM-THOOM-THOOM!»
THAT'LL DO. ALL'A'YEHS QUIET.

THAT'S YOU INSIDE, LIL' MARSTER?
YES, SIR.
SETTLING IN, THEN? GOOD MAN.

SPOKE TO MAJOR. HE SENDS DOWN HIS REGARDS...
ACTUALLY HE DON'T. NOTHING I'D BETTER REPEAT, ANYHOW.
OH.
IT'S ME FETCHED YOU, YOU KNOW, WITH THAT INJAN FELLOW.

YES, SIR. I REMEMBER BOTH OF YOU.
YA. AN' HERE I AM ON WATCH, FOR A REWARD. THAT'S ABOUT HOW PLEASED MAJOR IS WITH ALL THIS. AND THE LADS LIKE IT ABOUT AS MUCH.

YOU CAN TELL THEM, SIR, I'M QUITE USED TO CHORES. IF THEY NEED ANYTHING DONE–
OH, AYE? CAN YOU QUIET DOWN THESE LOONIES, THEN?
I DON'T THINK SO.
NO MORE CAN I.
«FTOO!»

AND CAN YEH TELL ME WHY YE'D NEED TWENTY MEN-AT-ARMS TO COME FETCH YOU ACROSS THE OCEAN, AN' NEAR DROWN AN' BURN DOIN' IT?
...NO?
NO, SIR.
AH. NO. THEN GO TO SLEEP, IS WHAT YEH CAN DO.
YES, SIR.

WE WERE MUCH ABOUT DELHI AT THE TIME, YOU KNOW, AND BUSY ALL THROUGH THE PUNJAB, WHICH WAS QUITE LIVELY THEN, AND WHERE MANY OF US COME TO SEEK OUT MAJOR. HE'D A REPUTATION ALREADY FOR TAKING GROUND FROM THE PATHANS, AND A MAN THAT DOES THAT KNOWS FIGHTING, I PROMISE YOU.

THE BOY I NIVVER SAW, THOUGH IT MAY BE MR. PRIDDISH DID, YOU MAY ASK HIM. THIS WAS IN THE NORTH, WHERE WE WAS STILL MARCHING IN YER LORD POMEROY'S COLUMNS LIKE IT WAS WATERLOO–WHICH WAS MADNESS–AND NO SURPRISE WE WERE DYING BY COMPANIES AND FAIRLY IN H–LL.

THIS TIME WE WERE BACKED UP TO LAHORE LIKE THE MUTINY REPEATING, AN' HELD THERE TILL YOU COULD WALK OVER THE RAVI FOR ALL THE BODIES IN IT, AN' YE'D HAVE TO FIGHT CROCODILES TO GIVE THE LADS BURIAL THOUGH WE DIDN'T GET TO HALF OF 'EM.

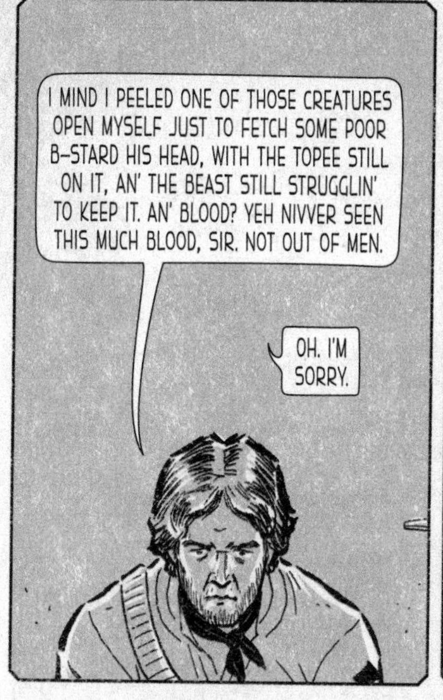
I MIND I PEELED ONE OF THOSE CREATURES OPEN MYSELF JUST TO FETCH SOME POOR B–STARD HIS HEAD, WITH THE TOPEE STILL ON IT, AN' THE BEAST STILL STRUGGLIN' TO KEEP IT. AN' BLOOD? YEH NIVVER SEEN THIS MUCH BLOOD, SIR. NOT OUT OF MEN.
OH. I'M SORRY.

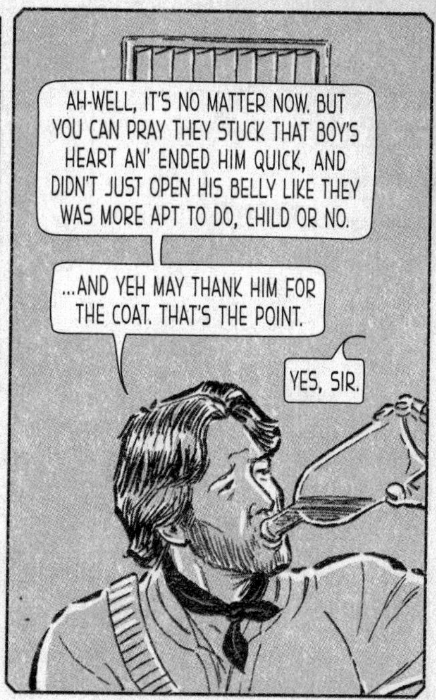
AH-WELL, IT'S NO MATTER NOW. BUT YOU CAN PRAY THEY STUCK THAT BOY'S HEART AN' ENDED HIM QUICK, AND DIDN'T JUST OPEN HIS BELLY LIKE THEY WAS MORE APT TO DO, CHILD OR NO.
...AND YEH MAY THANK HIM FOR THE COAT. THAT'S THE POINT.
YES, SIR.

YE'LL HAVE IT ON TOMORROW. LOOK SOMETHING LESS THE... VAUDEVILLIAN, I S'POSE, IF IT FITS.
SEE IF MAJOR DON'T LIKE YOU ANY BETTER THAT WAY.
YES, SIR. I HOPE HE WILL.

...GOOD NIGHT, SIR.
MM.

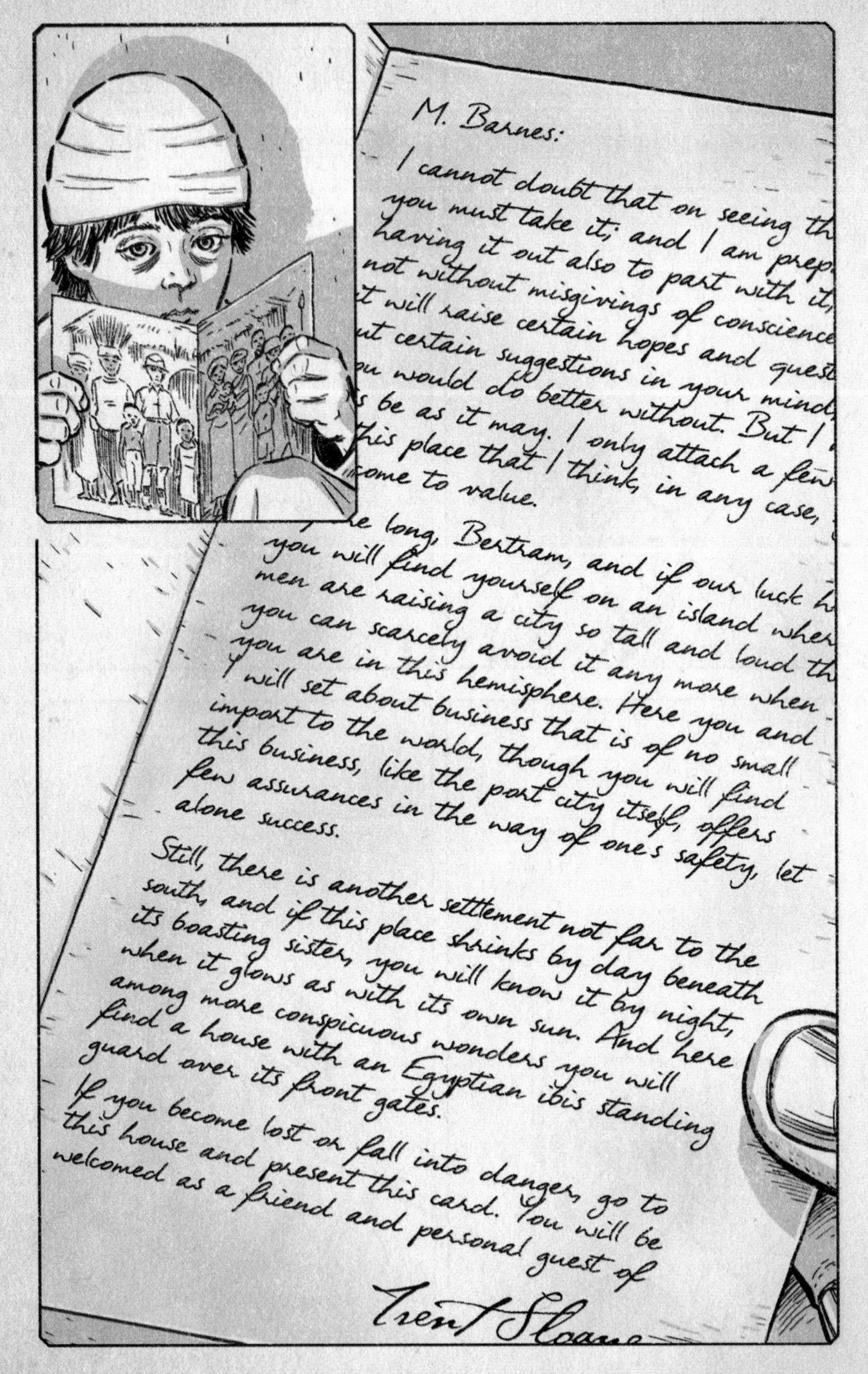
M. Barnes:
I cannot doubt that on seeing th
you must take it; and I am prep
having it out also to part with it,
not without misgivings of conscience
t will raise certain hopes and quest
ut certain suggestions in your mind,
u would do better without. But I
s be as it may. I only attach a few
this place that I think, in any case,
come to value.
e long, Bertram, and if our luck h
you will find yourself on an island wher
men are raising a city so tall and loud th
you can scarcely avoid it any more when
you are in this hemisphere. Here you and
I will set about business that is of no small
import to the world, though you will find
this business, like the port city itself, offers
few assurances in the way of one's safety, let
alone success.
Still, there is another settlement not far to the
south, and if this place shrinks by day beneath
its boasting sister, you will know it by night,
when it glows as with its own sun. And here
among more conspicuous wonders you will
find a house with an Egyptian ibis standing
guard over its front gates.
If you become lost or fall into danger, go to
this house and present this card. You will be
welcomed as a friend and personal guest of
Trent Sloan

As Bertram reads and re-reads Mr. Sloane's note, the knocking and yammering rise again through the passenger hold. These are not, unlike the noises of the sea, susceptible to any sort of rhythm or soporific pattern, but shrill and haphazard like an assault of insects. It seems unwise to try Sergeant Pensette just now with a request for cotton-wool. He must ask Mr. Renton, then, in the morning.

Bertram draws his legs up beneath the packing-cloths and sets the image of his parents between the small peaks of his knees, so he may study it while he stops his ears with his fingers. He sits like this for a long while, taking in the print through unblinking eyes, as a crease forms and deepens across his brow in unconscious imitation of his parents' sun-worried faces.

Really, he has no memory at all of the people in this print, and only the dimmest idea of what a father or mother would even *be* to a child, or he to them. But this image is proof of some greater, long-hidden dimension to Bertram's life, and the contemplation of its mysteries is novel to him in ways you and I cannot conceive. I say, for a soul so long starved of pleasures, this one is exquisite; and it is not yet edged with the longings or the worrisome questions Mr. Sloane has warned against....

I cannot tell you how long Bertram sits studying this print, but when he comes to again he must shake the use back into his hands and work at his stiffened limbs. Sergeant Pensette has taken up snoring in the hall, and it is a sound that would destabilize a lesser ship. The cries of the passengers persist as well, pricking deep, formless, dreadful associations in Bertram's mind. His eyes rove about the cabin, and there is the boy's pea-coat hanging limp from its peg. How horrid if he were to see it invested, suddenly, with the boy from Lahore, whom he can picture only too well now, rolling beneath the Ravi in the belly of a crocodile....Bertram blinks away these disjointed thoughts and tries to hold the gaze of the young lady in his photograph. The dusky infant wriggles and groans in her arms, but her eyes are untroubled. She meditates on a future where this weight is not another woman's child but her own, and her burden today is pleasant. The moans of the child grow louder, and they are the sounds of the ship's hull as it rolls in the black waves. Bertram recalls that he is below the ship's water-line, and it is an unpleasant thought. The noises excite more hoots and cackling from the *Virago*'s passengers. Bertram can see their dark and capering forms, now, flitting ahead of him, receding into the future, and he follows in spite of himself. He seems to be in some long hall of black-and-white checquered marble, with a lady's name wrought here and there in the stone and wooden scrollwork and embroidered on the furniture—*Lavinia* is the name... But the ship heels over again past vertical, and the rasping of Mr. Renton's tin tray on the floor recalls him to his tiny room in the present.

Bertram raises himself on his elbows and sees he has bent the print in his fist. He smooths it and tucks it into the folds of his shirt, rubbing an eye. The tray saws back across the floor, and his stomach gives an answering growl. He would like a sup of water, at least. He draws the cloth from his boots and lets them down toward the floor, careful not to look at the coat on its peg, and in this moment he becomes aware that there is someone else in the room with him.

Quietly, then, he slips back into the bed, inching away till he is stopped at the wall. A figure draws to the foot of his mat and rests a hand on it. It is small, a child's body, with shoulders narrow and bunched like Bertram's. There is an irregular bristling or nap to the figure's outline, as of animal fur, with tattered points for ears; but the thing moves undoubtedly like a human child, and is perhaps only wearing the costume of a little wolf or bear. Bertram sits wide-eyed, twisting the fabric of his shirt over the print of his parents, seeking it absently.

Bertram? Are you listening...? He seems to know the words before they are quite formed, as though reprising them from memory.

I'll show you, then. It's very important that you see this.... Bertram? The gardens are constituting around him, and the familiar light streaming through the cabin. He has been staring into a turn in a hedgerow, but the voice has its hold of him. *No—Not there. Bertram, you must wake up.* The gardens evanesce, pooling briefly about a path into the hedge. When his feet light beneath him it is on the ship's floor again. He is drifting toward the door of his cabin.

In the hall, Sergeant Pensette sits upright and stock-still beneath another hanging lantern, whether sleeping or sitting his watch it is unclear. But he is not outside Bertram's door, as the boy had judged. He is a long stroll away now, in an oval of light no greater than Bertram's thumbprint. It does not seem a shout could raise him at this distance, and he makes no sign of seeing as the boy flies up the companionway stairs.

In a moment more Bertram has come out onto the ship's deck, in the open air. The ship's engines thrum far below as he makes his way around the deck-house, listening out for the night's watches. When he gets to the forward gun-deck he stops: the little figure waits ahead, standing easily on a rail and looking out to sea, its black form visible only where it masks the stars in the sky beyond it.

Bertram approaches with a question forming in his mind, but the figure drops over the ship's side before he can speak. He lunges after it, scrambles up onto a cleat and pulls himself over the rail for a look below.... But there is nothing, not the figure that ought still to be falling, not a ripple where it might have entered the sea. Bertram waits like this, staring into the black water, first in distress, then held by an awareness that he will be shown something more.

One thing that strikes us (though less so Bertram) is this tiny filament of light in the western distance. We might take it for a beacon or a far-off storm, except it is neither. A little slit or flaw, then, in the blanketing darkness, right at the seam of ocean and sky: that is as nearly as I can describe it. And I can tell you it is nothing new or remarkable to Bertram. He has always known it to be there, whatever it is, fixed somewhere in the West. And there are certain times, as tonight, when he is led particularly to notice it.

At the same time, too, there is a glow gathering beneath the ship. He finds that his fingers are digging into the ship's rail, and that he is craning out for a look over the ship's side, against a powerful instinct of fear. A shape seems to be forming within or beneath the glow, incomprehensible at first for its size–But it is the body of a whale, proceeding with an awful slowness from under the ship's hull, wreathed in phosphorescence. The force of the vision is such that the ocean, the ship, the very night stagger back from it. Bertram is thrown from the cleat, and for a moment the sky and deck-boards are switching places over him. He regains his feet and fights back to the rail, but by now the whale is no more than a fading, greenish cloud a hundred yards off the ship's port side, with a few fainter shapes around it, presumably other whales at greater depths. All are heading toward the far-off spire of light, leaving Bertram to watch and to make what he can of this scene before his eyes.

He is still searching the western skyline when a man's voice breaks in upon his thoughts.

BIT HARDER'N YOU THOUGHT, IS IT? WELL: YE'VE GOT THE RIGHT IDEA, ANYWAY.
THERE'S THREE ALREADY DONE IT, YOU KNOW. MORE TRYING EVEN NOW, BELOW. THE ONES YEH DON'T HEAR YELLING, I SUSPECT.

THE LADS CURSE YOU FOR SUICIDES, BUT THEY DON'T MISS YOU, LAD, AND THEY'VE NOTHING AGAINST THE PRACTICE. IT'S ONLY THE TIME WE SPENT DIGGING YOU OUT'CHER HOLES. SEEMS A SH–TE RETURN FOR THE WORK.
BUT YOU KNOW WHAT I SAYS...? MM?
LOOK AT ME, BOY.

I SAYS WE OUGHT TO WATCH YOU AN' TAKE NOTE; FOR IT'S YOU THAT SEEN WHAT AWAITS US, AN' HERE YOU ARE HANGIN' FROM STRAPS AN' DASHIN' YER HEADS OPEN, WHICH TELLS US HOW MUCH YOU LIKE IT.
YE'R AWARE, I S'POSE, ALL THE WORLD'S AT WAR? AYE, SO IT IS. EUROPE'S ALREADY DOWN IN SMOKE AND ASH, AND THE REST GOIN' RIGHT UP THE LUM BEHIND IT.
THERE AIN'T A STOP WE MAKE BUT SOMEONE'S CROWING ABOUT THE END OF THE WORLD, AN' THE CROWDS GATHERED TO HEAR.

NOT THAT I TROUBLED TO LISTEN. THESE MEN ARE ONLY MAKING WORDS, I SAYS, AS I HAVE SEEN SOME CLEVER BIRDS DO.
NO, IF EVER THERE WAS REAL PROPHETS SENT INTO THE WORLD, WE'D NOT FIND THEM AMONG MEN, WOULD WE?

YOU'D NOT CONSENT TO LIVE AMONG GHOSTS, I THINK. AND MEN WOULD IGNORE YOU AND DRIVE YOU FROM OUR SIGHT, BECAUSE WE ARE VAIN CREATURES AND WE DETEST TO SEE OURSELVES IN BURLESQUE.
SO WHEN WE SEES YOU BOTCHED AND UNLOVED BODIES, IN YER MUD-HUTS AND DUSTBINS: HERE, I SAYS, IS MY SIGN COME AT LAST.
SIGN OF...WHAT, SIR?
WELL. THAT IT'S ALL UP WITH US AT LAST, FOR GOOD AND ALL.

AN' HERE SOME OF THE BOYS'D LIKE TO THINK YE'RE SENT AMONG US TO HELP FIX THINGS. ...MM?
BUT I SAYS, WHAT'S TO FIX? I CALL THIS A FINE HOUR FOR THE WORLD.
BUT IT DOESN'T REALLY SEEM–
OH, IT DON'T SEEM LIKE THERE'S VERY MUCH AFOOT TONIGHT, AYE. NOT FROM THE MIDDLE OF THE OCEAN, IT DON'T.

BUT I PROMISE YOU, LAD, ANYWHERE YE'D TOUCH LAND YE'D SEE GERMANS CUTTIN' UP THE ENGLISH AND THE FRENCH KILLIN' THE HUNS, AND TURKS KILLIN' SLAVS AND RUSSIANS KILLIN' PRUSSIANS, AND JAPS AT THE CHINESE AND INDIANS AT AFRICANS AND CATS KILLIN' DOGS I SHOULDN'T DOUBT...
AND IF YE'VE ANY DOUBT WHERE ALL THIS IS HEADED, YOU LOOK AT YER FRIENDS THAT'S DOWN THERE FIGGERIN' HOW IN A BARE ROOM THE NECK MAY BE CRACKED OR THE WINDPIPE SHUT.

AN' NO MORE IDEA O' WHY THAN HAVE YOU, WHO ARE ABOUT TO FEED THE MINNOWS BELOW.
BUT I TELL YEH, YE'R ALL SAVIN' YERSELVES FROM WORSE.

...THOUGH, IF YOU'RE SURE OF ALL OF THIS–
I AM.
THEN, WON'T YOU SPARE YOURSELF, TOO?
HA. GOOD BOY. AYE, I'VE TURNED THE THING OVER A BIT, I HAVE.
BUT: NO. I'M MEANT TO ENDURE THROUGH ALL OF THIS, Y'SEE. TO SIT IN WITNESS AND HELP THINGS ALONG, WHERE I CAN.

AND YOU WATCH ME, LAD: YE'LL SEE I BURY JOHN OGDEN, HARD A MAN AS THAT IS. OUTLIVE YOU, TOO, YOUNG THING THAT YOU ARE.
I WILL LIVE TO SEE THIS WORLD WITH NO MORE OF MAN'S SHADOW ON IT, AND WHEN THAT'S DONE, DO YOU THINK I'LL STAY ON AND ENJOY MY RUN OF THE PLACE?
HMPH. NOT A BIT OF IT.

I'LL PUT THIS GUN'S BARREL IN MY MOUTH AND PEN MY NAME ON THE GREAT LEDGER WITH IT, AS THE ONE THAT SAW THE JOB DONE.
AN' IF YOU THINK THIS IS MORE THAN MAN'S DESSERTS, I SUGGEST YOU RIDE ABOUT INDIA FOR A LONG YEAR WITH THE CEYLON COMPANY.
YE'LL SEE WHAT A LOT OF B–STARDS WE ARE, AN' KNOW HOW REJOICED THIS WORLD WILL BE WHEN IT'S RID OF US AT LAST.

...ANYWAY, THAT'S WHAT I LEARNED.
OI–YOU! BERTRAM–!

WHAT'S THIS, TOM?
ABOUT WHAT YEH SEE.
OH? I S'POSE YOU SET HIM UP THERE?
NO INDEED, SERGEANT. HAVEN'T MOVED FROM THIS SPOT, YOU MAY ASK THE BOY.

I ASK YOU, TOM. YOU THINK IT'S VERY SAFE FOR HIM UP THERE? AH?
WELL. NOW YOU MENTION IT–
I DO MENTION IT. AND IF YOU SEE HIM UP THERE AGAIN, YE'LL MOVE QUICK ENOUGH, WON'T YE?
AYE? ELSE WHAT, SIR?

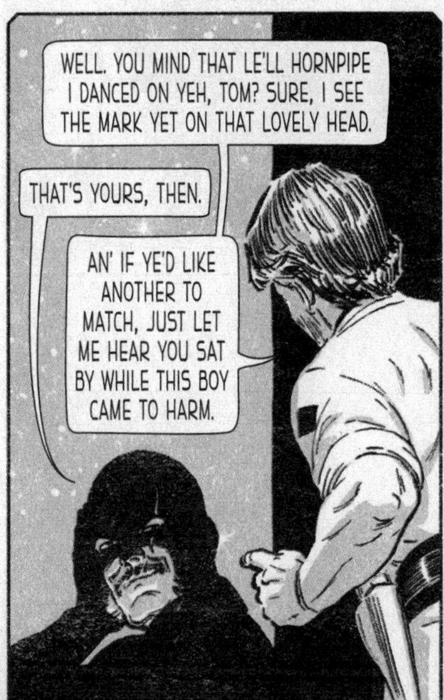
WELL. YOU MIND THAT LE'LL HORNPIPE I DANCED ON YEH, TOM? SURE, I SEE THE MARK YET ON THAT LOVELY HEAD.
THAT'S YOURS, THEN.
AN' IF YE'D LIKE ANOTHER TO MATCH, JUST LET ME HEAR YOU SAT BY WHILE THIS BOY CAME TO HARM.

AH, BUT DON'T YEH THINK I'D HELP MYSELF THIS TIME, SERGEANT? MM?
WHY DON'T YOU COME SEE?
...WELL. THE POINT IS–
–BERTRAM! CHR–ST, LAD!

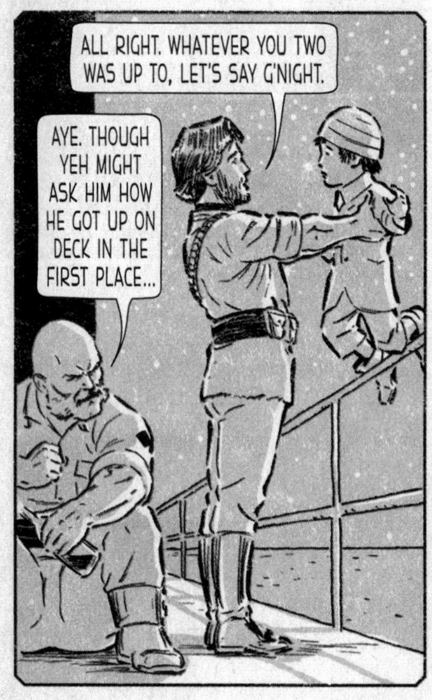
ALL RIGHT. WHATEVER YOU TWO WAS UP TO, LET'S SAY G'NIGHT.
AYE. THOUGH YEH MIGHT ASK HIM HOW HE GOT UP ON DECK IN THE FIRST PLACE...

...WHAT WITH HIS DOOR LOCKED FROM THE OUTSIDE, AND YERSELF POSTING GUARD.
BETTER LOOK OUT HE DON'T BECOME A HAZARD TO HIMSELF, WOT?
«PTOO!»

II.

40º 42' 16" N Lat | 74º 00' 34" W Long

New York City

. . .

May, 1918

...NO, SIR, THIS IS THIRTY-SECOND. STRAIGHT ON AND RIGHT, THEN LEXINGTON TAKES YOU SOUTH, AND YOU COUNT DOWN...
...BLEND IT IN. THAT OUGHT TO DO TILL WE GET YOU HOME. LET ME LOOK AT YOU...

ΕΧΕΤΕ ΑΔΙΚΟ. ΖΥΜΒΡΑΚΑΚΙΣ ΘΑ ΕΠΙΤΕΘΟΥΝ ΟΙ ΒΟΥΛΓΑΡΟΙ, ΜΕ Η ΧΩΡΙΣ ΤΟΥΣ ΓΑΛΛΟΥΣ.
ΕΥ–ΚΙΝΕΙΣΤΕ–KOSTAS, MOVE. MISS: I DON'T SEE YOU, YOU MUST SPEAK UP.
–OH, SORRY–
WHAT WILL YOU HAVE, *KOPELA MOU?*
THANK YOU. JUST THE ROYAL IBIS, PLEASE.

...I DON'T RECALL IF IT WAS HIS LEFT OR MINE, BUT ONE OF THEM IS GLASS. AND ONCE YOU SEE IT YOU CAN'T LOOK AWAY, AND THEN HE'S GOT YOU...
...SHE'D TURNED HER ANKLE AND COULDN'T COME DOWN FROM THE CARRIAGE. BUT OF COURSE WE'LL SEE THEM AT MONTAUK...

OH H–LL.

PARDON–PARDON ME, FATHER.
IT'S ALL RIGHT.

...THE OLDEST ARE MILITARY *IN MUFTI*, YOU MARK ME. AND WATCH 'EM ABOUT THE LITTLE ONE, IF YOU LIKE TO KNOW WHO'S AT THE TOP.
'DAY, MISS.

...CALLED QUAKING ASPEN, TO WHICH THE GROUSE ARE PARTIAL. MAGNIFICENT HUNTING ALL OVER THE GROUNDS, AND THE CANALS STOCKED WITH TROUT...
...NOT UNLESS THEY MOVED THE BURMESE BORDER BY A THOUSAND MILES OR SO...
...IN SILVER, OR RAILROAD BONDS, I DON'T RECALL. BUT HE TOOK A HIDING IN THEM, IS THE POINT...
...THOUGH I CHALLENGE YOU, UNCLE, TO FIND TWO MAPS OF THAT REGION THAT AGREE...

...NO, I WAS TOLD IT WAS INFLUENZA...
YES, BUT WHAT DO YOU THINK THE SPANISH FLU IS? IT'S ONLY INFLUENZA BY ANOTHER NAME...
...I WOULD BE GLAD IF YOU COULD NAME ME JUST TWO OF MR. WILSON'S POINTS...
...THEY'RE MADE TO LOOK EMPIRE, ONLY RUN YOUR FINGER OVER THEM: THEY'RE ALL FAKES...

...I WAS QUITE COMFORTABLE, BUT THE TALK IN THERE IS ALL POLITICS, LATELY.
I SHOULD SAY THE ATTEMPT IS TO TALK POLITICS. WHAT COMES OUT IS MORE LIKE ABSURDIST THEATER.

AH: BUT HERE ARE THE CIG-ARETTES AGAIN. LIKE MAGIC, WHEN THEY APPEAR.
GAD, YOU'RE RIGHT. I SHOULD LIKE A DISH LIKE THIS AT HOME.

OH IT'S ALL OF 'EM NOW, GASSING IN THERE THROUGH THE NIGHT, TO WHERE THEY CANNA' GET THEIR OLD BONES UP THE STAIRS TO BED. YOU ASK MR. NICHOLS IF HE EVER SEEN THE AULD MEN LIKE THIS, AN' HE SAYS NIVVER—NIVVER LIKE THIS.
...AND YELLED OUT LIKE SHE SAW A RAT, ONLY WHO DO YOU THINK IT WAS? BUT OLD BLAKE, ASLEEP ON THE LOVE-SEAT IN HIS DINNER-JACKET.

MISS...?
MAGUIRE, SIR.
CIGARETTES FOR THE GENTLEMEN, SIR.
THERE, PLEASE, ON THE CREDENZA. WE'LL SEE THEY GET THEM.
THANK YOU, MR. NICHOLS.

...SORRY, WHICH OF THEM?
ARTHUR. I DON'T BELIEVE JOHN HAS THE FIRST IDEA OF WHAT'S DOING, IN THAT HOUSE.
OR WOULD VOLUNTEER IT TO ANY OF US, IF HE HAD.

BUT WHAT LINE DO YOU TAKE WITH ARTHUR, THEN?
OH, IT'S SIMPLE ENOUGH: 'WE'VE BEGUN TO CONSIDER YOUR–EHH, YOUR "RESEARCH," PERHAPS–IN THE LIGHT OF SOME LATE DEVELOPMENTS, AND WE SUSPECT THERE MAY BE MORE TO IT THAN WE'D INITIALLY THOUGHT...'

–APPEAL TO HIS VANITY, YOU MEAN–
–WHICH HE'S GOT IN NO SHORT SUPPLY, IF MEMORY SERVES.
–NO, INDEED. AND IF YOU CAN SUPPRESS YOUR INSTINCTS AND MANAGE TO TAKE THE FELLOW SERIOUSLY, I THINK THERE IS NOT MUCH HE'D WITHHOLD.

THOUGH IF HE COULD PRODUCE THAT BIT OF JADE, BILL, I SUPPOSE HE'D ALREADY HAVE DONE IT.
STILL, WHAT HE COULD TELL US ABOUT IT MIGHT BE JUST AS VALUABLE. AND IT'S ONLY A SMALL POINT, THAT.
IT'S HIS PLANS I'D LIKE TO KNOW–WHAT'S HE BUILDING UP THERE, FOR ONE–?

ACH. YOU KNOW HE'S MAD AS A MARCH HARE, THOMAS. AND HE WAS THAT BEFORE HE LOST THOSE MEN.
WELL. I'M CERTAINLY NOT GIVING HIM THE LAURELS AND THE LECTERN DOWN HERE. WE'VE ENOUGH TROUBLE BEING TAKEN SERIOUSLY AS IT IS.

AND HIS HEALTH, AS I UNDERSTAND, WON'T PERMIT IT.
THEN YOU GO TO HIM, BILL. OR GET THAT MAN OF HIS. THE ONE– THE RUSSIAN. OR ROMANIAN. WHY CAN'T ANYONE FIND HIM...?

From the desk of Miss Anne Maguire, Maid of the Backstairs,
New York City Lodge of the Explorers Guild

• • •

Laura Catherine Molloy
In C/O Hotel Lavinia
Lowring-on-Hudson, NY

My Dearest Lolly,
You have my apologies first for this being so long in coming and I hope it finds you well. Weather in the city continues fine &c. but straight to business Lolly if you do not mind for there is much to tell and I am expected above soon.

I do not know the mood at Lowring but things here are surely drawing to a head and all to do with the arrival of your Mr. Ogden's brother. I told you he is coming by boat; well I understand he will dock with the Ceylon Company at a slip where your Mr. Ogden was accustomed to have his more discreet dealings if you take my meaning. If this be the case I know just the pier and I shall have to begin running errands to Fulton Market which is hard by. So there is my first item.

Now I suppose you remember these priests who have been hovering about the Guild & keeping an eye on our door and pretending to do anything *but*, well what I have done today I am not proud to relate but I slipped behind one of your black-gowns and let out an oath distinctly–and I will not say which only that no true man of the cloth would allow it in his hearing. And what do you think this man did Lolly: nothing at *all* is what. Proving what I have said from the first which is that these are no priests, and as I am resolved to learn just what they *are* I made an experiment today of rolling an orange past the old crow while he's at his breviary. Well. Not only does he watch me crawling past without twitching a finger to help (and fancy that in our good Father John) but he hoiks up that little book so I may not see it–& well he might Lolly for it is none of our Canon but some worm-eaten old heresy and the most outlandish scrawl on it too like Chinese mashed with Arabian and mind you I've a good eye for these things–Only let me return to this fellow's book in a moment when you know a bit more.

Next is the gathering at the Hotel Firenze next-door to us, and you may thank the doormen there for being such exemplary Italians and pitching their private conversation to the rafters as these Pantaloons will. By now we are all aware in this neighborhood that the Italians are hosting a delegation from India who have all come in disguise as English men of business and honestly Lolly there are Generals and diplomats of rank in this lot here on some secret errand and calling one another by their Christian names as though it were a fine joke indeed. There is one nabob in particular who seems to rule the rest, who is by the natural law of these things also the shortest, and exceedingly pleasant in his looks and manners but low-born for all his polish and with a malign cast to his eye or I am no judge. I think he must cut a tremendous figure in India if he is waited on by Generals like this, and though I have not yet divined the nature of his visit, still I doubt he has taken his lodgings at random. So you may class him with these other frauds across the street in that he is here most certainly to keep an eye on doings at the Guild, which leads me to what I suppose is the real business of this note.

Now, I have told you the serious-minded men of the Guild (and few there are) have locked themselves away with their books and old papers deep in the club, and have shunned food and sleep for nigh on three weeks now which is behavior I call reckless in men of *any* age, and instead they are havering on about what to do with regard to some imminent something, which thing I can hardly narrow down for you as it seems to involve quite *everything*: It is *this* jungle and *that* dark sea and this other desert plain which is of course meat and drink to the men of our club, but it is also the *War*, you see, and the ruination of the Planet and the looming *End of all Things* which is well enough for the unwashed to rave about in the street but quite a different thing to hear from lettered and dignified men as I believe these ones are.

There is some secret I am quite sure that binds all these sundry bits of argument together, but I have not yet struck upon it nor even close and the household for once seem wholly ignorant of it. I am in possession of a few stray facts and impressions only as you will see with nothing to explain or connect them, and if I relate these to you I hope you will not think me mad, my hope is rather that you are hearing talk along the same lines in your own house and that in putting my gabble together with yours we may get somewhere indeed. Here then Lolly is what I have:

First, I wonder if you have heard mention of a certain *City*, whose name I cannot tell you nor where it sits (some port of the Orient, it may be) but which subject gets the old men exercised I can tell you. They are bitterly at odds over what goes forth in this place and whether it be good or bad for us and what should be done about it, but it is agreed that *something* of great moment is taking place there anyway that may swing the War and carry our Race along with it. And what is more Lolly it seems your Mr. Ogden has had some dealings in this city on which point the old men of the Guild are keen to interview him, and you will see if he does not get a call to this effect and soon. He is even tied by some to a certain trespass or balls-up made in this city that either has or will yet bring a deal of harm to the world. Might he for instance have nicked a piece of Jade somewhere in his travels? I believe an accusation of the sort has been leveled against him in absentia as they say. For the life of me Lolly I cannot see what this means or how your Mr. Ogden's well-known travels and better-known misdeeds relate to the War or to the craters of Mars but I am retailing what I hear, and to judge from certain parties this man has gone wandering outside the circus of Humanity and quite unknowing kicked out one of the tent-pegs and perhaps this is something you would look into.

I should mention too that visitors to this City and emigrants from it are being sought and collected by some men and that at least one of these men is thought to be working for your Mr. Ogden, again to what purpose I cannot guess but I have heard the name Sloan repeated in connexion with the effort so if there is a Sloan in your Mr. Ogden's employ he might be the one to draw aside if possible or to listen in upon if not.

At any rate, while you are about this I will watch the docks against the arrival of John Ogden as I tell you & I will keep count of these new guests of the hotel and the long-robed heretics across the way, but more to the point I will continue to probe in the inner rooms of the Guild even though as of today this involves stealing round that old trout of a Mr. Nichols whom they have posted for guard (& this is done easily enough). Why just this morning I went in on pretext of bringing the old men cigarettes and espied some old papers on a secretary, and what is all over these but that very foreign writing I had seen on our pretend-priest's breviary outside! I shall have to get you a bit of this writing Lolly so you may examine it and perhaps help me to construe it.

Till then I shall hope there is nothing to any of this–or nothing too awful anyway–and it is only my imagination running riot, for who really would like to believe we are contemplating the End of our Days and that your employer has had a hand in the thing? It does seem wild I grant you. Still the old men of the Guild are stirred mightily by something as you would see if you could only visit, and the coming days or weeks ought to bring this thing closer to light, and if it should really be the Worst and we are all past praying for I am determined at the very least that the End should not take me by surprise (and then too we could all stop scrimping for war bonds as Mr. Lauderdale is forever at us to do).

And there is the bell again–Please do not worry overly about any of this Lolly till we know more, I am being ridiculous I am sure but it is all very curious I think you will agree. Please give my warmest regards to our Miss Frances and Mr. Faulk and Hattie and the rest & share no more of the above than you really must & keep a close watch over the old place dear Lolly for

Your loving cousin and correspondent,

Anne

& Best regards from Flossy who says she will go for a nurse in the Levant because I suppose we've not got enough to worry about as it is.

III.

IT IS TWENTY-TWO DAYS, by Bertram's count, since the *Girl of Safi* left his home in the Argentine, and we find him nested deep beneath her stern decks in one of these odd-shaped and out-of-the-way rooms designated for storage. This is not the closet he was shown to initially, and is less a room at all than a gap in the ship's plan, yet it suits his needs admirably. There is warmth here from the heating compressors on the floor above, and the eternal running of the propellor shaft to muffle the passengers' cries below. A porthole window near the ceiling marks the procession of day into night and gives some account of the weather. But more than anything it is a place unvisited by—perhaps unknown to—anyone but Bertram, and he has nosed it out and claimed it in the way the *Girl of Safi*'s rats have established themselves elsewhere in the ship.

Today (really the twenty-sixth since putting his home astern) young Barnes is roused by an echo of the engine-room bells and by an unwonted slowing of the ship. He is on his feet and heading down the dark and disused hall outside his room before he is quite conscious of waking, and he wonders if the rising commotion around him were a real living circumstance or only the continuation of a dream. In any case, there seems more urgency than real alarm in the thrum of footsteps, and in the voices swirling through the air and shrilling out of the speaking-tubes. He drifts to a porthole window, where a floating bit of debris proves to be a seagull keeping pace with the ship. The bird cries its warnings of landfall and fixes Bertram for a moment with a bulging, affronted eye, before peeling away from the ship's side, intent on other business.

The first men to pass Bertram are the young stevedores of the ship, who push through in their shore livery hauling baggage to the upper decks. Bertram is swept up the narrow stairs in a sweating, grumbling current of men, and he arrives in the open air to find the ship's crew and Ogden's dragoons and the ragged, squinting passengers all turned out *en masse*.

The clamor on the *Girl of Safi*'s decks—and there is a good deal of it—seems to be concentrated aft, where the six surviving passengers contend with their minders and where the horses emerge on trembling legs with scarves tied over their eyes. A chorus of shouts and a charge of wild-eyed stewards precede Mr. Mulcairn to the companionway door, and in the next moment it is Mulcairn himself kicking the Pasha's groom ahead of him and half-dragging, half-carrying the little Caspian nag he has somehow delivered alive from the Mideast.

Bertram dodges through legs and heaps of stores to the ship's waist, skirting around a giant, horsed figure that can only be Major Ogden. Ogden sits his charger square in the deck's center and pays no heed at all to a harangue, in French, from the first mate. The rest of Ogden's dragoons may be seen ranged about the forward decks, where they keep their distance from their commander and speak in undertones. Subadar Priddish smokes placidly, looking out over the port rail. It is not clear whether he is listening to Sergeant Pensette, who runs a rag over the same well-polished spot on a brass field-gun and cuts his eyes from the Sikh back to Ogden.

YOU MARK THAT, SIR. HE'S BEEN DRINKIN' STEADY SINCE THE ANTILLES, AND HAUNTING THE WATCHES DAY AND NIGHT.
MM.
WELL IF HE'S TOLD YOU SOMETHING, YOU MIGHT NOT MAKE IT SUCH A D—MNED MYSTERY.

IT IS NOTHING HE'S SAID, BUT...LOOK HERE: WE LEFT THE EAST ON A CERTAIN ERRAND, AND WHEN WE UNLOAD AT PORT, THERE IS THE ERRAND DONE. ORDINARILY, THAT WOULD MAKE AN END OF IT. DO YOU AGREE?
ORDINARILY? AYE. IF THEY GIVE US NO NEW ORDERS.

AH, BUT YOU SEE: THERE IS NO LONGER ANY 'THEY.' WE DO NOT SERVE THE CROWN OR THE COMPANY, WITH THEIR PRODIGIOUS WORKINGS, AND THEIR INSCRUTABLE DESIGNS. THERE IS ONLY A MAN WHO HAS BEGGED A BOON OF HIS BROTHER.
AND THE BROTHER, OUR MAJOR, HAS NOT EVER SOUGHT BEYOND THE LETTER OF HIS INSTRUCTION, SO FAR AS WE KNOW.
YET I FEEL HE PLANS TO MAKE AN EXCEPTION OF THIS CASE.

HE MUST LEARN WHAT WE HAVE DONE, AND WHY. HE DESIRES TO KNOW, AND INTENDS TO ASK.
WELL. I S'POSE HE'S GOT THAT RIGHT, AFTER ALL.
YES. SO YOU SEE OUR MAJOR, TODAY, AT THE DOOR OF ENLIGHTENMENT. AND YOU SEE HOW WELL THE PROSPECT SITS WITH HIM.

NA-AH. HE'S QUIET, AYE, BUT THAT JUST MEANS HE'S STORING FORCE, AND WHAT ELSE DOES A CAVALRYMAN DO AT SEA? WE BEEN A HARD YEAR CROSSING THE WORLD, AND NO MORE TO SHOW FOR IT THAN THESE HORRIBLE WITHERING MADMEN. I SAY HE'S QUITE READY TO THRASH SOME ANSWERS OUT OF HIS BROTHER, AND YE'LL CHEER HIM ON WITH THE REST OF US, SO GO AHEAD AND SHRUG.
AND WHILE WE'RE AT IT I MEAN TO ASK WHO SCUTTLED OUR LAST BOAT, AND I PRAY CHR–ST THAT MAN LIVES TILL I LAY HOLD OF HIM.

YES. IT IS INEVITABLE NOW THAT WE MUST ASK. AND WE MAY YET LEARN MUCH. THOUGH WE MAY FIND, WHEN WE HAVE OUR ANSWERS, THAT WE WERE BETTER OFF AS WE ARE NOW, WITH ONLY OUR QUESTIONS. OUR IDEAS OF THE WORLD ARE ABOUT TO CHANGE, MR. PENSETTE, AND NOT BY A LITTLE. YOU SHOULD NOT THINK THIS WILL BE AN AGREEABLE EXPERIENCE.
WELL. I S'POSE I'LL DECIDE THAT FOR MYSELF. AND IF YE'D TELL ME MAJOR'S AFRAID TO KNOW WHAT HE'S UP AGAINST–
I NEED ONLY LOOK AT HIM, TO SEE THIS IS TRUE.

NAH–WHAT RUBBISH. THAT'S JUST WHAT YOU ORIENTALS KNOW ABOUT IT. AN' SO YE'R AWARE, THAT PIPE AND BONNET DON'T MAKE YOU ANY MORE A SAGE THAN ME, SIR.

I SHOULD SAY THEY DON'T.

WULL: YOU HAD ENOUGH OF THE ROOMS BELOW, LITTLE MARSTER?
AYE, AND SEA-TRAVEL ALTOGETHER, I'LL BET. I'VE DONE WITH IT MYSELF, ANYWAY.
OH, I ONLY WONDERED IF WE'D GOT VERY CLOSE TO LAND, SIR.

ARE WE...?
OH: Y'SEE THERE, JACK, WHERE HE'S RIGGED A BIT LOW FOR LOOKOUT WORK.
OH, AYE. WHY DON'T YOU HAVE HIM UP ON THAT GUN, THEN?

THERE Y'ARE, LAD.
NOW WHEN I TELL YA, YOU LOOK THIS-A-WAY, AND TELL US IF YOU DON'T SPOT SOME TRACE O' LAND.

LOOK HARD, NOW, LAD.
HYEUGH-HYEUGH...!
AYE, YOU SEE 'IM, JACK?

40° 41' 04" N LAT
74° 00' 56" W LONG
MANHATTAN ISLAND,
UNITED STATES
. . .
MAY, 1918

IV.

THE PERFUME RIVER FISH COMPANY of Lung-doc Seaport, New York City, does, as I understand, purvey fish. But there is only the one distinctly low grade of salt cod on offer here, and it is not available for purchase. If you present yourself at the Perfume River Fish Company asking after *fish*, you will be turned away and watched narrowly by the old men in the front rooms as you retire.

Really, for the westerner, there is no getting into this place at all except by way of the *actual* Perfume River in French Indochina. There you must have met and impressed a certain Mr. Hsu, the founder and proprietor and governing spirit of the Fish Company; and you must have gained from him both an address and a letter of introduction. You must then, on your arrival at his New York establishment, make the old men a proper bow and offer them the courtesies of the East without expecting the same returned. You must show decorum and liberality of purse to the Chinese in the dark inner rooms while forbearing to judge their behavior; and you must sip tea and rice wine in rather a crude ante-room, often for a space of hours, without complaint. Only then will you be greeted and brought to a riverside courtyard, where you will realize some reward at last for these pains.

Our Mr. Hsu, you see, is a son of Hunan China, who as a young man was relieved of the Emperor's protection—and quite nearly of both his own *hands*—for his dealings in the opium trade. While Harry Parkes and his friends were going before the Board of Punishments and learning the tortures of the *Ling Chi*, Mr. Hsu was hot-footing it himself out of Canton Harbor, settling eventually with the expatriate population at Hué and reviving his business there. Within a year of his arrival he had built his now-famous gardens on the Perfume River estuary, and with help from Paris and the Ceylon Company (and such other concerns as were pleased to profit quietly under his name), he would go on to develop identical-looking posts in Java, Manila, Mogadishu, New York City, the Italian Riviera, and a rumored sixth location that I have not yet been able to place. Which is to say, he reproduced in each of these five (or six) port cities the courtyard in French Indochina that he found so excellently suited to the enjoyment of his stock-in-trade (which I remind you is not *fish*).

I have heard that Mr. Hsu describes his commerce as 'transport,' but that you cannot appreciate his meaning till you are seated at one of his satellite gardens, putting pipestem to mouth and looking out over the water. In New York, for instance, Mr. Hsu's guests will find a long stretch of the downtown waterfront sealed off by the curtain walls and tiered roofs of the Far East, and the grounds planted with Chinese cypress and flowering Empress trees, ginkgo and bamboo, dogwood and chrysanthemums, and all these stocked with crickets and caged larks and nightingales. The courtyard fronts the East River and not the South China Sea, inescapably; but Mr. Hsu has placed a few ornamental junks on the water and even moored a string of rafts at the mouth of his inlet, building bonsai forests upon these latter to suggest the islands of the Perfume Delta, perceived at a distance. Sit anywhere along this promenade, I say, and you are spirited out of the city to commune with Mr. Hsu himself in his pleasure-gardens of the East. And if there are flaws in the illusion, these vanish—or cease to matter very much, anyway—as one refreshes himself in the manner prescribed.

I warn you, the effect can disorient—or quite overwhelm—first-time guests of Mr. Hsu, particularly where they have gone too cavalier at the pipe. And we see an example of this today, in the miniature pagoda where our story continues.

We find two men seated in this pagoda, both facing out into New York Harbor, the one hidden behind a lorgnette with long legs crossed, and the other gripping his knees and staring ahead without comprehension, as though petrified in the receipt of vague and troubling news. A low lacquered table separates them, and this is set with Oriental serviettes and finger-bowls, and with various small dishes (the advertised salt cod among them) and a 'hubble-bubble' or water-pipe charged with Persian *shisha*, so far unsmoked.

Without lowering his glasses, the first man speaks quietly aside, and conjures a maid full-formed from the aether. The girl appears kneeling before them, presenting the man with a long bamboo pipestem and the crown of her head. She heats the pipe's old copper bowl with an oil-lamp and nods imperceptibly, at which the man–still watching the harbor though his glasses–takes a long and even draw from the pipe. He pronounces the words '*Gèng duo, xièxiè ni*' without exhalation, and the second man stifles a groan.

Silently, the maid resituates herself at the second man's feet and rolls another black pill in her fingers. She must guide the pipe to the man's mouth, as he will not let go his knees; but this done, he draws at the copper mouthpiece till the cords stand out over his knuckles and his trouser-cuffs lift over his threadbare socks. He vents smoke horribly then through his downturned mouth, like a masked demon of the Oriental stage, and closes his eyes–Though he pops them open just as quickly. I suppose the harbor, unpleasant as it strikes him just now, is still preferable to the pictures on view in his mind's theater.

There is a long spell of silence, then, before the first man mutters '*Hao nuhái,*' and quietly reverses the spell that brought the young lady and her pipe into being. When she has gone, he lets out his smoke through mouth and nose and adds, in the same offhand manner: 'This will be him.'

He sets the glasses on the table and we behold once more the drawn, patrician face of Mr. Sloane. The days and the distance have not altered his looks a jot: this is the same blank and bemused face we saw enveloped in flames in the Argentine. And he does no more now than stare out into the harbor. It is for his associate–whom we may as well start calling Mr. Kleitmann-Meyer, for that is his name–it is for this man to take up the glasses; but to do this he must release at least one of his knees, and he is not sure he can do *this* without flying up into the air. Still, the will of Mr. Sloane works implacably on him (for all that Mr. Sloane is only taking out a case of cigarettes and lighting one), and Kleitmann-Meyer lunges at last for the glasses. He puts them to his eyes hind-side-to and makes a sound in his throat that is not easily transcribed; but, reversing them, he takes a proper look at the harbor and its traffic of ships.

'…Which?' he says. 'Not the white one?' His English is pitched high with nerves and sharpened with the Austrian fricative.

'Recall,' says Mr. Sloane, 'the last time you saw an excursion steamer with an Indian field-gun mounted on her decks.' He breathes out smoke and places the cigarette case on the table. 'Upon my word, that's Ogden.'

'But he has wrecked his own vessel, *nicht wahr*?' says Kleitmann-Meyer. 'I suppose this other boat happens upon him, *tra-la-la*, just so, in the middle of the ocean. Mm? How lucky for him.'

'…Yes,' Mr. Sloane considers, after another long look. 'Though if not for that ship it would have been something else. You must bear in mind, the man is invincible.'

ON THE QUAY, SIR. UNDER THE PAGODA.
I TOLD MR. PRIDDISH, SIR: THAT'S THE SAME DEVIL FROM THE PUNJAB. AND YOU SEE IF IT AIN'T.

JUST YOU LET MAJOR CLAP EYES ON HIM, I SAYS.
AND CALLING HIMSELF 'SLOANE,' NOW.
...I S'POSE IT'S HIM, SIR?
WOT'S THIS?
QUIET, LAD.

ACH. HERE IS CAESAR RETURNED FROM GAUL.

WELL I AM D–MNED.
SO IT'S HIM, THEN? WHAT'LL YEH TELL HIM, SIR?
TELL HIM? I'LL TRY HIM WITH THAT REMINGTON, FIRST.
HA-HAAA! GOOD, SIR.

HERE IS SOMETHING: THEY'VE HANDED HIM A...*EHH*, I WONDER HOW YOU AND HE LEFT THINGS IN THE ARGENTINE...?

YOU'LL FIND THAT ONE THROWS HIGH AND RIGHT, SIR. I'D TRAIN IT ON THE LITTLE FELLOW'S FOOT.
HOLD STILL...
«CRRACK!»
«...CRRACK!»

«CRASH!»
GYAAAAH!

HRAW-HRAWW!
FINE SHOOTING, SIR.
IN WHAT WAY 'FINE'? IF HE WANTS TO SHOOT LI'L PAGODAS, I'LL TAKE HIM TO CHINA.
STOP YER MOUTH, LAD.

AUF DEM BODEN–SIR, YOU'LL BE KILLED–!
MM? OH: YOU DON'T REALLY THINK, WITH THE CHANCE TO CORRECT, THAT HE'D MISS A SECOND TIME? IT'S SOME SORT OF WARNING, I SHOULD THINK.
...THERE, YOU SEE? HE'S DONE.

I CONCEIVE A DEEP DISLIKE FOR THAT MAN.
YES. BUT YOU'LL KNOW HIM, NOW, BY SIGHT?
OH, RATHER.
GOOD. BECAUSE YOU'RE TO GO DOWN THERE AND HAND HIM THIS NOTE.

WHAT? OH: NO. NO-NO.
WHY DO YOU THINK YOU'RE HERE, MR. KLEITMANN-MEYER?
I–NO. HE WILL KILL ME, YOU SEE.
I DON'T THINK HE WILL. UNLESS BY SOME COINCIDENCE THESE ARE ORDERS TO DO IT.
WHAT? WHO WOULD WRITE ORDERS TO KILL ME?
WHO IS THIS FROM?

MR. SLOANE...? WHAT ARE YOU LOOKING AT?
...NOTHING. A TEAR IN MY COAT–
–THE NOTE IS FROM OGDEN'S BROTHER–BUT SEE HERE: YOU'RE WASTING TIME.
ON YOUR FEET, SIR.

AT THE CEYLON COMPANY PIER, A CERTAIN MAID STARES INTENTLY AT A PASSING CINEMA ACTRESS.
...YES, BUT THIS ANDREW—OR IS IT ARTHUR OGDEN? SORRY. I'M SURE HE'S GOT A NAME IN NEW YORK, I'VE JUST BEEN ABROAD, YOU SEE...
BUT ALL OF THIS IS HIS?
NOT—PRECISELY, NO. HE HEADS A GROUP...

OH THIS COULDN'T BE THE PLACE, PHILLIP. IT'S ALL SO SEEDY.
I TELL YOU, THAT'S THE POINT. NOTHING TO ATTRACT NOTICE. EVEN IF YOU HAPPENED TO WANDER IN CASUALLY, YOU WOULDN'T GET PAST THESE TWO.
BUT THEY'RE JUST LOAFERS.
NOT AT ALL. JUST YOU TRY TO COME HERE WITHOUT ME, AND YOU'LL SEE WHAT THEY ARE.
GENTLEMEN.
MR. FULLER, SIR.

THAT'S MY OFFICE RIGHT THERE, YOU SEE. I'LL SHOW YOU WHEN WE'RE DONE.
YES. THOUGH YOU KNOW, PERHAPS I'LL WAIT HERE AFTER ALL.
I ONLY WANTED TO SEE THE PASHA'S YACHT, AND THERE IT IS, AND IT'S VERY NICE. BUT I'D RATHER NOT GO ANY FARTHER, IF YOU DON'T MIND.

I DID TELL YOU THIS WOULD BE A BIT ROUGH.
YES, AND YOU'RE RIGHT AGAIN, AREN'T YOU? I SUPPOSE YOU CAN MAKE IT QUICK, WHATEVER YOU'RE HERE TO DO?
OF COURSE, YES. I JUST NEED THE CAPTAIN TO SIGN A MANIFEST—
THEN GO DO IT. I'LL FINISH MY CIGARETTE, AND IF I GET COLD I'LL STEP INSIDE.

–YOU'RE QUITE SURE YOU'RE NOT A SPY, PHILLIP?
OH–ME? HA! NO. I'M–REALLY JUST A JUMPED-UP CLERK FOR MR. OGDEN–
JUST WHAT A SPY WOULD SAY. BUT OFF YOU GO. THE LESS I KNOW, THE LESS I CAN TELL THE GERMANS.
OH, AND TAKE LION, WILL YOU? HE'D LIKE TO SEE THE HORSES, AND YELL AT THE GULLS.
WELL–YES, ALL RIGHT.

THERE'S THE CHASERS, TOO, SIR; THE ONE FORE AND ONE AFT. MR. MULCAIRN SAYS THEY'RE BOLTED, BUT THEY'D COME UP EASY ENOUGH.
GOOD. TAKE THEM, AND GET OUT ALL THE BRASS.

HAVE A LOOK BELOW, AT THE PUMPS. IF THEY'RE BRASS, TOO, LET'S HAVE THEM.
ANYTHING ELSE YOU NEED FROM THE SHIP, YOU'RE FREE TO STRIP IT BARE.

LOOK THERE, MARTIN: ISN'T THIS THE LITTLE ONE WE JUST SAW WITH OUR MR. DUROV?
–OR, SLOANE, NOW, I S'POSE?
EITHER WAY, THERE STANDS ONE VILLAINOUS-LOOKING LITTLE APE.
AYE. THAT IS THE CHIN OF A LIAR AND A REPROBATE OR I AM NO JUDGE OF A MAN'S FACE.

AND BLOCKING MAJOR'S WAY, WITH THE MOOD MAJOR'S IN.
HIDING A KNIFE, TOO.
HUH–? AH: SO HE IS. GOOD EYES ON YOU, HAVILDAR.
LOOK AWAY, BERTRAM. OUR MAN HERE MAY NOT HAVE ANOTHER MINUTE TO LIVE.

WHO ARE YOU?
NOBODY, SIR. A MESSENGER, SIR.

I'M TO WAIT WHILE YOU READ IT.
IT'S...ORDERS OF SOME KIND? SOMETHING TO DO WITH ME...?
YES.
OH...?

AN' WHAT'S THIS, AH?
NO-NO–I–!
AW, GIVE IT HERE, 'FORE YEH FALL ON IT.
QUIET, NOW: MAJOR'S TALKIN.'

THIS SAYS WE'RE TO LEAVE THE BOY WITH YOU.
IT–WHAT?

AH–OH. *HRM.* I SEE.
AND WHAT IS YOUR NAME, LAD?
NOT ME, YA BOOBIE. HE SAID A BOY.
SERGEANT: FETCH BARNES UP HERE.

AH–THOUGH YEH KNOW THIS PEEDY B–STARD COMES STRAIGHT FROM MR. DUROV, SIR?
MM.
–AN' YOU AS GOOD AS HAND BERTRAM OVER TO THAT DEVIL, SIR, LETTIN' HIM GO NOW?

I SAY, SIR–WE CANNA' JUST THROW HIM IN WITH BLACKGUARDS LIKE THESE, HEY?
ORDERS FROM MY BROTHER, SERGEANT. HE DOESN'T CONSULT YOU ON THIS. NEITHER DO I.
ANYWAY 'E'S SURROUNDED BY BLACKGUARDS NOW, IN'NE? DON'T SEEM TO BOTHER 'IM.

TRULY, I KNOW NO MORE ABOUT THIS THAN ANY OF YOU. BUT IF YOU CAN SHOW ME THIS BOY, WE'LL BE RIGHT OUT OF YOUR WAY–
–CAPTAIN SHAW?
SIR?
STRIKE THIS MAN WITH THE FLAT OF YOUR SWORD.
AYE, SIR.

–WHAT?
WAIT–!
«THWOKK!»

HOW YOU'VE GOT INTO MY BROTHER'S AFFAIRS, MR. KLEITMANN-MEYER, I DON'T KNOW. BUT I'LL SEE HIM TONIGHT, AND EITHER HE'LL EDUCATE ME TO SOMETHING I MISS, OR YOU AND MR. SLOANE CAN EACH EXPECT ANOTHER VISIT FROM ME.
...AND I'LL FIND YOU BEFORE THAT'S HEALED.
THIS IS NOT NECESSARY...

YOU TAKE THIS, NOW, LAD, AND NIVVER WORRY. WHEN THAT FELLA COMES FOR YEH, JUST STICK THE POINT OF THIS IN THE MEAT OF HIS THIGH AND DRIVE IT IN AS FAR AS IT'LL GO. WHAT DID I TELL YOU?
I'M TO STAB HIM IN THE LEG.
AYE, THEN WHAT? THEN YOU RUN OFF SCREAMING BLUE MURDER.
YES, SIR.
GOOD. THERE Y'ARE NOW.

AH: MASTER BARNES...? JUST A LITTLE THING, AREN'T YOU?
OI: YOU. LOOK AT ME, MY MANNIE.

JUST YOU LET ME SEE THIS BOY WITH ONE NEW SCRATCH ON HIM, HEY? I'LL TRAMPLE SEVEN COLORS OF SH–TE OUT'YA, NO MATTER WHAT YER STORY.
YES, I QUITE UNDERSTAND, SERGEANT. AND I SWEAR TO YOU, I WOULD NOT DREAM OF HARMING THIS BOY.

COME NOW, BERTRAM. THESE ARE BUSY MEN.
...UND JETZT DER TEUFEL KANN SIE HABEN.
HUH?
NOTHING. GOOD DAY, ALL OF YOU.

John Ogden is the first to leave the Ceylon Company slip, booting his horse to a gallop along the pier and plunging into the traffic of South Street. Not far behind him and nearly keeping up is Mr. Renton, who may be a tangle of spurs and coattails and overlong scabbard on two feet, but is as sleek and dogged as a hunting wolf when horsed. The two are watched out of sight by Miss Maguire, our maid from the Explorers Guild, who happens to be taking her lunch today on the East River esplanade. Miss Maguire considers, briefly, that these riders will be received tonight by her cousin, upstate. She must remember to ask Lolly all about it. Clearly there is some big news stirring, what with this Major riding out in such a hot haste.... But the thought slips easily through the web of Miss Maguire's thoughts. Really, since catching sight of Evelyn Harrow, she has been able to concentrate on little else.

She had recognized Miss Harrow at once, of course, from the society pages, and had known her for an actress, an occultist, and an object of the strangest speculation. She had heard her dissemble to her friend on the subject of Arthur Ogden, and had seen her feign and flatter her way onto the pier in what was really a marvelous performance. But what had struck Miss Maguire most was that the young lady, amidst all her other calculations, had turned to her and actually *noticed* her there on her bench. Beyond any doubt, this had happened.

Now, Miss Maguire does not claim any great advantage of beauty. She has not the strength of self-assertion. She has not learned a mastery of men, nor cultivated a very wide circle of friends. But she has always had, as a compensatory gift for her plainness, perhaps, a certain power of *invisibility*. She has become used to circulating freely through crowds, and watching and gathering intelligence without herself being noticed. And if this is not a faculty she is always conscious of in its exercise, still she recognizes—often with a jolt of alarm—when the veil about her is pierced, rather like a ghost when it is perceived by a 'sensitive,' to the horror of both.

And Miss Harrow had done more than spot her, she had intuited—hadn't she?—just what the maid was up to. She'd even flashed her a look of *encouragement*, as between conspirators. And why not? Perhaps in a sense they *are*, the maid reflects. Or they might become so. These are two young women, going each after the same object, differing only as to method. Why not help one another along, if it were possible?

It is a thing for the maid to consider, as she watches Miss Harrow and the others quit the pier along their various paths. As suspected, the actress does not stay long where her friend has left her. She takes a last, long draw on her cigarette and stalks away toward the Company storehouse. Mr. Kleitmann-Meyer, meanwhile, drags young Bertram north toward up-town, muttering obscenities through his clenched teeth. The dragoons finish their comprehensive looting of the *Girl of Safi*, as the workers on the quay receive and secure the incoming freight with the same practiced efficiency. The yacht's captain has fired her boilers, signaling his intent to leave port; while Phillip Fuller, agent to Arthur Ogden, anxious to find Miss Harrow again, pushes a few documents at random upon him, which the captain signs without reading.

Minutes later, Mr. Fuller is debarking with his bundle of papers under one arm and Miss Harrow's struggling Pomeranian under the other. The men of the crew, who have witnessed the spoliation of their ship and even been made to assist in it, heave at the gangway just as he steps to the pier, which action sends the agent sprawling ashore in a chorus of hoots and jeers. He is some time in collecting his papers, his spectacles, and the suddenly fearsome Pomeranian, and he stands to see the ship untied and backing from the dock. Her crew heaps insults on Ogden and his troop, on the ports of New York and on the New World generally, until Corporal Henty flings Mr. Kleitmann-Meyer's knife at them from somewhere on the pier. The blade sticks in the *Girl of Safi*'s radio mast, sobering the hecklers somewhat.

...And with this, Miss Maguire has spent up her hour's break. She gathers her effects as the dock workers close themselves into the Ceylon Company storehouse, and as Ogden's men head up the pier with a week's wages and a city to explore. She leaves Mr. Fuller calling and searching outside his office, next to Miss Harrow's fuming cigarette-end. Like the maid, Mr. Fuller returns to his work slowly, in an abstraction of thought. Though unlike him, Miss Maguire leaves assured of seeing Miss Harrow again. For the young lady's steps, she thinks, must inevitably bring her to the Explorers Guild.

...THIS WAS A BIT BEFORE WE MET MR. RENTON, Y'SEE, WHILE WE WAS STILL BUSY BRINGIN' THE PUNJAB TO HEEL. MISS OGDEN'D COME TO VISIT US THERE IN THE COMPANY OF A MISS GORDON, WHO WAS AFFIANCED AT THE TIME TO OUR MAJOR.
–HE MARRIED, THEN? OGDEN DID?

OH: AH-NO, NEVER QUITE. CARRIE WAS THROWN FROM 'ER HORSE INTO A IRRIGATION DITCH, AND DIED EITHER FROM THE FALL OR FROM NOT BEIN' DISCOVERED IN TIME. WHICH AN'T A THING I'D MENTION TO MAJOR–
–NO, CERTAINLY–
–BUT I WAS TELLING YOU ABOUT HAPPIER DAYS, AROUND JALANDHAR. WHICH–IT WAS COMMON THEN, YOU KNOW, FOR LADIES AND FAMILY TO JOIN THE MEN ON CAMPAIGN...

...AND SO MAJOR HAD HIS SISTER AND HIS LADY AT CAMP. AND THEY COME IN THAT WAY ON A MR. DUROV, WHO MADE THEM A FOURTH.
–NO–NO, IN POINT OF FACT, MAJOR AND MR. DUROV WAS ALREADY WELL-ACQUAINTED BEFORE THE LADIES COME.
AYE, THAT'S SO.

–WELL ARE YOU TELLIN' IT NOW, JACK, OR SHALL I?
I'LL KEEP YEH HONEST, BY G–D.
BUT NAH, YOU GO ON.
I WILL IF I LIKE, SIR. NOT BECAUSE YOU TELL ME.

...HRM. HOWEVER IT WAS, THEN, WE FIND THIS FELLOW DUROV. AN' THIS IS ONE O' YER NOBLEMEN'S SONS, SUCH AS YE'D FIND PLAYIN' KING ALL OVER THE OLD I.C.S.* AND DOWN AMONG THE TRIBES.
WE USUALLY HAVE NO TRUCK WITH THIS SORT, AS A RULE. ONLY THIS ONE CAN HOLD HIS LIQUOR AND HAS NO FEAR OF ANYTHING AT ALL, AND HE AND MAJOR BECOME ROARING GOOD FRIENDS, AS IT HAPPENS.
*THAT IS, THE INDIAN CIVIL SERVICE.

AN' I MIND HE SHOWED HORRIBLE METTLE IN A FIGHT, MARTIN, DIN'NE?
AYE, HE DID THAT. THOUGH UNHAPPILY HE SHOWS IT ON THE SIDE OF THE PATHANS, WHEN THEY UPROSE AGAINST US.
OH?

YAH. HE'D SOME IDEA OF MORALS, YOU KNOW—WHICH WAS FINE OUT OF A MAN TRADING IN OPIUM. BUT HIS IDEAS CLASHED WITH THE COMPANY'S, AND THERE WE WERE.
MAJOR'D HAVE HIS OWN TROUBLES IN THE SAME VEIN, OF COURSE, AND NOT LONG AFTER; BUT AT THE TIME HE WAS STILL A GOOD SERVANT OF THE LORD POMEROY'S, AN' HE TOOK THIS TREACHERY, AS HE CALLED IT, RATHER TO HEART.

AND DOUBLY UNFORTUNATE, OUR MAN JUMPS SIDES WHILE HE'S PAYING COURT TO MAJOR'S SISTER.
AND IS ONLY TOO SUCCESSFUL ON BOTH FRONTS, IF YOU TAKE MY MEANING.
–FOR A TIME HE WAS, AYE...

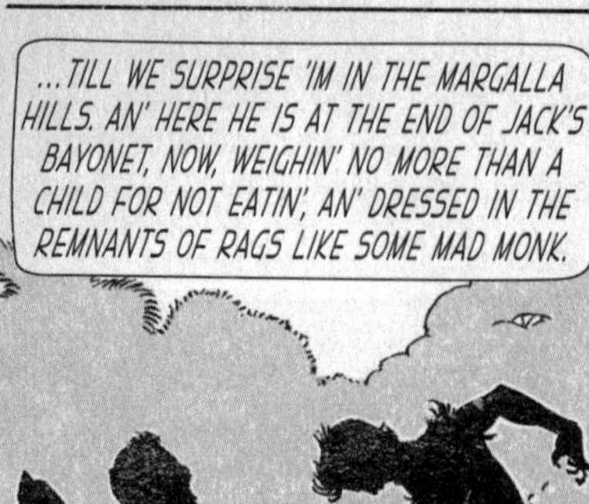
...TILL WE SURPRISE 'IM IN THE MARGALLA HILLS. AN' HERE HE IS AT THE END OF JACK'S BAYONET, NOW, WEIGHIN' NO MORE THAN A CHILD FOR NOT EATIN', AN' DRESSED IN THE REMNANTS OF RAGS LIKE SOME MAD MONK.

HOW HE LIVED TO MAJOR'S TENT I'M SURE I DON'T KNOW, AN' STILL LESS HOW HE LIVED TO MORNING. WE ONLY SAW HIM HORSED AND LEAVING CAMP NEXT DAY, BOUND WE THOUGHT FOR MISS OGDEN IN LAHORE.
HE WAS SPARED, Y'SEE, ON CONDITION HE TAKE HER FROM THE THEATER AN' MAKE HER HONEST.

BUT DO YOU KNOW? THE WH–RE'S SON DOES NEITHER.
WOULD'JA LET ME GET THERE, JACK? I NEARLY WAS.
AYE, HE DOES NEITHER, LAD. ONLY FLIES WITH HIS LIFE, AN' WE HEAR HIS NAME NO MORE IN INDIA OR ANYWHERE ELSE.
AN' THERE'S MISS FRANCES LEFT TO RUE THESE GODLESS SONS OF NOBLES, WITH HER HEART BROKE FOREVER BEYOND MENDING.

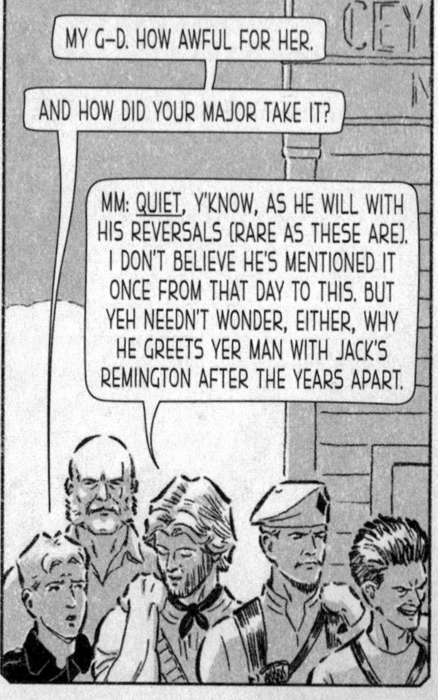
MY G–D. HOW AWFUL FOR HER.
AND HOW DID YOUR MAJOR TAKE IT?
MM: QUIET, Y'KNOW, AS HE WILL WITH HIS REVERSALS (RARE AS THESE ARE). I DON'T BELIEVE HE'S MENTIONED IT ONCE FROM THAT DAY TO THIS. BUT YEH NEEDN'T WONDER, EITHER, WHY HE GREETS YER MAN WITH JACK'S REMINGTON AFTER THE YEARS APART.

NO, THE WONDER IS WHY HE ONLY SPENT TWO BULLETS ON HIM. 'SPECIALLY ONCE HE'D CORRECTED FOR THE WAY THAT GUN THROWS.
AYE, THAT'S SO. I WONDERED MYSELF WHY HE DIDN'T PRESS THE POINT THIS MORNING.

BUT–IF IT'S REALLY THIS SAME MAN CALLING HIMSELF SLOANE, I DON'T SEE WHY HE'D LET HIMSELF WITHIN AN OCEAN OF YOUR MAJOR, LET ALONE FORCE HIMSELF BACK INTO THE MAN'S AFFAIRS.
HE CAN'T IMAGINE HE'D SURVIVE IT–PARTICULARLY NOT NOW–
NO. I CANNA' FIGURE IT ANY BETTER THAN YOU.
BUT HE'S COME LIKE NEMESIS, HASN'T HE? LIKE SOME GHOST, BENT UPON HAUNTING THIS FAMILY.

NAH–YOU SEE IF MAJOR AIN'T LET HIM LIVE, JUST TO SEE WHAT HE'LL SAY FOR HIMSELF.
AN' YE'LL SEE WE RUN HIM TO GROUND SOON ENOUGH. HIM BEIN' ONLY A MAN.
IS HE, TOM? I DON'T KNOW THAT. WHAT DID I SAY IN THE ARGENTINE, BUT THAT I'D SEEN THIS MAN'S GHOST–HM? AND SO I DID.

CHR–ST, WHAT RUBBISH YEH TALK, THOUGH.
YOU'RE NOT SERIOUS. SERGEANT...?
AN'T I? YOU MEET HIM, SON–ALL OF YEH, MEET HIM, AN' ASK ME THAT AGAIN. YOU TELL ME THIS IS ONLY THE MAN WE KNEW THOSE YEARS AGO, IN THE HILLS.

Miss Harrow ducks into the Ceylon Company storehouse just behind Subadar Priddish, and pauses to let her eyes adjust to the gloom. Her presence does not go unremarked by the workers here–I do not see how it could–but they do not think to stop or question her. In their view, she is only another of these exotic parcels from across the ocean, and so long as she is sure of her own business they need not trouble to *put* her anywhere, which is the extent of their concern with her.

She proceeds into the room and finds the air thickening with coal-smoke, and she sees that the crates and parcels that have sat here longest are mantled in soot. Noises begin to reach her, too, over the din of the workers: strange, muffled cries and rattling blows upon metal. She is drawn to a square of deeper shadow on the plank floor, and it seems these sounds–identifiable now as the cries of the insane–proceed from here. She can just make out a salt-eaten iron stair in the shadow at the square's edge, and without a moment's pause she lowers her foot to it.

The stairs–there are more, though not many–lead Miss Harrow down about six feet to a tin-walled catwalk that hangs along the underside of the pier. There is scarcely room in this passage for a man to walk upright, and Miss Harrow must wrap her mouth and nose against the choking coal-smoke. She presses on, losing light and air, and with the tin walls enlivened by the shrieks and laughter of the deranged souls ahead. It seems to her that hell in the industrial age would have ways of access like this.

The walkway leads to a short hall of iron-ribbed stone and another flight of stairs, and Miss Harrow descends these latter, slowing and pressing herself to a soot-grimed wall. Just ahead of her an archway gives in to a larger, gas-lit hall set at right angles to the stairs, with a low vaulted ceiling and a cinder floor laid with iron rails. A terrific grunt of machinery sounds from the hall and a gout of warm, sooty air rushes up against her as she steals through the archway, screening her eyes. A train is lurching into motion here, its old works coughing out steam and smoke in bursts that shake the room like cannon-fire. She slips back past the engine and into an unlit tunnel, rounding the last of the cars with a quick hop onto the tracks. The train is picking up speed, but she is able to catch a door-handle on the back of the rear car and hoist herself to a coupling. And crouching here, with no notion of the things ahead and only a reasonable guess that she is riding behind the Sikh and his party, Miss Harrow passes through the cinder-floored room and into the undercroft of the city.

We note in this place that these are not the better-known, publicly patronized tunnels of the Interborough Rapid Transit (where you would hardly find a coal-powered engine in operation). They are rather the legacy of a failed bid by George Westinghouse for the subway and elevated rail contracts of Kings County. Westinghouse had proposed to power his lines with a system of alternating current, and had laid model tracks beneath the city and offered free-to-the-public charters for a time, all to demonstrate the advantages of his grid over Edison's better-entrenched systems of direct current. We know from history, of course, that the contest did not go Westinghouse's way, and that he ordered his tunnels sealed rather than join them to the expanding works of his rival. What was not so well publicized is that Westinghouse's partners—among them the Honorable Ceylon Co., Ltd.—had already seized his trains and tunnels by this point, thinking him mentally unsound, and had placed him under guard at his home in Pittsburgh till a sale of these assets could be effected (and it is said one of his cars was found welded shut and loaded with casks of gunpowder beneath St. Patrick's Cathedral). In any case, the offers put forth by Edison and the IRT were deemed punitive, and a face-saving deal was struck at the last minute with Arthur Ogden, one of the venture's more prominent local partners.

Today Ogden maintains the Westinghouse lines privately, in partnership with cooler heads at the IRT. The old transformers have been pulled up and sold, but Ogden has fit his engines (he keeps two) to make use of direct current in the public tunnels, and to run on coal over the nonconducting lines, including where he has elevated the old rails to join those of the New York Central just north of the Harlem River. There are few better ways to introduce freight discreetly to the island and to route it through the city than Ogden's lines. And while I could no sooner catalogue all the system's uses than I could show you a map of the thing, I assure you that a cargo of six pop-eyed hermits and a Sikh deserter, with a vanished cinema actress clinging to the hindmost car, is not nearly the strangest thing these trains have carried, perhaps not even today.

Still, this is the shipment that concerns us, and we re-join Miss Harrow and the rest as they make their way south beneath Brooklyn. The actress has dropped a shoe and lost sensation in her arm and is finding the going, generally, horrid in the extreme. She has been wondering for some time now whether she mightn't have better luck following the train on foot, and as it eases into a bend she kicks off her remaining shoe and prizes her hand from the door-handle in preparation for a leap to the tracks. Yet she is no sooner set on this course than the train slows to a stop, and the tunnel fills again with the hoots and whistles of Mr. Priddish's friends, who appear to have done with this leg of their journey.

Miss Harrow stays for a moment on the coupling, frowning down at her shoe—more of a heeled Japanese slipper, really, a gift from someone or other, lying ruined now on the cinders—though she makes little of its loss. She is only waiting and listening and nursing her cramped hand while the cries diminish down another stone corridor. And then, as the train bestirs itself, she slips to the ground, steps over the rails and mounts a short flight of stairs onto the siding.

She feels her way along the puddingstone wall that backs the platform, rounds a rough-hewn column and climbs another dark flight of stairs. She is fidgeting with her scarf and patting soot from her jacket with the cries (as she judges) sufficiently far ahead, when she turns onto a landing and very nearly walks into a man waiting there.

She does not start or cry out, but there is a hitch in her breath, and she claps a foot down out of rhythm as though missing a stair with it. A quick 'Well: hello,' escapes her before she can quite check it.

The man is nearly half again as tall as the shoeless Miss Harrow, and he stands, smoking, in a well-traveled suit of excellent cut. There is a hinged wooden grate beside him, and beyond this more stairs. It is not clear what this gentleman is doing down here in the dark, and I should say it is his part, in such an encounter, to explain himself and to see he has not startled the young lady; yet he only stands smoking and preserving his silence. Miss Harrow finds she is avoiding his eyes and, worse, that she is the next to speak.

Miss Harrow skirts past the stranger and darts up the stairs, at a bit of a nonplus. Her conduct has surprised even herself, and she cannot quite explain it on grounds of exhaustion, or distraction, or being alone and without her shoes in an unfamiliar and doubtless unsafe part of the city... Well. She can examine all of this later, perhaps.

For now, she has reached the top of the stairs and found herself in a narrowing hallway, with the faintest streaks of light ahead that may or may not describe the outlines of a door. The light does mark the hall's end, anyway, and she gropes about until her fingers light upon a bolt, and then a handle. The bolt is rusted in place and the door held fast by a spring mechanism, but she works determinedly at these and succeeds, after a time, in moving the door from its frame. Seals of age and rot split open with a muffled cracking sound, and dirt and dust fall with a hiss and rise in whorls through a widening channel of light. She hooks an arm around the door and pries it open just far enough to get her slender body through.

A bit of caution–a quick look about, perhaps–might be in order. But the door has cost her time already and put Mr. Priddish and his party that much farther ahead, and–more to the point, though she would hardly admit it–there is this strange gentleman from down the stairs who might reappear behind her at any moment. She slips through the opening, therefore, without hesitation, and is little troubled when the door swings to behind her on its spring, with no latch on this side.

Miss Harrow must stand blinking for a moment, quite blind, and more than a little annoyed at her own helplessness. There seems to be nothing *but* light in this next place, whatever it is–a great luminous fog of it, as though she were suspended suddenly in a cloud.

She calls out once, and becomes

aware of murmuring voices only when these suddenly break off. She can make out little white, hexagonal tiles at her feet now, and feel through her stockings that the tiles are damp. She pads forward, rubbing at her eyes, until a slightly darker shape detaches from the light and resolves into the figure of a white-smocked valet. The man stands utterly still, and looks on Miss Harrow as he might regard the risen dead.

For her part, of course, Miss Harrow has already been intimidated once in the last few minutes, and this fellow had better make her some answers.

WHERE'D THE OTHERS GO?
...I'M SORRY?
A WHOLE MOB OF THEM CAME THIS WAY, AHEAD OF ME. OR DID YOU JUST GET HERE, TOO?
MISS–*HRM*–MISS: I'VE BEEN HERE SINCE ELEVEN THIS MORNING, AND EVERY DAY BUT SUNDAYS FOR EIGHTEEN YEARS.

I HAVE NEVER ONCE SEEN A SOUL PASS IN OR OUT OF THAT DOOR. I HADN'T EVEN KNOWN THERE WAS A DOOR THERE, UNTIL THIS MOMENT.
I TRUST YOU KNOW WHERE YOU ARE?
I BEGIN TO, YES.

WHO IS THAT, CARTER? I HEAR A YOUNG LADY?
MISS–I'M AFRAID YOU'RE NOT ALLOWED IN HERE.
OH, SETTLE DOWN. IT'S NOT AS THOUGH I'M LOOKING.

STEPPING AT LAST INTO THE OPEN AIR, MISS HARROW IS SEIZED BY A THOUGHT.
...THERE WAS ANOTHER DOOR.

THAT GENTLEMAN ON THE STAIRS HAD QUITE DELIBERATELY MISDIRECTED HER.

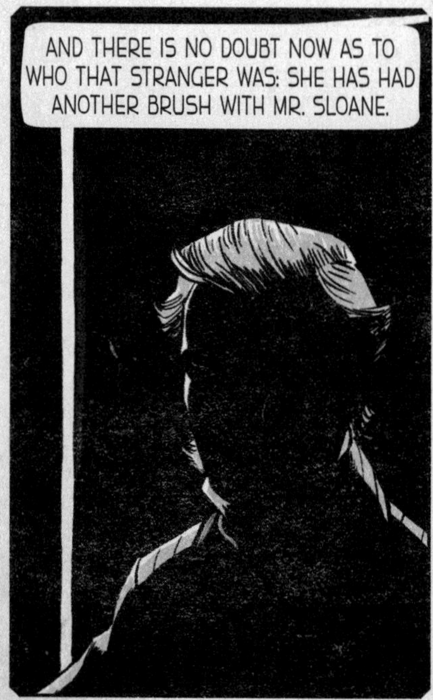
AND THERE IS NO DOUBT NOW AS TO WHO THAT STRANGER WAS: SHE HAS HAD ANOTHER BRUSH WITH MR. SLOANE.

WELL. I'D LIKE TO SEE YOUR MANNERS IMPROVE A BIT. BUT YOU'LL DO, WON'T YOU?
...I SUPPOSE YOU MUST.

Mr. Sloane, as I can tell you, is stopping only briefly at his house in Coney Island. He is here to receive the passengers of the *Girl of Safi*, to get some picture of their health and to see them into the hands of his associates. They will be brought upstate to the home of Arthur Ogden, together with a dozen or so fellow test-subjects and the various machines and chemicals used to test them, which arrangments Mr. Sloane is content to leave with his trusted staff.

If there is a wrinkle developing in the day's plan, it will have to do with another of his associates, a Mr. Kleitmann-Meyer, who has been left to take Bertram Barnes from the Ceylon Company slip to the rooms Mr. Sloane has hired in upper Manhattan. It is Sloane's intention to interview the boy there, at a safe distance from John Ogden, and then to conduct him personally out of the city. Yet with this appointment looming and Sloane concluding his business on Coney Island, we find Mr. Kleitmann-Meyer still struggling through the streets of downtown.

The Austrian, as we've seen, has taken substantially more opium today than is his habit. And the lingering presence of the drug in his veins, together with his rough handling at the docks and a natural aversion to crowds—not to mention the pressures associated with this errand and with Mr. Sloane's presence generally—these conspire to sink him into the blackest of moods. The streets and buildings of this hated city, too, have assumed an interchangeable aspect for him, and at the moment he is retracing his steps back to the pier, though Bertram does not dare point it out.

...THE REST OF THEM LAUGHING, TOO, AND WELL THEY MIGHT, ALL OF THEM TOGETHER, AND MYSELF ALONE–
–*PFUH!* PARDON–
CHESTNUTS! BAG OF CHESTNUTS, SIR...?

THERE'S A GIBBET BUILT FOR EVERY MAN IN THAT OUTFIT, YOU MARK ME. AND WHEN IT'S OGDEN SWINGING BY THAT GREAT BULL NECK, YOU WILL PERMIT ME A LAUGH OF MY OWN.
–*AHH VAI E FOTTITI,* SIR–AND THE BOY, TOO...
NEWS OF THE WORLD! LATEST FROM THE WAR! RUSSIANS NOT SO FOND OF IT AFTER ALL– PITCH THE ENTENTE OVER AT BREST-LITOVSK!

THREE-CENT EXTRA, TWO FOR THE DAILY! OUR EDITORS SPARE THESE PEOPLE NO INSULT!–'EY!
–THAT'S NEWS FOR GROWN MEN THAT PAYS FOR IT, NOT FOR LITTLE URCHINS BLOCKIN' THE WAY.
...THE BEAST IS RISEN INTO THE SKIES OVER EUROPE!
«*BOOT!*»

NEWS OF THE WORLD! BRIT-ISH TAKE JERICHO! GERMANS IN ESTONIA! EVERYONE FIGHTING EVERYONE ELSE–
–AND LO! HER CAPITALS BURN!
YOU–! AYE, YOU WILL FIND NO REFUGE HERE, BOY.
MUCH SAFER TO READ ABOUT IT AT HOME!

THIS LAND, TOO, WILL BE RAKED WITH FIRE, AND OUR CITIES THROWN DOWN–!
BERTRAM? COME–YOU MOVE THOSE LITTLE LEGS, OR YOU WILL WISH YOU HAD.
AH! YOU THERE!
YOU! THAT'S RIGHT. LOOK SHARP, NOW, OR YOU'LL LOSE A FARE....

...AND WHEN I'VE GOT YOU IN THERE, YOU'LL DO NO MORE OF YOUR SQUIRMING AWAY.

HERE–CAREFULLY, NOW. COME ROUND–*GAAH!* CAREFULLY, I SAY!
CAREFUL YERSELF, BROTHER.
OH-HO! IRISH. AND DRUNK, TOO, I'LL JUST BET.

NOW YOU MIND, THERE'S A BOY WITH...
...*EHM*, JUST BEHIND, *EH*, ME–BERTRAM?
NO, NO-NO-BERTRAM!

HE'LL KILL ME! HE WILL KILL ME FOR THIS I'M SURE!
NOW WHAT'S HE DOING?
HARD TO SAY, PAT.
SAYS SOMEONE'LL KILL HIM, THO.
OH, AYE?

WHY WOULD HE HAVE TRUSTED THIS TO ME?
WHY, INDEED, SIR.
CHILDREN LOATHE ME, YOU KNOW.
GRAB HOLD OF 'IM, PATRICK, CAN YOU?

NEVER WORRY, SIR. GET YEH RIGHT WHERE YOU'RE GOING.
AND WHERE'S THAT, FRANCIE?
HIM? MADHOUSE AT BELLEVUE, I SHOULD THINK.
OH, AYE. COME ALONG, SIR.
BELLEVUE? BUT I'M NOT MAD. SEE HERE:

THAT'S FOR THE EXPLORERS GUILD. MEMBER IN GOOD STANDING, YOU SEE.
SAYS HE'S A EX-PLORER, FRANCIE.
CERTAINLY, HE IS. MADHOUSES ARE FULL OF 'EM, PAT.

AH: HOLD 'IM NOW, PAT!
STEADY, SIR–!
NO-NO–I MUST FIND HIM–PLEASE!

WULL, THERE HE GOES.
YA. OFF EXPLORING SOME MORE.

A DESPERATE HALF-HOUR'S SEARCH LEADS MR. KLEITMANN-MEYER BACK TO THE PERFUME RIVER FISH COMPANY

AND FROM THERE TO A CERTAIN HAND-LAUNDRY IN CHINATOWN, THAT WE KNOW AS A SECRET MEETING-PLACE OF THE *JIA-DE* TONG.
...HE WILL NOT BE DIFFICULT TO SPOT, UNLESS YOU'VE GOT A LOT OF ORPHANS LURKING AROUND THE FULTON MARKET WITH THEIR HEADS WRAPPED IN GAUZE. DO YOU? I DO NOT KNOW, IT IS NOT MY CITY.

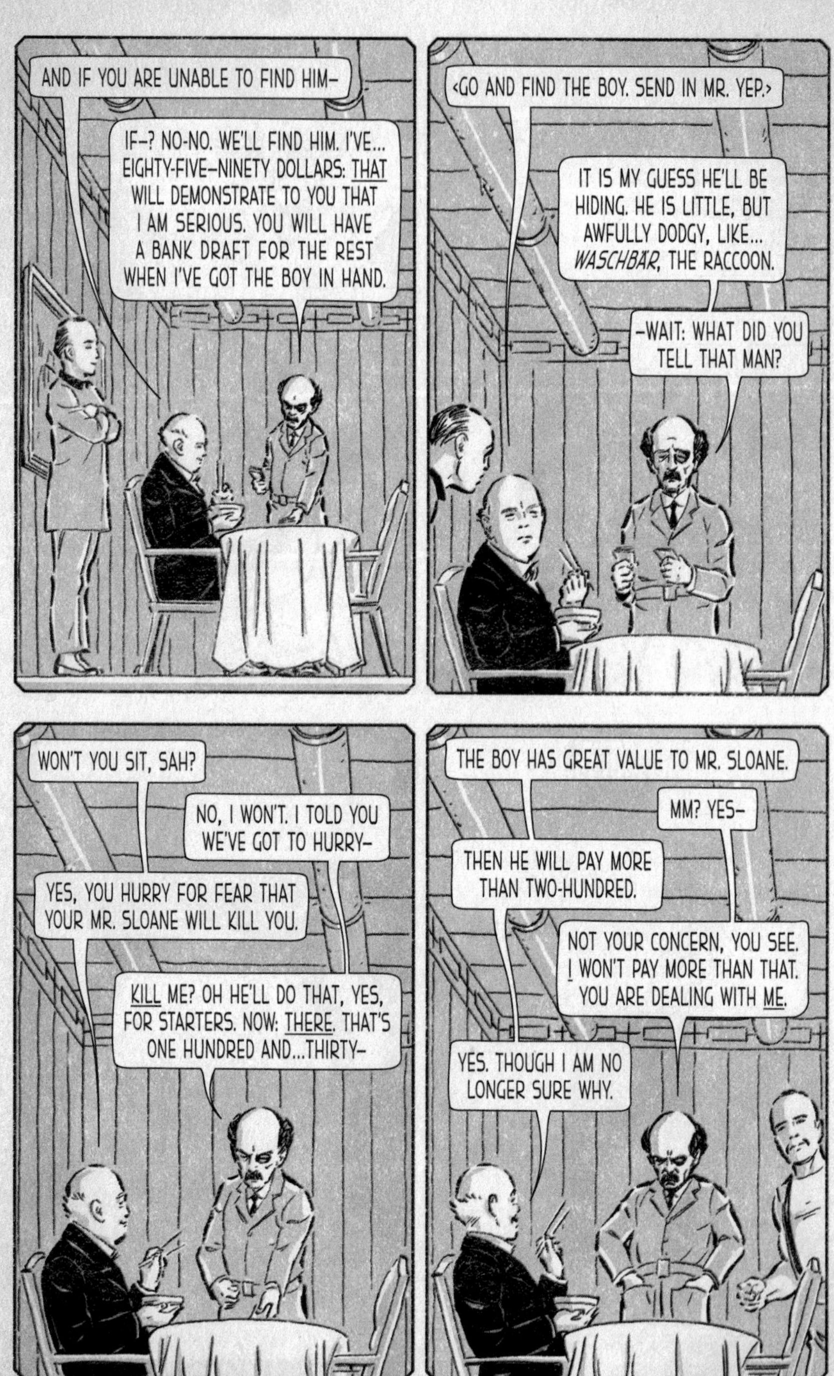
AND IF YOU ARE UNABLE TO FIND HIM–
IF–? NO-NO. WE'LL FIND HIM. I'VE... EIGHTY-FIVE–NINETY DOLLARS: THAT WILL DEMONSTRATE TO YOU THAT I AM SERIOUS. YOU WILL HAVE A BANK DRAFT FOR THE REST WHEN I'VE GOT THE BOY IN HAND.
<GO AND FIND THE BOY. SEND IN MR. YEP.>
IT IS MY GUESS HE'LL BE HIDING. HE IS LITTLE, BUT AWFULLY DODGY, LIKE... WASCHBÄR, THE RACCOON.
–WAIT: WHAT DID YOU TELL THAT MAN?
WON'T YOU SIT, SAH?
NO, I WON'T. I TOLD YOU WE'VE GOT TO HURRY–
YES, YOU HURRY FOR FEAR THAT YOUR MR. SLOANE WILL KILL YOU.
KILL ME? OH HE'LL DO THAT, YES, FOR STARTERS. NOW: THERE. THAT'S ONE HUNDRED AND...THIRTY–
THE BOY HAS GREAT VALUE TO MR. SLOANE.
MM? YES–
THEN HE WILL PAY MORE THAN TWO-HUNDRED.
NOT YOUR CONCERN, YOU SEE. I WON'T PAY MORE THAN THAT. YOU ARE DEALING WITH ME.
YES. THOUGH I AM NO LONGER SURE WHY.

IT DOES NOT SOUND AS THOUGH MR. SLOANE WILL MISS YOU, IN ANY CASE.
NO, THAT'S CERTAINLY TRUE.
WAIT: WHAT?

NN–NEIN–STOPP!

‹OUT OF THE WAY!›

‹‹POP! POP!››
GYAAAH!

I have mentioned that Ogden's dragoons—the eighteen who have made the crossing, at any rate—have been loosed today on an unsuspecting city. They are to wait here on word from Major Ogden, who is traveling upstate. Arthur Ogden, meanwhile, has arranged to board his brother's dragoons at the Hotel Firenze, which you may recall sits very near to the New York lodge of the Explorers Guild.

Now, the greater part of Ogden's troop are new to the States, and none are over-familiar with the city, and it was decided that they would establish a beachhead at the hotel and stage their incursions into the city from there. The men had filed inland accordingly, losing only a few bodies on the march to the public-houses and to other of the city's Sirens, with the rest surviving to look with lordly satisfaction on their rooms at the Firenze (which might not be the height of luxury, but neither are they the cabins of the *Virago*). They had readied themselves in 'evening dress' (reaching a further refinement, as though it were possible, of the strangeness of their day dress) and mustered in the hotel's parlor, which room had emptied quickly of other patrons. The men had stood some time admiring one another's turnout and planning adventures in the city, when they were visited by the *maestro dell'hotel*, who must deliver himself of a message, and who looked to have been pushed out at gunpoint to do it.

The man had swallowed hard, clasped his hands behind his back, and extended the compliments of Arthur Ogden. The *Signore*, he said, had arranged a generous, not to say *unlimited*, credit for his guests in the hotel's dining room. Which credit—and here the *maestro* might really have fainted—Which credit applied equally to the hotel's saloon *bar*.

Well. The news was brought before Ogden's men at a bit after four o'clock. At half-past seven, they have just settled down to eat in the hotel's dining room, and things are going much as you would expect.

THASSIT–SAVE YERSELF, LASS!
YOU FORGET HOW NIMBLE ARE THESE YOUNG YANKS, GEORGE.
NAH–JUST RUNNING TO FETCH 'IM THE INCENSE AND OILS, I EXPECT.

...A SLASH, CALL IT WILD, BUT IT CATCHES YER MAN RIGHT ACROSS THE THRAPPLE–
AND WITH THE OLD BOY STAGGERED, I BURY IT IN HIS RIBS–AND LEAVE IT THERE, WHICH IS WHY I CARRY THAT SABER NO MORE.
THE DEATH BLOW.
AYE, IT WAS...

...BUT THEN HE CAN'T BE IN H–LL QUICK ENOUGH TO SUIT ME–
STEADY, NOW.
AYE, MARTIN. ULTIMATELY IT'S A PILE OF FRUIT YE WAGE WAR ON.
CHR–ST, MARTIN...

YOU! WHAT'S KEEPING THE WINE?
A WORD, PLEASE, WITH THE *SIGNORE*...?
HEY–DON'T BOTHER HIM. WHAT'S THIS FOR?

THAT SPOON WAITS FOR THE SOUP, SIR. ORDINARILY, WE'D BE–
<<PLOINK!>>
WRONG! IT'S FOR FLINGIN' AT S–DS LIKE YOU, WHAT DON'T TAKE ORDERS!

AUGH. PLEASE, SIR. I HAVE BEEN ASKED TO REMIND YOU OF CERTAIN RULES OF CONDUCT–
MAN ORDERED WINE.
AH: OH. VERY GOOD, SIR.

THAT'S IT. OFF Y'GO.
DON'T TRAIN 'EM HERE LIKE THEY DO ABROAD, SIR, DO THEY?

HULLO...? HM?
...OH, HANG IT.

HA! GENNLEMEN: EVENING. GLASS FOR YOU, SIR; AND FOR YOU. COMPLIMENTS OF ARTHUR OGDEN.
WELL: AND OUR REGARDS TO HIM, SON.

HERE'S HOW!
...COMPANY HORSE, AREN'T YOU?

HUH?
OUT OF INDIA, I SHOULD THINK.
THAT'S RIGHT, YES.
ENJOYING A BIT OF LEAVE, YOU MEN...?
OR TAKEN THE FRENCH LEAVE, IS IT?*
EHH...
*THAT IS, HAVE THEY DESERTED?

WHY–NO–AS A MATTER OF FACT, WE–
NEVER WORRY, CORPORAL. WE'RE A LONG WAY FROM THE THEATER TONIGHT.
OH, RATHER.
BUT YOU'RE–MY G–D: GENERAL–
WHEEST, LAD. NONE OF THAT, NOW.

HERE *IN MUFTI*, YOU SEE.
WON'T SPOIL THIS, CORPORAL, WILL YOU?
NO, OF COURSE. BUT–
–BUT WHY THE TWO OF US IN THIS PLACE, HM? IN DINNER JACKETS? QUITE RIGHT.

BIT OF...DIPLOMATIC WORK, LET US SAY.
OH?
WELL. NOT...FULLY CLEAR ON WHAT THIS IS, OURSELVES. BUT HERE WE ARE.
AND BEATS RETIREMENT ALL TO H–LL, I SHOULD SAY.
AYE, THAT'S SO.

TELL YOU WHAT, LAD: THERE'S A MAN IN THIS HOTEL–JUST UP THE WAY, THERE–WAITING TO PUT YOU IN THE PICTURE, TOO.
SORRY–?
AYE: YOU, SON. SENT US DOWN HERE TO FETCH YOU, AS IT HAPPENS. WE'VE JUST BEEN WAITING OUR CHANCE.
COME. WE'LL HAVE YOU RIGHT BACK.

AND THEY CAN SPARE YOU, I SHOULD THINK.
LEAVE BEHIND US, WILL YOU, CORPORAL? AND HEAD TO THE W.C.
MEET YOU AT THE STAIRS.
AND PITCH THAT BOTTLE. OUR FRIEND'S GOT A WEST INDIA SHERRY HE'S KEEN TO SHARE WITH YOU.

AT THE SAME TIME, LIEUTENANTS OF THE *JIA-DE* SCOUR DOWNTOWN FOR SIGNS OF THE ORPHAN BARNES.

ZŬZHĬ TĀ. WŎ JIĀNG CĂIQŬ DE NÁNHÁI.

GRRR!
HUPP–!

«THWEEET–!»

PUHH–!

OUTTA THE STREET, LAD.
«THWEEE!»

HOW'S THIS, FRANCIE?
UH?

I SAY, THERE'S ANOTHER CHINAMAN GONE UNDER A STREET-CAR.
AH: SO IT IS.

LOOK THERE, PAT: YON URCHIN WOULD HAVE A WORD WIT' YA.
AH. YA: AFTERNOON, LAD. VERY NICE.

WOT'S HE GOT?
JUST SELLIN' OLD PITCHER-POSTCARDS, FRANCIE.
NAH—WE KNOW THIS ONE, DON'T WE? SURE WE DO.
OI: WHERE'S YOUR FRIEND THE EXPLORER, THEN?

LET'S SEE WHAT HE'S GOT, PAT. GIVE IT 'ERE.
FINE. THE TWO-A-YEH SORT IT OUT, AN' LET ME BE.

AH, Y'SEE? T'ROW HIM IN, PAT. HE'S A GOOD FARE.
AN' HOW DO WE KNOW THAT, FRANCIE?
'CAUSE I JUST TOL' YOU IS HOW.
MOVE IT, SO'S WE GET BACK AFORE DARK.

GEDDAP!
BERTR–BERTRAM? N-NO–WAIT!

On a certain cobblestone lane that tops a rise over the south-west point of Coney Island, a battered old post-chaise groans its way to a stop. Two men share a horse-blanket on the carriage's driving board, the one snoring with mouth opened to the heavens, the other holding rein on a bow-backed mare which, in terms of how it carries its years, looks of a piece with the decrepit chaise and the men themselves.

I would place the hour at about ten at night, though to see this group from the front you would guess they are facing into a wan sort of sunrise, so many and intense are the electrical lights of the settlement below. The driver, Francis by name, is forced to give the other man–his brother, Patrick–a thrust of elbow to the ribs. The latter responds with a bleary assurance that Monday, he will look for work. Francis, angering now, draws back a leg and deals his brother a kick to the knee that nearly sends them both from the driver's box on opposite sides, and does dislodge an empty bottle from beneath the blanket. As the bottle powders against the stones below, both men sit up and look daggers at one another.

CAREFUL, BOY. IF THE EYES ROLL OUTCHER HEAD, WHAT'LL YOU USE TO LOOK FOR 'EM? *HEH-HEHH.*
BUT IT'S A WONDER, FRANCIE, IN'NIT? FORGIVE ME IF I LOOK NO DIFFERENT'N HIM. I NEVER YET SEEN THE PLACE BY NIGHT, Y'KNOW.
OH SURE, LOOK AT THE PAIR OF YEH. PUT A PLUG OF TOBACCO IN THE BOY'S MOUTH AND YE'R TWINS.

...THOUGH I S'POSE THAT IDIOT LOOK O' WONDERMENT: IT'S YOUR FACE IN ITS NATURAL STATE, IN'NIT? LIKE A LANDED FISH, RATHER.
IT MAY BE THAT, FRANCIE. BUT I DO TAKE SOLACE, IN 'TWAS ME THE LADIES ALWAYS PREFERRED.
PREFERRED TO HAVE YOU LOCKED UP, YOU MEAN.
WHERE'S THE BOY GONE?

OH—HE'S FOUND THE HOUSE. AN' THERE'S YOUR PELICAN, FRANCIE.
...AND B'M'FAITH, THAT'S ONE AWFUL SPECIES OF BIRD.
IT'S A IBIS, I TOLD YE.
AND THE ONLY ONE OF ITS KIND IN ALL THE BOROUGHS, BERTRAM. YOU SHOULD SEE THE CROWD IT DRAWS BY DAY.
NOW GO IN THERE AND GET US PAID, PAT.

RIGHT. THOUGH...Y'KNOW I THINK WE'D HAVE A BETTER GO OF IT, FRANCIE, IF WE WAS TO HEAD IN THERE TOGETHER, AH?
OH, AYE? AND WHO'S WATCHING MOLLY, HERE? YOU'D LIKE FOR HER TO RUN OFF, I S'POSE?
SHE JUST TROD ALL OVER BROOKLYN, FRANCIE, PULLIN' US BEHIND. WHERE'S SHE RUNNING OFF TO?

Bertram's knock produces nothing at first but a bit of wait, and Patrick is near to abandoning the boy and taking his chances with his brother, when a hand begins drawing the door's many bolts and chains from within.

Moments later, an ancient footman stands before them in night-gown and sleeping cap and half-eye spectacles. He hunches forward with a candle guttering in a ring-handled holder before him, looking like some figure woken right out of the old serials.

WHAT IS IT? WHAT'S HAPPENED?
NOTHIN', FRANCIE. JUST A ELDERLY FELLA IN FANCY-DRESS.

WELL THAT'S WHO PAYS US, IN'NIT? UNLESS YOU WANNA ASK THE BIRD.
COME, BOTH OF YOU.

AH, THOUGH–SIR? WE BRUNG THE BOY, IS ALL. I'VE NO NEED TO GO IN THERE.
MM? OH, NO: I SUPPOSE NOT.
YOU–BOY–WAIT HERE, AND NO GOING ABOUT THE HOUSE, IF YOU PLEASE.

NOW: YOU'D LIKE TO SEE A PAYMENT, I THINK.
AYE, THAT'S IT EX-ACTLY, GRANDPA.
JUST SO. THOUGH I DO WARN YOU, I WAS TRADING IN THE BAZAARS OF EGYPT WHEN I WAS THAT BOY'S AGE...

MR. BUCHAN, BY THIS TIME, HAS MADE HIS WAY UPSTAIRS, TO THE FIRENZE'S STATE ROOMS
YOU'VE MET THE VICEROY, SON?
YES, SIR, AT BOMBAY.
...AND G–D HELP YOU, ARCHIE, WHEN WE DISCOVER HOW YOU ARE CHEATING.
HRAW-HRAWW!

WHERE HE IS PRESENTED TO HIS EMPLOYER, LORD POMEROY, VICEROY OF INDIA.
YOUR GRACE–
NO-NO, WE'LL SHAKE HANDS, LAD, AND BE DONE WITH THAT.
YOU MAY SIT OR STAND; I'LL BE SITTING DOWN THERE.

EITHER WAY, I'D LIKE YOU TO TRY THIS. AND NO MORE YOUR-GRACE-ING, IF YOU PLEASE.
THANK YOU, SIR.
OWEN IS MY NAME. MR. FITZMAURICE, IF YOU CAN'T BRING YOURSELF TO USE IT.

I AM PRESERVING THIS...DAYDREAM WHILE WE'RE HERE–IT ISN'T WORKING, BUT YOU SEE ME TRYING–THIS DREAM THAT I COULD ADMINISTER INDIA LIKE THIS, WITH ONLY MY FRIENDS ABOUT, AND OUR CALLERS BROUGHT IN WITH-OUT ALL THE FUSS AND FIDGETING. STRAIGHT TO BUSINESS, YOU KNOW.

IF YOU REALLY MUST BOW AND PULL A FORELOCK AND SO ON, BY ALL MEANS DO IT OUTSIDE AND GIVE THE RICKSHAW-WALLAHS A LAUGH.
YOU, MR. BUCHAN, WOULDN'T BE A WEEK AT THE COMPANY COURTS BEFORE YOU WERE KICKING DOWN ITS WALLS, AND I'M NOT SURE SOMEBODY SHOULDN'T.

OH NO, SIR. IT'S A FINE PLACE–
STILL BEING GRACIOUS, YES. BUT YOU LET THAT RICHELIEU DO ITS WORK.
MY THANKS TO YOU, GENTLEMEN. JOIN YOU IN A MOMENT.
SIR.

ANY RATE: I THANK YOU FOR AGREEING TO JOIN ME UP HERE, MR. BUCHAN.
–YES, OF COURSE–
WE'D QUITE LOST TRACK OF YOU, UP TO YOUR ARRIVAL AT PORT THIS MORNING. IF I HAD KNOWN I'D ONLY TO GO ABOUT MY BUSINESS AND WAIT, AND WE'D ARRIVE AT THE SAME HOTEL...
...WELL IT'S A STRANGE SORT OF COINCIDENCE, WOULDN'T YOU SAY?
MM? OH, RATHER.

BUT I AM A STUDENT OF THESE THINGS, YOU KNOW, THESE APPARENT FREAKS OF CHANCE. I HAVE FOUND MEANING IN MORE THAN A FEW, AND AMONG THE MEANINGFUL ONES, CERTAIN HINTS OF INTERCONNECTION.
OUR OWN RIDDLE IS SOLVED EASILY ENOUGH: DID YOU KNOW THAT WE'RE NEXT-DOOR BUT ONE TO THE NEW YORK LODGE OF THE EXPLORERS GUILD?
THE–? OH, NO, SIR.

YES. WE'VE GOT THE EARL, THERE, WATCHING THE PLACE THROUGH HIS GLASS.
WHOEVER PUT YOU HERE WAS AWARE OF THE FACT, TOO, I SHOULDN'T DOUBT. THAT DISPATCH YOU CARRIED FOR JOHN OGDEN CAME FROM THE GUILD, TOO. YOU RECALL THAT?
I–YES, I WAS SHOWN SOME MARKINGS ON THE CASE, AND TOLD THEY WERE THEIRS.

MM. I'D KNOWN ABOUT THEM IN INDIA, OF COURSE. BUT IT WASN'T TILL WE SAW THOSE ARMS ON YOUR DISPATCH THAT I THOUGHT I'D BETTER HAVE A LOOK.
I RODE WITH A FEW MEN TO MADRAS, AND WHAT DO YOU THINK I FOUND THERE? BUT THE VERY WORST CLASS OF BLATHERER AND BUFFOON–ODIOUSLY RICH MEN, OF COURSE, AND I KNEW THEM ALL–BUT NONE WITH ANY SECRETS THAT WEREN'T ALREADY KNOWN TO THE GOSSIPS IN BOMBAY.

I MIGHT REALLY HAVE LOCKED THEM UP, I WAS THAT DISAPPOINTED. BUT I ELECTED TO JOIN THEM, INSTEAD.
THEN YOU'RE A MEMBER?
WELL. I SHOULD SAY I'VE APPLIED. I DID DISCOVER AND MAP THE APATEAN ISLES IN MICRONESIA, YOU KNOW.
WE'D A BIT OF...TROUBLE WITH THE ABORIGINALS AT THE TIME, AND THE GUILD MAY NOT LOOK VERY KINDLY ON THAT SORT OF THING...THOUGH I'LL BE AMONG THEM YET, YOU MARK ME.

–BUT I LEFT MADRAS, IS MY POINT, IN SOME CONFUSION, OVER THE GUILD AND CERTAIN... OTHER IDEAS I'D BEEN REVOLVING, MOSTLY TO DO WITH THE WAR. AND I REMAINED THAT WAY, TILL THEY BROUGHT ME...
–ALEX, WE'LL HAVE THE...THANK YOU–
I SAY–TILL THEY BROUGHT ME THIS: YOUR NOTE FROM AL-SHAR.
AH–YES– ABOUT THAT–

–WAIT, THOUGH–I MUST TELL YOU: THIS NOTE OF YOURS EMBOLDENED ME TO LEAVE INDIA AT LAST. THIS TOLD ME THAT AT LEAST SOMEONE ELSE WAS CHASING THIS VISION I'D HAD MYSELF.
THIS TOLD ME IF I WERE READING SIGNS CORRECTLY, YOU AND I WOULD SEE ONE ANOTHER AGAIN. AND HERE WE ARE.
I SEE. THOUGH WHAT 'VISION,' EXACTLY–

WELL: I WON'T BOTHER YOU WITH ALL MY THEORIES JUST YET, BUT IN BROAD STROKES: I AM CONVINCED, MR. BUCHAN, THAT THERE IS A GOOD DEAL MORE BEHIND THIS WAR, AND BEHIND EVENTS OF THE WORLD GENERALLY, THAN IS MADE OBVIOUS TO MEN LIKE YOU AND ME.
I BELIEVE THE GUILD–OR CERTAIN ELEMENTS WITHIN IT, I SHOULD SAY–THAT THEY, AND YOUR NEW EMPLOYERS–THESE PEOPLE ARE ALL ATTUNED, SOMEHOW, TO THESE DEEPER CURRENTS OF INTELLIGENCE.

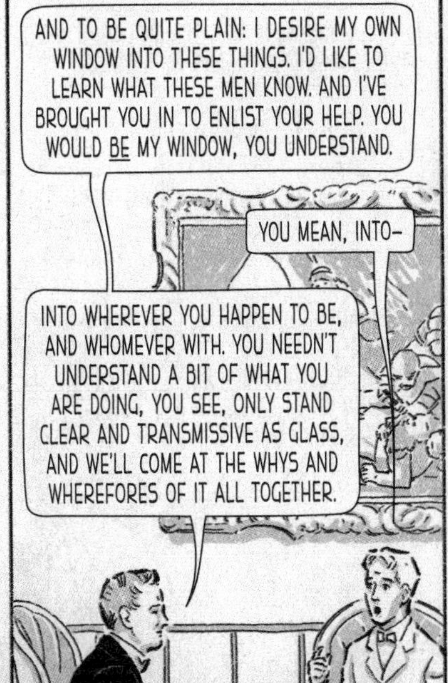
AND TO BE QUITE PLAIN: I DESIRE MY OWN WINDOW INTO THESE THINGS. I'D LIKE TO LEARN WHAT THESE MEN KNOW. AND I'VE BROUGHT YOU IN TO ENLIST YOUR HELP. YOU WOULD BE MY WINDOW, YOU UNDERSTAND.
YOU MEAN, INTO–
INTO WHEREVER YOU HAPPEN TO BE, AND WHOMEVER WITH. YOU NEEDN'T UNDERSTAND A BIT OF WHAT YOU ARE DOING, YOU SEE, ONLY STAND CLEAR AND TRANSMISSIVE AS GLASS, AND WE'LL COME AT THE WHYS AND WHEREFORES OF IT ALL TOGETHER.

IF I'M NOT MISLED, CORPORAL, YOU'RE A BIT CURIOUS ABOUT THESE THINGS YOURSELF. ELSE WHY WOULD YOU PUT YOUR NAME TO A NOTE LIKE THIS?
AH–YES, BUT, SIR, YOU KNOW THEY'VE SUSPECTED ME FROM THE START FOR AN INFORMANT.
IF I'VE LIVED UP TO THIS POINT, IT'S ONLY BECAUSE I HAVEN'T BEEN ONE.

QUITE, YES. WE'LL HAVE TO BE VERY CAREFUL IN OUR ARRANGEMENTS. I'VE FORESEEN THAT.
IF THEY KNEW I'D EVEN SEEN YOU, TONIGHT–
THAT WOULDN'T DO, I REALIZE. AND I SHOULD FEAR IN EARNEST, IF THEY LEARNED WE'D BEEN CORRESPONDING, YOU AND I.
CORRESPONDING?

WELL: WE'VE THIS. YOU'VE WRITTEN ME, MORE OR LESS, AND I'VE WRITTEN YOU–I HOPE I DON'T PRESUME ON OUR FRIENDSHIP?
OH–*EH*, NO. BUT–SIR, I DON'T SEE ANY SECRET ARRANGEMENT BETWEEN US AS BEING ESPECIALLY WISE, OR HONORABLE, SIR. FOR EITHER OF US.
YOU'LL UNDERSTAND IF I DECLINE. AND IF I MUST GIVE YOU ALL A QUICK GOOD-NIGHT.

HM? NO? ...WELL.
ALEX, I'LL HAVE THE REST OF THAT BOTTLE, IF YOU PLEASE.
GOOD NIGHT, THEN, ALL OF YOU. THANK YOU FOR THE...YES.

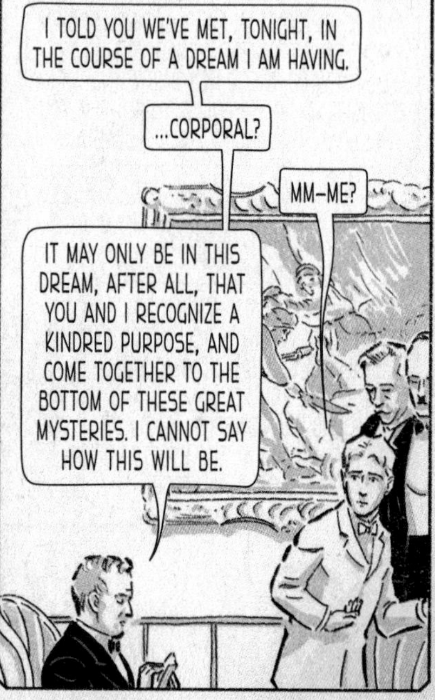
I TOLD YOU WE'VE MET, TONIGHT, IN THE COURSE OF A DREAM I AM HAVING.
...CORPORAL?
MM–ME?
IT MAY ONLY BE IN THIS DREAM, AFTER ALL, THAT YOU AND I RECOGNIZE A KINDRED PURPOSE, AND COME TOGETHER TO THE BOTTOM OF THESE GREAT MYSTERIES. I CANNOT SAY HOW THIS WILL BE.

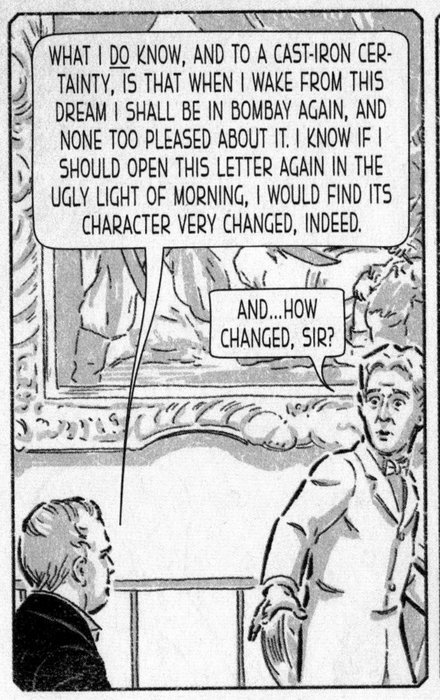
WHAT I DO KNOW, AND TO A CAST-IRON CERTAINTY, IS THAT WHEN I WAKE FROM THIS DREAM I SHALL BE IN BOMBAY AGAIN, AND NONE TOO PLEASED ABOUT IT. I KNOW IF I SHOULD OPEN THIS LETTER AGAIN IN THE UGLY LIGHT OF MORNING, I WOULD FIND ITS CHARACTER VERY CHANGED, INDEED.
AND...HOW CHANGED, SIR?

OH, I SUSPECT YOU KNOW: THIS IS AS BALD A CONFESSION TO TREASON AS WE GET AT OUR OFFICE. IT'S ALSO A RIGHT USEFUL INDICTMENT OF YOUR FRIENDS, IF THAT WERE EVER NECESSARY.

SIR, YOU COMMISSIONED ME YOURSELF, IN INDIA, TO–
–TO WHAT? I COMMISSIONED YOU TO DESERT THE COLONIAL ARMY?
WELL: I DON'T RECALL HOW YOU PHRASED THE THING–
VERY CAREFULLY, I AM SURE. SUBORNING TREASON IS A HANGING OFFENSE, YOU KNOW. IT WOULDN'T DO FOR THE INDIAN VICEROY.

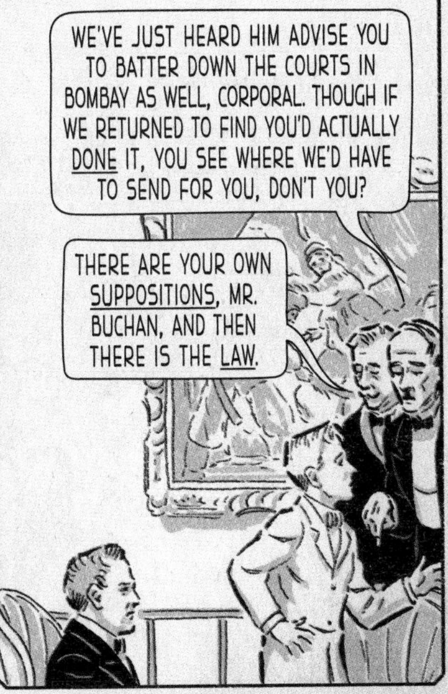
WE'VE JUST HEARD HIM ADVISE YOU TO BATTER DOWN THE COURTS IN BOMBAY AS WELL, CORPORAL. THOUGH IF WE RETURNED TO FIND YOU'D ACTUALLY DONE IT, YOU SEE WHERE WE'D HAVE TO SEND FOR YOU, DON'T YOU?
THERE ARE YOUR OWN SUPPOSITIONS, MR. BUCHAN, AND THEN THERE IS THE LAW.

YES. NOW: IF I'D THOUGHT AT THE TIME WE'D A CHANCE IN A MILLION OF OGDEN TAKING YOU, I MIGHT HAVE ARRANGED TO SEND YOU IN AS A SORT OF SPY.
BECAUSE I ADMIT, NOW THAT WE'RE CIRCUMSTANCED IN THIS WAY, IT PRESENTS US ALL WITH AN EXCELLENT OPPORTUNITY.

REALLY, THIS IS HOW I'D RATHER WE LOOKED AT THE THING, MR. BUCHAN: IN TERMS OF THE GOOD WE CAN DO ONE ANOTHER.
AND YOU REALIZE THERE IS MUCH I CAN DO FOR YOU AND YOUR FRIENDS, BEYOND SIMPLY FORBEARING TO HANG YOU ALL.

SIT, LAD. BEFORE YOU PUT A CRAMP IN HIS NECK.
YES, DO. AND BRING YOUR GLASS. ALEX: LET HIM TRY THAT MARAT, CAN YOU?

I'VE—THANK YOU, BUT I HADN'T OUGHT TO DRINK ANY MORE.
FILL UP, LAD. THEY'LL NEED TO FIND YOU LATER IN ONE OF THESE HALLS, SUCCUMBED TO DRINK. HELP TO EXPLAIN YOUR ABSENCE, YOU KNOW.
I'D DO IT, CORPORAL. THESE MEN KNOW THEIR BUSINESS. BIT FRIGHTENING, REALLY, HOW WELL THEY KNOW IT.

The Coney Island manor of Mr. Sloane, tonight, shows little sign of habitation, though there is a dull, pulsing sound rising through the floor-boards of the front hall. The house's butler–one Mr. Litchfield–has asked Bertram to stay by the front door, as, indeed, the boy's own better instincts would command; yet Bertram is drawn into the old house anyway, with Litchfield's voice dying behind him and a door, ahead, framed in murky light....

The door, as it happens, is unlocked, and it opens to a flight of stairs, which conduct Bertram down to a short passageway and a second door. The hissing of steam, the beating of a hammer on tin and the terse voices of men grow distinct ahead of him, through a blanketing hum of machinery. He finds after a time that he is standing on an iron landing with his hand on a rail, looking down over a vast underground train depot.

An engine vents steam into the darkness on Bertram's left, as workers couple passenger and flatbed cars behind it, these leading back to a turntable on Bertram's right, where a second engine draws new cars out from within a ring of sheds. But the greater part of the activity here is concentrated beneath Bertram, where a team of laborers and white-coated engineers are taking the innards out of a great iron machine and securing these in the open-roofed train cars beside it. The machine's framing stands more or less intact, and at its top, near the level of Bertram's own head, there is a wide iron node that looks something like the head of a great mosquito. A bundle of steel rods descend from this node to a chair beneath it that is bolted to a metal stalk and raised about five feet from the machine's base. The chair itself–incongruously–is a fine wooden

ladder-back piece with leathern cushions, presumably for the comfort of whoever should have to deal with these diabolical rods.

Bertram, taking this machine in from the landing, stands so transfixed that he does not notice the laborers pausing in their work, nor the engineers who are looking up at him, a few of them pointing. And he does not see Mr. Kleitmann-Meyer, who is seated beneath him with his back turned, and is still under the impression that Bertram is wandering through downtown Manhattan, irretrievably lost.

UH? ...SCHEISSE.

WAIT! WAIT-WAIT! HOLD RIGHT THERE–
JA, VERY GOOD!

MR. BARNES! WE ARE VERY–GREATLY RELIEVED TO SEE YOU, MY BOY. I MYSELF AM ESPECIALLY RELIEVED.

AH: CAREFUL, OR YOU ARE APT TO FALL. COME. YOU WOULD HAVE A CLOSER VIEW OF THE MACHINE, I THINK.

‹GENTLEMEN: HERE IS OUR PRODIGAL RETURNED, AND MY DIFFICULTIES SOLVED, I KNOW NOT HOW–BUT THIS IS LITTLE BARNES.›

‹AND HE IS A BIT FRIGHTENED. IF THERE IS ANY WAY YOU CAN LOOK LESS, PERHAPS, LIKE OLD WOLVES...?›

MY APOLOGIES. THEY ARE HARMLESS OLD MEN, REALLY. THEY LOOK AS IF THEY WOULD PREFER TO EAT YOU, *JA*, BUT ONLY BECAUSE THEY ARE SO THRILLED TO SEE YOU NOW. THE GERMANS HAVE THIS WAY OF ALWAYS BARING THE TEETH, YOU KNOW...
CLOSER, *HERR* BARNES. THIS IS VERY SAFE. COME.

MR. SLOANE HAS DESIGNED IT HIMSELF, YOU KNOW. HE HAD IT BUILT FOR YOU, BERTRAM.
JA–IT IS: IT'S FOR YOU. AND FOR YOUR FRIENDS, OF COURSE. THERE IS ANOTHER LIKE IT, TOO, WHERE WE ARE GOING.
YOU WILL SEE. THIS IS ONLY THE LATEST.

IT IS MADE—THIS WILL SOUND RIDICULOUS, I THINK—MAYBE LESS SO IN GERMAN—*EHH*, BUT IT LETS US PEEP INTO THE LITTLE CORNERS OF YOUR MIND, YOU KNOW.
THE MEMORIES HID BENEATH MEMORIES. THINGS YOU ARE NOT EVEN AWARE THAT YOU KNOW.

YOUR DREAMS AS WELL, BERTRAM. MR. SLOANE IS STUDIED IN THE MODERN SCHOOL, AND VERY MUCH LIKES TO KNOW WHAT YOU ARE DREAMING.

THE TRIALS OF COURSE ARE TO EVERYONE'S BENEFIT—YOURS MOST OF ALL. YOU WOULD LIKE TO FIND YOUR PARENTS, I THINK—HM? JUST AS WE WILL LIKE TO HELP YOU FIND THEM.
WE ARE TAKING IT NORTH IN PIECES, YOU SEE. MR. OGDEN IS CLEARING SPACE FOR US IN THE GREAT HALL, WHERE WE SHALL REASSEMBLE IT AND GIVE THE THING A GO.

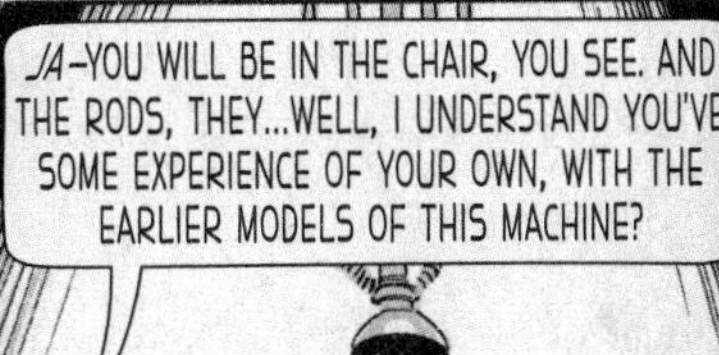
JA—YOU WILL BE IN THE CHAIR, YOU SEE. AND THE RODS, THEY...WELL, I UNDERSTAND YOU'VE SOME EXPERIENCE OF YOUR OWN, WITH THE EARLIER MODELS OF THIS MACHINE?

‹HE IS GOING TO FAINT.›

WHAT DO YOU THINK? HM? BERTRAM? THEY TELL ME IT IS QUITE PAINLESS NOW, THE WAY THIS IS DONE...

BERTRAM...?

V.

43º 55' 8" N Lat | 73º 36' 30" W Long
Lowring-on-Hudson, New York State

May, 1918

THE LORD OF THE KEEP at Lowring-on-Hudson maintains that his estate, in the feudal tradition, has lent its name to the surrounding town; yet the claim is specious, and no one else recognizes the estate by this name anyway. Now and forever, the citizens of this and the surrounding towns will call the estate the 'Lavinia' or simply 'the Hotel,' in reference to its foundation as a place-to-let for travelers of the leisured class.

I could–and I may yet–devote one of these histories entirely to the Hotel Lavinia and its ghosts. But our concern here is with its current ownership, and we note the arrival, in 1878, of Arthur Ogden III, father of the Arthur Ogden in these pages. The senior Ogden was so taken with the place that he secured its title in the following year, and he proceeded to dislodge or wait out his fellow guests until he could declare the hotel a private residence, which he did in 1881. He continued to run the estate as a hotel–even expanding its staff, its kitchens, and for a time its social menu–with himself and his family as its only permanent residents, and all others coming at his invitation and staying at his pleasure. Nor was this some late-developing eccentricity on Ogden's part (he was known, and not only by myself, as a sober and self-possessed man, right to the last). It was rather that he'd been raised in a suite of rooms at London's Connaught Hotel, and he looked to continue in this mode of living on what he deemed an appropriately American scale. And I am sure he is still rotating through bed-rooms and dining to orchestras and frequenting the downstairs bar today, if such things be practicable in the Hereafter.

It was at or about the millennium that Ogden's son took possession of the Lavinia, and if the changes he made to it were not immediate, they are by now unmistakable. Certainly it will no more be viewed as a place that invites the public. Roads and thoroughfares have been re-drawn and planted over for an area of miles around, and the forests of pine have been left to grow wild to the north, east and south. Within these boundaries, across what must be called the 'grounds,' there is only a great dull plain of stubble, with gardens and hedgerows, fountains and walks all removed or faded out of recognition by time, and an old gate with the hotel arms standing alone, denuded and bizarre. The few surviving trees seem to have been singled out for their grotesquery, all of them combed sideways by the winds off the river to haunting effect. And brooding over this splendor is the hotel itself, wide and squat as the Tuileries, with two great turrets suggestive of devils' horns at its center and an overall aspect of The Last Place on Earth.

If I may give my opinion, the estate has lost its claim to the gay name of Lavinia (which honors the architect's mother, by all accounts a gracious and spirited lady). No, the arguments of the good townspeople aside, I believe Arthur Ogden IV has at last earned the name of Lowring-on-Hudson for his dismal home on the river.

And I should think this view were shared by the two riders who emerge from the bordering woods, on this May morning in 1918, in the last hours before dawn.

The insides of the main building are a bit better preserved—or, at least, Ogden has not been so thoroughgoing in their neglect. But the below-stairs have never been a terribly attractive feature of the house, and the stark, half-lit servants' corridor in which we begin our stay would be at home in any city tenement. This is not the sort of hall one visits without good reason, and even servants of the house—the few who are left—have been requartered upstairs at their own request. If we are here ourselves it is only to follow, briefly, the hurrying figure of a lady.

And there is little enough to see of her under the sputtering gas-brackets, just a tall and angular body in a housecoat of white silk. Whatever her reason, she crosses this hall as quickly as she can, with hands knit before her and the white skirts of her gown swirling behind, like a ghost with an over-large house to haunt rushing between appointments.

Ahead of her, at the hall's end, there is a round, high-ceilinged crossing-room, and in it stands an unusually explicit marble of Leda and the Swan. I can tell you the sculpture is one of no little local notoriety, put here more or less in storage by owners who can agree neither to display nor destroy it. And this morning it is being rather actively admired by Mr. Renton, who has come in with his commander and clambered up onto it and, with boot-heels digging for purchase and hands busy about Leda's person, may be heard pouring improprieties into the giantess's unhearing ear.

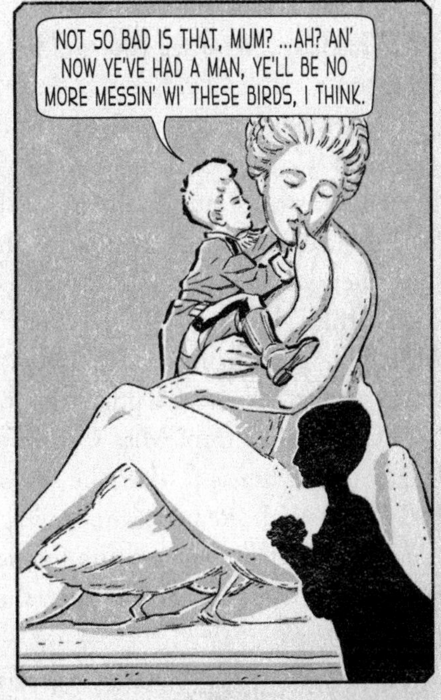

NOT SO BAD IS THAT, MUM? ...AH? AN' NOW YE'VE HAD A MAN, YE'LL BE NO MORE MESSIN' WI' THESE BIRDS, I THINK.

He is too absorbed in his suit to hear the light-footed approach of the lady in the hall, but he is quick enough to act when he sees her enter the room. He shinnies down the maiden's side, making, I think, to jump from the plinth with a sentry's challenge (or some Cockney corruption thereof). Yet as he jumps, his scabbard-point lodges in a crook of the swan's leg, and his sword-belt hangs in place while his weight carries him down through it. His tunic is shucked up over his shoulders, straightening his arms overhead and nearly strangling him. By the time he has wriggled free of his coat and belt, the lady has passed through the room.

She continues only a short distance ahead, stopping in the doorway of the under-servants' dining hall. Inside the room, John Ogden sits at a long, rough-hewn dining table. He has brought out his breakfast from the larders and sits reducing it, with remnants of a smaller meal opposite him, presumably left by Mr. Renton. The dawn has just begun to light the window-wells behind him, and a pot of water heats on a small hob. Ogden eats slowly, his eyes steady upon the lady's figure in the doorway.

If the two are struggling over introductions, they are not left very long at it. A fiendish little grunt announces the person of Mr. Renton, who shoulders past the lady and stands at his own impudent version of attention.

'This lady 'ere to see you, sir,' he announces, a bit belatedly, to the old dragoon.

Ogden blinks slowly, with a show of patience. 'Thank you, Mr. Renton,' he says.

Renton strolls into the room and selects an apple from a bowl on the table. He eyes the lady narrowly as he burnishes the apple on his sleeve, and then stops to point at her with a sudden surmise: 'Ye'd be Major's sister, then,' he says. 'One 'at wrote 'im in Meserpatamia.' He bites into the apple and chews for a moment, searching his memory. '...Ha!' he fairly shouts–'Frances Ogden, in'nit.'

Renton looks from Miss Ogden to her brother and back, fairly well-pleased with himself. '*Well*,' he says at length: 'I leave you people to it.'

Thus for Mr. Renton, who leaves, unnoticed, to stand guard in a little ante-room. Miss Ogden waits for her brother to take his water off the boil and sit with his tea, and then she speaks to him in suppressed tones.

...IT IS YOU, THEN. MISS MOLLOY SAID SHE'D SPOTTED YOU COMING IN ACROSS THE LAWN, BUT I...WE'VE BEEN AT THE MILL HOUSE. I'M SORRY NO ONE WAS HERE TO GREET YOU. MR. FAULK THOUGHT WE MIGHT FIND YOU DOWN HERE.
ARTHUR'S SOMEWHERE IN THE HOUSE...
HE IS, YES.
GOOD. I'VE TAKEN SOME TROUBLE IN COMING TO HIM.

HE'S...MOSTLY OFF IN THE EAST WING NOWADAYS. I CAN SHOW YOU. THERE'S A SITTING-ROOM HE USES FOR A STUDY, AND HE'S BEEN AT SOME NEW WORKS IN THE DINING HALL, WITH THE FURNITURE MOVED OUT...
YOU KNOW–HE SEEMS TO THINK WE'VE PUT YOU AT SOME RISK, WITH THESE... RATHER DESPERATE-SOUNDING LETTERS WE'VE SENT YOU.
NO.

–IT WAS DESPERATION, OF COURSE, ELSE I MIGHT NOT HAVE WRITTEN AT ALL. BUT I'D HARDLY HAVE ASKED YOU TO DESERT–
I'LL HAVE NO TROUBLE FROM THE ARMY, FAN.
...NO? THEN I'M GLAD. ARTHUR NEEDS YOU OF COURSE, BUT–

–OH, I'VE BEEN JUST SICK TO HAVE YOU HOME, JOHN. I'VE WANTED YOU OUT OF INDIA AND HERE WITH US VERY MUCH. I REALLY WOULD HAVE WRITTEN AT SOME TIME OR OTHER, I THINK, EVEN IF HE WERE PERFECTLY WELL. I'D HAVE INVENTED SOME OTHER REASON FOR IT.
WE'LL GET BOTH OF YOU SORTED, FAN. AND I'LL LOOK TO THE PLACE.
I MEAN FOR YOUR SAKE, TOO.

FIRST WE HEARD ABOUT MISS GORDON. IF IT'S TRUE, JOHN–
IT'S TRUE ENOUGH. I WAS SPARED THE WHOLE THING, BEING AWAY. HAPPENED RIDING, AS SHE WAS TOLD IT WOULD. I CAME BACK FOR RATHER A STARCHED SERVICE. THAT WAS ALL.
BUT JOHNNY, I WAS HEARTBROKEN OVER IT. AND YOU–
HUH-HUHH. 'JOHNNY.'

A MURDEROUS LOOK FROM OGDEN SENDS MR. RENTON OFF.
HUH? ...OH, H–LL.
MY G–D, JOHN. WHAT IS THAT BOY?
DON'T KNOW. WE FOUND HIM AFTER BERHAMPUR. DOESN'T APPEAR TO BE MUCH WE CAN DO ABOUT HIM.

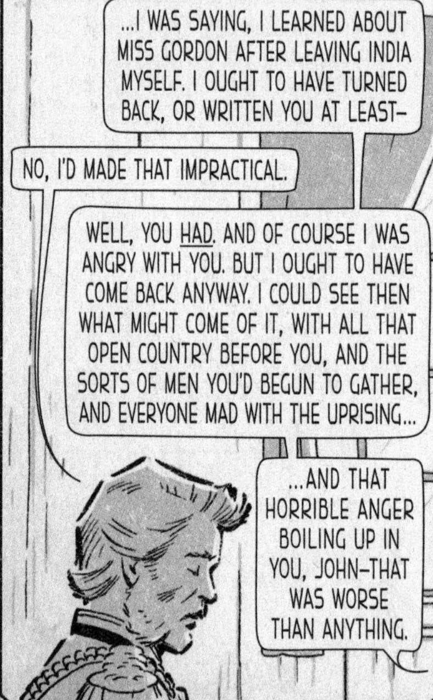
...I WAS SAYING, I LEARNED ABOUT MISS GORDON AFTER LEAVING INDIA MYSELF. I OUGHT TO HAVE TURNED BACK, OR WRITTEN YOU AT LEAST–
NO, I'D MADE THAT IMPRACTICAL.
WELL, YOU HAD. AND OF COURSE I WAS ANGRY WITH YOU. BUT I OUGHT TO HAVE COME BACK ANYWAY. I COULD SEE THEN WHAT MIGHT COME OF IT, WITH ALL THAT OPEN COUNTRY BEFORE YOU, AND THE SORTS OF MEN YOU'D BEGUN TO GATHER, AND EVERYONE MAD WITH THE UPRISING...
...AND THAT HORRIBLE ANGER BOILING UP IN YOU, JOHN–THAT WAS WORSE THAN ANYTHING.

I FELT IT WAS ONLY CARRIE AND I WHO EVEN CARED TO REMIND YOU OF YOUR HUMANITY. CERTAINLY THE COMPANY WEREN'T THERE TO HOLD REIN ON YOU AND THOSE MEN, NOW THEY'D SEEN WHAT YOU'D ALL BECOME.
I DIDN'T KNOW IT WAS ANYTHING QUITE SO–
–I HARDLY KNEW YOU BY THE TIME I LEFT. AND WHEN WE HEARD YOU'D LOST CARRIE, TOO...WELL. I SUPPOSE I WAS READY FOR THE STORIES, WHEN THEY CAME.

I ONLY THOUGHT IF I COULD GET YOU HOME, AND LOOK AT YOU, I WOULD KNOW THE WORST OF THOSE STORIES FOR LIES.
I TRUST MANY WERE.
YES–FORGIVE ME. I'VE JUST HAD SO LONG TO SIT WITH THESE WORRIES, JOHN.
YOU KNOW I STILL SEE YOU IN MY MIND'S EYE, YOU AND ARTHUR, COMING HOME FROM ST. JAMES THROUGH THE PARK. YOU RECALL THOSE GREAT FIGHTS YOU'D STAGE, IN WINTER?
I DO.

...ALL OF YOU DUG IN ALONG EAST DRIVE. THERE MUST HAVE BEEN A HUNDRED OF YOU BY THE TIME THEY MADE YOU STOP. OLDER BOYS, TOO, FROM THE WORST PARTS OF THE CITY, AND OVER THE RIVER...
YES, AND YOURSELF.

WELL–YES, ME, TOO, FOR A TIME. UNTIL THINGS REACHED SUCH A PITCH.
THEY STARTED WEIGHTING THEIR SNOWBALLS WITH STONES, SOME OF THEM–DO YOU REMEMBER?–AND YOU MARCHED RIGHT OVER, DEMANDING TO KNOW WHOSE IDEA IT HAD BEEN, AND NATURALLY IT HAD BEEN ARTHUR'S.
THAT'S RIGHT.

AND THEN YOU, FOR WHATEVER REASON–WAS IT FATHER, WHO FORBADE YOU TO BEAT ARTHUR?
NO. I'VE JUST NEVER HIT HIM.
WELL, I REMEMBER YOUR THRASHING SOMEBODY HORRIBLY FOR IT. PROBABLY ALL THE WORSE, IF YOU WOULDN'T LET YOURSELF HIT ARTHUR.

MM. THOUGH YOU'RE WRONG ON THE POINT OF MY BEATING ANYONE. I PICKED THE UGLIEST OF ARTHUR'S CAPTAINS, AND I HADN'T SEEN FIGHTING LIKE THAT YET, NOT LIKE WHAT THESE BOYS WERE USED TO. I DON'T KNOW THAT I'VE EVER TAKEN WORSE.
STILL–YOU WERE ALL OF...EIGHT? OR NINE?
EIGHT. THE BOY HAPPENS TO BE WITH ME STILL. IRISHMAN CALLED MULCAIRN. I BELIEVE HE'S THE UGLIEST MAN ALIVE.
BUT MY POINT, JOHN, IS YOU'D ALWAYS SUCH A SENSE OF JUSTICE, DIDN'T YOU. THE FIGHTING I COULD NEVER ABIDE, BUT I COULD UNDERSTAND IT WHEN I SAW IT CAME FROM THAT SAME INSTINCT OF YOURS, OF SETTING THINGS TO RIGHTS.
...THOUGH I MUST WONDER NOW, IF YOU TOLD ME ALL YOU'VE DONE OUT IN THE WORLD, HOW MUCH I COULD FORGIVE?
AND IF THIS WERE REALLY A CONCERN OF YOURS, AFTER ALL?
I DO NEED YOUR HELP WITH ARTHUR. I JUST DON'T INTEND TO BRING IN WOLVES, TO CHASE OUT MY MICE. I HOPE YOU UNDERSTAND THAT.
...MM. I WONDERED WHAT I'D DONE, THAT MY SISTER WOULDN'T TAKE MY HAND, AND KISS ME.
I SUSPECT I KNEW.
...FAN, I OUGHT TO SEE ARTHUR.

FAN...?
THERE'S ONE MORE THING. I'VE PROMISED LOLLY–
–WHO?
SORRY: THERE'S A MISS MOLLOY WHO WORKS WITH US–
THE ONE THAT SPOTTED ME COMING IN?

YES. SHE'S GOT A COUSIN, A MISS MAGUIRE, WHO HELPED US ALONG IN INDIA. I DON'T KNOW IF YOU'LL RECALL HER...
MM. WITH HER DAUGHTER. FEARS ME NOW AS WELL, I SUPPOSE–
FEAR YOU? ANNIE? NO, I SHOULDN'T THINK SO.
SHE WAS ALWAYS TERRIBLY FOND OF YOU.

THEN WHAT–
–ARTHUR'S GOT HER A SITUATION AT THE GUILD NOW, IN THE CITY. SHE'S BEEN LISTENING, THE WAY SOME OF THEM DO, TO THE OLD MEN DOWN THERE. AND SOME OF WHAT THEY'VE BEEN WHISPERING ABOUT IN NEW YORK HAS COME UP TO US HERE, THROUGH LOLLY.

NOT THAT WE CAN MAKE VERY MUCH OF IT. BUT MISS MAGUIRE IS HOPING VERY MUCH TO SPEAK TO YOU, WHILE YOU'RE HERE.
I SEE.

I PROMISED LOLLY I'D TRY TO PUT YOU THROUGH TO HER. OR I'D MENTION IT, ANYWAY. I SUPPOSE YOU'LL GO BACK THROUGH THE CITY AT SOME POINT...?
IT'S POSSIBLE I WILL. BUT, FAN, REALLY–
FIRST YOU'D SEE ARTHUR.
LET ME SEE WHAT SHAPE HE'S IN, CAN YOU? THEN I'LL SPEAK TO WHOMEVER YOU'D LIKE.
YES, OF COURSE.
HE'LL BE AWAKE, YOU THINK?
HE'LL...I SHOULD THINK SO, YES.
YOU'LL SEE.

The filament of light is there, fixed and everlasting. Whether it is literally in Bertram's sight or perceived in some other wise, it is all one to him. Increasingly it works as an irritant, like a fleck of sediment in the corner of his eye. It sounds, wearyingly, its note of alarm, persistent and piercing, though like no sound of this world it grows louder as he increases his distance from it, and like no light, he stares right into it to relieve the ache of it and to ease the strain it places upon him. There is an alignment of his body, and a direction of movement that he naturally seeks, in consequence. And when he is well-oriented, then the world is not so cluttered and confused about him; then he can move with something of vigor and decision. In these moments he is not facing into this light but projecting it. His beacon, so far removed from him over the sea, stirs a companion light within him, and the way before him is vivid and brightly hued.

But he is not often left to orient himself, and still less to direct his own movements, and these spells of peace and clarity have become increasingly rare. By day, he is moved from one keeper to the next, a prey to greater designs that, so far, have brought him farther into the North, farther from this thing that sits somewhere to the south and west of him, over the broad curve of the earth. Behind him he perceives the lights to wane, as ahead the darkness only deepens, and as his anxieties grow, and even the common objects of the world begin to worry and oppress him. In his dreams he is a bit freer to go about where he will, and it seems these travels are bringing him steadily closer to some sort of realization. But he has not been able to carry much yet out of his dreams into his waking life, only a few confused impressions of an overgrown garden and a girl in a wolf's hide, and of great glowing bodies moving through the sea toward the eternal lights in the South....

Tonight, the clattering motion of a train and a worn and frantic voice beneath him call Bertram back from his dream-wanderings, and he wakes in a small, elevated berth, once more among the surviving passengers of the *Girl of Safi*.

...THIRTY-FOUR...
...THIRTY-FOUR...

MEINHERR? ...HERR SLOANE? AUGHH.
WHUH? WHO'S THAT?
D—MNED CLEAREY BOY! IN THE AZALEAS.
...THIRTY-FOUR...

HELLO...?
...THIRTY-FOUR...
COULD—SIR, MAY I ASK YOU WHERE WE'RE GOING?

...THIRTY-FOUR...
SIR...?
I'M COUNTING THEM UP! I'M COUNTING THEM UP! I'M COUNTING THEM UP—!
QUIET! ALL OF YOU: QUIET!
IT'S OUTRAGEOUS! I WILL FILE SUCH A COMPLAINT—!

YOU CAN COUNT UP, SIR, OR DOWN; BUT YOU MAY NOT STICK AT THE SAME NUMBER! I WON'T HAVE IT!
AHH! HE'S TEARING UP THE PRIVET, D–MN HIS EYES!

SCHNELL, BITTE. FOLGEN SIE MIR.
I'M COMING. HULLO THERE, BERTRAM.

...IN WHICH CASE YOU ARE NOT COUNTING, SIR, YOU'RE ONLY REPEATING A NUMBER; IN WHICH CASE YOU'RE MAD, SIR, AND SO I TELL YOU PLAINLY!

...HOW CAN ONE RELAX, MR. SLOANE, WITH THESE ZANIES AT HER BACK? THE TRAIN HITS THE SLIGHTEST BUMP AND THEY ALL WHOOP LIKE COMANCHES.

IT CAN'T BE BORNE. THIS'LL GO ON FOR HOURS, YOU SEE.
DO SEEM RATHER WROUGHT-UP THIS MORNING, DON'T THEY.
THEN IT WILL OUTLAST OUR TRIP; WE'RE NEARLY THERE.

AH: AND IS...THE BOY HUNGRY? HM? HE COULD DO WITH A BIT OF ROAST, I THINK, JUDGING BY HIS LOOKS...
MISS VAN DOESSLER IS CONVINCED SHE'S BEING POISONED, BERTRAM.

OH. HO-HO. NO, THAT'S NOT AT ALL WHAT I—*HRM.*
BUT YOU SEE WHAT I'M UP AGAINST. I TRUST THAT... MAN IS STILL THERE?
YOUR FOOTMAN?

MM. THAT'S HIM. HE'D LIKE TO KILL ME, I'M SURE. WAITING HIS CHANCE. A MAN WHO'D TRY THIS WOULD TRY ANYTHING.
HERR SLOANE: BITTE.

OH, GO ON. I CAN SEE THIS IS OF NO INTEREST TO YOU.
ONE OF US WILL SEE YOU UPSTATE, ANYWAY. GO ON. OUT, OUT.
YES. WELL. GOOD LUCK, BOTH OF YOU.

...THAT, BERTRAM, IS A JUSTIFIED LADY. A PARANOIAC WHO REALLY IS BEING FOLLOWED.
FOLLOWED BY WHOM?
BY THE BLACK ROBES, I SHOULD THINK.
OH...
THIS TRAIN IS FULL OF PEOPLE THEY'D LIKE TO MEET. SOME THEY DON'T KNOW ABOUT, SOME THEY DO BUT HAVEN'T BEEN ABLE TO FIND–LIKE MISS VAN DOESSLER.

...OR MR. DEVANG, OVER THERE–HE'S BEEN STARING AT YOU FROM BEHIND THAT POTTED PALM. NOT SURE WHAT HE'S UP TO.
...BUT YOU'RE GOING TO HELP US SOLVE A GREAT PROBLEM, BERTRAM. YOU, AND THE PEOPLE ON THIS TRAIN.
OH? HAS IT ANY-THING TO DO WITH–

–YOU RECALL MAJOR OGDEN? WE'RE GOING TO SEE HIS BROTHER, AT A GREAT, SPRAWLING HOUSE THEY'VE GOT IN THE COUNTRY. TREMENDOUS FUN.
SORRY, YOU HAD A QUESTION?
OH: WHEN WE GET THERE, THAT MACHINE I SAW: YOU'LL PUT ME IN IT?
WE'LL TRY EVERYONE IN IT. ALL THESE PASSENGERS TODAY, AND ANYONE ELSE WHO WANTS A GO. I'LL SEE IF WE CAN'T GET YOU A TURN IN IT TONIGHT.

BUT LET'S SEE WHAT THIS IS...
CAREFULLY, NOW.
HERR RIEBLING, YOU MUST STOP THIS AT ONCE–!
GRLLK!

SIR–LET HIM GO, I SAY, OR WE'LL HAVE TO SHOOT YOU!
–SHOOT HIM!
YOU SEE HOW IT IS, *HERR* SLOANE.
YES: COLONEL RIEBLING? I WONDER WHAT YOUR PROGRAM IS, WITH THIS MAN. YOU TWO APPEAR TO BE AT A STALEMATE.

THE REST OF YOU: PUT UP THOSE GUNS, WOULD YOU? IT TOOK US SIX YEARS TO FIND THIS MAN, AND ANOTHER YEAR TO BRING HIM THIS FAR...

IF YOU SHOOT HIM NOW, IN THE LAST HOUR OF THIS TRIP, I WILL PERSONALLY–
«THUNK!»
ALL RIGHT: WHO'S LENT HIM A KNIFE?

AH–SIR, YOU SEE–
NEVER MIND. THAT'S HIS KEY?
«SNAP!»

HERR SLOANE, I MUST WARN YOU–

«THUM-THUMM!»
«KER-CHUNK–!»

THIS MAN NEEDS A SHAVE AND A CHANGE OF CLOTHES.
THERE'S HIS KNIFE. DON'T GIVE HIM ANOTHER, IF YOU PLEASE.
THANK YOU, SIR.

COME IN, BERTRAM. YOU'RE QUITE SAFE.

I'D MEANT TO INTERVIEW YOU THE OTHER DAY, RIGHT OFF YOUR BOAT, THOUGH MY ASSOCIATE MANAGED TO SET YOU AT LARGE IN THE CITY BEFORE YOU'D GOT TO ME.
I FEARED WE'D MISSED OUR CHANCE WITH YOU, BUT, HAPPILY, HERE YOU ARE. AND I DON'T SEE WHY WE SHOULDN'T TALK, WHILE WE'VE GOT A MOMENT.
WHAT IS THAT?

THIS? OH, I KNOW AN OLD WATCH-MAKER'S SHOP IN ZURICH THAT MAKES THEM. I THOUGHT YOU MIGHT LIKE IT. LOOK HERE:
TWO LEARNED APES TURN'D TO THE CLOT

BERTRAM FOLLOWS THE GLOWING ORBIS CRUCIGER BACK AND FORTH WITH HIS EYES. HIS VOICE GROWS DISTANT.
YOUR FRIENDS FROM THE BOAT, THEY SEEM TO ENJOY LOOKING AT IT WHILE WE TALK. WHAT DO YOU THINK?
MR. RENTON SAID THEY'VE ALL SEEN SOMETHING, AND IT'S MADE THEM MAD.

...WELL. THEY DO APPEAR TO HAVE SEEN SOMETHING, A FEW OF THEM. A THING THEY'RE AT A LOSS TO EXPLAIN.
BUT I HAVEN'T SEEN IT.
NO? OR, NOT THAT YOU RECALL.
NOT THAT I RECALL.

JUST AS YOU DON'T RECALL BEING KNOCKED ON THE HEAD, THOUGH I CAN SEE PLAINLY YOU HAVE BEEN. I SHOULD SAY ONE'S MEMORY WERE A TRICKY THING.
HOW ARE YOU FEELING, NOW? YOU'RE VERY RELAXED...?
YES.
GOOD. HOLD STILL.

I HAVE HEARD THAT A MAN CAN SEE SHAMBHALA AND STILL HOLD ONTO HIS WITS, IF ONLY HE CAN FORGET WHAT HE'S SEEN.
SHAMBHALA...?
YES. THE FORGETTING PART, AS I UNDERSTAND, REQUIRES A NASTY BIT OF DRILLING. BUT, THANKFULLY, HE DOESN'T REMEMBER THAT, EITHER.

WHICH IS ALL VERY WELL IN THEORY, OF COURSE. I'VE JUST NEVER...
...I HADN'T YET SEEN IT DONE.
«THOONK»

IT WAS MISS MAGUIRE WHO DUG THESE UP FOR US, AT THE GUILD. SHE THOUGHT, WITH THE LOOK OF THEM, THE RUNNERS MIGHT NOT TAMPER WITH THEM. THIS MIGHT SEEM LIKE SOME VERY IMPORTANT BUSINESS.
AND–DO YOU KNOW?– I'M NOT SURE IT ISN'T.
I REALIZE YOU DON'T THINK MUCH OF ARTHUR AS AN ADVENTURER, JOHN. BUT HE'S UNEARTHED SOMETHING. EVEN IF IT WAS PURELY BY ACCIDENT.
WE'VE HAD A NUMBER OF THEM CALL, ALREADY, FROM THE GUILD–NOT THOSE RIDICULOUS TYPES ARTHUR USED TO BRING HOME, BUT SERIOUS-MINDED MEN. AND THEY'VE GOT SO INSISTENT, LATELY.
THEY'VE EVEN INTERVIEWED WITH ME, FOR ALL I CAN TELL THEM. ARTHUR'S BEEN TURNING THEM ALL AWAY, OF COURSE, ON MR. SLOANE'S ORDERS.
FAN: I SAW THE MAN THEY'RE CALLING SLOANE, IN NEW YORK. YOU MUST HAVE KNOWN, HE'S–
...WHAT?
IT'S TRUE, THEN, YOU HAVEN'T SEEN HIM, YOURSELF?
MR. SLOANE? NO, I HAVEN'T. YOU KNOW HE ONLY CAME FOR A SHORT TIME, TILL HE'D GOT HIS DOC-TORS IN PLACE. HE AND ARTHUR SPEAK MAINLY BY POST.

IF HE VISITS AT ALL I WOULDN'T KNOW. WE'RE HARDLY EVER IN THE MAIN HOUSE, AND THERE'S NOT MUCH STAFF LEFT TO REPORT ON THINGS–ARTHUR'S LET THEM ALL GO. YOU SEE HOW IT IS...
I DO, YES.
HEE-YAHH!

MR. RENTON?
OHH: THAT'S EASILY FIXED, Y'KNOW.
THERE'S AN ASH TREE OUT BY THE KIOSK. SOMEONE'S MOTORCAR BENEATH IT.
AYE, SIR. WE'LL HAVE A LOOK.

FAN: I'M GOING TO INSIST YOU MEET THIS MR. SLOANE WHEN HE RETURNS FROM THE CITY. WE THREE ARE GOING TO TALK, AND SET A FEW THINGS IN ORDER.
YES, ALL RIGHT. BUT WHY–?

A SCURRYING NOISE FROM DOWN THE HALL ALERTS THEM BOTH.
WHAT WAS THAT?
...NOTHING. THERE'S ALWAYS SOMEONE FLITTING THROUGH THE SHADOWS IN THIS PART OF THE HOUSE. I USED TO HEAR LITTLE SCRAPING FOOTSTEPS ALL THROUGH THE NIGHT.

'AT'S IT. YOU KEEP YER EYES ON THE HOUSE, JUST LIKE THAT...

...THEY'RE USUALLY THAT WAY, AROUND TO THE LEFT. YOU'LL SEE THEM BEFORE YOU REACH THE DINING HALL. THEY WON'T LET YOU THROUGH TO ARTHUR, BUT YOU OUGHT TO BE ABLE TO PERSUADE THEM, AS HIS BROTHER.
PROMISE ME YOU'LL ONLY TALK TO THEM, JOHN, AND NO MORE.
I'LL FOLLOW YOU, THEN. YOU SPEAK FOR US.
OH: BUT I'M NOT LET IN THIS WING, YOU KNOW.

AND I DON'T WANT YOU GETTING ANGRY ABOUT IT, EITHER.
MM. I THINK IT'S POSSIBLE I WILL.
–WELL, DON'T. JOHN? LOOK AT ME.
YOU'RE NOT ODYSSEUS, COME BACK TO BLOODY HIS OWN HOME. IF YOU CAN'T KEEP YOURSELF IN HAND WHILE YOU'RE HERE–

YOU DO IT, FAN. COME. YOU KEEP ME IN HAND TILL YOU CAN TRUST ME TO DO IT MYSELF.
I'LL SEE ARTHUR IN ANY CASE. I THINK IT BETTER IF YOU WERE THERE.
YOU'LL LISTEN TO ME, THEN, AND DO NOTHING RASH?
I WILL.
ALL RIGHT. ...ALL RIGHT.

ACH–YOU...
ANSCHLAG, BITTE. VERZEIHEN SIE MIR.

YES–DOCTOR: THIS IS JOHN OGDEN, ARTHUR'S–
JA I AM SORRY. ARTHUR IS HAVING PRIVACY FOR HIM, NOW.
VERLASSEN SIE.
WE'LL JUST HAVE A LOOK, THEN–

SH-H-H. WAS IST DAS? WER SIND SIE?
-NEIN-SO HE IS WITH HIS DOCTORS, AND YOU ARE NOT CRASHING IN, NOW, YOU SEE.
-JOHN-

MEINHERR?
FAN...?
YES, ALL RIGHT.

«CRRASH!»

«POP! POP! POP!»

JOHN. HOPE YOU'RE HAVING LESS TROUBLE WITH THE WAR THAN WE'VE GOT HERE.
ARTHUR: MY GOODNESS.

Arthur Ogden's body, in contrast to the portrait above him, has the ravaged look of a consumptive's. Much of his skin is covered with plaster and bandages, and these are sodden through as though the wounds were suppurating all over him. His eyes bulge from deep within their ashen sockets, and a long-toothed grin completes the picture of an animate skeleton. Mr. Ogden's manner is anxious and distracted, and he lets out quick, intermittent laughs as he speaks, rather in the way of a nervous tic.

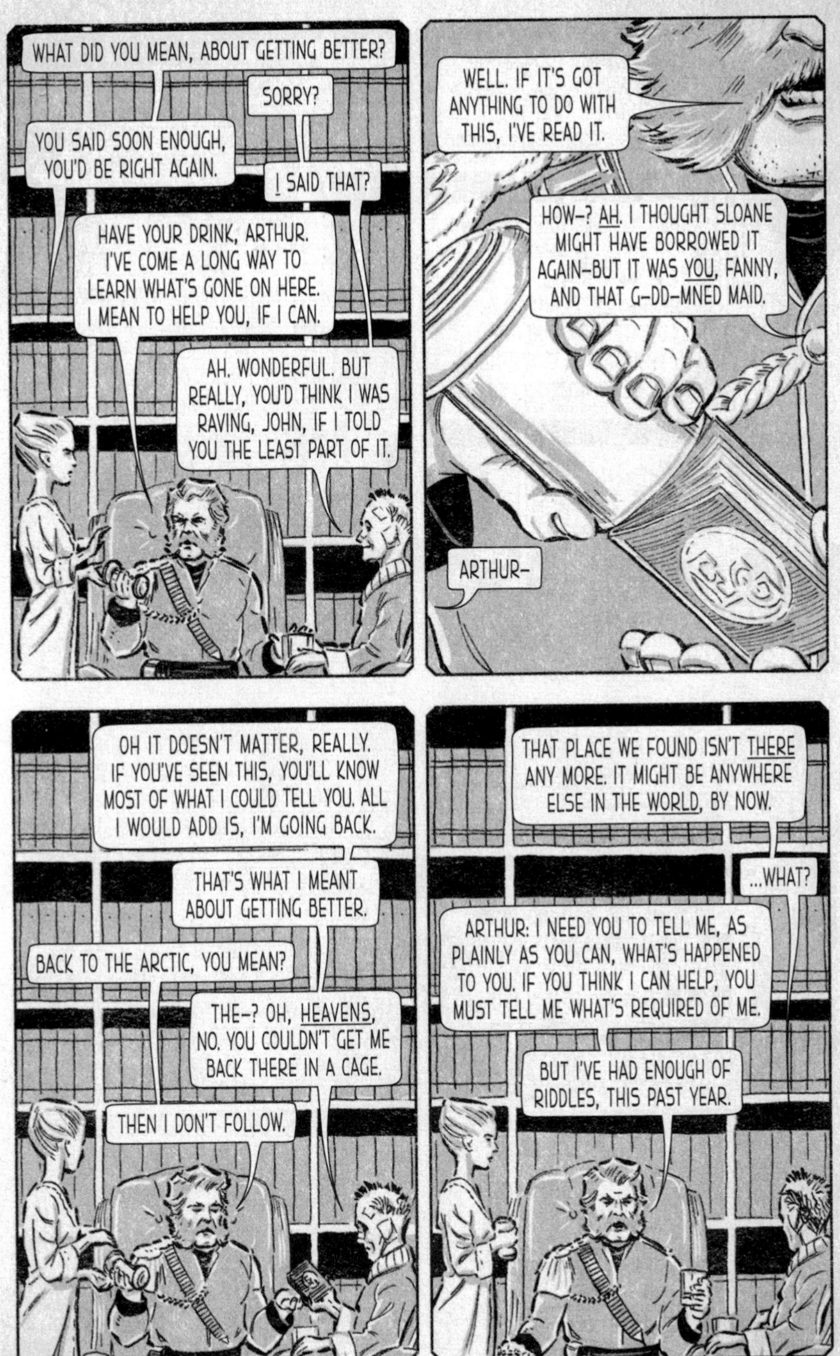
WHAT DID YOU MEAN, ABOUT GETTING BETTER?
SORRY?
YOU SAID SOON ENOUGH, YOU'D BE RIGHT AGAIN.
I SAID THAT?
HAVE YOUR DRINK, ARTHUR. I'VE COME A LONG WAY TO LEARN WHAT'S GONE ON HERE. I MEAN TO HELP YOU, IF I CAN.
AH. WONDERFUL. BUT REALLY, YOU'D THINK I WAS RAVING, JOHN, IF I TOLD YOU THE LEAST PART OF IT.
WELL. IF IT'S GOT ANYTHING TO DO WITH THIS, I'VE READ IT.
HOW–? AH. I THOUGHT SLOANE MIGHT HAVE BORROWED IT AGAIN–BUT IT WAS YOU, FANNY, AND THAT G–DD–MNED MAID.
ARTHUR–
OH IT DOESN'T MATTER, REALLY. IF YOU'VE SEEN THIS, YOU'LL KNOW MOST OF WHAT I COULD TELL YOU. ALL I WOULD ADD IS, I'M GOING BACK.
THAT'S WHAT I MEANT ABOUT GETTING BETTER.
BACK TO THE ARCTIC, YOU MEAN?
THE–? OH, HEAVENS, NO. YOU COULDN'T GET ME BACK THERE IN A CAGE.
THEN I DON'T FOLLOW.
THAT PLACE WE FOUND ISN'T THERE ANY MORE. IT MIGHT BE ANYWHERE ELSE IN THE WORLD, BY NOW.
...WHAT?
ARTHUR: I NEED YOU TO TELL ME, AS PLAINLY AS YOU CAN, WHAT'S HAPPENED TO YOU. IF YOU THINK I CAN HELP, YOU MUST TELL ME WHAT'S REQUIRED OF ME.
BUT I'VE HAD ENOUGH OF RIDDLES, THIS PAST YEAR.

WELL. PLAINLY, THEN: YOU CAN SEE I'M NOT IN THE PINK OF HEALTH, JOHN. YOU UNDERSTAND THAT MUCH.
I DO.
THEN I'LL TELL YOU, THIS ISN'T FROSTBITE, OR ANYTHING LIKE IT. I'D MADE A FULL RECOVERY BEFORE I LEFT CANADA. THIS... CONDITION OF MINE–IT ALL STARTED AFTER I'D GOT HOME.
IT STARTED WHEN MR. SLOANE ARRIVED.
–UNRELATED. ...AT LEAST, HE DIDN'T BRING OUT MY SYMPTOMS. I'M NOT SURE THEY DIDN'T BRING HIM.
GO ON.
WHAT I FOUND IN THE NORTH IS MAKING ME ILL, JOHN. AND I'M GETTING WORSE RATHER QUICKLY. IF I DON'T GET BACK TO THIS THING, I WILL DIE. THAT'S AS PLAIN AS I CAN MAKE IT.
AND YOU'RE QUITE SURE IT'S NO LONGER IN THE ARCTIC.
IT ISN'T. I SENT A RECOVERY PARTY, BUT THEY ONLY BORE OUT MR. SLOANE ON THIS POINT. IT LEFT A SORT OF...SCAR ACROSS THE ICE, NOTHING MORE.
THE MEN ARE STILL THERE, TAKING UP MISSIONARY WORK, OF ALL THINGS.
BUT YOU AND MR. SLOANE, YOU'RE ENGAGED IN FINDING IT AGAIN.
AND YOU, TOO. YOU'VE BEEN A TREMENDOUS HELP ALREADY, JOHN. DON'T SEE WHY YOU SHOULDN'T SHARE, ULTIMATELY, IN THE DISCOVERY.
IN...THE DISCOVERY OF SHAMBHALA, YOU MEAN.
...YES. THAT'S WHAT I MEAN. WHEN WE'VE FOUND IT, I WILL ASK YOU TO FETCH ME THERE. IF YOU'VE COME WITH A MIND TO HELP–IF YOU'D SAVE ME–THEN THAT IS WHAT YOU CAN DO.

YOU CAN SEE ME, OR WHAT'S LEFT OF ME, SAFELY TO THE CITY. THAT–PLAINLY–IS WHAT I'D REQUIRE OF YOU.
SOMEONE'S COMING...
THEN–WHAT?–YOU REACH THIS PLACE AGAIN, AND MAKE YOUR RECOVERY? JUST LIKE THAT.
OH, NO–NO, JOHN: IT ISN'T JUST LIKE ANYTHING.

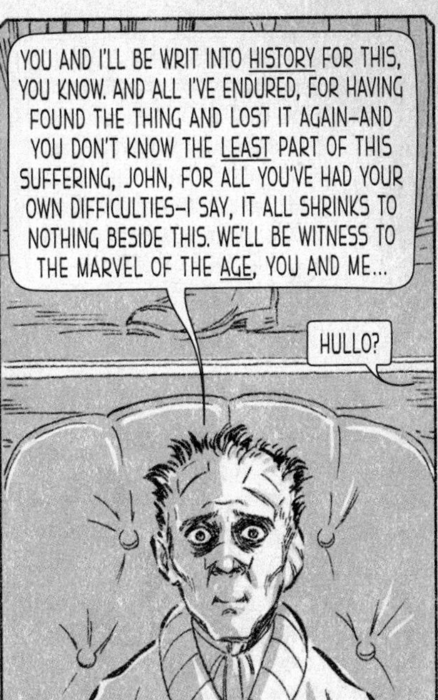
YOU AND I'LL BE WRIT INTO HISTORY FOR THIS, YOU KNOW. AND ALL I'VE ENDURED, FOR HAVING FOUND THE THING AND LOST IT AGAIN–AND YOU DON'T KNOW THE LEAST PART OF THIS SUFFERING, JOHN, FOR ALL YOU'VE HAD YOUR OWN DIFFICULTIES–I SAY, IT ALL SHRINKS TO NOTHING BESIDE THIS. WE'LL BE WITNESS TO THE MARVEL OF THE AGE, YOU AND ME...
HULLO?

SOMEONE 'ERE TO MAKE A FOURTH.
ASKIN' AFTER A MR. SLOANE. I TOL' 'ER SHE'D THE WRONG ADDRESS AGAIN.

WELCOME, MISS.
...I SAY: CAN IT BE YOU AND I'VE MET BEFORE NOW?
OH: NO, ARTHUR. YOU'RE RECOGNIZING HER FROM THE PAPERS. MISS HARROW, AREN'T YOU? THE ACTRESS?
MM. AT ANY RATE, I WAS.

...NO, IT WASN'T THAT. IT WAS IN THE ARCTIC...
SHE COME IN EASY ENOUGH, SIR, THOUGH I DID HAVE TO CHASE THE HUNS OFF HER. THEY'RE IN THE HALL, AND MORE GATHERIN'. DON'T KNOW HOW MANY MAKES THE INVASION OFFICIAL–
SEE THEY DON'T GET IN.
MR. RENTON? GO ON.
...I HADN'T THOUGHT OF IT TILL THIS MOMENT, BUT...MISS HARROW, I BELIEVE YOU WERE ONE OF THOSE WHO LOOKED IN ON ME AT FORT DEFIANCE, AFTER MY ACCIDENT.
I SEE. WELL, IT WOULD HAVE BEEN FOR A FEW MINUTES ONLY. AND THE STATE YOU WERE IN, MR. OGDEN...THIS IS FLATTERY, REALLY.
HMPH.
YOU WERE...RATHER FRUSTRATED AT THE LITTLE I COULD TELL YOU. I THINK I'D NEVER SEEN A GIRL SO LOVELY, IN SO EVIL A HUMOR.
WELL. WE CAN'T BE BLAMED FOR OUR LOOKS, CAN WE, ARTHUR?
EHH...NO.
WHAT ABOUT YOU, MAJOR? OR WILL YOU GO ON PRETENDING I HAVEN'T ENTERED THE ROOM.
WE RESCUED YOUR BROTHER AT SEA, YOU KNOW.
DID YOU?
HASN'T HE TOLD YOU? WELL: YOU SEE ME ASTONISHED.
WHAT'S YOUR BUSINESS HERE, MISS HARROW?
MINE? ONLY THE SAME AS BEFORE. STILL AF-TER MR. SLOANE. HOPE YOU WON'T HAVE HURT FEELINGS, ANY OF YOU.

YOUR BROTHER'S TOLD YOU, HE TOOK A SHOT AT MR. SLOANE THE OTHER MORNING? IN NEW YORK?
YOU DID WHAT?
FORTUNATELY FOR ALL OF US, HE DID MISS.
BUT—I CAN'T HAVE THAT, JOHN. DO YOU UNDERSTAND? I CANNOT ALLOW IT.

I'VE GOT A HISTORY WITH HIM, ARTHUR. THOUGH I'D SOONER NOT DISCUSS IT IN FRONT OF STRANGERS.
IN FRONT OF—? PLAINLY, MISS HARROW AND I'VE MET, AND SHE'S A GUEST NOW IN MY HOME. WE CAN ALL BE CIVIL, AT THE VERY LEAST.

QUITE RIGHT. YOU OBSERVE, I'M NO MORE A CAPTIVE AT SEA, BUT IN THE HOME OF A GENTLEMAN.
AND YOU KNOW, ARTHUR, IF YOUR BROTHER HAS FEELINGS ABOUT OUR MR. SLOANE, I'D ADVISE HIM TO GET RID OF THEM. THEY WILL PLAY H—LL WITH ONE'S JUDGMENT, THESE FEELINGS.

I SHOULD THINK THAT WERE GOOD ADVICE FOR YOU, MISS.
FOR ME. WELL. YOU MAY KNOW LESS ABOUT THAT THAN YOU THINK.
I KNOW IT ISN'T SAFE TO DISCUSS HARMING MR. SLOANE, IN YOUR HEARING.

–PLEASE–BOTH OF YOU. NO ONE'S TO HARM MR. SLOANE. AND I'LL SHOW YOU WHY NOT.
COME–I MUST SHOW YOU WHAT HE'S BEEN DOING FOR US. IT'LL GIVE YOU A BIT OF PERSPECTIVE ON THE WHOLE AFFAIR.
YOU, TOO, JOHN. YOU REALLY MUST SEE THIS.

HADN'T WE OUGHT TO GO, JOHN? I'D LIKE TO SEE.
WE CAN DO WHATEVER YOU LIKE, TILL MR. SLOANE ARRIVES. THEN I'LL TAKE THIS UP WITH HIM.

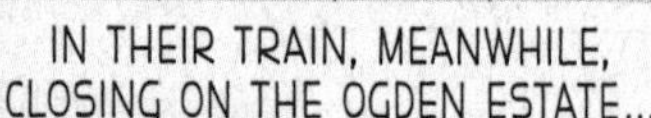
IN THEIR TRAIN, MEANWHILE, CLOSING ON THE OGDEN ESTATE...

...THE MIND, BERTRAM, HAS JUST TOO MANY PLACES FOR YOUR MEMORIES TO HIDE. YOU CAN'T POSSIBLY DRILL THEM ALL OUT. HERE–FOR INSTANCE, THE LAST TIME WE SPOKE, I SHOWED YOU A FIGURE–A SNAKE DOUBLED ON ITSELF, BITING ITS OWN TAIL, THUS. YOU MENTIONED YOU'D SEEN SOMETHING LIKE IT IN A DREAM.
YES.
SEEMS AN UNUSUAL DREAM FOR A BOY, DOESN'T IT?
I DON'T KNOW.

WELL. I CAN TELL YOU IT IS. THOUGH I WONDER, AS YOU RELAX AND CONCENTRATE, IF YOU COULD DESCRIBE THIS DREAM FOR ME.
...BERTRAM?
IT FLOATS OVER MY HEAD, MOSTLY.
THE...SYMBOL DOES. IN YOUR DREAM.
YES.
INTERESTING. AND IT'S SMALL, OR VERY LARGE?
LARGE. I CANNOT SEE THE ENDS OF IT.

ALL RIGHT. YOU CAN CLOSE YOUR EYES, AND WE'LL PUT THIS AWAY. I'D LIKE YOU TO PICTURE THE SYMBOL FLOATING OVER YOU, THE WAY YOU'RE USED TO SEEING IT, UNTIL YOU'RE QUITE SURE IT WILL BE THERE WHEN YOU OPEN YOUR EYES. ...HAVE YOU GOT IT?
YES.
GOOD. NOW... OPEN YOUR EYES.

WHERE ARE YOU, BERTRAM?

IN THE GARDENS.

THE GARDENS, I SEE. THOUGH YOU'LL HAVE TO TELL ME ABOUT THEM. I'M STILL BACK HERE IN NEW YORK, YOU KNOW.
THERE ARE...MOUNTAINS, AND THE LAKE. MY SISTER IS IN HER COSTUME, HIDING. IT'S A GAME...

...THE EVENT OF SEEING SHAMBHALA, WHEN IT'S NOT FATAL—AND I GATHER IT IS, MOST OF THE TIME, SO I WAS QUITE LUCKY—BUT IT IMPRESSES ITSELF DEEPLY ON THE SUBCONSCIOUS. THE CONSCIOUS MEMORY IS UTTERLY VOIDED.
IT'S JUST TOO MUCH FOR US TO ASSIMILATE.
IN MY CASE, I RECALL THE LIGHTS, THEN MAKING THE ENTRY IN MY LOG AND CRAWLING OVER THE ICE...AND THEN'M WAKING AGAIN IN THE YUKON. ALREADY IT'S 1916. NOTHING IN BETWEEN, YOU SEE.

I RECOVER BITS NOW AND THEN—AND YOU SAW ANOTHER FALL INTO PLACE WHEN I RECOGNIZED MISS HARROW. BUT I CAN'T RECALL WHAT I MIGHT HAVE SEEN, BENEATH THE ICE.
NOTHING ABOUT THE REST OF YOUR PARTY?
NO-NO. ALL VERY MUCH A BLANK.
AND YOUR EXPLORERS GUILD: HAVEN'T THEY BEEN ANY HELP?
THE GUILD? OH, NO. THEY'RE COLLECTORS OF INTELLIGENCE, JOHN, AND DITHERERS. ACADEMICS. I'M NOT CONVINCED THE GUILD DO MUCH OF ANYTHING. AND WE'LL NEED THINGS DONE, NO MISTAKE.

BUT THEY KNOW ABOUT YOUR CITY, AT ANY RATE.
THEY ARGUE IT ALL DIFFERENT WAYS—I CAN'T BOTHER TO KEEP TRACK. I DON'T NEED THEIR THEORIES, OR THEIR WARNINGS, ONLY THEIR MATERIAL SUPPORT. AND I MAYN'T EVEN NEED THAT, WITH YOU HERE.
WHAT WARNINGS?
REALLY, I DON'T KNOW. THEY'VE BEEN A D—MNED NUISANCE, IS ALL I CAN TELL YOU. AND WHO DID THEY SEND UP FIRST, WHEN THEY GOT WIND I'D COME HOME? BUT OUR COUSIN CYRIL!

THEY'D MADE HIM A SECRETARY OF THE TRANSEPT, IF YOU CAN IMAGINE THAT.
WHAT DID CYRIL TELL YOU, ARTHUR?
OH, HOW SHOULD I KNOW? WE NEVER LET HIM IN. HE'S GONE TO ENGLAND NOW, BUTTONING LLOYD GEORGE'S TROUSERS FOR HIM, AND WITH THE IDEA I'VE MADE SOME GREAT DISCOVERY FOR HIS GUILD.
HOW DO YOU LIKE THAT, JOHN? I HOPE THEY FIND SOME TRENCH TO STICK HIM IN, WHERE HE CAN THINK LONG UPON MY ACHIEVEMENTS.
ANYWAY: HERE WE ARE.

MY...
YES. THEY'VE BUILT A SECOND MACHINE TO GO RIGHT THERE; IT'S COMING UP WITH THEM TODAY. I'M TOLD THIS FIRST ATTEMPT WILL LOOK RATHER QUAINT NEXT TO THE NEW ONE.
WHAT DO THEY DO, ARTHUR?

WELL. FOR RECOVERING <u>MEMORIES</u>, AREN'T THEY? MR. SLOANE AND HIS FRIENDS HAVE WAYS OF DRAWING THESE FORGOTTEN THINGS OUT FROM THEIR HIDING-PLACES IN THE MIND. MESMERISM, MOSTLY, AND THEY'RE ALL ADEPTS–TO THE POINT WHERE I MUST HAVE THEM ANNOUNCE WHEN THEY'RE PUTTING ME UNDER–TOO MUCH WAKING UP ALL ABOUT THE HOUSE, WITH HOURS MISSING...

EHH, BUT THE POINT IS, THESE METHODS GET THEM ONLY SO FAR. TO GET RIGHT IN AMONG THESE DEEPER MEMORIES, THE'VE GOT TO DELVE–<u>PHYSICALLY</u> DELVE–INTO THE SUBJECT HIMSELF.

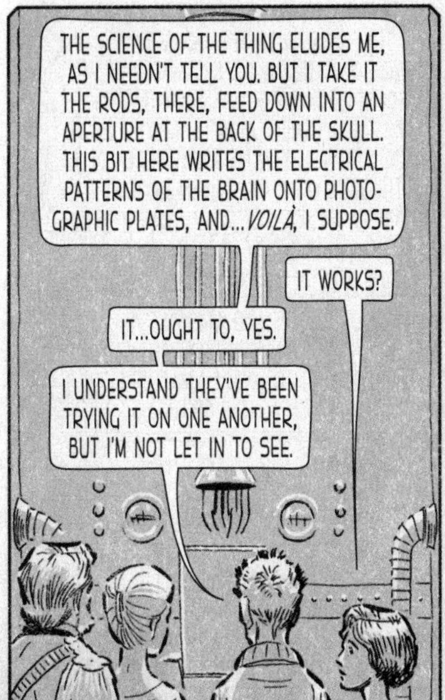

THE SCIENCE OF THE THING ELUDES ME, AS I NEEDN'T TELL YOU. BUT I TAKE IT THE RODS, THERE, FEED DOWN INTO AN APERTURE AT THE BACK OF THE SKULL. THIS BIT HERE WRITES THE ELECTRICAL PATTERNS OF THE BRAIN ONTO PHOTOGRAPHIC PLATES, AND...*VOILÀ*, I SUPPOSE.
IT WORKS?
IT...OUGHT TO, YES.
I UNDERSTAND THEY'VE BEEN TRYING IT ON ONE ANOTHER, BUT I'M NOT LET IN TO SEE.

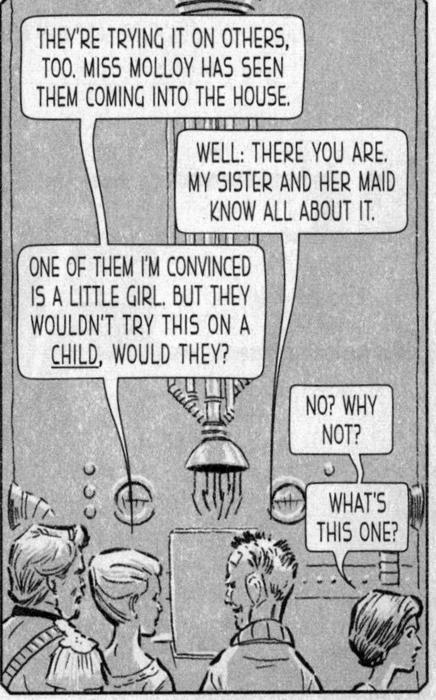

THEY'RE TRYING IT ON OTHERS, TOO. MISS MOLLOY HAS SEEN THEM COMING INTO THE HOUSE.
WELL: THERE YOU ARE. MY SISTER AND HER MAID KNOW ALL ABOUT IT.
ONE OF THEM I'M CONVINCED IS A LITTLE GIRL. BUT THEY WOULDN'T TRY THIS ON A CHILD, WOULD THEY?
NO? WHY NOT?
WHAT'S THIS ONE?

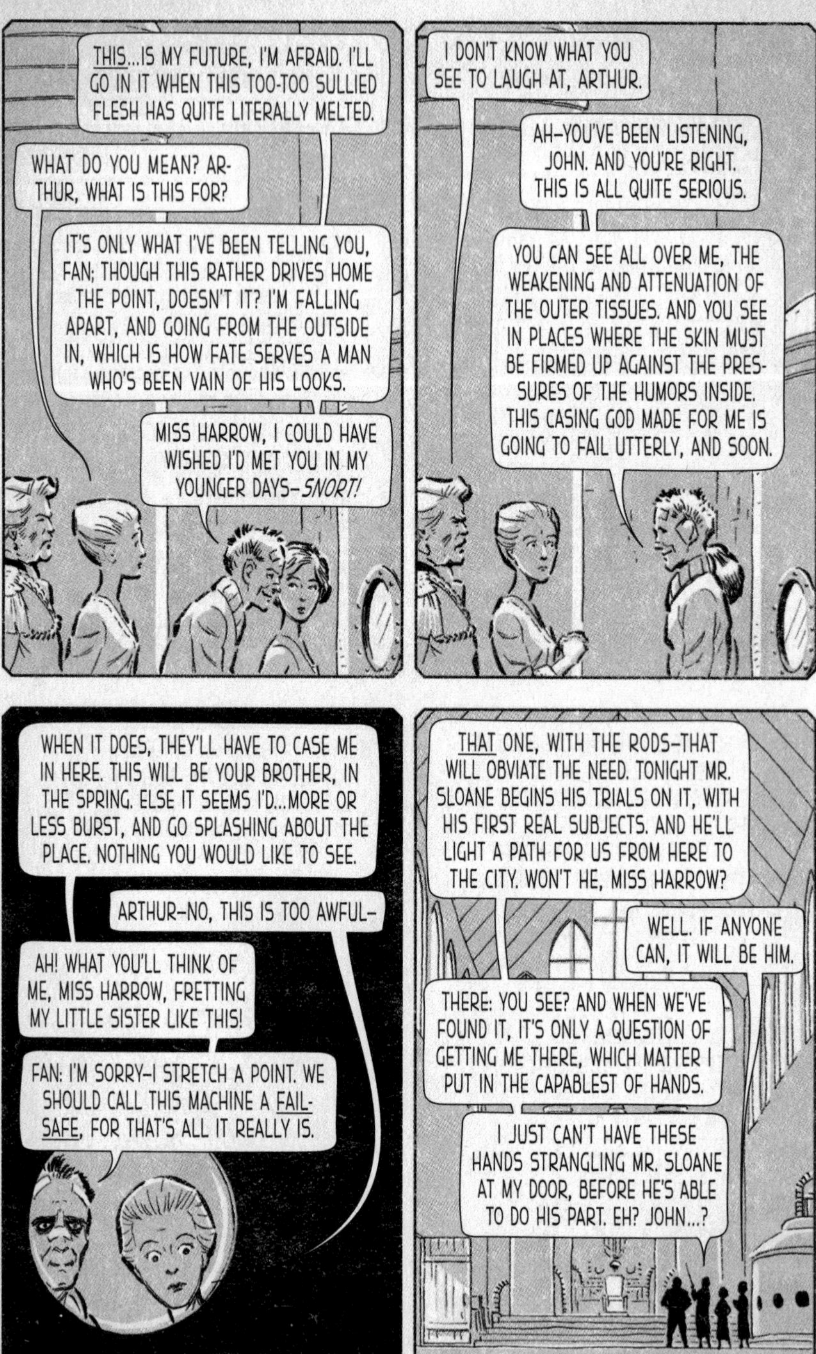
THIS...IS MY FUTURE, I'M AFRAID. I'LL GO IN IT WHEN THIS TOO-TOO SULLIED FLESH HAS QUITE LITERALLY MELTED.
WHAT DO YOU MEAN? ARTHUR, WHAT IS THIS FOR?
IT'S ONLY WHAT I'VE BEEN TELLING YOU, FAN; THOUGH THIS RATHER DRIVES HOME THE POINT, DOESN'T IT? I'M FALLING APART, AND GOING FROM THE OUTSIDE IN, WHICH IS HOW FATE SERVES A MAN WHO'S BEEN VAIN OF HIS LOOKS.
MISS HARROW, I COULD HAVE WISHED I'D MET YOU IN MY YOUNGER DAYS–SNORT!
I DON'T KNOW WHAT YOU SEE TO LAUGH AT, ARTHUR.
AH–YOU'VE BEEN LISTENING, JOHN. AND YOU'RE RIGHT. THIS IS ALL QUITE SERIOUS.
YOU CAN SEE ALL OVER ME, THE WEAKENING AND ATTENUATION OF THE OUTER TISSUES. AND YOU SEE IN PLACES WHERE THE SKIN MUST BE FIRMED UP AGAINST THE PRESSURES OF THE HUMORS INSIDE. THIS CASING GOD MADE FOR ME IS GOING TO FAIL UTTERLY, AND SOON.
WHEN IT DOES, THEY'LL HAVE TO CASE ME IN HERE. THIS WILL BE YOUR BROTHER, IN THE SPRING. ELSE IT SEEMS I'D...MORE OR LESS BURST, AND GO SPLASHING ABOUT THE PLACE. NOTHING YOU WOULD LIKE TO SEE.
ARTHUR–NO, THIS IS TOO AWFUL–
AH! WHAT YOU'LL THINK OF ME, MISS HARROW, FRETTING MY LITTLE SISTER LIKE THIS!
FAN: I'M SORRY–I STRETCH A POINT. WE SHOULD CALL THIS MACHINE A FAIL-SAFE, FOR THAT'S ALL IT REALLY IS.
THAT ONE, WITH THE RODS–THAT WILL OBVIATE THE NEED. TONIGHT MR. SLOANE BEGINS HIS TRIALS ON IT, WITH HIS FIRST REAL SUBJECTS. AND HE'LL LIGHT A PATH FOR US FROM HERE TO THE CITY. WON'T HE, MISS HARROW?
WELL. IF ANYONE CAN, IT WILL BE HIM.
THERE: YOU SEE? AND WHEN WE'VE FOUND IT, IT'S ONLY A QUESTION OF GETTING ME THERE, WHICH MATTER I PUT IN THE CAPABLEST OF HANDS.
I JUST CAN'T HAVE THESE HANDS STRANGLING MR. SLOANE AT MY DOOR, BEFORE HE'S ABLE TO DO HIS PART. EH? JOHN...?

VIELLEICHT, JA. WENN ES NICHT PASST.

EXCUSE ME–SIR? SORRY: HAS THERE BEEN A FIRE?
AH?
I HEARD A CRASH. I THOUGHT THERE MAY HAVE BEEN A FIRE...
ER SAGT: 'ES IST EIN FEUER?'
SIE IHN HIER RAUS.
MR. SLOANE HAS GONE TO THE HOUSE. THERE IS NO FIRE. THEY ARE WAITING FOR YOU. GO UP THOSE STAIRS, THAT WAY. YOU WILL SEE THEM.
ALL RIGHT. THANK YOU, SIR.

OI! GRAB HOLD'A THAT GIRL!
WHAT YA STARIN' AT? TRIP 'ER UP!
KNOCK 'ER DOWN, LAD! YA DEAF–?

AUGH, FER CHR–ST'S SAKE!
OI! WHA'D THAT MAN TELL YA?
HE SAID, KNOCK HER DOWN.

AYE. THUS:
LOOK SHARP, FRANK! SHE'S DOUBLED BACK!
DOOFH!

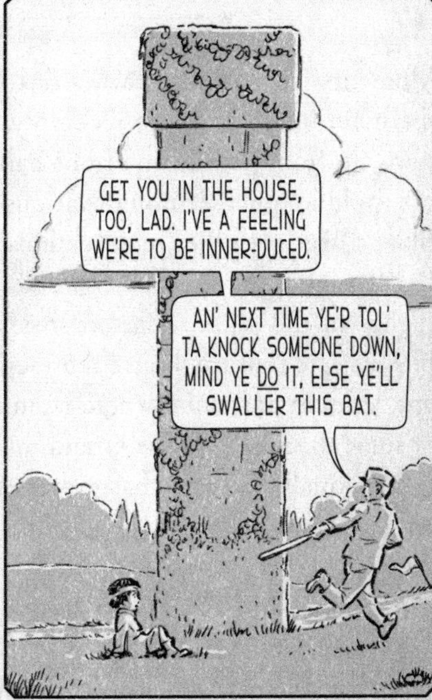
GET YOU IN THE HOUSE, TOO, LAD. I'VE A FEELING WE'RE TO BE INNER-DUCED.
AN' NEXT TIME YE'R TOL' TA KNOCK SOMEONE DOWN, MIND YE DO IT, ELSE YE'LL SWALLER THIS BAT.

Moments later, young Barnes has slipped through the opened door of the main house and into its empty, marble-flagged vestibule. It is a few steps up from here to the front hall and its satellite rooms, and we find him poking quietly through various parlors and saloons in search of Mr. Sloane or some other representative of the house.

He rounds an old concierge's desk and hears, through the formidable silence of the place, a far-off shriek and an answering trill of laughter. He is aware that the house represents a danger to him, and that there is one room in particular where he must not go; yet he comes as the vessel of some *warning*, and his errand must be done. He drifts steadily along, going equally without haste or hesitation, searching the long halls as one would study the channels of his own subconscious in a state of lucid dreaming.

He pauses at one point to study a deformity in the shadow of an urn, when that shadow springs to life and runs giggling to another room farther down the hall. This is followed by a larger form—one of the blue-jawed orderlies, with his cricket bat—breaking cover with an oath, and loping from behind a bust of the Marquis de Lafayette to a different side-room. The chase continues with the orderly, his companion, and the shadow—this little girl we have seen in the strait-jacket, arms thrust over her head and sleeve-ends flapping behind her—bolting from one room to the next, crisscrossing the hall in various combinations, with at least once, positively, the girl pursuing the two men. The three take little heed of Bertram, who trails them deeper into the house until the girl doubles back upon him, sprinting straight down the center-line of the hall. She has neared almost to the point of colliding with him when she cuts to her right and dives through a parting in two sliding doors, and Bertram follows her into what we will recognize as the ante-room to Arthur Ogden's study.

Here we find Frances Ogden sitting and the girl huddled now, panting, on her lap. An ancient footman called Mr. Faulk and a lady's maid called Miss Molloy stand pressed to the doors of Arthur's study, making no attempt to conceal what they are doing, which is eavesdropping on Miss Ogden's brothers.

YOU GUARD THE EGRESS, PAT.
WHICH? THIS ONE HERE?
HE MEANS, STAND BY THE DOOR.
OH. AYE. DON'T SPEAK GAELIC, DO I?

ALL RIGHT: TIME FOR YER BATH, MISS, AND NO MORE DELAY.
YOU'LL STOP THERE, MAN. AND YOU'LL STOW THAT CRICKET BAT, BEFORE I USE IT TO BREAK THE HEAD OF YOU.
APOLOGIES, GUVNER. THIS IS NONE O' YOUR AFFAIR.

I SHOULD SAY IT'S NONE OF YOURS, SIR, WHEN MY LADY BATHES.
UH? OH, NOT HER, GUVNER. 'AT ONE.
AH: MY MISTAKE. OFF YOU GO, LASS.

NO-NO, DEAR. IT'S ALL RIGHT.

YOU–BOTH OF YOU–OUT.
ONLY DOIN' OUR JOB, MISS–
AND WHO PAYS YOU TO FRIGHTEN THESE CHILDREN? MR. FAULK, SEE THEM OUT, PLEASE.
IF IT'S ONLY BATHING 'EM, WE'RE WELL UP TO THAT, GENTLEMEN.

AH-WELL. I'LL WISH YIZ LUCK, THEN.
AND YE'LL BE FIXIN' THAT LADY'S BROKEN NECK, TOO, ELSE I MISJUDGE YON CURTAIN-ROD.
UH?

NO-NO-NO–! YOU MUSTN'T DO THAT, MISS!
AYE, MUM. THEY DON'T RIG UP THE DRAPES WITH THIS IN MIND.

HOLD STILL, NOW. THERE'S A GIRL...
OH, MISS FRANCES–DO COME DOWN...!

THERE. GOT YOU.
DRAW THE CURTAIN OUT INTO THE ROOM, PLEASE, AND GATHER IT TIGHT. WE'LL SLIDE HER DOWN.

THAT'S IT. RIGHT DOWN TO THEM, DEAR. I'LL COME AFTER YOU.
WELL DONE, MISS! AN' YOU NEXT...

MY G–D–
I SAY–MISS OGDEN?

«SNAP!»

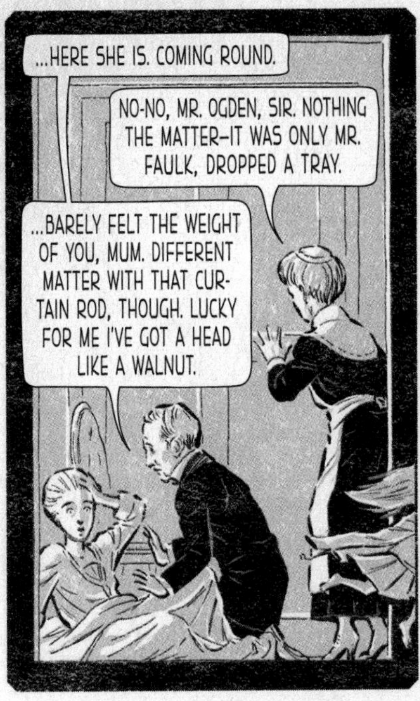
...HERE SHE IS. COMING ROUND.
NO-NO, MR. OGDEN, SIR. NOTHING THE MATTER–IT WAS ONLY MR. FAULK, DROPPED A TRAY.
...BARELY FELT THE WEIGHT OF YOU, MUM. DIFFERENT MATTER WITH THAT CUR-TAIN ROD, THOUGH. LUCKY FOR ME I'VE GOT A HEAD LIKE A WALNUT.

AH-AH: SLOWLY, MUM. MAKE SURE SHE'S ALL RIGHT, MR. FAULK–
YOU'LL HAVE TO EXCUSE ME–
MISS OGDEN–?

DIE SCHWESTER VON HERR OGDEN.

MISS OGDEN? TRENT SLOANE.

ALAIN? WHAT IS THIS?
SORRY?
...YOU DON'T KNOW ME, THEN.
WELL. ONLY BY NAME, IT'S TRUE. AND I REGRET IT'S TAKEN US THIS LONG TO MEET.

I'M AFRAID YOU CATCH US AT RATHER AN INOPPORTUNE–
ARE YOU VERY WELL, MISS?
BRINGEN SIE MORPHIUM, MISCHUNG SIEBEN PROZENT.
JAWOHL.

IS THERE A CHANCE, MISS OGDEN, THAT YOU AND I'D HAVE MET BEFORE THIS? I CAN'T THINK IT WOULD HAVE ESCAPED ME. BUT THEN, STRANGE TO SAY, I'M NOT ALWAYS THE AUTHORITY ON HOW I'VE SPENT MY DAYS, NOR WITH WHOM.
NO. I BELIEVE THAT'S TRUE.
BUT I DINE WITH YOUR BROTHER TONIGHT. IF YOU COULD JOIN US, I SHOULD BE GLAD OF THE CHANCE TO RENEW OUR FRIENDSHIP.

…OUR FRIENDSHIP, YES.
–AND YOU CAN ASK ME WHATEVER QUESTIONS YOU'D LIKE. I RATHER HAVE MY OWN QUESTIONS, ABOUT OUR ACQUAINTANCE.
MM? OH: YES.
GOOD. TONIGHT, THEN. IF YOU'LL JUST WAIT HERE, MR. VOGT WILL…WILL SEE TO YOU.
…IS THAT BARNES?

BERTRAM: YOU'RE TO BE UPSTAIRS, SON. DIDN'T THEY BRING YOU IN WITH THE OTHERS?

THE TRAIN IS DESTROYED, SIR. AND THE DEVICE YOU'VE BUILT. THERE'S BEEN A FIRE.
OH?
INSIDE THE HOUSE, TOO. THE MACHINES YOU'VE GOT HERE: THEY'RE ALL GONE.
THEY'RE–? NO, BERTRAM. THEY'RE RIGHT HERE, IN THE DINING HALL. I'LL SHOW YOU–
ACH–MEINHERR:
ICH HABE BRANDY, ABER KEIN MORPHIN–

«THOOOM!»

GEHEN SIE ZURÜCK! BRINGEN SIE WASSER! SCHNELL–UND TEPPICHE!
WO IST SLOANE?

JOHN...?

IT WASN'T HIM. ...MR. SLOANE?
JOHN WOULDN'T HAVE DONE THIS, IN HIS OWN HOME.

NO? THEN WHERE DO YOU SUPPOSE HE'S FLEEING, MISS OGDEN?

MISS OGDEN CATCHES UP TO HER BROTHER IN THE STABLES.
YOU'RE NOT RESPONSIBLE FOR THAT FIRE IN THE HOUSE, JOHN. ARE YOU?
NO.
MR. SLOANE WILL THINK YOU ARE, I'M SURE.
THEN YOU'VE MET HIM.
YES. I SEE, OF COURSE, WHAT YOU'D WARNED ME AGAINST.

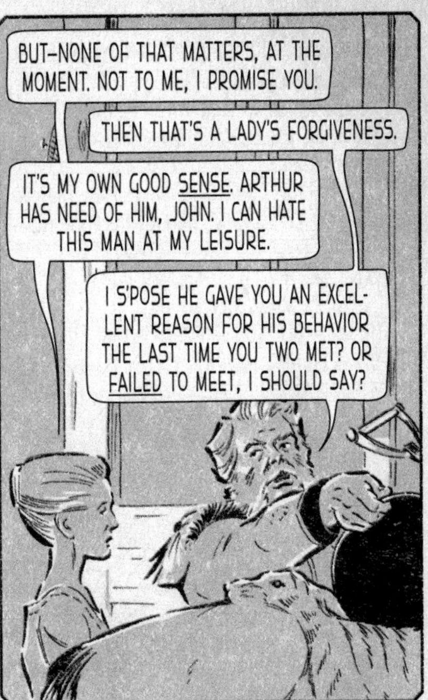
BUT–NONE OF THAT MATTERS, AT THE MOMENT. NOT TO ME, I PROMISE YOU.
THEN THAT'S A LADY'S FORGIVENESS.
IT'S MY OWN GOOD SENSE. ARTHUR HAS NEED OF HIM, JOHN. I CAN HATE THIS MAN AT MY LEISURE.
I S'POSE HE GAVE YOU AN EXCEL-LENT REASON FOR HIS BEHAVIOR THE LAST TIME YOU TWO MET? OR FAILED TO MEET, I SHOULD SAY?

HE APPEARED NOT TO REMEMBER ANY OF IT.
AH.
AND I BELIEVE HIM, JOHN. HE'S ANOTHER MAN, SOMEHOW.
YES, OF COURSE. THE ONE I KNEW WAS CALLED DUROV.

I MEAN, YOU RECALL HE DIDN'T JUST LEAVE INDIA–HE VANISHED UTTERLY. THERE WEREN'T EVEN RUMORS OF HIM–NOTHING–TILL HE APPEARED AT OUR DOOR. AND HE WOULDN'T HAVE DONE THAT–WOULD HE?–IF HE REMEMBERED A THING FROM INDIA? I DON'T SEE HOW HE COULD INTRODUCE HIMSELF SO GRACIOUSLY, AS HE'S DONE....
MM. I'M SURE HE WAS NOTHING SHORT OF CONVINCING.
BEHIND 'JEH, MISS.

NONE OF IT'S TO THE POINT, ANYWAY. IT'S ALL BECOME AWFULLY SIMPLE, JOHN. SEEING ARTHUR'S MADE IT THAT WAY. I FIND I DON'T CARE WHAT MR. SLOANE IS. AND, REALLY, I–
YOU DON'T CARE WHAT I AM. I KNOW. SO LONG AS WE CAN HELP ARTHUR.
I CAN'T SEE HIM LIKE THIS, JOHN. I THINK I'D MISJUDGED MY OWN STRENGTH. BUT YOU'VE PROMISED TO HELP HIM, HAVEN'T YOU?
I HAVE.

CHR–ST. HOW LONG'S IT TAKE YOU TO SADDLE A HORSE?
MR. RENTON SPOTTED TWO MEN RUNNING FOR THE WOODS, JUST AFTER THE CHARGES WENT.
ANYWAY, ARTHUR WON'T HAVE ME IN THE HOUSE WITH YOUR MR. SLOANE. WE'LL LEAVE FROM THE CITY, IF HE AND SLOANE CAN DECIDE WHERE TO SEND US.

IF THAT'S THE CASE, FAN, THIS'LL BE GOOD-BYE.
YES.
YOU THINK IT'S ALL MADNESS, I KNOW. ARTHUR AND HIS SHAMBHALA...
BUT I GAVE MY WORD TO YOU. WE'LL DO ALL WE CAN FOR ARTHUR. WHAT I THINK DOESN'T REALLY SIGNIFY.
...AND YOU WON'T HARM MR. SLOANE, WILL YOU, IF YOU DO SEE HIM AGAIN?

PERHAPS NOT.
...I MAY JUST HAVE TO HATE THAT MAN AT MY LEISURE, AS YOU SAY.

VI.

FOR ALL THE OTHER ADVANTAGES they may possess, the grounds of the old hotel are not a good place for a man to come under fire. And the fields south of the free-standing gate—where we find John Ogden and Mr. Renton booting their horses to a gallop—are particularly bad in this regard. If you were chasing, say, a pair of black-robed saboteurs across this lawn, and found they had left the woods full of gun-men to cover their retreat, you would appreciate very quickly the disadvantage of your position. And if Ogden has any doubts on this point, the little flash from the darkness ahead drives it home. Mr. Renton has just turned back to him with a few heated words apropos of their delay at the stables, when the bullet cuts past him, snicking up one of his shoulderboards.

The shot seems almost to have rolled him from his saddle, so quickly is the boy down at the horse's side. But he has only hopped down to use the beast for cover, and he hustles it along with one hand on its girth strap and the other pulling a pistol from his coat. Ogden has drawn his own trench-gun from its scabbard, meanwhile, and got down behind his horse's ears. He mutters a calming word to the horse and fires into the trees. Not that there is much chance of his hitting anything, but there is no sense either in letting his attackers draw a steady bead on him. Indeed, the half-dozen rifles and fowling pieces ahead pop off to little effect, and Ogden has crashed into the wood before any of them can fire again.

There is a moment's confusion, then, as horse and rider grope about in the dark for a trail, with figures darting at a crouch between the trees and bullets zipping past them at all angles. From somewhere ahead comes the snarling of an automobile engine: this, Ogden thinks, would be the black-robed men making for the cart-path. The rest of these figures are apt to be local woodsmen, hired and put here to frustrate pursuit, and he mustn't lose time to them. He spurs his horse toward the automobile and sees Mr. Renton weaving through the trees with apparently the same thought. The woodsmen have tied off their horses but, unwisely, they have left them bunched together, and Mr. Renton drops one of them with a pistol-shot as he cuts past the group. The remaining horses shriek and rear against their leads, and the woods behind Ogden fill with the enraged shouts of men and another crash of gunfire. He ought, he knows, to spray these other horses with shot from his unused barrel as he passes them. But he sheathes his weapon instead, and makes all possible speed after the fleeing car.

This lapse of Ogden's—or this stirring of humanity, if you like—tells quickly against him. The woodsmen are right up on their mounts, and the panic that might have scattered the horses only gives them greater impetus as they come thundering onto the path behind him. The horses have been standing idle for some hours, too, where Ogden's charger has already covered half a mile and is straining beneath his weight. Ahead of him, the black roadster has found its high gear, and as the cart-path gives way to a packed-earth road the car careens out of sight, round a curve. The men behind him will have to be dealt with before he can continue the chase.

Ogden pulls his horse away from the river and hugs the stone wall to his left, whistling ahead for Mr. Renton. The slope descending to the river makes this a blind turn, and it is fortuitously placed. Ogden reins his horse to a halt, wheels it around and steadies it with his knees, as he checks his pistols. Renton—good lad—has somehow heard his whistle and guessed his design. The boy checks his own horse, leaps from the saddle and scampers up into the brush on the hill. It is for Ogden now to wait, and to listen....

HYAHH–!

«CRACK-CRACK!»

«POP! POP!»

Thus for Major Ogden and the woodsmen. Now, I would like to describe a thrilling scene of chase for you, where our man closes on the roadster and trades fire with its drivers and so forth. But I am bound to say that outside the cinemas, a horse burdened with a rider can maintain a four-step gallop for a few miles at most. Ogden's hope had been to overtake the automobile quickly on the rutted paths south of the estate, but, failing this, he and Mr. Renton must settle into a long and dogged pursuit at a more practical trot. And they are still bouncing along hours later, with the sun dipping to the Hudson, and their prospects of overtaking the car dimming likewise with the miles.

Just south of Staatsburg, the road pulls away from the river again and zigzags through a hilly stretch of woods. Mr. Renton, by now, has ridden ahead and out of sight, and it is with some surprise that Ogden finds the boy's claybank mare tied up in these woods, absent its rider. The spring rains have filled the old moss-lined stone troughs that dot this stretch of road, and the horse has been left to drink at one of these troughs. Ogden guides his own horse toward Renton's and looks up to see the boy himself, sprinting down from a low rise ahead and waving his arms as though to ward him off. Renton greets his commander in a fierce stage-whisper: 'You and that beast,' he hisses, 'yeh make a bigger noise than the Mongol army.' He ties Ogden's charger off and slips away, back up the rise, without another word.

Ogden swings down from his horse, cups a drink out of the trough and laves water over his head. He ambles toward the wooded slope and finds he has pulled a shoot from an overhanging branch almost without thinking. The black-robed men will not be run down today, he thinks, and it is a long way to New York. While they rest the horses, he may as well address these manners of Mr. Renton, which have grown a bit wild from a want of tending.

He strips his shoot clean, then, as he walks, with thoughts of applying it to that purpose—that is, of applying his stick to the person of Mr. Renton. And after a climb of about a hundred paces he comes upon the boy again, lying prone this time and scanning over a ridge with his spyglass. Ogden can see, unaided, from this height, that the road has bent gradually west with the river, and that both cut back sharply after the rise. Where the path straightens again he sees a pair of dark figures pacing around what certainly looks like a stalled automobile. He calls for Mr. Renton's glass and raises it to his eye, allowing, privately, that the boy's instruction may have to wait.

'It's only the lanterns, I think, on the front,' Renton whispers to him. 'Either they can't get 'em lit, or the things're broke. But they must doubt they were followed this far, else they wouldn't be laggin' around like this.'

WE CAN HEAD 'EM OFF, AS Y'SEE, BUT I LAY YOU THAT CART STILL RUNS. SO WE GOT TO STEAL UP ON 'EM QUIET.

«SCHUNK!»

YOU'RE JOKING, AH? NEXT TIME MAYBE YE'LL JUST SEND A BUGLER AHEAD AND SAVE US THE BOTHER. ...MAJOR?
«POP!»

OI! I'M THE ONE FOUND 'EM! –AUGHH!

The driver of the automobile—as perhaps you have guessed—is one M. Polisson, a man of advanced age and of no little standing in this order of black-robed men, whom we first met at sea off the Cape Verde Islands. It had been M. Polisson's ill luck, on that occasion, to have been booted from the decks of the *Virago* by the man now pursuing him, and to have cracked the bones of his hip in the fall. He had been so impatient afterward to leave the islands by aeroplane that he had not allowed the breaks to set properly. And he did, as we recall, anticipate Major Ogden in the Argentine, walking then with the aid of a stick, and in no inconsiderable pain. Yet in place of the hoped-for reckoning with Ogden, M. Polisson was only bound by Captain Shaw and beaten with staves by the orphans of the place, till one of his eyes was struck out from his head.

Ordinarily, you would not think a man of M. Polisson's age and infirmities very well qualified to chase a commander of cavalry across the globe. But you will observe that this is no longer the mild and deliberate man who boarded the *Virago* six months ago. His many trials and leagues of travel have stoked an implacable hatred in him, and he at least views himself as perfectly fit to pursue and torment Ogden—Indeed, he would not let

the job fall to anyone else. And this is all well, except that something else has risen in him, too, since the Cape Verdes, a thing he might not have appreciated in its full force till now. For with Ogden thundering after him and earing back the hammers of his shotgun, we find Polisson's hatred shrinking beneath an overpowering *fear* of this man. Polisson winds the steering wheel and mashes the gear-box of his roadster, crying out some misremembered verse from the Book of Luke. In steadier hands, the car ought to have distanced Ogden, and easily. But I suppose his passenger points this out to him in vain.

...AND HOW WE LIKE THIS TURN OF EVENTS, HEY?
MY–. SOMETHING IS TERRIBLY WRONG...
AYE, YOU STATE A FACT, FATHER.

BAH.

VII.

40º 44' 57" N LAT | 73º 59' 04" W LONG

HOTEL FIRENZE, BACK TERRACE & GARDENS

. . .

MAY, 1918

ON THREE, NOW: UNO...DUE–
«POP!»
«POP!»
«CRACK!»
CHR–ST, WILL YOU LET HIM PICK THEM UP? WHERE'S THE SPORT IN THAT?
«SMASH!»
«SMASH!»
ALL RIGHT, THEN–GO ON–

WATCH IT, LAD!
GYAHHH–DIO!
«POP!»
«POP!»
«POP!»
«CRACK!»
EY! CAPTAIN!
UH? OH–HOLD UP, LADS– IT'S MR. RENTON...

WULL–HULLO THERE, SIR!
'ZIS MEAN MAJOR'S COME AS WELL?
MM. 'E'S NEXT-DOOR, AT THE EXPLORERS GUILD.

SAYS YE'R ALL WANTED, READIED FOR TRAVEL.
SEE IF WE CAN'T FIND YE SOMETHING BETTER TO SHOOT AT THAN THE HOTEL PLATE.

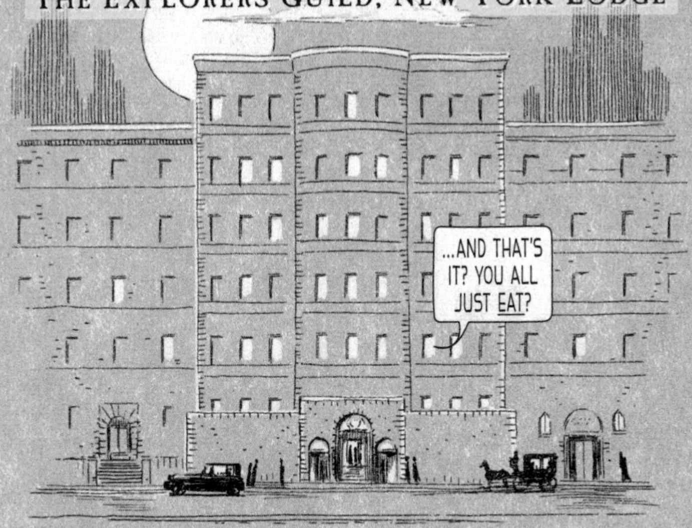
40º 44' 59" N Lat | 73º 59' 08" W Long
The Explorers Guild, New York Lodge
...AND THAT'S IT? YOU ALL JUST EAT?
Evening of 22nd May

A DINNER AND LECTURE, TONIGHT, AT THE GUILD, WITH A GOOD SHOWING OF THE NEW YORK MEMBERSHIP.
WELL: GENERALLY THERE ARE TOASTS–AND QUITE CLEVER, SOME OF THEM...

...AND THEN THE MEAL IS EXCELLENT, OF COURSE.
I TOLD YOU THAT'S THE CHINESE PREMIER...?
MISS HARROW HAS INVEIGLED HER WAY IN ON THE ARM OF CHARLES WHITMAN, GOVERNOR OF THE STATE.

WHERE ARE THEY GOING?
WELL. DON'T APPEAR TO BE MEMBERS. I SHOULD THINK NICHOLS IS SHOWING THEM BACK TO THE STREET. ...WHAT?

OH, WHAT A LOT OF NONSENSE, CHARLES. MEN HAVE BEEN SLIPPING IN THAT WAY ALL NIGHT. THERE'S SOMETHING INTERESTING HAPPENING BACK THERE, AND YOU'RE EITHER FIBBING TO ME OR YOU'RE TOO LAZY TO ASK.
DARLING, I PROMISE YOU–
OH, BE QUIET.

FOR ALL I KNOW YOU'RE NOT A MEMBER, EITHER, AND YOU FOUND YOUR LITTLE BUTTONS IN A CHRISTMAS CRACKER.
–BUT, YOU SAW THE PHOTOGRAPHS–
YOU AND YOUR BICYCLE IN SOME CLOUDS, YES–AND I TOOK YOUR WORD FOR IT YOU WERE ON KILI-MANJARO. WHAT A FOOL I'VE BEEN.

ANYWAY, I HAVEN'T HUNG ABOUT THESE OLD GOATS ALL EVENING JUST TO HEAR MORE TOASTS AND LOOK AT CHINAMEN.
EVELYN, PLEASE–
GOOD NIGHT, CHARLES. YOU MAY KEEP YOUR PASTE EARRINGS, TOO.

...THEY FOLLOWING US?
INDEED NOT, MA'AM. TRYING TO RECOVER YOUR EARRINGS, I SHOULD THINK.
MISS HARROW COLLARS A FOOTMAN ON HER WAY OUT OF THE ROOM.

GOOD. YOU'VE A MISS MAGUIRE, I THINK, SOMEWHERE IN THE HOUSEHOLD?
MAID OF THE BACKSTAIRS, MA'AM. YES.
GIVE THIS TO HER, PLEASE. TELL HER, HER COUSIN'S FRIEND, MISS HARROW, IS WAITING AT THE CLOAK-ROOM, AND WILL PRESENT HER COMPLIMENTS THERE.
VERY GOOD, MA'AM.

GENTLEMEN–I BEG YOUR PARDON–!
MR. SUTHERLAND? BLOCK THE DOORS, PLEASE. THESE MEN'LL HAVE TO TURN ROUND.
WE-ELL. COMFY IN 'ERE, WOT?

SIR: YOU'RE AWARE, THIS IS A PRIVATE CLUB, AND–WHY: YOU'RE HERE IN VIOLATION OF THE LAW, AREN'T YOU–?

WHAT IS THIS, GENTLEMEN?
FORCING THEIR WAY IN, SIR. IF YOU'D LOCK THE DOORS–
THANK YOU, NICHOLS.

...WELL. THERE WON'T BE ROOM TO SEAT ALL OF YOU.
WE'LL STAND.
THIS WAY, THEN.

HOLD ON. FEW MORE, FOR THE LADS.

THEY'VE BEEN COMING IN ALL DAY...

...FROM ALL OVER, MISS.

MR. BLAKE–FELLOW IN THE FANCY ULSTER–HE'S BEEN AT THE MAGIC LANTERN, THERE...
I S'POSE HE'LL MAKE A SHOW WITH IT ANY MINUTE.
AN' THERE'S THE LODGE PRESIDENT, MR. BIDDLE.

IF YOU TAKE A STATION, THERE, WHEN IT GOES DARK, YOU'LL HAVE A LOVELY VIEW O' THE PROCEEDINGS.
EVENING, ALL OF YOU. –*HRM.*
GENTLEMEN...YES, AND LADIES, THANK YOU–I'M TOLD WE'VE A FEW OF YOU NOW, G–D HELP US...
HRAWW-HRAWW!
BUT IF YOU'D ALL KINDLY TAKE YOUR SEATS...

ALL RIGHT, NED: LECTERN'S YOURS.
THANK YOU, MR. BIDDLE. LET US HAVE THE FIRST FRAME, PLEASE.

THERE WE ARE.
ST. PETERSBURG, RUSSIA...

Explorers Guild

INTERLUDE

The Search for Shambhala

- or -

A Smattering of Facts and Surmise touching upon this Search

EG

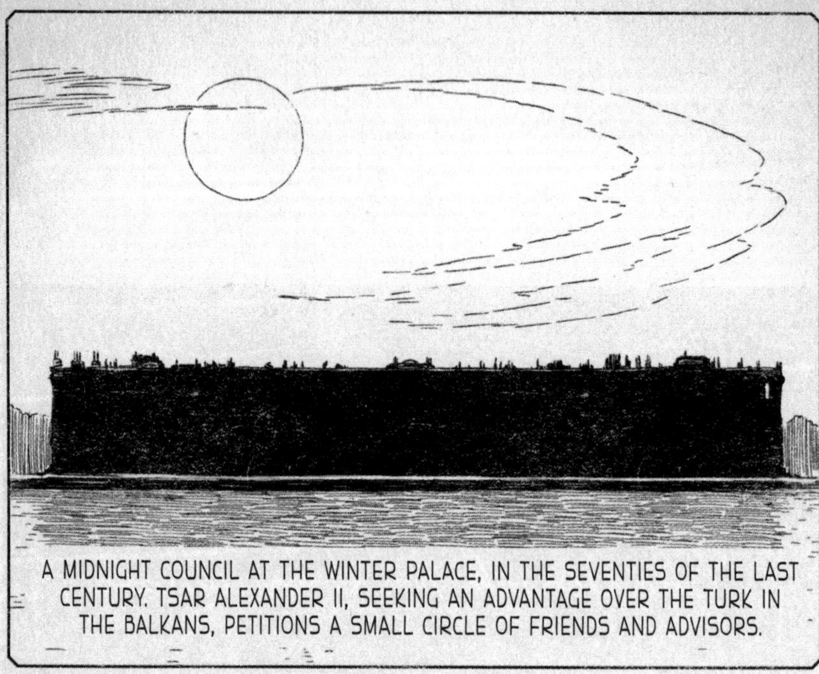
A MIDNIGHT COUNCIL AT THE WINTER PALACE, IN THE SEVENTIES OF THE LAST CENTURY. TSAR ALEXANDER II, SEEKING AN ADVANTAGE OVER THE TURK IN THE BALKANS, PETITIONS A SMALL CIRCLE OF FRIENDS AND ADVISORS.

AT DAWN, ELEVEN MEN AND TWO WOMEN SET OUT LIKE KNIGHTS OF CAMELOT ACROSS THE ASIAN CONTINENT...

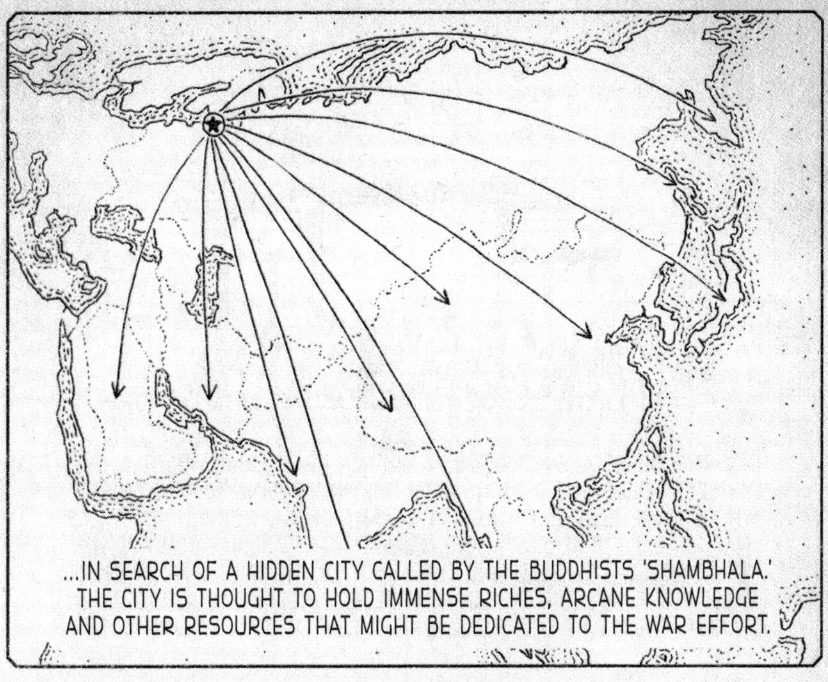
...IN SEARCH OF A HIDDEN CITY CALLED BY THE BUDDHISTS 'SHAMBHALA.' THE CITY IS THOUGHT TO HOLD IMMENSE RICHES, ARCANE KNOWLEDGE AND OTHER RESOURCES THAT MIGHT BE DEDICATED TO THE WAR EFFORT.

MANCHURIA
TIBET
AMONG THOSE COMMISSIONED TO FIND THE CITY IS ROMANIAN COUNT AND GENERAL GRIGOR SELESCU, HERO OF BALACLAVA.

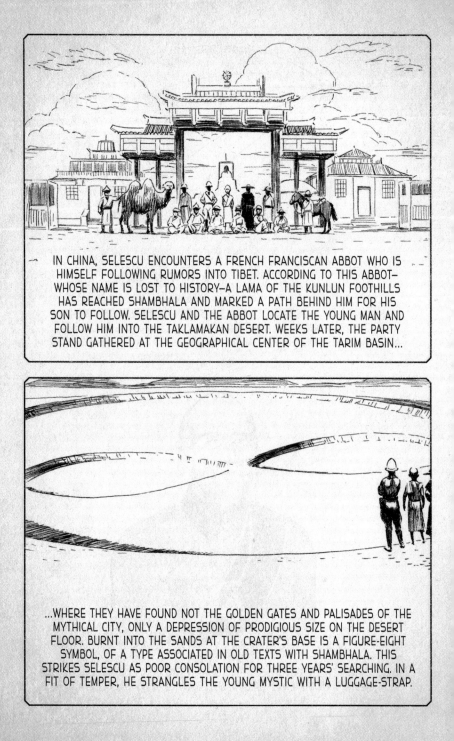

IN CHINA, SELESCU ENCOUNTERS A FRENCH FRANCISCAN ABBOT WHO IS HIMSELF FOLLOWING RUMORS INTO TIBET. ACCORDING TO THIS ABBOT—WHOSE NAME IS LOST TO HISTORY—A LAMA OF THE KUNLUN FOOTHILLS HAS REACHED SHAMBHALA AND MARKED A PATH BEHIND HIM FOR HIS SON TO FOLLOW. SELESCU AND THE ABBOT LOCATE THE YOUNG MAN AND FOLLOW HIM INTO THE TAKLAMAKAN DESERT. WEEKS LATER, THE PARTY STAND GATHERED AT THE GEOGRAPHICAL CENTER OF THE TARIM BASIN...

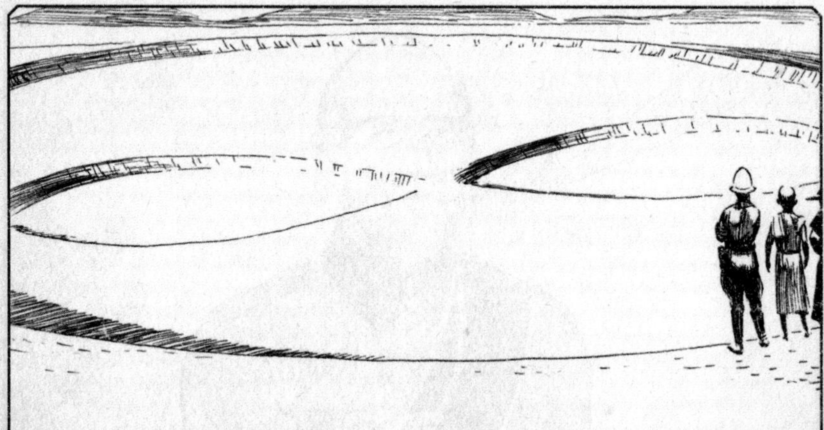
...WHERE THEY HAVE FOUND NOT THE GOLDEN GATES AND PALISADES OF THE MYTHICAL CITY, ONLY A DEPRESSION OF PRODIGIOUS SIZE ON THE DESERT FLOOR. BURNT INTO THE SANDS AT THE CRATER'S BASE IS A FIGURE-EIGHT SYMBOL, OF A TYPE ASSOCIATED IN OLD TEXTS WITH SHAMBHALA. THIS STRIKES SELESCU AS POOR CONSOLATION FOR THREE YEARS' SEARCHING. IN A FIT OF TEMPER, HE STRANGLES THE YOUNG MYSTIC WITH A LUGGAGE-STRAP.

SELESCU'S MOVEMENTS, AFTER THIS, ARE DIFFICULT TO TRACE, BUT HIS ASSOCIATION WITH THE FRENCH ABBOT CONTINUES. A TINTYPE PORTRAIT FROM THIS PERIOD SHOWS THE ABBOT SEATED WITH SELESCU'S SON, PRESUMABLY IN THE COUNT'S CASTLE ON THE BLACK SEA.

THE ABBOT IS THOUGHT TO HAVE TAKEN UP RESIDENCE HERE AFTER THE TAKLAMAKAN EXPEDITION. AND HERE, AS WE ARE TOLD, HE DEVOTES THE NEXT THREE DECADES TO HIS STUDIES OF CELESTIAL MOVEMENTS, AND TO THE FOUNDATION OF A NONRELIGIOUS ORDER OF UNKNOWN PURPOSE.

AT THE SAME TIME, THE SYMBOL DISCOVERED BY SELESCU'S PARTY IS
REPORTED SEEN IN THE KALAHARI DESERT, IN THE MARIANA ARCHIPELAGO,
IN THE AFRICAN JUNGLE AND IN THE TREE CANOPIES OF THE AMAZON...

...AND–LESS PLAUSIBLY, PERHAPS–PROJECTED ONTO CLOUDS OVER THE
TIBETAN PLATEAU AND GLOWING ON THE SURFACE OF THE NORTH SEA.

SEEMINGLY, NOT ONE OF THESE REPORTS IS BROUGHT BEFORE THE PUBLIC. THE ERA WITNESSES A STEADY DISAPPEARANCE—NOT TO SAY ORGANIZED SUPPRESSION—OF ALL ACCOUNTS RELATING TO THE SHAMBHALA 'MYTH.' SCHOLARLY AND SPIRITUAL TEXTS, TRAVEL DIARIES AND LETTERS OF CORRESPONDENCE GO MISSING, WHILE THEIR AUTHORS ARE DISCREDITED AND DEFROCKED. LAMASERIES ARE FIRED AND ARCHIVES LOOTED. JOURNAL AND NEWSPAPER ENTRIES ARE WITHDRAWN AND RECANTED.

THE TSAR'S CIRCLE FROM THE WINTER PALACE HAVE ALL PERISHED BY THE TIME AN ASSASSIN'S BOMB CLAIMS THE TSAR HIMSELF. AND THOUGH IT IS WHISPERED HERE AND THERE THAT SELESCU'S ABBOT AND HIS FOLLOWERS HAVE HAD A HAND IN THESE DEALINGS, NO ACCUSATION IS EVER BROUGHT OUTRIGHT, MUCH LESS PROVEN.

THIS, AT ANY RATE, IS THE SHAPE OF THINGS AS THE MILLENNIUM ARRIVES. AND MORE THAN A DECADE WILL PASS BEFORE THE SUBJECT OF SHAMBHALA IS REVIVED, IN THE HALLS OF THIS GUILD.

70° N LAT

IT IS THE FALL OF 1912. AMERICAN ADVENTURER ARTHUR OGDEN TRIES FOR THE NORTHWEST PASSAGE, REPORTEDLY ON A DARE FROM HIS COUSIN, THE BRITISH AMBASSADOR.

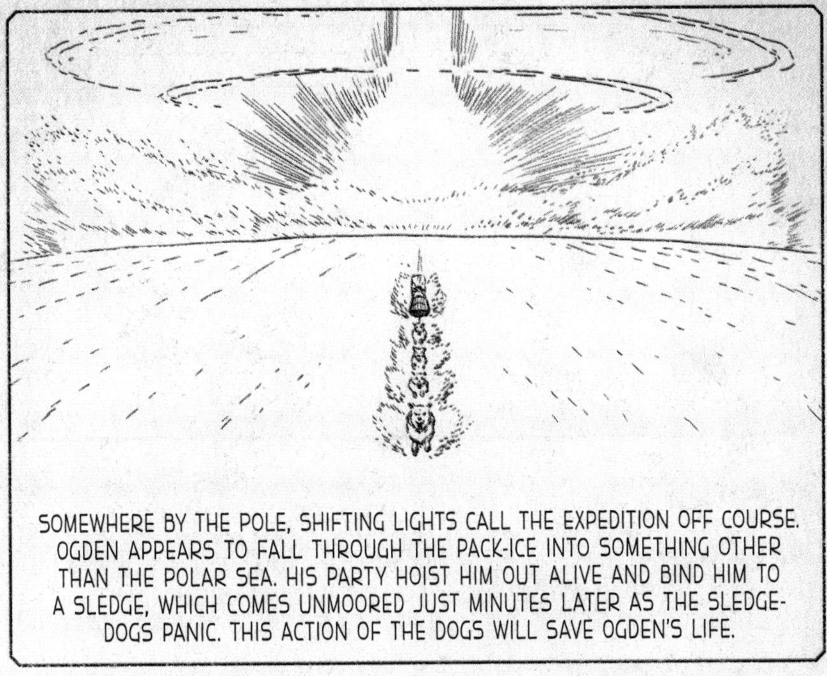
SOMEWHERE BY THE POLE, SHIFTING LIGHTS CALL THE EXPEDITION OFF COURSE. OGDEN APPEARS TO FALL THROUGH THE PACK-ICE INTO SOMETHING OTHER THAN THE POLAR SEA. HIS PARTY HOIST HIM OUT ALIVE AND BIND HIM TO A SLEDGE, WHICH COMES UNMOORED JUST MINUTES LATER AS THE SLEDGE-DOGS PANIC. THIS ACTION OF THE DOGS WILL SAVE OGDEN'S LIFE.

LA VILLE... JE L'AI VU...!
AT FORT DEFIANCE, OGDEN RAVES TO SENTRIES ABOUT GOLDEN TOWERS BENEATH THE ICE. HE PRODUCES A JADE ARTIFACT...

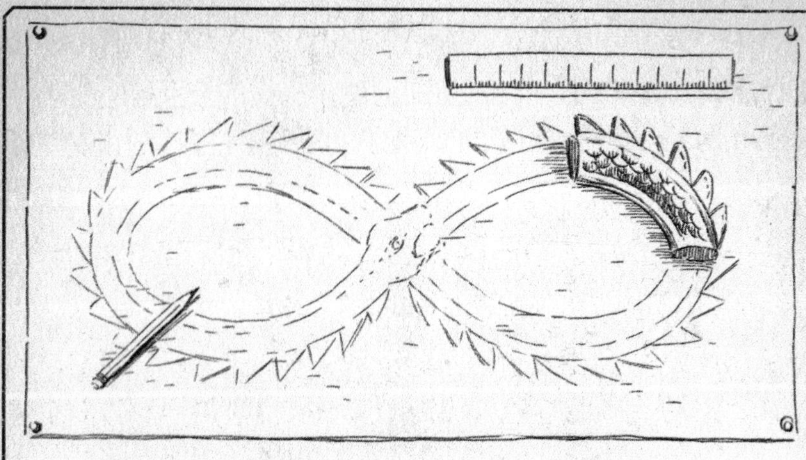
...THAT IS THOUGHT TO BE A FRAGMENT OF THE OUROBOROS, OR SERPENT DEVOURING ITS OWN TAIL. IN THIS CASE, THE FIGURE IS DOUBLED ON ITSELF, IN THE MANNER WE HAVE SEEN NOW IN VARIOUS FORMS, FROM OUTER MONGOLIA TO THE AFRICAN INTERIOR, AND FROM THE JUNGLES OF THE SOUTH TO THE ICE FIELDS OF THE NORTH.

WHAT, ULTIMATELY, TO MAKE OF THIS SYMBOL? IS IT A NATURAL OCCURRENCE, OR THE WORK OF AN INTELLIGENT HAND? A GRAFFITO—A MESSAGE, PERHAPS—LEFT BY SOME LOST CULTURE? OR CAN IT BE THAT WE'VE PENETRATED TO THE VERY GATES OF SHAMBHALA? HAS ONE OF OUR NUMBER, QUITE BY ACCIDENT, MADE THE DISCOVERY OF THE AGE...?

...YES. MR. OGDEN HAS VISITED THE UPPER STRATA OF SHAMBHALA AND RETURNED WITH PROOF OF HIS DISCOVERY. THIS IS OUR CONCLUSION.
AND WHERE'S HIS PROOF, NOW? I ASSUME YOU MEAN THIS BIT OF JADE...?
I'M AFRAID IT'S VANISHED. STOLEN FROM FORT DEFIANCE. MR. OGDEN WOKE WITHOUT ANY MEMORY OF IT.
HRM. THAT'S ALL OUR MR. BLAKE COULD TELL US, TOO.

WHAT ABOUT THESE SIGHTINGS IN THE AMAZON, AND MONGOLIA AND AFRICA–?
ALL VALID, SO FAR AS WE KNOW.
BUT WHAT ARE THEY? THIS FIGURE-EIGHT GLYPH–
MOSTLY, THEY ARE REPRODUCTIONS, BY HUMAN HANDS. THE RECORDS OF WITNESSES, IN SOME CASES.

THEY SEEM COMPELLED TO RE-DRAW THE FIGURE, OVER AND OVER, MANY OF THEM. THE LARGER OCCURRENCES–THE ONES MR. BLAKE REFERRED TO: THESE MARK ACTUAL SITES, WHERE THE CITY MAY HAVE BEEN FOUND AT ONE TIME.
SIGNPOSTS, THEN.
RATHER A SORT OF SCAR, OR A RESIDUE IT LEAVES WHERE IT HAS BEEN.
THEN YOU'RE TALKING ABOUT SEVERAL CITIES.

THERE HAS ONLY EVER BEEN THE ONE THAT WE KNOW OF. IT'S JUST THAT ITS LOCATION IS NEVER FIXED FOR VERY LONG.
YOU DON'T MEAN TO SAY–
YES. IT MOVES.

THE CITY HAS BEEN SHIFTING LOCATIONS FOR AS LONG AS WE'VE RECORDED HISTORY. AND LIKELY, FOR FAR LONGER THAN THAT.
THEN THESE CAN'T BE THE FIRST SIGHTINGS.
THEY'RE NOT. THE GREEKS SAW THE SAME THING AND CALLED IT *HYPERBOREA*. IT WAS *AZTLÁN* TO THE AZTECS, *OLMOLUNGRING* TO THE BÖN MYSTICS, *EL DORADO* TO THE SPANISH, *UTTARAKURU* TO THE INDIANS, *TIRNANOG* TO THE CELTS. THE TIBETANS ONLY GIVE US OUR MOST RECENT AND ACCURATE RECORD, SO WE ADOPT THEIR NAME.

PAH. PLACE THAT BIG, YOU SAY, JUST PULLS UP STAKES AND MOVES? B–LLOCKS, SIR.
WELL. IF IT DIDN'T, MR. OGDEN COULD HAVE BROUGHT US BACK TO CANADA AND POINTED THE PLACE OUT.
HE DID. IT WASN'T THERE.
BUT–WHAT IS IT, MR. SLOANE, AFTER ALL? ISN'T THAT THE QUESTION? SHAMBHALA, OR WHATEVER NAME YOU GIVE IT–WHAT'S INSIDE IT, I SHOULD LIKE TO KNOW?
I'M SURE I'VE HEARD THE SAME THEORIES YOU GENTLEMEN HAVE–
BUT YOU DON'T KNOW.
NO MORE THAN ANY OF YOU, I'M AFRAID.

HMPH. I SHOULD THINK THESE BLACK-ROBES OF MR. BLAKE'S KNEW SOMETHING–WHAT, NED?
YES: WHAT ARE THEY? THEY'VE GOT A NAME, I SUPPOSE?
I'VE HEARD THEM CALLED THE 'NOVITIATE,' OR *LES CANOTIERS*, IN REFERENCE TO THE HATS THEY WEAR. BUT THEY HAVEN'T GOT A NAME FOR THEMSELVES, THAT I'M AWARE OF. UNLESS MR. SLOANE KNOWS IT.

I SAY–AREN'T YOU ONE OF THEM YOURSELF, MR. SLOANE?
ME? I'M ONE OF YOU.
I WILL THANK YOU NOT TO BE GLIB ABOUT IT, SIR.

WE TAKE IT THEY'VE BEEN CONSTITUTED UNDER THIS FRENCHMAN TO LEARN WHAT THEY CAN ABOUT THE CITY, AND TO KEEP THE REST OF US FROM DOING THE SAME. IS THIS YOUR IMPRESSION, TOO?
AND BL–DY GOOD THEY'VE BEEN AT IT, WHAT?
WELL. YES. THEY'RE RATHER GOOD AT KEEPING THESE STRAY BITS OF INTELLIGENCE FROM US, AND PROMOTING A GENERAL IGNORANCE ON THE SUBJECT OF SHAMBHALA.
...BUT THEY ARE NOT OF THE CITY, YOU SEE. WHAT THEY DO, THEY DO OFF THEIR OWN BAT. THEY ARE ONLY APOSTATE CHRISTIANS, AFTER ALL, AND NO MORE PRIVY TO THE CITY'S SECRETS THAN YOU OR ME–BEYOND WHERE IT MIGHT BE FOUND, OF COURSE. AND WE ARE ON POINT OF LEARNING THAT OURSELVES.
ARE WE?
WELL–HE IS, ANYWAY.
YES, I DO WISH YOU'D LET US IN ON A BIT MORE OF YOUR OWN WORK, MR. SLOANE.

WELL, WE'VE BEEN GRASPING AT STRAWS FOR YEARS NOW. AND THEY ARE STILL, UPSTATE, RUNNING OUT VARIOUS LINES OF INQUIRY.
BUT I AM CONCENTRATING MY OWN EFFORTS ON A SINGLE SUBJECT. I BELIEVE HE CAN UNLOCK A GOOD BIT OF THIS MYSTERY FOR US.
OGDEN, YOU MEAN?
AH–NO. A BOY.
LIKE MR. OGDEN, I'VE REASON TO THINK HE'S BEEN INSIDE THE CITY. UNLIKE OGDEN, HE'LL SUBMIT TO TESTING.

AND WHAT SORT OF 'TESTS' DO YOU MEAN TO TRY ON HIM?
I'D SHOW YOU, ONLY WE'VE BEEN... INCOMMODED JUST NOW, AND BY THESE SELFSAME BLACK-ROBES.
HRM, YES. WE'D HEARD ABOUT A FIRE, UPSTATE. ALL'S WELL, I HOPE?
OH, YES. IF BY FIRE, YOU MEAN EXPLO-SIVES, DELIBERATELY SET; AND IF BY WELL, YOU MEAN MY WORK OF THE LAST YEARS RUINED BEYOND RECOVERY, AND MY ASSOCIATES DEAD AND MAIMED: THEN WE'RE ALL QUITE WELL, YES.
–I SAY, THOUGH–NO NEED TO GET SNAPPISH ABOUT IT–

–WITH THE FURTHER BENEFIT, THAT THERE IS ONLY ONE APPARATUS LEFT IN ALL THE WORLD FOR CONTINUING OUR WORK. AND THIS SITS IN THE HANDS OF MR. BLAKE'S BLACK-ROBES, IN ROMANIA.
AND WHAT ABOUT THAT, MR. SLOANE? YOU CAN'T MEAN TO GO THERE...?
I DO. WE VISIT YOU ON OUR WAY TO THE BLACK SEA.

–YOU MEAN THIS SELESCU FELLOW'S CASTLE?
–MIGHT WE HAVE A TALK WITH YOUR BOY, OURSELVES?
–IT'S THE VERY DEN OF THESE LIONS, ISN'T IT? YOU'LL GO RIGHT UP AND KNOCK, I SUPPOSE?

CAN'T VERY WELL GO TRAIPSING AROUND EUROPE NOWADAYS, CAN YOU, SLOANE? UNDERSTAND THEY'VE GOT A WAR ON, OVER THERE.
MAYBE MR. OGDEN COULD CALL IT OFF FOR YOU.

MR. SLOANE: THE KALACAKRA TEXTS DESCRIBE SHAMBHALA AS A CITY FOR THE SPIRITUALLY ELECT. FOR PILGRIMS ON THEIR WAY TO NIRVANA, YOU KNOW. IS THAT WHAT YOU ARE?
BECAUSE IF YOU'RE NOT, THE SAME WRITINGS PROPHESY AN AGE OF WAR AND MORAL DECLINE, SUCH AS WE ARE IN NOW, YOU'LL AGREE...

...AND IN THESE TIMES, THEY SAY, AN INVADER–A BARBARIAN–FINDS AND PENETRATES THE KINGDOM, NOT BY SPIRITUAL BUT BY SCIENTIFIC MEANS. AND IT IS HIS TRESPASS INTO SHAMBHALA THAT SIGNALS THE END OF OUR TIME ON THIS EARTH. IT IS THEIR VERSION OF THE APOCALYPSE.
I SEE. AND YOU'RE ASSIGNING ME THE ROLE OF 'BARBARIAN,' IN YOUR SCENARIO.

GENTLEMEN–I POINT OUT TO YOU THAT THE TRESPASS HAS ALREADY BEEN MADE. IT WAS OGDEN'S, YOU SEE. WE ARE ENDEAVORING TO RIGHT THIS WRONG, BEFORE MR. BLAKE'S WAR AND DECLINE GROW VERY MUCH WORSE.
YOU AGREE, THEN, THERE'S SOME INTER-RELATION BETWEEN OUR DEALINGS IN THIS CITY AND THE COURSE OF THE WAR?
WE CONSIDER IT A POSSIBILITY.
AND WE SAY IF THERE WERE A CHAIN OF EVENTS LEADING TOWARD ANY GREAT CATACLYSM, IT WAS BEGUN WITH MR. OGDEN'S INCURSION INTO THE CITY, AND IT WILL END WITH HIS RETURN.

WELL–WHICH IS IT, NED? IS IT SAFE FOR THEM TO PURSUE THIS WORK? OR, INDEED, IS IT VERY SAFE TO KEEP THEM FROM IT?
I CAN'T SAY. THOUGH NEITHER CAN THEY, NOR ANYONE ELSE. THAT'S RATHER THE POINT.
WHAT ABOUT THAT, SLOANE? YOU'VE GOT RATHER QUIET.

...WELL. IT'S NOT FOR ME TO PRONOUNCE ON THE TIBETAN SCRIPTURES. THEY DO STRIKE ME AS A BIT WILD. BUT THIS, I REALIZE, FROM A MAN WHO'S DESCRIBED TRAVELING CITIES TO YOU.
HRM. IT'S A GOOD POINT.
HAPPILY, FOR ME, THE CALCU-LATION IS PLAIN ENOUGH. MY EMPLOYER IS DYING. IF I CAN GET HIM TO THE CITY I BELIEVE HE CAN BE SAVED. THIS IS WHAT I'VE BEEN ENGAGED TO DO, AND THIS IS MY INTENT.

I SAY–IT'S ALL A BIT CAVALIER, ISN'T IT, FAVORING ONE'S OWN INTEREST OVER ALL THE REST? PARTICULARLY IF THERE'S ANYTHING IN THIS APOCALYPSE BUSINESS.
IT'S NO GOOD RUNNING OFF HALF-COCKED, IN ANY EVENT. TOO MANY UNKNOWNS, AND A DEAL TOO MUCH RISK ALL ROUND. YOU'LL SEE, MR. SLOANE, WHERE I CAN AUTHORIZE NO ACTION ON THIS BODY'S BEHALF, TILL WE'VE HAD A GOOD LOOK INTO THINGS.

I DON'T EXPECT YOU CAN, MR. BIDDLE. BUT YOU SHOULDN'T THINK WE'D WAIT FOR YOU, EITHER.
MR. OGDEN HOPED WE MIGHT FIND SOME USEFUL KNOWLEDGE HERE, OR SOME HELP AT LEAST IN ALL THE TRAVEL AND TRANSPORT, SO I'VE COME AT HIS REQUEST. BUT HE IS EQUALLY PREPARED TO MOVE FORWARD WITHOUT YOUR BACKING.
OH? WHAT ABOUT OUR OPPOSITION? HOW WOULD HE DEAL WITH THAT?
HE'D DEAL WITH IT THROUGH MYSELF, MR. BIDDLE.

ANY OPPOSITION, BEYOND THE THEORETICAL, FROM THIS OR ANY OTHER BODY: THIS BECOMES MY CONCERN.
I...SEE.

THERE YOU ARE: TALK TO HIM. I'M AFRAID I DON'T HAVE THE LUXURY OF DEBATING THIS ANY FURTHER.
I UNDERSTAND AND ACCEPT YOUR POSITION, GENTLEMEN. AND I GIVE YOU ALL GOOD EVENING.

BEGGING YOUR PARDON, SIR?

THAT'S YOU, IS IT? MAJOR?
COME A BIT INTO THE LIGHT, I CAN'T–
AH: MISS MAGUIRE. I WAS TOLD WE MIGHT FIND YOU HERE. AND HOW ARE YOU, DEAR?

OH: TOLERABLY WELL, SIR, FOR THE SHAPE I'M IN, I THANK YOU.
AND YOUR...YOU'D A DAUGHTER, DIDN'T YOU, IN INDIA–
AH! HE REMEMBERS, BLESS HIM! AYE, SIR, SHE'S QUITE WELL ALL THANKS TO YOU, AND UPSTAIRS SAWIN' LOGS AT THE MOMENT–THOUGH I'VE A MIND TO WAKE HER NOW YOU'RE HERE–HER VERY PRINCE COME IN FROM THE EAST!

SEEM TO RECALL YOUR SUFFERING A GOOD DEAL, ON THAT CHILD'S ACCOUNT.
ME? OH...NO, SIR. NEVER A MOMENT OF IT. AND IF WE TWO DIDN'T HAVE WORSE, THERE'S YOU TO THANK, ISN'T THERE? NOT AN EVENING PASSES, SIR, BUT WE RECOMMEND YOU TO THE ALMIGHTY, AND I BELIEVE YOU'LL FIND HIM WELL-REHEARSED IN YOUR ACCOMPLISHMENTS, FAR OFF AS THAT MEETING-DAY WILL BE.

WELL. I THANK YOU FOR THAT.
...AND WE TRY, AS A PRACTICAL MATTER TOO, SIR, TO KEEP AN EAR COCKED FOR ANY USEFUL BIT OF INTELLIGENCE HERE-ABOUTS. I HAD SOME TO TELL YOU TONIGHT, YOU KNOW, ON THE SCORE OF SHAM PRIESTS AND OLD TIBETAN WRITINGS AND LORD KNOWS WHAT ELSE–

–FAN MENTIONED IT, YES–
–BUT I SEE YOU'VE ALREADY HEARD MORE THAN I'D BEEN ABLE TO GUESS MYSELF. I ONLY ADD THAT THE MEN WHO TOOK YOU INTO MR. BIDDLE'S STUDY TONIGHT, SIR, ARE NOT THE FOOLS AND DEBTORS AND BLOWN BLADDERS OF OUR OUTER ROOMS. THOSE ARE GENTLEMEN, SIR, LETTERED AND TRAVELED, AND SUCH WARNINGS AS THEY GIVE YOU, YOU MAY TAKE SERIOUSLY.

I PLAN TO, MISS MAGUIRE. FOR THE MOMENT, THOUGH–
–BUT YOU'RE OFF ABOUT YOUR BUSINESS, AREN'T YOU? AND I WOULDN'T KEEP YOU, SIR, NOT FOR WORLDS. QUITE ENOUGH JUST TO SEE YOU, AND TO SEE YOU WELL, AS I SHALL BE GLAD TO TELL FLOSSY.
YOU'LL REMEMBER ME TO HER, THEN?

OF COURSE, SIR. GOD KEEP YOU ALL, NOW.
...AND WHEN YOU MEET OUR FRIENDS IN THE BLACK GOWNS, YOU MAY LET 'EM KNOW THEY'RE NOT HALF SO CLEVER AS THEY MAKE OUT TO BE, HM? NOR THE REST OF US HALF SO DIM.

MISS HARROW, MEANWHILE, PUTS HER CASE TO OGDEN'S DRAGOONS.
...BUT YOU WON'T RUN THE BLOCKADE IN ANYTHING HALF SO POSH, YOU KNOW.
THEY'RE STOPPING EVERYTHING NOW. YOU'LL BE BACK ON ANOTHER TRAMP STEAMER, DINGIER AND DRAFTIER THAN THE FIRST. JUST YOU SEE IF IT ISN'T SO.

GENTLEMEN–PLEASE: MADAME'S COAT–
AYE, GIVE IT 'ERE–
NO–I REALLY MUST ASK–*OOF!*
NEVER MIND WHAT YE'LL ASK. I SAYS GIVE IT.

WHEEST, JACKIE. LADY'S SPEAKING.
YOUR FRIEND THE DUKE, THOUGH: TRAVELS IN STATE, DOES HE?
OH, YES. BY AIR, YOU SEE. WITH HIS COOKS AND STEWARDS–AND THESE CUNNING LITTLE BALINESE MASSEUSES WHO CAN POSITIVELY RAISE THE DEAD WITH THEIR TOUCH...YOU'LL SEE, HE RETAINS THE STAFF OF A FLOATING HOTEL.
AH: HERE'S MR. SLOANE.

...MISS HARROW. YOU'VE GOT OFF SHIFT.
THEN, YOU NOTICED.

I'VE BEEN GOING ABOUT THE PLACE DRESSED AS A MAID, LIKE I DID IN 'MAN AFTER MIDNIGHT.'
I'D HAVE INVITED YOU TO SIT, THOUGH IT WASN'T MY PLACE, YOU UNDERSTAND.
YES, OF COURSE. I HEARD IT ALL ANYWAY, YOU KNOW. AND I TELL YOU: WHATEVER YOU'RE PLANNING, MR. SLOANE, IT WON'T DO.

AND HOW IS THAT?
YOUR TRANSPORT, I MEAN. I'VE BEEN NOSING AROUND OUTSIDE AS WELL.
YOUR AGENTS HAVEN'T HAD ANY LUCK GETTING A SHIP, HAVE THEY? OR NOT ONE THAT CAN GET YOU ALL QUIETLY ACROSS.

AND HOW WOULD YOU GET OVERLAND THROUGH EUROPE, ANYWAY–PARTICULARLY NOW, WITHOUT THE GUILD BACKING YOU? I'D SAY YOU'RE STUCK.
WE ARE QUITE CAPABLE OF MAKING OUR OWN ARRANGEMENTS, MISS. I THANK YOU FOR YOUR CONCERN.

OH? WHAT ABOUT TRANSPORT FOR ALL OF YOU, BY AIR, LEAVING TO-NIGHT? ALL PERFECTLY LEGAL AND FREE OF CHARGE, AS IT HAPPENS. WHICH OF YOU CAN ARRANGE THAT?
INTERESTING. WALK ME TO THE STOOP, WOULD YOU? I BELIEVE THESE MEN ARE WAITING ON MR. OGDEN.
OH–*EHH*, YES. EXCUSE US.

I MIGHT NOT HAVE THOUGHT YOU'D BE SO READY TO TAKE UP WITH THESE MEN AGAIN, MISS HARROW. AND SO QUICKLY. PERHAPS I'VE GOT THE WRONG IDEA OF YOUR FIRST CROSSING WITH THEM.
I DON'T KNOW WHAT YOUR IDEA OF IT IS, MR. SLOANE.
BUT I WOULD BEAR A GOOD DEAL WORSE, IF IT BROUGHT ME AT ALL NEARER TO YOUR CITY.

ANYWAY, I DON'T INTEND TO TRAVEL WITH THEM ON THE SAME FOOTING AS LAST TIME.
NO, OF COURSE. THOUGH YOU MAY FIND YOU WERE SAFER AMONG THEM AS THEIR CAPTIVE.
WELL. WE'LL JUST HAVE TO SEE.
AND YOU KNOW, I WOULDN'T THINK YOU'D BE SO KEEN YOURSELF TO TAKE UP WITH JOHN OGDEN. MM?

NO. QUITE RIGHT. THOUGH I'D BEAR A GOOD DEAL WORSE, AS YOU SAY.
I SUPPOSE WE'LL HAVE TO LOOK OUT FOR ONE ANOTHER, MR. SLOANE.
MAJOR SAYS WE GO DIRECT FROM HERE, MISS, FOLLOWIN' YOU. UNLESS–

...WE'VE NO OBJECTION TO THIS, DO WE, MILOR'?
AN' WHAT IF HE DID, JACK?

WHY: IT'D JUST ABOUT SPOIL THE TRIP, WOULDN'T IT, IF WE HAD TO MUDDLE THROUGH WITHOUT HIS HIGHNESS?
OH, COME, YOU BOYS. YOU'RE ON THE SAME SIDE NOW. I WON'T TAKE ANY OF YOU ANYWHERE IF YOU'RE GOING TO BORE ME WITH THIS.

WELL. JUST YOU WAIT HERE, MUM, WHILE WE COLLECT THE KITS AND LITTLE BARNES. MAJOR'LL BE OUT PRESENTLY.
MR. BUCHAN, YOU STAY ON AND WATCH THESE TWO. GIVE US TEN MINUTES.

...YOU HEARD THEM MENTION THIS IDEA THAT...IF THE WRONG MAN WERE TO BREACH THE CITY, IT MIGHT GO RATHER BADLY FOR ALL OF US.
MM. BUT THERE WAS HARDLY NEWS IN THAT, WAS THERE. I'VE READ THE OLD TEXTS, AS I SUSPECT YOU HAVE.
I SEE. AND YOU'RE REALLY THAT ANXIOUS FOR THE END OF THE WORLD, MISS HARROW?
NO. ONLY CURIOUS TO KNOW WHICH OF YOU IS RIGHT. AND I MEAN TO SEE FOR MYSELF, AFTER ALL.
COME....

OH, THEY CAN TRACK PEOPLE, CAN'T THEY, YOUR FRIENDS? LET THEM CATCH UP. IT'S JUST A BIT THIS WAY.
MISS–?
NO, WE'RE TO WAIT–
–BUT YOU WON'T LET ME WALK ALONE, WILL YOU?
AND YOU, TOO, MR. SLOANE. COME. I'LL INTRODUCE YOU TO FRIENDS OF MINE, AND HAVE A TALK WITH CHARLES EDWARD. ANYWAY, IT'LL BE GREAT FUN.

END *of* BOOK THREE

IN BOOK FOUR:

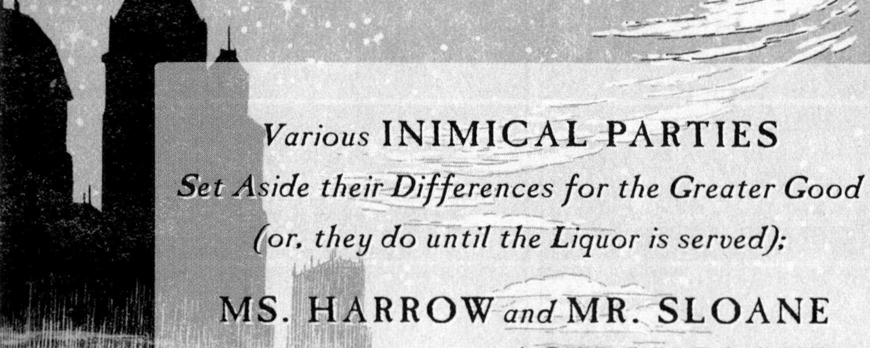

Various INIMICAL PARTIES
Set Aside their Differences for the Greater Good
(or, they do until the Liquor is served);

MS. HARROW *and* MR. SLOANE
Meet Fatefully on the ASTRAL PLANE;

M. Polisson Returns PARTWAY
from the DEAD; *while*

The EUROPEAN ARISTOCRACY
bid us Farewell, in Song; and

The ABBOT *Disproves that Adage*
that No Man is an Island.

— Also —

Flaming OCTOPODES

Launched from the Woolworth Building;

Proof of the Volatility of Hydrogen Gas;

— *And* —

An All-Round ESCALATION *of*

INTRIGUE *and* MAYHEM.

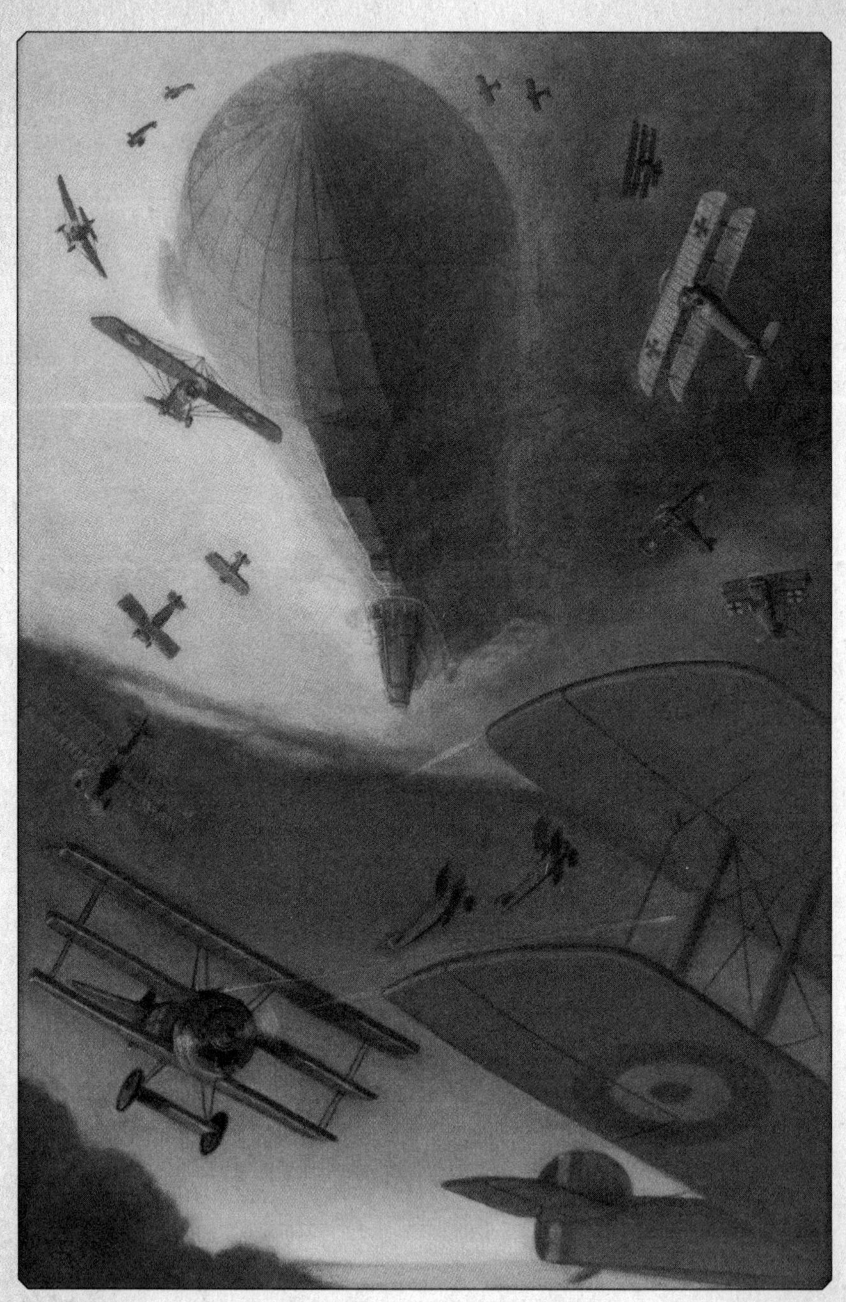

THE *LUFTSCHIFF METTERNICH*,
HARRIED OVER THE BLACK SEA.

BOOK FOUR

- of Five -

I.

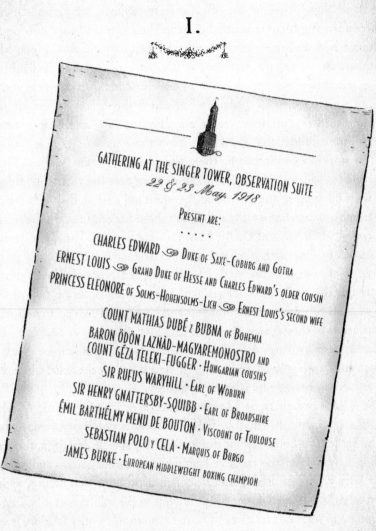

GATHERING AT THE SINGER TOWER, OBSERVATION SUITE
22 & 23 May, 1918

PRESENT ARE:

. . . . .

CHARLES EDWARD — DUKE OF SAXE-COBURG AND GOTHA
ERNEST LOUIS — GRAND DUKE OF HESSE AND CHARLES EDWARD'S OLDER COUSIN
PRINCESS ELEONORE OF SOLMS-HOHENSOLMS-LICH — ERNEST LOUIS'S SECOND WIFE
COUNT MATHIAS DUBÉ z BUBNA OF BOHEMIA
BARON ÖDÖN LAZNÀD-MAGYAREMONOSTRO AND
COUNT GÉZA TELEKI-FUGGER · HUNGARIAN COUSINS
SIR RUFUS WARYHILL · EARL OF WOBURN
SIR HENRY GNATTERSBY-SQUIBB · EARL OF BROADSHIRE
ÉMIL BARTHÉLMY MENU DE BOUTON · VISCOUNT OF TOULOUSE
SEBASTIAN POLO Y CELA · MARQUIS OF BURGO
JAMES BURKE · EUROPEAN MIDDLEWEIGHT BOXING CHAMPION

MISS HARROW RAISES HER HAND to knock, but hears the low murmur of voices and the hiss of a clarinet recording from within the room, and thinks better of announcing her arrival. She passes through the door, down a hallway of mirrored walls and black marble columns, into a tobacco-fogged parlor where guests of the Duke lounge and slump and totter about in advanced states of drunkenness. The few wives who remain here lie sleeping in untidy heaps, while the mistresses and spongers and party-crashers dance listlessly in pairs and trade unmannerly bits of gossip. None, it seems, are of concern to the men, who sit puffing on cigars or staring blankly at the liquor in their glasses, quiet but for the exchange here and there of a remark and a throaty chuckle. Here, Miss Harrow reflects, are the last sons of Europe's noble and royal houses, idling away their evening in exile, in the provisional luxury of a rented hall, in a nation they all disdain; while across the Atlantic their subjects rid the world comprehensively of one another. And she must concede with a little shudder that she knows all of these men.

The storklike gentleman by the gramophone is Count Mathias Dubé z Bubna of Bohemia. The Count stands bent over the turntable, fidgeting with his glasses and following the spinning shellac disk obsessively, as though anxious lest a moment's quiet should break in upon the music. Six times, when she and Count Mathias were living in Paris, Evelyn had consented to dine with him at Les Ambassadeurs; six times she forgot the appointment. On the sixth, the Count had proceeded with dinner as though she really were seated across from him, ordering two *entrées*, two *plats*, two bottles of champagne and so forth. And he'd conducted a conversation throughout the meal that was charming at first but sank gradually into a string of heartfelt pleas, angry recriminations, sarcastic retorts and howling sobs. Or so Evelyn had heard weeks later, while dining at Les Ambassadeurs with Saxe-Coburg.

Near Count Mathias, on a low cushioned bench, sit Sirs Rufus Waryhill and Henry Gnattersby-Squibb, Earls of Woburn and Broadshire, respectively. Sir Henry holds several dozen slips of paper in his thick fingers—betting tickets from the races at Empire City, earlier today—and reviews these with a look of dismay and disbelief for insights they refuse, apparently, to yield. Meanwhile, Sir Rufus attends to the rolling and re-rolling of a cigarette in what he conceives to be the American frontier fashion, learnt from the day's outing at the cinema. Both men are heirs to dwindling fortunes and acreage, and both were rivals for Miss Harrow's hand before the war. Their contest had drawn to a head on a rotting balcony at Boodle's, where they'd bellowed and grabbed and slapped ineffectually at one another in a sort of living allegory of the aristocracy in decline, till Sir Henry had spotted Miss Harrow leaving on the arm of a third gentleman, whereon the earls had shaken hands; and they have been all but inseparable since.

The third gentleman, as ill luck would have it, is represented next to them in the person of Émil Barthélmy Menu de Bouton, the taciturn Viscount of Toulouse. The Viscount stands against a mantel with his arms folded over his chest, and he may or may not notice when Evelyn flits by without a word for him. A bit farther on, Sebastian Polo y Cela, Marquis of Burgo, has cornered Saxe-Coburg on the subject of the rumored marriage between Viscount Émil and the Archduchess Margarita von Stromberg. Never *mind* the monster they create politically, he is saying—It is a torment to him that a being so *lovely* should be dragged off into wedlock, and so young: a *torment*, he repeats, but vaguely, as though undecided whether the injured young being were the Archduchess or the Viscount.

Beside this pair, Count Géza Teleki-Fugger paces back and forth beneath the steep slope of the windows, biting his lip and murmuring to himself. He is rehearsing a confrontation with his twin brother, Asbòth Teleki-Fugger, who has accepted a military commission from Franz Josef and is hanging about the family estate at Keszthely, plotting no doubt to rob Count Géza of his portion of the inheritance, or whatever might remain of it once the killing and the political realignments are finally done.

And there, on the balcony, peering through a pair of field glasses, stands Teleki-Fugger's cousin, the Baron Ödön Laznàd-Magyarmonostro, an aging bachelor who had been one of the louder voices in favor of war on the British and French after Sarajevo. He has since become one of the conflict's bitterest opponents, it having dumped him ungraciously with his friends in these hovels of the New World and put off the grouse hunt for three seasons running.

Yes: here are the fading stars who once made up the eternal constellation of Old Europe; and Miss Harrow regards them coldly. They are no more to her than dissipated old ghosts, mooning over their lost kingdoms and revolving their pointless schemes, persisting in a world that had evolved past their comprehension. She regrets, now, having rushed ahead of her own party, and having left Mr. Buchan in the lobby on the pretext of adjusting her toilette. She will be glad of the soldiers' intrusion now, if only to rattle these sleepers awake, and to make them confront something real and ineluctable in the present.

Till then, she is content to wander idly through the Duke's hired rooms, accepting nods from one gentleman and another and taking drinks from the passing trays. She stops by a viperish group of ladies and shows them her back until they quit the room with a *harumph*. Really she is only studying a tapestry she recognizes from the Duke's apartments at Veste Coburg. And that bench, too—the one supporting the earls: this was once a pew in a Bavarian country church, as Saxe-Coburg was fond of telling her. It had been carried out by a Protestant mob in the Thirty Years' War, and borne along over centuries of upheaval to a flea market in Batavia, where the Duke's great-uncle Fritz, ambassador to the Dutch East Indies and collector of rarities, had found it and added it to the family estate, along with…with actually a good deal of the rugs and paintings and antique weaponry surrounding Evelyn now. Even the stone flags around the hearth have been imported. The Duke has not just hired these rooms, she thinks—he has *stopped time* in them. Here, he and his fellows-in-exile can sit and smoke and dream they are only waiting out the war till the madness overseas should run its course, till their children wake to the enormities they have done and cry for a return of the Old Order. It seems the Duke has taken great pains lest his dreamers be woken, bringing Veste Coburg piecemeal over the Atlantic, right down to the porcelain chamber pot with its chain of pink-cheeked cherubs decorating the rim, which Sir Rufus holds uncertainly now in his upturned hand like a second-rate Hamlet who has forgotten his climactic lines.

And who can say but they're not all better off like this, floating high over the city in these rather harmless pantomimes, secure in the idea that there is still some place for them—some *use* for them—in the dark world below? Maybe they could even be exhibited to the public, after a time….

Miss Harrow is in the midst of these reflections when a young lady's scream and a crash of glass announce, unmistakably, the arrival of the Fifth Dragoons in the next room. She sets off toward the disturbance, but it seems the crash has started the men in the room from their own dim trains of thought and, looking up, they all seem to notice her at once. Drinks are mis-drunk, then, and spouted forth through royal noses. Drowsing women are rolled from laps. The English earls give simultaneous gasps, then turn to growl murderously at one another. Evelyn is dodging a sweeping, courtly bow from Viscount Émil, when she collides with Saxe-Coburg himself.

MISS HARROW!
-OH-
–I SAY! WE'D NO IDEA YOU WERE IN NEW YORK. IT'S BEEN–WELL SINCE COWES, HASN'T IT?
AND–OF COURSE WE'VE ALL...
–YOU'VE BEEN HEARING THE STRANGEST RUMORS, I KNOW.

-WHY, YES-
WHATEVER YOU'VE HEARD, CHARLIE: I PROMISE YOU I'VE DONE MUCH WORSE.
WHY: JOVE! I BELIEVE YOU HAVE! AH–YOU'RE DELIGHT-FUL, MISS HARROW.

COME, I'LL INTRODUCE YOU TO–
NO, YOU'LL NOT.
-MM?
LISTEN, CHARLIE: I NEED TO BEG A FAVOR, AND I'M IN AN AWFUL RUSH...

OOH– CAREFUL, DEAR.

AH–THEY SPEAK! HERE IT IS...
'GREETINGS, THOU FILTHI-
EST AND FATTEST OF ALL
POSSIBLE BARONS...'

VILLAINS! MISCREANTS!
I'D RATHER NOT KNOW,
BUT: WHAT IS HE DOING?

OH, SOME OTHER PARTY HAVE SET UP IN THE
WOOLWORTH BUILDING. ÖDÖN, POOR FELLOW,
SENT OVER A CASE OF BOLLINGER THINK-
ING THEY MIGHT BE A LOT WE KNEW. THEY
ANSWERED THIS MORNING WITH A CRATE OF
OCTOPUSES–DEAD ONES–LONG-DEAD–CAN'T
IMAGINE HOW THEY'D HAVE COME BY THEM.
STILL CAN'T GET THE...BOUQUET OF
THEM OUT OF HERE, YOU NOTICE.
RATHER A GRUESOME SHOW. AND HE'S
BEEN KEEPING HIS VIGIL EVER SINCE.

BOLSHEVIKS! REVEAL
YOURSELVES!
SORRY: YOU WERE SAYING,
ABOUT A FAVOR...?

...CAN'T SAY WHAT THE DUKE'S FRIENDS MIGHT HAVE BROUGHT IN FOR THEMSELVES. AT THE BAR WE'VE ONLY GOT CHAMPAGNE, IN HONOR OF THE KING'S NAME-DAY.
MISSED THAT, DIDN'T YOU? THAT WAS APRIL.
THE HUNGARIAN KING'S, SIR
AH.

...AYE, MUM. GUESTS OF THE DUKE'S.
WELL THAT'S THE DUKE'S COUSIN, GRAND DUKE OF HESSE. I THINK HE'D KNOW IF YOU WERE FRIENDS OF CHARLES'S.
S'POSE IT'LL HAVE TO DO, THEN. LET'S HAVE YER BEST CHAMPAGNE.

AN' WHAT'S THAT?
GETTING YOU YOUR CHAMPAGNE, SIR.
HA-HAA! NO I MEANT WE'RE TAKING YOUR CHAMPAGNE, LADDIE.

MR. BUCHAN? MR. RENTON? BACK THERE, AND START HANDING OUT BOTTLES.
BUT THAT'S GOOD!
JACKIE, YOU SAW THIS? HE GIVES ME THE GLASS!

YOU CAN STOP THERE, YOU.
CAN'T VERY WELL COME IN LIKE MARAUDERS, CAN YOU–AND NO INVITATION–AND GO LOOTING THE PLACE–

DON'T THINK? WELL, YOU STAND THERE, MUM. SEE IF THAT AIN'T WOT 'APPENS.
AND YOU–CROSS ME WITH THAT STICK AGAIN, GRANDFATHER. GO ON.

...NO-NO, I'M ONLY SAYING, THE ENVE-LOPE'S RATHER FRAGILE, YOU KNOW. IF YOU WERE TO PUNCTURE IT–
BUT, WHY WOULD I DO THAT?
NOT THAT YOU WOULD–NO, OF COURSE. BUT IF IT HAPPENED–IT'S FULL OF HYDROGEN GAS, DEAR–
CHARLIE? IF YOU'RE GOING TO BE A BORE ABOUT ALL THIS–
OH: NO-NO. NO. ONLY TRY-ING TO HELP, YOU SEE...

YOU–NEVER MIND THAT. YOU TELL ME IF THAT AIN'T JIM BURKE I SEE?

WHO, CAPTAIN? THE SMALLISH ONE?
AYE, THERE'S 'JIMMINY' JIM BURKE, ENGLISH MIDDLEWEIGHT.
UNLESS I MISTAKE HIM, WOT?
I'M SURE I DON'T KNOW.

BUT YOU'RE RIGHT, CAPTAIN. THERE STANDS JIM BURKE, EUROPEAN CHAMPION. 'THE SOUTHAMPTON HERMES.'
THE WHICH?
AH: DREADFUL NICKNAME.
SOUNDS LIKE A AILMENT.

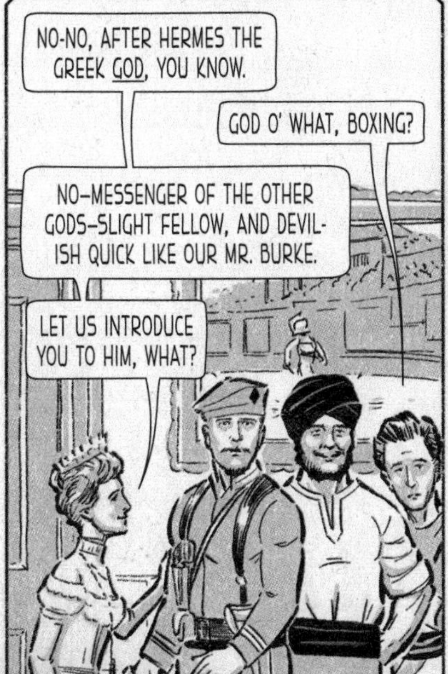
NO-NO, AFTER HERMES THE GREEK GOD, YOU KNOW.
GOD O' WHAT, BOXING?
NO–MESSENGER OF THE OTHER GODS–SLIGHT FELLOW, AND DEVILISH QUICK LIKE OUR MR. BURKE.
LET US INTRODUCE YOU TO HIM, WHAT?

YOU'RE FEELING WELL ENOUGH, BERTRAM?
YES, SIR.
WELL. ALL RIGHT. STAY HERE A MOMENT, THEN. LIE DOWN ON THOSE COATS IF YOU LIKE. I'LL SEE WHAT'S KEEPING THE OTHERS.
CAN WE GET YOU ANYTHING?
NO, SIR. THANK YOU.

...BEEN HELPING LOCALLY WITH THE WAR EFFORT, YOU KNOW. ON THURSDAY HE FIGHTS SOME LIGHT-HEAVYWEIGHT JEW AT THE ATHLETIC CLUB, THEN IT'S BACK TO THE FRONT.
WHAT SAY WE GIVE THEM A BIT OF WHAT YOU SHOWED THE BOYS THIS MORNING, AH? MR. BURKE?

JA—A DEMONSTRATION. *GUT.*
DEMONSTRATE ON ONE OF THEM, WHY DON'T YOU.
WELL, IT WOULDN'T BE QUITE FAIR—

PAH! THEY'RE ALL USEFUL ENOUGH WITH THEIR HANDS, I HOPE?
SURE, WE ARE. YOU SHOW 'IM, JACK.
YAH? IF YOU THINK HE WOULDN'T MIND...
THIS YOUNG MAN? NOT IN THE LEAST.

GOOD SHOW, CAPTAIN.
BUT—HE'S BOTTLED, ISN'T HE?
OH, RATHER. I SHOULD SAY THEY ALL ARE.
THEN YOU CAN SHOW THEM THE DANGERS OF THAT, AS WELL. GO ON.

ALL RIGHT. SOME OF THE RUDIMENTS, ANYWAY.
GOOD. THE RUDIMENTS. LET 'EM HAVE THOSE.
MIND THEY TAKE THE GUNS OFF HIM, SIR RUFUS.

YOU KNOW THAT MAN, SAHIB, SPEAKING WITH MR. SLOANE?
MM. ANOTHER OF VICTORIA AND ALBERT'S. DOES SLOANE KNOW HIM, I WOULD ASK.
I ONLY KNOW AT SANDRINGHAM THEY THOUGHT HE CHEATED AT CARDS.

THE LEFT IS JUST PROBING, YOU SEE... DRAWING OUT TENDENCIES...TILL WE GET AN OPENING FOR THE CROSS–THERE.
«–PIFF!»

CHR–ST, JACK. COVER YER CHIN, MAN.

BEG PARDON–HEY! YOU'RE NOT TO BE IN HERE, YOU KNOW.
SORRY. I'M WAITING FOR MR. SLOANE, SIR.
WHO? DON'T KNOW ANY SLOANES.
WE WON'T BE LONG, ANYWAY. I WON'T GO IN. I PROMISE.

NO YOU BL–DY WILL NOT. YOU'LL GO DOWN TO THE STREET THIS MINUTE. HERE–UP-UP–
GO ON–HM?–WON'T YOU?
«RAPP!»

WELL. SOMEONE'S GOING TO COME OUT AND SEE ABOUT YOU. I DON'T WANT YOU SCARING OFF THE GUESTS.

...WHEN YOU THROW THE BIG RIGHT, THAT OPENS THE BODY.

–AND WE GO FROM THERE TO THE HEAD, AND BACK, ANTICIPATING YOU.
IT'S ALL THESE COMBINATIONS, YOU SEE.
«CRRACK!»

...HE'S ALL RIGHT?
OH, HE'LL HARDLY NOTICE THIS.
JACKIE? HOW'S IT, LAD?
STRAIGHTEN 'IS LEG, WHERE 'E'S ON IT.

MAY'VE GOT A BIT CARRIED AWAY–
NOT AT ALL, LAD. A GREAT BIT OF SPORT. AND AN EDUCATION FOR THOSE MEN.
THERE'S A VERY PARTICULAR ART TO IT. THAT'S WHAT I LIKE TO SHOW THEM.
SO YOU HAVE, SO YOU HAVE...

CHAMPAGNE FOR THE CHAMPION! AH, BUT HE DOESN'T TAKE IT!
'SCUSE US–

YOU KNOW, SON: THAT MAN ONCE CARRIED AND DRAGGED ME SIX DAYS THROUGH THE HILLS INTO FORT SALISBURY, WITH A MATABELE SPEAR THROUGH ME.
OH? SORRY, I DIDN'T REALIZE.
HOW WOULD YOU? LET US SEE YOUR HANDS.
NOW: SAY HE'D TOOK HOLD OF YOU LIKE THIS. WHAT THEN?
STEADY ON, SERGEANT...
–BUT–
–NOW-NOW–HE WON FAIRLY–
–ALL IN SPORT, YOU SEE–
–YOUR MAN CAN TAKE HIS GRUEL, CAN'T HE?
AYE, HE CAN–IT'S ME, SIR, THAT WON'T WATCH HIM TAKE IT. NOT FROM THIS ONE, ANYWAY, WHO DINNA' EVEN HELP JACK UP.
–HYEK–
SEE THERE: CAN'T SET HIS FEET WHEN HE'S RUN BACK LIKE THAT.
DON'T CARE WHO Y'ARE: CAN'T THROW A PROPER PUNCH IF YOU CAN'T SET YOUR FEET.

YOU, SIR–!
SOMEBODY STOP THEM!

OUGHT TO OF KNOWN SERGEANT WOULDN'T LIKE TO SEE THAT. THEY ARE RATHER FRIENDS, THOSE TWO.
WELL. YOU MIGHT HAVE LET US KNOW, BEFOREHAND.
NAH, HE'S JUST WORRYING THE BOY, IS ALL. YOU'LL SEE, HE'LL–

...AH: STAND CORRECTED.

YOU THERE–SERGEANT! YOU'VE DONE MURDER, MAN!

OH KEEP YER HAIR ON, FATHER. THERE'S A BALCONY JUST BELOW.
THOUGH I DON'T THINK HE KNEW TILL HE HIT IT.
GET BELOW AND FETCH HIM UP. GOOD G–D.

CAN YEH STAND, JACK?
AYE, SURE. BOY'S AW-FUL QUICK, WHAT?
...WHERE'S HE GONE?

CHARLES: WHAT IN THUNDER IS THIS? WHAT ARE THESE MEN DOING HERE?
OH, THEY'RE NOT WITH ME.
YES, WE'VE JUST ASKED FOR THE LOAN OF THE *METTERNICH.* WE'LL HAVE IT BACK, YOUR GRACE, RIGHT WHERE IT IS NOW, BY FRIDAY NEXT.

BUT–I TOLD THEM, THE *METTERNICH* ISN'T–
OH FOR G–D'S SAKE, CHARLES, GIVE IT TO THEM. I WON'T HAVE THESE MEN HERE ANOTHER MINUTE.

LADIES? BEG YOUR PARDON, HE'S BUSY JUST NOW.
AND YOU'RE BETTER OFF DOWNSTAIRS, REALLY. THIS ONE HASN'T GOT A FARTHING FOR YOU.

I WANT YOU TO USE BETTER JUDGMENT, MR. BUCHAN. YOU CAN'T JUST GO ROUND TALKING TO THESE STRANGE GIRLS. LEAST OF ALL HERE.
BUT THEY SEEMED–
AUGHH. AND YOU'D KNOW, I SUPPOSE?

MISS HARROW–?
CHARLES–REALLY, DEAR–THIS IS ENOUGH OF YOU AND YOUR LONG FACE. YOU'LL HAVE YOUR BALLOON RIGHT BACK, YOU KNOW.
BUT IT ISN'T–DARLING, MY CONCERN, IS ENTIRELY FOR YOUR SAFETY.
THEN GIVE US A KISS, WON'T YOU? AND WISH ME LUCK.

YES. THAT'S ALL WELL. BUT–SUPPOSING YOU DON'T JUST EXPLODE OVER EUROPE, YOU KNOW THEY CAN STILL MAKE IT RATHER HOT FOR YOU ON THE GROUND.
YOU THINK I DON'T KNOW, CHARLIE, WHAT A MESS YOU'VE LEFT FOR US OVER THERE? I WOULDN'T BE TROUBLING YOU IN THE FIRST PLACE, IF IT WEREN'T FOR THIS G–DAWFUL WAR.

OH? I HOPE YOU DON'T THINK I'M SOMEHOW RESPONSIBLE FOR IT?
AREN'T YOU? I'D SAY AS A MAN, AND A EUROPEAN, YOU'RE AS GUILTY AS ANYONE.
AND THE WAY YOU'RE ALL HUDDLED OVER HERE, LIKE BOYS UNDER A TABLE WITH THEIR ROOF ON FIRE: IT DOESN'T DO ANY OF YOU MUCH CREDIT, YOU KNOW.

BUT–WHAT WOULD YOU HAVE US DO, RATHER?
I DON'T KNOW. BUT IF IT WERE ME, AND MY COUSIN WERE THE ENGLISH KING, I SUPPOSE I'D HAVE WIRED HIM BY NOW. I'D BE DOING SOMETHING TO KEEP MY HAND IN IT.
MISS? PLEASE. *WIR MÜSSEN GEHEN.* WE ARE UNDER WEIGH.

In the Duke's apartments below, the last of Ogden's men are marching out cock-a-hoop with the last of the Duke's liquor, as the partygoers watch, benumbed and impotent, like villagers lining the funeral route of a monarch of whom they had been vaguely fond. 'My *G–d*,' the Earl of Broadshire murmurs. Sir Rufus lets his face fall into his hands. Baron Ödön stands astride the balcony threshold, his attention divided between Ogden's men and the Woolworth Building, where flares of fire signal some new mischief to come. Count Mathias redoubles his own attentions on the whirling phonograph disk, though he is seen to ball his fists when Captain Shaw whisks a bottle of sherry from an occasional table beside him. When Mr. Renton carries a long sable duster past Count Géza, the Count digs in his pocket and dazedly holds out a coat-check ticket and an American dollar. The ticket is a year old, from the cloak-room of the Union Club, and it is for the jacket Count Géza is wearing; but Renton is happy to pocket the Count's dollar and, naturally, to carry on with the stolen coat.

The rest of the gathering wilt in their seats and scowl with goggle-eyed faces, as though the very air were being siphoned from the room; else they pace and seethe and mutter imprecations, pointedly ignoring the looting of the Duke's rooms. And what more, really, would you have? What gathering of civilized men in a peaceful city is equipped for a raid of cavalrymen? And such lunatics as these?

With the liquor gone, now, and the last glimmers of good cheer snuffed in the general malaise, there is little to hold the Duke's bright young things, and the ladies gather their effects and slip away unnoticed. 'Jimminy' Jim Burke is carried up from the floors below, the worse for various breaks and twists and for a terrific shock of nerves, to be laid out in a sitting-room till a physician can be summoned from bed. Nor is this the worst of it for our aristocrats: for here comes the Duke's airship, drawing its gangway and nosing into the air off the building's eastern façade.

There is not a man or woman left in these rooms who will not feel, at the sight of the east-bound ship, a pang of loss, and a sudden and hopeless longing for the salons and races, the seaside walks and hillside châteaux and the peaceful, cosseted spheres of the Old World, which must seem more remote from them now than ever. It is not as though any of our partygoers had actually *planned* a return passage on this ship, any more than its departure closes the way home for them; yet these people are sentimental and sensitive to symbols and, if I've not yet made this clear, they are a good deal *drunk*.

Their sorrows will seem childish, of course, to those of us with worries of our own. And how really can we pity men like these, who have squandered the riches and good faith of a civilization so that they, heirs to age upon age of History, might inhabit a state of ease on an otherwise remorseless earth? Our radicals may reason that it is these dissipated and inbred old creatures who are to blame for the wreck of Europe, and that they should praise their luck when they are only plundered of their liquor and cursed and jeered at and dropped onto balconies, when they manifestly deserve worse.

It is not a point I care to argue. I only note that our radicals are not always as bold as their own speeches, and that craven and selfish behaviors were never the province of any one class of men. I should say, too, that if the Duke and his guests aren't quite the paragons their fathers were, why then, neither really were the fathers themselves.

You'll observe, at any rate, that whatever else they may be, the Duke and his lot are not altogether bad *sports*. For here is Saxe-Coburg returned to his rooms, helping his cousin's wife to her feet and admonishing the others with a just-audible: '*Hrm*: ought at least to . . . *watch*, you know.'

This brings the rest of the gathering out to the balcony, with the exception of Count Mathias, who must twist his neck and roll an eye horribly to watch the phonograph and the night sky both at once. A hush falls on the men and women who have stepped into the spring air, beneath the great form of the *Metternich*. The ship, of course, has been commandeered by an untitled little adventuress—what is worse, an *actress*—and her murdering friends; but few on the balcony can sustain feelings of antipathy for very long, not with the ancient moon in full phase and this wondrous airship, glory of modernity, rising before it like another, superior celestial body. Sighs, you may be sure, are vented into this night, and water stands in more than one eye. Sir Rufus is moved to render 'Auld Lang Syne' in his wavering, limp-lipped baritone, as the others, ever susceptible to song, take up the tune after their own fashion. And who will care that no two versions of the song agree, or that the mismatch of

German and English throws it quickly out of meter, and the whole thing peters out and ends in a confused silence? The singers—helpless, bereft and abandoned on their tower in the New World—are linking arms now, waving and bidding *bon voyage*, raising empty glasses.

As the dirigible floats away toward the harbor and the sea, a small orange orb takes flight from the top of the Woolworth Building. Our aristocrats wave for a moment longer, holding out against despair, with fading smiles and dreams evanescing of long-ago appearances on far-off balconies…And still the point of light grows larger, clearly nearing them.

'Attack!' screams the Baron, hurling himself against the parapet. An undignified cry escapes the Viscount, and the Grand Duke of Hesse ducks behind his wife as the flaming missile strikes the building and drops to the balcony with an ugly, wet report. The bartender—whom no one had noticed among them up to this point—douses the flames with his soda-bottle. The others gather round and the Baron flips the thing over with his boot: it is a kerosene-soaked octopus, smelling unspeakably. The partygoers lift their eyes to the Woolworth Building, where several dozen points of light are rising even now into the air.

'Inside, then?' the Duke opines. He moves the gathering swiftly into the apartment and secures the French doors behind them as the balcony and building-side fall under a barrage of flaming bodies. The volley is followed by another, and a third. The partygoers stare without comment, as at some bizarre but ultimately harmless turn of weather, until the last of the fires smolders out. Even Baron Ödön seems to have exhausted his catalogue of blasphemies. He has been robbed of a fine moment by this incomprehensible insult, and can only sit, like his colleagues, at a loss as to what to do next.

'Anyway: I'm having a drink,' states the Earl of Broadshire, standing with decision. 'You? Rufus? Charlie…?' He surveys his friends, and follows their eyes back to the empty shelves and dashed bottles. '…Ah: right,' he says. He thrusts his hands into his pockets and wanders from the room, whistling some meaningless, anodyne tune.

Meanwhile, the jazz recording, having run its course, crackles like a forlorn and inarticulate ghost on the gramophone, and Count Mathias collapses to the floor.

II.

THE PASSENGERS ABOARD the *Luftschiff Metternich* gather to the windows, and not to return the parting waves of the Duke and his guests. There is little thought spared for the party diminishing below, and no regrets in any case. The old men still had their money and titles and a comfortable spot in which to sit out the war. And if the party had come to a complete smash, why, the Duke and his guests could always haul their old bones down to the street, into that great glittering riot of arc lamps and theater marquees and billboards and restaurant signs beneath them. They could take in *Business before Pleasure* or *Polly with a Past* or *The Kiss Burglar* and then a late supper at the Knickerbocker or what-have-you. It is the *everlasting* party down there, after all, and the city that stretches beneath the airship is like a map of infinite diversions, a display of all modernity's jewels heaped upon the earth's black baize and shining with a ferocity to stave off the night. Even the flaming mollusks from the Woolworth Building pass unnoticed beneath the *Metternich*, lost against the vastly greater spectacle of Manhattan. And what a spectacle! The ship's passengers may have seen a good deal of

the world, but not (excepting Miss Harrow and Mr. Sloane) much of what we would call *civilization*; and none have beheld, from the air, such a sprawling and ungodly beauty as this.

Of Ogden's original forty (and the number was never more than approximate), we have *Messrs.* Priddish, Shaw, Pensette, Mulcairn, Renton, Gurung, O'Hara, Pandit and Henty left tonight on the *Metternich*'s observation deck, with Ogden himself, of course, Mr. Buchan and Mr. Sloane, Miss Harrow and Master Barnes to round out the group. All shuffle quietly astern, their silence punctuated here and there by a blistering oath, as expressing some mix of concern and admiration for the gathering might of the New World. There seems to be a comfort for these travelers in watching the bright city out of sight, in seeing it lessen and wink out altogether, against the greater profundities of night and ocean.

The sight places a cap on their American adventures, too, and the darkness works on all of them to immediate and sedative effect. The dragoons have been drinking more or less steadily since making landfall in the States, and they are content to doss down, snoring, where they stand. Bertram yawns, folds his arms onto a rail that lines the bank of windows, and gently lowers his head. Mr. Buchan makes a few last notes in his book and dims the lamp beside him. Only Major Ogden stands and quits the room with Subadar Priddish attending him, leaving Mr. Sloane to stare in his quiet, feline way at Bertram, while Evelyn smokes and keeps her eyes on Sloane. The actress is working herself up to some comment when Mr. Sloane stands and slips from the room with a quick bow.

They had all been introduced, on boarding the *Metternich*, to a cabin boy called Heiner. And a bit of an odd specimen, this boy, with the skeletal frame and hooded eyes and pallor of a little risen corpse (or, as Sergeant Pensette had remarked, of a lost son of Mr. Sloane's). Sloane finds the boy standing now in a long corridor of white doors, staring at nothing in particular. The boy makes no sign of hearing when he is asked about a berth for Bertram; he only waits until Mr. Sloane has drawn to a halt and finished speaking, at which he relates in monotone that his name is Heiner, and he will be pleased to serve *Meinherr*.

As Mr. Sloane clears his throat into his fist and repeats his request, the head of Evelyn Harrow may be seen peeping round a corner of the hall behind him. She's a bit far away and her German is hardly perfect, but she picks out the phrase '*Radium-Krankheit*'–or radium sickness–more than once in his inquiry. The cabin boy stands, possibly listening, with hands clasped behind his back and eyes level on the space next to Mr. Sloane, until once more the gentleman falls silent. Without speaking, Heiner extends an arm to the door nearest him and pushes it open. Inside is a neatly appointed child's room with a goose-down duvet over a low twin bed, a pair of woolen slippers tucked beneath a reading desk, a freshly filled Benares ware basin on a stand and an adult-sized rocker by the heating grate. Heiner accepts, without comment, a pat on the head and a quiet confirmation that the room will do.

Evelyn hurries back to the observation deck and has just re-seated herself when Mr. Sloane enters and crosses over to Bertram. There is a moment's pause as he stands frowning down at the boy, clearly at a nonplus. He's arranged a bed for Bertram, and the boy must be taken there; but the lifting and carrying of sleeping orphans seems a bit outside his repertoire. A throat-clearing and a few taps of his foot go for nothing. He prods Bertram's shoulder, then, gingerly, as you might try a wild animal under sedation or a dud land-mine, and still with no result. He looks an appeal, finally, to Miss Harrow, who has been watching these efforts blank-faced, with her head at a slight tilt. She is no better versed in the handling of children, of course, but she stubs out her cigarette, crouches to Bertram and speaks a few words in the boy's ear, and in the next moment he is following her quietly from the room. Mr. Sloane falls in behind them, completing the picture, as they head into the hall, of a queer sort of family.

At Bertram's room they find the door has been left open, and Mr. Sloane bids Evelyn wait by it in the hall as he ducks inside with Bertram. He points the boy up into the bed and draws the duvet over him, boots and all, and Bertram grows still again instantly. Sloane waits over the bed, then, gnawing on a finger with his back to Miss Harrow, for perhaps a five-count; but it is no more than this. In the next moment he is bending to check the heating vent, and his face betrays no more than its habitual, bemused look of calm.

She steps aside to allow him into the hall, and is easing the door closed behind him when she finds herself nose-to-nose with Heiner the cabin boy. It seems Heiner has been standing here all along, behind the opened door, with his dead eyes more or less on Miss Harrow's. And he appears so abruptly to her, and so close, that she cannot suppress a little scream; though for his part, Heiner does not show the slightest change of aspect whether it is a door directly in front of him or a young lady screaming or what-have-you. Mr. Sloane looks from the cabin boy to Miss Harrow with a not un-Heiner-like passivity of face.

'We can help find you a suitable room,' he states. 'Or, if you'd like to talk, I'm not feeling especially tired.'

I would guess the *Metternich* were floating somewhere over Georges Bank at this hour, though it may be, for once, that our longitudes and latitudes do not hold a great deal of meaning. I should rather say that we are suspended above and between two stops on the globe, and two points in our story, between campaigns past and planned, and that this night is an opportunity for calm, and surcease, and a taking of stock.

Major Ogden and Subadar Priddish have established themselves in the second officer's quarters, which officer had woken to see them poring over a map of Europe at his desk, and had quit the room in his nightshirt, waving a fist and promising reprisal. Mr. Mulcairn, meanwhile, has brought his little Caspian nag to a two-storied ballroom amidships and hobbled it there, and the horse has been nosing through the leavings of its master's late dinner while Mulcairn beds down under canvas at the room's center. On the observation deck, the dragoons wage their campaigns through various dream-realms (Sergeant Pensette is scouring the Maharani's catacombs in Johor, for instance, where Bertram lies somewhere sealed in a box); while in his own dream, Bertram follows a familiar rustling sound into a hedgerow and comes awake screaming in his bed. He recomposes himself for sleep only to wake again later in terror, and so on through the night.

Farther forward on the ship–and well out of earshot of Bertram's cries, Miss Harrow and Mr. Sloane have found a stateroom where they can speak at last in seclusion (discounting Heiner, who stands just without the door he has closed, with his hand still on the latch). Miss Harrow takes up subjects of one kind and another–the Duke and his colleagues, her last crossing on the *Metternich*, the fall of the German mark–seemingly at random, and so far Mr. Sloane is the picture of polite interest. It is only when she pauses to take a swallow of brandy that he asks, in his musing way, whether she weren't holding back some other question.

Well. Of course she *is*, and there is really no reason why she shouldn't have asked it already. But Miss Harrow does not like being anticipated like this, any more than she likes this sense, generally, that Mr. Sloane is in among her thoughts. She finds she has been jumping from one unintended remark to the next and that now, rather than ask about Shambhala or radium poisoning, she only lets out a deprecating laugh and says: '...A question? No, not that I'm aware. Though there *is* a story I ought to tell you, if you really are in a mood to listen.'

Mr. Sloane indicates that this is precisely his mood, and she blinks at him in a way that would remind him, if he were in any doubt, that she is still a nineteen-year-old girl, and rather beautiful.

'I suppose,' she says, offhand, striking a match and setting it to a new cigarette, 'I suppose this *does* end in a question. But you'll guess it before I'm done.' She drops the spent match into an ashstand, vents a little smoke and settles back into her chair. 'Listen, now,' she says, 'and tell me if any of this sounds familiar to you....'

When the war came through Europe (Miss Harrow begins), I was glad of it, perverse as that will sound. For one thing it let me out of my contract with Mr. Sprague–or it did as far as *I* was concerned. I was already quite done with the cinema, you see, if I'd ever really been in the thing, and it wasn't just to do with the acting. I felt I'd been raised from the depths of want and obscurity and flung to heights of renown without seeing very much good in either. I was still young, of course, and tended to see things in the *wildest* extremes. But I felt I'd taken the world's measure and I was little pleased with the place, and if war meant the ruin of the *status quo*–and increasingly it was looking that way–well, I was entirely for it. (I'm afraid that's as far along as my ideology ran, but it seemed to suit my age and the age of the world, and I'd seen enough of the new radical groups to know I wouldn't be the first featherheaded young person in any of them.)

Anyway, this was the period where–as you'd say–'she took up with *low company*,' and that's rather a kind portrait of my new friends. Really my behavior was execrable, and it was all that my *old* friends could do to keep it out of the papers. By 1916, in the summer, I was still legally engaged to promote *The Pharaoh's Mistress* with Wegener. And they'd got me as far as New York, but I was making a point of running out on whatever they wanted me to do. There were scenes of chase, and private investigators–all much more fun than it sounds. At one point I found myself sprinting out of the Waldorf and jumping without thinking into someone's lovely new Darracq, and who should be inside but Oleg de Turbie, the bastard Romanov? I introduced myself and asked if he might not break his plans for the evening. He said he'd been waiting on an aunt–they had been shopping in town before some gala or other on Long Island–but what he'd really wanted was an excuse to chuck the whole thing; so off we went.

This was the start of a two- or three-month fling, and my first really prolonged disappearance from the genteel world. Oleg and I took up rooms at the Hotel Albert under assumed names and in elaborate disguises, though I suppose these charades were more fun than they were strictly necessary. The Albert in those days was a great asylum—in both senses of the word—for revolutionaries and anarchists, nihilists, provocateurs and assassins, crackpots, and every kind of exile you can imagine; and painters and poets, too, carrying on with their muses and models on the upper floors; and brilliant minds and lost souls and idlers like me just poking around for diversion, who had tired of the usual things...But all types of castoffs and refugees from civilization, anyway, who for whatever reason didn't wish to be seen by anyone but one another. And spiritualists? I should say the Albert was *lousy* with them at the time. Just beneath Oleg and me there was a Madame Anacharsis, who worked out of her rooms. She was a tremendous draw—and an even greater *fraud*, of course, but an amusing one. The first time Oleg and I sat with her I recall she brought over the relative of some Marquis, and they were looking after a lost deed to a château in the Dordogne and all going just mad over it....

But we'd the real article, too: Rudolf *Steiner*, you know, was a neighbor of ours for a time. He knocked on our door once wanting to know about an odor, and later we helped him chase a bat out of his room. He was the one who first made me aware of Shambhala, which is of course what I'm getting to.

It was...I think in the basement of the Brevoort, where Oleg and I ran across Steiner one night. He was sitting in a corner over a cup of tea, alone, observing the crowd. I never once saw him touch alcohol, but he did like to sit where others were taking it and to observe them. 'Drink is driving them away from the aetheric body,' he told us when we'd sat down. 'They are losing their spiritual memory.' Rather awkward, as we're sloshing our Dresden Sours over him, yet he didn't seem put out in the least. He was warm, jovial—and quietly *expectant*, as I thought, though I say it now with the benefit of hindsight.

He was known to everyone at the Brevoort, anyway, and people made a point of passing our table to shake his hand or offer one of those over-formal bows you do when you've drunk too much. He wasn't making space for any of them, either, not till a certain gentleman came to present himself. And—just to give you a sense of this man—the first we saw of him was a little mummified animal head advancing out of the crowd. It was the handle of a walking stick, as we found, and he came rapping this stick on our table by way of a hello. He was called Ainsley, and I think he was the seediest man I have ever seen. He stood a little under six foot, and as thin as an unwrapped mummy. And he wore an old frock coat that I doubt he ever took off, with parti-colored thongs and ribbons holding the thing together and a sash about his waist and a silk stocking binding his shirt-collar to his neck. He kept bouncing from one foot to the other and flipping up the tattered ends of his coat so that overall he presented the appearance of a ruined harlequin. And *talk*? I should say he did nothing *but*, from the moment he called us to order. Whether it was the clocks stopping simultaneously at Lens and Bitburg, or the Archduke's motor failing next to his assassin, or the hail in summer that grounded the R.A.F. in Gaza or what-have-you, he scarcely allowed himself a breath. It was as though his long body were conducting a clash of wireless signals and he must give vent to this noise whether he would or no.

And Steiner listened to all of it, you know, perfectly charmed. He smiled and nodded and interjected here and there a thoughtful 'Yes, I see...,' as he sipped his cold tea and let Ainsley into our booth. Oleg was trying to get a drink down the man just to quiet him, but there was no hope there. Ainsley must let us know about the saints floating in procession over Seville, and the lost populations of Central Europe, and the amnesiacs wandering the Asian strands–till you could almost trick yourself into hearing some hidden language or code in what he was saying, some larger message made up of these stray bits of nonsense...And I think this was probably *true*, again in view of what came later; but my greater sense at the time was that his eyes were falling increasingly on me, and that the evening had come to a complete frost, thanks to him. Oleg was sagging quietly under the table with his fingers stopping his ears, and I was on point of making our excuses and dragging him to the street, but it turned out there was no need. Ainsley quite abruptly clapped his jaws shut, stood and bade us all good evening.

Well: do you know? Steiner would not hear it. We would all follow the gentleman out, he said. And before we could vote this up or down he was handing me out of the booth. Ainsley rapped his stick on the floor and presented me with a bony elbow, as though he'd lead us from the Brevoort into some Victorian dinner-party. He had assumed a sudden dignity—which was absurd to witness in a man dressed like that—but I did set a hand on that oily coat-sleeve and let him walk me out, because by now, quite in spite of myself, I was curious to see where this all might lead.

Moments later he was marching me up Fifth Avenue and over onto Tenth, with Steiner half-leading, half-carrying Oleg behind us. It was borne in on me—slowly, I'm afraid (I tell you we'd been drinking since noon)—but I noticed our steps were tending back toward the Albert, and I sensed that Steiner had known this all along for our destination. He and Ainsley were certainly colluding on *something*, I thought. It flashed on me that Steiner was no longer living at the Albert, and that he was rumored bankrupt, and I supposed they might be leading me home to *rob* me. But—I admit this to you—the possibility only spiked my curiosity. You must know I didn't care *what* they were about, except that the whole thing had the savor of some iniquity. And in those days I didn't keep anything of my own at the hotel and didn't even carry *money*, so if robbery were really their intent, I'd have had the better laugh of it anyway.

So: here was Ainsley, leading us on in that quiet, dignified manner he'd assumed, and that somehow suited him even worse than his mania at the Brevoort. He broke his silence only here and there, leaning in toward me with some little *mot* like: 'Frankly, I don't think there's much to be gained from human sacrifice. At least nothing that is apparent to me.' Steiner was keeping up a conversation in undertones with Oleg, meanwhile, and this continued as we entered the Albert and crossed the lobby. I could not catch what they were on about until we stepped into the lift and the operator closed us in, and Steiner muttered something about a 'midnight séance.' I thought I must have misheard. But when we were let out on the sixth floor I could no more doubt it: they were taking us to that run-down fraud of a Madame Anacharsis!

Oh, I had *greatly* overestimated these men, that was all. I stamped my foot and positively refused to go farther—for all the good *that* did: they were already a good way down the hall by now, dragging Oleg. I stormed off after them, determined at least to see them hoaxed for wasting my time, and when that got boring I would pinch Oleg awake and make him drive me to the Plaza. And I suppose I was still too angry and too busy with my plans, just then, to notice the changed atmosphere in Madame's hallway.

For one thing, there was no one lagging about, and there were *always* loafers and inebriates in the halls of the Albert. Someone had put out the lights, too. There was only the one lamp glowing over Madame's door, beneath a shade of ruby-glass. And in the faint cone of light I could just make out Steiner in conversation with a little figure on a stool–a greeter, I supposed, though Madame did not typically use these in her sittings. He wore an outsize seaman's cloak, this man, and it was like some magic had shrunk him without also reducing his clothes, and he must look up out of his collars now like a rabbit from its hole. Certain of his features strengthened the impression, too, of a burrowing animal–his long teeth and nails, tiny glittering eyes, his turned-up nose; and I gathered on drawing up to him that this was an animal of aggressive nature. He'd apparently let Ainsley pass, but Steiner was having some difficulty and must shift Oleg to the little man while he dug in his wallet. The guard hopped down from his stool with eyes ablaze, one hand easily steadying Oleg and the other drawing a sap out from that vast coat. He let out really a *wonderful* string of obscenities in his little Scouse accent as he advanced on poor Steiner, and Steiner had to retreat a step, out of the light, till he struck at last on what he was digging for: a card marked with a crude symbol, which item he raised in a trembling hand like an old saint defying the Devil. The imp snatched the card away and left Steiner and me to catch Oleg, while he ran up his stool to examine the card in the light. I caught a bit of the thing myself, too: there was a circle surrounded by strange writing, with crooked crosses in the middle–the 'Black Sun,' as I'd come to know it, and I'm sure you've run across the thing yourself. But it was good enough at the time for our admission and, on my part, for a delightful little thrill of dread. The guard battered the door twice with his fist and pocketed Steiner's card with obvious disappointment. As Madame's door opened and we crossed her threshold I began to think the evening might not be beyond salvage after all.

Inside, Steiner took a moment to gather himself. He explained that these were new friends of his, and they'd hired Madame for one of these private gatherings they'd been staging about the city and in London. He had helped to arrange certain terms with her–they would bring their own table, for one–and though she had raised objections, he'd overwhelmed each of these with more *money*. This done, his friends had set about their preparations, sending Steiner to the Brevoort to await a summons. He had just begun to wonder if they'd perhaps tricked him out of his hundreds when, happily, Mr. Ainsley had appeared, and now here we all were (and Steiner not a bankrupt after all). It seemed to Steiner that we were here to debunk Madame Anacharsis, and I conceded, again with this sense of deflating hopes, that he was probably right. There were cynics all about in those days, you see, making sport of these sham spiritualists, and in general I was all for it. But I could not help thinking I'd seen enough of these things already, and my thoughts were reverting to Oleg and the Plaza when I caught sight of Mr. Steiner's *friends*.

There were about two dozen of these, I would say, in a range of types not uncommon in the occult and seditious circles of the day–reduced aristocracy and bastards of the upper class, lesser academics and out-at-elbows intellectuals and ladies passing as men and so forth–with perhaps more than the usual want of grooming and one or two legitimate maniacs wandering through the group, undetected by the others. But what distinguished these people was a *look* they all shared–a vacant, hungering look, I thought. They were all so intensely preoccupied and restive, and though they were grouped around cocktails in the conventional way, I saw no one paying the least attention to what was being said, not even by themselves. Naturally I supposed they were all drunk, because I'd been drinking myself and that's how you account for anyone's behavior when you are like that. But really–and this I would come to understand in the weeks and months that followed–these were men and women in the grips of *obsession*.

Ainsley of course was fully one of this lot, and he went right in yammering and pacing around with the rest. Steiner kept back with me by the door and seemed more or less aloof from this madness (though I hadn't examined him closely yet, either). And Oleg: if I say no more about *him*, it is because he went belly-down behind a sofa as soon as we were announced, and I don't know *how* he got out of there later. But we'd timed our arrival neatly, anyway, for we'd just got our champagne when the lights flickered and failed, and Madame Anacharsis, with the spirits upon her, summoned her company to the table.

The table itself was an unusual article (and you will recall Steiner's friends had wheeled it in and insisted on its use). It was large and round and made of old lacquered wood, with an illuminated surround of glass or crystal about the top, and this was carved with symbols of an exotic and…really a *disturbing* character, as you examined them. There were long-robed men with the heads of animals, rendered flat-footed and in profile like Egyptian Hieroglyphs, and they were hauling at leashes or whips, leading other crouching, half-formed men along, with sloped heads and fish scales and idiotic sharp-toothed grins. There seemed to be monkeys got up like priests, too, and tall, callipygian figures that I took to be girls, with their bodies swollen out of all human proportion… All these horrible beings, anyway, in procession about the tabletop. And then here came our own group, looking scarcely less demented, rushing in to take their seats now that Madame had signaled her readiness.

The ten or so chairs at the table went quickly, and none who took them were inclined to make room, not even for a young lady. But Steiner drew two folding chairs and a hassock together behind the inner circle, and put me between himself and Ainsley as Madame warmed to her performance.

And I should say, as someone who threw in briefly with acting herself, that Madame's commitment to the farce was *utter*, even impressive in its forlorn way. She fairly shook the spirit-plane with her greetings and invocations, pitching these in the wildest Bohemian accents (though she was no more Bohemian than I am, only a banker's daughter out of Connecticut). And she built upon these preliminaries as her 'spirit controls' came gusting through her. You must imagine how exercised a woman becomes as she makes loan of her person to Kublai Khan, then John the Baptist, and a Nautch dancer out of Calcutta, Martin Van Buren, some male lover of Lord Byron's, and a 'savage of Borneo' who spoke only in clicks and grunts.…Really she did the work of a vaudeville troupe singlehanded, making use too of a black glove to float 'apports'–jewelry, a straw doll, scrolls of paper and even a live *pigeon*–from the folds of her robe to the tabletop, and setting off phosphorescent patches all about the room as further proof of the spirits' 'coming through.'

Steiner, I could see, was missing none of her tricks, though he looked on without judgment or any certain emotion at all. To Ainsley and the others she was invisible. They only gripped the edges of the table (or pulled at their trouser-legs, the ones who hadn't got a seat) and rocked and moaned. Their quiet and desultory grunts fell gradually into a rhythm, and then into a horrible chanting. Whether encouraged by this or only trying to hold the stage, Madame pushed herself to even greater absurdities: the murdered Abby Borden strove against her daughter–the latter not even *dead* yet, I believe–for possession of the medium, while the spirit lights flashed about us like Chinese New Year and ribbons of ectoplasm streamed from Madame's wig on black wires…It was *madness*, and still the chanting rose. In one flash I saw another sitter had joined us late–a lean, bearded man beneath a painting I hadn't noticed at the back of the parlor, telling rosary beads and chanting with the rest (though more about him in a moment). Some of the other men, now, were breaking the chant to yip out words in English, words bereft of meaning and pitched toward no one, drawn involuntarily from them as it seemed to me: 'Come Mechizedek!' they cried. 'Come Marduk! Come Manu, Great Progenitor! Halgadom–Vril–Vattan…!'

Madame Anacharsis, nothing if not game, chucked the Misses Borden without farewell and took up her own version of the cry, foregoing even her gypsy accents: 'Yes,' she shouted to the the ceiling-beams, 'Play our human harps! Show us Mechizedek! Show us Thule!' and so forth. She had put her ring-fingers to her palms, in accordance, I suppose, with her ideas of the Eastern divinities. 'Open the hidden books of the Essenes!' she said, echoing the chanters: 'Lift our eyes to the White Island. We are on pilgrimage to the Great City of Temples–The Imperishable Sacred Land–'

Here there was a loud rap on the table, and I say *loud* but really I thought the thing had *split*. And with this all other noises in the room stopped dead. Madame popped one eye open and scanned faces: her own table was rigged to spin and bounce and let out various sounds and scents, but that great knock was something novel and I think she'd like to have known who'd produced it and how. And there was something else: for the first time in the sitting, she had gathered all the eyes in the room. I saw her calculating–she must furnish some answer or other from this 'White Island' place, you know–and she'd parted her lips to give the thing a go when she halted again, and this time it seemed that something were truly wrong with her. The sitters were positively leering at her now, tipping forward in their seats like things magnetized. Even Steiner put by that gentlemanly diffidence to gape at her with the rest. Madame shuddered and her hands flew to her temples, and her face went pale beneath whatever dye she used. These were no more of the hoary old pantomimes. She had experienced a genuine stab of pain, and when her eyes flicked open they saw none of us, for they were filled now with the purest *horror*.

I drew in a breath and seized Steiner's arm, and…and I'm afraid the whole thing gets a bit odd from here. I don't know if I shall be able to describe it, quite.

...It all ended (Miss Harrow continues) in a fair degree of chaos. Poor Madame went ramrod-straight in her chair, and was...*vibrating*, else it was the air in the room shifting around her, I don't know. And then... Well. First, a *man* appeared. The table let out its great cracking noise, the door to the apartment swung open and there he was–A very *strange* man, I should say. A great moving mound of flesh, a head taller than any of us and as wide around as any three together. His head was shaved but for the one long lock like a horse's tail swinging from the front, and he wore a shapeless white gown or shift with crude woven sandals on his feet and his bare, hairless stubs of legs in between, thick as wine-casks. His arrival drew looks of terror and outrage from the sitters, not that he could be bothered to notice. His mood was jovial, almost mocking. 'Thule! Thule!' he barked back at us, chuckling. He scanned the room with an expression suddenly fierce, till he spied an unfinished glass of champagne on a bookshelf, and then he broke into his broad grin again, snatched up the glass and drank it off in one tilt.

Ainsley, meanwhile, was fondling some object that hung from his neck on a leathern cord. I heard him mutter 'the *Great Beast,*' but he would not amplify on the statement for all that I whispered aside to him and pulled on his sleeve. He would not take his eyes off the thing, either, as indeed none of us could. Even the long-haired stranger at the back of the room put away his rosary beads to take this phantasm in. The Beast drew closer to the lights of the table, throwing a tangle of orchids to the floor and guzzling the water out of their vase. I saw that his hands were stained with red paint, and he had an eye painted on his forehead, a black eye with long lashes and a band of cobalt over it in the Egyptian style. One of the more senior men at the table stood and demanded that he account for himself.

'I am Boleskine,' said the Beast, drawing a sleeve across his lips. 'To my friends Ananda Vigga. You, on the other hand, may call me *Lord* Boleskine.' He found a tray of honey-cakes (a friend of Madame's kept bees and would send her these, laced apparently with some opiate) and he was forcing them down several at a time, as he pointed to his forehead and grumbled, 'You will know me by my eye.'

It struck me this was a routine with which the men and women of our party were not unacquainted, though they were anxious still to have it done. 'We have not invited you, nor your magic,' the old man railed at him. 'Go back, whatever you are, and send for your masters.'

'I am Perdurabo,' the Beast continued, between mouthfuls. 'If I'd masters and they wished your society, you would not see me. And it's "magick," with a "k."'

This proved to be more than one frail-looking woman could bear. She leapt to a chair and tore off her false beard in an access of rage. 'What in *Chr–st* is the difference, in pronunciation?' she cried. 'There is no way on *earth* to know if it is spelled with a "k" or not, when the word is spoken!'

The Great Beast pointed again at the eye on his forehead. '*I* know,' he said, simply. He took a long swallow of *eau de vie* and gestured past us with the bottle-neck. 'Look, now, who comes through,' he said.

And here is where a second thing happened, stranger even than the advent of the Great Beast. Madame Anacharsis let out a shriek and we turned to her all at once. Her...her *features*, you see, seemed to have *flattened*–it seemed they were being shone onto some unidimensional plane over her face, and they were holding still while her head vibrated most awfully, thrashing about in a blur. Her shrieking went on and intensified, growing deeper in pitch and less definitely human. And then she...

Well. I was in a picture, once–*The Automata of Jericho*–Basil called it 'Expressionist'; it was a disaster–but he arranged in the climactic scene for me to shed a mechanical skin I'd been wearing. It all flew into pieces about me, each castoff part drifting out of frame in its own direction on a wire. I won't tell you what torture it was to rig the thing up, but I mention it because I saw Madame's face do more or less the same thing. Her features–and I know how this will sound–they *broke apart* and proceeded in all directions through the room, dissolving slowly into the dark. Not that her actual *flesh* went anywhere–the pieces were more like projected images, but *vivid*, and real enough to anyone there. The others saw it, too. They had all fled to the far end of the room by now and Steiner, who'd taken cover behind a potted palm, was motioning me quite vigorously back to him. Except it was no good, you see. I was rooted to my chair now, powerless even to breathe. It was like the catatonia one experiences in a nightmare, and none of these men bold enough to come collect me. That awful howling and gurgling kept up as the last details left Madame's face and the lights of the table faltered beneath her, and through it all the Great Beast, left in possession of the room, went lumbering about, quite enjoying himself. He fetched another bottle from a cabinet and dropped to one of the chairs as if taking in a show.

...And then, quite suddenly, it stopped. The noises sank beneath our hearing, and the lights shone steady upon Madame's face again. Only it was no longer her face, it was an *old man's* face, etched and drawn with incalculable grief. The voice that rose out of it, too, was no longer the medium's–and this was *quite* beyond Madame's talents of mimicry, I swear to you. It was an old man's voice, halting and feeble. 'Where is my son?' it asked, as two black and deep-set eyes roamed fearfully about the apartment. The men and women of our party shrank from this gaze, desperate not to be taken for the son of *anything*. 'Where is my son? Where is my *son*...?' it intoned, over and over, and apparently without hope of answer. It was the voice of a deep and irremediable sorrow–and with an accent of the Balkan states, as I could not help but notice.

The pleas went on unheeded, anyway, as the men and women of our party held conference at the back of the room. I might have listened in, too, but just then I felt a pain in my head like the worst neuralgia, and this shut out all else. It was like an electric current passing between my temples on a wire, and my hands flew to them in reflex as I had seen Madame's do. I thought I must faint, and then I was convinced I *had* fainted, for there was a flash and an enveloping darkness, and then without any *physical* sense that I'd opened my eyes the room was revealed to me again, and I felt–oh it's no stranger than the rest, is it?–I felt I had somehow been removed outside *time*. The sitters were gone from the room and their chairs left empty. That awful Madame Anacharsis old-man *thing* was maundering on at the table, but he was of no importance now, like a supernumerary in a dream. All else was stillness and suspension. There was no light but the glowing table. The very dust seemed to have frozen in the air. And then...there was another being in the room. I suppose I felt it quite before I saw it, beside me, where Ainsley had been sitting: it was that thing Ainsley had called the Great Beast, but cleaned up a bit in appearance. There was no more paint on him or lock of hair, and he had traded his nightshirt for a wine-colored monk's robe, edged with gold bullion. I understood (though I cannot explain how) that his 'Perdurabo' character was only some guise he took on to deal with Steiner and his sort. He was the same great heap of flesh when he appeared to me alone, but he was transformed into some ideal of himself, serene and dignified.

As I came out of my fugue I found him chanting quietly, coaxing me perhaps to his level of consciousness, readying me for our interview. His voice–if you may call it that–came in a soft, rumbling *basso profondo*. And I could see his mouth forming words: 'Peace grant you peace; I am come with news,' he was saying. 'And if it pleases you I will beg a boon.' But the words constituted directly in my *mind*, you see, without the slightest ring or echo from the room (which is how I understand disembodied voices will visit the mad). My own voice, too, as I found when I tried it, had that same dead quality as his. It was as though we were trading words in a vacuum. And then I really despaired, because I felt the madness of the other sitters had touched me as well.

But he would not call it madness. He told me rather that these others had been *tried*. They had been let out from their houses, he said, and had muddied their boots in the garden, and now they could not be let back in to tread on the carpets... Or something to that effect. It was the veriest nonsense, I am sure, and I might have laughed, except I was clinging to my *sanity* just then, and I shuddered to think what my laughter might sound like in our little vacuum. I asked instead if I weren't also being 'tried,' and he said I was. And shouldn't I muddy your carpets, too? I asked, to which he replied, very gravely indeed, in the negative.

My friends in this room, he said (misjudging who were my *friends*), were full-formed creatures of the world, and whatever their pretensions they would make no profit in spirit that they would not turn to the gratification of their grosser appetites. Whereas I–he said–*I* was young and only half-formed, and had not the world's imprint on me; I had not yet any real *stake* in the place. Had I not, he asked, always sensed what vain offerings were these fruits of the world? Had I not *proved* it, who had gathered them all, and only heaped emptiness on emptiness? Had I not always looked on my fellows, in their toil, from without, as I might look at some absurd bit of theater?

Well, that's not *exactly* true, I said—I don't always *look*. But he was warming to his subject and would not be put off with jokes. I had known these mortals, he said, to be busy at nothing. I had sensed a brighter sun over their bunched backs and lowered eyes. I had seen past the works and rewards of this life to a greater purpose, and I had held myself in wait for it.

...Now, you'll say this was no great penetration on his part. What girl of seventeen does *not* feel a ghost in her own world? Which does not think there is some special destiny reserved for her, to which all others are blind? These are feelings as universal as they are felt to be exceptional by every girl who has them. But I tell you I *was* a bit of an exception. For me, this disaffection with the world was no passing phase of youth. I was *christened*, for G–d's sake, by a Franciscan friar who'd just flogged his horse to death in the street—How in conscience do you take such a place seriously? And indeed I had not, and *could* not, to the point where after seventeen years I'd begun to think this might represent a problem. It's all well to laugh at the world, you see, but to laugh so persistently at anything feels like madness, and it is horribly *wearying* besides. Sooner or later you've got to take *something* in earnest, don't you? And here was this...this great white *being* putting his finger on the very spot, on that emptiness or want in me that I had felt so young, and carried so long. And more than that, he was *filling* it. He had filled it already.

He said he was the Bodhisattva, the pedagogue, earthbound, and he had marked a path for me. I had awoken to a cosmic mystery, and would be filled with a new purpose. And though he said no more about it—and I am sure he declined to name *Shambhala*—that is most certainly what this purpose was. The City's outlines were before me even then. And it would call on me, pulling irresistably, from that moment forward, like my own magnetic North.

Now: just how he'd have brought all this into my understanding, and without words, I cannot say. But it was a power of his, just as it was in his power to cloud the minds of those he *didn't* want treading his path (the madness of the other sitters seemed to be his doing, you see; I take their condition to be some milder and purely cerebral form of the Complaint, and serving much the same purpose). But we discussed none of this. The next I was conscious of his speaking, he was giving me the task of 'bringing the son before the father.' This was the boon he had said he'd beg of me, earlier. He indicated the old man at the head of the table (who was already relinquishing his spot to a rather worse-for-wear Madame Anacharsis), and he called this man the Father. 'And there sits the Son,' he said, pointing to the back of the room, where the bearded, gangle-limbed drifter had sat beneath the painting. Only now, as the lights came up and Steiner and the rest stood from their places of hiding, I saw the stranger and the painting both had gone–I supposed he had stolen it. I ran after him, past the imp at the door and down into the street, but I saw no more sign of him from then to this day. By the time I returned to the Albert they'd fixed the lights in Madame's hall, too, and her apartments were empty but for a pair of hotel maids. A rumor came up some time later that she'd been left at Bellevue under the name 'Mary Morgan,' but I saw no evidence of her on the hospital rolls and indeed I never saw her again. Soon they were letting her rooms at the Albert to a nihilist couple from Scotland.

But my own efforts from there forward were put against this new task of mine, and I've been quite busy since, between the research and travel and perhaps a hundred more sittings, as I hardly need tell you. I didn't know–I still don't–whether this job of uniting 'father and son' had been given to me literally to do, or if it were just some koan-like riddle meant to steer me toward Shambhala. But if there *is* a Father, and my clue to him was the old man who'd invested Madame Anacharsis, then I'm quite sure this man is Count Selescu, the Romanian general who'd quested after the City on orders from Tsar Alexander (and whose accent would have had some savor of the Balkans). I am convinced too that the Great Beast (or the Bodhisattva or what-have-you)–this was almost certainly some projection of Selescu's advisor, the 'Abbot,' the one who'd led him through Mongolia. Selescu *did* have a son, you know, brought up in the Abbot's care. And it's not so wild to think they'd have led this boy into the mysteries of Shambhala, this being more or less the family business in the last century. I've not been able to find much record of this boy, but he…I suppose he'd have grown to about *your* age by now, Mr. Sloane. And you *do* recall my saying this story ended in a question….

MR. SLOANE...?

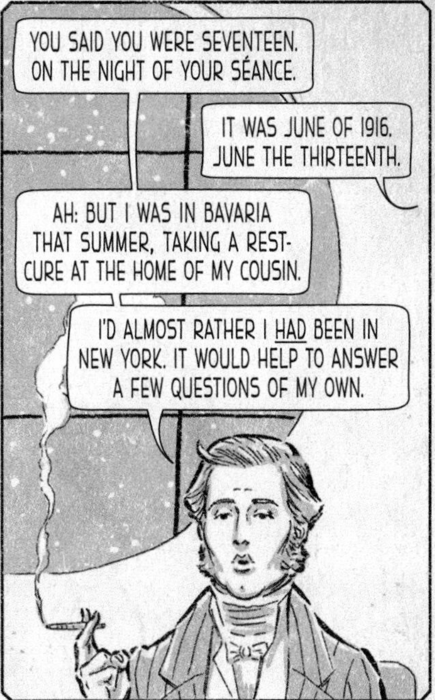
YOU SAID YOU WERE SEVENTEEN. ON THE NIGHT OF YOUR SÉANCE.
IT WAS JUNE OF 1916. JUNE THE THIRTEENTH.
AH: BUT I WAS IN BAVARIA THAT SUMMER, TAKING A REST-CURE AT THE HOME OF MY COUSIN.
I'D ALMOST RATHER I HAD BEEN IN NEW YORK. IT WOULD HELP TO ANSWER A FEW QUESTIONS OF MY OWN.

AH, WELL. IT WAS ONLY A THEORY. TOO NEAT, PERHAPS.
SIR? I'M SORRY–MAJOR'D LIKE TO SEE YOU.
ANYWAY, THE COUNT'S DEATH IS WELL-DOCUMENTED. I DON'T KNOW WHAT BRINGING ANYONE TO HIM WOULD EVEN MEAN NOW.
HERE–LOOK:

SELESCU'S SON. THIS IS ALL I'VE BEEN ABLE TO FIND OF HIM. BUT THE ABBOT, THE MAN SITTING WITH HIM: THIS IS DECIDEDLY THE THING THAT CRASHED OUR SITTING IN NEW YORK.
I AM TOLD HE CAME BACK FROM THE EAST WITH THE DROPSY, OR WITH SOME VARIANT OF THE COMPLAINT, AND THAT HE'S CONTINUED TO EXPAND LIKE THIS THROUGH THE YEARS.

I CAN'T IMAGINE HE'S STILL ALIVE, BUT I'M TOLD HE IS, AND THAT HE'S GOTTEN TOO BIG TO MOVE FROM THE CASTLE AT FERITIVA. MEANING HE'D BE THERE TODAY, IN SOME FORM OR OTHER.
...INTERESTING.
AND IF HE IS, IF IT'S ALL TRUE, THEN I MEAN TO SEE HIM.

I DON'T KNOW HOW WE'LL BE GREETED, BUT...WELL, I SUPPOSE IF IT COMES TO FORCING OUR WAY IN, THAT'S RATHER IN MR. OGDEN'S LINE, ISN'T IT?
THOUGH I THINK I'D PREFER IT IF HE'D BROUGHT A FEW MORE OF HIS MEN.
OH, I SHOULDN'T THINK THE NUMBERS WOULD ENTER INTO IT. MAN'S INVINCIBLE, YOU KNOW.
FORGIVE ME, MISS HARROW.
MR. SLOANE, SIR–?

COME AND HAVE A DRINK.

MISS HARROW, YOU'LL EXCUSE ME. IT APPEARS I'M SUMMONED.

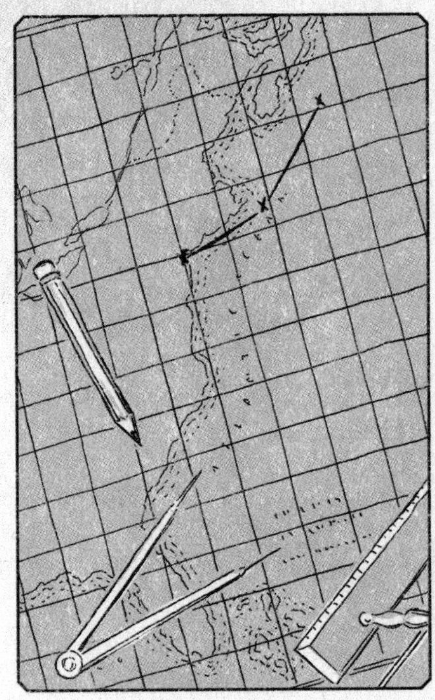

THANK YOU. I UNDERSTAND THEY'RE HAVING SOME WEATHER, OVER ENGLAND.
DIDN'T SAY, 'COME HAVE A TALK.'
AH. NO, YOU DIDN'T.

MR. RENTON.
SIR?
TWO MORE LIKE THIS. REST OF YOU: GO ON.
AYE, SIR.

IT'S IN THE EAST, THEY OPEN DOORS FOR PRIVACY. YOU'VE BEGUN TO THINK LIKE THEY DO.
SIT, MR. SLOANE

YOU DON'T RECALL ANY...ASSOCIATION WITH MY SISTER. SOME YEARS AGO.
SORRY? ...NO, I DON'T. AS I TOLD MISS OGDEN HERSELF IN NEW YORK.
SO FAR AS I KNOW, OUR 'ASSOCIATION' IS LIMITED TO THAT ONE INTERVIEW, AT YOUR HOME.

WOULDN'T RECALL ANY DEALINGS WITH ME, THEN, EITHER. IN INDIA.
I DON'T KNOW THAT I'VE EVER BEEN TO INDIA, MAJOR.
YOU DON'T KNOW?
FIGURE OF SPEECH. I BELIEVE I HAVE NOT BEEN THERE.

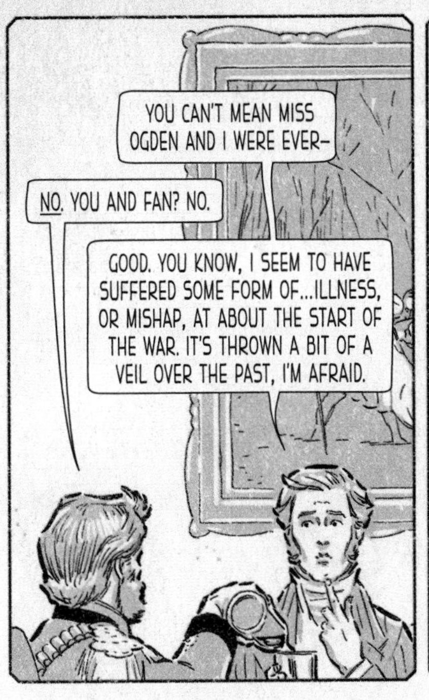
YOU CAN'T MEAN MISS OGDEN AND I WERE EVER–
NO. YOU AND FAN? NO.
GOOD. YOU KNOW, I SEEM TO HAVE SUFFERED SOME FORM OF...ILLNESS, OR MISHAP, AT ABOUT THE START OF THE WAR. IT'S THROWN A BIT OF A VEIL OVER THE PAST, I'M AFRAID.

...BUT IT DOES SEEM, FROM THE WAY BOTH OF YOU HAVE ASKED ME NOW, THAT I MUST HAVE KNOWN HER–
I PROMISE YOU, YOU AREN'T A THING TO FAN.
YES, BUT IF WE'D ANY ASSOCIATION, YOU KNOW– IF YOU OR SHE COULD TELL ME ANYTHING I MIGHT HAVE BEEN UP TO...

YOU'RE ONLY SOMEONE SHE THINKS CAN HELP OUR BROTHER, POOR GIRL.
OUGHT TO TELL HER IT'S YOU THAT LED HIM INTO THIS, IN THE FIRST PLACE.
THAT I DID?
NOT THAT IT'D SWAY HER ONE WAY OR THE OTHER. SHE'D ENLIST THE DEVIL'S OWN HELP FOR ARTHUR AT THIS POINT. AND SO SHE HAS, WHETHER IT BE YOU OR ME.

YES, BUT WHAT DO YOU KNOW ABOUT–
MR. SLOANE: THERE'S NOTHING I CAN TELL YOU TONIGHT THAT WILL HELP YOU.
FAN WON'T SEE HER BROTHER SUFFER. THAT'S ALL WE NEED TO KNOW, YOU AND I.
...REST CAN WAIT.

THEN MISS OGDEN'S BOUND YOU TO WORK WITH ME. FOR HER BROTHER'S SAKE.
I SHOULD SAY, IT'S GOOD OF YOU TO HONOR HER WISH, MAJOR. I KNOW YOU HAVEN'T GOT MUCH TASTE FOR MY COMPANY. THIS CAN'T BE EASY FOR YOU.
OH? AND WHAT FAMILY DO YOU HAVE, SIR?
–SORRY?
YOU'D TELL ME IT'S GOOD FOR A MAN TO ACT AGAINST HIS PRINCIPLES, WHERE HIS LOVED ONES ARE CONCERNED. ONLY, WHAT WOULD YOU KNOW ABOUT THAT?
I DON'T THINK I'VE SAID ANYTHING VERY STRANGE.
TELL ME WHAT'S IN THERE, THAT YOU'D SPEAK TO ME ON MATTERS OF THE HEART. GO ON.
I PERCEIVE I AM MOCKED.
NO. I ONLY WANT TO KNOW HOW TO STRIKE AT YOU, MR. SLOANE.
WHAT ABOUT THE YOUNG LADY?
THE–?
SEARCHED THE WORLD FOR YOU, DIDN'T SHE? SEEMS RATHER TAKEN WITH YOU. I IMAGINE THERE WERE OTHER WAYS TO EUROPE, FOR BOTH OF YOU.
YES. WELL. THOUGH NOT MANY QUICKER, FOR ME.
I DON'T SUPPOSE THE YOUNG LADY'S CHARMS ENTERED INTO IT, FOR YOU.
WOULDN'T THEY?
NOT FOR YOU. NO. I THINK YOU'RE STILL COLLECTING PEOPLE. SHE SEEMS TO KNOW A GOOD DEAL ABOUT SHAMBHALA. YOU DON'T LIKE THAT SORT GOING ABOUT ON THEIR OWN, DO YOU?
THAT'S TRUE, I DON'T.
...LIKE YOUR BLACK-ROBED FRIENDS DON'T.

NO, THEY DON'T EITHER. I SUPPOSE WE HAVE THAT IN COMMON.
STILL, IT'D BE A HARD-HEARTED MAN WHO DIDN'T NOTICE MISS HARROW'S–
HE'D HAVE NO HEART AT ALL.
HE'D...I SEE. AND NOW YOU'LL MAKE YOUR POINT, I HOPE?

I SHOT YOU FROM THAT BOAT. WITH A BORROWED GUN, FACING INTO WIND, AND THE DECK AND THE HORSE MOVING BENEATH ME. YOU'D FORGIVE A MAN FOR MISSING UNDER THE CIRCUMSTANCES, BUT I DIDN'T MISS. I PUT A BULLET RIGHT...THERE.

I SAY THERE'S NO HEART IN THERE, BECAUSE I KNOW THERE ISN'T.

NO, YOU'RE RIGHT, MAJOR. THOUGH I HADN'T ANY REASON TO SUSPECT MY... MORTALITY, UP TO THAT MOMENT. YOU CAN IMAGINE MY SURPRISE.

YOU DON'T EVEN KNOW WHAT YOU ARE.
WELL. BIT OF THE UNIVERSAL CONUNDRUM, ISN'T IT.
BUT THEN, WHETHER YOU'RE A GHOST, OR THE RISEN DEVIL, AS THE MEN SEEM TO THINK, OR JUST SOME SHARED INSANITY OF OURS–I DON'T SEE IT MATTERS. I'VE GOT HOLD OF YOU NOW, MR. SLOANE. AND I'LL KEEP YOU TILL I'VE LEARNED WHERE WE'RE TAKING ARTHUR. AND THEN, HOWEVER IT'S DONE, I'LL RID THIS WORLD OF YOU.

AH. THEN I KNOW WHERE THINGS STAND, DON'T I.
SO YOU DO.
ALTHOUGH...I'LL OFFER YOU ONE MORE REASON WHY YOU WOULDN'T KILL ME, JUST YET.
OH?
OTHER THAN PER-HAPS YOU CAN'T.

...AND I'VE PROMISED FAN.
WELL. IF YOU'D LIKE TO MAINTAIN THAT AS YOUR REASON, YES.
BUT I THINK YOU'RE CURIOUS YOURSELF, TO KNOW WHERE I'M GOING. MM? AND I'D SOONER STAKE MY LIFE TO THAT, THAN TO ANY PROMISE YOU'VE MADE YOUR SISTER.

IF YOU DON'T KNOW WHAT A POWERFUL INSTINCT YOUR CURIOSITY IS, MAJOR, I THINK YOU WILL BEFORE LONG. FOR YOURS IS WOKEN NOW. AND YOU'LL SEE IT BEGINS TO SHOUT DOWN ALL ELSE–HONOR, FEAR, LOVE–ONCE IT'S GOT IN A MAN'S EAR.
I SEE. THIS FROM A MAN WHO KNOWS SO MUCH ABOUT LOVE AND HONOR.
I KNOW THAT ONCE A MAN GOES SEEKING HIS OWN ANSWERS IN THIS WORLD, HE MAY AS WELL HANG IT UP AS A SOLDIER.

MM. THOUGH MY OWN DESERTION HAD MORE TO DO WITH A CERTAIN LETTER, AS PERHAPS YOU KNOW.
OH, I DON'T MEAN THAT. THE COMPANY YOU'VE SHED WITHOUT MUCH BOTHER, HAVEN'T YOU–WHETHER OR NOT THEY'RE DONE WITH YOU, AS PERHAPS WE'LL SEE...
NO, I SHOULD THINK THE GREATER STRUGGLE FOR YOU WOULD BE LEAVING YOUR OWN MEN.
WHAT?

YOU'RE IN THE MIDST OF TRANSFORMATION, MAJOR. SOON YOU'LL HAVE NO MORE NEED OF THEM, IF YOU HAVE ANY NOW.
YOU CAN'T THINK IT'S ANY ACCIDENT, THAT YOU'RE DOWN TO HALF A DOZEN OF THEM ALREADY–
THAT'LL DO, MR. SLOANE.

The state rooms on the *Metternich* have each, at a minimum, two porthole windows, one of them looking out from the bed-chamber to the surrounding skies, and the other giving sitters in the sitting-room some view or other of the ship's interior. In Miss Harrow's rooms, for instance, the cabin-door window lets out on a long passenger corridor. And this suite being one of many appointed for distaff use, the window is screened on the inside by a little valance or swag of eyelet lace.

Now, I have no doubt this curtain was an expensive article, and I admit that as decoration it does nicely; but as a device for privacy the thing is effectively worthless. Where it is not pierced by holes or recessed from the window-frame, it gives only the sheerest cover of loose-woven silk, so that any passing body in the hall, being so motivated and of average adult height, can see the better part of Miss Harrow's sitting-room and make an educated guess about the rest. Add to which, when the cabin is lit and the corridor dim—as is generally the case—the voyeur stands all but invisible to anyone inside. It is a deplorable circumstance for the cabin's occupant, you will agree. And it is one of which, almost continually since discovering it in Miss Harrow's case, Corporal O'Hara has been pleased to take advantage.

Up to a moment ago, and for the reasons of lighting mentioned above, Miss Harrow had not seen nor even suspected her admirer in the hall. But she had emerged tonight from her bed-room, dressed in—let us say, in a sort of article for which we may thank the French and this liberated age—and with a copy of Bambach's *Rambles in Austrian Tyrol* raised before her face. She had heard a moan from the hall, and thought that either a man had had his foot trod on out there, or else...

Comprehension had rushed upon her all at once. She had dodged over to a hassock by the cabin door (this being out of the voyeur's sight-line), and here she has stayed from that moment till now, with knees drawn to her chin and a thumbnail wedged in her teeth. It is not that she objects particularly to being spied upon. She has grown quite used to it, and I can name instances where she has gone out of her *way* to give admirers—even mobs of them—these privileged views of herself. No, if she has an objection in the present case it has to do with the admirer himself. For assuredly it is Corporal O'Hara out there, and the man's attentions have lately become odious to her.

The Irishman had pursued her, she knows, from the moment he'd slunk aboard the *Girl of Safi*, and his suit had been of an especially irksome kind. Quiet and skulking was the Corporal's *modus operandi*. His was that dark little presence in the tail of her eye, ever watching, hungrily, waiting his chance. Like some jackal in human form he fled easily when she gnashed her teeth, only to appear right back at her heel in the next moment, undeterred, with his staring eyes. She could not even summon a proper fear of him, which might at least have been useful. Even now, with that hideous eye roving the cabin and herself pinned to her hassock, there is no more in her than a deep and wearying annoyance, and a hateful indecision. What good to cry out for help, she thinks, when he would only steal back into the dark with his private little snicker? What good to throw open the door and lay into him, when he'd like nothing more than a scolding from herself, in undress? She would not acknowledge him now for worlds, and she would no sooner gratify him with a second look at her, which rules out fleeing to the bed-room. So she must sit and gnaw at her thumbnail and wait till he gives up his vigil, without any real expectation that he will.

It is some time after midnight when a voice reaches her hearing from far off down the hall. It seems almost, to her grasping imagination, as though she has willed this sound into being.

MR. BUCHAN–?

GO ON, CORPORAL. THIS IS NO MORE YOUR POST.
HA! YOU THINK I NEED GUNS FOR A MITE LIKE YOU? ON'Y HOPED I WOULD'N HAVE TA SET DOWN MY BOTTLE–

GRKK–!

ENOUGH–BOTH OF YOU–REALLY–STOP THIS.

MR. BUCHAN, WHO IS THAT?
IT'S–NO ONE–
SEE THERE, SON? NEXT TIME I RING YOUR SKULL WITH THIS.

HRM! IT'S ON'Y YER SERVANT, MUM, CORPORAL O'HARA, SITTIN' A WATCH 'ERE ON MAJOR'S ORDERS. THO WHAT THE BOY'S UP TO HERE IS MORE'N I CAN SAY–
WELL I DIDN'T ASK FOR A GUARDIAN, MR. O'HARA, AND YOU CAN TELL MR. OGDEN THAT. TELL HIM I DON'T WANT ANY MORE OF YOU SQUATTING OUTSIDE MY DOOR AND TROUBLING MY SLEEP, DO YOU UNDERSTAND?

AH–HRM. IF THAT'S WHAT YE'D HAVE–
IT IS. NOW, GO ON.
MR. BUCHAN, YOU'LL STAY, IF YOU PLEASE, AND SEE HIM GONE.
OH, AYE? WULL. 'NIGHT THEN, AND GOOD DREAMS T'YA.

PTHTHTPH!

...WELL THAT WAS SOMETHING, WASN'T IT.
YES, I'M TERRIBLY SORRY–

OH YOU NEEDN'T APOLOGIZE FOR HIM. I'M GLAD HE'S BROUGHT YOU HERE, ANYWAY, AND...WELL, I SUPPOSE WE'RE ALONE NOW?
YES, HE'S GONE. I'LL GIVE HIM A BIT OF LEAD AND SAY GOOD NIGHT MYSELF–
NO-NO. I'M POURING A GLASS OF WINE, MR. BUCHAN, AND THEN I WANT YOU TO COME IN AND LOOK AT SOMETHING.
UNLESS YOU'D PREFER NOT TO?

EHH: IF–YES, OF COURSE.
THEN COME. AND CLOSE THE DOOR AFTER YOU.

THERE YOU ARE: MY SAVIOR.

...THOUGH, I SUPPOSE YOU WERE JUST AS MUCH MINE–
OH LA. YOU'RE IN NO DANGER FROM A CREATURE LIKE THAT, ARE YOU?
WELL–I SHOULD THINK I AM NOW, IF I WEREN'T ALREADY. AND IF HE'S TROUBLING YOU, I OUGHT TO BRING IT TO MAJOR.

NO-NO. THAT MAN WILL NOT HAVE THE PLEASURE OF SEEING ME VEXED. WE'LL IGNORE THE WHOLE THING.
GIVE EVIL NOTHING TO OPPOSE AND IT'LL DISAPPEAR ALL BY ITSELF– DIDN'T SOMEONE SAY THAT?
SOMEONE AWFULLY PATIENT, IF HE DID. AND LIKELY HE WAS WRONG.

ANYWAY, THAT'S ENOUGH OF MR. O'HARA. ANY MORE AND YOU'LL PUT ME OUT OF MY MOOD.
APROPOS: JAMES, YOU KNOW I'VE BROUGHT YOU IN AND HERE YOU HAVEN'T LOOKED UP AT ME ONCE. I SAY THAT'S EXHIBITING BAD MANNERS.

YES OF COURSE; BUT YOU'RE–
OH YOU'VE...STOOD CANNON-FIRE AND THOSE THINGS, HAVEN'T YOU? THIS CAN'T BE MUCH WORSE.
JUST FOLLOW MY VOICE AND...

...YOU SEE: THERE I AM.
SOMETHING LIKE HOW PERSEUS FOUND ANDROMEDA, ISN'T IT?
DON'T KNOW IF THE GREEKS MADE SUCH...CLEVER THINGS FOR THEIR CAPTIVE GIRLS TO WEAR–

NO, YOU'RE RIGHT. COME AND HELP ME OFF WITH IT.
THAT'S ALL RIGHT: YOU MAY, NOW THAT I'VE ASKED YOU.
...G–D. I'M NOT USED TO WORKING SO HARD AT THIS.

YOU KNOW WHAT THIS IS, I HOPE?
I...YES. I HAVE SOME LITTLE EXPERIENCE OF IT.
GOOD. YOU KNOW, I'D WONDERED.
–A MOMENT, THOUGH.

AH. THANK YOU, JAMES.
NOW, COME: LET US SEE WHAT THESE GIRLS IN BOMBAY ARE TEACHING YOU MEN.

ELSEWHERE ON THE SHIP, A HOWL-
ING CRY DISTRACTS HEINER FROM HIS
CONTEMPLATION OF THE MOON.

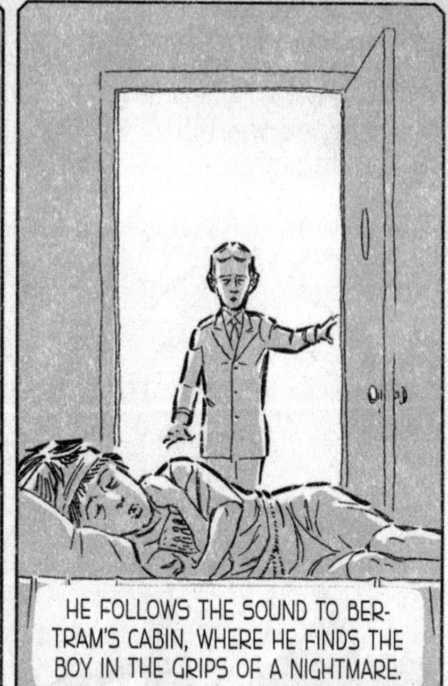
HE FOLLOWS THE SOUND TO BER-
TRAM'S CABIN, WHERE HE FINDS THE
BOY IN THE GRIPS OF A NIGHTMARE.

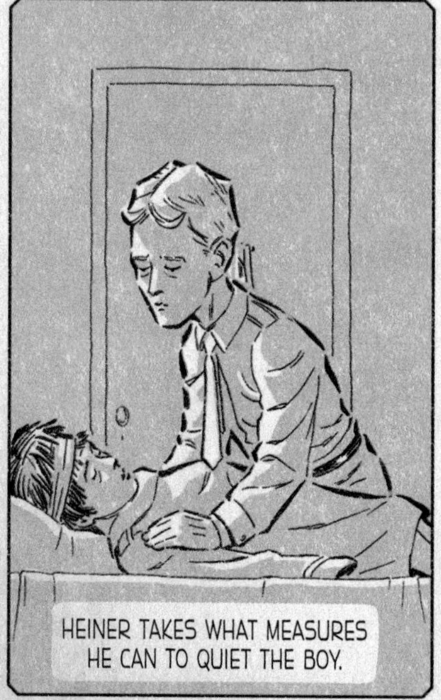
HEINER TAKES WHAT MEASURES
HE CAN TO QUIET THE BOY.

BY THE TIME HIS HAND IS FREED, DAWN HAS GATHERED IN THE WINDOWS AND HIS KNEES ARE ACHING HORRIBLY.

BERTRAM WAKES WITH A TEA-SERVICE AND A SET OF AUSTRIAN NURSERY BOOKS ARRANGED BESIDE HIM. THE BOOKS ARE HEINER'S MOST VALUED POSSESSIONS, AND HE HAS NEVER LET THEM INTO ANYONE ELSE'S CARE.

THEY ARE LOVINGLY INSCRIBED TO A BOY CALLED RUTGER, A ONETIME PASSENGER ON THE *METTERNICH*.

WE WON'T TAKE UP AS LOVERS, JAMES. YOU DIDN'T THINK WE WOULD, DID YOU?
NO, MA'AM.
GOOD.
...WHAT DID YOU THINK?

WELL: ONLY THE USUAL THINGS ABOUT GIFT HORSES. AND I SAW WHERE A YOUNG LADY MIGHT GET LONELY, TRAVELING SO LONG, AND IN SUCH COMPANY AS YOU'VE GOT.
YES, BUT YOU DIDN'T THINK MY INVITATION HAD ANYTHING PARTICULARLY TO DO WITH YOU...?

OH-NO, NOT THAT I'D CONSIDERED. I DO HAVE A NUMBER OF FINE QUALITIES, OF COURSE–
–OH, STOP–
–BUT AS FAR AS THAT GOES, NO. I THOUGHT IF THERE WERE ANY OF US FOR YOU, IT MIGHT BE MR. SLOANE.
MM. I MIGHT HAVE THOUGHT SO MYSELF. I SUPPOSE I DID, FOR A NUMBER OF YEARS. BUT NOW HE AND I'VE TALKED...

...ANYWAY, YOU'RE A NICE YOUNG MAN, JAMES, AND I LIKE YOU, AND THERE IT IS. YOU MUST TELL ME YOU WON'T GET YOUR HEART BROKEN OVER THIS, WILL YOU?
WELL–DO MY BEST NOT TO–
–AND IT WOULDN'T DO, EITHER, TO LET THIS OUT AMONG THE MEN. I'M THINKING LESS OF MYSELF HERE THAN OF YOUR OWN SAFETY.

NO, QUITE RIGHT. YOU CAN TRUST THE DESPATCH-RUNNER TO BE THE SOUL OF DISCRETION.
HM. YOU KNOW, IT STRIKES ME YOU'RE BEING TERRIBLY REASONABLE ABOUT ALL THIS. I'M NOT USED TO MEN BEING REASONABLE, ONCE THEY'VE GOT THIS FAR.
SHOULD I BE SUSPICIOUS OF YOU, MR. BUCHAN?

SUSPICIOUS?
–I'VE KNOWN THESE LITTLE FLINGS TO LIGHT A SORT OF SLOW-MATCH IN A MAN'S BRAIN. HE LEAVES ME PERFECTLY COMPOSED AND GETS ON NORMALLY FOR DAYS, AND THEN: BANG! HIS REASON BLOWS ALL TO BITS. HE RUNS BACK TO ME, RAVING.

IT'S NOT FUNNY, THOUGH, IS IT?
NO, IT SOUNDS D–MNED AWKWARD FOR YOU BOTH.
BUT IT HAPPENS, YOU SEE.

–OR: THERE WAS A MAN IN MY ACTING DAYS, WE WOKE AT THE IMPERIAL IN VIENNA AND I LET HIM GO ON VERY MUCH THE SAME TERMS AS I HAVE YOU, AND HE SEEMED TO TAKE IT NO WORSE. HE PECKED MY CHEEK, TOOK A PRIMROSE FROM THE BREAKFAST TRAY FOR HIS LAPEL, AND LEFT THROUGH THE WRONG DOOR. I WAS ABOUT TO RAG HIM FOR IT WHEN I HEARD SCREAMING IN THE PLAZA. HE'D WALKED RIGHT OFF MY BALCONY.

MISS HARROW: I'M NOT VERY PRACTICED IN THESE THINGS, AS YOU'LL HAVE GUESSED. BUT I DO APPRECIATE THE...TERMS UNDER WHICH I WAS BROUGHT IN, AND I'M VERY FAR FROM COMPLAINING ABOUT ANY OF IT.
IF OUR FRIENDSHIP FROM HERE FORWARD ISN'T ALL I'D LIKE, I SHALL JUST HAVE TO BRAVE MY DISAPPOINTMENT. I'VE STOOD TO CANNON-FIRE, AS YOU SAY; PERHAPS THIS WON'T BE MUCH WORSE.

WELL. ALL RIGHT. I'LL TRUST YOU MEAN ALL THAT. GIVE US A KISS, NOW.

STAY AWAY FROM THE BALCONIES, AND BE THE GENTLEMAN YOU ARE NOW, AND WE'LL LOOK INTO EXTENDING THESE TERMS OF YOURS.
I'M EASILY FOUND. GOOD DAY, MISS HARROW.
GOOD DAY, YES.

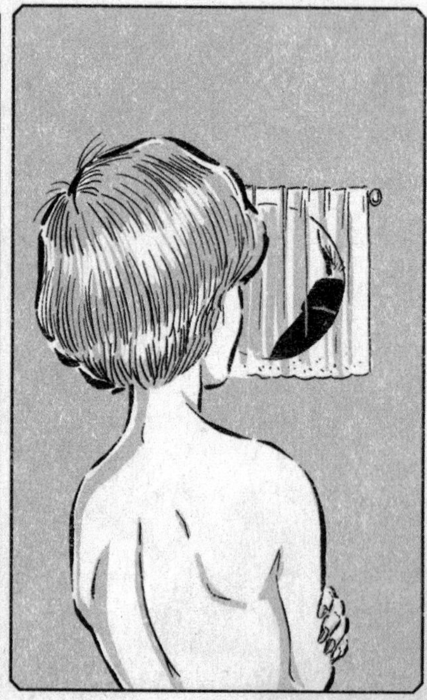

On the *Metternich*'s observation deck, the ship's stewards are clearing the last of the breakfast service. Mr. Sloane sits aside from the dining tables in a lounger, reading a badly out-of-date *Tatler* and penning notes in a little steno pad. His interview with Major Ogden is about three days gone, making this the morning of 27 May, 1918.

The intervening days, I should say, have been quiet ones, given mostly to private recuperation and reflection. Ogden's men have finished off the ship's liquor, which point was not reached without a few frantic searches of the saloons and demonstrations of displeasure, for which the *Metternich* is visibly the worse. But the men have emerged from the fogs of inebriation, and whether fit and clear-headed now or gravely ill, they are all as subdued in manner as we are likely to find them.

Ogden himself has stayed closeted with Subadar Priddish in the second officer's quarters, poring over his maps and weather reports. The Sikh feels his commander is struggling with some question or concern that hasn't anything to do with the weather or the landing, and he has caught Ogden measuring him now and then with an anxious eye. But their conversation deviates little from the necessities of travel and their strategies of approach, and Mr. Priddish offers counsel on these things with his habitual patience.

Miss Harrow, meanwhile, has divided her time between the *Metternich*'s library and Bertram's bedside. Her visits to Bertram's cabin were prompted at first by hopes of coinciding there with Mr. Sloane (in which hopes she had been consistently disappointed); but she has discovered an unexpected pleasure now in arranging for Bertram's comforts, and she has developed a certain fondness for his society, particularly where he is such a good listener. And if some of her stories are ill-chosen for a boy of seven, if her ministrations are tentative and amateur—or applied more to her benefit than his (she has been rouging his cheeks, for instance)—still we cannot fail to notice an improvement in the boy's health and spirits, and we must credit at least some of this to Miss Harrow's agency.

This morning, too, she will be found in her rocker by the heating grate, where she reads while Bertram sleeps. She has not yet noticed Heiner, the wraith-like cabin boy, who stands in the doorway staring in. And when she happens to look up between pages, she flinches and pulls a little frown—it cannot be helped. Yet Heiner is here by compact today.

And he needn't speak, only point, to indicate that Mr. Sloane has surfaced again on the *Metternich*, this time somewhere aft.

Moments later, Miss Harrow is rushing along a corridor, flipping to a dog-eared page in her book and marking the place with her finger. Heiner stands ahead with one arm holding back a door to the observation deck and the other raised to point, unnecessarily, through the opened doorway. Inside sits Mr. Sloane with his *Tatler*, in sole possession of the room, as told. He stands with a gracious nod to Miss Harrow as she enters.

MR. SLOANE. WE WEREN'T SURE WHAT MAJOR HAD DONE WITH YOU.
NO? I WASN'T ENTIRELY SURE MYSELF. I THINK I MAY HAVE SURVIVED SOME FORM OF DUEL.

...THOUGH YOU MAY WANT TO TAKE CARE WITH FIRE AROUND ME. I'M STILL RATHER EXUDING WHISKEY, THREE DAYS ON.
MM. I WOULDN'T TRY MATCHING DRINKS WITH HIM AGAIN.
HERE: I'VE FOUND THIS FOR YOU.

THIS IDEA OF MINE, THAT I'D SEEN YOU AT MY SÉANCE, THOSE YEARS AGO: I'VE BEEN SO CONVINCED OF IT FOR SO LONG THAT I'VE FOUND THE IDEA RATHER HARD TO LET GO.
EVEN WHEN YOU'D PROVED IT WASN'T YOU, STILL I FELT IT MUST BE.
AND–YOU KNOW–I'VE ALWAYS FELT THAT THE PICTURE I SAW BEHIND YOU MIGHT PROVIDE SOME CLUE...

THERE. THE DOMES OF PASSAU CATHEDRAL, OVER THE INN RIVER. YOU DON'T KNOW HOW MANY OF THESE BOOKS I'VE HAD TO LOOK THROUGH.
I SEE...

THAT PAINTING AT THE ALBERT: IT WASN'T A PAINTING, IT WAS A WINDOW. YOU WERE SITTING IN PASSAU WITH THAT VIEW BEHIND YOU, WHILE WE HELD OUR SÉANCE IN NEW YORK. YOU WERE NO MORE PRESENT THAN THE ABBOT, OR SELESCU.
BUT I SAW YOU, MR. SLOANE.
YES. MY COUSIN'S, AT INNSTADT.

YOU'RE SELESCU'S SON, AND OUR ABBOT'S PROTÉGÉ. WHICH MEANS YOU'RE LEADING US TO YOUR HOME.
I WONDER HOW MUCH OF THAT YOU KNEW.
MY GOODNESS. I OUGHT TO SIT.
MR. SLOANE FEELS A MOMENT'S WEIGHTLESSNESS...

WIR GEHEN NACH UNTEN.
WE BEGIN OUR DESCENT.
...WHICH IS IN SOME PART LITERAL.

UP, LADS. GET UP. WE'RE STORMING THE CASTLE.

BIT HIGH UP FOR BIRDS, IN'NIT?

HOW'S THIS BELOW, JACK?
HUH. MAJOR COME OUT YET?
LOCKED IN WITH 'IS INJUN.
GO KNOCK ON HIS DOOR. SEE IF THERE'S A OATH HE AIN'T USED YET.
STILL, WE MIGHT GET HIM...

<–RUDDERS ALL TO STARBOARD, CAPTAIN–WE CAN'T COME AROUND IT. THEY'RE STILL CLOSING.>
<THEN CUT ENGINES, OPEN THE VALVES–WE'LL DROP THROUGH LIKE A STONE.>
<EVERYONE IN LIFE-VESTS, MR. HENNINGER.>
<AYE, SIR.>
*FROM THE BAVARIAN.

MORNING, SIR. WHO WE DECLARING FOR?
FOR THE AULD MOTHER, IN'NIT?
ENGLAND? SHE AIN'T MY MOTHER.
AN' IT'S A HABSBURG VESSEL, JACKIE. HER ALLIES OUT THERE ARE THE HUNS.
AYE, TILL WE FIRE ON 'EM. THEN WE TAKE ON THE WHOLE FIELD.
THIS IS MY POINT.
GENTLEMEN: MAY I SUGGEST NEUTRALITY?
YOU MAY NOT.

WELL. OVERHEAD, YOU KNOW, THERE ARE ABOUT HALF A MILLION CUBIC FEET OF EXPLOSIVE GAS. A GREAT BOMB, AND YOU'RE TIED TO THE BELLY OF IT.
THEN SO ARE YOU, YER HIGHNESS.
SO AM I. WHICH IS WHY I'D HESITATE TO PROVOKE AN ATTACK.
GIVE ME THAT. THOUGH IT AIN'T GONNA WORK.
AND IT'S AGAINST MY PRINCIPLES, BESIDES.

STEADY, LADS.
NAH, IT'S NO GOOD, JACK.
MAJOR? SIR, ARE WE FIRING--?

THAT DEVIL YOU MAY SHOOT, MR. PRIDDISH.

MISS HARROW–
YOU GO AHEAD. I'LL TELL YOU WHAT HAPPENS.

SUBADAR PRIDDISH'S BULLET FINDS ITS MARK.
<<CRRACK!>>

BUT AS THE SOPWITH NOSES DOWN, ITS RUDDER BLADE GASHES THE *METTERNICH*.

HOW MANY BULLETS TO SET OFF YOUR BOMB, SIR? SHE'S TAKEN SEVERAL HUNDRED.
I WOULDN'T MIND THE BULLETS– IT'S INCENDIARIES WE CAN'T HAVE. I IMAGINE THEY'D HAVE USED THEM, IF THEY BROUGHT ANY.

‹LEVEL HER OFF, MR. STANGL, AND FULL AHEAD. GET US TO THE STRAND.›
‹AYE, SIR.›

‹‹CRRASH!››
WHAT'S SLOANE SAYING?
SAYS IT'S ALL RIGHT, SO LONG AS WE DON'T HAVE ANY...

...ABOUT TO SAY, 'FIRE.'

'OW'S YER WEATHER PORT-SIDE, MA-JOR? OVER 'ERE IT'S RAININ' BAVARIANS.

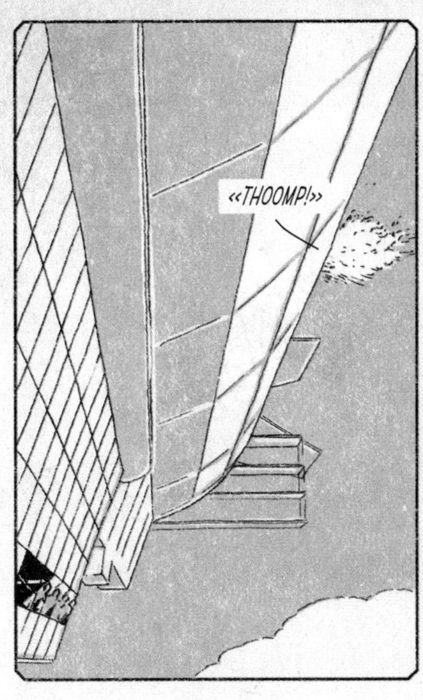
«THOOMP!»

ALL OF YOU–OFF!

BERTRAM–!
HE'LL BE ALL RIGHT.
LET GO NOW, EVELYN.

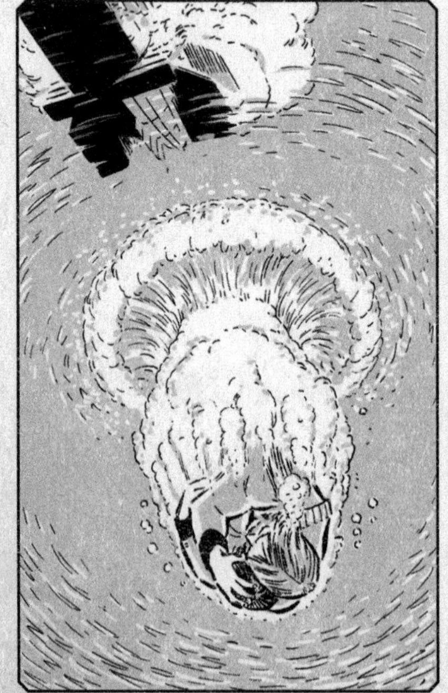

‹YOU! HE'S DROWNING. BRING OVER THAT BENCH—QUICKLY!›
WHO, HIM? YA, HE'S NO SWIMMER, IS HE?
OI—TOM: KICK OFF YER BOOTS, MAN. YE'LL BOB UP LIKE A CORK.

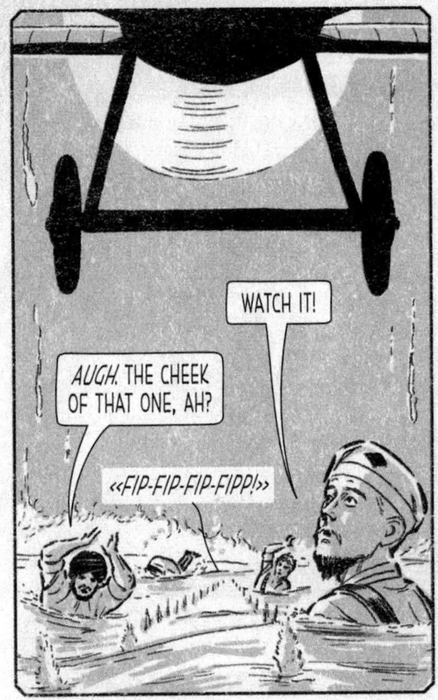
WATCH IT!
AUGH. THE CHEEK OF THAT ONE, AH?
<<FIP-FIP-FIP-FIPP!>>

<<BAP-BAP-BAPP!>>
GO ON AND CHEER, YA SONS-A-BELIAL! THAT WAS ONE OF OURS!

OH DEAR–NO-NO-NO...

THE LITTLE BODY IS NOT BERTRAM'S, BUT YOUNG HEINER'S.
THE CABIN BOY'S FACE, GENERALLY EXPRESSIONLESS, IS GRAVEN NOW WITH THE INTENSEST HORROR AND GRIEF.
AS THOUGH FINALLY BROUGHT, IN DEATH, TO SOME STRANGE APPROXIMATION OF LIFE.

HEAD UP, LAD. STAY UP HERE WITH US.
BERTRAM...?
BERTRAM HIMSELF HAS SURVIVED THE FALL, THOUGH HE MUST STRUGGLE TO STAY CONSCIOUS IN THE WATER.

...THERE YOU ARE. GOOD BOY.
SERGEANT, YOU STAY HERE. HE'S COMING ROUND.
AYE, SIR.
HE WAKES SOME TIME LATER, ON THE SHORE.

...THAT'S TWICE NOW, AH?

ALL THE YEARS WE FOLLOWED MAJOR, AND NEVER SAW SO MUCH AS A HORSE SHOT FROM UNDER HIM. AND LOOK NOW: HE CAN'T SET FOOT ON NOTHING WITHOUT IT EXPLODES.

III.

FOR REASONS THAT WILL BE PLAIN to the reader, the mustering of the Fifth Dragoons at Feritiva is not the quick and routine affair their commander would have envisioned just hours ago. Still, as I am pleased to record, all our passengers from the *Metternich* have washed up on the strand more or less fit to push on.

The last to report had been Private Mulcairn, who was sloshing about on an ottoman in search of his horse and had refused an order to kick in to shore. We might, indeed, have seen no more of the man, but that his game little Caspian was spotted rounding a headland beneath a wounded French pilot (which pilot, relieved of the horse by our dragoons, had given a terrifically Gallic shrug of the shoulders and wandered off on foot). Captain Shaw had then won the job of fetching Mulcairn through a drawing of lots, and had delegated the same job to Corporal Buchan, whereon Buchan had put to sea on an improvised raft, aping the French pilot's shrug, to applause.

Some hours later we find the sun sinking behind the Balkans and a fog stealing in after it from over the sea. Mr. Mulcairn has returned to shore and reclaimed his horse, and may be seen grazing it now on a bluff. His fellows have dragged together all useful salvage from the *Metternich*, and a slim inventory it is. They are barely provisioned for a hike to the Castle Feritiva, let alone armed for an attack on it. But we find the dragoons scrounging and mending and re-rigging all in good cheer, as men who've returned to a more suitable mode of work after months of chasing ghosts and zanies and languishing on ships of one kind and another. No, if there is a concern in the camp today, it is over a different matter entirely: somewhere in the morning's chaos, you see, Mr. Sloane and Miss Harrow seemed to have slipped away with little Barnes.

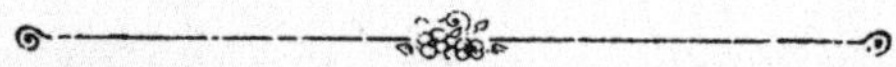

By the time their absence is noted, Mr. Sloane has led Bertram and Miss Harrow over a shoulder of rock and out along the Durere promontory. Their steps fall gradually onto an old road that connects the hamlet at Feritiva with the larger feudal settlement and castle ahead, and they continue without speaking or looking back, making steady progress but gazing each, perhaps, over a different terrain of thought.

I should think Miss Harrow would have put a pointed question or two to Mr. Sloane by now, or that she'd have picked up at least on the conversation they'd been forced to abandon on the *Metternich*. Yet she has barely spoken since she climbed out of the sea. She follows along in a dazed, hangdog silence most uncharacteristic of her, with her mouth compressed and brow lined, and her eyes flicking up to Bertram's back and falling again into abstraction, over and over. For all the uncertainties swirling around Mr. Sloane and all the dangers manifest in this quiet hike to the castle, Miss Harrow cannot pull her thoughts back into the present. In her mind, you see, she is still drifting in the wreckage of the *Metternich*, reaching through the cracked beams and balusters and scraps of canvas, turning over the little figure of the cabin boy. Only that vacant, waterlogged little face is not his own, it is Bertram's....

A few steps ahead of her (as she seems compelled to check, continually), Bertram walks with his head tipped forward and his gaze skimming along the grass, taking two steps for each one of Mr. Sloane's. Bertram's thoughts, too, are circulating far from the present, and we may trace them among the wildgrown gardens and distant spires of light, the green-glowing whales and the young girl in costume with her whispered warnings, and other such places and pictures as we have seen before on his mind's stage. It is not that he seeks these things out with a view to ordering them or examining them for meaning. They are simply and persistently *there*. These are the places—the images, symbols, sensations—memories, perhaps—to which his mind reverts when it is left idle. They do not admit interpretation yet, these visions. But he feels his life's arrow to be pointed toward a time of epiphany, when each will materialize before him and make its own definition plain. It is only for him, for now, to know these pictures and to remain alive and observant, so that he might recognize them at the appointed hour.

Of the three travelers, anyway, only Mr. Sloane maintains a view of the castle ahead. Though to say he 'sees' it in its present state is to miss certain cues in his behavior. His eyes are a bit *too* fixed, for one thing. Here he'll lower a hand absently, just in time to brush a fencepost; there his feet edge around a crumbled block of paving or skip over a water-filled rut, seemingly of their own accord. This is the way a blind man might proceed through a familiar place, consulting the maps of his memory. And indeed, I should think the eyes of Mr. Sloane were projecting as much as they take in. To him these weedgrown fields are nodding with summer wheat, and the empty cart-paths teem with visitors and vendors. Ahead, where the old stone structure blears with the fog and merges into the coming night and might really be *anything*, he can see the soaring lines of the Castle Feritiva. And just as plain are the cypress trees sprouting from the cliff ledges, the long white strip of sand girding the bay, the peasant houses clustered like limpets beneath the old walls and battlements, and the high seaward fortification dropping straight into the surf....

What effect these visions have on Mr. Sloane, what changes they will work in him, I cannot say. But he has not come solely to wake the ghosts of his memory. He is here with a larger, pressing purpose: Bertram must be got into the castle's undercroft, and without delay. So he must wonder why he has found himself suddenly paused at the gate of a thatch-roofed hut, still a good distance from the castle and well off the road.

Moments later he stands at the hut's gaping front-door frame, and looking in he can see its hearth is smashed and its mantel bowed. There are swallows nested in its eaves, too, and the packed-earth floor is littered with husks of fruit and blacked all over by the fires of squatters. Yet here, Mr. Sloane thinks, were once a woman and an invalid man. They were favorites of the Count's–domestics, perhaps, in their retirement, with their own children grown or killed or anyway absent. They'd a fender too big for this hearth, either borrowed or stolen from the castle, with a coal-scuttle and irons beside it, and a table and chairs and cups on hooks, hatchments and little reproductions of the castle arms and other tokens of service, and a cedar-wood box with mementos of travel inside–a rattle-drum from China, a carven mask from Capetown, folded Mideast textiles and Shetland wools. And here more than any of it were the treasured days of Mr. Sloane's childhood. Here, he thinks, when he had lingered too late in the evenings, they would put out a tick for him, and then there would be honeyed tea and *vingt-et-un* with English playing-cards, and the parlor games he'd taught them, and a reprieve from the long hours cloistered among books and somber men....

Strangely, he cannot seem to conjure the old couple themselves. They are all disjointed flashes and mannerisms and snatches of speech, with even their names effaced. But the loss is rather welcomed by Mr. Sloane, who finds in these elusive and inchoate figures an analogue for his own fractured being.

STAY RIGHT THERE, DEAR.

MR. SLOANE...?
YES, SORRY. COME HELP ME, WOULD YOU?

COME ON, THEN. IT'S NO GOOD, YOUR STAR-ING FROM OVER THERE.
BUT: WHAT ARE YOU DOING?

MM? OH: I'LL SHOW YOU.
THAT'S IT. RIGHT TO ME...

WHEN I LIFT, IF YOU'D WEDGE THAT BEAM IN AFTER ME...
AH: GOOD. THANK YOU. OUGHT TO BE ABLE TO GET IT FROM HERE MYSELF.
BERTRAM, COME LOOK.

ESCAPE TUNNEL FROM THE CASTLE, YOU KNOW. BELIEVE I WAS SHOWN THE DOOR AT THE OTHER END, WHEN I WAS A BOY.
I'D TAKE A CANDLE, SOME NIGHTS, DOWN INTO THE UNDERCROFT TO STUDY IT.
AND I'D STOCK MY NIGHTMARES WITH THE THINGS I IMAGINED LIVING IN HERE, SEALED IN THE DARK THROUGH THE AGES.

SOONER OR LATER OF COURSE I MUST TRY THE DOOR, AND THEN VENTURE IN, AND ULTI-MATELY BECOME STUCK ON THIS END. THEY'D PLANKED IT OVER AND PUT A BED ON TOP.
I SUPPOSE THAT WAS HOW I MET THE OLD COUPLE WHO LIVED HERE, WHEN THEY HEARD ME KNOCKING BENEATH THEIR BED, AND SOMEHOW GOT ME OUT.

AT ANY RATE, I OUGHT TO BE ABLE TO SHOW YOU WHERE NOT TO STEP. IT JOINS THE CATACOMBS NOT FAR FROM HERE.
YOU DON'T MEAN YOU'RE CLIMBING IN?
I THOUGHT WE MIGHT, YES. OR YOU CAN WALK UP TO THE GATES AND KNOCK, IF YOU LIKE.
I JUST CAN'T SAY WHO'D ANSWER.

MAJOR–?

...THIS RAGAMUFFIN'S BEEN CAMPED UP THE ROAD ASKING FOR YEH, AN' DON'T SAY MUCH ELSE.

THINK HE MEANT TO DELIVER THIS INTO YER HANDS, SIR. SINCE HE D–MNED NEAR PULLED OFF MR. HENTY'S EAR, TRYIN' TO KEEP IT.

SEE THAT? YEH MAD B–STARD?
THAT'S ALL WE'RE DOIN,' IS HELPIN' YOU DELIVER IT.

C CO COMMERCIAL CABLE
TELEGRAM
BDB929 ORIG
NY 01 USA
25 MAY PM 6 44
FILING TIME SHOWN IN DATE LINE IS STANDARD TIME AT POINT OF ORIGIN.
TIME OF RECEIPT IS STANDARD TIME AT POINT OF DESTINATION.
FRIEND IN SERVICE HOTEL FIRENZE WAITS UPON
TWO SOZZLED OLD GENTLEMEN OF CEYLON CO
HEARD TO SAY CO HAS QUOTE EYES ON J OGDEN =
CONSTRUE TO MEAN SPY IN YOUR NUMBER YOU ARE
SO ADVISED =
ALL BEST ANNE MAGUIRE =
PS SMALL CONSIDERATION FOR BEARER OF CABLE I
YOU PLEASE WHO HAS RODE FAR TO DELIVER -0-
AM 4 18

...FROM NEW YORK, SIR?
GO ON, LAD. IT'S NO AFFAIR O' YERS, IS IT.

AIN'T YERS EITHER, THEN.
AYE. JUST MY POINT.

A BIT FARTHER UP THE ROAD, CAPTAIN SHAW HAS BEEN RE-CONNOITERING THE CASTLE.

STILL THREE EACH ON THE LOWER WALKS, SIR, AND SIX MORE ACROSS THE TOP. THEY'VE STOOD THEIR POST SINCE WE LANDED, AND HARDLY MOVED.

QUEER THEY'D PUT NO ONE AT THE BRIDGE, SIR. YOU'D THINK A DOG THERE, MEAN ENOUGH, COULD HOLD THAT CASTLE HIMSELF.
P'RAPS YE'LL ADVISE THEM ON THAT POINT.
I ONLY REMARKED HOW QUEER IT IS, THAT NO ONE'S THERE. AND LUCKY FOR US, RATHER.

YOU ARE QUITE SURE THE SENTRIES HAVEN'T MOVED, MR. SHAW?
YES, SIR.
ALL RIGHT. SERGEANT, CORPORAL: BOTH OF YOU AHEAD WITH MR. RENTON.

HYARRHH! SERGEANT, THEY GOT ME! –OOFH!
HOLD IT, LAD! TURN 'IM OVER THE EDGE!
DOWN, MR. BUCHAN.

AHH! HAVE AT YOU NOW! THERE! AND THERE! HYAA!
«PIFF!»

CLEAR OUT BELOW, YOU MEN!
ACH FER CHR–ST'S SAKE.
«THUNK»

YOU, SIR–BACK! –*EN GARDE!*–AN' SOME FOR YOU, AH? HA! –*LA VOILÀ–HAWR-HAAARW!*
OI–STOP YER MOUTH, LAD!
MEET US DOWN AT THE WICKET DOOR, NOW, AN' QUIET.

'WHY, YE'VE COME THROUGH FOR US AGAIN, HAVEN'T YOU, MR. RENTON? IN YOUR HANDS THE LIVES AND HONOR OF THIS UNIT!'
AN' WHEN THEY COME TO DECORATE BOYS FOR CUTTIN' UP MANNIKINS, THEY'LL SAVE YEH THE LEGION OF HONOR, SIR.

DIDN'T KNOW THEY WAS MANNIKINS GOIN' UP, DID I?

FIND ANY LIVE BODIES YOU CAN. IF THEY AREN'T SLOANE, THEY OUGHT TO KNOW WHERE HE IS.
AYE, SIR.

Subadar Priddish, with a touch on Ogden's sleeve, has alerted his commander to some other presence in the hall, and Ogden sends his dragoons away with a view not just to searching the castle but to quieting the room around him. He sees Priddish withdraw to the eastern wall, and judges by this that the eavesdropper is somewhere in the gallery over the Sikh's head.

Ogden fills and lights a pipe with a show of nonchalance. He has picked out the sound as well, now—a rattling, sibilant breathing in the darkness around them. He strolls around a corner and back, consulting an old repeater, and hears the spy shifting with him. There is a familiar quality in this lurching about, in the irregular breathing and the involuntary chirps and grunts: one can hardly have spent the last year as Ogden has and not recognize, from their sounds alone, the fevered activities of a madman.

The repeater in Ogden's hands, as Mr. Priddish will know, is a gift inscribed by Carrie Gordon, Ogden's onetime fiancée, and it has not kept time since it was dropped in the Yangtze River several years ago. If Ogden has brought it out, it is so he can point with the fingers beneath it into the adjoining hall, where he has found a stair that leads up into the gallery. Priddish slips away, then, quiet as a cat, but it appears the opportunity is already lost: for no sooner is he gone than the hallway fills with the shouts and whistles of the returning dragoons. The noise spooks the stranger in the gallery and he scurries away into the castle, Priddish giving chase but with little hope now of catching him. Ogden is left to frown into the gloom with a palm on his pistol-butt until, presently, *Messrs.* Buchan and Pensette arrive, pushing a black-robed captive ahead of them.

MAJOR OGDEN–
–QUIET.
HERE WE ARE, SIR: A LIVE ENOUGH BODY FOR YEH. FOR THE TIME BEING.
PLEASE, ONE OF YOU, TAKE A CANDLE.

AND YOU HEAR THAT? AMERICAN, SIR. OR DOES A FAIR IMITATION OF ONE.
HE WAS WALKING TOWARD US, SIR, WHEN WE FOUND HIM. HE SAYS THEY'VE BEEN WAITING FOR US.

...THOUGH HE SAYS HE DOESN'T KNOW WHERE MR. SLOANE IS.
NO, BUT I IMAGINE HE'S SOMEWHERE BELOW.
GIVE ME THAT.

CERTAINLY. IT'S FOR YOU. BUT THERE'S SOMEONE ELSE YOU OUGHT TO SEE, SIR, BEFORE YOU GO LOOKING FOR YOUR FRIEND.
...MAJOR?
I KNOW YOU. YOU'D BE TOM MALTHROP.

I...WELL, I AM. YES. NOW, YOU MUST TELL ME HOW YOU–
FRIEND OF MY BROTHER'S. SIX YEARS AGO, YOU AND HE WENT TO THE POLE.
WE...WE DO KNOW ABOUT ARTHUR OGDEN AND HIS TRIP, YES. THOUGH I DON'T KNOW THAT HE AND I EVER MET. I WONDER IF YOU'RE MISTAKING ME FOR–
–SIR?

–SORRY. IF YOU DON'T MIND...

WHEN SERGEANT TOOK HOLD OF HIM, HIS HAT WAS THROWN OFF. I SAW HE'D THIS, HERE–RATHER LIKE THE BOY'S. YOU SEE?
MM. GIVE HIM HIS HAT.

LOOK AT ME. HEY: TWICE, IN THE YEARS SINCE ARTHUR WENT FOR THE POLE, TOM, I'VE SEEN THESE GHOSTS–MEN I KNEW TO HAVE DIED IN THE ARCTIC. I'D ONLY GLIMPSES OF THEM, AND I FELT I MUST BE MAD, TILL RIGHT NOW.

For a place rumored to be a headquarters of the black-robed men, there don't seem to be many of these characters about. Here and there we see a body turning a corner or withdrawing into shadow, but these are mostly pages and guards and lamplighters, all of them schooled, apparently, in the tradition of staying out of their masters' sight. There has been no more trace of the spy from the front hall gallery, either, and Mr. Priddish has returned from his pursuit alone and saturnine. The rest of the dragoons have fallen in as well, and we see them walking in close formation behind the agitated figure of Mr. Malthrop.

Castle Feritiva is built on such an imposing scale, and is so pervasively dark and stripped of ornament that one tends to go about it—consciously or no—in a penitent sort of silence. Not but that Mr. Buchan must *try* to make conversation. He offers up a string of questions and remarks, getting no particular response until, at his dozenth-or-so mention of the castle's missing tenants, he hears Mr. Malthrop quietly observe that the men here have all gone off on *pilgrimage*. '...Where,' Malthrop adds, 'with any luck, you lot will follow.' Mr. Buchan nods knowingly, but after a few more paces his brows converge again. 'And...what does that *mean*, really?' he asks. Malthrop, in answer, only puts a finger to his lips and gestures ahead to a pair of iron-studded oak doors.

You might recall, dear reader, a message being run to these same doors a year ago, when they were watched over by a pair of long-robed guards. Tonight one of the doors hangs open, and there is just the one older man, without a hat and in a robe of the seedier variety, standing beside it. 'Come...come; come-come-come,' this man is saying, bowing in the repeated, fervent manner of the East-Asians at court. 'You're expected inside, gentlemen–Come.' Malthrop takes up a position beside this man, and seems not a little gratified as the dragoons shuffle past, silent and slack-mouthed, each getting his own first view of the castle's white inner sanctum. Only Ogden arrives studying Malthrop instead of the room beyond the doors, and there is a moment's pause as the old cavalryman stands looking down at his brother's friend, sawing a finger across his scarred chin. 'I don't know, Tom,' he mutters, 'but that you had all better died in the North.' With no more to add, he plods off after his men.

The next room–the Abbot's court–is an enclosed atrium or sun-parlor with the look of an ancient bath, floored with white porcelain tiles and giving out above through a ceiling of glass and ironwork. The walls to right and left cannot be seen at all, and what seems to be the far wall is really the curving edge of some immense, free-standing structure at the room's center. There are right-triangled joists, two stories high, bracing the structure along its convex face, and these are held in place by rivets the size of cartwheels. The thing might be a quarter-mile around altogether, and would not look out of place in the shipyards at Belfast or on the Clive, though it is built to an even greater scale than these works and is, of course, enclosed. On seeing this wonder, the dragoons must struggle against an idea that the castle's innards are somehow larger than the castle itself.

By now, Mr. Malthrop has closed the door behind them and receded into the castle, and they are left in the care of his bare-headed colleague, who begs to be called 'the Chamberlain.' This man catches up to the group and nods to each of them, searching faces until he finds what looks like a suitable interlocutor in Mr. Buchan. Somewhat to the young man's surprise, he takes Buchan's elbow and pulls him toward the structure ahead, motioning for the rest to follow.

'If you'll permit me,' he says, 'I will guess this is your first visit to the Castle Feritiva, and your first audience with the Abbot?' Mr. Buchan nods here in the affirmative. '*Ah*. Then as we've a bit of a walk yet, I ought to give you a word or two on this fellow you are about to meet.' Buchan raises no objection to this. 'Good. Very good. Let us see...' The Chamberlain coughs into his fist and affects to cast about for some suitable words of introduction.

'...The Abbot,' he begins, 'whose Christian name is one of a *few* castle secrets, came to us from France by way of Mongolia in the year 1883. He was the invitee of Count Selescu, lord of this house, who'd had dealings with him in the East and had returned about a year ahead of him. When the Abbot did come it was overland through Russia in the largest coach-and-eight many of the castle staff had ever *seen*, and with a body of physicians and attendants all in the black gowns and hats that have since become more or less *de rigueur* about the place. A *breathtakingly* obese man, this young Abbot. I am told he was greeted with a fairly uniform dropping of jaws, and this in a place where not much used to pass for novelty.

'He was kept at first in the courtyard behind the kitchens while his rooms were being prepared, though this placed a dreadful tax on the kitchens and the larder and only made the job of moving him that much more difficult. How they ultimately *did* move him through the castle is still anyone's guess—Rather like moving the pillars of Stonehenge, I am told, most of it done under cover of night and no doubt by real druids.'

'He suffers some...ailment?' asks Mr. Buchan.

'Well. His physicians have always been vague on the subject, and their mutterings are as dark and open to question as are the men themselves. They mention this and that about an imbalance of humors and a perpetual and overmastering appetite, with virtually nothing eliminated (if you can envision *that*). A wholly unexampled metabolic aberration, they say, and not without a note of pride. For a time they called in experts from as far off as word of the Abbot would reach, but all to little avail. And—really—I think you'll find him quite content nowadays to remain as he is. There are no more advisors brought in, anyway, and he has relegated his own doctors to fighting the side-effects and complications of the disease, which is quite employment enough for a staff of thirteen. One early concern, for instance, was the tremendous *strain* the Abbot's mass placed upon his heart: well, you'll see what they've done is to shore up the old walls and flood the Abbot's bed-chamber with the man still in it—Letting his natural buoyancy counteract gravity, you see. You'll have heard no man is an island—hm?—but I'll show you one who *is*, Mr. Buchan. They've arranged it so you can row out to him in a little skiff.'

'In a—? People row out to him?' Young Buchan struggling, for a moment, with the image of this.

'Yes, and oftentimes spend the day. If it's incredulity causing you to ask, it's only because you cannot appreciate the *scale* of the man till you've actually clapped eyes on him. He's been growing unchecked for decades now, to the point where, if they took the roof off from over him, he'd feature on area *maps*—Do you understand?'

Buchan nodding, though not with what I would call a look of understanding. 'And, people spend the day doing *what* on him, exactly?' he asks.

'Well—I'd say mostly hiking. He mayn't be the attraction he was in the last century, and lately we've been too busy to admit any guests at all. But they've fit him with a swing and a bowling green. There's a topiary and a pitch for battledore and shuttlecock (too small for adults, though we used to invite the children to play), and there were always musicians and performers…Still I *do* think, for the greater part of our guests, the idea of walking about on a man's body was a day's entertainment in itself.'

Here the Chamberlain reaches a staircase that climbs diagonally up the face of the Abbot's retaining wall, from the foot of one joist to the top of the next. He takes the stairs without slowing, as do Buchan and Mr. Renton, behind him. But Mr. Henty, on reaching the stairs, offers to mount a guard at their base, and a few others volunteer to join him with perhaps more than the usual alacrity. Ogden eyes these men from beneath his brows for a moment, but leaves Captain Shaw to stand with

Henty and sends Private Mulcairn back to watch the doors to the hallway. The Chamberlain waits just long enough to see these arrangements made, and then continues his climb and his monologue together.

'...Above the water-line,' he says, 'they treat the Abbot with a decoction not unlike the beechbark they use in tanneries, and they've worked his skin to a leathern toughness. There are special gum-soled brogans we encourage visitors to wear on him, though we did have an especially drunk sportsman tromp out there in his golfing spikes once, and I don't believe the Abbot sustained any serious injury, if indeed he noticed at all.

'As to the water in his tank, it is mostly that–distilled tap-water–though you will see his assistants tippling this or that phial into it at all hours of the day. And you'll find it stocked with bright-colored fish, most of them brought back from the tropics. They are there not just to amuse the guests but to feed off the algae that gathers on the Abbot's skin. And he in turn reports the sensation of their feeding to be an agreeable one, which I suppose is what the naturalists mean by *symbiosis*.'

Buchan, with a finger raised: 'You mean to say, he voices opinions?'

'Oh of *course* he does. Quite a lot of them. In fact, the real attraction on the island is the Abbot himself–which is to say, his speaking parts. These sunk from view some years ago, beneath what is still technically his shoulder-line. But they've fixed a length of stovepipe over his upturned face so he can be fed, and in between feedings he's able to converse. You've seen the brass duct-work, haven't you, running all through the castle? There's a removable length of it that joins the Abbot's speaking-tube to the greater network of pipes, so he can project his voice all about the castle, rather like a ship-captain using his paging system.

'And he hears through it every bit as well, you know. There's really nothing in this castle that escapes his notice, which gives him rather a high perch over the world. We've all our own eyes and ears out there, of course, and you'll see us bringing intelligence into this castle as the bees gather pollen for their hive. Over the years he's amassed a good deal of it–A good deal of *intelligence*, that is, not pollen. Though they do keep bees on him, as well. What was I saying?'

'...All sounds very impressive,' offers Mr. Buchan, vaguely. He is only half-listening himself, awaiting the view at the top of the stairs, now that they've drawn close.

'*Impressive?* I should say so. I can name you quite a few prominent men who've taken this walk before you—princes, archbishops, ministers, even an American president—and none of them so grand but that they will sit and profit—humbly, mind you—from the Abbot's counsel. And do you know? He's an entertaining fellow, to boot. Drop an ocarina down there, and they say he'll play it for you.'

'But'—Buchan's incredulity, woken at last—'a man needs use of his fingers, doesn't he, to play the ocarina?'

'He does, yes. Which is why that saying falls under the heading of *Castle Jokes*.'

'Ah.'

The lights of dawn are gathering in the upper reaches of the court, and the Chamberlain leaves his lantern on a hook at the top of the stairs as he leads Buchan through an archway and into the structure's interior. There is a gruff exchange behind them, and only *Messrs.* Renton, Priddish and Ogden continue through the arch. It seems the rest have come as close to this Abbot as they intend, and will not be coaxed any farther by words alone. Mr. Renton keeps pace with Ogden, heckling the others behind him, per his habit: '*Ach!* 'E's a bl—dy monster! Run, you men!'—and so forth.

The Chamberlain leads them out onto a white marble platform that runs cantilevered along the wall's inner face and is fitted with a row of miniature iron cleats. The first of these cleats sits unused, while the rest moor dozen-man dinghies as they might at any lakeside pier. A man in thick spectacles and a uniform of nautical bedecking waits beside the last dinghy with hands clasped behind his back for Corporal Buchan to acknowledge him; only Buchan, eyes stretched over the water, has to be led to within reach of the man and turned bodily to face him before introductions can be made.

'Mr. Buchan: Mr. Boyanov,' says the Chamberlain, as the two men shake hands. Boyanov's English extends no further than a few standard words of greeting, but these suffice as he guides Mr. Buchan to the last of the skiffs and seats him astern. Boyanov slips away then, ducking and grinning, and Buchan cranes over to read the legend *SMS Tyrolean* painted across the bows of the skiff, beneath a little bowsprit of gilt wood. These carnivalesque little boats, Buchan thinks, and Mr. Boyanov himself, with his seagoing coat and his elaborate courtesies, and these stories of illustrious men and all the bygone amusements on the island–these must belong to some sunnier day when the castle lay open to the world. Today, they seem like the vestiges of a dream, fading in the growing darkness and secrecy of the castle, isolated and absurd....

In a moment more, Boyanov has seated Ogden, Priddish and Mr. Renton each at his own thwart in the boat and stepped in behind them. Birdsong may be heard rising now over the island, though by 'song' I mean these African birds are shrieking as though they're being roasted alive. Buchan can see them over his shoulder, these fugitive dabs of primary color against the backdrop of palm-leaves. The Chamberlain looses the bowline from its mooring and hands the coiled rope to Boyanov, who settles himself at the oars and signs to be cast off. He brings the little *Tyrolean* about, and the Chamberlain comes swirling toward Buchan like a man standing by a carousel. Buchan asks him if this Bulgarian will be his guide on the island.

'Not necessary, sir,' says the Chamberlain.

'Then we'll find your man's...speaking-tube without much trouble, I hope?'

'Head directly to the center of the island.' The Chamberlain cups a hand to the side of his mouth as the distance grows between him and the soldiers: '...You'd see it now if it weren't for the mist–There's a steel cylinder at the island's highest point, within that stand of palms! Good day, you men!'

He offers a deep and elastic bow and strolls off through the archway. Buchan resituates himself to face forward again, and to resume staring at what he must struggle to remind himself is a man.

The Abbot's body, he considers–notwithstanding that it *is* a man's body–is fairly nondescript, being a smooth and mound-shaped mass, rather like the old barrows of western Europe as he has heard them described. It has been fitted with tracts of sod and potted trees and hedges, and elsewhere with carpets and runners and odd bits of furniture. But these efforts seem to have flagged as the island grew, and the greater part of it today–of *him*, I suppose–is bare and featureless, a leathery-brown color above the water and a light mauve beneath.

Another skiff like the *Tyrolean* is returning from the Abbot, with another fancifully garbed seaman at its oars and a thin, round-shouldered man in tinted spectacles composed dourly amidships. The latter would seem to be one of the Abbot's assistants, and he looks a good deal like Mr. Sloane's associates at Lowring-on-Hudson (Mr. Buchan is not sure he hasn't seen this very man, in fact, in New York). But Buchan gives the matter scant thought, for sitting in the bows of the little boat is Evelyn Harrow.

Miss Harrow sits with her back turned to him and an arm dangling over the boat's side, and her fingers trailing along the water's surface. She does not stir when Mr. Buchan calls to her, and he must wait till the boats are passing to see her face.

'Miss Harrow...?' The boats have drawn close enough now to where he can nearly reach her, and perhaps give her a shake. Boyanov and the other rower exchange nods and some form of joke, in German. Mr. Renton elbows Ogden in the ribs, pointing to the young woman and making some comment aside, but Ogden stands unmoving in the bows of his own boat, waiting only to disembark. Miss Harrow's eyes light briefly on the group and she seems to recognize at least Mr. Buchan, though to judge from the lilt of her voice, her thoughts are not anywhere in the present.

'...You've made it, then, you boys.'

'Yes–Miss Harrow, you're all right?'

'They gave me a moment to come see him,' she says, disregarding the question. 'I rather had to. But...I've got to look in on Bertram downstairs. Come and get us–would you?–if we don't come up on our own.'

'We will, yes. But–You've seen him, this Abbot? Miss Harrow? What's he told you...?'

But Miss Harrow is done with her end of the exchange. She fades from view behind the shadows of the retaining wall, and Mr. Buchan can only return to his own contemplation of the island. Boyanov has got them to within twenty yards now of a jetty, whose near end floats on pontoons and whose landward struts rest in little depressions on the island's surface. The gum-soled shoes mentioned by the Chamberlain have been set out on the jetty in ordered pairs, but Ogden lights from the ship and stalks right past them in his boots, with Renton and Priddish following suit behind him.

Buchan, the last from the boat, must fight off a moment's imbalance as the jetty sinks beneath his weight–This greatly to the amusement of Mr. Boyanov, who may have seen men before Mr. Buchan stagger about the dock with arms pinwheeling, but will never tire of the joke. Buchan is not above a grin at his own expense, either, and he sits smiling on the dock as he trades his boots for a pair of the brogans, sized just a little tight. He nods to Boyanov, who is motioning him forward.

'Yes. I'm going, yes.' Buchan a bit overloud here, as though to make his English understood. 'And you'll wait where you are? Mm? Till we return…? Right *here*?' He points to the jetty beneath him, and Boyanov, nodding with increased vigor, points to the floor of the skiff.

'All right. Excellent. Thank you.' Buchan stands and rubs his palms together, and eyes the hill before him with obvious trepidation. Certainly, it is difficult to picture American presidents and village-green bands and children at badminton on such an unprepossessing lump as this. '…All ashore, eh?'

As expected, the surface of the island gives underfoot, but slowly, rather like clay. Walking and balancing become less difficult at a quickened pace, but the going is hardly easy, and from here to the palms above is a climb of two hundred yards at a not-inconsiderable angle. Young and fit as he is, Buchan finds himself bleary-eyed and stooping for wind as the grade beneath him eases, and he draws level with the man-made bower at the island's summit.

The bushes and trees here are all potted in terra-cotta urns and troughs, and these seem arranged at random, either imitating the haphazard plans of nature or else expressing the indifference of the Abbot's gardeners. Buchan weaves his way in through the pots, ducking and pushing aside the low-hanging branches. A clearing ahead is ringed by four long, quarter-turned benches, like a circle of white marble evenly broken and expanded around the island's central object.

And if the Chamberlain was not strictly accurate in calling the Abbot's speaking-tube a 'stovepipe,' he was not very far off, either: the thing is no more than a simple–not to say homely–length of extruded steel, three feet across, reaching about eight feet up from the island's surface and polished to a shine. A gum collar has been fitted to its base, possibly to guard against infection (being sunk, as Mr. Buchan must again remind himself, into living tissue), and a line of rivets up the tube's height show where braces have been set inside it to shore it up against collapse. Buchan finds Major Ogden pacing around the tube, deep in thought, while Mr. Renton and Mr. Priddish make use of the benches. The young Corporal has just begun to wonder when (and of course *how*) they will hear the voice at the nether end of this tube, when he realizes he has been hearing it for some time.

The Abbot's 'voice,' you see, is really more of a deep rumbling that rises through the soles of one's feet and sets the very air about him in vibration. It is only at the island's center, where the speaking-tube adds a bright overtone to the rumbling, that the sound is at all clarified, and shaped into something like intelligible speech. Mr. Buchan is not able to catch quite all of what is being said, particularly at first. But what he hears as he seats himself at the edge of the clearing is roughly this:

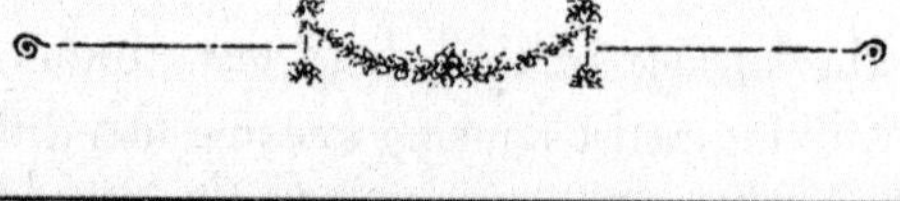

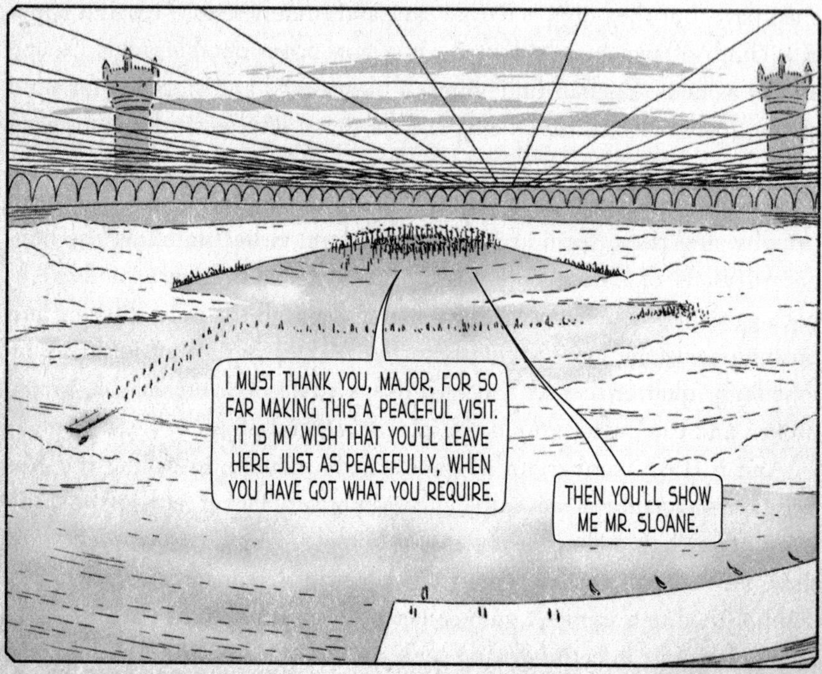

I CAN. THOUGH I WONDER IF HE WERE REALLY WHY YOU'VE COME.
I THINK WE'D BOTH RATHER SEE MR. SLOANE LOCKED SAFELY AWAY, HM? I THINK YOU'D RATHER I SHOWED YOU A WAY TO THE CITY, AS I AM ONLY TOO GLAD TO DO.
YOUR INTERESTS AND OURS ARE VERY MUCH ALIGNED, YOU SEE.
AH. THOUGH YOUR FRIENDS HAVE LEFT ME IN SOME DOUBT, ON THAT POINT.

YES—THIS AFFAIR WITH YOUR BROTHER THE EXPLORER HAS CAUSED SOME DIVISION IN MY HOUSE, AND YOU HAVE MY APOLOGIES FOR IT.
WE'RE AGREED—ALL OF US—THAT ARTHUR MUST BE BROUGHT BACK TO THE CITY. THERE WAS ONLY A QUESTION AS TO WHETHER OR NOT IT WERE SAFE TO HAVE YOU INVOLVED IN THIS. AS THOUGH WE'D ANY CHOICE IN THE MATTER.

MOST OF US RECOGNIZE THAT YOU ARE INVOLVED, MAJOR, AND THAT YOUR BROTHER WILL BE SAFEST IN YOUR OWN HANDS. WE FEEL IT IS OUR DUTY NOW TO MARK A PATH FOR YOU, AND TO RENDER WHAT AID WE CAN.

AT THE...EXPLORERS GUILD, IN NEW YORK, THEY WERE CONNECTING SHAMBHALA TO THE WAR, AND TO PROPHECIES OF A...HYSTERICAL BENT. THEIR IDEAS OF THE APOCALYPSE HAD SOMETHING TO DO WITH AN 'IMPURE SOUL' WINNING HIS WAY INTO THE CITY.
THEIR FEAR WAS THAT ARTHUR MIGHT BE THIS IMPURE SOUL.
AH. AND IS THIS YOUR FEAR, TOO?
WELL. YOU SEE ME TRYING TO GET HIM THERE, REGARDLESS.
PERHAPS YOU'LL TELL ME WHAT YOU KNOW ABOUT IT.

I CAN TELL YOU WHAT WE BELIEVE, MAJOR. WE BELIEVE THE CITY EXISTS IN BALANCE WITH OUR OWN WORLD, AND IN ACCORDANCE WITH CERTAIN RULES.
CHIEF AMONG THESE RULES IS THAT NO MAN MAY ENTER OR EVEN LOOK ON THE CITY, WHO IS NOT SELECTED AND CALLED BY IT.
AND HOW DO YOU KNOW WHICH ARE CALLED, AND WHICH ONLY HAPPEN TO FIND IT?
YOU NEED ONLY LOOK AT THE RESULT, MAJOR. A SCORE OF PILGRIMS WILL ENTER THE CITY'S GATES THIS YEAR, AS QUIETLY AS THEY MIGHT CROSS A THRESHOLD AT HOME.
OF THE REST—OF THE UNBIDDEN—I SHOULD SAY THE HAPPIEST ARE THE ONES WHO FALL DEAD ON THE SPOT.
A FEW OTHERS WE MIGHT FIND AND HELP, BEFORE THEY BECOME A HARM TO THEMSELVES AND TO THE REST OF THE WORLD—
—THE WAY YOU'VE HELPED MY BROTHER'S FRIEND MALTHROP.
YES. THAT'S QUITE RIGHT.
AND I S'POSE YOU'D HAVE 'HELPED' ARTHUR IN THE SAME WAY, IF YOU'D GOT HOLD OF HIM.
OH—NO: YOUR BROTHER HAS NOT JUST SEEN SOME HINT OR REFLECTION OF THE CITY, MAJOR. HE HAS ENTERED IT, AND STOLEN AN ARTICLE OF JADE FROM IT.
THE JADE WE'VE RECOVERED AND SENT AHEAD, FOR WHAT GOOD THAT WILL DO.
BUT THERE IS NO LITTLE CONTAMINANT WE CAN ROOT OUT OF ARTHUR. HE IS QUITE BEYOND OUR HELP. WE MUST GET HIM BODILY TO THE CITY, AND HOPE HE DOES NOT GO TOO LATE.

AND–QUITE AS IMPORTANT–NO ONE MUST TRY TO ENTER WITH HIM. NOT YOU OR YOUR MEN, OR MISS HARROW. CERTAINLY NOT OUR MR. SLOANE.
DO YOU UNDERSTAND THIS? MAJOR?
WHAT HAPPENS TO ARTHUR WHEN HE GETS THERE? SEEMS YOU'D PUT HIM IN LINE FOR SOME PUNISHMENT, AFTER WHAT HE'S DONE.

PUNISHMENT? NATURALLY THERE WILL BE PUNISHMENT. DO YOU NOT SEE HIM PUNISHED ALREADY?
DO YOU NOT SEE THE WORLD IN IMBALANCE, AND ALL THIS WORSENING WHILE HE REMAINS ALIVE AND ABROAD?

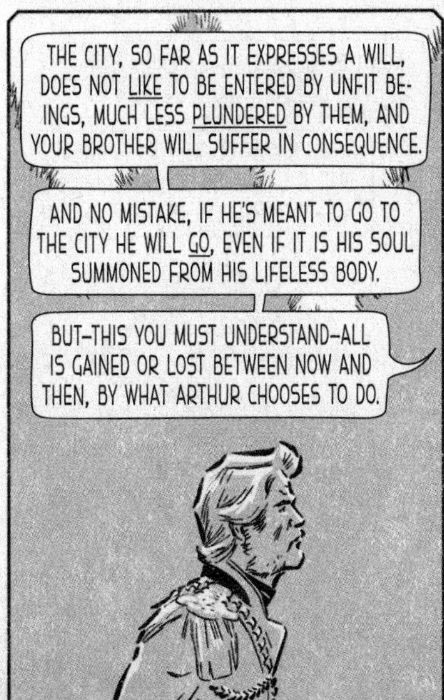
THE CITY, SO FAR AS IT EXPRESSES A WILL, DOES NOT LIKE TO BE ENTERED BY UNFIT BEINGS, MUCH LESS PLUNDERED BY THEM, AND YOUR BROTHER WILL SUFFER IN CONSEQUENCE.
AND NO MISTAKE, IF HE'S MEANT TO GO TO THE CITY HE WILL GO, EVEN IF IT IS HIS SOUL SUMMONED FROM HIS LIFELESS BODY.
BUT–THIS YOU MUST UNDERSTAND–ALL IS GAINED OR LOST BETWEEN NOW AND THEN, BY WHAT ARTHUR CHOOSES TO DO.

IF HE GOES TO THE CITY WILLINGLY, HUMBLY, AS A PENITENT, I BELIEVE HE MAY YET BE SAVED. OTHERWISE HE WILL BE GROUND UTTERLY OUT OF EXISTENCE.
AND I CANNOT SAY BUT THAT AS HE GOES, SO GOES THIS WORLD OF MEN.

WILL I BE ABLE TO BRING HIM HOME, THEN, AT ALL AS HE WAS?

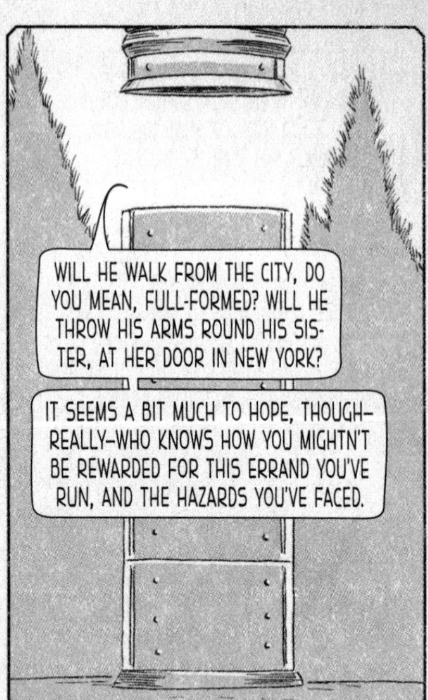
WILL HE WALK FROM THE CITY, DO YOU MEAN, FULL-FORMED? WILL HE THROW HIS ARMS ROUND HIS SISTER, AT HER DOOR IN NEW YORK?
IT SEEMS A BIT MUCH TO HOPE, THOUGH–REALLY–WHO KNOWS HOW YOU MIGHTN'T BE REWARDED FOR THIS ERRAND YOU'VE RUN, AND THE HAZARDS YOU'VE FACED.

I DO KNOW, MAJOR, THAT YOUR SUCCESS WILL BRING A RENEWED LIFE TO YOUR BROTHER. THAT YOU MAY BELIEVE.
I JUST CANNOT SAY ON WHICH SIDE OF THE CITY'S GATES HE WILL FIND IT.

NOW I'VE TOLD YOU WHAT I CAN, AND TIME DOES NOT WAIT FOR US.
I CAN SHOW YOU THE WAY FORWARD, BUT IT IS FOR YOU TO SEE YOUR OWN FATE–AND ARTHUR'S–IN THIS DIRECTION.

OI! YOU COME FROM THE ARM'RY, LAD, OR TH'MUSEUM?

AH: WOULDN'T DO THAT, FATHER. NOT SAFE.
'AT'S MR. MULCAIRN'S.
YES, BUT HE'S ONLY LEADING IT. THAT'S HIM ON THE GREAT DUN, ISN'T IT?
AYE, BUT HE'D RATHER CARRY THE PACK HIMSELF THAN PUT IT ON THIS ONE, THE MAD BAST–RD.

MR. O'HARA: UNCRATE THOSE CARBINES AND TRY THEM. KEEP ONLY THE ONES THAT FIRE TRUE, OR THAT YOU THINK WE CAN TRADE.
AYE, SIR.
YOU TWO HELP HIM. AND NO BULLETS IN THESE CAISSONS THAT AREN'T MATCHED TO A GUN WE CARRY.

...BY NOVEMBER...? NOT OVERLAND, SAHIB. I CANNOT SEE IT.

MURAT'S CAVALRY MADE THIRTY MILES, AND WE ARE NOT THEY. WE SHOULD DO HALF THAT AT A FORCED MARCH. THAT IS HUNDREDS OF DAYS TO NEPAL.
WHERE'S THE BOY? SIR?

WHAT IF IT WERE MESOPOTAMIA, INSTEAD?
–AND MISS HARROW SAID SHE'D BE ALONG–

HELP THEM WITH THAT COUPLING. MR. BUCHAN, YOU, TOO. WE'RE DONE ESCORTING WOMEN AND CHILDREN.
NAH, WE DURSN'T LEAVE BERTRAM IN THERE, SIR. NOT WITH MR. SLOANE AND THESE OTHERS MINDING HIM.
...WHAT IS IN MESOPOTAMIA FOR US?

MAJOR: LOOK AT ME, SIR. THEY TELL YOU WHERE HE IS?

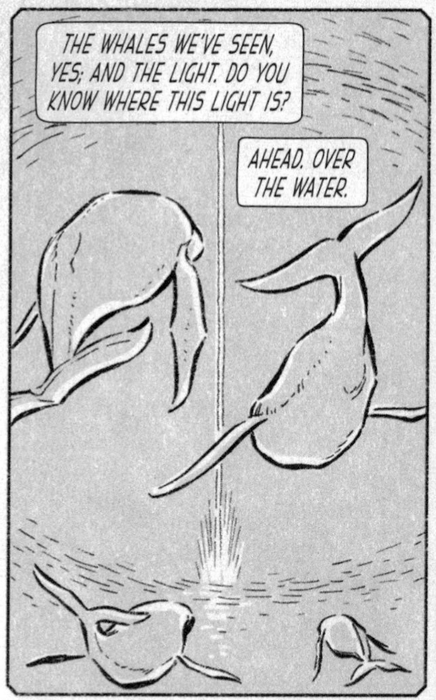
THE WHALES WE'VE SEEN, YES; AND THE LIGHT. DO YOU KNOW WHERE THIS LIGHT IS?
AHEAD. OVER THE WATER.

–YES. GOOD.
YOU KNOW, I SEE WHAT YOU ARE SEEING; I AM ONLY A LITTLE BEHIND. I IMAGINE THAT LIGHT IS THE CITY.
...DO YOU THINK IT IS?

I DON'T KNOW. THE WHALES ARE GOING THERE.
I CAN SEE THEY ARE.
I'LL HAVE TO GO THERE, TOO.

PERHAPS, YES. BUT NOT RIGHT NOW. I'D LIKE TO RETURN, IF WE CAN, TO THE WATER, AND LET THE REST SEEP AWAY. CAN YOU DO THAT, BERTRAM? ONLY THE WATER, NOW, AS FAR AS WE CAN SEE...
YES, SIR.

THERE IT IS. GOOD. I REMIND YOU, THIS IS NOT THE OCEAN BUT A VAST, STILL POOL OF CLEAR WATER, AT JUST THE TEMPERATURE WE LIKE, WITH NO COLOR AND NO SHAPE, MIRRORING A NEUTRAL SKY. IF THE WATER AND SKY WERE TO SWITCH PLACES, THE PICTURE WOULD BE NO DIFFERENT...

THERE. YOU'VE GOT IT EXACTLY.

YOU ARE PERFECTLY AT PEACE, AND COMFORTABLE....
IS HE IN ANY PAIN?

IS MISS HARROW THERE?
EHH...SHE–YES, SHE'S COME BACK. SHE'S FINDING ALL OF THIS VERY INTERESTING.
I'M FINDING IT HORRID.

MISS HARROW–?
–SHE CAN'T HEAR YOU, SON. BUT WE BOTH NEED YOU TO RELAX, AND TO CONCENTRATE.
...YES, SIR.
TWO LEARNED APES

GEBEN SIE IHM MEHR.
JAWOHL.

PLEASE, MISS HARROW. IT IS BETTER YOU WAIT TILL WE'RE DONE.
COME: SIT.
NO, I'LL STAND HERE, THANK YOU.

...MUCH BETTER, BERTRAM. THERE IS NOTHING AROUND YOU NOW BUT THE WATER, AND NO SOUND BUT MY VOICE...

NOW: YOU'LL FIND, AS YOU LOOK OUT FOR A HORIZON–THERE, LOOK: YOU'LL SEE THERE ARE MOUNTAINS AT THE FAR END OF THIS POOL. THEY ARE ONLY PALE SHAPES NOW. YOU CAN JUST MAKE THEM OUT. BUT WHEN YOU'RE FEELING READY, WE'LL DRAW NEARER TO THEM.

THERE...GOOD. AND YOU SEE WE CAN MOVE ANYWHERE WITHOUT EFFORT, AND WITHOUT HURRY...JUST SO, STEADILY CLOSER...AND YOU BEGIN TO SEE THEM RISE INTO DEFINITION.

NOW, I'LL TELL YOU: JUST BEYOND THE MOUNTAINS THERE IS A CERTAIN MOMENT, A SPACE OF TIME YOU HAVE KNOWN ALREADY, AND WILL BE PLEASED TO SEE AGAIN. WE'RE GOING TO ENTER BACK INTO THAT MOMENT, JUST AS RELAXED AND OBSERVANT AS WE ARE NOW.

I'LL REMIND YOU, TOO, THAT NO HARM CAN COME TO YOU WHILE WE ARE HERE. WE ARE ONLY LOOKING AT PICTURES...AND IN THIS CASE, A PICTURE VERY FAMILIAR TO YOU. A LOVELY LAWN AND GARDENS.

YOU'VE BEEN PLAYING HERE WITH YOUR SISTER, AND SHE'S COME DRESSED AS A LITTLE WOLF. THERE IS A LAKE IN THE DISTANCE, AND A HEDGEROW NEARER TO YOU WITH A PATH LEADING INTO IT. DO YOU KNOW THE PLACE I'M DESCRIBING?
...YES.

GOOD. WE'RE NEARLY THERE. WE'LL SLIP OVER THESE MOUNTAINS, THROUGH THE TWO CENTERMOST PEAKS, RIGHT THERE... YES. ALREADY I THINK I CAN HEAR YOUR SISTER'S VOICE. DO YOU HEAR IT?
...INGRID.
INGRID

THAT'S RIGHT. JUST THROUGH HERE, AND...YOU'RE IN THE...MY G-D: IN THE GARDEN. THIS IS VERY GOOD.
BERTRAM, ARE YOU ALL RIGHT?
IS HE ALL RIGHT?

SOMETHING'S TROUBLING YOU, BERTRAM?
YES. I OUGHT TO— INGRID'S CALLING.
WHAT'S SHE SAYING?
'BERTRAM: NOT THERE.'
WHAT DOES SHE MEAN? NOT WHERE?
IN THE HEDGES.

ER IST MEHR ÄNGSTLICH.
ER IST IN ORDNUNG. RUHIG.

THERE WAS A NOISE. SOMETHING MOVED. I'D LIKE TO GO, BUT I'M NOT SUPPOSED TO.
NO-NO: I TOLD YOU, YOU'RE QUITE SAFE. WHATEVER THIS IS, I'D LIKE TO SEE IT WITH YOU. I'D LIKE YOU TO SHOW ME.

MR. SLOANE: I'M SORRY, THIS IS ENOUGH.
GO ON, BERTRAM. IT'S JUST ALONG THE PATH, ISN'T IT?
PLEASE...I DON'T LIKE IT.

ENOUGH–BERTRAM, I'M TAKING YOU OUT OF HERE–
BEWEGEN SIE.

I MUST SEE THIS, MISS HARROW.
WHAT–? GET YOUR–

BERTRAM: GO ON.
I'M SORRY–THIS IS THE END OF IT–IT'S GOING TO WAKE ME UP–
NO-NO–YOU'RE DOING QUITE WELL. BUT YOU MUST HOLD STILL, OR I WON'T SEE WHAT THIS IS.

KOMM HER UND HALTEN SIE IHN–DRAW THE STRAPS IN.
MR. SLOANE, FOR G–D'S SAKE–!

WHAT IS THIS? MISS HARROW?
PLEASE–STOP HIM, CAN'T YOU?

IT'S THAT BIT OF SHADE ON THE HEDGE WALL, ISN'T IT? YOU'VE GOT TO MOVE CLOSER, BERTRAM–WE'VE GOT TO SEE THIS–
BUT IT'S NOT SHADE.

OFF HIM! ALL YOU– F–CK OFF'A HIM!
CHR–ST, LAD, WE'LL HAVE YEH OUT–

MR. BUCHAN, HOLD THAT ONE BACK.
SIR: PLEASE.

WHAT ARE YOU DOING?
LEAVING, SIR. WE'VE GOT TO BRING THESE TWO, AS WELL.
BRING THEM WHERE?
EAST. I THINK. YOU CAN ASK THE ABBOT WHERE, EXACTLY. HE'S TOLD MAJOR.

YOU'RE LEAVING ON THE ABBOT'S RECOMMENDATION? AND WHY ON EARTH WOULD YOU DO THAT?
WELL. MAJOR'S ORDERS, SIR.
AND IT HASN'T OCCURRED TO HIM—OR TO ANY OF YOU—THAT THIS ABBOT MIGHT DELIBERATELY MISLEAD YOU?
THEY WANT YOU ALL COLLECTED AND PUT OUT OF THE WAY, CORPORAL. AND HERE YOU ARE, HELPING THEM DO IT.

COME ON, BOY. DON'T LET 'IM WORK THAT JADOO ON YEH.

REALLY, MISS HARROW: YOU WON'T RECONSIDER...?
...WELL.

BEWEGEN.

BERTRAM? WAKE UP, PLEASE.
COME, WE'RE ALL RIGHT NOW.

AH! CORPORAL–ONE OF YOU, PLEASE–
GET SOMETHING FOR HIS HEAD!

END *of* BOOK FOUR

IN BOOK FIVE:

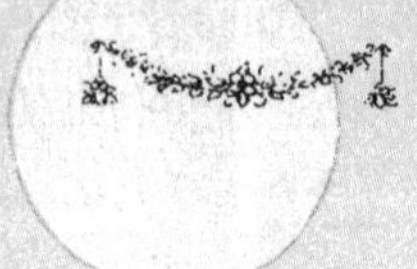

The WAR-BALLAD
of Wrenfrappe and Phixston-Higgs;

A Company of GURKHAS *Choose Precisely the* WRONG HORSE *to* STEAL;

— and —

MR. BUCHAN *Shows His Resolve at an* INOPPORTUNE MOMENT.

. . .

— While —

MR. RENTON *Upends a City's* ECONOMY *with an* AMERICAN DOLLAR; *and*

MISS HARROW, *in her Grief, Measures her* STAKE *in this* WORLD.

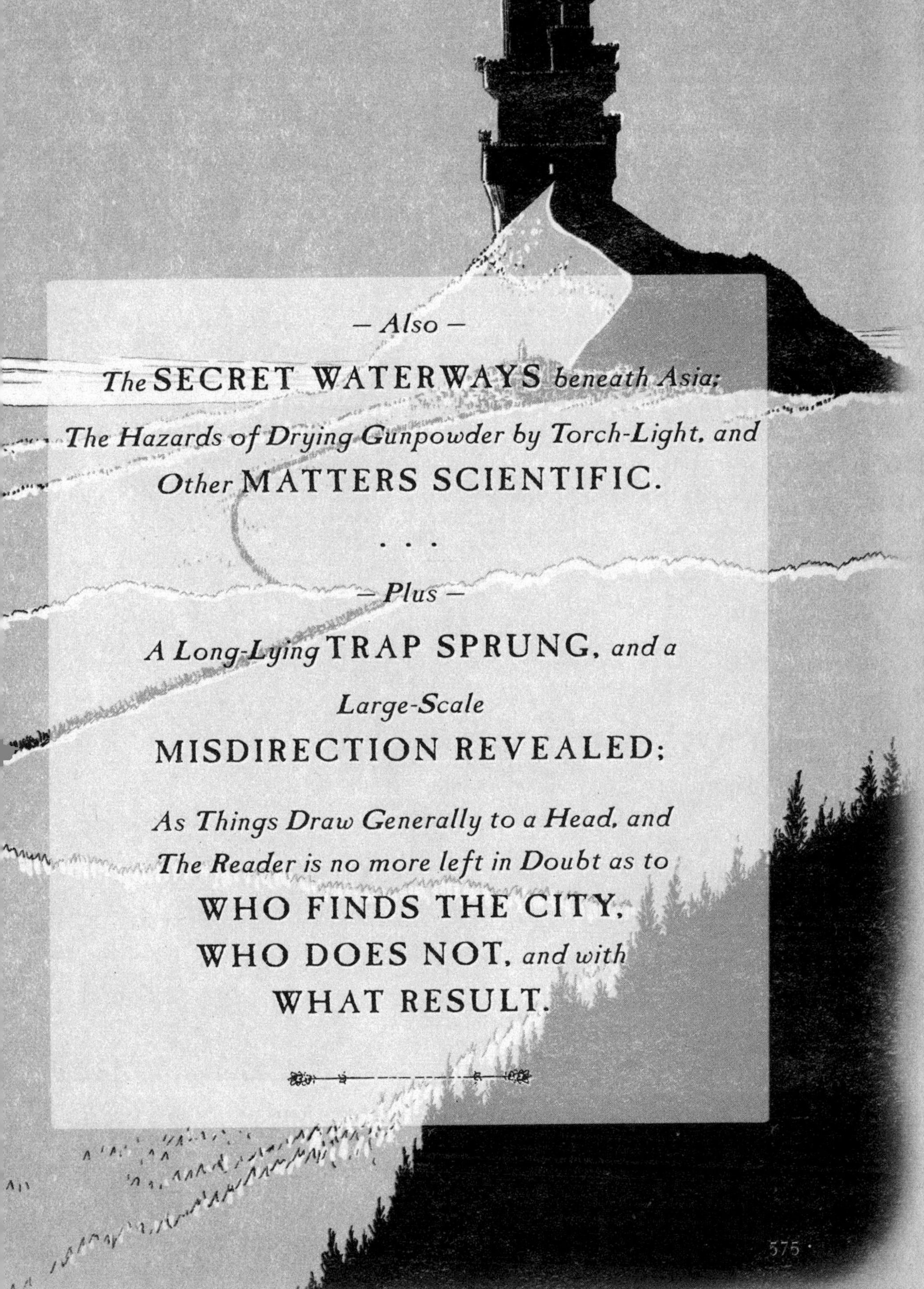

— *Also* —

The SECRET WATERWAYS *beneath Asia;*
The Hazards of Drying Gunpowder by Torch-Light, and
Other MATTERS SCIENTIFIC.

. . .

— *Plus* —

A Long-Lying TRAP SPRUNG, *and a*
Large-Scale
MISDIRECTION REVEALED;

As Things Draw Generally to a Head, and
The Reader is no more left in Doubt as to
WHO FINDS THE CITY,
WHO DOES NOT, *and with*
WHAT RESULT.

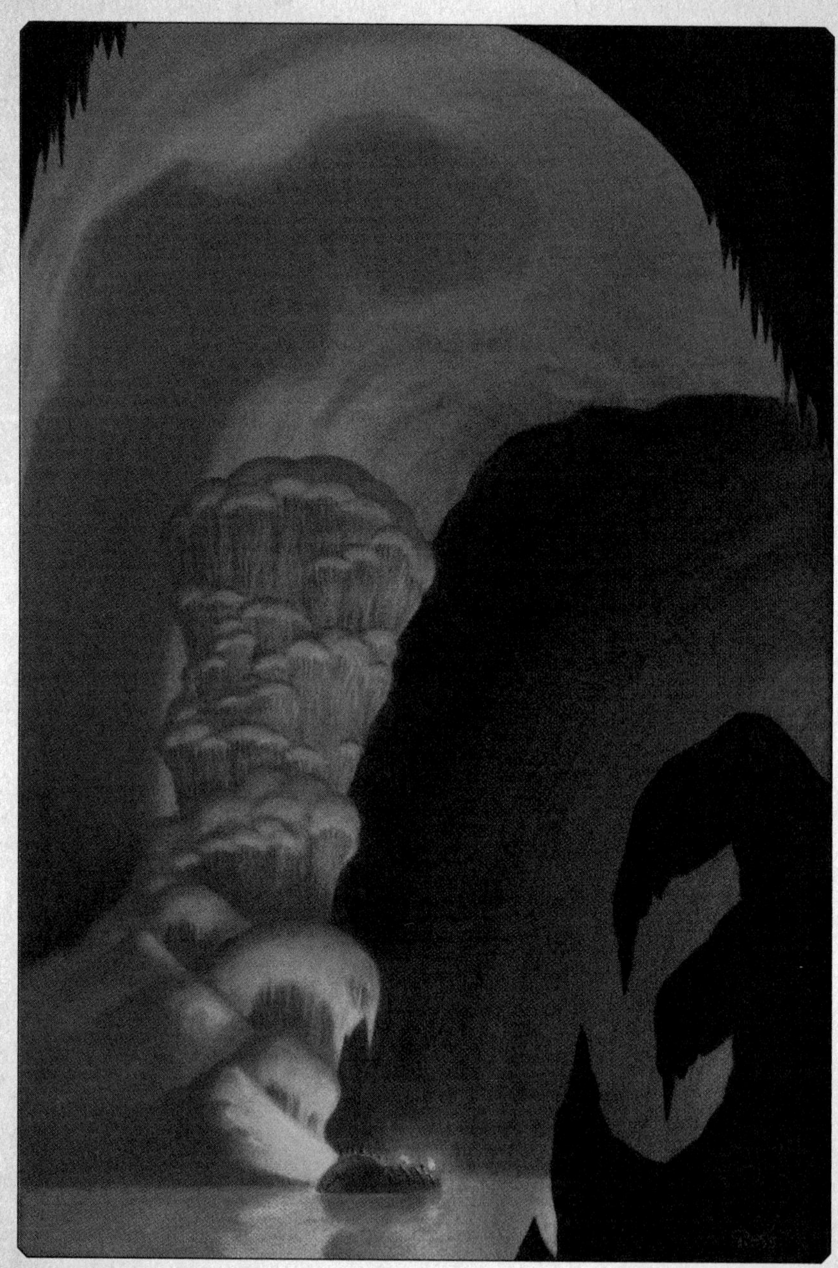

'ALL ABOUT THE EAST, IN THE PLACES WHERE THEY RETAIL NO END OF NONSENSE, YOU HEAR STORIES OF THE LOST RIVERS THAT RAN BETWEEN THE CAPITALS OF THE ANCIENT WORLD.'

BOOK FIVE

- of Five -

I.

TWO NAMES YOU ARE NOT LIKELY TO FIND in the war annals are those of Jeremy Wrenfrappe and Cassius Phixston-Higgs, and the reason for this—also the reason they feature in our own history—is that the fortunes of both men were tied for a short time to those of John Ogden and his dragoons.

As fellows in archaeology at Jesus College, Wrenfrappe and Phixston-Higgs missed T. E. Lawrence by some five years, though by 1915 the latter's exploits were ringing across England, and not least of all in the halls of his alma mater. It was supposed by the fathers and benefactors of *Messrs.* Wrenfrappe and Phixston-Higgs that the young men, left at

Oxford, must soon go the way of Lawrence and expressly to their deaths; while it was heard by these same fathers and benefactors that the boys were already gone far in the direction of Apollo and Hyacinthus, for which the college stood likewise to blame. It was determined that the young men would be sent to opposite poles of the earth, Wrenfrappe to look after family mining interests in the Americas and Phixston-Higgs to authenticate relics at a dig in Hamunaptra, India.

Yet for all the connivances of fathers and benefactors, Christmas holiday in 1917 saw both young men returned to London and drinking themselves legless at the Athenaeum. In a scene that might have made an excellent barrack-room myth had only it and the war gone differently, Wrenfrappe stood declaiming over a tintype of Roosevelt at San Juan Hill that he'd brought back from the States, while Phixston-Higgs shouted him down with a leaf from *The War Illustrated* showing Lawrence (apocryphally) decorated at Aqaba. It seemed the years of separation had only hardened the two in their resolve to face down the Kaiser and his dupes, and by the time they were turned out of the Athenaeum to shout their school songs and war slogans at the waking city, they had more or less arrived at their *plan de guerre*.

Now, the less said the better, I think, of their initial exploits on the Continent. Half their British recruits failed to show for the crossing, and the other half deserted between Calais and the Aegean coast. Yet the two men continued to look east with all the resilience and optimism of their youth, and why not? It was August of 1918, Ludendorff had stalled outside Paris, and all across Araby, from Budapest to the Arabian Sea, the rotted pilings of the Ottoman Empire lay exposed in the receding tide of Pax Germana. Arab revolutionaries and the Ceylon Company Expeditionary Force were folding up Ottoman interests throughout the Mideast, and there were dispossessed young men everywhere willing to take a British regular's wage to go raiding in the Levant. Wrenfrappe and Phixston-Higgs were able quickly to replace their faint-hearted Britons with enough Greek privateers and Balkan deserters and Mideast refugees to justify, in at least one respect, their chosen name of 'Jenkins's Own Welsh Irregulars.' All they seemed really to lack in this flurry of recruitment was a bit of veteran leadership to shape their rabble. And here fate stepped in once more to meet their need: for it was said that a British cavalry commander of some reputation was dodging and fighting and bribing his way through Bulgaria with the remnants of his old company (and a Russian film actress besides). They had been turned back at the Turkish border and were trying to make Stamboul again through Greece, and were supposed to pass within a few miles of the Oxford company's camp at Alexandroupoli (by which I mean their hotel there). All in all, it was decided that the young adventurers could do a good deal worse than to try this Major Ogden on his way by, as indeed they did.

Their finely phrased note of introduction made little impression, I am afraid, on the old trooper, who was still for bulling his way through Turkey per his original plan. But it was argued by Mr. Priddish that Bulgaria had been rough going and Asia Minor only promised more of the same, and that any potential sea-routes into the Levant ought to be explored. The Sikh had led an embassy to Alexandroupoli, therefore, and had tried to arrange terms with the young men; though in the event he proved a shade too clever for them (not to mention a shade too *swart*), and his fellows came off much too loud and boorish, and not any less so as they got into the ouzo. Even Miss Harrow's charms, for once, were seen to lack effect. Out of all of them it was Mr. Buchan who got the kindest reception, and, seeing how matters stood, Mr. Priddish and the others had withdrawn, leaving the young runner to represent their interests.

The council had lasted well into the next day, and concluded with Buchan's appearance, at Ogden's tent, in one of the slouch hats affected by the Oxford company. Buchan (between draughts of bicarbonate) explained that the hats were worn in imitation of Roosevelt's Rough Riders by all but Phixston-Higgs, whose own hat had fallen into the sea during a recruiting trip to Thasos. As acting quartermaster of the company, Wrenfrappe had denied his friend a replacement on grounds that Phixston-Higgs had let his go *intentionally* and had, indeed, not ever approved of the hats. ('They are either worn tied under the chin or else folded and secured beneath the shoulder-strap, and in either case the hat doesn't just *blow overboard* without yanking the wearer with it, though you know there are times, Cassius, when I wish yours *had*.' Thus Wrenfrappe.)

More to the point, and after some patient questioning on the part of Mr. Priddish, it was learned that Phixston-Higgs had bought a lot of Bikaner camels through an Indian associate, and that these camels were being held at an American mission on the Beyrouth peninsula. Wrenfrappe had met the pilot of a troop-ship who would be returning from Macedonia by way of Alexandroupoli and who was willing, for a consideration, to bring the Oxford company south through the Mediterranean to their camels. From there, depending on the complexion of things (they'd still rather an inexact picture of events in the theater), they might either continue south into the Jordan Valley and help with the demolition of the Hejaz Railway, or, if that work were already done, they could raid east toward Damascus. The goal in any case was to distinguish themselves in some action or other before finding Lawrence and offering him their swords. Until then, they'd more than enough credit to feed and salary Ogden and his men, more than enough room on their troop-ship for the company and their mounts, and they would be leaving for Beyrouth within the week.

Wrenfrappe and Phixston-Higgs were composing another letter to Lieutenant-Colonel Lawrence when Mr. Buchan presented himself at their hotel with return word from Ogden (really, from Mr. Priddish): Ogden, he said, would accompany the young men as far as Beyrouth, and would advise them there after an inspection of their camels, making no promises.

Which offer struck the young men as eminently fair, not to say sporting. They woke the *maître d'hôtel* straightaway to toast their success, and they were still toasting with Mr. Buchan when their conveyance drew into port some days later (though the promised troop-ship was more of a convoy of merchant barges; no matter). Mr. Buchan went on drinking the Oxford company's health and regaling them with stories of adventure as they made their way southeast across the Mediterranean, till at last they raised Mount Sannine and the domes and spires of Beyrouth.

And there, in the quiet hours after the landing celebration, Mr. Buchan had been loaded into a cart behind one of the purloined camels, as Ogden's men helped themselves to the fittest beasts and drivers and the best-preserved weapons, leaving the Abbot's arquebuses and ribauldequins to the Oxford men, who after all were admirers of antiques.

One can imagine the desolation on the face of Wrenfrappe as he opened a gritty eye on the scene of Sergeant Pensette, creeping through camp, showing the young man one of his own Martini-Henry rifles (loaded now) and pressing a finger to his lips, while Corporal Buchan went bouncing along feet-first behind Wrenfrappe's own dreams of Arabian adventure, out into the alien dawn.

It is twelve days after the Beyrouth landing when we re-join Ogden and his dragoons, and it has been a quiet ride for the better part of it.

We do note that another cable has come in from Miss Maguire, this by way of a groom in the household of one Mr. Spitz-Walton, a trader with the Anglo-Persian Oil Company living near the deposits at Mosjed-Soleiman. The prevalence of Miss Maguire's friends in these far-flung places is a cause of wonder for Ogden, and the willingness of these messengers to strike out across great distances at her request is no less remarkable. In this case, the rider has brought Ogden word about a Miss Gordon, his friend from India, whom the careful reader will understand to have died long ago in a riding accident. Well: in the first place, it seems we've been misled on the point of Miss Gordon's decease, for according to this note she has been removed (*alive*, we assume) to a 'ladies' home' in Bankipore. There is mention of a 'condition' in the young lady that has 'greatly worsened,' and we might catch another word or two before Ogden balls the note in his fist. But we have not quite reason, yet, to scare up this particular ghost, and until we do and can deal with it properly I would as soon let it lie. I only remark that we find Ogden more than usually taciturn on the road to Mesopotamia, and that his mood has communicated itself to the men and even to the beasts behind him.

Nor is he the only rider left on this road to mull the missteps of his past. Mr. Buchan has had the better part of two weeks to consider their hard use of the Oxford company, and he has had occasion to hear, more than once and not in the politest terms, the reason he was chosen over the rest of the company to liaise with the Oxford men. He is not, of course, under any illusions about these knights-errant he travels with. He knows Wrenfrappe and Phixston-Higgs are lucky to have mixed with them and come out just a few guns and camels the poorer. He understands what has been gained by the ploy, and knows he would only have queered it if he'd known too soon where things were heading. But what use, these arguments? The matter is simply not sorting well with Mr. Buchan's conscience. He can bring himself neither to wear the slouch hat given to him by Wrenfrappe in Greece, nor to throw the thing off into the surrounding desert. He only rides with the hat folded over his pommel, feeling himself reproached by it. And he is still sitting in private dialogue with the hat when shouts begin blowing back to him from the front of the group. Captain Shaw must lean over and quirt the young man's horse before Buchan goes galloping up the line, to where his commander has summoned him.

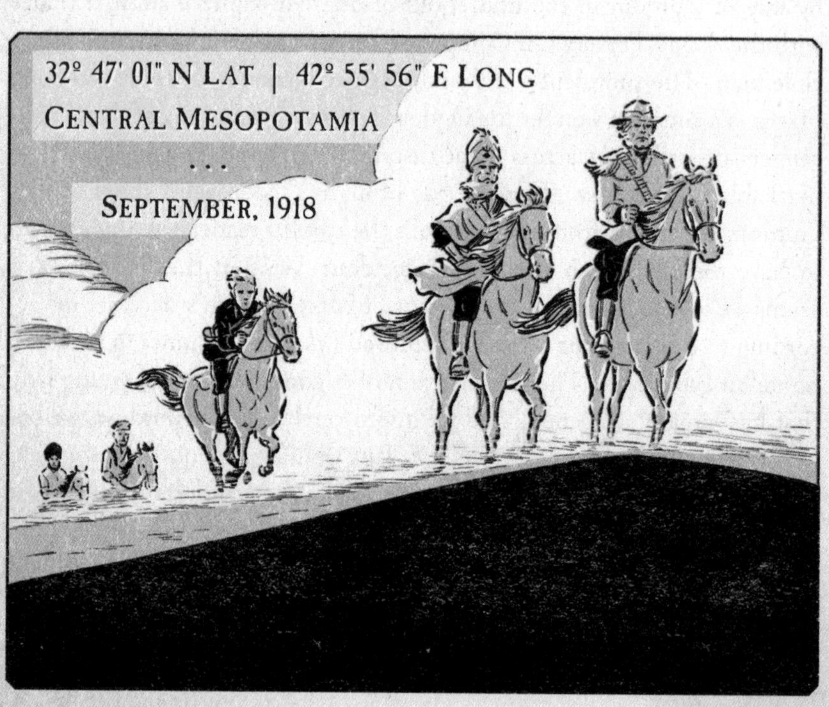

32º 47' 01" N LAT | 42º 55' 56" E LONG
CENTRAL MESOPOTAMIA
. . .
SEPTEMBER, 1918

I SUPPOSE YOU KNOW THIS ROAD, CORPORAL.
YES, SIR.
A YEAR AGO WE WERE A HUNDRED MILES EAST OF HERE, ON A TERRACE AT THE AL-SHAR CITADEL. THERE WAS A MOSAIC, AND YOU MADE A SKETCH OF IT.
YES, SIR.

THAT SOMETHING YOU'D STILL HAVE?
THE SKETCH? I OUGHT TO.
YOU'RE NOT...SENDING THESE RECORDS OF YOURS ANYWHERE, FOR INSTANCE.

OH—NO. NO, I'VE GOT IT. GIVE ME A MOMENT.

THAT'S THE ONE, ISN'T IT, SIR?
MM.
YOU RECALL WE HAD THE SHARIF WAITING FOR A QUESTION FROM ME. FROM POMEROY, REALLY.
YES, SIR.
'WHAT IS THE GODDESS OF AL-SHAR CASTLE?'
THAT'S WHAT THE VICEROY DESIRED TO LEARN.

IT IS NOT ANYTHING IN THE HINDU CANON. MUCH AS IT IS MADE TO LOOK THAT WAY.
IT'S NOT A GODDESS AT ALL.

I THOUGHT IT MIGHT BE A CONSTELLATION–THE STONES, IF THEY WERE GREATER AND LESSER STARS...
THOUGH THERE AREN'T CONSTELLATIONS LIKE THESE. I'VE LOOKED.

NO. ALL ABOUT THE EAST, YOU KNOW, AND IN AFRICA, IN THE PLACES WHERE THEY RETAIL NO END OF NONSENSE, YOU HEAR STORIES OF THE LOST RIVERS THAT RAN BETWEEN THE CAPITALS OF THE ANCIENT WORLD.
MAJOR'S UNCLE ONCE CAPTURED A MAN AT LAHORE WHO CLAIMED TO KNOW A DOOR TO ONE OF THESE RIVERS. HE HAD SEEN IT, HE SAID, BENEATH A TEMPLE IN THE CITY, ON A DOOR MARKED WITH A CERTAIN SYMBOL– A COIL OF SNAKES, AS IT STRUCK HIM.

SOMETHING PERHAPS LIKE THIS.
WE PAID HIM LITTLE MIND, THIS MAN. BUT IT IS A LONG- AND WIDELY HELD BELIEF.
IT'S A MAP. THAT SYMBOL– THE MOSAIC–IT'S A MAP.

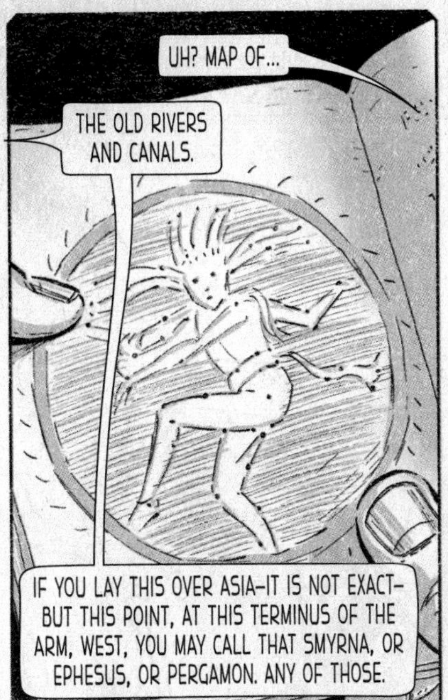
UH? MAP OF...
THE OLD RIVERS AND CANALS.
IF YOU LAY THIS OVER ASIA–IT IS NOT EXACT–BUT THIS POINT, AT THIS TERMINUS OF THE ARM, WEST, YOU MAY CALL THAT SMYRNA, OR EPHESUS, OR PERGAMON. ANY OF THOSE.

THIS, GOING EAST, WOULD BE BAGHDAD. SOUTH, THE RIGHT LEG, IF YOU FOLLOW: THERE IS MECCA. AND SO FORTH. QAZVIN, SAMARKAND, LAHORE, UNTIL...FARTHEST EAST: KATHMANDU.

YOU SEE IT? WHERE THERE ARE THE STONES, THESE ARE THE CITIES OF THE OLD WORLD. THIS TOPAZ YOU NOTE, JUST BENEATH BAGHDAD, ON THE GODDESS'S BELT–PRESUMABLY IT IS AL-SHAR.
INTERESTING.
'INTERESTING...?' IMAGINE THE OLD RIVERS ARE NOT GONE, MR. BUCHAN, BUT ONLY LOST.

I SEE. AND HOW DOES ONE 'LOSE–'
HE DOES NOT. WHAT HE LOSES ARE HIS POINTS OF ACCESS. THE RIVERS ARE NOW WHERE THEY HAVE ALWAYS BEEN. THEY ARE DEEP BENEATH THE GROUND.

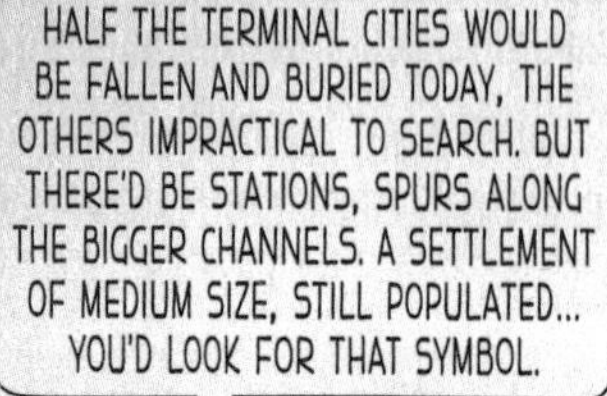

HALF THE TERMINAL CITIES WOULD BE FALLEN AND BURIED TODAY, THE OTHERS IMPRACTICAL TO SEARCH. BUT THERE'D BE STATIONS, SPURS ALONG THE BIGGER CHANNELS. A SETTLEMENT OF MEDIUM SIZE, STILL POPULATED... YOU'D LOOK FOR THAT SYMBOL.

THEREFORE YOUR LORD POMEROY'S INTEREST IN AL-SHAR, YOU SEE? THE SYMBOL IS NOT JUST A MAP BUT A SIGNPOST. WHERE IT IS FOUND, IT YIELDS THE OLD WATERWAYS.
HE TOLD YOU THIS WAS HIS REASON FOR ORDERING YOU TO AL-SHAR?

HE WAS NOT IN THE HABIT OF GIVING REASONS. BUT WE HAVE HAD LEISURE TO GUESS.
I ASKED MY UNCLE'S RISALDAR ABOUT THE MOSAIC AND THE OLD RIVERS, BEFORE HE WAS KILLED. MAN THOUGHT I WAS MAD.
WE WERE CALLED AWAY, AND I THOUGHT NO MORE ABOUT IT UNTIL WE HAD TO CROSS THIS CONTINENT AGAIN.

THEN, YOU MEAN TO SEARCH THE CASTLE AGAIN, ON THE STRENGTH OF AN OLD STORY YOU JUST DESCRIBED AS NONSENSE–
IT WOULD NOT BE IN THE CASTLE, BUT AT THE FOOT OF THE ROCK. A DOOR. WE WOULD LOOK FOR YOUR GODDESS.
IF A RIVER COULD BE FOUND, AND A MEANS TO NAVIGATE IT...WELL.
IF NOT, WE WON'T HAVE GONE VERY FAR OUT OF OUR WAY.

Mr. Priddish's door is not ultimately a door, but the least anomaly—a dab of mortar in a cleft of the rock, twice passed by the party and tried on the off chance—at the base of the Al-Shar height. Rather unlike their last visit here, the dragoons have come quietly, by torch-light, in peasants' rags, and there is little in this hour of night to distinguish them from the work crew they've scared up from the village, except I suppose that Ogden's men are the ones standing back and steadying torches while the locals have at the earth with their picks and shovels. The dragoons watch with a bored sort of cynicism that has half to do with the work efforts they see on display, half with the enterprise as a whole—all of them, that is, but for Mr. Buchan, whose looks will require a bit of explanation.

A thing has happened to the young Corporal, you see, quite unrelated to the digging or to ancient waterways or any of it: a girl has come up from the village begging alms, and has slipped him a note. Which note (indubitably Pomeroy's) has sat buttoned in the Corporal's tunic, with its seal unbroken, for the better part of an hour.

Now, it is six months since Mr. Buchan left New York, and he's been inclined to forget—sometimes even to doubt—that he is working in the Governor-General's secret employ. There had not been the least sign of any such arrangement, and really, as Buchan reflects, he'd not seen much *at all* of the Company in the last half year (nor considered that this might be a sign of something in itself). It is true that in Bulgaria the men had muttered about an unseen 'presence' shadowing the camp, and that more than once they'd come upon scenes of rout and massacre, of Ottoman companies and insurrectionists and the ubiquitous highwaymen killed and cleared, apparently within days of their arrival. They had found bridges reformed and rocks and timber hauled away and more than the usual stares of fear and wonder, but nothing in any of it to say it was the Company's doing, and still less to implicate Buchan even if it were. He'd felt an unpleasant pang of conscience a few days west of here, when Ogden had asked him if he weren't 'sending these notes of his somewhere.' But he had produced his sketch, and the moment had passed. If Ogden had had any grounds for accusing him, he wouldn't have bothered to ask. And really, what grounds were there? What had Buchan done, up to now, that any of them could object to? A conversation with Pomeroy while drunk. That seemed the extent of it.

Returning us to this note in Mr. Buchan's pocket. This, you'll appreciate, is a certifiable cause for worry. He has accepted a private dispatch from the Viceroy, you see, and is not sure but the quick-eyed Mr. Renton scowled at him as he took it. With each minute that passes now, with each opportunity missed, through inaction, of destroying the note or having out with some confession, Mr. Buchan finds himself sunk deeper into self-accusation and paralysis. The note might not literally be burning into his side, as it seems to him, nor glowing for the others to see; but I cannot say it isn't flashing out *some* incriminating message through the window of the young man's face. And all in all I should hope he takes care in this secret enterprise of his. For if he is discovered in it by Ogden or any of the dragoons, there will be no help for him.

The work crews eventually clear the earth and brush from what appears to be a wind-carved niche, sealed long ago with stones and gypsum cement. There is no goddess exposed for Mr. Priddish in the digging, though he allows the symbol would likely be on a door, beneath the seal. The point is taken as academic. Ogden is not after symbols but a waterway, and is not for lingering here any longer than they must. He orders charges set against the rock, and clears the workers out from the pit they have made.

The day has nearly risen by now, and a few dozen villagers have gathered to spectate. There is the briefest suspension in their murmuring as the charges are tripped, and as the dust plumes out over the plain like an ancient exhalation. Some of the men look skyward, as though to see if the palace might not come crashing to earth at last. But the old structure holds, the debris settles, conversations are resumed, and the chanting of the crews rises again over the striking and scraping of their picks and shovels.

The end of *Fajr*, or sunrise prayer, brings villagers up to the site in increasing numbers, and Buchan is set on watch over them with his back to the citadel. It is unclear what these men make of the digging, and unclear, too, whether any recognize the dragoons from their last visit to Al-Shar. They seem content just to look, squatting on their haunches in the lengthening shade of the escarpment, as young ladies in the *hijab* circulate among them, ladling out water from terra-cotta pots. Now and then boys from the village will appear next to one of the elder spectators and dart away again, in the manner of boy runners the world over, and this, certainly, strikes Mr. Buchan as a sign of mischief. He manages to catch the eye of Sergeant Pensette, who has been detailed with him and stands fifty paces to his left with hands folded over his rifle's muzzle. The Scotsman, too, is watching the runners and the swelling crowds with concern, but on meeting Buchan's stare he only frowns and jerks his head toward the villagers, as to tell the younger man to mind his watch.

Some time before noon the picks and shovels fall silent, replaced by the voices of the workers themselves, raised in argument. Ogden has left them a camel and wagon in payment, which items are not so easily divided, it turns out, among a score of men. Buchan chances a quick look at the workers behind him, and finds the dragoons have all gone–likely slipped through a black aperture he sees now in the rock. Even Sergeant Pensette has quietly left his post, as he notes with a flutter of stomach. Strange that Miss Harrow would not have called to him, or that Mulcairn would not be left to guard the rear. Behind him there is just one of the veiled young ladies, who bends over the seemingly needless task of gathering stones into a tin scuttle.

'It is not safe, *effendi*,' the girl mutters to him, in English.

'I'm sorry?' asks Buchan, his voice ramping up a bit in pitch.

'Look away, if you please,' the girl whispers. Buchan turns from her, eyes roving the crowd of men, as she continues with her back to him. 'They are only watching,' she says, 'that you might not leave without their knowing, while the rest hold council in the village. We are busy among them, but they will not have the *farangi* soldiers much longer. Go and tell your friends they must come out. I do not know that the rock has a door but the one, and the old men would seal you in.'

'But who...? How do you–?'

'Quickly–look.' The girl pulls her scarf down over her chin, and Buchan gets the briefest glimpse of an almond-eyed face–something of the southern Indus and younger even than he had thought–before the *hajib* is up again over her nose.

'This isn't more of you from the Viceroy...?'

The girl vents a pretty sort of grunt and asks, in lowered voice: 'You do not know me, eh? But you know the old *khanoom* by the rock, I think.'

He follows her eyes to a sturdy-built older woman with her back to the escarpment and her scarves–all pristine white–drawn back from her face. Buchan must take a prolonged look, but then he has placed her: only paint that shrewd face, he thinks, and lay a pike in her hands and it is the old *haseki* who chased him out of her harem not a year since. And what had her experience been from that day to this, he wonders, that she would be down from the castle today, presiding over this gathering of villagers with her long cigarette, now bending to hear some patriarch's joke, now scanning a note brought down from the castle, now dispatching a boy to the village, and with all the workings of this ancient settlement seemingly under her watch...? Buchan looks all these questions to the girl beside him, and she answers with a smile from her own eyes. But she is just as quickly back to business, collecting her stones and affecting not to notice him.

'Kindness rewards you,' she says, 'as we acquire merit who know and reward a kindness. When *Khanom-eh* Hediyeh, our mother, hears the great *effendi* is returned, she has us down among the old men to hear what news. Some, we learn, are for taking the *effendi*'s party and currying favor with the Turk, or winning a ransom from the English. As the *effendi* lingers under the castle these voices grow bold in the village, and we are sent with opium and perfumed brandy for those who take them, and with certain other arts to work upon those who do not. And the voices are quieted now, and the worst of the instigators left snoring in their huts.'

'But–Your "great *effendi*," that's our Major Ogden, hey? Fellow with the'–a terrible glower, here, from Buchan–'and the whiskers–'

'–*Sah*, yes–'

'And what kindness, exactly–'

'Ah: then you do not remember. We are found with our mother Hediyeh on the night the castle is entered, and the *effendi*, your Major, forbids his men to enter the baths where we are hid. It is a singular kindness in our experience with men, and one she does not permit us to forget, as though we would. Even you, who would find us quite by accident–you forbear to trouble us on the next day (though my sisters laugh that on another day we will have you in and lock the doors behind you)–Ah! and see how the color rises to your face? It is just so on that morning.'

'–*Hrm*–yes–'

Here the girl is admonished with a sudden, rather forceful '*Tch*–!' from the white-scarved Hediyeh; though it is only a bit more feigned work for the girl before she goes on, in her stage-whisper:

'We hear such stories of the *farangi* devils,' she says, 'but when you come, it is only to deliver us from the devils of our own house. And do you know? In his wisdom, the *effendi* sends our sister Neda to judge that great *Shaitan*, our Sharif. You saw her, I think, on that day…'

'Yes, there was a servant girl–'

'Ah! The Sharif makes her *çikadar* to the court of the Vizier, but only that he might have her out from under Hediyeh's protection and treat her shamefully after the tradition of men in these parts. I would not tell you the list of his perversions, but it speaks loudly to them that our gentle Neda should send the man in a thousand pieces to *Jehannum*. We say the *effendi* chooses well who sends Neda to that garden, though he might pick out any young lady of the castle with the same result, and most of the boys withal.'

'I see…' Buchan eyes the castle behind him with a little shudder. 'And what's become of you all now, without your Sharif?'

'Ah: now we are all quite happy, *Alhamdulillah*. The men of the court are dead and scattered, and the ones who stay help our mother and the Sharifah to make this a resting place for our war-wounded. And Neda is gone to her family in the Nineveh hills, with her tales of wickedness in the river settlements. Do you not see, then, the kindness you have done? That is what I tell you.'

'Yes, I–though, you know–it may all have been incidental–'

'This matters not. We have reason to help you now, as you have reason to trust us. And do you see? Already you have let me talk too long. The old men will wonder why I am only shifting stones from here to there. This is no good place for you, *effendi*. You are all at the back of the lion's den, no mistake, and he is but sleeping. It is for you to go out quietly as you came, for *ya Allah*!–we can do no more for you when he wakes.'

With this, the veiled young lady takes up her burden and quits the camp. Buchan has just time to stammer out a thanks, and she pauses, risking a last look at him. '*Jazak Allahu khair*,' she says, and is gone.

Buchan is careful then not to follow her with his eyes, much as he would like to. And he allows a bit of time and a good deal of pacing and throat-clearing so her withdrawal will not seem to have occasioned his own. But this done, he halts himself and raises a finger, as a man does who is seized by a thought. He jogs then through the camp, half-walks and half-skids down into the depression the workers have left and ducks into the black breach in the rock. There may look something amiss in this little pantomime, and the villagers may, like all predatory beings, be tempted to chase wherever there is sign of retreat. But he has these young ladies and their wise *haseki* behind him for a rearguard, and better these than a column of the Company foot.

Not that he is strictly in the clear, just yet. Mr. Buchan must grope his way blind into what is probably a dead-ended cave *at best*, and with no living sign of his friends anywhere about. Nor has he forgotten this note he carries in his pocket. It is possible, he thinks, that the dragoons have left him quite deliberately behind, and that one of them is waiting in the dark to cut his throat for a traitor. And it is just as possible they've fallen into a pit or become trapped or lost or otherwise preyed upon by the castle spirits. The very air around him might be fatally tinged with poisons from inside the earth.... Yet there is *just* that chance, too, he thinks, that all is well, and that Ogden has made some discovery farther on in the darkness. And really, against the certain hazards behind him, it is the open possibilities of the way ahead that hold the more powerful attraction (and there, if you like, is the optimist in miniature).

The young man's feet, at any rate, maintain their steady march forward, around what seems to be a slight bend, till a dull point of light floats into view. He calls ahead without hearing an answer, but on approaching the light's little ambit he sees it is an air-starved taper in the hand of Mr. Renton. The boy greets him with a word of thanks for 'taking his *feechting* time.'

'It's you, Mr. Buchan?' Pensette's voice follows Renton's, from a few steps past him.

'Yes, sir.'

'An' jest you, lad?'

''Course it is.' Renton cuts in. 'Any o' those wogs look like they was takin' up archaeology?'

'*Quiet*,' Pensette hisses. 'Help us shift this back into place, would you, Mr. Buchan? That beast Mulcairn opened it on our way in, an' he's gone on now after his bl–dy horse.'

He motions Buchan toward a slab of stone that has been pushed aside to expose a crude archway. Buchan takes an involuntary look back to the tunnel's mouth, though there is only darkness that way.

'You're…sealing yourselves in?' he asks.

'Keepin' the rest out, rather.'

'Then–there's some other outlet farther on?'

'What's farther on is Major, an' there's his orders left for us, an' so much I know.'

'–Because,' Buchan presses, 'they seemed to think, outside, that our better chance lay in riding back out on the Basra Road–'

'Aye, no doubt they did.' Pensette has set himself to the rock again and begun to push. 'But it's for'ard for us, lad, an' where we go we burn our ships like yer man Cortés. Yeh may choose one side of this rock or t'other, now, but ye'll needle me no more about it.'

The answer suffices for Mr. Buchan. He ducks through the arch and feels along the rock for a purchase. '…Not worried you'll lose your air, doing this?' he cannot help but add.

'Take it yeh can draw breath now?' Pensette asks him.

'Yes, sir.'

'Good. An' ye'll keep at it, long as you follow orders. Come this side, and shoulder to it with me. You too, Mr. Renton…'

With a great effort the three are able to force the slab back over the opening, and Mr. Renton is just able to slip through the breach as it closes. The boy does not wait for the others to recover their wind, either, but goes sprinting ahead with his taper, and Buchan and Pensette must lumber after him, wheezing oaths.

Mulcairn's Caspian horse has been left about twenty paces ahead, and where Renton has gone past it like a shot, it is no simple matter for two grown men to edge past a frightened horse in such a dark and narrow space. By the time they are clear of the horse, Renton and his light are quite naturally gone. It is by the merest chance that Pensette stops short at a waxy square of light on the floor, this being an opened hatchway and nearly, for the cavalryman, a career-ending fall.

Pensette lowers himself to hands and knees and thrusts his head through the opening, as though to vent some thundering threat onto the head of young Renton. But he pauses instead, swings his boots around and slips through the hole himself, muttering the word 'ladder.'

It is indeed an ancient sandalwood ladder, half-petrified and missing two rungs out of every three, that conducts him and Mr. Buchan to a shelf of rock some thirty feet below. And it is just as well that they descend with their eyes on the treacherous old ladder and their backs to the stone chamber behind them. The room, and more particularly the vessel hanging at its center, are better taken in with one's feet planted squarely beneath him. And even then, your newcomer to the subterranean port at Al-Shar is most often obliged to sit.

II.

THERE ARE STILL TORCHES AND LANTERNS being kindled below as Mr. Buchan lights on the shelf of rock and hops down more ledges and stairs to the cobblestone floor. Shouts rise out of the semi-dark as he crosses the room, but he is too absorbed to hear them until Ogden snaps out his Christian name. It seems he is being told to mind a *pit* at the room's center, just beneath the hanging ovoid he has been studying so fixedly. Like Sergeant Pensette a moment ago, Buchan comes very near to a fatal fall, and there is a sickening moment where he stands with arms flapping and his innards carrying over the pit's rim; but he keeps his balance and retreats a step, and the dragoons, cursing him lustily for a fool, return to their own inspection of the strange vessel.

Now, by way of picturing the thing yourself, you must imagine a snub-nosed marine vessel about forty feet in length and nearly that many wide, with its iron keel and framing bolted to the *outside* of a hull of polished wood. Imagine this hull, then, with rudder removed and everything shorn off over the main deck, overturned onto a second, identical hull, and the whole thing banded together by thick rings of iron, all symmetrical but for a pair of round quartz windows over the bows. For Captain Shaw, the vessel calls to mind the image of a rugby ball with stunned eyes; to Miss Harrow it is a Fabergé egg resting on its side; to Private Mulcairn a stuffed partridge, less the legs. It seems likely to all that it is a marine vessel, yet it is equally clear that it has hung here, perhaps for centuries, so far innocent of the water.

Holding the vessel aloft is a massive, straddle-legged crane, whose block-and-tackle pulleys are toothed like gears and reeved with iron chains.

A second crane has been left in front of the first with its chains hanging empty in the air, and both stand over the long rectangular slot in the floor into which we nearly just lost Corporal Buchan. As Buchan skirts round the hole now, he notes it is not a straight vertical drop but a steep-angled shaft cut into the rock, lined lengthwise with wood planks as far down as he can see (which is not very far). A disagreeable smell floats out of this opening into the room along with the faint but unmistakable sound of rushing water.

He is backing away from the pit and the vessel toward the ledges at the far end of the room, when he is passed by O'Hara and Mr. Renton, who are headed down from above with a length of rope. It seems Mr. Renton will be put down the shaft with a lantern, and he is perversely eager to carry out the order; though not so eager that he does not stop and turn at the sight of Mr. Buchan. Renton sidles up to the young man, leering and clicking his tongue, and whispering something about Mr. Buchan's 'admirers.' It is unaccountable behavior even in such an imp as this.

'My–?'

'*Shoor*, governor–Don't these peasant girls just find yeh all over the world–mm?–An' they talk to yeh right close, an' normally so shy wi' the bad *farangis*....'

'Oh–no,' says Buchan, 'those were the same young ladies Major found and helped, the last time we–'

'–I don't mean 'em trulls from up the palace,' Renton hisses. 'I mean 'oo's the ones passin' yeh scraps o' paper, mm?' Then, noting the evolution of Buchan's face: '*Ah*. An' din' I hear just now about'cher friend in Africa, too?'

'Don't know what you mean,' Buchan returns, woodenly.

'Huh? Oh, no: *shoor* yeh don't.' Again with the leer. 'I played dumb wit' the lads, too, never worry. This is for *us* to know, in'nit. Least for *now*, it is.'

O'Hara clears his throat and scuffs at the cobblestones, and Renton withdraws, eyes on Buchan and a finger pressed to his nose. A look of pure devilment lights the boy's face, but he suppresses this with a determined effort. He shows Buchan a mask of innocence and snaps him a wink before turning and carrying on with O'Hara.

'Oi! Ye'r all right, Mr. Buchan?'

It is Captain Shaw calling down from one of the ledges. Buchan waves airily and hobbles to a stair, to sit.

'Aye that's jest a stitch, lad,' Sergeant Pensette opines. 'Must remember to take water, thirsty or no, in these dry places.'

'Aye, that's it.' Shaw nods, and falls back to work. 'Man through it, then, and come help us.'

Mr. Shaw has wedged his torch into a staple on the wall and is milling with Pensette through heaps of old weapons and stores. In the faint light we can see a Korean *hwacha*, or fire-cart, slouching drunkenly on a broken axle, next to piles of powder-tipped arrows and Chinese thundersticks and other antique firearms and missiles of Eastern provenance. A miscellany of daggers and short swords, bows, lances and spears bristle from casks and crates, and other, sealed barrels are shown to contain desiccated fruits and meats and rancid water. The two cavalrymen have been separating the useful items from the less-so, with an argument developing as to which pile is which.

Not far from these two, on the same ledge, Miss Harrow and Bertram sit on rattan mats in the light of an old lamp, poring over a romance novel Miss Harrow has picked up on the road from Beyrouth. The book had begun with a flash of adventure and some perfunctory notes on the North African culture, but had settled quickly to its main points of business, which are the frowned-upon lusts of an archaeologist's wife among her Zouave captors. Miss Harrow looks up from her reading as Mr. Buchan climbs toward them, but a little tug at her sleeve reminds her she has stranded Bertram in the courts of Algiers, and she must repair for now to that wild place.

The dragoons, otherwise, are concentrated on the next ledge up, at the near end of a gangway that reaches to a hatch at the top of the vessel. Ogden and Subadar Priddish have crossed the gangway and may be heard bumping through the ship's innards while the whole thing sways gently on its chains. Ogden has barred the others from adding their weight to the ship, which prohibition had not wanted repeating. The men seem fully content to monitor things from where they stand and to consider what a queer pass this trip has reached.

Before long, too, the dragoons are treated to a promising bit of comedy, courtesy of *Messrs*. Renton and O'Hara. O'Hara, you see, has braced himself next to the pit at the room's center, where he holds a monkey-rope over what is presumably Mr. Renton, gone down into the darkness below. The Irishman has been letting out just enough line to duck the boy into the black water beneath him, and is affecting not to hear the oaths and howls echoing up through the shaft. The noise does alert the dragoons on the ledges above, and they send down their own hoots and jeers, which O'Hara acknowledges with a broad wink. He continues to pay out his line and draw it in, whistling to himself, till he feels Mr. Renton will have got the joke. Then he hauls the boy up, and is ostensibly shocked to find him soaked and shivering, with his lantern doused.

Renton coughs and splutters and rolls gasping to the floor, although—and oddly enough—he seems to take the mistake in good part. He waves off the dragoons' laughter, smiles and motions O'Hara over to him. He has *found* something, he whispers, and he's brought it up from below—something the others mustn't see. O'Hara (who really ought to know better than this) stops coiling his rope and cranes in for a look. Renton motions him down just a bit farther, and then lets drive with an algae-slicked cobblestone straight into the Irishman's skull.

The wet clap of the stone against the head of O'Hara may be heard throughout the chamber, and you may guess with what thundering approval it is received above. The blow stretches O'Hara out to his full length on the floor, and here is Mr. Renton standing over him now, soaked and shrieking and seeming even more than usual like a mad animal up on its hind legs. Nothing will do but that the Irishman must go down the hole himself, and Renton is kicking him that way, forgetting perhaps that they are still bound together by the line. The dragoons realize—slowly, but still—what is going forth, and they see they will not be able to reach the floor in time to stop it (assuming they would). They can holler down all they like, too. The boy is quite beyond hearing.

What ultimately brings Mr. Renton around, and saves him and Mr. O'Hara from the worst, is a short whistle from their commander. The dragoons have heard this sound over Mughal cannonfire and Zulu war-cries, it has rallied them in chaos and summoned them all out of dreams and it seldom fails, as it does not fail now, to draw them up stiff as posts.

Even Mr. Renton freezes with his boot-heel on O'Hara's shoulder at the very edge of the pit. All look up to see Ogden crossing the gangway with Priddish trailing him. The two have done their inspection, and Ogden says he will hear Captain Shaw's report on supplies and Mr. Renton's report on the waterways as soon as the men can quit whatever game they're at and get that b–stard O'Hara to his feet.

A short while later the soldiers are messing together with Bertram and Miss Harrow, with only Corporal Buchan absent. Ogden shares his and Mr. Priddish's view that the vessel overhead is some variety of submersible and says they've deduced, from this, that certain spans of this underground system will be navigable only from beneath the water (which news is met with a chorus of groans). If Mr. Renton be correct, he adds, the journey will *begin* underwater, after a blind descent through the pit behind him (more groans, this time silenced by a look from the speaker). Ogden and Priddish have got a rough idea of the ship's operation but only the crudest map of the waterways, and their only hints as to the going ahead are the piles of armaments around the ship and the hidden gun-ports along its sides, which make it seem unlikely they will be cheered all the way to Kathmandu.

The remark brings a strangely solemn Mr. Buchan out of the shadows, with his slip of paper held out before him. His expression is so uncharacteristically grave that it silences the company, and Miss Harrow whispers his name and reaches for his hand. Buchan, heedless even of this, gives his note to Ogden and announces that he has received a secret communication from the Ceylon Company. And it seems he cannot help himself now but he must detail in trembling voice all his dealings with Lord Pomeroy, from his original commission in India and his confession at Al-Shar, to the note in Jatum and his meeting with Pomeroy in New York and, finally, his receipt of this message today.

Renton is up with a pistol out of his belt before Buchan is done. 'I *seen* 'im!' the boy shrieks, hopping from foot to foot. 'I seen 'im take 'at note *myself*–A *f–cking* spy I says, an' din' I just *know* it!' It is unclear which is the greater outrage, Mr. Buchan's spying or the chance that Renton might not get credit for discovering him first. In any case the dragoons are up beside him, having out their own weapons and denunciations. But Mr. Mulcairn is up as well, with his back to Buchan, and Miss Harrow has stood with her arms leveled between the two groups.

'You see me, don't you?' Mulcairn roars to the company. He takes hold of the nearest dragoon–which happens to be Mr. Henty–and rattles him by his shirtfront. 'You see me in front of you? You'll talk to that man through *me*.' He points back to Mr. Buchan, and snaps Mr. Henty's head with another emphatic shake.

'Stop it! Just–*Stop*.' Miss Harrow has been pushed aside in the exchange but she scrabbles her way back and seizes Mulcairn's oaken arm. 'Mr. Ogden, don't you see this? Get *up*, please.'

Ogden has so far sat unmoved next to Mr. Priddish, and he has not taken his eyes from Buchan's note. But he looks up at Mulcairn now, and waits for silence.

'Aye, we see you standing in front of him, Tom,' he says. 'That'll do. You may sit.'

Mulcairn stands just long enough to let the other dragoons sit before him, just long enough to draw a hard stare from Ogden. If he stands any longer, or if he should meet Ogden's eyes, the dragoons know the situation will have evolved. But he takes his seat again, manifestly to their disappointment, and Ogden returns to his note.

'There's an encampment,' Ogden says, clearing his throat into a fist, '–an encampment, where this spur meets a…what they call a "western artery," somewhere under the Zagros Mountains. All vessels taken and crews pressed or killed. None let past. We're told to watch for their lights.' He hands the paper to Mr. Priddish and surveys the company. 'You see how many we are. And now you've some idea of what we're going against, with the Viceroy's compliments. I don't see any way at this but by putting our backs together. All of them, and his included.' A nod here to Buchan. 'So that's what you'll do, and d–mn all else.'

Ogden does not wait for signs of assent, but moves straight to issuing orders: Gurung and Henty will climb up and fetch three more casks of powder out of the tunnels; Shaw and Pensette will load the ship with any of the old arms that can be made to serve; Mr. Buchan will advise on the ship's operation; Mr. Mulcairn, working alone, will bring his horse down from the tunnels and make it fast in the ship else he will decide between the horse and the expedition. The rest will provision the ship under Mr. Priddish's eye.

With this, the men file away and turn, grumbling, to their work. All but Buchan, who is kept by a gesture from Ogden, and Mr. Renton, who, like a terrier latched onto a joint of meat, cannot seem to let the subject of spying drop.

'I've heard you–In Africa, too, yes,' Ogden is saying over the boy's racket–'But consider, if he were a trained spy of Lord Pomeroy's, he wouldn't have let you catch him at it, and certainly wouldn't have confessed to it.'

'Then yeh excuse 'im on the basis of 'e's *bad* at it?' cries the boy.

'We're done debating the point,' Ogden growls. 'You have an order now to help Mr. Priddish, and you'll by G–d do it.'

Renton is ready with another comment but Ogden stands, and the boy must skip out of arm's reach. Renton makes a last, unspeakable gesture at Mr. Buchan and carries himself off into the dark, and the two men look after him with–it must be said–not a little amazement.

'Sir,' Buchan stammers, when the moment has passed, 'I ought to have come right out with this long before now, I realize–and–Well, it hardly bears saying, does it, that any letters from here on, from Bombay or from anywhere–'

Ogden waves him to silence and sits again, digging in his coat pockets. He draws out his pipe and bag of tobacco, and crosses one boot over the other.

'...I regretted taking you in,' he says, at length, 'first because I'd felt pressed by time and hadn't fathomed you yet, the way I'd known these other men in India. That's how I viewed it at first, anyway. But I believe that's wrong. I believe I took you in because I knew you straightaway for a man of character.' Ogden scrapes the bowl of the pipe, and drums out the loose ash on a stone. 'The others,' he says, 'will know you've put their safety ahead of your own, if you'll allow them time to understand that. Perhaps you'll see a chance, too, to remind them.'

'Yes, sir.'

'It's true, as I told Mr. Renton: a better spy might have warned us without endangering himself. Though I suppose you must have it all off your chest. Anyway, I'll advise against your carrying secrets around, in future. You're not built for it, if anyone is.'

'No, sir.'

'Good. For now, you're not really inspecting that ship. You'll shut yourself in the orlop till I'm sure these men will fight with you.'

'Yes, sir,' says Buchan. And he is as pleased as any man ought to be, who has been ordered into confinement.

Ogden sits for a moment more, charging his pipe and observing the dragoons at their work. He sees Mulcairn hauling his ape-like body up the ladder, back into the tunnels. 'Any rate,' he says, 'your parting with that horse has paid you a good dividend.'

Subadar Priddish has given Bertram and Miss Harrow the task, meanwhile, of counting out rations, though I am not sure either is making a good job of it. They sit on a tarp surrounded by sacks of meal and biscuit and loose piles of cured meats. They dig desultorily in one place and another, but really they are watching the interview below, until Buchan snaps his commander a salute and marches away. They have listened closely and seen, even from this distance, the swift improvement of Buchan's mood, and it is difficult not to smile at the young Corporal as he hops up toward them, with elbows swinging high. Yet if his confession has relieved Mr. Buchan of this particular worry, it has also brought a greater concern to the mind of Miss Harrow. And her face, I am afraid to report, only hardens as the young man draws near.

'What have you been *doing*, James?' she demands, when he's got close enough to hear.

'I–Nothing. What?' This is a bit less than the welcome he had hoped for.

'You *know* they've been whispering since New York about someone or other *following* us, or clearing the way ahead, or anyway interested in what we're up to. And what if it were *true*, James? What if it's your Ceylon Company after us and *you're* the one who'd brought them along?'

'Well: I don't know I'd call them *my* Company–'

'Do you know the *risk* you've put us all to? If they were to track us to the City…? What are their interests there, anyway?–Oh, don't answer. I *know* you don't know–But I'm sure they're not *good*, whatever they are.'

'I…' Buchan scans about the room, to Miss Harrow's increased annoyance.

'They're not here *now*, James. That isn't the point. They can wait till we surface again. Even if we sent you off, they've already had a good look at us *all*, haven't they? They could follow any one of us.'

'I could ask them to stop–'

'No, it's *done*, you see.'

'–Though I don't know who I'd even speak to, at this point. I'm not allowed contact with them anyway.'

'Oh, there's nothing *anyone* can do, is there, but wait and hope against the worst.' She picks up another black, stick-like scrap of meat, but cannot seem to make sense of it. 'Ah, James! You couldn't have told *me*, at least, what you were doing…?'

As poor Mr. Buchan fumbles for an answer, a pair of men tromp by. The first of these is Corporal O'Hara, going to get his head sewn by the second, which is Captain Shaw. And I should think O'Hara were feeling a bit emboldened by events at camp, for he squares right up to Buchan and drills him in the chest with a forefinger.

'Well done, man,' he says, with his jackal's grin, and the blood running over his temple. He is pleased to see Miss Harrow, too, kneeling in her heaps of provisions.

'An' well done to *you*, mum,' he says, dipping her a quick nod: 'This le'll c–ck-up of a spy for yer friend, wot?'

'All right, Hugh.' Shaw moves him along, though O'Hara must give her another courtly bow and leave cackling.

'Don't worry about that one–,' says Buchan, with his fists balling.

'–I don't,' Evelyn returns, flatly. 'But I can thank you for the remarks anyway. I don't guess that will be the last of them.'

'Miss Harrow, if any of these men–'

'But they *will*, James. And then what? You'll be locked up under the ship. Thank you, but I'll see to my own preservation.' She clucks her tongue at the little piles around her and falls back to work. 'Go on,' she says. 'I'm very angry with you at the moment, and it's probably best all round if you were hidden away.'

In two hours' time the submersible has been loaded with all the weapons and stores it will be made to carry, and the party have closed themselves in as tight-packed as the bodies in an old slaving barque (in view of which, perhaps, one of them has daubed the name *HMS Black Joke* across the vessel's bows, in pitch). The ship has been fitted all through its interior with iron rings, and there are chains and leather straps depending from these, so that the supplies for the trip—from great hogsheads of water and salt-pork to loose sidearms and tools—may be made fast on the walls and decks and between the transverse beams overhead. And the look of all these articles, I should say, hovering at random, in the dark, is something like a military depot caught in mid-explosion. For the passengers there are larger iron rings wrapped in embroidered padding and arranged in pairs, the lower ring serving for a seat and the upper for a brace about the ribs, with straps that may be cinched about the waist and crisscrossed over the shoulders (though we note only Bertram and Miss Harrow are using them

as intended). Ogden has secured himself in the bow behind the quartz windows, next to an hourglass in a gimbal. The hourglass's use he cannot fathom, and he can see nothing through the windows but a bleary darkness, but he must look assured of his business in any case.

Behind him, Mr. Priddish skitters about the cabin making a last check of straps and hatches, as somewhere beneath them Mr. Mulcairn struggles to calm his horse, and G-d alone knows how they are faring. Lower still, in the belly of the ship, Mr. Buchan sits in darkness between the ship's pumps. And the whole vessel, bottom to top, is filled with the cries and oaths of the dragoons as they snug themselves into place. It does not seem to Mr. Priddish that he can leave these men much longer in wait. They will face all manner of danger in the field of course, and gladly, but they have not got the nerve for this sort of venture, where they must go blind and constricted into dangers unknown. Not even Ogden can keep the strain from his voice.

'Mr. Priddish?' the old trooper snaps, from the bow. 'What's your impression of *these*, sir?' He sits with his feet on a pair of treads, and an iron lever–something like a railroad brake–in his fist. 'Their *operation*, in particular.'

'You may let them be for now, Sahib,' Priddish explains. 'The lever lets us guide the rudder to some degree, once we are underwater. But during the descent all fins and rudders are retracted and sealed, and there is no need of steering. When we have surfaced, we'll assemble the ship's wheel in the stern, and steer the vessel from there.' Priddish has withdrawn into the ship and is securing himself on a raised seat beneath a hanging lantern. 'You see the winch over you, and the clasp on the underside of the hatch?'

'Mm?' Ogden barks. '...Oh: yes.'

'When you are ready, sir, you may try the winch. I would angle us forward, so we will rest nose-down along the declivity.'

'All right.' Ogden pulls on the winch's handle, and when it won't turn, he pushes, cranking it counter-clockwise, and the ship answers with a jarring drop of its bows. The men are thrown forward against the rings girding them, and a loose spade drops and clatters across the deck. The cries grow louder and more insistent, and more than one dragoon calls for Ogden to stop the descent, as though it were possible.

'Quiet, you men,' Ogden snarls, over his shoulder. Priddish has begun working his own winch, and the ship bounces down on its chains like a cart descending stairs. 'And the clasp?' Ogden calls back to the Sikh.

'That releases the chain, Sahib.' Priddish's voice has thickened a bit, as Ogden is privately pleased to note. 'We will let go the forward and after chains together, and then we must close the hatch and set the pins. From there we will let gravity and the current do their work–'

The jolt of the ship's landing is enough to start a yelp from the majority of its passengers, all at once. 'It's a insterment o' torture!' cries Mr. Renton, in a voice he'd ordinarily be ashamed of. 'The *feechtin'* Black Hole o' Cahlcotter!' opines Mr. Henty. Sergeant Pensette, insanely, is trying to wriggle out of his seat. Clearly it is time for Ogden and Priddish to release the chains, which they do, counting down from three. And well-coordinated as the action is, it releases hell inside the *Black Joke*.

For one thing–as not even Mr. Priddish had thought to expect–the ship rolls to its side as soon as it sets down. And it continues to spin and carom freely as it picks up momentum on its way down the shaft. The grinding of the ship's hull against the hardened old planks is loud enough to vibrate skulls, but still not sufficient to smother the cries of the men, which are now truly the howls of the damned. Ogden, who's had the presence of mind to twist the handle overhead and to set the hatch's pins, nevertheless goes stamping on the treads and hauling at the handle beside him for all he is worth. Barrel-tops pop open and water and flour and rice and knives go wheeling through the cabin and pour over the men, and Mr. Priddish is sickened to see the lantern's glass flecked with gunpowder. Mr. Mulcairn's horse, belowdecks, can be heard shrieking and staving in planks with its hooves, while Mulcairn, desperate to calm the beast, must hammer it unconscious with his fists. Loud as the struggle is, the Irishman's sobs and pleas for forgiveness are scarcely less audible above, and no less awful to hear.

The ship strikes the black water with a hideous crash, and it shudders and spins violently hind-side-to as all its cracked old seals spring at once, sending jets of fetid water in at every angle and snuffing the lights. The current rakes the vessel against the stone ceiling of the canal, though as it fills with water the ship settles into the depths, and it no longer sounds, at least, as though it will be ground apart. Mr. Priddish strikes

a match and rekindles his lantern, and tries not to look at the horror-stricken faces rising out of the dark around him. He finds an evacuator tube and screws it into a coupling over the stern, and pulls a lever to open a valve in the coupling. From here he tumbles and gropes his way belowdecks, loosing the rudder and fins from their recesses outside the ship, all in less time than it takes to describe. The ship, marvelously, rights itself and spins bows-forward, though the motion sends all the water it has taken on into the bilges and Mr. Buchan must be fished, gasping, through the hatch of the orlop. The young man is not so addled but he can hold a lantern, and he does this as Mr. Priddish ducks into the bilges, throws the valve beneath one of the pumps and hands the pump back up through the hatch. From here the work is plain enough: 'Pump like *be-d–mned*,' as the Sikh puts it, this being the first oath Buchan has ever heard him employ.

The pump is worked by a two-handled arm like the walking-beam of a railway handcar, and the men fall each on one of the handles, forcing the water in the ship's hull up through the valve Mr. Priddish has opened over the main deck. The water is already running about their knees, and with the ship's leaks only widening it is all they can do to slow the water's rise; though with a second team called down and a second pump in operation the men are able to gain ground and even to regulate, roughly, the submersible's depth. Ogden has got a feel for the tiller now, too, and after a few knocks off the tunnel's roof and sides, he manages to keep them bows-forward in the current. Mr. Mulcairn has lashed down his horse and climbed to the main deck, where he helps the others light lanterns and re-secure loose articles. Ogden asks if he has not killed the horse, and the Irishman, hearing the note of sympathy in his commander's voice, says he hopes not, but that he's hit the beast hard enough to

where he might have. Ogden gives him a quick but meaning nod, and both fall back to their work. There is a sense, or very nearly, that the men have pulled through the worst, and that they've got matters in hand. This just as the submersible shoots off a shelf or cataract at the end of the Al-Shar tributary.

The fall comes wholly without warning, and it is not at once clear what has happened. The decks are simply beneath the men's feet in one moment and gone in the next. Feet and coattails fly up, guts heave into mouths and heads split on roofbeams as the ship and crew drop freely through the air and crash about fifteen feet below. Bodies fly pell-mell into the forward half of the ship, then, and another miscellany of items–this time including the uncrated lanterns and the heavy brass pumps–drop painfully onto the men where they lie heaped; and then all slide aft again as the ship heaves back to level. Mr. Priddish stands, finally, nursing a new-cracked pair of ribs. He calls his crews back to the pumps, and the soldiers manage, with a frenzy of effort, to surface again in the great, swirling underground river.

They are pumping still when Ogden calls down to announce that the main deck is no longer taking on water, and that the dim outlines of a tunnel have risen in the forward windows. It seems they have come to a wide and navigable watercourse, perhaps this 'western artery' of Lord Pomeroy's, and he orders Mr. Priddish up to refit the ship accordingly. The dragoons, who have shouted themselves out of voice, nonetheless manage three cheers for their commander and three more for Mr. Priddish (and though Ogden would ordinarily have found the man who'd raised these cheers and had him whipped, today he allows the matter to pass).

The top and bottom halves of the submersible are held together by iron clamps, and Mr. Priddish details a pair of men to release these as two others draw down the hinges that link the ceiling-beams. This done, he and Mr. Mulcairn push back the transverse beams as they might retract the canvas top of a cabriolet, and with not much more effort. The whole thing fits neatly into a cavity in the stern, and the men are left, if not in the open air, then in the greater enclosing darkness of the underground cavern, to marvel at the ingenuity of the ship's makers.

And for the moment it is all of them ranged about the deck. Even Bertram has climbed down from his seat to see the cavern walls limned about him in the water's dull phosphorescence. The men stare and stretch, grinning and thumping backs, nursing all manner of little wounds, chaffing one another over the unmanly screams that had minutes ago filled the dark. Mr. Henty demands, of no one in particular, a 'tot of rum' for his own display of nerve, and is cried down good-naturedly. Mr. Priddish is not proof against a bit of giddiness himself (nor, I dare say, above a private bit of self-congratulation). He offers his own views as to which indignities belonged to which of the company, and is so absorbed in the debate that he fails to notice the ship settling back into the canal. It is Miss Harrow, of all people, tossing a spent match overboard, who sees the water risen to within arm's reach of the gunwales. She is loath to break up the party on deck—particularly where Mr. Buchan is in among the dragoons again, his sins against the fraternity pardoned or at least forgotten in this latest escape from death. But she must ultimately ask who is manning the pumps. And at about her fifth repetition of the question, Mr. Priddish frowns over the ship's rail and shouts the men back into action.

For Ogden, too, the moment's

elation and reprieve from worry are quick to pass. If they are in this western artery—and it seems they are—then so much the better; but this is also where they must run upon Mr. Buchan's pirates. And the devil in it is that the enemy might be days ahead, or only past the next bend. The Zagros Mountains are useless to him as a point of reference now, though he knows Al-Shar is not very far from the Persian border and the current bearing them east is strong. It is more apt to be a matter of hours, he thinks, than days before this enemy is met. They are a single craft, battered and not very large, with a pitifully small complement of men, and a woman and child to protect besides. And *still* the old trooper might like his chances if only his men had a pinch of dry powder between them.

He paces the deck in a fever of calculation. They must slow the ship, he thinks, and discover a way to salvage gunpowder in this dripping, airless tunnel. The men see this mood on their commander and fall quietly to various tasks—working the pumps, helping Mr. Priddish to cable the ship's wheel, assessing damage to the ship and the stores and so forth. Sergeant Pensette has gone head-down in a scupper, neither drunk nor sick as you might suppose, but clearing items from the netting below. Hoisting himself back to the deck, the Scotsman is surprised to find his commander behind him, turning one of the freed items in his hands.

'A…baking-sheet, sir,' says Pensette, as though an explanation were needed. 'From the galley, I should think.'

But his commander's thoughts are elsewhere. Ogden hands the sheet back to the Scotsman and paces another half-dozen turns across the deck.

A quarter-hour later Ogden has given new orders, and the ship's company have bent to their work with a renewed urgency. Belowdecks, they man the pumps in shifts of four. Above, Subadar Priddish stands at the wheel, while Mr. Pandit increases the ship's drag by tying loose planks and weights and empty casks to its stern. Bertram has been set up on a stool at the ship's bow, where he scans the tunnels for possible places of mooring. All others have been ordered to clear the main deck and to bring up every flat bit of metal that can be found or made on the ship. Copper sheeting has been pulled from the galley walls and tin plates and trays emptied from its lockers. There are pre-Roman shields from the weapon-room and cups and bowls and ammunition crates hammered flat, and of course there is Sergeant Pensette's baking-tray, which he had been carrying around as proof of his own cleverness till ordered to set it down with the rest.

As these articles are brought to the deck and made ready, Ogden orders them set on props and made level, and stopped around their edges with water-damped wadding. The flat surface is spread, then, with every loose gram of powder that can be recovered from below. The hundred little pouches from the *hwacha*'s arrows must be pierced and emptied; the powder cask that had held its top must be scooped clean and its powder-caked staves broken up and laid out; any likely-looking black sludge is poured out on the chance it will fire; waterlogged cartridges are stood wherever there is room. Fires are kindled then beneath the metal trays and tended by men with buckets of water handy. The rest of the dragoons stand guard along the gunwales, watching for that stray risen spark that would blast them all into atoms, as Ogden cuts his eyes continually from the drying powder to the darkness ahead. It is, as you will imagine, rather a trying hour for them all.

With these preparations made and little point in staring at the powder, willing it to dry, Ogden's mind jumps to a new conundrum: even if the *Black Joke* should forbear to explode, he thinks, and if they can recover enough powder to meet their enemy, there is still this matter of the ship's taking water. He cannot have men working the pumps who could otherwise fight, and much less can he have the boat *sinking*. He goes with Mr. Priddish therefore into the dark below, and drags out a hogshead of a hard black substance he'd spotted in his search for powder. After a bit of heating the stuff and working it in with water it proves, as he'd hoped, to be a sort of gum or resin in preserved form. Mr. Priddish finds, too, that the ship's old cables twist easily apart for the making of oakum. The men who can be spared from above, then, are called down and put to work pulling fibers from the ropes and soaking them in the reconstituted gum, then prying up the old caulking from the hull's seams and forcing in the new with chisel and adze. The work is slow going for men unused to a ship's maintenance, but it seems that gains are made and held against the flooding of the bilges, and the lower decks are nearly pumped dry by the time a new call comes down from above.

MAJOR?
THE WATER IS EDDYING, SAHIB. A BEND IN THE RIVER, PERHAPS.

...SIR, CAN WE HAVE YOU ON DECK?

ALL RIGHT. PUT OUT THE FIRES. TAKE THE CARTRIDGES FIRST; THEY'LL NEED TO COOL.
CAPTAIN SHAW, BRING ALL THAT BELOW. READY THE SIX-POUNDERS WITH YOUR MEN AND KEEP THE PORTS CLOSED.

MISS HARROW, YOU CAN HELP MR. BUCHAN TIE OFF THESE ARROWS. SERGEANT PENSETTE AT THE FOR-WARD CHASER. QUICKLY, ALL OF YOU, AND NOT A SOUND. WE DON'T KNOW BUT THERE ARE SENTRIES ABOUT.

ПОМЕДЛЕННЕЕ. КТО ТАМ?
؟يش ىلوک يربخ رثبنپ مپ مث اي

ОТВЕТЬ МНЕ. БЫСТРО.
...HULLO?
КТО ТАМ?

PLEASE...WATER...
АНГЛИЙСКИЙ. НАЙТИ Г-ЛЕЧМИР.

ENGLISH, HM? YES? AND HOW MANY ARE YOU?
WATER...
THERE'S WATER HERE. IT'S ONLY YOU?
YES, MILOR'.
IF YOU'RE HIDING ANY-ONE ELSE, YOU KNOW, WE'LL CUT THEM UP.

ПДПТЕ МЕДЛЕННО.

HSST–! IL EST COUCHÉ.

I SAY: THERE'S SOMEONE UP HERE CALLED *L'IGUANE*. HE THINKS YOU'RE UP TO SOMETHING, AND HE'S A GOOD JUDGE OF THESE THINGS.
WHAT ARE YOU UP TO, BOY?
NOTHING, SIR–WE HAD A 'ORRIBLE ACCIDENT–TRULY, SIR. AN' NONE BUT ME LEFT.

HEAVE TO, WILL YA? AN' THROW OVER A LINE.
YES, COME. I'LL SHOW YOU WHY HE'S CALLED THE IGUANA.
LITTLE BOYS WHO LIE TO US ARE FED ALIVE TO HIM, YOU KNOW.

HOLD, MR. RENTON. NOT YET.

Mr. Renton, by now, is insensate to Ogden's command. The boat is drawing slowly to a stop, and the boy is brought up level with the twisted little figure on the quay. And there is nothing else for it: Mr. Renton's hand must reach inside his coat for the pistol at his belt. The sight of *Monsieur* the Iguana, at such close range, simply cannot be stood. His wet lips and stooped back, his rolling eyes and scaly, leprous skin, these are provocation enough; but he has raced down from the height and skipped over the rat-lines with some little object raised before him. And as he waves it over the *Black Joke* in an attitude of listening, there is no mistaking what the thing is. Renton follows the gnarled little ear in its last sweep of the main deck as his own hand works his pistol free. *Monsieur* has got his boot up on the ship's rail now, and he calls some direction or other over his shoulder while he re-attaches the ear to his hair with a jeweled clip. Ogden is hissing something, too, but he can no more stop the boy's hand than can Renton himself. The Iguana turns to see the bore of Mr. Renton's pistol about three feet from the tip of his own misshapen nose.

There is a click as Renton's cartridge misfires, and the Iguana's lips part to reveal the carious stubs of his teeth, all of them filed to points. He gurgles a few more words aside—*'Je vous l'ai dit—Tuez-les'*—with the severed ear dangling directly in front of Mr. Renton. The boy does not look away or stir in the least, he only thumbs the pistol's hammer back and, to the surprise of all, his second cartridge answers. The pistol's report echoes in a wet, smacking sound, indescribably awful, as the ball zips through the Iguana's ear and scatters the rest of his head in a dark red jam. There follows a strange, suspended moment, where the men of the encampment look to the gun-shot, and the Iguana stands with arms straightened and fingers splayed and no head over his shoulders. There is just the eternal rush of current for sound, until a bark from Ogden is answered belowdecks by Captain Shaw. The dragoons on the main deck stand with rifles leveled over the rail, and Sergeant Pensette pulls a tarp from over the *hwacha*. The pirates haven't time to raise their own weapons before a last order is called and the port-side cannons of the *Black Joke* erupt in flame.

«THOOOM!»

MR. MULCAIRN–HELP HIM FACE THAT GUN FORWARD–
MR. HENTY, STAY AT THE CHASER; CLEAR US ROOM AHEAD.
YOU MEN–GET AT THOSE LINES!

The lagoon, as it happens, is not very well fortified against attack. The settlement's main batteries all face upstream, and most ships come in hobbled and in a state of surrender. After Captain Shaw's six-pounders sweep the dock into the canal and the *hwacha* sets the rest of the quayside ablaze, the pirates can bring little but small arms to bear on the *Black Joke*. What fighting there is is concentrated farther on, where a bridge spans the channel's outlet and men are able to swing in on lines or to drop from overhead onto the deck; though even then, few of these men arrive in any shape to fight. They seem to be leprous, most of them, or to suffer some similar, wasting disease, something unique perhaps to this settlement. Their skin is black and shining where the affliction has taken root, and a fist landed on these patches will tear through the flesh as it would through overripe fruit. Some bodies are run fully through with the disease, and these land on the deck with legs bursting beneath them while others, pricked by a blade, vent their insides like overfilled sacks of wine. It may be imagined with what distaste the dragoons meet an enemy like this. The decks and rails of the *Black Joke* are soon slicked with gore and the fragments of dead men, and still the attackers arrive by dozens. Few have even the wherewithal to raise their ancient weapons, but they march idiotically into the guns and swords of Ogden's dragoons, as though to smother them by a sheer weight of numbers.

Ogden, for his part, tries to keep the ship's guns trained forward and his men alert to the hooks and snares falling out of the dark. The ship gathers way slowly through the channel, though as it breasts the archway, a new danger may be seen materializing on the settlement's downstream slope.

SERGEANT?
AYE, SIR, ALMOST GOT IT–
I TOLD YOU SEND MULCAIRN TO ME, G–D D–MNIT!

SAHIB, WE'RE PASSING THAT POINT. MR. MULCAIRN, YOU KNOW, DOES NOT SWIM.

HOLD IT–CORPORAL–!

WHAT IS THIS, MR. BUCHAN?
YOU SAID, SIR, THE MEN COULD STAND A REMINDER.
AH. ALL RIGHT. THEN YOU GIVE THEM ONE, SON.
THERE'S A CHINESE JUNK AT THE CENTER OF THIS INLET, AND BEHIND THAT YOU'LL SEE THE MAGAZINE. YOU'VE GOT TO FIRE IT BEFORE THEY CAN LOAD THAT BATTERY, ELSE THEY'LL SHELL US FROM BEHIND.

YES, SIR. GET THERE AS QUICKLY AS I CAN.
MR. BUCHAN? WE CAN'T SLOW THE SHIP.
NO. I REALIZE.

ALL RIGHT–DOWN, D–MN YOU, AND GIVE HIM COVER.

WELL. THE MAD B–STARD.
AYE. IT WAS YOU, Y'KNOW, MEANT TO GO UP THERE. AN' MY OWN MISTAKE YEH DIDN'T.
WHICH IS JUST YOUR EVIL LUCK, IN'NIT, TOM?

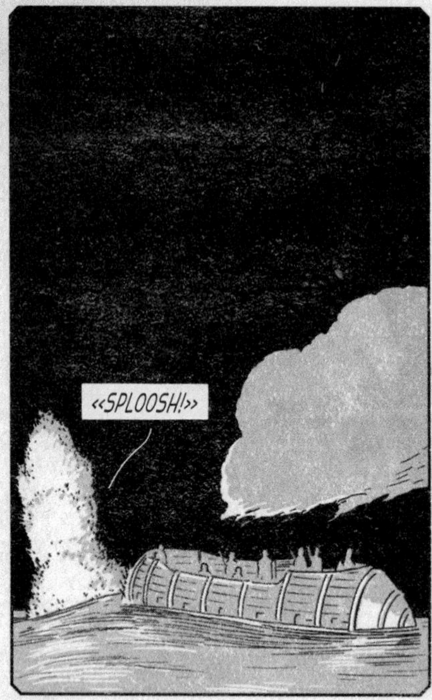
«SPLOOSH!»

HOAH! WIDE ABOUT THIRTY FEET, SIR.
–MOUNTING ANOTHER–
STAND INTO IT. THESE ONES COULDN'T HIT A HAY-RICK.

AH! BOY'S MADE IT OUT, SIR. ALONG THERE–THE RIDGE–

MR. PRIDDISH, COME AFT–MR. GURUNG, GIVE THAT RIFLE TO HIM AND HOLD THE WHEEL.

THERE. MAKING FOR THAT GALLEY, OVER THE GAP–MEANS TO JUMP IT.

HE'S RUN OUT A WICK, SIR–OR POWDER–SOMETHING'S SPARKED BEHIND HIM ANYWAY–THEY'RE ALL MAKING FOR IT–

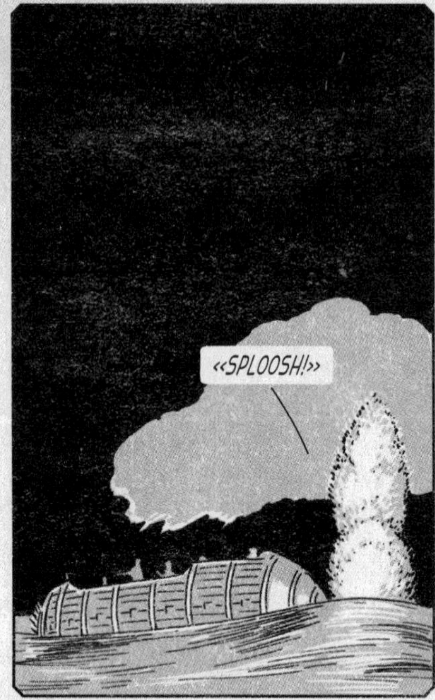
«SPLOOSH!»

–SIR, THEY'RE BRACKETING US.

GO ON, LAD–JUMP IT…JUMP–!
GOOD BOY! QUICK, NOW…

BUCHAN IS HALFWAY ACROSS THE GAP WHEN A BULLET STRIKES HIM AND SPINS HIM OVER. HE DROPS FROM SIGHT.

...AH, THE POOR
F–CKING–

«SPLOOSH!»

CHR–ST! THAT'S A THIRD GUN UP,
SIR–TWENTY-FOUR-POUNDER. WE
CAN'T TAKE ONE OF THOSE DIRECT–

«THOOOMM!»

HA! LAD'S DONE IT, SIR.

...WULL. GOOD BOY.

ALL RIGHT–ALL THIS GETS WASHED AND STONED BEFORE WE HAVE THE BOY UP. MR. SHAW, DETAIL TWO MEN AND LOOK OVER THE SHIP, LET US KNOW THE WORST OF IT, AND CHECK THE BILGE.

...AND PRAY WHATEVER THESE MEN HAD ISN'T CATCHING.
GET HER BELOW, MR. PRIDDISH.
I'LL GET MYSELF BELOW, THANK YOU.
GO ON WITH...WHATEVER HE'S GOT YOU DOING.

MUCH DOING JUST NOW, WASN'T THERE, HUGH?
SIR?
I'VE BEEN A MOMENT SORTING IT OUT.
YOU CAN STOP, NOW, AND STAND UP. NO POINT IN YOUR DOING THAT.

OH? YOU TELL ME WHY NOT.
BECAUSE THIS IS ALL THE HEARING YOU GET. MOST WOULD HAVE IT STANDING.
A HEARING? AH-NO. I'LL HAVE TO KNOW WHAT THIS IS ABOUT, MAJOR.

MM. IF WE WERE TRYING YOU IN INDIA, HUGH, I MIGHT NOT PUT A VERY GOOD CASE. I'D HAVE TO SWEAR TO KNOWING YOUR SNIDER'S REPORT IN A HUNDRED, AND HEARING IT BEHIND ME IN THE MOMENT THAT BOY FELL.
IT'S TRUE, OF COURSE. BUT IT'S JUST AS WELL I NEEDN'T PROVE IT. DON'T KNOW HOW I WOULD.
STAND UP, HUGH.

STEADY, MAN. YOU'LL HAVE JUSTICE.
AYE, SIR. AN' YOU WONDER I'M NOT STEADY?

SIR? WE CAN'T–
IT'LL BE ARGUED WE CAN'T SPARE ANY MORE MEN, AND IT'S TRUE. WE CAN'T. BUT IT'S BECAUSE WE'RE SMALL, HUGH, THAT I CAN'T KEEP ANY LIKE YOU. I CAN'T HAVE YOU ONE MINUTE MORE.

OH–YOU WEREN'T WATCHING, BERTRAM?
I SAW MR. BUCHAN–
AUGHH. YES, IT'S TOO AWFUL, ISN'T IT. LET'S GET YOU AWAY FROM THERE.

«POP!»

IT WAS MR. O'HARA, WASN'T IT.
YES, OF COURSE.

JAMES SEEMED TO KNOW HE WOULDN'T SEE US AGAIN. IT ONLY SEEMED, FOR A MOMENT THERE, AS THOUGH HE MIGHT...

FORGIVE ME, BERTRAM. I'M ONLY TALKING. WHAT A HORRID PLACE, THESE TUNNELS.
I'M SORRY, MISS HARROW.
I'M—ME, TOO. YES.

...YES. THAT POOR BOY.

AT THE SAME TIME, MISS HARROW IS BEING DISCUSSED IN THE ABBOT'S COURT AT FERITIVA.
...THERE WAS A YOUNG LADY WITH US, WHO FELT YOU'D VISITED HER THROUGH SOME PARLOR-MEDIUM IN THE STATES...

SHE HAD A SHORT AUDIENCE WITH YOU HERE, WHILE I MADE MY PREPARATIONS BELOW.
I'VE WONDERED SINCE IF I HADN'T BETTER KEPT HER WITH ME. IT STRUCK ME SHE CAME BACK TO US SOMEHOW CHANGED.
AH. HOW MANY YEARS GONE, *CHELA*, AND HOW MANY DAYS HIDDEN AWAY FROM ME IN THIS CASTLE; AND YOU COME ASKING ABOUT A GIRL?

I HAVE QUESTIONS OF ONE KIND AND AN-OTHER. I WONDER MOSTLY, THESE DAYS, WHAT YOU AND I HAVE WROUGHT IN THIS WORLD, AND WHAT MAY STILL BE DONE ABOUT IT.
BUT SINCE I'VE ASKED YOU ABOUT MISS HARROW, PERHAPS YOU'LL INDULGE ME THERE FIRST.
MISS HARROW, THEN...
SHE'S ONE OF THOSE YOU ANOINTED TO HELP BRING ME HERE.

...WHICH, APROPOS, I TAKE TO BE YOUR DESIGN IN RAZING THE MACHINES I'D BUILT IN NEW YORK. SO I'D BE FORCED TO MAKE USE OF THE ONE HERE.
YES, OF COURSE.
MM. IN MISS HARROW'S CASE, SHE FOUND AND TRANSPORTED ME IN RETURN FOR SOME GUIDANCE ON YOUR PART. YOU HAD PROMISED TO SET HER ON A 'PATH' FROM HERE, PRESUMABLY TO THE CITY.
JUST SO.

THOUGH ALL YOU'VE REALLY DONE IS TO DI-VERT HER, ALONG WITH THE REST OF THEM.
AH: SO WE COME TO WHAT TROUBLES YOU. I ASSURE YOU, *CHELA*, I HAVE DONE NO MORE WITH YOUR FRIEND THAN THANK HER FOR THIS OFFICE SHE PERFORMED, AND SWEAR TO IMPOSE NO MORE UPON HER.
BUT I IMAGINE SHE FELT OWED FOR THIS 'OFFICE.'

SO SHE DID. BUT CONSIDER THIS GIRL. I FOUND HER QUITE CHANGED FROM THE SEALED LITTLE CREATURE I MET JUST A FEW YEARS AGO. SHE HAD BEGUN TO DEVELOP TIES TO THIS WORLD. SHE HAD BEGUN TO COMMUNE WITH CERTAIN OTHER SOULS. WAS THIS YOUR IMPRESSION ALSO?
I–YES. SHE HAS DRAWN VERY CLOSE TO LITTLE BARNES.

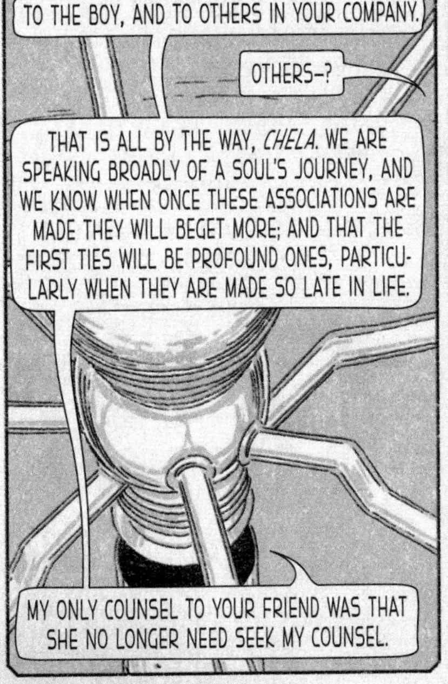
TO THE BOY, AND TO OTHERS IN YOUR COMPANY.
OTHERS–?
THAT IS ALL BY THE WAY, *CHELA*. WE ARE SPEAKING BROADLY OF A SOUL'S JOURNEY, AND WE KNOW WHEN ONCE THESE ASSOCIATIONS ARE MADE THEY WILL BEGET MORE; AND THAT THE FIRST TIES WILL BE PROFOUND ONES, PARTICU-LARLY WHEN THEY ARE MADE SO LATE IN LIFE.
MY ONLY COUNSEL TO YOUR FRIEND WAS THAT SHE NO LONGER NEED SEEK MY COUNSEL.

SHE WOULD FIND HER PATH BY LISTEN-ING TO THE PROMPTINGS OF HER OWN HEART, NOW THAT IT HAD FOUND ITS VOICE. I ADDED SHE MIGHT DO SO, VERY OFTEN, IN DEFIANCE OF REASON. NOR DO I THINK SHE WAS VERY LONG IN PUTTING THAT LESSON INTO PRACTICE.
NO. DIRECTLY SHE CAME BELOW, SHE WAS GIVEN A CHOICE: SHE COULD EITHER LEAVE BERTRAM TO ME, AGAINST THE IMPULSE OF HER HEART; OR CARRY HIM OFF AGAINST THE...THE RATHER HARD LOGIC I MUST HAVE REPRESENTED.
YOU'D HAVE ANTICIPATED HER HEART MISLEADING HER, IN JUST SUCH A CASE.

OH: I DON'T SAY SHE WAS 'MISLED'–
–NOT FOR YOUR PURPOSE, NO. BUT SHE IS GONE THE WAY YOU WOULD HAVE, AND SHE THINKS SHE HAS GONE THERE OF HER OWN WILL.
PERHAPS, YES. BUT YOU MUST UNDERSTAND, THESE ARE VERY CLEVER, AND VERY WILLFUL PEOPLE WITH WHOM WE DEAL–MISS HARROW, MR. OGDEN–EVEN YOURSELF, *CHELA*–AND LOOK AT ME: I HAVEN'T EVEN POWER TO FEED MYSELF.

I LIE STRAITENED IN THIS TANK AND WILL NEVER MORE MOVE FROM IT. SUCH FRIENDS AS I HAVE ARE FORCED TO SLINK AROUND THE WORLD BENEATH THE GAZE OF MEN, LIKE THEY WERE RATS.
WE CANNOT COMMAND YOU, WE CANNOT PUT YOU FORCIBLY WHERE YOU MUST GO...WE CANNOT EVEN FIND YOU MUCH OF THE TIME.
I MUST USE WHAT MEANS I HAVE AT HAND.

YES, OF COURSE. AND YOU MUST BE VERY IMPRESSED WITH YOUR OWN SUBTLETY. MM? I THINK YOU ARE LIKE THE CHRISTIAN DEVIL, IF THE EARTH WERE REALLY FOULED BY SUCH A THING.
HYEUGH-HYEUGH. YOUR FRIEND OGDEN MIGHT DESCRIBE YOU IN THE SAME TERMS, SO PERHAPS WE ARE WELL-MATCHED. AND OF COURSE WE KNOW THINGS THEY DO NOT, *CHELA*.

BUT I TELL YOU: IF YOU PERCEIVE YOUR FRIENDS ARE IN DANGER, YOU MUST GO TO THEM. YOU MAY STILL MEET THEM AT KATHMANDU, FOR THAT IS WHERE THEY ARE BOUND. AND THERE IS STILL TIME, IF YOU WOULD ACT TODAY.
ONLY TELL ME, AND I WILL ARRANGE IT.

...NO. IT WOULD BE A DREADFUL MISTAKE, AS YOU'RE AWARE.
WE ARE SEALING THIS BORDER BETWEEN OUR WORLD AND THE OTHER AND WE ARE SETTING OUR BACKS TO IT AND PRAYING WE ARE NOT ALREADY TOO LATE. THAT IS ALL. THE FATE OF YOUR FRIENDS–OF ALL OF THEM BUT THE BOY–IS CLOSED TO QUESTION. WHAT REMAINS IS TO LEARN WHAT YOU MUST DO, AND TO SETTLE, IN YOURSELF, HOW IT IS TO BE DONE.

THIS IS REALLY WHAT YOU HAVE COME TO ASK, *CHELA*, AND I WOULD PREFER WE SPEAK OF THAT.
OH? I THINK I'D RATHER, MATTHIEU, THAT YOU DID NOT USE THESE WORDS OF THE LAMAS. YOU DON'T UNDERSTAND THEM, AND YOU PROFANE THEM. YOU MAY CALL ME SLOANE.
AH. AND WHERE DID YOU COME BY THAT NAME?

WHERE? I DON'T KNOW! I MUST HAVE HEARD IT SOMEWHERE, OR SOMEONE TOLD IT TO ME. IT IS AS EMPTY OF MEANING AS THE REST OF ME.
AH! AND HERE I WOULD SAY YOU ARE ONE OF TWO CONSEQUENTIAL PEOPLE IN ALL THE WORLD.
...I WAS INVOLVED, IN SOME FASHION, WITH A YOUNG WOMAN IN INDIA. DID YOU KNOW THAT?
YES.

I SAW HER MORE RECENTLY IN NEW YORK, AND HADN'T THE LEAST STIRRING OF MEMORY AS WE TALKED. CAN YOU IMAGINE?
I'D ARRANGED TO SPEAK WITH HER AGAIN, TOO, BUT...I WAS TORN AWAY BY THIS 'BUSINESS' OF YOURS. AS I SUSPECT I WAS CALLED AWAY ONCE BEFORE, IN INDIA.
BUT WE MUST HAVE CARED SOMETHING FOR ONE ANOTHER, AND HAD AT LEAST SOME EXPECTATION OF HAPPINESS...

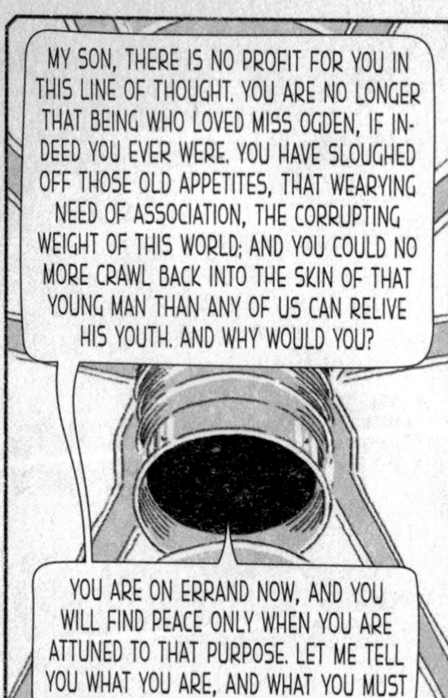
MY SON, THERE IS NO PROFIT FOR YOU IN THIS LINE OF THOUGHT. YOU ARE NO LONGER THAT BEING WHO LOVED MISS OGDEN, IF INDEED YOU EVER WERE. YOU HAVE SLOUGHED OFF THOSE OLD APPETITES, THAT WEARYING NEED OF ASSOCIATION, THE CORRUPTING WEIGHT OF THIS WORLD; AND YOU COULD NO MORE CRAWL BACK INTO THE SKIN OF THAT YOUNG MAN THAN ANY OF US CAN RELIVE HIS YOUTH. AND WHY WOULD YOU?
YOU ARE ON ERRAND NOW, AND YOU WILL FIND PEACE ONLY WHEN YOU ARE ATTUNED TO THAT PURPOSE. LET ME TELL YOU WHAT YOU ARE, AND WHAT YOU MUST DO, SINCE YOU HAVE COME TO LEARN.

...NO.
NO? THOUGH I THINK YOU HAVE GUESSED MUCH OF IT ALREADY.
THAT MAY BE. AND IT MAY BE INEVITABLE THAT I'LL LEARN THE REST.
BUT I CAN LIVE ONE MORE DAY IN IGNORANCE.
YES, OF COURSE. IF THAT IS YOUR WISH.

IT'S...ALL I CAN THINK OF, ANYWAY.
I SUPPOSE I'VE CHERISHED SOME HOPE, TO THIS POINT, THAT I MIGHTN'T BE UTTERLY LOST.
TOMORROW YOU MAY TELL ME THAT I AM.
LOST? NO-NO. YOU SHOULD CONSIDER, RATHER, THAT YOU ARE FREED FROM THE WHEEL OF THINGS.

IT IS A STATE TO WHICH THE WISE OF THIS WORLD ASPIRE, YOU KNOW.
YES? THEN THEY OUGHT TO ASPIRE TO SOMETHING ELSE.

...THERE'S NONE THAT AREN'T SOAKED THROUGH AND SPOILT, SIR, THOUGH I'VE GOT GURUNG SORTING OUT THE BAD FROM WORSE.
THE GREATER CONCERN IS WATER, WHERE WE'VE LOST TWO OF THE CASKS AND A THIRD SPLIT.

WE'RE TESTING THE THIRD ON MR. MULCAIRN, ONLY BECAUSE HE WON'T LET THE HORSE TAKE IT.
IF THAT WATER PROVES GOOD WE'LL HAVE TWO, PERHAPS THREE DAYS' RATION, BUT NO MORE.
–QUIET. DO YOU HEAR SOME-THING...? A MAN'S VOICE, BEHIND US!

...AYE, THERE: SAYIN'–'GO TO THE SMALLER' SOMETHIN'-OR-OTHER...HEAR THAT?
FELLA'S SHOUTED HISSELF HOARSE.
WULL. IT'S ENGLISH, ANYWAY.
SMALLER WHAT? I WONDER.

AH! SMALLER OF THEM CHANNELS, I SHOULD THINK.

SIR, WE'VE SOMEONE BEHIND US, SUGGESTS WE TAKE THE SMALLER OF THOSE TWO PASSAGES.
DOES 'E? AN' IF YE CAN TRUST ANYONE, IT'S THE BEGGARS LIVIN' DOWN IN THIS JAKES, IN'NIT?
MOOT POINT ANYWAY, JACK. WE CANNA' GET OVER AGAINST THIS CURRENT.

THE SMALLER ONE! MAJOR– THE SMALLER ONE! LEFT, SIR!
...THAT'S JAMES.

AH, BUT MISS, Y'CAIN'T KNOW THAT...
IT'S MR. BUCHAN, I PROMISE YOU.
...LEFT ONE, SIR!

MR. PENSETTE, GO DOWN AND SECURE THE BOY. MISS HARROW, YOU WITH HIM, PLEASE.

CLIMB TO THE PORT RAILS! MR. PRIDDISH, GET BELOW AND GET US BALLASTED!

WELL, IF WE AIN'T ROLLED OVER WE'RE BROUGHT INTO YON ROCKS, AND JUST AS THAT DEVIL BEHIND'D HAVE IT–
LORD GRANT WE SEE HIM, THEN. JUST ONCE, JUST THE GLIMPSE, AND LET ME GET THE F–CKING SHOT OFF–

«CRRASH!»

...WELL I AM D–MNED, SIR, IF IT AN'T YER MAN HIMSELF! COME IN A LITTLE WHERRY, WITH ANOTHER PULLIN' AT THE SCULLS!
AND MORE BOATS BEHIND THEM, IT LOOKS LIKE.

WHAT-HO, CORPORAL! WHO'VE YOU GOT, THERE, LAD? OR'VE THEY GOT YOU?
OH–NO–THESE ARE CAPTIVES FROM THE SETTLEMENT.
THERE WAS A GAOL AT THE FOOT OF THE HILL, MOST OF IT CAGES HUNG IN THE WATER–I FELL RIGHT ONTO IT WHEN THE MAGAZINE WENT–

COME UP ALONGSIDE, MR. BUCHAN. WE'LL HAVE YOU ON-BOARD, BUT I CAN'T RISK DISEASE FROM ANY OF THESE OTHERS.
NO, SIR. I'VE TOLD THEM.

...I MADE AS THOUGH TO HELP THEM DOWN WITH THE POWDER–IT WAS ALL SUCH A SCRAMBLE, YOU KNOW–BUT I WAS ONLY LAYING A TRAIL OF IT BE-HIND ME TO IGNITE THE REST. WHEN I'D GOT FAR ENOUGH AWAY, I LIT IT AND RAN FOR THE WATER–
AND SHOT MAKIN' YER JUMP, AS WE ALL SAW.
–THOUGH FORTUITOUSLY, I THINK. I MIGHT HAVE BURNED WITH THE REST IF I'D MADE THAT JUMP. AND THE BULLET WENT CLEAN THROUGH, AS YOU SEE.

AT ANY RATE, I FOUND THESE MEN IN THEIR CAGES, AND AFTER THE BLAST THERE WAS NO ONE REALLY TO STOP US FROM PRYING UP THE OLD LOCKS. THEY SHOWED ME TO THE BOATS AND GAVE ME–
–HERE, THIS: A ROUGH MAP OF THE WATERWAYS. AND WE HAD TO ROW AFTER YOU THEN LIKE MADMEN–WHICH, HELP-FULLY I THINK, MOST OF THEM ARE.

BUT YOU SEE HERE, AT THE FORK, HOW THE WIDER CHANNEL GOES STRAIGHT SOUTH, INTO THE SUBCONTINENT. YOU'D NEVER HAVE MADE NEPAL THAT WAY, SIR.
HRM. JUST AS WELL YOU CAUGHT US, THEN. ASSUMING THE MAP IS GOOD.
WELL: WE'LL BE ABLE TO CHECK IT ON AT LEAST ONE POINT–THIS, THERE, WHERE THEY MARK A CITY. THEY SAID WE OUGHT TO RAISE IT IN A DAY, OR TWO AT MOST.

A CITY?
–OR, A SETTLEMENT, ANYWAY, APPARENTLY OF SOME SIZE, AND THE ONLY ONE LIKE IT ON OUR WAY. IF WE'D ANY IDEA OF REFITTING, OR PROVISIONING THE SHIP–AND I THOUGHT WE MIGHT–THIS WOULD BE OUR LAST CHANCE BEFORE THE ORIENT.

CORPORAL? THERE'S ONE HERE'D LIKE TO MAKE CERTAIN YE'RE REALLY YERSELF.
IT WAS NO GOOD, MY TELLIN' HER.

WHAT A STUPID THING YOU DID, MR. BUCHAN! AND LOOK AT YOU, FILTHY AND BLOODIED NOW–AND SHOT–AND LETTING US ALL THINK YOU'D DIED–
OOF!
–GENTLY, PLEASE, MISS–

–AUGH! THEY COULDN'T FIND YOU DIRTIER RAGS TO DRESS THIS? I SUPPOSE YOU'D LIKE TO LOSE THE ARM ALTOGETHER, TO IMPRESS THESE MEN?
–'AT'S IT, MUM. YOU LAY INTA 'IM, WORRYIN' US SO!

AN' WOT A LOVELY PITCHER OF FAMILY YE-ALL MAKE, AH? YOU THAT TWO DAYS AGO WAS JUST AS HAPPY TO PICK THAT MAN'S BONES.
OH? SO WHAT'S THE POINT OF BRINGIN' THAT UP, MR. RENTON?
«PTOO!»

IT'S TRUE, IS THE POINT. NOT TO MENTION HE CAN FIRE TEN MAGAZINES AND STILL BE A BL–DY SPY.
–WHEEST, LAD.

III.

FOR SOME NUMBER OF HOURS and days (we will need to allow a degree of imprecision from this point on, as regards time) we find the *Black Joke* faring forward on the old waterways. Here and there it must negotiate a sudden drop or turn in the route, or a rush of current; here and there one of the crew will point out a stray thread of sunlight or a strange glyph on a cavern wall. But in the main this is a period of resting and healing and waiting on events. At about the third day, Mr. Buchan is called on deck to observe an elbow in the river and a fissure in the rock at the elbow's point. These are features he has anticipated through the use of his cinder-drawn map, and he regards them now with no little excitement. To the others, of course, the smaller channel looks far less promising than the waterway easing past it. But Mr. Buchan heads them toward the split in the rock, and it seems the dragoons have come a bit far to begin doubting him only now.

The ship tosses over rills of foam, through a little gap and into the calmer waters beyond, where the fissure widens to about a cable's length across. The temperature of the surrounding air takes an abrupt drop, to where the walls are streaked with runnels of icy water and one's breath may be seen drifting out into the dark. Mr. Henty, at the forward lookout, announces lights ahead, though he might have saved himself the effort. There is no dragoon on deck who has not already spotted this sure sign of habitation, nor begun checking, subconsciously, the action of his guns, and the hang of various belts and pouches.

The current draws them forward through a second choke-point and into a vast vaulted grotto, where a few torches, set along the walls in niches, begin picking out the remains of ancient mosaics: a half-image of Christ raising a crumbled hand in benediction, fragments of hunters galloping across an arid landscape, a nomad leading a disintegrating zebra on a leash. Ridges of hand-carved rock stand over the water in zigzagging ramps and level tiers, and human figures may be seen treading these footpaths, unmindful of the vessel with its deckful of staring men passing beneath them. A beggar hurries along with his face concealed in the hood of his cloak, dodging past an old woman who quirts her donkey, mechanically, in the opposite direction. Others walk with jugs perched on their heads, in the African manner. Stalls and lean-tos made of rotted planks and scavenged ship-parts begin dotting the footpaths, and these gather, farther along, into what might be called rival slums on either side of the channel. The dark alleys and sagging domiciles in this neighborhood do not invite very close scrutiny, but one may see, at a glance, over here an urchin girl worrying a wounded beetle with a stick; and there a boy smearing provocations on a wall with a fistful of wet ash. A toothless couple quarrel in some ugly hissing tongue, while a band of toughs in tight leggings threaten a peasant who clutches, by its neck, a limp form that might have been a seagull. Alcoves have been cut into the rock walls ahead, some of these with doors and some of the doors painted, and in these alcoves are the inevitable young ladies making merchandise of themselves. One especially drowsy-looking siren parts her skirts to exhibit a ghostly leg to the crew of the *Black Joke*, and I do not doubt, but for the presence of their commander, that a dragoon or two must brave the swim, at least to inquire after the young lady's rates. Yet Ogden has business ahead, and we may be thankful this time that he will not be kept from it.

The crew settle for blowing kisses to the bright-colored ladies of the shore, as the slums diminish into the gloom and a bustling port district comes into view. The watercourse here is filled with small craft, no two of them even remotely alike, and Ogden must take care at the wheel. The little boats jostle for position, their crews and captains hectoring one other in a babel of shouts, or else drawing up close to trade gossip. Nearer to the docks, sailors and stevedores load and unload the boats under the eyes of the port's officials, these stout men in braided waistcoats who stride the quayside and puff officiously at their clay pipes. There are fishing boats, too, compounding the commotion as they work their trade among the freighters. Mr. Buchan waves, without response, to a Malay crew who are hoisting a net of fish, eels and garbage out of the canal, while pariah dogs circle round the dripping heap, whimpering and thrusting their noses through the netting. An odor of rotting sea life rises palpably over the *Black Joke*, and Bertram must bury his nose in his sleeve. The dragoons go from affecting not to notice the smell to acknowledging it with jokes, and then to making a quiet show of braving it; but each man must cover his nose and even clamp his eyes, in turn, against the assault. Ultimately John Ogden is left to stand alone at the ship's wheel with his jaw set and eyes streaming as he guides the submersible through the port, under a series of sandstone arches and into a public square.

Here the smell has abated a bit, and the men are able to leap from the ship's bows and to secure it, nose-in, among other passenger vessels at a stone landing. The swarm of activity above and ahead of them suggests they have come to the city's central marketplace or bazaar, and Ogden orders what tradable goods they have left brought up in barrels, to be bartered for water and provisions. The men will be sent with their allotted goods and two hours' leave up the long ghat into the square.

Nor will Miss Harrow be dissuaded from joining them. After a spirited argument with Ogden she is given *Messrs.* Mulcairn and Buchan for escort, and ninety minutes in which to scour out quinine and fresh milk for Bertram. Only the boy himself is left behind, with Sergeant Pensette to mind him and to keep watch over the ship. Thus do our travelers enter the great, teeming city, whose name they will not bide long enough even to learn.

Gryzba, I should say, is the name of this underground settlement. Not that the name will mean very much to you, or that even a preponderance of its own citizens would identify the port by that name. But I enter it into our record, along with a few other details that may serve to illustrate this especially strange stop in our journey.

I should say that at first, from its fringes, there seems nothing terribly unusual about the marketplace at Gryzha, and least of all to men of H.R.H.'s Colonial Army. The merchants and peddlers here–like their counterparts all across the world–come struggling to market beneath rugs, bolts of cloth, trays of flatbreads, bundles of wine-skins hanging from wooden yokes and so forth. Even the 'livestock'–if that is what you call these rheumy-eyed skeletons being pulled and goaded and heaved in cages toward the square–these would not look entirely out of place in a Moroccan ghetto market or in the Chandni Chowk. It is only as we pass on a bit and enter the marketplace proper that we begin to revise this first impression of normalcy.

The shopkeepers, in particular, may be seen cajoling and harassing passersby in the accepted manner, but also singing and weeping and forcibly grabbing them; and there is at least one fellow doing all of these things at once, while stopping intermittently to perform a Cossack dance on a little scaffold. Women tear at a pile of linens spread across a table while the stall owner cowers on the ground beneath them, screaming and clawing at his customers' ankles. One grinning gentleman in a horsehair suit steps out of an alley with a tray of pastries only to have a waiting boy launch himself crown-first into the man's gut. The man doubles over, gasping for air, as the boy and his accomplices sprint into the crowd with his pastries and the tray elevated in triumph. Elsewhere a turbaned man inspects a bicycle wheel with disgust, dashes it to the ground and enacts some violent sort of pantomime *vis-à-vis* the wheel's owner. In the scuffle that develops, a band from the buyer's turban snags in the harness of a passing donkey, and the frightened ass dashes off into the crowd with the turban unspooling behind it. The long white cloth stretches through the plaza, where it entangles a group of peasant women and drags them, wailing, to the ground. Captain Shaw has been watching these proceedings with head cocked, and he asks Mr. Priddish what on earth the two men are about. Mr. Priddish points and states, rather simply: 'That one is buying a bicycle wheel.' And indeed, the bare-headed customer has calmly picked up the wheel, shrugged, and dropped a few coins into the merchant's palm. The two men shake hands and embrace, each kissing the other's cheeks as the dragoons lose track of them in the throng.

Shortly after this incident a bell in a clock-tower begins pealing, and all eyes turn to a temple at the edge of the marketplace. A column of bearded men issues from beneath the temple's Assyrian arch and descends its marble stairs, striding with purpose through a crowd of alms-beggars, who seem to know better than to impede them. At the base of the stairs, where towering statues of winged, human-headed bulls stand sentry, the column splits and the bearded men disperse to platforms at the corners and intersections of the marketplace, there to wait out the tolling of the hour with eyes piously closed. In the hush that follows the bells–for the whole marketplace has grown still by now–the men draw out scrolls of pinkish parchment and begin reading in booming voices, as buyers and vendors below scribble on their own scraps of paper, trying feverishly to keep pace with the announcements.

Now: the Gryzhan monetary system, on which we spare a few words, dates to antiquity, with the arrival of the first Wu Zhu coins and Athenian drachmas in the hands of the canals' nomadic traders. As the trading-post grew into a port of note, other currencies found their way into circulation: the Babylonian shekels and Roman denarii and Spanish reales of the city's founders mixed with the thalers, rubles, francs, lira, pesos, rupees, escudos and pounds of successive ages. An *ad hoc* monetary system evolved, in which all these various coins and notes were assigned a value based on their relative abundance or scarcity in the port, and on their perceived strength in the superterranean world. It is a system that is still in place today: whenever a currency is recognized and authenticated by the Ministry of Finance–our bearded gentlemen with the scrolls–it becomes legal tender in Gryzha, and all her merchants, shopkeepers, and customers are obliged to accept it. And because the prices of Gryzhan goods are tied to the values of these currencies, it is necessary for the ministers to keep scrupulous account of the various sums in its reserves, figures which they present to the public every hour, on the hour, over the course of the business day.

Their calculations are, to say the least, complicated, and fluctuations in exchange rates have on more than one occasion led to catastrophe, as when a barge of Sitric pennies crash-landed at the port, setting off the so-called Panic of 1847 and wiping out half the city's fortunes. But there is no law so widely or heartily endorsed in Gryzha, and none so expressive of the city's political ethos, than the one that honors all the world's currencies past and present, and assimilates them into the Gryzhan money supply. Every decade or so, the chief finance minister will recommend the adoption of a single currency; every decade or so, the chief finance minister of Gryzha is assassinated. So it has gone through the centuries, and the freaks of the Gryzhan monetary system are not just an accepted fact of life here but a particular point of pride.

Not that any of this is helping our dragoons in their own negotiations: quite the reverse. We find them possessed of great piles of dubious-looking coins and notes but no closer to the basic goods for which they came, and most have begun already to perceive the problem in this. Mr. Buchan, for instance, had left a district of weapons-dealers just moments ago in high spirits. A German trench knife had fetched several times its weight in Egyptian piastres; and a tiny, secretive fellow in a red fez and dark glasses had given him a hundred Danish kroner for a Siamese kris. He'd had similar 'luck,' too, in unloading the rest of his old weapons and even his spoilt provisions. He had paused on his way back through the market, then, to watch the bearded men in their bit of theater, little knowing these men were degrading wholesale the value of his coins. And now he finds himself at the stall of a general-goods dealer, mooning over the returns from this morning's efforts, which are scarcely enough to buy him a box of matches and a pint of kerosene. His queries about fresh milk and medicine are received with laughter. And his best hope, in the view of the not-unsympathetic shopkeeper, is to keep hold of his coins until the new rates are released.

Mr. Mulcairn, seated not far behind Buchan, has notched one of the dragoons' few successes on the day, having eschewed money and traded a bag of dud bullets straight-out for a jar of Silesian vodka. You will recall that he and Buchan have been detailed to keep Miss Harrow out of harm; yet as Mulcairn sits with his prize he is quite content to let Miss Harrow go poking about through the stalls as she will. It is the young Corporal–the very picture of misery, seated before his worthless old coins–who presents a picture much more to the Irishman's taste.

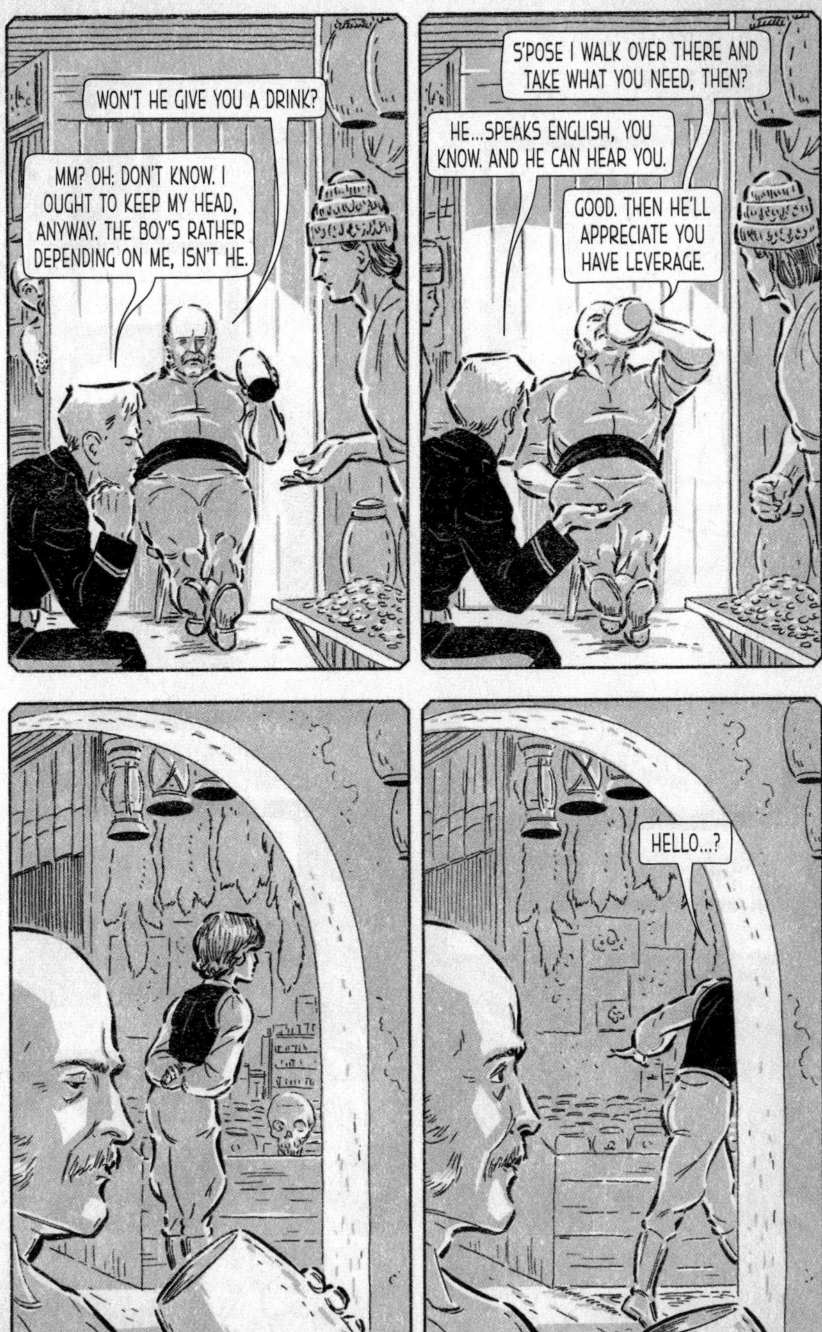
WON'T HE GIVE YOU A DRINK?
MM? OH: DON'T KNOW. I OUGHT TO KEEP MY HEAD, ANYWAY. THE BOY'S RATHER DEPENDING ON ME, ISN'T HE.
S'POSE I WALK OVER THERE AND TAKE WHAT YOU NEED, THEN?
HE...SPEAKS ENGLISH, YOU KNOW. AND HE CAN HEAR YOU.
GOOD. THEN HE'LL APPRECIATE YOU HAVE LEVERAGE.
HELLO...?

WAS WOLLEN SIE?
SORRY? I WAS JUST LOOKING AT THESE. RIGHT HERE.

AINGLICH? AH? GUT. COME.
BUT: DO YOU KNOW WHAT THESE ARE? DO YOU KNOW WHO DREW THESE SYMBOLS?
JA: WE KNOW, OF COURSE. COME.

BACK AT THE DOCKS, SERGEANT PENSETTE MUST WARD BEGGARS OFF FROM THE BLACK JOKE.
ALL WE GOT IS THIS RIGHT HERE FOR YA. SEE THIS?
...CHR–ST IT'S NOT TA GIVE YA, YA EEDJETS.

THOUGH: TELL YA WHAT–LOOK 'ERE, YOU CAN HAVE ONE-A THESE–
THERE Y'ARE. PUT ONE RIGHT IN YER BELLY, AND YEH CAN CARRY IT TO MARKET. AH?
F–CK OFF, NOW.
<<POP!>>

Ogden and Subadar Priddish, meanwhile, have run across a Russian trader—more accurately a *hoarder*—of arms called Ublyodok, and followed him to a hangar-like storehouse in a district of giant tin-sided buildings. Like Mr. Mulcairn, they have resisted the lure of coins in great piles and persuaded Ublyodok to take their old weapons in direct exchange for water, spirits, pine pitch and a cartload of what the Russian calls 'ship's biscuit' (ordered to sample one of these, Mr. Renton had pronounced it 'good enough' and begged for water). The three men sit now in a little ornamental garden outside the storehouse, consecrating their trade with a bottle of Dutch brandy. Ublyodok is delivering himself of a typically dark and baroque Ukrainian toast when he stops, and his lip curls over some rather startling bridgework. Ogden and Priddish follow his eyes to a delegation of city police, who are coming on from the direction of the plaza with a rabble of onlookers.

'*Nichoova*,' says the Russian, throwing back his drink. 'It is formality.'

As his boys clear away the brandy and glasses, Ublyodok walks out to the iron planters at the edge of his garden and receives the Commandant of police. The latter comes up grinning and nodding his head, and I should call this one of the haler and cheerier specimens we have found so far in the dismal port city. He is built nearly to Ogden's proportions, with a neat crop of blonde hair and a guileless, egg-shaped face. His uniform, alone among his fellows', appears *in toto*: jodhpurs and tunic of grey broadcloth with black facings and leg-braids, black top-boots and shoulderboards, and a black *kepi* in the French style, worked with silver bullion. The four other '*gardiens*' have perhaps a uniform between them, and it is an early ancestor of their Commandant's, much the worse for wear.

The detail draw up outside the iron planters while the Commandant and Ublyodok exchange greetings in the local lingua franca (which seems to be a compound of Slavic dialects, spoken in someone's idea of a French accent). Ublyodok indicates his guests with a sweep of his palm, and the young man clicks his heels and delivers a sort of welcoming address to Ogden.

'*Monsieur* the Commandant,' Ublyodok translates, 'gives welcome from…from many people you must avoid. He begs to know the reason of this visit.'

'Provisioning my ship,' Ogden says, answering from his chair.

'I tell him, yes,' says Ublyodok. 'If you will please to follow him, *Monsieur* the Commandant will add you to the port register. Is formality.'

Ogden takes a quick look aside at Mr. Priddish, and returns his eyes to the Commandant. 'Begging *Monsieur*'s pardon,' he says, 'I have engagements to keep and a poor experience of "formalities" in these port cities. I give *Monsieur* good day.'

He nods to the Commandant, who gives him an answering nod, apparently without comprehension. Ublyodok tries a few more words of explanation, and the Commandant answers these with his smile unaltered, his brows still raised in that same mode of pleasant expectation.

'Is thus,' says the trader, finally, to Ogden: 'He count seven of you in the plaza, three here. Is ten to show to the Magistrat, and the ship for inspection, too; and is maybe taking a long, long time waiting. Or…' He gives a distinctly Russian tip of his head, as to say, these things must be borne. 'Is formality,' he states once more, this time with an air of conclusion.

There follows a stretch of silence, wherein the Commandant stands frozen at a slight list, while Ogden and Priddish stare off at nothing, and Ublyodok wonders if his guests have not taken too much brandy on their empty stomachs. *We* know, gentle reader, that if Ogden should elect to crack this Commandant's neck, Mr. Priddish would see his associates dead just as quickly; and I suppose they are both making calculations to this effect. But Ogden has already shot and slashed and scorched his way through one port in the last twelve hours, and we will forgive him, I hope, if he'd make at least the *attempt* to leave this one peacefully.

In any case, his next action is to offer clipped instruction to Ublyodok, *vis-à-vis* the transport of his supplies back to the docks. He says he and his men will be assembled on the *Black Joke* and ready to cast off as soon as these goods are secured in its hold, and he bids Ublyodok to repeat this in translation to the Commandant, so the young man will have no misconceptions on the point of their staying. The Commandant listens with his same attentive half-smile, and conveys his understanding in a few quick bows. He clicks his heels then, and invites Ogden out of the courtyard with a pass of his upturned palm, rather like a conjurer waving a volunteer up to the stage.

Here and there, as the port *gardiens* lead Ogden in a wide circuit around the plaza, an onlooker will detach from the surrounding darkness and keep pace with the group. These tagalongs are mostly drunks and alms-beggars and urchin boys, who in a block or two will spend their little energy and get their laugh from the crowd (or their cut from the Commandant's stick) and make an end of the performance there. But before long an exception comes to the notice of Mr. Priddish: there is a little man gliding almost invisibly in and about the group—now at the Commandant's heel, now skirting the crowd of onlookers, now paused beside a lamp-post ahead. He wears a long claw-hammer coat, this man, keeping both hands behind him in its tail-pockets, and he walks with his back bent and head advanced so that, in motion, he looks something like a skater on the Dutch canals in the old engravings; except that he is swart-skinned and soot-grimed from top to bottom. There is no telling how long he has been with the group, though as Priddish now sees, Mr. Renton has been shadowing *him*, being a bit of the same species as this man. The boy, too, grows impatient of this man's having the drop on Ogden, and gives his commander a clipped, '*Oi!*'

Ogden looks over his shoulder and scans about, till Renton points at the dark figure beside them.

'Who is that?' Ogden asks, and the boy fires back a typically, needlessly affronted, 'How would *I* know?'

After a few more steps, though, the little man coughs into his fist and makes his own answer:

I AM *MONSIEUR* KHOREK, SIR. PORT *FONCTIONNAIRE*, AND YOUR SERVANT.
...ENGLISH, AREN'T YOU? HM, YES. WE MUST HAVE A MAGISTRAT WHO KNOWS THAT LANGUAGE...
WE HAVE MORE OF YOU ENGLISH EVERY YEAR, I THINK. DON'T WE, *MONSIEUR* COMMANDANT?

...HM-YES. THE OLD MOTHER COMPASSES THE WORLD WITH HER GREAT ARMS, AND STILL SHE MUST POKE AND PRY AND TWIST HER LONG FINGERS INTO THE EARTH, AS AFTER SOMETHING LOST. WHAT IS IT? SHE MIGHT NOT KNOW HERSELF. THOUGH I WARN, THERE ARE MEN DOWN HERE WHO LIKE TO PRICK THOSE FINGERS.

YOU ARE COME OUT OF THE MIDDLE-WEST DISTRICTS, I THINK? HM? MAJOR?
–THE GATES ON THE TIGRIS, OR THE GULF OF PERSIA: YOU HAVE RE-OPENED ONE. HM? AND HOW DID YOU LEAVE OUR LORD LECHMERE?

...MAJOR, YOU ARE GOING BEFORE A COUNCIL OF THREE PORT MAGISTRATS. THEY HAVE NO MORE TO DO TODAY THAN ASK YOU QUESTIONS, AND THEY HAVEN'T YOUR INTEREST IN BEING QUICK ABOUT IT. I ANTICIPATE THEIR QUESTIONS FOR YOU, SO I MAY HASTEN YOU THROUGH THE COUNCIL-ROOM.
HOW, THEN, DID YOU LEAVE M. LECHMERE?

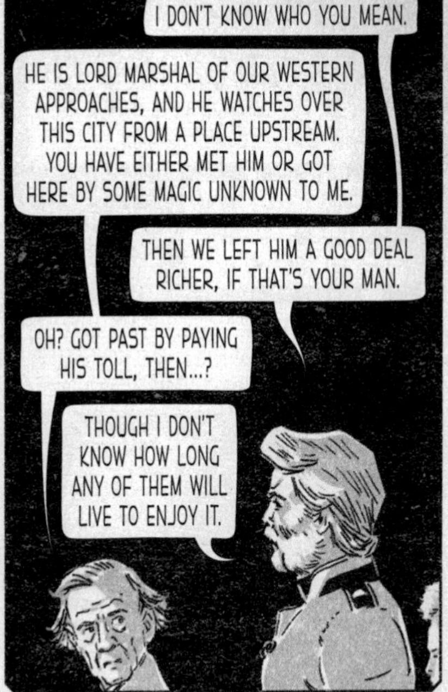
I DON'T KNOW WHO YOU MEAN.
HE IS LORD MARSHAL OF OUR WESTERN APPROACHES, AND HE WATCHES OVER THIS CITY FROM A PLACE UPSTREAM. YOU HAVE EITHER MET HIM OR GOT HERE BY SOME MAGIC UNKNOWN TO ME.
THEN WE LEFT HIM A GOOD DEAL RICHER, IF THAT'S YOUR MAN.
OH? GOT PAST BY PAYING HIS TOLL, THEN...?
THOUGH I DON'T KNOW HOW LONG ANY OF THEM WILL LIVE TO ENJOY IT.

AH. NO. VERY TRUE. THE OUTPOSTS ARE AREAS OF QUARANTINE, YOU KNOW, WITH AN AILMENT SPECIFIC TO EACH.
YOU HAVE HEARD OF THE SERPENT-MEN OF PATELA AND BHOGAVATI...HM? NO? THEY WERE KNOWN IN INDIA FOR A TIME. NOT ANY MORE, PERHAPS, OUTSIDE OF BAD DREAMS. BUT THE PORTS AND THE MEN ARE QUITE REAL, AND THERE ARE MAYBE A HUNDRED MORE POPULATIONS LIKE THESE.
WE ARE CONSTANTLY UNDER THREAT IN THIS CITY, YOU SEE–INCURSIONS FROM WITHOUT, DISEASE WITHIN–AND THE OUT-POSTS SERVE DOUBLY IN OUR DEFENSE.

OUR SICK ARE TRANSPORTED AS SOON AS THEY ARE FOUND OUT, AND THE OUTPOSTS ABSORB THEM. RETURN IS THEN IMPOSSIBLE.
BUT THE QUARANTINED ARE ALLOWED TO ENRICH THEMSELVES IN THE MANNER YOU'VE DISCOVERED, AND ON DYING THEY SETTLE A PORTION OF THEIR ESTATE ON LEGATEES AT HOME. IT IS A BARGAIN THEY ALL MUST MAKE IN THE OUTER SETTLEMENTS, THOUGH SOME GO INTO IT QUITE WILLINGLY.
THERE ARE EVEN INSTANCES OF DELIBERATE INFECTION AMONG THE POOR, IN THE CITIES–CHILDREN EXPOSED TO DISEASE, THAT IS, IN ORDER TO ENRICH THE PARENTS.

NASTY EXPEDIENTS ALL ROUND, HM? AND THIS WILL LOOK NO BETTER THAN EXTORTION AND BRIGANDAGE, IN YOUR VIEW. BUT YOU ARE ALIVE, AFTER ALL, AND YOU MAY COME THROUGH THIS YET.
WHERE DO YOU GO FROM HERE, MAJOR—HM? CHINA? OR IS IT THE SOUTH?
SOMEWHERE BETWEEN. MY BROTHER IS ILL, AND HIS CURE IS IN THE MOUNTAINS OF NEPAL.

HE'S ILL, THEN?
HE DOESN'T TRAVEL WITH US. HE PRECEDES US BY AEROPLANE.
AH. GOOD. VERY GOOD. MUSTN'T MAKE HIM WAIT, THEN. AND YOUR DEALINGS WITH THE RUSSIAN HAVE BEEN SATISFACTORY? HE HAS PROVISIONED YOUR SHIP FOR THE WAY AHEAD? ALL IS MADE READY...?
I'LL TELL YOU THAT WHEN I'M BACK ABOARD MYSELF.

AH. YES-YES, SO YOU WILL. BUT I...WELL I DON'T SUPPOSE HE LET YOU INTO THAT STOREHOUSE OF HIS, DID HE? M. UBLYODOK?
NO.
NO. PERHAPS HE WAS WORKING HIS WAY UP TO IT. HE WAS NOT BORN AMONG US, YOU KNOW. HE ESCAPED A CHARGE OF ANARCHY IN THE UKRAINE BY FLEEING INTO THESE CANALS, AND HE WAS BROUGHT TO GRYZHA BY THE MANY UNCLES AND COUSINS WHO HAD BEEN FORCED UNDER-GROUND IN THEIR OWN TIME.

IT IS SAID WE CAN THANK THE HOUSE OF ROMANOV FOR HALF OUR POPULA-TION, AND I THINK IT IS TRUE. BUT I UN-DERSTAND UBLYODOK AND HIS FRIENDS ARE ARRANGING THEIR OWN THANKS. HE MENTIONED NONE OF THIS TO YOU...?
NO.
...NO. WELL. HE IS GATHERING WEAPONS AND MEN FOR A RAID UP THROUGH ODESSA, WITH SOME IDEA OF KILLING THE TSAR.

HE'S–WHAT?
I SAY, HE'S PLOTTING AGAINST THE RUSSIAN TSAR. I WASN'T AWARE HE TALKED OF ANYTHING ELSE.
BUT–HOW LONG'S 'E BEEN WAITING TO HAVE AT THIS?
OH, HE'S BEEN... TWELVE OR THIRTEEN YEARS IN HIS PREPARATIONS.

HA! AND DON'T ANY OF YOU GET THE PAPERS?
THAT WILL DO, MR. RENTON.
–WHY DO YOU ASK THAT?
ONLY BECAUSE YOU CAN TELL THAT BOOBY HE'S ABOUT A YEAR LATE. THERE'S NO MORE TSARS IN RUSSIA, AS EVEN I KNOW.

YOU DON'T SAY...
THEY DRAGGED 'EM INTO A BASEMENT AND SHOT 'EM; THE GIRLS, TOO. I'LL GO TELL HIM–
YOU WILL NOT.
YOU'RE QUITE SURE ABOUT ALL THIS?

AM I SURE? THE LITTLE GIRLS PACKED THEIR DRESSES SO FULL OF JEWELS THE BULLETS WERE BOUNCING OFF. THEY HAD TO BAYONET 'EM IN THE END–
MR. RENTON.
G–D. ALL RIGHT. BUT NO ONE TELLS HIM WITHOUT ME THERE.
YOU EITHER.
NO. NO, OF COURSE I WON'T. NO, THAT...WOULDN'T DO.

In Mr. Buchan's corner of the plaza, meanwhile, we see the rest of the dragoons gathered, and none too happily. Like Mr. Buchan they have dealt away their trade goods and come shuffling in with long faces and heaps of worthless coins. The latter have been pushed into a communal pot, with the dragoons milling behind it, sharing stories of the day's frustrations and putting increasingly pointed questions to Mr. Buchan's merchant. They appear to be closing ranks in order to bargain as a body, and there is every indication of this business's growing ugly. The questions rise quickly to shouts, and weapons are fingered as eyes narrow and grins widen. Nor are the locals insensitive to this darkening of the atmosphere. Merchants from neighboring stalls gather and mutter in their many languages, and a boy is dispatched to bring gendarmes from the square. Haggling in the Gryzhan manner is one thing, you see, but these dragoons are well-armed and, to judge from their looks, not above plain robbery or worse.

«THWEET!» SIE–FINDEN HORST. SCHNELL.

WHY DON'T YOU LEAVE THAT OPEN? MA'AM...?

AH. HORST IS COMING. MY SON. HE WILL HELP YOU. COME SEE HIM.

I...WAS ONLY ASKING ABOUT A SYMBOL SOMEONE'S LEFT ON YOUR DOOR...
ENGLISCH. SIE IST ALLEIN. TUN SIE DIES LEISE.
JA.

...BUT: YOU DON'T KNOW ANYTHING ABOUT IT, DO YOU?
GO. I FOLLOW YOU DOWN.
EHH...A SYMBOL? NO-NO. IT IS THERE A LONG TIME. THE MARKTSTÄNDE, THE BOOTHS, THEY ARE ALWAYS TRADING HANDS.

THEN, REALLY, I OUGHT TO GO—
NEIN, MISS. THERE IS ANOTHER BOOTH TODAY. ANOTHER MARKET I WILL SHOW YOU. MEN YOU WILL MEET, JA?

I SEE...AND I GO VEDDER I LIKES IT OR NUTT, IST DAT ZO?
JA. I AM GLAD IS VERY FUNNY.
I SUPPOSE I'M BEING TAKEN HOSTAGE? MY GOODNESS. AND BY YOU TWO DUMMKOPFS? OH, IT'S TOO MUCH!
SAGEN SIE NICHT, 'DUMMKOPF.'

IT IS TRUE. YOU SHOULD NOT SPEAK LIKE THIS.
WELL I'M SORRY, BUT I CAN'T GO. I'M WITH BRITISCHE SOLDATEN, YOU UNDERSTAND. MANY OF THEM, AND VERY NASTY. THEY WOULD GLADLY KILL YOU, JUST FOR THAT ACCENT.

HELFEN SIE IHR DIE LEITER HINUNTER.
–I SHOULD SAY IT'S NEARLY WORTH IT, JUST TO SEE WHAT THEY'D GIVE FOR ME. BUT, YOU KNOW, AS SOON AS I RAISE MY VOICE TO THE MEN OUTSIDE–
JA, IT IS A GOOD POINT.
SIE KÖNNEN ES TUN.
–SORRY?

YOU ARE NOT IN OUR USUAL LINE, YOU SEE. BUT WE MAKE ALLOWANCES, HYEUGH-HYEUGH.
«THWOK!»

MOMENTS LATER, MISS HARROW LIES INERT ON A MARBLE SLIP, BELOW.
RUHIG. SIE, UND DANN ICH.

SIR...?
HALLO?
SORRY: I'M LOOKING FOR MISS HARROW. IS SHE THERE?
EHH: SHE IS THE YOUNG LADY? JA, COME.

BUT–WHO ARE YOU? I CAN'T SEE MISS HARROW.
IT IS ONLY MYSELF, AND MY SON. COME. WE WILL SHOW YOU YOUR FRIEND.

BRINGT IHN.

NO, I CAN'T SEE ANYTHING DOWN THERE. I HAD BETTER GO.
ACH–NO! COME.
HORST: SHOW HIM.

IT IS ONLY A LADDER, YOU SEE. QUITE SAFE. COME.
ALL RIGHT. JUST A MOMENT, THOUGH.

AHH: THE SWALLOWS FLY TO THE CAT, TODAY, *HYEUGH-HYEUGH!*
BERTRAM? NO...

GYAAAHH!

«*THWAPP!*»

From a distance, the tower at the far western point of Gryzha calls to mind a many-humped tree, like some hulking, Gothic cousin of the willow. On nearing it, though, Ogden can see that each of the many humps is a separate enclosure, with each component piece reflecting some new type of design or construction and many reproducing great works of the superterranean world in miniature. Here, for instance, are the onion domes of St. Basil's, striped with sheets of hammered bronze and tin; there is the rotunda at Monticello, cut out of bleached wood; here a railway station of Empire design separates a Georgian English country estate from a Bavarian château with a clock-tower. One full level of the building re-creates the Temple of Karnak, complete with priestly colossi and an avenue of sphinxes; nearby, a multistoried structure of stainless steel, built to resemble a New York skyscraper, clings like a theater sign to the corner of the building. A floating replica of the Taj Mahal hangs from a roof cornice, accessible only by ladder.

The tower might not appeal, aesthetically, to men of simpler tastes, like our Major Ogden; but really the thing is a marvel, both in the design of the individual enclosures and in the harmony of the aggregate. The effect is only spoiled in one place, over the tower's entrance (the portico of St. Paul's Basilica, wrought exquisitely in Sienna marble), where someone has hung a crude, hand-lettered sign marking this the *Fonction Publique*. But there the sign is, and it calls us back to the business at hand.

The Commandant of police whisks Ogden and the others inside without a word for the doormen, and leads them through a press of bodies to an unmanned stone desk and directory. Whatever the tower's exterior, its insides might be those of any Central European tenement, and there are people simply *everywhere*, filling all the tiled concourses and landings. Khorek vanishes into the press of bodies—gone to get his English-speaking Magistrat, we presume—and there is a bit of delay before he is showing himself again at the head of a stair, beckoning to his Commandant.

Four flights up, in a slate-paneled council room, three bewigged *fonctionnaires* sit before a small gallery of witnesses. Yet M. Khorek has no sooner poked his head into this chamber than he is hissing some word or two at the senior councillor, and the room is emptied. There is comedy, undeniably, in the haste of these three *fonctionnaires*, who sit one moment immotile and tremendously dignified, and in the next must scoop up their dockets and gavels and nameplates and scurry past the little Inspecteur with these items clutched to their chests and robes trailing behind. Renton is not above a laugh at their expense, either, but Ogden and Mr. Priddish take advantage of the moment's confusion to peer into the room.

'There,' says the Sikh, pointing: a painting hangs at the back of the room—a map, it seems, of the underground waterways and greater port cities. The rendering is at once complex to the point of abstraction—a great, many-layered, reticulated mass—but it is also, notably, incomplete. Many of the twisting routes trail off into nothing, and there are patches all over where the bare canvas shows through, as though not even the artists and cartographers of this city were aware of their world's extent, and the picture were still evolving as word came in from the outposts.

I should not doubt this map were the reason M. Khorek has found the room unsuitable, and he nearly squeals with impatience when Ogden draws back from the Commandant to take a second look at it. Khorek darts between them to secure the doors himself, and orders the group ahead with some of the uglier-sounding words in the Gryzhan lexicon.

After a bit more shuffling and shouting and doubling back, Ogden and Mr. Priddish are let into a second, smaller room (a magnificent representation of the *Gare du Nord*, if they could but see it from the outside). There is barely space in here for the council's desk and standing room for the others, but there are excellent window views of the upstream caverns to the west and the plaza and waterfront below and to the east. Ogden, with a few of the *gardiens*, notes the growing disturbance below them in the marketplace. 'I need to know what that is,' he says quietly, aside, to Mr. Renton, and the boy slips away without further instruction.

The *gardiens*, meanwhile, have dragged out a pair of jalousie screens and portioned off a corner of the room with them. In this corner a boy stands working a windlass, whose cable runs down through an aperture in the floor into the open air. Every so often, as we see, the boy raises a metal tray from below, digs a folded slip of paper from the tray and hands it to a clerk seated beside him. The clerk reads these notes and scribbles in a memorandum book, occasionally dashing off replies to be lowered back on the tray. This activity–with the concomitant scratching of the clerk's pen, the grinding of the chain and the creaking of the winch and so forth–this runs on through the scene I am about to describe, though none but Ogden and Priddish pay it any mind.

At the moment, all eyes have turned to the senior Magistrat, who raps on the desk with his gavel till he has got quiet from everyone but the boy and his windlass. He pens some heading, then, across a new sheet in his ledger and addresses Major Ogden in the following terms:

WOULD YOU CARE TO GUESS WHICH GROUP IS YOURS?
...*MONSIEUR?*
I BELIEVE THE QUESTION WAS PUT RHETORICALLY.
SO IT WAS, YES.

I WON'T KEEP YOU WITH A FULL TAXONOMY OF BLUNDERERS, *MONSIEUR*—I HAVE KNOWN SEVERAL DOZEN SPECIES IN MY TIME WITH THIS COUNCIL—BUT I SEE BROADLY TWO TYPES:

THERE ARE THOSE WHO COME KNOWINGLY TO DO US HARM, AND THOSE WHO WILL DO IT UNWITTINGLY.
YOU MAY SAY—AND I HAVE HEARD—THAT SOME TRAVELERS FIND THEIR WAY TO US WITH INTENT TO HELP OR TO BETTER THIS PLACE. I SAY ONLY GIVE THESE MEN TIME, AND THEY WILL EARN MY SECOND DISTINCTION.

WE ARE A CLOSED SYSTEM, *MONSIEUR*, A FRAGILE SYSTEM, AND THERE ARE INNUMERABLE WAYS FOR YOU TO DO US HARM, WHETHER YOU WOULD OR NO.
AH-YES. *MERCI.*

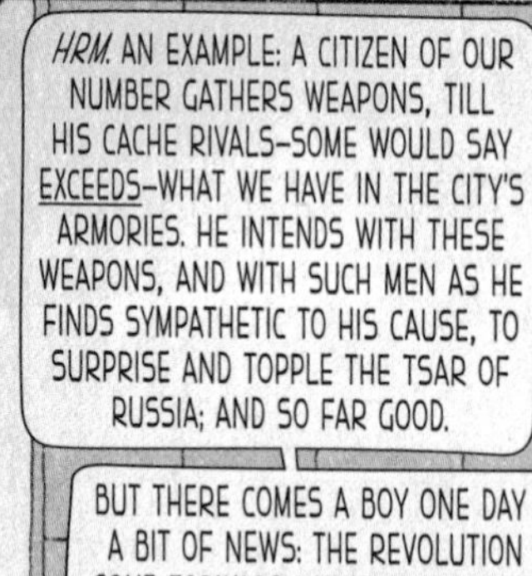
HRM. AN EXAMPLE: A CITIZEN OF OUR NUMBER GATHERS WEAPONS, TILL HIS CACHE RIVALS–SOME WOULD SAY EXCEEDS–WHAT WE HAVE IN THE CITY'S ARMORIES. HE INTENDS WITH THESE WEAPONS, AND WITH SUCH MEN AS HE FINDS SYMPATHETIC TO HIS CAUSE, TO SURPRISE AND TOPPLE THE TSAR OF RUSSIA; AND SO FAR GOOD.
BUT THERE COMES A BOY ONE DAY WITH A BIT OF NEWS: THE REVOLUTION HAS GONE FORWARD WITHOUT HIM. THE TSAR IS DEAD AND THE MONARCHY ENDED. MM?

ÇA VA. WHAT HAVE WE NOW? A MAN GIVEN TO DRINK AND TO FLIGHTS OF TEMPER–A KNOWN ANARCHIST–SITS ON A MOUNTAINOUS STORE OF GUNS AND POWDER AT THE CITY'S CENTER, WITH NO MORE CAUSE TO DIVERT HIM.
PERHAPS, YOU KNOW, HE SETTLES INTO A QUIET TRADE, OR DUMPS HIS GUNS INTO THE RIVER...
BUT I CAN ENVISION OUTCOMES FAR WORSE. I CAN SEE THIS PORT BURNING AND A CITIZENRY IN ARMS AND THE HEADS OF THIS COUNCIL RAISED ON STICKS.

AND WHY? BECAUSE A BOY DESIRED TO SEE THE EXPRESSION ON M. UBLYODOK'S FACE WHEN HE LEARNED HE WAS A YEAR LATE FOR HIS OWN REVOLUTION.
HOW DOES THAT ALL STRIKE YOU, MR. OGDEN?
WHEN YOU HAVE A QUESTION FOR ME, I'LL ANSWER IT.
CAREFULLY, *MONSIEUR.*

NO–AGAIN HE IS RIGHT. I AM MAKING A POINT, AND IT IS THIS: OF ALL THE CANCERS BROUGHT DOWN TO OUR CIVILIZATION FROM ABOVE, THERE IS NONE SO PERNICIOUS AS THE CANCER OF INFORMATION.
AND OUR INSPECTEUR DOES WELL TO BRING YOU HERE BEFORE YOU LET ANY MORE OF IT ESCAPE YOU. YOU MAYN'T LEAVE THIS COUNCIL A HIGH INITIATE, *MONSIEUR,* BUT WE CAN EDUCATE YOU TO A FEW THINGS.

SO LONG AS YOU DO IT QUICKLY.
...BEG YOUR PARDON?
OUR SHIP LIES STOCKED AND WE ARE LATE FOR APPOINTMENTS IN THE EAST. IT SOUNDS AS THOUGH OUR QUICK DEPARTURE WOULD SERVE YOUR INTERESTS AND MINE EQUALLY.

GO ON. *C'EST BIEN. ALLEZ.*
AH–YES. WE OUGHT TO PASS YOU ALONG, TO BE ANOTHER PORT'S PROBLEM–*ÇA VA?* SOME WOULD, I DO NOT DOUBT. I DO NOT DOUBT IT.
BUT LET US SEE: ACCORDING TO M. THE INSPECTEUR'S REPORT YOU HAVE ENTERED THROUGH THE MIDDLE-WEST, COME BY WAY OF LORD LECHMERE'S STATION, AND WERE ALLOWED PASSAGE THERE BY LEVY. I SEE.

YOU ARE HERE TO PROVISION YOUR SHIP, AND IN THE CANALS GENERALLY TO...EXPEDITE AN OVERLAND TRIP. YOU WILL WARRANT TO THE COUNCIL THAT THIS IS YOUR TESTIMONY, AND THAT THESE FACTS ARE CORRECT.
I WILL.
GOOD. GOOD. THEN LET ME TELL YOU IN THE FIRST PLACE, MR. OGDEN, THAT OUR CIVILIZATION DOES NOT EXIST AS A CONVENIENCE, OR AS A SYSTEM OF TRANSIT, FOR YOURS. I CANNOT ALLOW THAT IT WOULD BECOME SO. DO YOU UNDERSTAND?

I DO. AND I WOULD CALL THIS AN ISOLATED CASE OF USE, BORNE OUT OF EXTREME URGENCY. WE HAVE BEEN CAREFUL TO SEAL THE ENTRANCE BEHIND US AT AL-SHAR, AND WILL TAKE THE SAME PRECAUTIONS ON LEAVING.
AH. GOOD.
–S'IL VOUS PLAÎT?
BEGGING THE COUNCIL'S PARDON...?

A QUESTION, M. KHOREK?
ONLY A CONCERN, THAT *MONSIEUR* HAS NOT BEEN FULLY FORTHCOMING. THE COUNCIL WILL PLEASE ASK HIM ABOUT HIS AFFILIATIONS WITH THE BRITISH CEYLON COMPANY, AND WITH THE EXPLORERS GUILD.
WELL. WHAT OF THAT, M. OGDEN?
THE CEYLON COMPANY HAS LONG EYED THESE WATERWAYS AS ROUTES OF TRADE, YOU SEE, AND AS LINES OF SUPPLY FOR THEIR ARMIES. AND NO DOUBT THEY WOULD SOONER ANNEX US TO THE ENGLISH COMMONWEALTH THAN PAY FOR USE OF THESE CANALS. WE TAKE THAT TO BE THE COMPANY'S *MODUS OPERANDI.*
AS TO THE EXPLORERS GUILD, THEY WILL NOT STAND TO HAVE ANY BLANK AREAS ON THEIR MAPS OF THE WORLD, AND WE SEEM TO OCCUPY RATHER A LARGE ONE.
THEY IMAGINE THE SECRETS OF AGARTHA, ATLANTIS, LEMURIA, SHAMBHALA–EVEN OF THE CHRISTIAN HELL–TO BE KEPT SOMEWHERE WITH US, AND I AM TOLD THEY WOULD OPEN OUR HALLS TO THE EYES OF THE WORLD ABOVE, WITHOUT REGARD TO CONSEQUENCE. HM?
YOU CAN SEE, PERHAPS, THAT THE LEAST INCURSION BY EITHER BODY INTO OUR WATERWAYS WOULD BE RUINOUS TO US. AND WE MUST THEREFORE KNOW WHAT YOUR AFFILIATIONS ARE WITH THESE BODIES.
I AM A DESERTER OF THE CEYLON COMPANY ARMY AND WOULD CONSIDER THAT AFFILIATION ENDED. I HAVE NO AFFILIATION WHATEVER WITH THE EXPLORERS GUILD.

I SEE. I SEE.
HM. YES. AND THE SCUTCHEON ON YOUR BOY'S COAT: THAT IS NOT THE ARMS OF THE EXPLORERS GUILD? WHERE IS HE?

THE COAT IS STOLEN, AS I IMAGINE THE BUTTON TO BE. THE BOY IS NO MORE A PART OF ANY GUILD THAN I AM.
SAHIB–?

PERHAPS IT IS AS YOU SAY, YES. BUT– YOU KNOW–THIS GUILD, OR YOUR CEYLON COMPANY, IF EITHER WERE TO LEARN YOU'D COME THROUGH OUR WATERWAYS, THEY WOULD BE MOST ANXIOUS TO KNOW HOW YOU HAD FOUND THEM, AND WHAT YOU HAD SEEN. THERE IS THAT DANGER, AS WELL.
I HAVE NO WISH TO BE FOUND BY EITHER BODY, MUCH LESS TO HELP THEM.

NOT EVEN IN EXCHANGE FOR LENIENCY– HM?–FROM THIS ARMY YOU'VE LEFT?
YOU LITTLE KNOW THE CEYLON COMPANY, IF YOU IMAGINE THEY BAR-GAIN WITH DESERTERS.
INSPECTEUR–? YOUR ATTENTION TO THIS, PLEASE?

SIT. I BEG THE COUNCIL, SIT.
ON THE MATTER OF LORD LECHMERE AND HIS TOLL, *MONSIEUR* OGDEN–
IN A MOMENT, INSPECTEUR. COME: SEE WHAT THIS IS. M. COMMANDANT?
YOU ARE NOT ALLOWING ME TO HELP YOU, *MONSIEUR*. INSTEAD YOU MUST WITHHOLD, AND SHADE THE TRUTH, AND FLOUT THIS COUNCIL'S AUTHORITY. THIS IS VERY BAD. BUT...
...HERE WE MAY HAVE YOU ON A POINT OF FACT.
DO YOU KNOW THERE ARE MEN RUMORED IN FROM LECHMERE'S STATION–HM? AND THEIR ARRIVAL COINCIDES MORE OR LESS WITH YOURS.
WHEN THEY ARE FOUND AND QUESTIONED, WHO KNOWS BUT THEY WILL HAVE A DIFFERENT VIEW OF HOW YOU LEFT OUR FRIENDS, HM?
PERHAPS THEY WILL SAY, AS I KNOW FOR FACT, THAT LECHMERE DOES NOT LEVY TOLLS ON STRANGE VESSELS, AND DOES NOT WILLINGLY LET THEM PASS IN ANY CASE.

AND I SAY HE DID.
OH—YES, OF COURSE—YOU HAVE SWORN TO IT. BUT WE SHALL HAVE TO SEE...

IT IS YOUR MEN AT THE CENTER OF THE DISTURBANCE, *N'EST-CE PAS?*

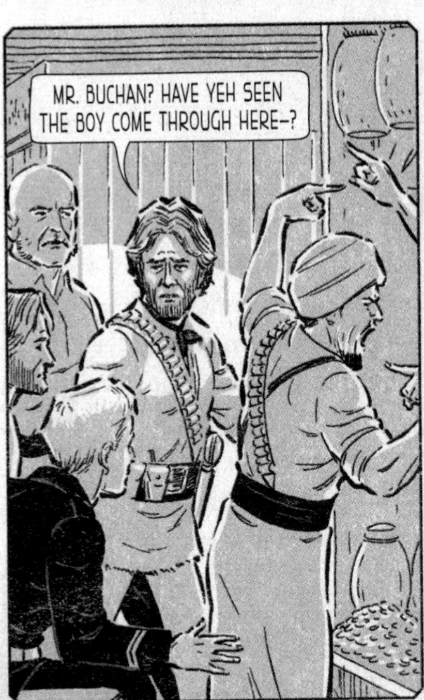
MR. BUCHAN? HAVE YEH SEEN THE BOY COME THROUGH HERE—?

AH—THERE. BERTRAM, WHAT IS THIS, LAD?
OH, HE WAS ONLY WANDERING AGAIN, IN SOME KIND OF...FUGUE, I SUPPOSE. YOU MUST REALLY KEEP A BETTER WATCH OVER HIM, SERGEANT.
WULL—YES, BUT I—
LUCKY FOR US, HE CAME STRAIGHT TO ME.

Buchan would keep Miss Harrow and the boy with more questions, but the shouting and jostling in this corner of the plaza are building into frenzy, and it is well they are leaving it. Buchan's shopkeeper is standing silent now in the center of the fray with his arms folded over his chest, refusing absolutely to make any deals until the new exchange rates are cried. This in defiance of Mr. Pandit, who is on his feet yelling at the man and menacing him with a fistful of piastres. The cavalrymen shove their coins across the counter as merchants leap into the booth and shove them back. Captain Shaw appeals uselessly for an offer of credit. The gendarmes wheel their knob-kneed mounts around and ready their whips, while a grinning Mr. Mulcairn tosses his empty jar aside and joins his fellows at last.

It seems the exchange is going in a too-familiar direction, and I've no doubt we'd be hearing the crack of guns next except that, with the shouting at its highest pitch, Mr. Renton comes ambling in from the fringes of the crowd. He roots through his pockets, draws out the bank-note given to him in the Singer Tower last spring, and slaps it on the counter in front of Buchan. The shopkeeper picks up the slip of paper and eyes it curiously.

'That's the American dollar,' the boy tells him, impressively. 'Quite valuable.'

'Dollar,' the shopkeeper echoes, rolling the strange word over in his mouth and drawing the bill right to the bridge of his nose for inspection. '*Dol*-lar…' His voice trails off, and he walks out of his shop with a few merchants following him. The dragoons pause and let go the wrists and lapels they have grabbed. They watch as the shopkeeper wanders into the plaza and stops one of the bearded ministers. 'Dol-lar,' he whispers, showing his bill to the minister. 'American.' His tone is at once puzzled and reverential.

The minister snatches the bill out of the man's hand. 'A dol-lar?' he bellows, incredulous.

The shopkeeper nods fearfully. More merchants are drifting in from their own stalls to view the strange note. 'A dollar…*dol*-lar,' they murmur, with mounting agitation.

Captain Shaw is wondering aloud what these men are doing, when one of the merchants tears away from the group and goes streaking across the plaza. 'A *dol*-lar!' he screams, crashing into passersby. And the market, suddenly, breaks out in a havoc beyond anything we have seen here–which is saying much: customers retreat into the alleys and side streets, a row of textile stalls collapses, a fire erupts outside the temple. Shouts of 'Dol-lar! Dol-lar!' echo through the square. A solemn man strips off his dark robes and climbs naked to the top of a street-lamp, where he begins shrieking at the top of his lungs.

The shrieking man and the riot generally (I think it time we apply the term) are gathering eyes all across the port, and not least of all in the tower where we've left Major Ogden. The hearing has been suspended, in fact, while the Magistrats, the police and the gallery of witnesses all jostle for position at the windows. And it is important to note sight-lines

in the room: most, as we say, are directed east into the plaza, with only Ogden and Priddish standing as before, facing west. *Monsieur* the Inspecteur circles them, needling Ogden on one point and another with his eyes on Ogden's face. He seems to be coming slowly round to some final argument that will keep these two in the port for good, and he takes no small pleasure in goading his captives as the snare tightens around them. Mr. Priddish lowers his eyes to the canals and more or less maintains his air of calm, but inwardly he must see the prospects of a nonviolent exit from this city dimming. It is at this juncture that a body, burned and mangled and already gas-bloated, comes drifting into port on the dark water below.

A hand, now, seems to run across the harp-strings in Mr. Priddish's chest, and he grips a little concealed *kirpan* in his belt. There is no question the body has floated down from Lechmere's encampment. No question, either, that if it should be spotted by anyone else in the room, this would seal the dragoons' fate. Yet there is this distraction in the plaza, and all backs are turned, for now, to the river. The boy goes on cranking his windlass as the Inspecteur demands a list, from Ogden, of the items he's paid in toll Lord Lechmere. Even below, outside, the few *gardiens* and civilians dawdling on the promenade have turned away to watch the disturbance. As if by miracle, too, the swirling bundle of rags and waterlogged flesh rolls to its *left* and disappears into the pilings beneath the city, when it could as easily have gone right and tumbled all along the crowded waterfront.

It is not until the body is gone that Mr. Priddish spares a look at his commander, and he judges from the tensing of the latter's jaw that Ogden has seen the body as well. The quick-eyed Inspecteur notes Ogden's reaction, too, and darts a look back over his own shoulder, but there is no more to be seen on the black water. The Magistrats are still calling him to the window (and there is this repeated mention of their heads on sticks, a thing for which there must be precedent in Gryzha); yet they call him in vain. M. Khorek is focussed entirely on Ogden, and finally, for the first time since the two met, Ogden returns the little man's stare. The Sikh, too, has taken a step toward them both. The Inspecteur looks quickly, instinctively, behind him, and whirls back with a wildness in his hard little eyes: three more bodies have come bobbing down the canal after the first. There is no more chance that these will go unseen, and nothing remains for the dragoons to do but act.

Khorek does not quite get out a cry to his Commandant before Priddish has him, and has opened his throat with the little dagger. In the next moment the dragoons have whisked him on his heels into the hall. They are gone so swiftly and quietly that only the boy at the windlass sees them leave, and he must point and hop madly for half a minute before he is recognized by the men at the windows. In this time, Ogden and Priddish have already got the Inspecteur down to a mezzanine walkway, where they pitch him over a rail into the crowded lobby and flee to an exit in the opposite direction.

Truly, the dragoons could not have arranged a better cover for their retreat than this uproar in the square. Their path from the tower to the waterfront is a black swirl of humanity—something, Ogden reflects, like their first plunge into these awful canals—and it is all he and Mr. Priddish can do to hop between currents and angle through the heart of the mêlée toward the remaining dragoons. If there is any pursuit from behind, it, too, is swallowed up in the chaos, and the only signs of police in the market are the mounted gendarmes, who will not notice just now if their city is short an Inspecteur or two.

The turmoil is so great that neither Ogden nor even Mr. Priddish notice Renton darting back through the crowd toward the tower. The boy, to be sure, marks his commander and the Sikh, but declines to call out as they pass him. He seems bent on some other business at the *Fonction Publique*, and this does not seem the place for explanations.

Meanwhile, the rest of the dragoons–and quite naturally–have used the riot as their cue to begin looting in earnest. At Captain Shaw's cry of '*Go!*' they dive over various counters and grab whatever they can lay hands on–lanterns, lemons, cured meats, canisters of fuel, helmets and pick-axes, not forgetting Bertram's milk and medicine–and they stop only when they hear Ogden whistling to them. Our impression is that, absent this signal, they would go on fighting and looting and would end up wandering lost through the port like children abandoned at a fair. But Ogden *has* come, as he invariably does, through what dangers they needn't know, and the men run after him now, shouting and hauling their stolen provisions and booting the crazed Gryzhans aside.

At the docks, all stores are thrown onto the *Black Joke* and all neighboring watercraft are boarded, cleared with a spray of gun-fire (or just a menacing look) and cut free. Ogden and Priddish gather dock-lines from the other boats and wind them round bollards on the *Joke*, and tug and steer the whole bumping mass along as best they can toward the harbor's narrow outlet. Here, on Ogden's orders, the men shoot and bore holes through all vessels but their own, sinking them in a great heap behind the *Joke*. In a few minutes more they have hopped back over the improvised blockade to their own boat, and Sergeant Pensette is pushing them out into the current with his boot-heel.

The retreat, as it happens, is witnessed by only a few fist-waving merchants on the ghat and a few ousted fishermen struggling in the black water. The port is still consumed in riot, and the gendarmes can still be seen bucking through the marketplace, firing pistols into the air and lashing the crowds with their whips. It will strike a few of the men as anticlimax that they are not trading fire with the port and watching ships founder on the blockade and so forth, and it does seem a shame to leave a full-blown riot in progress; but no matter. The dragoons have taken in their fill of the Gryzhan life and economy today, and are quite content to leave the whole benighted mess astern.

There is just one last matter of concern for Ogden, who has noted Mr. Renton's absence and is calling the boy's name over the harbor. But he is not very long awaiting an answer. A shrill '*What?*' sounds from behind him, and there is Mr. Renton turned out on deck, apparently unharmed. He has been rooting through the ship's provisions and may feel he is in line for reprimand, but Ogden only mutters something about counting off the company and ruffles the boy's hair. Renton ducks his hand and glares at him, then slips away and returns dragging a crumpled roll of canvas. He pushes the bundle on Ogden and stands shifting for a moment, scratching at the back of his head.

'Some nervy b–stard's blood on it,' he says, 'and that bit's burnt. But it oughtta serve, wot?'

Ogden, with Priddish craning over for a look, unfolds the painted map of the canals he had seen at the *Fonction Publique*. Mr. Renton had apparently got back into the tower and found the council-room locked and guarded; he had slipped out a transom window in the hall, edged along a bit of molding on the tower's face and into the empty room, cut the painting from its frame and fled with his prize to the *Black Joke*. It is not the first nor maybe the greatest act of cleverness Ogden has seen out of his men, but he is nonetheless a moment in summoning words.

'*Hrm*. Well,' he says, spreading the map carefully over a hatch cover, 'good work.'

The commendation is lost on Mr. Renton, who is already up on the stern rail, staring at the dying lights of the port and gnawing on a pilfered apple. But the map will indeed serve, as Ogden has indicated, and he will be quite careful with it while it is in his possession.

. . .

{I am told, by the way, that you may see this map today at the Vienna lodge of the Explorers Guild. That is, you would see it, if you visited that lodge as a high-ranking member. I should hope that even in Vienna they will know not to display the thing. –E.W.B.}

IV.

JOHN OGDEN RARELY DISCUSSES A COMMISSION with his men, and he has not suddenly acquired the habit in the course of this adventure. Even Subadar Priddish has been left in doubt as to where they will go after Kathmandu, though he knows–as they all do–that the mountain city is not their destination. The dragoons, per their own habit, are content to leave these matters in Ogden's hands. But if you are curious yourself, gentle reader, we can revisit an earlier setting of our story and pick out some clue as to where they might all be headed....

I would show you, in particular, a certain phrase inscribed on the inner wall of the Abbot's tank in Romania, just above the water-line: *Mons Tria Millia Passuum Latuit Bene*, or 'A three-mile peak, well-hid.' We find this phrase amid a great volume of writings and mathematical symbols that encircle the Abbot, all of it descriptive, as he says, of the thirty-seven locations where the City is known to manifest. The 'hidden peak' is where he and his followers anticipate the City occurring next, in November of 1918. Or at least, he had said as much to John Ogden in their interview here, some months ago. And he had not needed to add that this was the last occurrence Arthur Ogden could expect to see, in the short time that remained to him.

The Abbot had described certain strange pockets or valleys formed aeons ago, when the Indian subcontinent drifted into Eurasia and raised the Himalayan plateau. At the center of one of these pockets, apparently, sat *Channa-achala*, the Sanskrit name for 'hidden mountain,' known locally as *Sumeru*, or Mount Meru. Here the winds racing down from the north ran through little channels in the Sagkata glacier and stirred unceasingly round the base of the mountain, raising a cloud of icy vapor nearly to its summit, at the level of the surrounding plateau. Viewed from a distance, the cloud appeared to be a solid extension of the glacier, with just the tiniest anomaly at its center. It was only on approaching the rim of the valley that one descried the floating peak–That is, the little mountain suspended on a lake of cloud, with a lamasery clinging to its summit. Apparently the thing was rather a wonder, and did not need a lamasery to proclaim its sacredness.

At any rate, the little peak was really the uppermost tip of a much greater mountain, and one must descend the glacier and cross the valley in order to gain the mountain's base, which crossing was made next to impossible by the valley's winds. The trek would be no small challenge, but pilgrims and hermits had been making it barefoot from time out of mind, and a hearty specimen like Major Ogden, operating with his brother's life (and possibly the health of the *world*) at stake, could surely manage it. As to finding Channa-Achala, this was represented as a simple matter of getting to Kathmandu and asking for the peak by name; though the Abbot had foreseen that by the time Ogden reached the Nepalese capital, he would have no need to ask.

Ogden had had this destination wired to Lowring-on-Hudson and had gathered his men and lit out into the East, as told. But this last riddle of the Abbot's had not, from that day on, been very far from his thoughts: How was it, exactly, that he and his purpose would be recognized in Kathmandu, so that he needn't ask for his mountain? Who would have prepared the way for him, and to what end...? These questions had come to mingle in his mind with uncertainties greater still–your mystical cities and the fate of civilization and so forth–to create a general, creeping anxiety in him, of which, up to the last year, he'd had little experience indeed. Even Mr. Priddish's counsel, ordinarily a great comfort, had offered few of the practical solutions Ogden might have preferred (beyond that he must wait on events and trust to his instincts and other such things that had begun to strike him lately as platitudes). He had sought distraction in drink, and in those salutary bouts of violence of which the trip had provided a few. But what had truly kept him from falling, as he conceived it, into an endless and paralyzing meditation were these thousand smaller and more pressing questions of the day: how, for instance, to keep the men fed and moving, and Bertram and Miss Harrow safe; where to light cook-fires or how to caulk their ship; where to dispatch men to scout for water or haggle for horses.... In these endless little puzzles, Ogden can often forget those vaster, vaguer riddles waiting to get between him and his sleep.

Not but some of these quandaries of leadership are deeper and thornier than others. It is about seven days since the *Black Joke* left Gryzha, and we find the ship grounded in an anonymous little inlet, with Mr. Mulcairn turning the bowline round a stalagmite and the rest of the crew waiting on board, looking out from the forward decks. Ogden and Mr. Priddish have gone ahead with their map, and are stooping with it to a little stone obelisk at the foot of a long switchback trail.

Now: I would not have you picture this 'map' as some tidy little device, like the local rail chart in your borough of today. The waterways, for one thing, are rendered in brush-strokes on canvas, so that any bulge or flutter in these lines is just as apt to be a tic in the artist's hand or a stray dollop of pigment as any real feature of the underground system. Add to which, each network of lines is its own bramble-patch of forks, branches, and spurs tapering at its outsides to nothing. And there are at least five of these networks discernible, all intertwined and layered one over the other. These lines might breast the lakes and seas above or descend to the world's core; currents might be flowing in one direction or the other. There is no key to any of it nor any indication of scale, and the colors and glyphs meant to mark out specific ports and hazards clarify little for those not already versed in this code.

The map, in fine, is as intricate as it is hopelessly approximate. Yet here are Ogden and Mr. Priddish holding it to the little fingerpost by the cave, looking from the symbols and colors on one to those on the other, back and forth, over and again. After a long space of calculation, Mr. Priddish voices the thoughts of both men: 'It would seem this is the way, Sahib. Though I could not swear to it.'

Ah: very good. And all well for Mr. Priddish, who needn't swear to anything. It is *Ogden* who must decide if this is the place, or if they have not reached it yet, or if indeed they are already past it. And he must stake the expedition on his choice. Draw up too soon and the foot-path might lead them anywhere, with no certain way back to daylight; fail to stop in time and they would run irrecoverably off-course (as they had nearly washed down into India a week since). Hesitation, of course, would not look well to the men, and the boat cannot sit much longer in any case, as he will not risk its discovery by anyone trailing them on the water. He must make a quick judgment on whatever imperfect basis, and hand it down with conviction, that is all.

Ogden takes a last hard stare at the obelisk and rolls and binds the map. 'Bring them up, Mr. Priddish,' he says. And we are reminded once more of Cortés burning his boats on the shores of Mexico: there is now, as ever, but the one line of march, and that way is forward.

After the better part of a day's climb (which they might call the worse), the party reach a shelf of rock backed by a narrow cave. They bring their lanterns into the cave and find a wall at its far end, where a bamboo ladder stands flanked by paintings of Hindu mountain gods and multi-armed monsters with forked tongues. Overhead, a little square is outlined in slivers of light, and footsteps and muffled voices may be heard from somewhere above this. Ogden tugs at one of the bamboo rungs to test it, and climbs to the square, which gives easily on its hinges when he pushes it. Well. If he must come up from a position of disadvantage, best to do it quickly.

He throws open the hatch and scrambles out, hopping to his feet on a floor of dust-filmed wood planks. All around him, as he sees, there are somber young men hunched on benches, working at metal frames. The air reeks of smoke and grease. A boy rolls a flock of spoked wheels past him. In some other age, long-past, the bamboo ladder may have conducted travelers up into a great temple or a castle of the Nepalese monarch. Today it lets Ogden into a workshop where bicycles are being made.

The remaining dragoons come up behind Ogden, each of them marveling, perhaps, as he has never marveled before at the assembly of bicycles. Their arrival does not cause the least stir, either, though it cannot be every day that a band of murderous westerners appears in these workers' midst (can it?). Ogden is on point of hauling one of the workers to his feet and shaking *some* sort of acknowledgment out of him, when a squat, pug-nosed foreman comes striding down one of the aisles, barking some Nepali phrase. Mr. Buchan asks Mr. Priddish aside what the man has said; the Sikh points out, patiently, that he is not Nepalese. But I suppose it is beside the point. The little man is off before Ogden can respond, leading them all across the workshop floor.

When the foreman gets to a station in a corner of the shop, he puts his heels together and presents Ogden with a military sort of pantomime. This for the benefit of an old man in wire-rimmed glasses, who sits tightening a bolt over a brake cable. To Ogden's surprise, the old man speaks in unaccented English, without looking up or pausing in his work.

MY BROTHER WILL DESCRIBE TO YOU THE ARRANGEMENTS HE HAS MADE. YOU ARE FOR THE CHANNA-ACHALA, IS THAT SO?
YES.

THEN IT IS ALL WELL. YOUR OWN BROTHER HAS COME THROUGH HERE, MAJOR, NOT SIX DAYS BEFORE YOU. MY BROTHER HAS SENT HIM AHEAD. I AM AFRAID HE WAS IN NO CONDITION TO WAIT.
MY BROTHER'S COME? ARTHUR OGDEN?
INDEED YES. HE WAS DRAWN UP FROM THE RIVER IN A CRATE, ON THE CONVEYOR LINE, AHEAD OF THE BAGGAGE.

I AM TOLD HE IS SEALED IN A STEEL TANK INSIDE THE CRATE, ALIVE BUT IN A VERY BAD WAY. THERE ARE THIRTY-FIVE COOLIES NOW IN HARNESS, TAKING HIM INTO THE MOUNTAINS. YOU WILL BE MAKING BAD PROGRESS INDEED IF YOU DO NOT OVERTAKE THEM.
HOW'S THIS, GENNLEMEN? YOU HAD A GOOD LOOK, HAVE YEH?

PLEASE, CALL YOUR MAN BACK, MAJOR.
WHO'S HE TALKING TO? I DON'T LIKE THE LOOK OF THAT LOT.

NO MORE SHOULD YOU. THEY ARE LATE OF THE SIXTH GURKHA RIFLES, TOO UNRULY EVEN FOR YOUR OWN MAJOR ALLANSON. NOW THEY ARE HOME FROM THE DARDANELLES WITH NO MORE COMMISSION. THEY KEEP THEIR UNIFORMS ONLY BECAUSE THE WAR OFFICE DARE NOT RECLAIM THEM. THEY ARE VERY BAD MEN.

THESE? NAH, YE'RE MISTAKEN, SIR. THESE AN'T BAD MEN. ARE YA, SWEETHEART?
MAJOR: PLEASE. WE HAVE NOT GOT TIME FOR DELAY.

...JUST THE TYPE WE'D TRY WHEN WE WAS BORDERERS OURSELVES, SIR, IN'NIT?
COME, MR. PENSETTE.
–THAT, OR ASK 'EM TO JOIN ON.

THESE LOST SOULS HAVE BEEN LOITERING ABOUT SINCE GALLIPOLI, STEALING MONEY AND ARMS FOR THEIR RAIDS INTO INDIA. IT IS JUST AS WELL YOU'VE NOTHING THEY THINK WORTH TAKING.

The unassuming door in the Durbar Marg is opened by a Mr. Tamang, brother of the old man from the bicycle shop. *Twin* brother, I should say, right down to the wire-rimmed spectacles; and with the one brother fled before the second appears, Ogden is not sure he isn't prey to some puzzling Eastern joke.

'*Vitra auhu Huss*–Good morning, you men, and welcome,' says this pleasant old creature, waving them in with a sweep of his arm, and reappearing ahead of them with a lamp. Ogden answers these pleasantries with a flood of questions, which is all well with Mr. Tamang. His is that impenetrable good cheer the western traveler finds in the East, and takes either for cordiality or reserve, for wisdom or idiocy, arrogance or servility, according to his own prejudices. In this case, the old man hears what questions he is disposed to answer and happily ignores the rest. On the subject of accommodations and the arrangements made for the party's travel, his answers are direct and precise; though on the point of Arthur's health he is immovably vague, to where Ogden cannot tell if his brother is alive or dead. When asked who has alerted him to the dragoons' arrival and underwritten the expedition, the old man makes no reply at all until he reaches a door at the end of a narrowing hall. He waves his lamp over the door's carvings, to reveal more of these Hindu deities slashing at each other with long swords, demons ravaging rice paddies with thunderbolts, hunters chasing deer through a forest and, cut through the midst of all this, the Latin word *Cognoscere*.

He has surprised Ogden into silence, as he notes with a feline sort of pleasure. He snuffs his lamp and pushes the door open to the baths and guest apartments, on which cue the servants of the house come padding out from their places of hiding. Tamang floats ahead and spreads open the doors to a balcony, and trades a few words to a pair of grooms outside. Mr. Mulcairn has arrived and is seeing his horse brushed and fed in a courtyard below, as the old man desires Ogden to see. Ogden gives a brief thanks for this, and asks Mr. Tamang if he is a member of the Explorers Guild. The Nepali answers, in his equivocal way: 'Yes, I am a friend of that society.' And he mentions lightly that the Guild have taken an interest in Ogden's doings, viewing him as a 'man of potential.' Yet before Ogden can press him any further on this head, the old man bows and is gone.

OGDEN HAS LONG CEASED TO VIEW THE APPEARANCE OF MISS MAGUIRE'S TELEGRAMS AS MIRACULOUS.

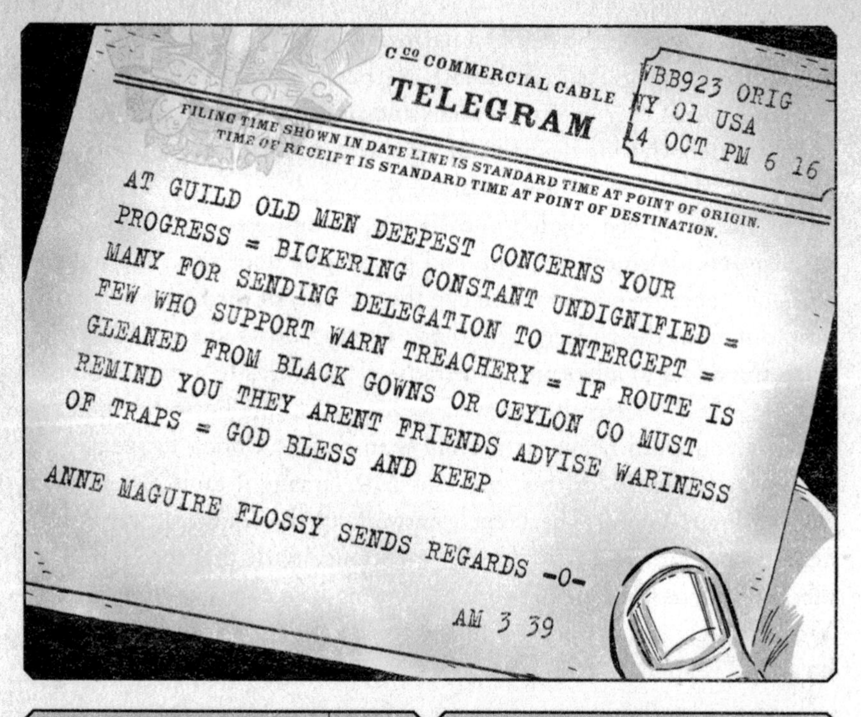
C.º COMMERCIAL CABLE
TELEGRAM
FILING TIME SHOWN IN DATE LINE IS STANDARD TIME AT POINT OF ORIGIN.
TIME OF RECEIPT IS STANDARD TIME AT POINT OF DESTINATION.
WBB923 ORIG
NY 01 USA
14 OCT PM 6 16
AT GUILD OLD MEN DEEPEST CONCERNS YOUR
PROGRESS = BICKERING CONSTANT UNDIGNIFIED =
MANY FOR SENDING DELEGATION TO INTERCEPT =
FEW WHO SUPPORT WARN TREACHERY = IF ROUTE IS
GLEANED FROM BLACK GOWNS OR CEYLON CO MUST
REMIND YOU THEY ARENT FRIENDS ADVISE WARINESS
OF TRAPS = GOD BLESS AND KEEP
ANNE MAGUIRE FLOSSY SENDS REGARDS -0-
AM 3 39

THERE IS NO QUESTION, FOR OGDEN, OF ALTERING HIS COURSE AT THIS LATE DATE. NOT WITH ARTHUR GONE AHEAD.

LITTLE POINT, TOO, IN TROUBLING THE MEN WITH ANOTHER ILL-DEFINED WARNING.

AS TO STAYING ALERT FOR TRAPS,
WHAT ELSE HAD HE BEEN DOING
SINCE LEAVING ON THIS EXPEDITION?

Evening finds our travelers settled in a paper-paneled sitting-room, all of them bathed, fed, and lounging—or sleeping outright—in the silken robes of the house. Mr. Tamang continues to host after his fashion, being no less gracious than he was on welcoming his guests and no less evasive on points he feels disinclined to treat. Here and there he does let an interesting detail slip: Arthur had arrived in the company of his hermits and lunatics from New York; black-robed men and spies from the Ceylon Company had been rumored in the city. But there is no more mention of the Explorers Guild, nor of which members might be discussing Ogden's 'potential.' And Mr. Tamang will not comment on Shambhala, nor on any worlds that may or may not be opening over his mountains, viewing this sort of speculation as unseemly and possibly heretical. On the subject of Mr. Sloane, he says (stifling a yawn) that no one of Sloane's description had entered the city, so far as he knew; and if this man had promised to see Ogden once more before his journey's end then, why, perhaps he would. Mr. Tamang reiterates that he is only their host and outfitter, and that their way is clear into the mountains. All necessary arrangements have been made. They will have use of a sherpa called Netra, and they will depart Kathmandu at first light. It is to these points that the old man recurs, repeatedly, with a beatific smile, until there are no more questions from his listeners. And only then does he venture two questions of his own: might Bertram be woken, and might he and Mr. Tamang converse?

Ogden grants the request with a hard stare and a grunt (I cannot say he has enjoyed the interview overmuch) and goes off to seek a bed. It is Miss Harrow who leads the sleep-dazed Bertram in and seats him on a cushion, facing the old man. She recedes with a bow and sits with Mr. Priddish and Mr. Buchan to listen in. Not that there is much for anyone to hear: Mr. Tamang's idea of 'conversation' proves to be a long and silent communion with the boy, with only a Nepalese phrase, or an anodyne comment about the journey, escaping him now and then. Mostly he sits with his eyes half-lidded and his smile fixed and knowing, while Bertram stares up into the serene and sun-wrinkled old face without the least nod of his head or shrug of his little shoulders.

So it goes, into the small hours of the night. The breathing of Mr. Priddish grows deep and regular, and a soft rattling rises out of Mr. Buchan's throat, and still the boy and the old man sit in this strange interview. Miss Harrow does not think Bertram has spoken once since he was brought in and introduced. Though she seems to hear his whispering voice from somewhere, as she lets go the scene in Mr. Tamang's sitting-room and falls into a dreamless sleep....

A NOISE IN THE COURTYARD WAKES PRIVATE MULCAIRN. IF, INDEED, HE'D BEEN SLEEPING IN THE FIRST PLACE.

«CRRACK!»

You may have guessed, gentle reader, that these visitors are the Gurkhas we saw earlier in Durbar Square, and that they have come to take Mr. Mulcairn's horse. Certainly, the Irishman is clear enough on both points. He arrives to see one of their arms carrying back in the dark, and to feel the beaded end of the man's stock-whip crack against his brow, cutting a welt down his face and spilling an eye out of its socket. Yet Mulcairn, in answer, only shakes the blow off, covers the courtyard at a bound and buries his knife to its hilt in the Gurkha's belly. I suppose the others had thought to see him turned back or at least staggered by the whip, and they stare at something of a loss as he hoists his knife from just over the man's groin to the underside of his chin and leaves it lodged there. The whip-handler is no less surprised by this turn than the others, and he rests his free hand almost gingerly on Mulcairn's wrist, this while his innards break out through his tunic.

Mulcairn has off his robe, then, and turns square to this man's fellows, as they set themselves to him. A recognition flashes between the big Irishman and these twenty dark, grinning faces across the courtyard. All parties have an idea of what will follow, and they are all suited excellently to this sort of work.

Now: I hesitate to show you very much of this encounter, dear reader. We have looked in on scenes of violence before, I realize, but none quite so brutish or close-fought as this. The swiftness of Mr. Mulcairn is horrible to see, as he vaults from one Gurkha to the next like a panther in among hunting dogs, snapping up live bodies and leaving them mangled beneath him. His hands, his teeth, his unshod feet go groping through the press of men, each relentlessly at its business: here a thumb hooks in a mouth and turns a jaw, there a heel stomps a knee to a backward angle and the bones come bristling out like kindling wood. These are no more men once they enter Mulcairn's grasp, they are only packets of bone and sinew and blood, and against hands that can flatten a skull between them there is little a body can do to preserve the life inside it. So the gouged and bent and cracked shapes accrue beneath him, with now and then a yelp expressive of pain, or an eyeball rolling in mortal fear, or the weakened pawing of a hand as life is extinguished to remind us, awfully, of their humanity. Unceasingly this work continues, under the moon.

Still, through all this, the Gurkhas are making progress of their own. They have closed on Mulcairn without firearms, or if they have them they'll not use them for fear of waking the house. But they are armed with the traditional curved knives of the Gurkhas, called *kukris*, some carrying several of these and many with longer knives and *Tulwars* besides. And where not every man is able to get a blade in Mulcairn before his own life is snatched away, many of them do; and gradually, inevitably, the cuts begin to tell on the Irishman. His attackers are simply too many. His limbs grow sluggish, or cease to answer where their nervous cords are cut. Increasingly he must pause to pant as more little knives go into him. He will rise in spasms and shed the men from his back, grip throats and limbs with hands like blacksmith's tongs, cracking bones and windpipes...yet two of the Gurkhas rush in for each he has dispatched, and he falls again with ever more gathered on him.

The scene has not quite ground to its finish (though I cannot believe it will be much longer now) when the moon picks out another body flying to the courtyard from the balconies above: it is Sergeant Pensette, who had stumbled outside in his stockinged feet to drain his body of the house rice-wine, and had seen the commotion below. He'd seemed at first to be dreaming, or looking into some pocket of hell with the noises off, but he had blinked the scene into focus and is taking the stairs a flight at a time now with his pistol out.

By the time Pensette reaches the snow-dusted flags there are three Gurkhas left over Mr. Mulcairn and they have been working their knives freely on him for nearly a minute. Pensette looses four shots running and rolls the Gurkhas off the great inert body, and skids in to stanch and tie off what he can, whistling the while for the house. As he works, he is a bit thrown to see Mulcairn staring up at him. And there is something more worrisome now in the Irishman's one placid blue eye, than in the other that has been ruined by the Gurkha's whip.

AH SWEET CHR–ST, TELL ME MY ESCORTING ANGEL HAS NOT THE FACE OF MARTIN PENSETTE.
AN' WHO'S SENDING ANGELS, TOM?

AH. HELL'S GOT THE BETTER CLAIM ON ME, IS IT? –*HRM.* WELL. IN ANOTHER MINUTE WE'LL KNOW WHO'S RIGHT.
...ANYWAY, I WILL.
WHAT BUNK YEH TALK, TOMMY. NEXT FOR YOU IS A SEAMSTRESS WITH THE FACE OF A YELLA APE; AN' YOU MAY ASK HER FOR LIFE'S MEANIN' IF YEH LIKE, AN' GIVE US BOYS A LAUGH.

...TOM.
–MM?
I SAY, YOU BIDE A MINUTE. I CANNAE SHIFT YEH, YE BEAST, BUT WE'VE RAISED THE HOUSE NOW.
AYE, SO THEY MAY COME AND CROW.
WHEEST, MAN.

NAH, IT'S ALL WELL. YE'VE SEEN I DIDN'T GO FOR ANY POXY KING, ANYWAY. NOT FOR MAJOR AND HIS BROTHER AND HIS DREAM-CITIES EITHER. HUH? STANDS THAT BRAVE BEAST OVER THERE, MARTIN, AN' I BELIEVE I SAVED HER FROM MEN WORSE THAN ME–*HRM.*
AN' IT'S QUITE ENOUGH IF THAT'S ALL I MEANT AT LAST.
YOU LOOK AT HER AND TELL ME IF I LIE.

INDEED NO, TOM. BUT YE'LL STOP THAT TALK, FOR IT BREAKS THE HEART OF ME.
AH! *HRM.* THIS FROM HIM WHO'S STAMPED HIS BOOT-SOLE ALL OVER MY SKULL. *HRM. HEH-HEHHH.*

AYE, AN' YE'LL UP AND HAVE BETTER OF ME, TOM.
YOU SEE 'EM THERE? YE'RE SAVED, MAN.
...TOM?

MM...AH-YES. BETTER YOU THAN ANY OTHER, MARTIN. BETTER YOU.
ONLY FOR ONCE BE A SCOT, WOULD YOU, AND FORBEAR TO SPEAK. I'D SET MYSELF IN ORDER, AND I COULD USE THE–*HRM*–USE A BIT OF QUIET.

AYE, ALL RIGHT. YOU REST, BROTHER.

STAY. PUT THEM DOWN.
I WANT YOU TO LOOK ON THIS. ...ALL OF YOU, BY G–D.

YOU OUGHT TO REMEMBER WHAT WAS DONE HERE.
YOU WON'T LIVE TO SEE A THING LIKE THIS DONE AGAIN. NOT WITH TOM GONE.

...THIS CAME ABOUT OVER HIS HORSE?
AYE, SIR.
WELL. THEN I THINK HE CAN'T BE ENTIRELY D–MNED.

MR. RENTON? YOU MAY TAKE THAT HORSE FOR YOUR OWN. YOU SEE WHAT IT MEANT TO TOM. PERHAPS IT'LL MEAN SOMETHING TO YOU.
AYE? AN' YOU CAN GO F–CK IT.
...WHAT?

THIS MAN WAS A BLACK-HEARTED B–STARD, AS YE WELL KNOW.
AN' HIS HORSE WAS NO SACRED ANIMAL, IT WAS A F–CKIN' HORSE. YOU MAY'A NOTICED THEY DON'T EVEN USE 'EM UP HERE.

ALL RIGHT, LAD. ALL RIGHT–
IF IT'S MINE I'M'A SEND IT DOWN TO HELL TO LOOK FOR TOM.

Without excusing Mr. Renton's behavior, I imagine he is speaking, in his way, for the rest of these dragoons. Even Ogden falls into a brooding silence on the boy's departure. The rest will have to make shift with the terse eulogy he has given Mulcairn, for there is no more coming.

No loss, of course, is easily stood in such a small and close-knit company as this. But there is more represented in this scene, to these dragoons, than the loss of a man. There is an offense here to the *order* of things. A man cannot stop the planet's turning, they know; there is no halting the tides nor staying the weather; the sun is hot and the nights dark and there is no power on this earth that will kill Tom Mulcairn. These are the faiths they have long carried, who haven't gods in the traditional sense but who have seen the world and know its workings. It is unthinkable–it seems monstrous–that this Irishman of the Connaught Rangers will not stand and grunt some blasphemy at them all, as he has stood from fights and marches all over the earth, reliably as the sun's rise, times out of counting. That the great body should only lie still and silent now, beneath them, strikes them as a horrible incorrectness. And there is nothing so much in these faces as a naked disbelief, with outrage and even a hint of fear kindling beneath it.

It will not do, Ogden knows, to leave his men very long like this–In an hour they will have burned the house of their host and perhaps declared war on the city–But there is remedy for all of them in action. He calls Mr. Tamang to the courtyard and consults briefly with him and with Mr. Priddish. The men are ordered inside then to gather their kits, while a dray ox is put in harness and Mulcairn's body is haled off to a grain shed. Mr. Tamang will order affairs at his home and see to the disposition of Mulcairn, so long as Ogden can get his men into the mountains without delay. And this Ogden does, careful to direct the dragoons around the courtyard and out through the mews, quietly, with the dawn spreading before them. The events of the morning, he thinks, must settle as they will in the minds of his men. All that is beyond doubt is that they–and so our story–will carry past the end of Tom Mulcairn.

Of the following days there is not much to note, beyond the tedium of foot-travel through the mountain paths and roads, from one undifferentiated village outpost or way-station to the next. On another day, in different circumstances, we'd consider a ramble through the Nepalese interior of quite enough interest to fill its own volume. But we have an appointment to keep in these mountains, and it is difficult to see the trek from here to there as much more than a routine business of marches and rests, of one boot set before another *ad infinitum*. Certainly it is so in the mind of John Ogden.

Even as the party reach the Channa-Achala Valley, a place well-described as a lake of cloud, with the sacred peak floating at its center–a sight wondrous, surely, even to the Nepalese guides–even here, as a practical matter, there is little use in standing to marvel while a valley remains to be crossed and a three-mile mountain stands to be summited. The rigors of travel, the nearness of his destination, and a hundred lingering questions (not least of which, why have they failed to overtake his brother's party?) have left Ogden ill-disposed to admire the scenery just now. And he has no sooner arrived at the rim of the valley than he orders his men down into it.

The descent is among the more difficult passages in a journey that has not lacked in difficulties, and the valley itself is an endless slog through biting winds, under a low-lying sun whose powers seem rather magnified by the whirling cloud of ice overhead. Our travelers are two days plodding through this hellish landscape, mazed and stupid from hunger and inanition, lifting and plunging their feet with the steadiness of animals, before Netra, their lead guide, descries a figured archway in the rock wall ahead.

V.

THE SUN FOLLOWS OUR DRAGOONS for only about ten or fifteen paces into the tunnel, and by the time the men have stamped the snow from their boots they are walking in darkness. The winds still groan across the tunnel's mouth like the music of ancient gods, though even these can reach only so far into the mountain. The clamor dies gradually beneath the footfalls of men and beasts, and the grinding of cartwheels and the jangling of the animals' tack, and the men—I do not exaggerate—could almost weep for the relief of it. A similar, better-known wind—the *mistral* of Provençal France—is recognized as a defense for murder in that country, and whatever one's feelings on the French jurisprudence I think it does illustrate the distance to which a high and relentless wind will go in scrambling a man's wits. Certainly, having made two days' march across the Achala Valley, Ogden's men would make excellent advocates in the Provençal court. And they shuffle through the dark now, tongueless and euphoric, till the day's first rest is called, and they sleep where they fall.

Netra has gone bandy-legging ahead and may or may not have abandoned them here. This is impossible to judge, though neither does it matter very much. There is nowhere for anyone to go but forward, and when Ogden rises again he needn't call an order. He only presses ahead in silence as the rest kick one another awake and fall in behind him.

The men who do gradually find their voices seem to be whispering and hushing one another like schoolboys behind their master's back, till one of them is nudged forward by the others. This spokesman feels his way past the guides and drivers, up to Bertram and Miss Harrow, where, steadying himself on the rear gate of their cart, he begins his address:

'Bert–*hrm*–Bertram'–the voice identifying this as Sergeant Pensette–'S'pose that's you, then.'

'...Yes, sir,' sounds faintly, from the dark.

'Ah-weel. I hope I an't woke yeh...?'

Bertram stirs on his pillows and sits up. 'No, sir,' he says, and Miss Harrow allows this lie with a little frown.

'Good. Good....' After a pause, and another throat-clearing, Pensette continues at graduated volume: 'See here, then: *ehh*, the lads've been on about, they'd like to know are yeh *feelin'* altogether well, son.'

'Oh. I think I've been a bit tired.'

'Ah.'

'But it's only that. I hope they're not worried. I ought to be right again with a little rest.'

'If you'd let him rest *now*, for instance,' Miss Harrow suggests.

But Pensette must unburden himself. 'Yah, yah,' he stammers. 'Y'see though, it's the opinion o' certain of us, since the canals at least, an' I canna' say where I'm one o' these m'self, an' I hardly allow it's possible–'

'–Go on,' says Miss Harrow.

'Well: they wonder if the boy an't begun to *shine*, just the least bit.'

'Beg your pardon?' Miss Harrow, again.

'Oh, aye. It's the trip, surely, the queerness of it, an' the strain it's put on the lads. There's some begun to see a greenish *light* about the boy, which is madness, sure, but *you* try tellin' em. It come up again while we took our rest just now, an' they sez Martin if you're so sure it's untrue whyn't you ask the boy flat-out, which is why yeh see me now–Or I s'pose yeh *hear* me, anyway–'

'He's told you he's tired, Sergeant,' says Miss Harrow, without quite the command of her voice that she would like.

'Ah *rubbish*!' shouts Mr. Renton, who seems to have come up with Pensette, to the general surprise. 'I'm run-down myself and ain't we all, but nivver have I got so tired that I start to give off a Chr–stin' *light*–!'

His answer is a swing of the Scot's paw at a well-practiced height, clapping against the boy's ear and spilling him against the stone wall in a clatter of hilt and scabbard and pistol-butts. Renton hops up with a screeching oath for Pensette, who tries to find the boy again for a kick.

'Stop it–Please, that's enough!' cries Miss Harrow. The two are still scuffling when Bertram speaks, just audibly:

'Sergeant? It might be true, though.'

And now Renton and Pensette grow still. The whole party have quieted, actually, and are straining to hear what is being said. I should think the tunnel would carry Bertram's little voice even up to Major Ogden, though I cannot be sure.

'At the place where they kept me,' Bertram says, 'in the Argentine, we'd ink that shone in the dark, and we put it on the clocks and pocket-watches. They said we weren't to play with it, and they would know the boys who *had* because they would glow, and they would become sick and have to stay by themselves, and we all saw boys led away very ill who were glowing like the ink. But I promise I never played with it. Really, I didn't.'

''*Course* not, lad,' growls Sergeant Pensette, as though he'd like to see the man who would challenge Bertram on this point.

'…So, I can't be sick like the others. And really I don't feel ill. Only tired.'

'*There*, Sergeant,' says Miss Harrow, no longer able to restrain herself. 'He's *tired*, and that's the *fifth* time you've heard it, so will you let him *rest* now, or do you think it better to stand here and wear him out with your *questions*?'

'No, indeed, miss.'

'No *which*?'

'I'll leave him be. Only trying to look after him–'

'–Then do it. Go away, and let him alone.'

'Aye, then.' Adding, too softly even for Bertram to hear: 'Sorry, lad.'

Miss Harrow, trembling now, helps Bertram back into his rugs, while a hush falls over the party. They proceed without speaking for some time, and Miss Harrow is on point of sleeping herself when they pass a sputtering little torch in an iron bracket. Here, in the faltering light, she sees that Sergeant Pensette has not left them. He has been walking all along with his hand on the gate, staring into the cart. Nor has she the heart at this point to order him away.

Another march follows, quiet and long—an hour or several, it is difficult to say—before the tunnel opens onto a vast clearing with the night sky above. At least, that is how we interpret this landscape on first seeing it: a clearing or a fog-covered lake ringed by settlements. The dragoons are shuffling in from the dark and spreading across a fire-lit terrace, blinking and yawning and stretching limbs. To either side of them, beneath tapering flights of stairs, there are pagoda-roofed walks leading to more rock-cut chambers and verandahs. From somewhere past these hidden walks we can hear the now-familiar grunting and milling of men and yak and oxen and the shouted transactions in Nepali and Sherpa, along with—as our India-bred men cannot fail to note—the less-typical sounds of *elephants* being wrangled. The noises roll together and rise through the dark, ringing on the ancient stones and echoing over the immense clearing, though it is hardly the clangor of the Kashgar market-stalls. The greater sense we have as we emerge from the tunnel is one of peace and welcome, and the dragoons know without asking that they have entered a sacred space.

Mr. Priddish supposes the station to be an ancient *vihara*, or sanctuary for itinerant monks. He says the clearing is man-made, or at least shaped by men, and that if they could only see it they would find it quadrangular, like the courts in the cave monasteries at Ajanta and Karli. Mr. Buchan suggests they scout the place out in the light of day, to which Priddish says, cryptically, that the day is already long-risen.

Well. This would seem to be another Sikh riddle, else a rare lapse in Mr. Priddish's English. But Buchan sees several of the men pointing into the night sky, and he follows their gaze to where the stars have arranged themselves in concentric squares overhead.

'...*Sumeru*,' Ogden pronounces. He and Mr. Priddish are reading from the texts of the Theravada cut into the stone columns around them.

'Your Mount Meru,' says the Sikh. 'Center of the physical and metaphysical universes. Unusual only in the scale of the representation.'

'"Representation?"' says Ogden. 'This would be *it*. This would *be* the center.'

'...To men of faith, that may be,' Priddish qualifies, as though to say it is not a faith he shares.

Netra reappears and announces, to any who'll listen, that their elephants have been readied for the ascent. Captain Shaw asks when exactly they'll be shown a mountain to ascend, and Netra cocks his head, and looks from Shaw to Ogden. The little guide surveys the clearing, then, grins and opens his arms, and clucks some Nepali phrase whose meaning is unmistakably, '*Voilà!*' It appears that riddles are to be the order of the day.

Now: it will not naturally occur to a man, who has once set out to summit a mountain, that he might scale the thing from the *inside*. And certain of Ogden's men are still struggling with the concept as they boot their elephants up the endless rock-cut ramps and stairs that line the mountain's interior. A debate rises among them as to whether the Channa-Achala were naturally hollow–some species of derelict volcano, for instance–or carved out by men. The latter view strikes Captain Shaw as insupportable: where to *put* all the discarded rock, for one? Mr. Henty suggests the Captain's own mother has secreted it, while Sergeant Pensette points out that the 'cousins' of the Nepalese had thrown up China's Great Wall, and that these people were so numerous as to be 'capable of anything.' The guides and mahouts, so far as they can be understood, attribute the work to various of the mountain gods, which is of course no help to anyone.

With the exceptions of Miss Harrow and Bertram, who have been put up in a canopied howdah, the party travel one man to a beast, on rugs and leather mats through which every joint of the animals' spines may be distinctly felt. The men are not able to sleep nor even rest properly as they might on horseback, and after the initial exhilaration of the

climb they lapse back into an aggravated silence. Channa-Achala, as we have mentioned, is a peak of just three miles, but the elephants are trekking around and around a square perimeter that shrinks only gradually from a base measure of eight miles, and the going uphill is perforce slow. The howdah must be unbuckled from one bull elephant and thrown over the next at each of the stage-stations, too; and Miss Harrow adds further delay when she asks her mahout at one point if he might not stop pricking his beast about the mouth and ears. The boy's response is to shoulder his bull-hook, on which his elephant lumbers to a halt, and the rest of the procession are brought up short behind him. The elephant misplaces a foot and shudders, as though noting suddenly how narrow is this ledge beneath it and how hideous the drop; and soon all the elephants are grunting and stamping, tossing their heads, cleaving to the rock wall or else staggering out toward the darkness. 'Oh G–d,' Miss Harrow drawls, gripping her hand-rails. 'Go on, then.' The boy, who has not turned to her or spoken, reapplies his hook, and the climb continues as before.

And so, on and on, this upward journey. There is a grinding repetition to the climbing and pausing, the inclined and level runs, the switching of elephants. The wonder is gone from the torches and fire-lit shrines and stupas that the men took only this morning for stars in the celestial vault. Time stretches further out of calculation, and the days seem remote that were not filled with climbing, resting, changing, climbing, and the endless drift between sleep and waking. Bertram alone is able to sleep through the ascent with his head on Miss Harrow's lap, though there is no telling what dark distances the boy is covering himself, nor how far he has yet to go.

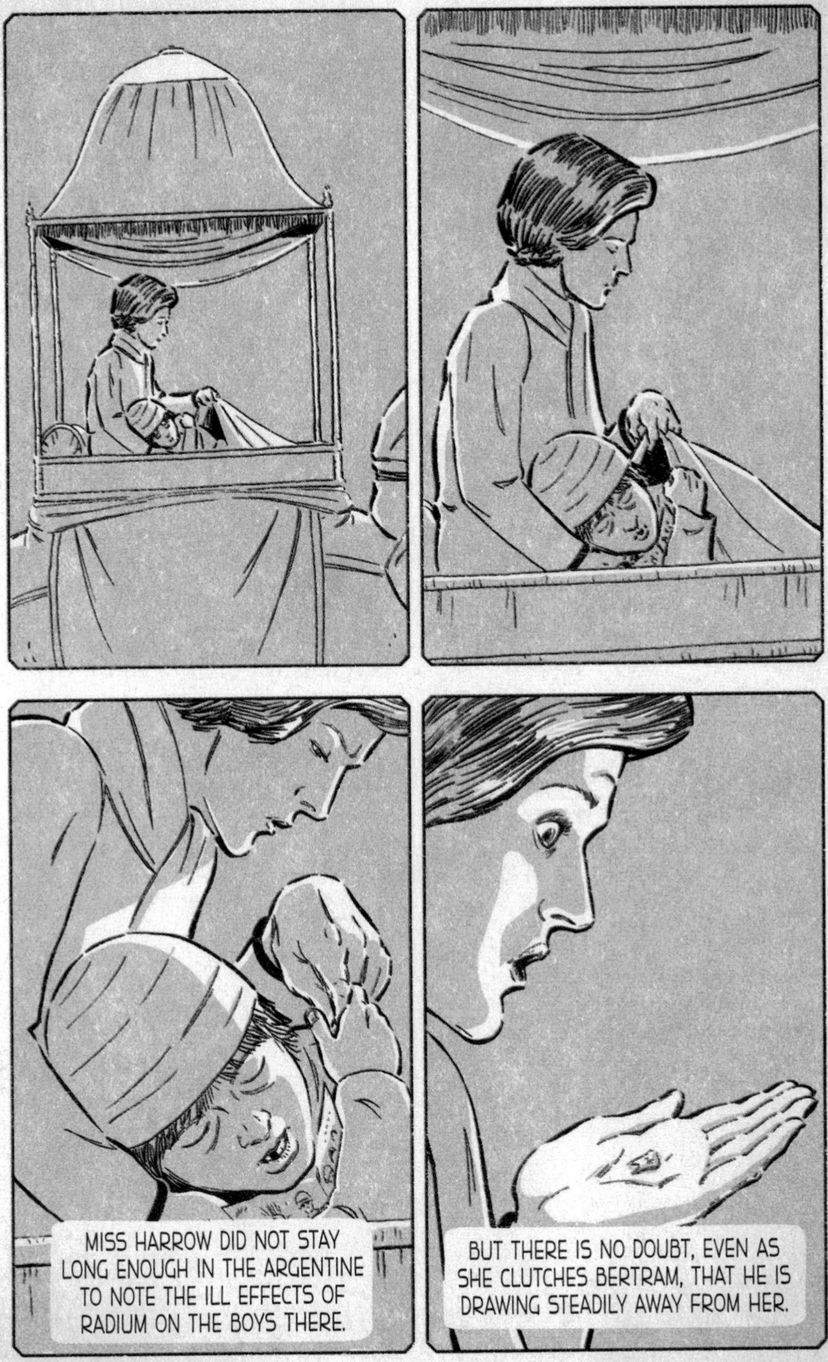

MISS HARROW DID NOT STAY LONG ENOUGH IN THE ARGENTINE TO NOTE THE ILL EFFECTS OF RADIUM ON THE BOYS THERE.

BUT THERE IS NO DOUBT, EVEN AS SHE CLUTCHES BERTRAM, THAT HE IS DRAWING STEADILY AWAY FROM HER.

...IT IS BETTER THAN A YEAR NOW SINCE WE LEFT OUR VICEROY'S SERVICE.
MANY AND MANY A MILE WE HAVE GONE, BACK AND FORTH ACROSS THE WORLD'S FACE AND BENEATH AND ABOVE IT WITHAL.
WHAT HAVE WE SEEN, SAHIB?

MM. ALL SEEMS A BIT OF A DREAM, DOESN'T IT.
YES.
AND NOT MUCH LOGIC OR CONNECTION TO IT, BUT ONLY A DREAM-LOGIC. FROM MY BROTHER'S NOTE AND HIS STORIES OUT OF THE NORTH, TO THE DELUSIONS OF THESE HERMITS AND OUTCASTS, AND THE RIDDLE OF THIS BOY, AND LATELY THESE MEN WHO ARE ISLANDS AND THE OTHERS LIVING ON THESE RIVERS UNDER OUR FEET...ALL TENDING TO WHAT?

THERE'S SOME GOLDEN CITY FLOATING OVER THIS MOUNTAIN, I SUPPOSE? WE BRING ARTHUR IN AND HE SPRINGS FORTH, WHOLE AGAIN, OUT OF HIS BOX...?
THE FUTURE REMAINS AS CLOSED TO ME AS IT EVER WAS, MR. PRIDDISH. AND I AM NOT SURE THE PAST IS ANY LESS A MYSTERY.
QUITE SO, YES.

THE WORLD IS CONSUMED TODAY IN WAR–AND WHERE IS IT? STRANGE THAT WE SHOULD BE SO REMOVED FROM IT, WHO WERE SOLDIERS ONCE. BUT I THINK WE ARE THROUGH SOME BARRIER. WE ARE IN THE DREAM. AND I CANNOT TELL IF WE ARE ON TO THE GREATER AND DEEPER WORKINGS OF THE WORLD OR ONLY LOST IN SOME MADNESS.

...YES, SAHIB.
WELL: I WISH YOU'D SAY SOMETHING, IF YOU'VE GIVEN THIS ANY THOUGHT.

I...YES. THERE IS MUCH IN WHAT YOU SAY. LATELY MY THOUGHTS ARE RUNNING IN THESE SAME CHANNELS.
BUT I WAS COME JUST NOW TO THINK OF YOU.
OF ME? AND HOW'S THAT?

OUR ASSOCIATION ENDS WITH THIS JOURNEY, DOES IT NOT?
WHAT? I HAVEN'T SAID THAT.
NO. IT IS A PRESENTIMENT I HAVE HAD SINCE OGDEN MEMSAHIB'S NOTE CAME TO US. BUT I WAS STRUCK ONLY NOW, IN OUR CLIMB, BY THE CERTAINTY OF IT.

...THERE IS A DRAWING IN A BOOK BY A MAN CALLED FLAMMARION, WHERE A MISSIONARY HAS CRAWLED TO THE EDGE OF THE WORLD AND PUT HIS HEAD OUTSIDE THE ARCH OF SKY AND STARS, INTO THE MACHINERY OF THE UNIVERSE...
DO YOU KNOW THE ONE?
NO.

WELL. I WAS SHOWN IT AS A REPRESENTATION OF THE MISSIONARY'S FOLLY WHEN I WAS A BOY. FOR, WHO CAN MAKE SENSE OF THE WHEELS OF FIRE AND CLOUD AND ALIEN SUNS, AND WHAT GOOD TO GRASP AT THESE MYSTERIES WHEN YOU MIGHT ONLY LOSE YOUR FOOTING IN THE WORLD, AND PROFIT NONE IN WISDOM?
I WAS TOLD THAT GOOD DEEDS AND REMEMBRANCE OF GOD ARE THE PILLARS OF THE RIGHT LIFE, AND THAT ONE'S WORK IS TO ORDER HIS SOUL ON EARTH AND TO TRUST THE REST TO THE GRACE OF VĀHIGURŪ. AND SO I HAVE DONE, AND BEEN CONTENT TO DO.

I SEE. AND YOU'D CALL ME THE MISSIONARY, IN YOUR LESSON?
WE ARE ALL HE, SAHIB, WHO HAVE TAKEN THIS COMMISSION AND THOUGHT UPON WHAT WE HAVE SEEN. AND I DO NOT THINK IT AN EVIL TO MEDITATE ON THE DESIGNS OF THE UNIVERSE. IT IS ONLY THAT I FORESEE A DIFFERENT WAY FOR YOU, FORWARD FROM THIS POINT.
AND WHICH WAY'S THAT?

YOU ARE WOKEN, AND NO MORE FIT TO BE A SOLDIER. JUST AS YOUR DRAGOONS, AND MYSELF— WE ARE FIT TO BE NOTHING MORE.
MM. THOUGH I THINK YOU'RE A GOOD DEAL MORE THAN A COMPANY SOLDIER, MR. PRIDDISH. AND I THINK YOU CAN NO MORE RETURN TO THE SERVICE NOW THAN I CAN.

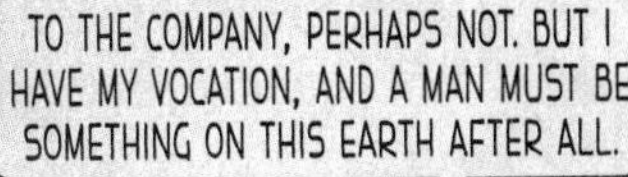

TO THE COMPANY, PERHAPS NOT. BUT I HAVE MY VOCATION, AND A MAN MUST BE SOMETHING ON THIS EARTH AFTER ALL.
AND...SOMEHOW THAT WOULDN'T APPLY TO ME?
I DO NOT KNOW WHAT YOU'LL BECOME, SAHIB. I ONLY BELIEVE THAT, IN SOME, THE JOURNEY TO A GREATER CONSCIOUSNESS PROCEEDS IN THE ONE DIRECTION, LIKE TIME'S ARROW.

AND A MAN WHO IS INTREPID OF MIND AND HAS NOT THE STRICTURES–NOR THE SOLACE–OF MY FAITH CAN GO VERY FAR IN THIS DIRECTION.
I THINK YOU WOULD NOT WAKE ONLY TO FALL BACK INTO THE SAME DREAM OF IGNORANCE. WHEREAS I WILL MEDITATE ONLY SO LONG ON GOD'S PLAN, WHO CAN LIVE BY IT WITHOUT KNOWING IT.

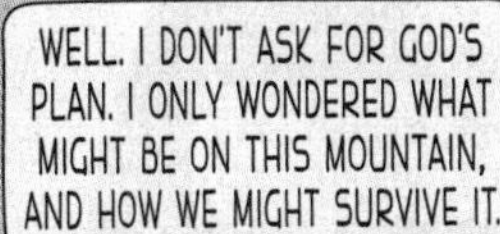

WELL. I DON'T ASK FOR GOD'S PLAN. I ONLY WONDERED WHAT MIGHT BE ON THIS MOUNTAIN, AND HOW WE MIGHT SURVIVE IT.
YES. FORGIVE ME. IT IS AN EVIL TO STRAIN AGAINST THE CURRENTS OF THE WORLD, AND TO WORRY OVER THESE ASSOCIATIONS BETWEEN MEN, THAT WILL QUITE NATURALLY GROW AND DIMINISH.
YOU ONLY ASKED AFTER MY THOUGHTS, AND I WAS REFLECTING IN THE MOMENT THAT OUR PARTING MIGHT GO ESPECIALLY HARD WITH MR. RENTON...

I HAD BETTER ASKED WHAT YOU THINK WE'LL FIND AT HOME IN THIS LAMASERY. THAT SEEMS A SUBJECT WORTHIER OF OUR CONSIDERATION, JUST NOW.
QUITE SO, SAHIB. I SHALL THINK UPON IT.

HERE. YOU MAY HAVE THIS, IF YOU'D LIKE.
WHAT?

I THOUGHT YOU'D HAVE IT AS A TROPHY, OR A MEMENTO.
AT THE VERY LEAST, YOU COULD GET A GOOD PRICE FOR IT.
BUT, I GAVE IT TO YOU.
AND IT'S SERVED ITS TURN–
–ANYWAY KEEP IT. OR LEAVE IT HERE. I AIN'T CARRYIN' IT.

WE DON'T GIVE OUT RIBBONS OR ORDERS, YOU KNOW. AND WITH YOU IN PARTICULAR I FEEL WE'RE MORE APT TO CLIP YOU FOR YOUR MISTAKES THAN POINT OUT WHERE YOU'VE DONE WELL.
BUT THIS–YOUR FINDING IT, AND BRINGING IT TO ME: IT WAS WELL DONE. I DON'T KNOW YOU HAVEN'T SAVED US ALL, WITH THIS.

WULL–ONLY IF 'AT'S SHAMBHALA UP THERE, WOT? AS REMAINS TO BE SEEN.
MR. RENTON–LOOK AT ME. I SAY YOU'RE A GOOD SOLDIER, LAD. AND SO YOU ARE. AND YOU'VE PROVED IT ENOUGH.

YOU'RE A D–MNED LITTLE IMP, TOO, THOUGH I KNOW A GREAT MANY GOOD MEN WHO STARTED THAT WAY.
I SUPPOSE I DRIVE YOU HARDER AND PUT YOU IN MORE DANGER THAN I MIGHT ANY SON OF MINE. BUT I SEE THE GOOD IT'S DONE YOU. AND I'M PROUD OF THIS YOUNG MAN I SEE.

...HM? I AM. I'LL HAVE YOU KNOW THAT.
-ALL RIGHT-
DO YOU KNOW IT? I'LL HEAR IT FROM YOU.
AYE, SIR. CHR–ST.

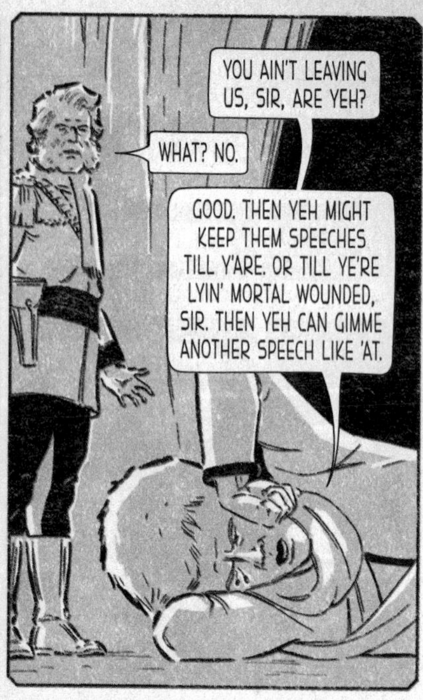
YOU AIN'T LEAVING US, SIR, ARE YEH?
WHAT? NO.
GOOD. THEN YEH MIGHT KEEP THEM SPEECHES TILL Y'ARE. OR TILL YE'RE LYIN' MORTAL WOUNDED, SIR. THEN YEH CAN GIMME ANOTHER SPEECH LIKE 'AT.

IT'S ALL TOO SICK-MAKIN', IF I'M BEIN' HONEST.

Ultimately, after a climb of days, Bertram finds himself smiled upon by the Buddha, and strangely enough this is not just another dream-occurrence. His elephant has actually found the head of the stairs, and he is being handed out from beneath the howdah's canopy. He would like, he thinks, to lie in contemplation of the deity a bit longer—that serene, unlined face, as free of concern as the Four Kings are watchful and wary around him—but there is not time for it. Bertram is tipped upright and stood on his feet, and led off into another torch-lit hallway with his hand clasped in Miss Harrow's.

A corps of Nepalese, meanwhile, disperse themselves along the line of elephants, not to unburden the animals but to keep them back from the inner edge of the stairs, which they do with staves of figured bamboo. There is a man in lama's robes standing at the head of the stairs, too, ringing his own staff on the flags and waving the beasts up one at a time with a great air of ceremony. The dragoons are made to wait for some time, particularly those farthest down the stairs; though they are too tired by now to complain of the delay and the last of them—Mr. Buchan—scarcely notices it. He is bent over a sketch of the ceiling fresco, noting with his usual care the Buddha, the Kings surrounding him, the square shaft cut into the deity's navel at the apex of the rock... He is still adding details when he is called down from his elephant. There is something in the urgency of the voices that makes him leap with pad and pencil in either hand before he has quite gauged the drop or shaken the blood back into his legs. The result, of course, is a horrible spill on the stone platform, though the expected chorus of laughter and jeers fails to materialize. The dragoons seem to be too far ahead, and the Nepalese too busy for jokes. He has just time to snap up his notepad as the guides raise him and prop a forked branch beneath his underarm, and then he is being pushed ahead after the others.

He has been aware, possibly since the elephants first stopped, of a dull light and a little tremor, both repeating intermittently. He had been too absorbed in his sketch to consider these properly, but now, from deep within this firelit hall, a heavy grating sound drums upon his breastbone, and a viscid white light gathers and wanes, and he recalls at last what he has come here to see.

'Is this *it*, then?' he demands of the men steadying him: 'We're here?'

There are several dozen Nepalese lining the tunnel's sides, all bobbing their heads, whether understanding him or no. Mostly they are waving him on, tugging at his arms and his tunic. He gathers he is being rushed ahead against another occurrence of this sound and light.

'Yes, all right, but how to *behave*, now?' This he seems suddenly anxious to know. Bowing and penitential, is it? Not really possible at the pace they've got him keeping. Hand over the heart? Seems absurd, this far out from the Occident. Exhibit the crown of the head, then…? He hands his crutch aside and smoothes his hair, tugs his coat straight and shoots his cuffs. The tunnel takes a right-angled turn into an even narrower channel, crowded with yet more bodies. Four blows sound from a stone door at the end of the passage: something has beat upon it from the far side. The door is heaved open by long-robed Nepalese, and the tunnel dissolves in white light. Starved and exhausted and half-lame, and far from certain any of this is really happening, Buchan goes forth as many of his race do when they are called back to the Almighty's side–That is, bothering mightily over the *protocol* of the thing. What had Mr. Priddish done in this spot? he wonders. Is there some Nepali greeting or another, or some holy text he ought to recite…? It is his Englishman's way of bearing up in the face of the imponderable, by looking to oneself and one's own readiness. Not, 'What is Shambhala?' but, 'How does one present himself, when he has found it at last?'

…And–also, sorry–this as a second, undeveloped thought: but, why in this sacred place, at a moment when some bit of reflection and ritual are surely in order: why is everyone suddenly in such a tearing *hurry*?

VI.

NN–HOLD A MOMENT–!

OUGHH–
KGLCKK!

28º 07' 58" N Lat | 85º 04' 17" E Long
Channa-Achala Mountain Lamasery, Central Nepal
November, 1918

YES, GOOD. THIS IS ALL OF THEM...? GOOD.
KEEP THE GUNS TRAINED ON THEM.

THANK YOU, BROTHER.
SABBE SATTA BHAVANTU SUKHITATTA.

GENTLEMEN: I OFFER YOU THE CONVENTIONAL GREETINGS.

DO YOU KNOW, MAJOR, IN THE ABBOT'S COURTYARD, IN ROMANIA, THE FULL INSCRIPTION READS, 'A THREE-MILE PEAK, WELL-HID BENEATH THE SEA.'
THE MAN'S INCREASE OVER TIME, YOU SEE, HAS DISPLACED THE WATER IN HIS TANK, AND RAISED THE WATER-LINE OVER THE SECOND HALF OF THE PHRASE.
FITTINGLY, I SUPPOSE.

BUT IT'S PUT YOU ON THE OTHER END OF THE GLOBE FROM WHERE YOU OUGHT TO BE. PRECISELY THE OPPOSITE END, AS A MATTER OF FACT.
HERE, INSTEAD OF THE CITY, THERE IS A THING CALLED AN 'ANTIPODAL OCCURRENCE' COMING IN A FEW DAYS' TIME.

THESE MEN–THEY MEAN TO SEE WHAT EFFECT IT WILL PRODUCE ON YOUR BROTHER.
THEY'VE GOT HIM UP THERE, WAITING.

I DON'T KNOW IF IT WILL ANGER YOU OR RELIEVE YOU, MAJOR, TO LEARN THAT ARTHUR HAS NEVER REALLY FIGURED INTO ANY OF THIS, EXCEPT AS A SORT OF CAT'S PAW.
HIS RESOURCES DID GIVE US BERTRAM, THOUGH, AND BERTRAM GETS US INTO THE CITY–SO IF HE DERIVES ANY BENEFIT FROM HIS TREATMENT HERE, HE CAN TAKE IT AS A...KARMIC REWARD OF SOME SORT.

WHILE YOU MEN, FOR LEAVING US IN ROMANIA, AND PUTTING THE BOY TO NEEDLESS RISK, AND GENERALLY CAUSING NO END OF TROUBLE: YOU MUST PREPARE TO RECEIVE YOUR OWN REWARD.
I ANTICIPATE THEY'LL TRY TO MAKE YOU A USEFUL PART OF THIS ORDER, LIKE YOUR FRIEND MALTHROP, OR ELSE...
...OR ELSE I DON'T KNOW. YOU'LL HAVE TO FIND OUT.

BE OFF, MR. SLOANE. YOU HAVEN'T TIME TO LINGER OVER BUSINESS.
UNLIKE MYSELF, AND THESE GENTLEMEN, WHO HAVE ONLY TIME.
YES, THOUGH: I WONDER IF THIS WERE STRICTLY NECES-SARY, BROTHER POLISSON?

NECESSARY? NO, I DOUBT THAT IT IS.
BUT...YOU'LL DO IT ANYWAY. I SEE.
WELL: YOU SHOULD KNOW I DON'T APPROVE.
THOUGH I CAN'T HELP, EI-THER, MAJOR, THE ENEMIES YOU'VE MADE.

MIND YOU, SIR–LET THE GURKHAS DO THAT.
AH-AH: STAY WITH US, NOW...
OH, IT'S SAFE ENOUGH. NOT BUT THAT A MAN COULD DIE RIGHT HERE, FROM THE ILL-WILL ALONE.

ADIEU, MAJOR. WE MIGHT HAVE ARRANGED THINGS BETWEEN US, YOU KNOW.

ALL RIGHT, THAT'S DONE. BRING THEM UP, NOW. UP! THAT'S IT.

WHAT HAVE YOU TO SAY TO THIS, MAJOR? MM? NOTHING...?
MY G–D, MR. SLOANE. GET THEM DOWN–
AFRAID WE CAN'T, DEAR. AND YOU WON'T DO THEM MUCH GOOD BY WATCHING.
MISS HARROW? COME. PLEASE. I'D RATHER I DIDN'T HAVE TO DRAG YOU.

THEY'RE KEEN TO SAY SOMETHING, HM?
...DON'T KICK, YOU OVER THERE– YOU'RE MAKING IT WORSE.
EVELYN–HE'LL BE ALL RIGHT...

THERE–THAT'LL DO. LET THEM DOWN.
BUT ONLY TO GET YOUR BREATH, GENTLEMEN; THEN YOU'RE GOING BACK UP. AND I WARN YOU, WE MAY BE AT THIS A WHILE...
I'LL EXPLAIN THIS TO BOTH OF YOU–
BERTRAM? DON'T LOOK, SON.

In whatever other ways my youth may have followed convention [*thus Mr. Sloane, to Bertram*], it was decided I would be educated from birth to certain mysteries. The greater part of this schooling took place at home, where my father's spiritual advisor—this 'Abbot' fellow, though I knew him as *Père* Sourire—where this man was my tutor and confessor. And there were outings, too: I would be called away every so often to witness, in one corner of the world or another, the appearance of a great column of light. This was simply a condition of my life, and I never knew a time when it was not so. A rather dreary life of reading and charting the cosmos and making various heretical devotions, interspersed with brief and dreamlike flashes of desert and jungle, and gatherings on the polar ice and on flotillas at sea. And it was not only the lights, for often I would see the summoned going toward them in procession, these pure souls who went in a kind of ecstasy with their feet trailing along the ground or even the water. And there were the impure, too, driven away, harried into death or lunacy or rotting in their sanatoria and hermits' retreats. And everywhere, compassing all of it, watching, were the black robes in their growing numbers. One can only imagine what a boy makes of these things.

Still, I was not given very much to

do on these outings. I was led there only to watch, like the others, from what was thought to be a safe distance. Yet it must have become obvious that I was not developing the complaints of mind and body that so often visited the men around me—that caused, for instance, the increase in Sourire's person that confined him eventually to his courtyard in Feritiva. It was thought I'd developed a sort of tolerance to the lights through a limited and early exposure, as children may be inured to some forms of disease. And Sourire must have wondered at his luck, to have discovered this resistance in a young man already under his protection. I was singled out for special use, though it would take Sourire and his circle some years to decide what this use might be.

One can learn only so much about anything, you see, from a safe remove. Sourire knew how to anticipate, through his readings of the heavens, the City's movements, and so how to find it. He knew who might approach it and who might not, and how close the impure might come, and various other rules that governed its appearances among men. But he was no more enlightened than you or me as to what the City actually *is*, in its essence: Why should it appear at all? Who were its aboriginals? What was its construction? Had it any plans with regard to our own race...? He'd nothing after decades of study and travel but his 'rules' and these questions. His stewardship of the City's secrets—which duty he conceived and imposed on himself, you know—this seemed to pass without the City's notice. There was not the least bit of privileged knowledge tossed over its walls, in all those years, to the black-robed men waiting outside. They were all in the rather ridiculous position of safeguarding a thing that was not theirs, and of which they were wholly ignorant. (You might say this put them on a footing with most religions of the world, though I would take care who I said that to.)

Anyway, there was a turn in our affairs just before the war, and this came about quite by accident, as these things will. Sourire had developed a practice of luring travelers toward the City, and letting them approach as close as they might before he'd recapture them for study. I had helped him in more than one of these affairs, and I was there in Canada when Arthur Ogden penetrated the City and brought out his fragment of jade. It was revelatory, of course, this mishap of Ogden's; and we began that night to plot our own attempts on his model.

Over the next two years there were new travelers sent in, unwitting and coerced. There were volunteer teams of our own. There were colored lenses and pressurized envelopes and great contraptions like diving-bells, but all to little gain. If we got a man in at all, if he didn't die outright on the descent, he would become blinded, disoriented, useless for identifying and gathering artifacts. A man must be able to keep his wits in this environment, you see. He must be proof against the wasting air of the City, whether it be through some natural power of his constitution, or–the thought came inevitably–through some resistance developed in him, over a long and measured exposure to the place....

Well. I could see of course where all this was heading. Though I think it was my own impatience, more than prudence, that drove me to lead a trial myself.

I tell you all of this at second-hand, Bertram. I recall none of it, only what Sourire has told me long after the fact. I *do* know what brings a man to forsake himself in his search for the City, though, and I know because I've felt it in me these last years, as I have seen it in Sourire and his order, and in Miss Harrow. It has to do with the loss or renouncement of one's ties to the earthly life, or the failure to develop these in the first place. One conceives that his world and its pursuits are illusory, without point; its people are shades, incomprehensible and bizarre. And if he lives at all in this world he is only waiting in the belief that his life is a prelude to some greater and truer existence....And do you know? It is all perfectly *true*. I think it's the great irony of this irreligious age that our cynics and all these clever men of science are actually the ones in error: there really *is* a higher existence that one may discover, to which he may aspire, against which his world is a crude sort of farce. I was raised, you see, not just in this belief but with certain *knowledge* of it. Yet I was mistaken to think this was all one could take or learn from this world, that this was the extent of its use, that the place was but a waiting-stage for us, and a humiliation.

To live in this view, Bertram, as I appreciate now—this is to miss a greater point. I think we cannot be put here only to vault past this world into some unknown Other. There ought to be a meaning as true as any in how we negotiate this life, and a value in mixing with our fellows, in loving and enjoying love's receipt, and in being content to have done so. The rest, I feel, is what will ultimately prove meaningless. And if developing ties to this world and exercising love and compassion are not the very *point* of us—I cannot presume to know—then we are at least better occupied in this way, I feel, than with the riddles of other worlds, which only prove impossible for us to solve and unhealthy even to ponder.

...But I stray from my point. It is enough to say that I ought to have learned these lessons sooner. A man without a stake in this world loses the guiding light of his humanity, and he will drift down any number of dark paths. Which is how I found myself circumstanced in June of 1914, on the eve of this trial I've mentioned.

I do not know if I'd loved very often up to that point (I rather doubt it), but I know I was called away from a young woman in India just as we prepared to wed. Sourire desired that I should be in the Americas, and that I should arrive with no more connection to this world than a *rope*, binding me quite literally to a few of his black-robed colleagues. And this is how it was. This is how I breached the City in the last days before the war.

We had trekked a hundred miles into the Honduran forest, and found the lights over a hidden *cenote*. I am told I finished off a drink (I had been in liquor since we'd docked at Punta Patuca), muttered some black imprecation and stepped from the shelf of rock in the manner of a suicide. And then it was down into the great cavern with me, down through the water, past old Mayan offerings to the lords of Xibalba and into I know not what.

In another thirty minutes they were stretching me out insensate on a reed mat, prying a little bundle out of my arms. And what do you think this bundle was? What do you think I'd snatched from this other world, and brought into ours? ...It was *you*, Bertram.

Mr. Sourire and his associates recorded your parents' entry into the City in the winter of 1904. I believe they'd taught in missionary schools in Africa and the South Pacific up to that point, and, more meaningfully for us, I believe they went to the City without children. That is to say, your parents were beings of this earth, while you and your sister were conceived and born inside the City's walls. Whatever your life was there, whatever place or stratum you occupied, it was—it *is*—your home. And when we took you from it, Sourire likened the feat (rather grandly) to the theft of an angel from heaven.

Not that he was to profit very much by it. You came into our world like an infant pulled through the trauma of birth, scarcely alive and wholly disoriented, and without use of your senses. They restored you, somewhat, to health and function, and you recovered your speech (you spoke in English, your parents having been British colonials); but like anyone arrived from anywhere about the City, you came utterly void of memories. There was only the palest flicker of your parents' faces in your first regression, and even this could not be called up a second time. They could not draw the least detail of the City from you, nor learn the smallest secret of your being, for all they ran you through their tests and trials—the horrors of which, I think, could only have compounded the harm we'd done you. And when the last of these men had taken his crack at you, when he had cleaned his instruments and given you up for a bad job, you were discarded at last, shut away in your workhouse at the southern end of the world, where if nothing else you would expire quietly with your secrets.

And it appears I wasn't much more help to Sourire and his friends than you were. I'd come awake, like you, without recall of our adventure or of anything leading up to it, though I suffered no other ill effects. I was—as the black-robes in Honduras put it—rather *enhanced* by the experience, and not in a way they found pleasant to behold. I suppressed the light around me, they said. I spoke warnings to them in languages they could not comprehend.

And I vanished from a stone chamber, sealed and guarded. I was simply there one moment and gone in the next. They called me a revenant, a ghost. And I do not think, in the final review, that they were very far wrong.

Our friend Mr. Ogden was pleased to point out once that I do not know what I am, and of course he is right to say so. I know that I'm *not* Mr. Sloane, particularly—or Durov, or Selescu, or whoever was lowered into the City—much as I may still hold in common with these men. I am not so much a man at all, I think, as the extension of a purpose. I exist—or I am given lease in this world—to accomplish something, the operative problem being that up to recently I hadn't known what this thing *was*. Whatever instruction I received in the City was left there, lost with all else on my way back up to the forest floor. I returned with just an instinct, or a guiding sense, of when I was nearing my object or drifting farther from it.

It needn't have been any great mystery, either. I think if I'd had the first hint of my dealings with Sourire, or if they'd told me my reasons for trekking into Honduras, I'd have filled in the rest myself.

I am on an errand, you see, to redress the wrong I've done. I was meant to find you, Bertram, and to return you to your home.

HM? ...MISS HARROW? YES: WE'VE SAID OUR GOOD-BYES, AND LEFT HER QUITE WELL. YOU NEEDN'T WORRY.
I KNOW THAT WILL PAIN YOU; AND CERTAINLY IT DID HER. BUT THERE WAS NO QUESTION OF HER COMING ALONG.

I TOLD MISS HARROW ALL THAT I'VE TOLD YOU, BERTRAM, AND A BIT ABOUT THE ARRANGEMENTS I'VE HAD TO MAKE.

I FELT SHE WAS OWED SOME EXPLANATION, AT LEAST, OF WHAT HER SEARCH HAD BEEN ABOUT, AND WHAT IT HAD COME TO.
AND SHE SEEMED TO GRASP THE GENERAL SHAPE OF THINGS.

...THOUGH I DON'T THINK THE REALITY OF IT, OR THE FULL WEIGHT OF WHAT MUST COME, STRUCK HER UNTIL SHE SAW MY AEROPLANE, WITH ITS SINGLE SEAT.

I THOUGHT THIS MIGHT BE THE APPREHENSION, FINALLY, OF HER FAILURE–SHE WOULD NOT EVER SEE HER CITY, AFTER ALL.
OR THAT, AFTER SO LONG A DEVOTION TO HER SEARCH, AND SO MANY YEARS OF TRAVEL, SHE COULD NOT CONCEIVE THAT SHE WOULD BE STARING AT JOURNEY'S END.

BUT IT WAS NONE OF THIS.
MAY I...

BERTRAM...? SWEETHEART, CAN YOU HEAR ME? COME FOR A MOMENT, WOULD YOU?

IT'S ALL RIGHT.
I'M GOING?
MM-HM. HOME, DEAR.

HERE:
YOU'RE GOING TO YOUR MUM, AND YOUR FATHER.
BUT, WHERE? ...NO, I THINK I OUGHT TO STAY.

NO, DEAR. THIS PLACE IS TOO, TOO AWFUL FOR YOU. YOU'LL GO TO YOUR HOME AND YOUR FAMILY...AND DO YOU KNOW? YOU'RE GOING TO HELP US ALL.
WHAT?

OH—I DON'T KNOW HOW, THIS TIME, BUT MR. SLOANE SAYS IT'S QUITE TRUE. IF YOU GO WITH HIM, AND ONLY STAY WELL TILL YOU ARRIVE, YOU AND HE'LL PUT THINGS RIGHT AGAIN.
YOU'LL SAVE ME, DEAR, LIKE YOU DID BEFORE. YOU REMEMBER THAT?
THE...MM. THEY WERE GOING TO HURT YOU.
YES. MY LITTLE GUARDIAN.

ALL IS WELL NOW. I PROMISE YOU.
...GOOD BOY.

OH, IT'S TOO MUCH. REALLY, I DON'T THINK I CAN BEAR IT.
I'M SORRY, MISS HARROW.
THOUGH YOU KNOW, YOU DESPAIRED ONCE THAT YOU'D NOT FOUND A PLACE FOR YOU IN THE WORLD. I MIGHT SEE EVIDENCE TODAY THAT YOU HAD.

A LOT YOU'D KNOW ABOUT IT.
...PERHAPS NOT. BUT I AM TOLD, BY A MAN BETTER-VERSED IN THESE THINGS, THAT ONE'S SOUL TENDS TO GROW IN COMMUNION WITH OTHERS. AND THAT THE CONNECTIONS BETWEEN US, ONCE MADE, TEND TO MULTIPLY.

WELL THAT'S LOVELY.
I WAS TOLD THAT IN RELATION TO YOU, MISS HARROW.
BY A MAN WHO FELT THAT OTHERS, TOO, HAD GOT A PLACE IN YOUR HEART.

MEANING...? OH. YES, I SUPPOSE.
I DON'T KNOW WHAT CONSOLATION YOU'LL FIND IN YOUR YOUNG CORPORAL, OR FOR HOW LONG. BUT I THINK YOU'LL FIND THE WORLD'S ASPECT CHANGED A BIT, OWING TO THIS CHANGE IN YOU.
...UNLESS YOU REALLY DO MEAN TO RENOUNCE ALL THAT, AND KEEP AFTER YOUR FLOATING CITIES FOREVER.
MM. IT'S A THOUGHT, ISN' T IT.

MR. SLOANE: PLEASE–YOU WON'T LET HIM...THAT IS, I CAN'T BEAR TO THINK HE'D SUFFER, OR BE TOO MUCH AFRAID. YOU'LL...YOU MUST AT LEAST TELL ME HOW IT ENDS WITH HIM. CAN YOU?
BUT...YOU KNOW I WON'T BE–
I KNOW. YES. BUT FIND A WAY, PLEASE.

MISS HARROW, YOU WON'T NEED ME TO TELL YOU. IF IT ENDS WELL WITH BERTRAM–AND I TRUST IT WILL–YOU'LL SEE SIGN IN THE WORLD.

YOU OUGHT TO STAY WITH THESE MEN FOR NOW, AND DON'T GO ANY NEARER THE LAMASERY. I DOUBT YOU'LL HAVE VERY LONG TO WAIT. GOOD-BYE.

<FATHER? LOOK.>
<YES. COME. HAND HIM UP.>

I DIDN'T PLAY WITH THE INKS. PLEASE DON'T TELL THEM I DID.
...BEG YOUR PARDON?
WE WEREN'T ALLOWED TO. I PROMISE YOU I DIDN'T.
SORRY, I DON'T—BERTRAM?

LET'S STAY AWAKE, CAN YOU?
BERTRAM...?

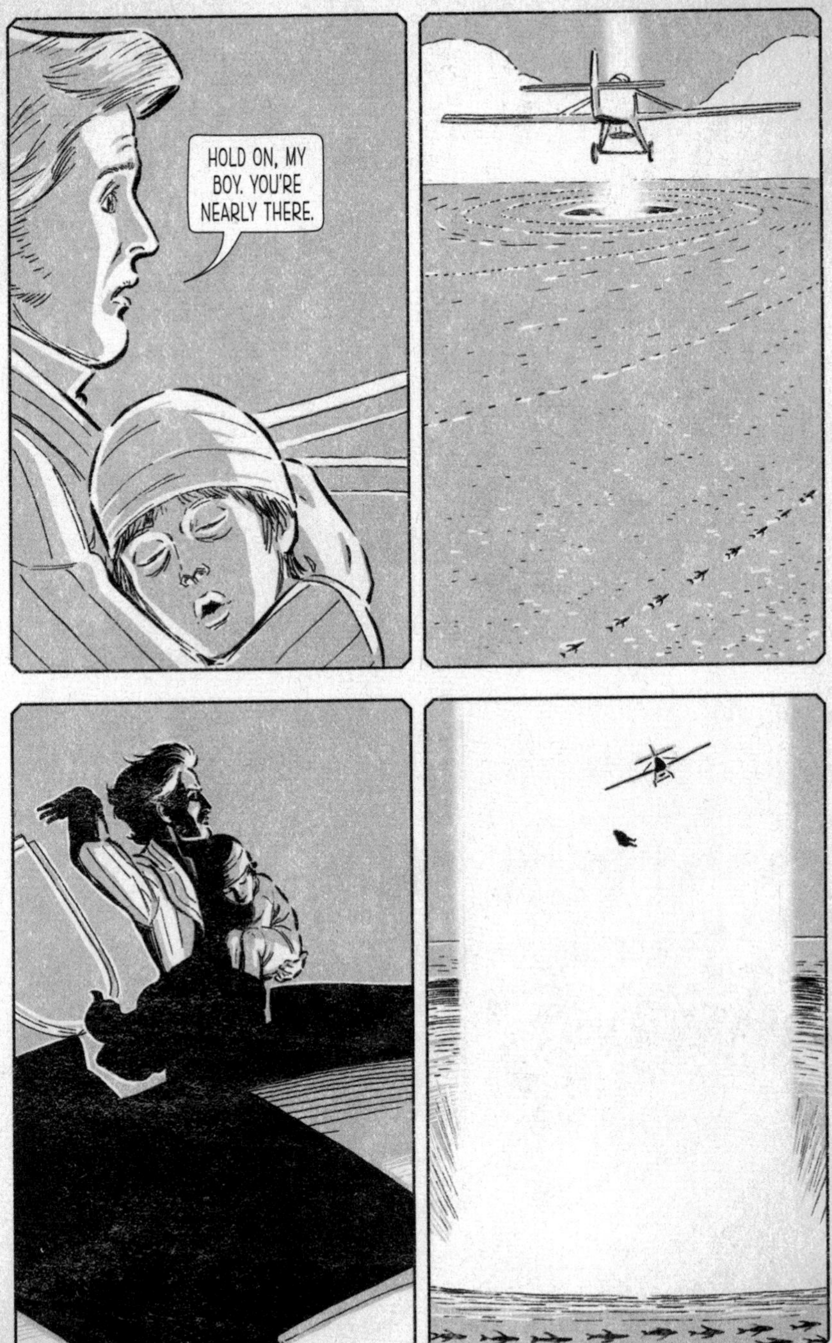
HOLD ON, MY BOY. YOU'RE NEARLY THERE.

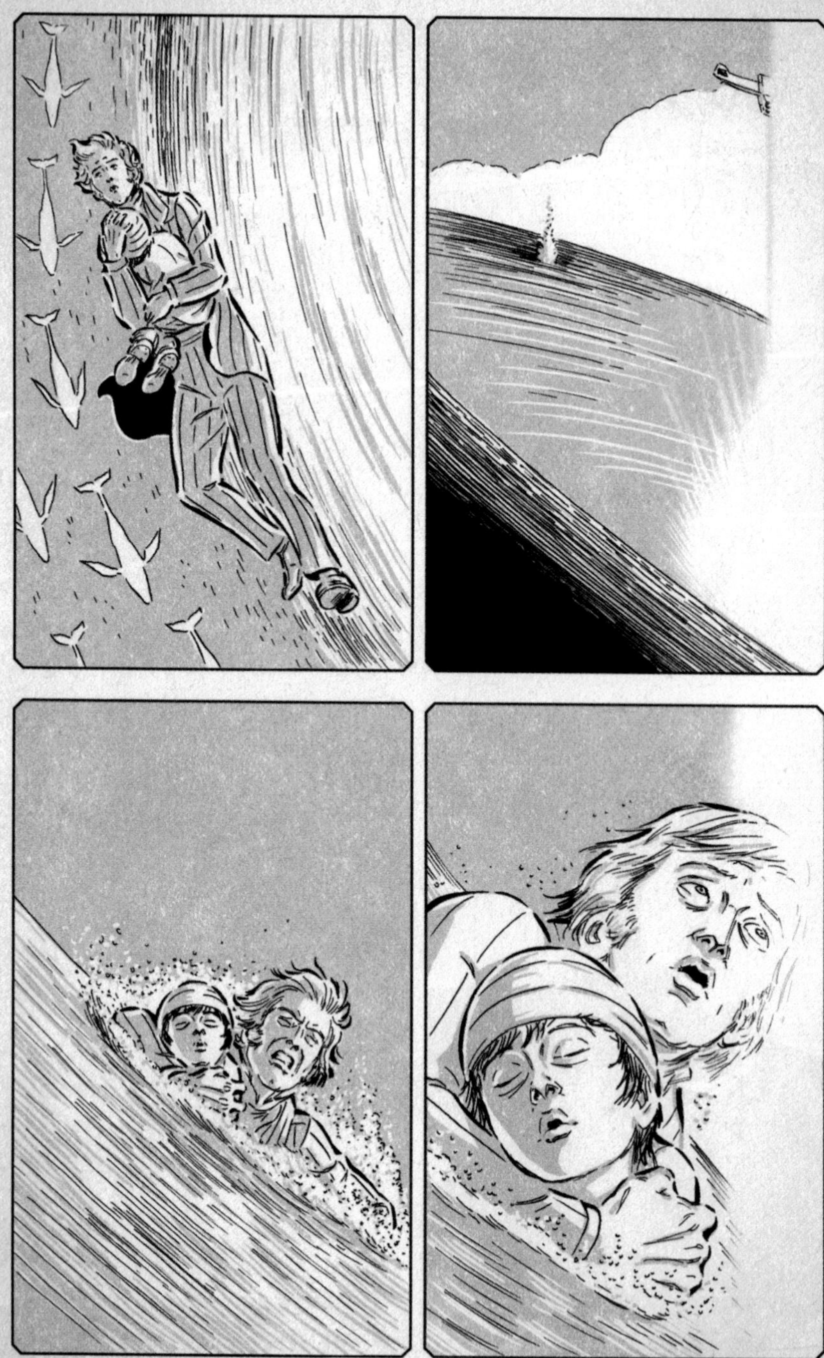

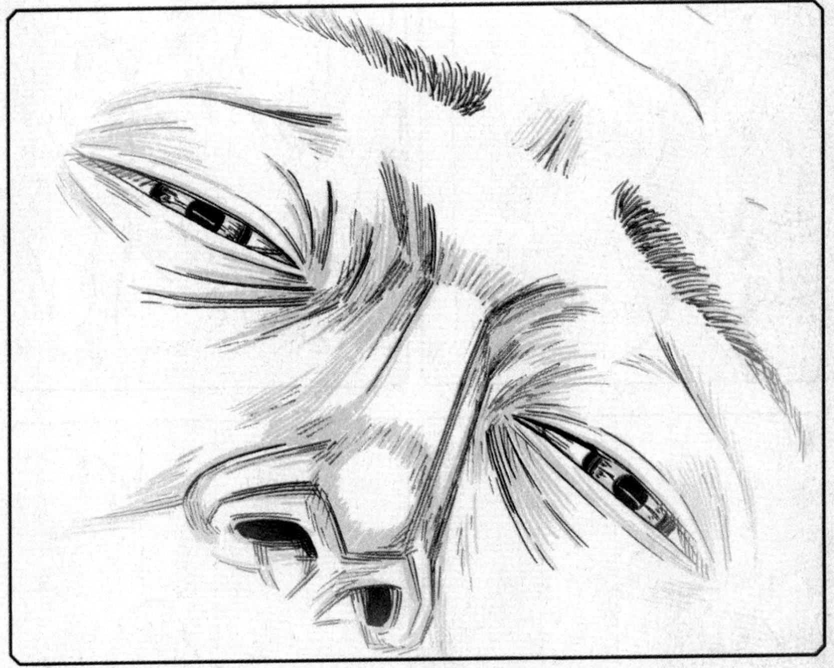

BERTRAM, I'M AFRAID I'VE...TO GET US HERE, YOU KNOW, I'VE HAD TO MAKE CERTAIN CONCESSIONS.
FOR MY SAFE PASSAGE TO NEPAL, AND AWAY FROM THERE WITH YOU, I'VE PROMISED THEM OGDEN, AND THEN WHATEVER REMNANT THERE IS OF ME.

AND–THOUGH I SUPPOSE IT'S RATHER UNCHARACTERISTIC OF ME–I DO MEAN TO HONOR THESE COMMITMENTS.

...OR, MOST OF THEM, I DO.

SIR? ...MAJOR?

...KEYS. FROM MR. SLOANE. IMAGINE THIS LARGER ONE WILL FIT THE DOOR.
BUT–
I DON'T KNOW. MIGHT HAVE...RECOVERED SOME MEMORY OF INDIA. IT MAY BE HE SERVES OTHER MASTERS THAN THESE BLACK-ROBES. OR SERVES NO ONE AT ALL.

...ANY RATE. IT'S NOTHING WE'LL LEARN SITTING HERE. LET US SEE YOUR HANDS.

HOW ART THOU FALLEN FROM HEAVEN, O SON OF THE MORNING? *HEH-HEHHH...!*

«POP!»

AH: GOOD, SIR.
AN' WHEN I FIND YEH BELOW, MY MANNIE, I'LL GIVE YEH A SIGHT WORSE THAN THAT.

WE'RE HOLDIN' HERE, THEN?
AYE, YOU'D RATHER WE CATCH MORE OF 'EM COMING OUT, SIR?
MAJOR...?
SAT SRI AKAL, SAHIB. PEACE GRANT YOU PEACE.
WHAT'S HE MEAN? HEY–?

I'M FOR THE SUMMIT, AND I GO ALONE FROM HERE.

YOU MEN ARE FREE TO...
...TO WHICH, SIR?
HOLD A MOMENT.

HUH. COMPANY, IN'NIT.
AYE. AND POMEROY HIMSELF UP T'FRONT, IF I DON'T MISTAKE 'IM.
...AND HERE I'M GONE THROUGH MY LAST CARTRIDGE.

WHAT HAVE YOU LEFT US, MAJOR? NOT VERY MUCH, HM?
...THOUGH ONE NEVER KNOWS.

GO ON, GENERAL. FIND US SOMETHING THEY HAVEN'T BURNED.

I CAN SEE WE'RE JUST PASSING, MAJOR, BUT I'VE BEEN MULLING A PROPOSAL FOR YOU, AND WHILE I'VE GOT YOU I THINK YOU SHOULD HEAR IT.
WELL...?
YES: I'D LIKE YOU TO RE-FORM THIS COMPANY AND MAKE CAMP OUTSIDE BOMBAY. SEND ME YOUR OFFICERS IN THIRTY DAYS, AND I'LL HAVE A NEW COMMISSION PREPARED FOR YOU.

WE'LL AGREE TO PUT THIS...LATEST ADVENTURE UNDER THE LAST COMMISSION, AND HAVE AN END OF IT THERE.
HOW WOULD THAT SUIT YOU, THEN? BECAUSE IT STRIKES ME AS RATHER MORE THAN FAIR.
AYE, THOUGH–MILORD, SIR: IF ANY MAN OF US SHOULD FAIL TO REPORT–?
–WHY? IS ONE OF YOU PLANNING NOT TO REPORT?

...BECAUSE I SHOULD BE CLEAR: IF YOU HAVEN'T GOT ALL OF YOU ROUNDED UP AND QUITE READY TO SERVE THE COMMONWEALTH, YOU SHOULDN'T SHOW YOURSELVES ANYWHERE NEAR INDIA.
IT'S THE WHOLE COMPANY OR NONE OF YOU, MAJOR. I'D LIKE TO BE UNDERSTOOD ON THIS POINT.
AYE, SIR. VERY GOOD.
...MAJOR? I'LL HAVE YOU SAY IT.
I UNDERSTAND.

GOOD. THEN I SHOULD RATHER SEE YOU ALL IN A MONTH, THAN OTHERWISE.
GOOD DAY, YOU MEN.

GO, SAHIB. WE WILL FIND OUR WAY FROM HERE.

NO. WAIT FOR ME.
WON'T BE A MINUTE.

WHAT'S THIS, HAVILDAR?
FOUND THEM, SIR, ABOUT TO CARRY THESE CHESTS AWAY. STARTED RUNNING BACK AND THROWING THE BOOKS ON THE FIRE, AS SOON AS THEY'D SPOTTED US.

WE GOT TO MOST OF THEM, SIR, BEFORE THERE WAS VERY MUCH DAMAGE.

AH: SO YOU DID. EXCELLENT.
WE'VE THE SORT OF MEN WHO CAN WORK OUT A CYPHER LIKE THIS, SURELY?
YES, SIR. WE'VE GOT OUR BEST AT BOMBAY.
GOOD. EXCELLENT.

PUT THESE MEN UNDER GUARD, HAVILDAR, AND CONTINUE LOOKING.
WELL DONE, ALL OF YOU.

...ARTHUR?

UH? OH, YES: IT'S ME, JOHN. AND HOW DO YOU LIKE THIS? BIT MORE MY OLD SELF, WHAT? THESE SURROUNDINGS AND THE... THE COMPANY HERE NOTWITHSTANDING.

YOU JUST STEPPED FROM YOUR BOX LIKE THIS?
MM? OH: YOU'LL HAVE TO ASK THEM.
BUT I SUPPOSE IT WAS SOMETHING LIKE THAT. IT'S ALL THE LIGHTS, YOU KNOW.

...THOUGH I WOULDN'T GET MUCH CLOSER, JOHN. THEY'VE A WONDERFUL EFFECT ON BROKEN OLD BODIES LIKE US, THESE LIGHTS. BUT I DON'T THINK THEY'LL DO YOU ANY GOOD.

CAN YOU GET OVER TO ME, THEN? WE'D LIKE TO HAVE YOU OUT OF HERE, ARTHUR.
OUT OF HERE? OH: NO, THAT WON'T BE POSSIBLE. I THINK YOU MUST KNOW THAT, JOHN.
EVEN IF YOU HADN'T CONSIDERED UP TO NOW WHY YOU'VE COME.

...WELL YOU'RE HERE TO SAY GOOD-BYE, AREN'T YOU.

SORRY, JOHN. HATE TO WORRY YOU–
ME? I SHOULD HOPE YOU'RE BEARING UP, ARTHUR.
MM? OH, I AM, YES. THOUGH IT'S STRANGE, YOU KNOW–I'VE BEEN LIVING IN THESE OLD MEMORIES, LATELY, THESE SHINING OLD DAYS–NOW THAT I'M...NOW THAT IT'S ALL PAST, YOU KNOW.
I THINK THERE WAS ONE EASTER, JOHN, WE'D OUR COUSINS IN, AND THEY TAUGHT US NEEDLE'S EYE AND WE WERE AT IT TILL DARK, RUNNING ALL THROUGH THE WOODS...

...AND ALL THOSE DAYS AT THE SHORE. CLEAN AND SIMPLE SOULS, WE WERE, AND LITTLE RUNNING LEGS TO CARRY THEM AND NOT MUCH MORE.
I SUPPOSE THE SHAME OF IT IS WE'D HAVE TO RUN SO LONG, TILL THESE DAYS ARE GONE OUT OF MEMORY, AND WE'RE COVERED UP IN THESE WASTING OLD BODIES...
BUT YOU AND I WERE BOYS, ONCE, JOHN. I WAS YOUR OLDER BROTHER. I DO HOPE YOU REMEMBER HOW IT WAS, WITH US.
I DO.

WELL. I SUPPOSE I HAVEN'T MUCH MORE TO SAY ABOUT IT; ONLY THAT. YOU SHOULDN'T WORRY, I HAVEN'T SUDDENLY GOT PHILOSOPHY, JOHN.
AND YOU'RE NOT AFRAID?

NO. NO, IT'S MORE THAT...WELL, YOU SEE, ALREADY THE LIGHTS ARE FAILING. I'D RATHER YOU WEREN'T HERE WHEN THEY GO OUT. REALLY, YOU SHOULDN'T HAVE TO SEE WHAT WE ARE...

...AND THINK OF SOMETHING TO TELL FAN, WON'T YOU? NOTHING REALLY LEAPS TO MIND.
I WILL.

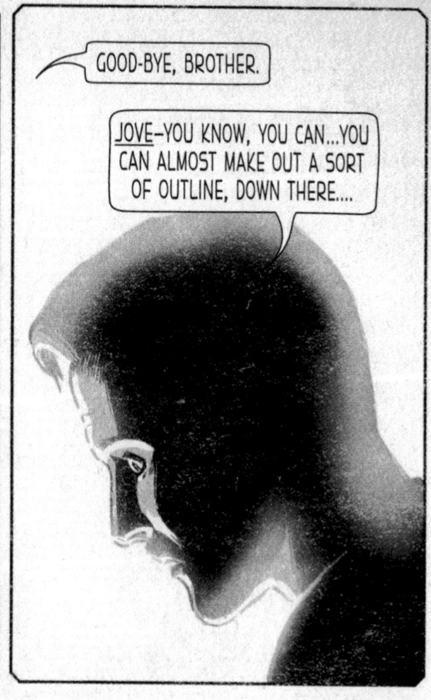
GOOD-BYE, BROTHER.
JOVE—YOU KNOW, YOU CAN...YOU CAN ALMOST MAKE OUT A SORT OF OUTLINE, DOWN THERE....

IT'S A FINE PLACE, BERTRAM, AND A FIT HOME FOR YOU. I PROMISE YOU, I'LL KEEP IT SAFELY HID.

THANK YOU, DEAR, FOR SHOWING ME. I HOPE YOU'LL FORGIVE ME EVER FOR COMING.

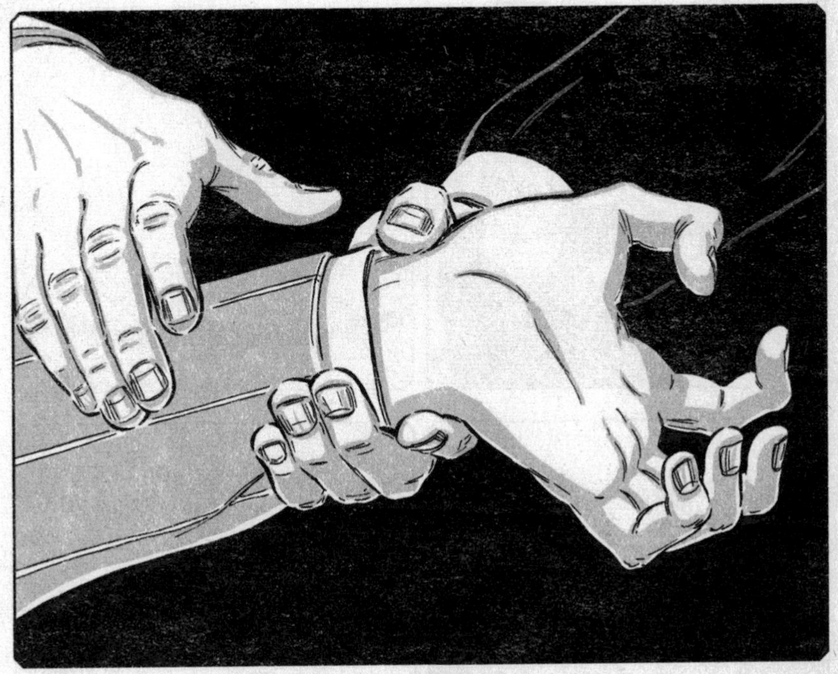

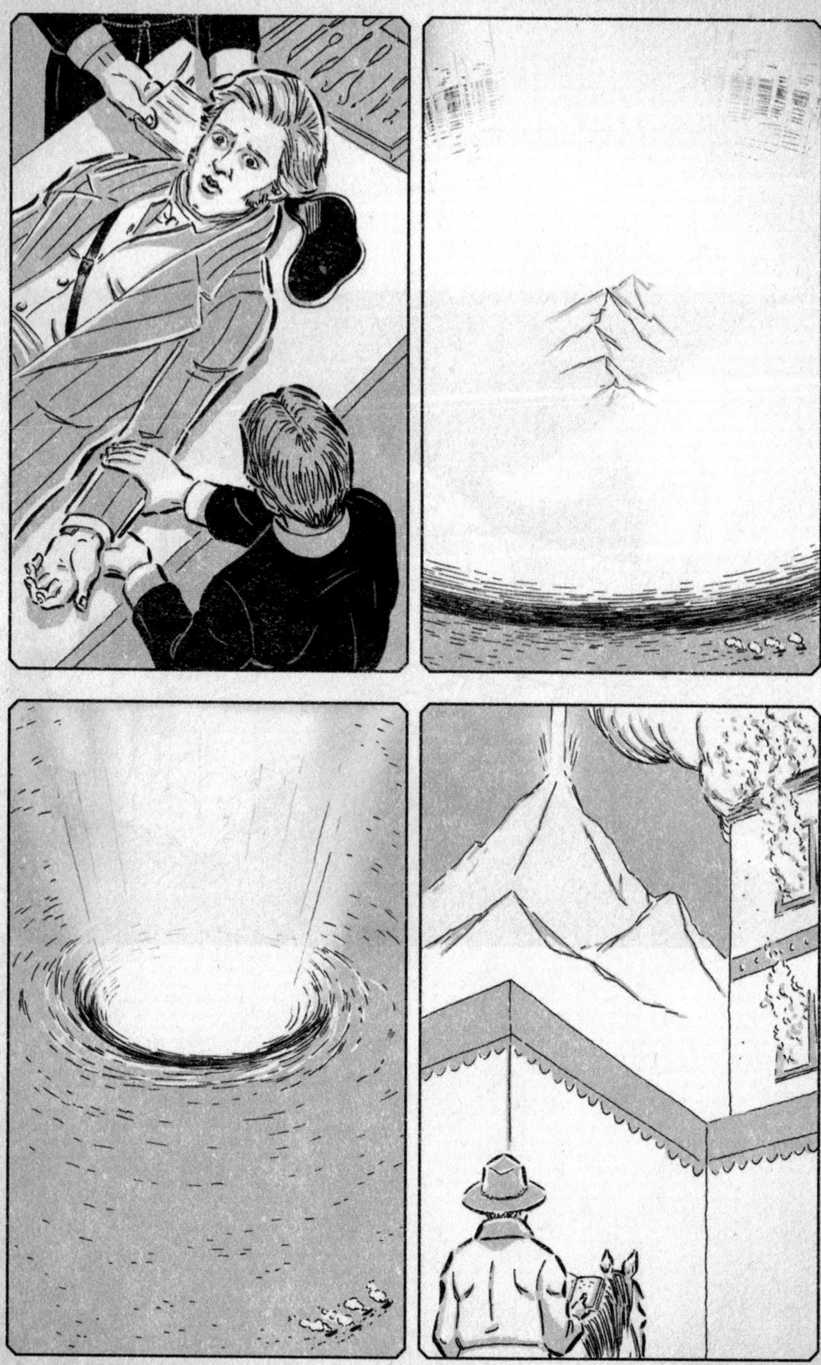

...I SAY, MR. RENTON: I TOLD MAJOR YOU WOULD NOT SO EASILY LEAVE HIM. BUT HERE YOU'RE TAKING THIS RATHER IN STRIDE.
WHAT? WHAT MAKES YEH THINK I'D LEAVE 'IM?

MM? OH—WELL: HE'S GONE BACK THAT WAY, HASN'T HE?
AYE, AN' WHEN HE'S DONE, WHERE DOES HE GO? TO INDIA'S WHERE.
YES, BUT SO WILL WE ALL. AND INDIA IS A BIG PLACE.

AYE, BUT I KNOW RIGHT WHERE HE GOES, DON'T I? AN' THERE HE'LL FIND ME. HE CAN DO ALL HE LIKES TILL THEN.
I CAN WAIT.
I SEE. VERY GOOD, SAHIB.

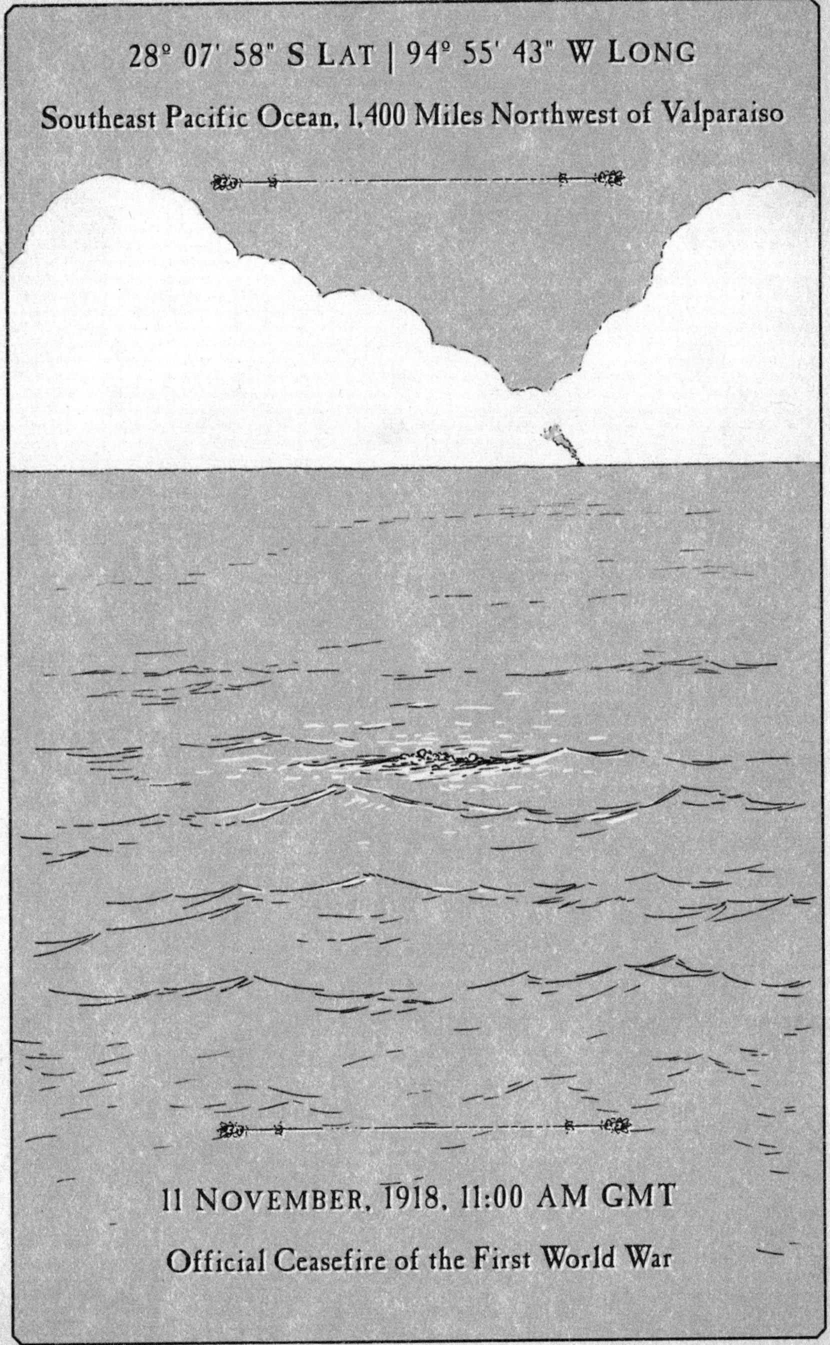

28º 07' 58" S LAT | 94º 55' 43" W LONG
Southeast Pacific Ocean, 1,400 Miles Northwest of Valparaiso
11 NOVEMBER, 1918, 11:00 AM GMT
Official Ceasefire of the First World War

END *of* VOLUME ONE

A Few Final, *Possibly* OVERHEATED, *but* *Nonetheless* HEARTFELT *Words of* ACKNOWLEDGMENT

...AND HERE WE ARE. You know, I'd turned to this thinking I might dash off a few names and survey a bit of who's done what, and then I'd send it along and maybe break for lunch. Well. A week has passed now, I've got piles of notes and drafts and I've twice been to the Mount to hear what Kevin makes of all this. I've thought long on the meaning of *acknowledgment* and on the people I'm about to name and, of course, on the unseemliness of wading into this section on a note of self-reference (conclusion there: it can't be avoided). Really, these are things I've been revolving since Keith Quinn floated the idea of a fictionalized Explorers Club in the first place. And in all the time since then, through all the last week's focused efforts and all the floundering and false starts, I haven't come away with any good answers, only a few hard realizations, which are roughly these: one, this won't be a business of a couple or three neat paragraphs, or a few hours or weeks or years of consideration. I don't know if I can even sort out, at this point, after such a long and arduous and communally joined process, exactly who's done what and when, let alone how they've done it or in God's name *why*. Worse, these are real people who've taken action in real life, and there is a standard in reality I'll have to measure these words against. There is a real and palpable weight of gratitude I feel, that I'll carry to the end of my life. "Thanks," as Kevin says, begins to sound like a terribly small word; and here it's all I've really got. I suppose this will have to stand for my answer, then, for now. And if I can't properly—or even remotely—"acknowledge" all or any of the people who've played a part in this book, I do at least mean to go down trying.

So—*Ahem*:

EIGHT YEARS AGO I WAS IN A HOTEL ROOM with my brother, CHRIS BAIRD, and friend KEITH QUINN, the three of us waving sketches and scraps of written material, pointing and grunting like Early Men, all for the—maybe you'd say *benefit*—of KEVIN COSTNER and his associate ROBIN JONAS, the latter having brought the five of us together. We conjured shamelessly with names like Conrad and Kipling and Edward Gorey. We brought out stories and maps and concept drawings of men and women with great misshapen heads. We should, by rights, have faced all the familiar, scolding questions—Yes, but what else is this *like*? How do you *sell* it? Why isn't it *finished*? What are you even *asking us for*?—and then shown to hotel security. But there was Kevin with a print of the steamship *Virago* in his hand, pointing out details in the rendering, asking about weathering on the ship's sides, and getting—I hope it isn't too corny to say—right on board the thing with us. This was—is—a born storyteller and enthusiast, and you learn this immediately on meeting him. Somehow that fascination Kevin felt as a boy when running across Walt Disney (as in, physically colliding with him) or outlasting his friends to see all of *How the West Was Won* in the original Cinerama—&c. &c.—somehow this wonder and openness to inspiration has stayed with him, and hasn't diminished but only burned brighter through his decades of hard-won success. In my own experience you meet either the visionary or the doer, but very seldom do you find the two paired in the same person; and if ever a body has these qualities and adds *success* to them, this inevitably spells the end of one quality or both. Those who've claimed the heights rarely seem eager to climb back down and start over; they become disinclined to work, they'd rather not look small again. But, as it happens, none of this seems to be a part of Kevin's calculations. Once he seizes on an idea he goes in on it full guns, and he *stays* in it unwaveringly and for good. And from our own first meeting forward he has proven to be one of the few constants in *The Explorers Guild*, helping variously as its writer, editor and art director, its proselytizer, patron and mentor and, as frequently needed, the best of all possible cornermen.

What he has done for *Explorers* has, in short, become unclassifiable. But in strict terms of authorship, he has dictated passages and points of story that are now too numerous to list (the through-line of Mulcairn and his horse, as one example, is entirely—and quintessentially—Kevin's); and where he's not speaking directly from the page it is his influence shaping things, everywhere. I've been eight years working with him on one project and another, watching how he acts and how he treats people; I've taken in his unique slant on the world and processed comments, continually, like "Yeah, but you know Buchan would never *say* something like that." I've seen Kevin weather setbacks and criticisms, both cheap and legitimate, with patience and humility, and I've seen him take our wins with equally good grace. I've listened to his thoughts on story and his remembrances and musings, for all that I'm jabbering the whole time myself and seeming, I think, not to listen (and for some picture of how this works, I point out that Ogden and Renton are, to some degree, the two of us in caricature). But all this has gone to the expansion and refinement of our own story, is my point. Kevin has taken a flighty sort of fairy tale and matured it, sewn it together and grounded it in a language of humanity. So how, ultimately, to quantify an influence like this? I'm not sure I can. His contribution has grown too amorphous now, too encompassing, too much the essence of this book. I might have played some of the notes, as they say, but this music is all Kevin's. And what great fortune on my part to have met a friend (as I hope to say) and coconspirator like this! In a better world I think more of us would.

With Kevin, anyway, we came to the Tig offices and joined our efforts with those of JASA MCCALL—still one of the shrewder and more committed souls I've found in this city—and with AUSTIN GILMORE, a great talent in his own right. There is no way to count or characterize all the hours Jasa and Austin have logged with us or the miles we've traveled, and I don't know that I'll get to work down my debt to either of them. But I do hope they get some reward or recognition worthy of their efforts, something even grander than, say, a fumbling mention in the back of this book.

On which—our book—for all the contributions of the above-named creators and allies, our Volume One would never have reached daylight without the support and vision and the persistent efforts of our extraordinary partners. And this may sound like a generic line of praise, but really: try hustling some unorthodox new property around to the gatekeepers of our popular culture. You'll get to know just how resolved you and your friends are, and you'll appreciate what a unique sort of individual it is who raises a hand from the other side of the table. We'd been many years kissing frogs before FONDA SNYDER ventured to say she might know what to do with this project. Fonda we now know as a rare sort of artistic spirit who seems to circulate everywhere in a cloud of goodwill, and deservedly. It was through Fonda that we met the almost frighteningly competent ROB WEISBACH; and I imagine, even as you're reading this, Rob is out there solving, fixing, distilling, enhancing, explaining, or otherwise making something better, or else just teaching some hapless soul to speak intelligibly. Together Fonda and Rob have agented this project, which I realize might mean any number of things, but I can say in this case there isn't much they *haven't* done. They were there early on to help Keith and me craft our pitch, and to shape the piece generally, and they're with the project still as guiding influences. And anyone who's had to beg and harass an agent into showing the *least* interest in what they're doing will appreciate what a rare find we've made in Fonda and Rob.

From our new footing in New York, anyway, with Fonda and Rob, the project made its next big leap, and this time it was JUDITH CURR and her team at

Atria Books providing the landing place. SARAH DURAND and DANIEL LOEDEL helped to usher us in, and to settle us with the levelheaded and many-armed PETER BORLAND, our steady and gentlemanly hand at the helm, whom we might shorthand as this book's editor, though, again, the word hardly covers his contribution. Peter enlisted the help of one PETER GUZZARDI, who fell right in with our egos-at-the-door policy and brought his immense talents to all aspects of our story; and it is another credit to Peter Borland that he'd have found and tapped this wise and veteran soul. I can't imagine editors being much better suited than Peters B. or G. to the project's needs or to my own. DANA SLOAN and JIM THIEL dove headlong with me into hazards of design and production past counting and, if you're holding this, they've come through with solutions on all fronts. DANIELLA WEXLER helped Peter Borland carry things forward and kept all parties connected for three-plus years, across four time zones. ALBERT TANG, taking inspiration from our favorite old books, gave us this lovely cover design. JESSICA CHIN fought through our tangled mess of words and helped to comb it as straight as it was going to get. PAUL OLSEWSKI and ANDREA SMITH have helped us unleash this project on a formerly unsuspecting–and now I think fairly well-prepared–world. And for all of you at Atria who have yet to play your part at the time of this writing: you, too, have my sincerest thanks. This team has improved our book in all the ways it could be improved. And while any one of you, at any time, might have begged off, lost heart, reversed course, or just not known what to do, by some miracle none of you have. All this book's failings and miscalculations I will own myself. What Judith and this team have done, in Kevin's words, is to help our book become what it wanted to be; and I don't think you can ask any more from your publisher.

And I still, somehow, haven't touched yet on the work of contributing author STEPHEN MEYER. Stephen's "one foot on the road and one in the ditch" sensibility came as a perfect complement to Kevin's and my own, though I suspect Stephen's ditch runs a good deal deeper than mine, and his intellect and grasp of history loom at similar scales. Stephen tucked right into the world of *Explorers*, and his ideas and his prose have been worked frequently into this story, giving it dimensions both of strangeness and solidity that it would have suffered greatly without. If there is justice in the world you'll hear more from Stephen directly, and before too long.

The work of colorist PAUL CONRAD also appears in places throughout this volume, and I can think of no higher praise than that I can't pick it out, where it does appear, from Rick Ross's own. We relied a great deal, too, on the talents of letterists/balloon artists JOHN TRAUSCHT and KEN REYNOLDS, and if I make it to the UK I mean to hunt Ken down and thank him personally for his excellent work and his ever-prompt, frictionless communications (a too-rare thing in this world of widespread and unseen coworkers).

Which leaves RICK ROSS himself...though, how on earth do I cover this one? Rick did no less than all the art in this book. *All* of it. What kind of maniac even *tries* something like that? I happened to catch Rick in a classified search four years ago, and how he managed to be available at that moment, within range of our ad, and why he'd have taken this leap with us, knowing as little as any of us where we'd land: I don't know if I'll ever understand this. But the Fates smiled on us or what-have-you, we found Rick, he signed on and now he's done what he's done, God love 'im. I think his gifts will be obvious enough on the preceding pages; but I would add, for my own part, as someone who's toiled long in illustration and knows very well his limits in that discipline, that I have about as deep and profound an admiration as anyone can for Rick's art (and no more jealousy, I hope, than is becoming between friends). And to match Rick's tremendous talent–as perhaps you'll have guessed from the volume of work in this book–there is that dreadful, tireless, Calvinist work ethic of his. Rick: you know what these last four years have been. You know the unique understanding we share of this book and of life and work in general. I just don't know if you appreciate fully what a comfort and a motivation it has been for me, these last four years, to know there's always another light burning in another room across town, as I'm weathering these seasons of loneliness and fatigue and self-doubt. I hope you're proud of what you've made, and I hope we see you today on the eve of the great acclaim you deserve.

Finally, to my family, I'm afraid I may have to re-introduce myself, and reassure you that this hunch-backed figure in the garage is actually the husband of one of you and the father of the other two. I reserve this most special thanks for you three, who keep me going just by being your own unique and busy selves, and by allowing me now and then to run in your gang. Without you guys none of what I'm trying to do would be possible, or at least, what would be the point? Ali: twenty years into this I still feel like we're the kids who've slipped out while the adults weren't looking, and I can't wait to continue our adventures together in the wide world. Ben, I've promised when I turn this thing in that we're having a sleepover in your room, and I think I'm about to make good on that promise; I propose we drag Winnie in, too, and have us a time. Please continue to hold a place for me at the table, you guys, and one on the sofa, and a chair in the dining room where I swear we're going to finish that puzzle before summer's out. And please be patient with your husband and dad. I love you all so dearly.

–JB

JON BAIRD is the author/illustrator of the novels *Day Job* and *Songs from Nowhere Near the Heart*. He is a codeveloper, with Kevin Costner, of the *Horizon* miniseries.

BAIRD

. . . .

KEVIN COSTNER is an internationally renowned filmmaker. Considered one of the most critically acclaimed and visionary storytellers of his generation, Costner has produced, directed and/or starred in such memorable films as *Dances with Wolves*, *JFK*, *The Bodyguard*, *Field of Dreams*, *Tin Cup*, *Bull Durham*, *Open Range*, *Hatfields & McCoys*, and *Black or White*, among many others. He has been honored with two Academy Awards, three Golden Globe Awards, and an Emmy Award.

COSTNER

. . . .

RICK ROSS is an artist and filmmaker whose first widely recognized work in graphic fiction was illustrating the Image Comics series *Urban Monsters*. He was the lead artist for the graphic novelization of Spike TV's *1000 Ways to Die*, and he has also created artwork for numerous animated motion comics, including for the Cinemax television show *Femme Fatales*. He publishes the online graphic fiction anthology *Agitainment*.

ROSS

W